DANGEROUS LESSONS

Chin had always thought of Rebecca as his teacher—an instrument to help him learn the ways of the alien race that he had to master if he was to amass still greater wealth and power.

But now, suddenly, she was more, much more.

She was woman, abandoning her mouth to his, letting his hands work his will on her body, stripping her clothes away, wondering at the beauty they discovered.

Yet she was a teacher still, her hands showing him what she expected, her body demanding more of him than had any other woman before her, her expertise leading him to ecstasy he never had dreamed possible.

But even as Chin plunged into the vortex of this new pleasure in the new world, he dared not think what the price would be. . . .

THE
YOUNG
DRAGONS

Recommended Reading from SIGNET

- [ ] **EMERGENCY (Mid-City Hospital #1) by Virginia Barclay.** (#AE1070—$2.25)*
- [ ] **HIGH RISK (Mid-City Hospital #2) by Virginia Barclay.** (#AE1071—$2.25)*
- [ ] **THE KILLING GIFT by Bari Wood.** (#E9885—$3.50)
- [ ] **TWINS by Bari Wood & Jack Geasland.** (#E9886—$3.50)
- [ ] **A GARDEN OF SAND by Earl Thompson.** (#E9374—$2.95)
- [ ] **TATTOO by Earl Thompson.** (#E8989—$2.95)
- [ ] **CALDO LARGO by Earl Thompson.** (#E7737—$2.25)
- [ ] **THE WORLD FROM ROUGH STONES by Malcolm Macdonald.** (#E9639—$2.95)
- [ ] **THE RICH ARE WITH YOU ALWAYS by Malcolm Macdonald.** (#E7682—$2.25)
- [ ] **SONS OF FORTUNE by Malcolm Macdonald.** (#E8595—$2.75)*
- [ ] **THE EBONY TOWER by John Fowles.** (#E9653—$2.95)
- [ ] **DANIEL MARTIN by John Fowles.** (#E8249—$2.95)
- [ ] **COMA by Robin Cook.** (#E9756—$2.75)
- [ ] **THE CRAZY LADIES by Joyce Elbert.** (#E8923—$2.75)
- [ ] **THE FINAL FIRE by Dennis Smith.** (#J7141—$1.95)
- [ ] **SOME KIND OF HERO by James Kirkwood.** (#E9850—$2.75)
- [ ] **KINFLICKS by Lisa Alther.** (#E9474—$2.95)

*Price slightly higher in Canada

THE
YOUNG
DRAGONS

J. Bradford Olesker

A SIGNET BOOK
NEW AMERICAN LIBRARY
TIMES MIRROR

PUBLISHED BY
THE NEW AMERICAN LIBRARY
OF CANADA LIMITED

Publisher's Note

This novel is a work of fiction. Names, characters, places, and incidents are either the product of the author's imagination or are used fictitiously, and any resemblance to actual persons, living or dead, events, or locales is entirely coincidental.

NAL BOOKS ARE AVAILABLE AT QUANTITY DISCOUNTS WHEN USED TO PROMOTE PRODUCTS OR SERVICES. FOR INFORMATION PLEASE WRITE TO PREMIUM MARKETING DIVISION, THE NEW AMERICAN LIBRARY, INC., 1633 BROADWAY, NEW YORK, NEW YORK 10019.

First Printing, April, 1982

2 3 4 5 6 7 8 9

 SIGNET TRADEMARK REG. U.S. PAT. OFF. AND FOREIGN COUNTRIES
REGISTERED TRADEMARK - MARCA REGISTRADA
HECHO EN WINNIPEG, CANADA

SIGNET, SIGNET CLASSICS, MENTOR, PLUME, MERIDIAN and NAL BOOKS are published in Canada by The New American Library of Canada, Limited, Scarborough, Ontario

PRINTED IN CANADA
COVER PRINTED IN U.S.A.

To Tom, my brother—would that
every man could have one like him.

ACKNOWLEDGMENTS

To the memory of A. S. Burack, Editor of *The Writer*, who gave countless writers so many years of inspiration and education when they were so desperately needed. .

To my agent and good friend Peter L. Ginsberg, who had a sustaining faith in this novel and its author.

To my longtime friend, Ron Smith, who was of invaluable assistance in matters of linguistics.

And most of all, as always, to my precious Susan, who was more than a little help with this one.

BOOK ONE

BOOK ONE

Chapter 1

The child was screaming loud cries of pain, had been screaming since Kung Lee Wong carried her from the old woman's house. The old woman had pulled too tightly on the bandages while binding his daughter's feet. Kung Lee knew this because he had heard a distinct snap when his daughter's foot had broken.

He pulled up on the reins and the leathery old ox that pulled his cart slowed to a stop. Kung Lee tied the reins, took a long, tired look out over the endless stretch of rice fields, and turned to look at his daughter in the back of the cart.

Her face was contorted, wet with tears, her eyes wide with pain. She was three years old. Kung Lee's face was a yellow mask, devoid of emotion, and his voice conveyed this to the young child.

"Be still, daughter. You have cried long enough. It will do nothing to help your pain. It will only make it worse."

He sighed as she shrieked louder and he wondered, briefly, if her convulsions had grown in intensity because of the pain or because she wanted to hold his attention.

Kung Lee clicked his teeth. "One would think you had never been bound before."

He looked at the neat white bandages wrapped and knotted around what would someday be called "golden lilies." His eyes paused on her feet. Their growth had been successfully halted at an inch and a half. Her left foot had been broken three times in as many years. Her right foot had suffered the fate only once before.

Stuffed into shoes no longer than a peanut shell, her feet would grow no more than another two inches in all the days of little Ling Wong's life. What would grow, Kung Lee thought, was the price she would fetch should he decide to sell her.

He pondered that question for a moment, wondering whether it would be wisest to sell her or wait for a well-placed family to approach him with a contract. The corner of

3

his slitted mouth curled. It was time to start thinking about such things.

Still the child cried, and now his voice grew stern and sharp as his patience grew thin.

"Be quiet, child, or I shall provide you with ample reason for tears."

And then, her fear overcoming her pain to a degree, Ling's sobs subsided and Kung Lee turned back around, poked the ox's rump with his stick, and settled back as the cart lurched forward.

It was nearly sundown by the time Kung Lee pulled the cart to a halt in front of the small baked clay hut that was house and home to him and his family. He jumped down off the cart, his legs aching more this year than they had the last, walked around to the rear, and pulled Ling out of the flatbed.

She was still whimpering from the pain, but Kung Lee could see that she was making an effort to control her tears as he carried her in his arms. He would carry her this first day of the fracture. But afterwards she would have to make do with the small cherry-tree branch, which served as a crutch, that her father kept in the house for such purposes.

He opened the cracked oaken door of his house and pushed inside. Kung Lee crossed the dirt floor of the house's single room and deposited Ling on one of the three bunks against the far wall. She sniffled several times, looking up at her father for consolation. But when she saw that it was not forthcoming, she laid her head on the straw mattress, with pain her only companion.

It had been a long trip to and from the old bondage woman's house and, too, his daughter's crying had set him on edge. As he lit the peanut oil lamps in the house he thought about having a smoke on his pipe. But he was concerned that the opium would leave him too senseless to enjoy his dinner, and his hunger was greater than his craving for a smoke so he dismissed the idea.

Kung Lee walked to his bunk on the other wall and sat on it, giving a soft moan, grateful that Ling had drifted off to sleep. He was glad to be rid of her caterwauling for a while.

From outside he could hear the rapidly approaching footfalls of his sons coming from the rice fields in which they had toiled daily since they were old enough to walk, the same rice fields in which he had toiled since he had been old enough to

4

walk, in which his father and his father's father and all their ancestors had toiled for more than forty centuries.

The door of the hut opened and Kung Lee Wong's two sons hurried in, both of them out of breath. He looked at the two young men—as opposite as any two young men could be.

Yang, eighteen and born a year before his brother Chin, seemed to have made the most out of being born first. He towered over his younger brother, both in height and physical mass. Yang's features were broad, his shoulders wide, and his arms, even through the fabric of his collarless dark blue work-jacket, could be seen rippling with muscles that had been cultivated with religious determination; he followed a rigorous daily exercise regimen after his work in the fields had been completed.

His face, as if to match the character of his body, was wide and filled with expression. It was a face unlike that of most Chinese, and Kung Lee had pondered that fact many times, wondering if perhaps there had been a raped ancestor somewhere in his distant past.

Yang's cheeks twisted and wrinkled about the scar on the left side of his face. The three-inch scar was a badge of honor, a mark of pride he had acquired in winning the village martial arts tournament two harvests ago. The scar distinguished him from other young men in much the same way his victory in the tournament had distinguished him from the other combatants.

All his life Yang had stood out from other youths through his strength, size, and courage. This had been a source of pride to Kung Lee and had established him, within the village, as a man with a son who was capable of bringing honor to his family name.

And yet, he thought, looking at Yang, there was something missing in the boy; it was almost as if because of his size and great physical strength, the gods, in their wisdom, had chosen to make him deficient in other areas, as if to decree that no man had a right to all of their gifts.

Kung Lee had observed, many times, that the boy lacked the ability to use reason and calculation in his dealings with his peers. It was as if Yang was so impressed with his own strength that he felt it unnecessary to arbitrate, debate, and discuss. And Kung Lee knew, unfortunately, that Yang's feeling had often proven to be true. More than a few of

Yang's fellows had been coaxed into submission by the youth's mighty blows.

Kung Lee, on the other hand, was aware of the power of discussion, compromise, and diplomacy. It was the more diminutive Chin who had availed himself of these latter virtues. Chin had watched with curiosity as his brother labored to build his body and his martial arts skills. Through the years of listening to Yang's grunts and groans and smelling the sweat of his efforts, he wondered what was the purpose of it all if the mind, too, was not exercised.

To Chin's way of thinking it was a far simpler matter to use the brain in one's head—surely, he thought, an organ capable of far greater feats than could be accomplished by the mere muscle in one's arm—to circumvent whatever challenges should oppose a man.

That Chin's brain was as developed as Yang's muscles was an irony which Kung Lee had often contemplated. He decided that the gods had once again shown their wisdom in bestowing the gift of strength on a young man with little intellect and the gift of intellect on a young man with little strength.

Both his sons were puffing from their frantic run and Kung Lee smiled slightly at their excitement, knowing in advance what it was that had sent them scampering home early from the rice fields.

He suppressed a smile as he feigned ignorance. "What is it? What is it, my sons? Are there dragons in pursuit? Or perhaps rebels from the south?"

They fought to control their gasps and it was Yang who first recovered, shaking his head furiously.

"No, no, father. It is our honorable Uncle Ah Wan from Hong Kong!"

"My brother Ah Wan? From Hong Kong?" He fought to contain his amusement. "Surely you are mistaken, Yang. Not Ah Wan. He lives in that great city by the sea. You saw a face from a distance . . . only a man who resembles your uncle." He turned to his younger son. "What do you say, Chin?"

Chin shook his head wildly in assent, still drawing long breaths, exhausted from the mile sprint from the paddies. When he broke into speech it was in a rasping voice that sounded older than his seventeen years.

"It's true, father . . . it's true! Yang is right. It *is* Uncle Ah Wan!"

Now the smile broadened on Kung Lee's face as he abandoned the ruse. "Well, then," he declared, standing up from his bunk, "we'd better prepare a feast worthy of the occasion."

Chin smiled in return. "You knew, father; you knew he was coming."

Yang turned to look down at his brother, then back to his father. "Chin is right," he added excitedly. "You *did* know, didn't you, father?"

"Yes, yes, I did." He walked to the small cupboard on the far side of the room and began taking out the foods he had been holding for the arrival of his brother—a fine, crisp head of *bok choy,* a half-dozen dried sections of cuttlefish, and a plump duck which had cost him almost a full day's labor.

Ling awoke from the commotion caused by the arrival of her brothers and, finding the pain in her foot waking with her, began crying anew.

Chin looked at his sister, then to his father. "What's wrong with her, father?"

"Her foot," Kung Lee said, laying the *bok choy* on the countertop and halving it with a knife. "I think it's broken."

"Again?"

Kung Lee glanced at Chin. "She'll recover."

Yang frowned at his brother's concern. "I think she pretends to be hurt to get father's attention."

Hearing his remarks, Ling began wailing louder.

"See," Yang accused, "she seizes on concern as an owl on a mouse."

Chin crossed the room and knelt at the side of his sister's bed. He stroked her head for a moment. "Does it hurt badly, Ling?"

She nodded.

He turned back around to face his brother. "I'd like to see what you would do if they bound your feet, Yang."

Yang laughed loudly, holding his stomach for a moment. "Bound *my* feet? Can you imagine such a thing?"

Kung Lee smiled slightly, the thought amusing to him.

Yang said, "They don't tie men's feet, brother!" He paused, then added, "But by the looks of the way you fawn over her perhaps *your* feet should be bound."

Chin glared icily at him. "There is no sin in compassion."

"Why feel compassion about something that will benefit her later in life? Would you rather she be a big-footed woman?"

7

Chin looked to his father for support, but Kung Lee occupied himself with the preparation of the dinner, pleased to see Yang using his brain in combat for a change.

Chin turned back to his sister. "I feel compassion because she is my sister and she is in pain."

Yang pulled off his jacket. "You would do better to wash yourself and help make the house fit to greet our uncle."

"Your brother is right," Kung Lee said. "Your uncle will be here in a moment and the house needs tending. Your sister shall survive. Women have suffered worse pain than having their feet bound. So it has been for centuries." He paused, then added, "It is their lot in life."

Chin patted Ling on the head for a moment, then rose. He thought about countering, about saying that he could not imagine pain to be anyone's "lot in life." But he glanced at his father, saw that Kung Lee was waiting to see if he would reply to the remark, and decided against it.

Kung Lee was pleased to see his son remain silent. He knew that the sensitive boy opposed the remark and he knew that it was in him to say so. But wisdom—far advanced for one so young—and a respect for his father's word had prevented him from doing so.

There was a knock at the door and Yang flew to open it. Yang smiled widely, then bowed forward from the waist, rubbing his hands rapidly together.

"Uncle Ah Wan, your humble nephew greets you."

Wearing a fine, cream-colored tunic, his head cleanly shaven, his long queue gleaming black with expensive oils and extending down the middle of his back, Ah Wan returned the bow.

"It warms me to see my nephew a full-grown man," Ah Wan said, rubbing his hands in a circular motion.

Yang beamed for a moment, then stepped aside to let his uncle enter.

Chin approached his uncle, bowing and gesturing in the same manner his brother had. "I have sorely missed you, uncle, in the year since your last visit."

"And I have missed you, Chin. Not since that visit have I engaged an opponent who presented me with a challenging chess match."

Chin smiled under his uncle's praise, then moved aside.

Kung Lee drew in front of his brother and both men bowed at each other, wringing their hands together.

Kung Lee said, "My brother honors my house with his presence."

"It warms my heart to once again look upon you, Kung Lee."

Kung Lee straightened and appraised his brother, his clothing, the damask cloth satchel he carried, the gold ring on his finger.

"It is good to see that my brother is prosperous."

Ah Wan smiled. "I have fared well, though I am hardly a mandarin yet. But my prosperity pales beside the fortune brought to you by your fine family."

Kung Lee laughed. "Being a bachelor was a choice of your own making."

"Yes. And a choice which pleased neither of our parents."

"You have made the most of that decision, Ah Wan."

He nodded. "The life of an adventurer is not one to be shared with a woman." Ah Wan looked toward the bed where Ling was now sitting up. "And how is little Ling?" he said, approaching the bed.

She smiled slightly as he bent.

"You don't remember me, do you, child?" He smiled widely. "I am your Uncle Ah Wan. When last I saw you, you were no larger than a turtle's egg."

She laughed briefly, then winced as the pain lanced through her foot.

The smile left Ah Wan's face. "What is it, little one?"

"My foot," she said.

He looked down at the bandages, then nodded knowingly. "So," he said, "the golden lilies." His features softened. "I know it is painful, child. But someday, when you are in the house of a well-born gentleman, wearing rich clothes and eating fine food, you will look back and bless your father for it."

Kung Lee clapped his hands together. "Yang, Chin; the food awaits you. Begin preparing dinner for your uncle who has journeyed so great a distance to visit."

The two boys leaped to the task. Working at the wooden counter, Chin chopped the *bok choy* into shreds and sliced the cuttlefish into bite-sized pieces while Yang placed first kindling, then logs in the fireplace over which hung the blackened cooking kettle.

Kung Lee and Ah Wan walked out of the house and stood in the cool night air. For a long time they said nothing, but each held his own thoughts. They watched a cart rumble by, listened to the shrieks of children playing in the streets, heard the barking of a dog as it questioned the approach of a stranger.

Finally Ah Wan said, "The boys are growing into men."

Kung Lee nodded. "Not without attendant difficulties, however."

His brother turned to look at him. "How so?"

"I worry about Yang." He crossed his arms. "He seriously injured a boy in winning the tournament last season."

"It is the nature of martial arts. It is a harsh contest."

"True. But I saw the match." Kung Lee looked into his brother's eyes. "Yang had already won the contest. The boy was no match for him. The injury was an unnecessary infliction. I fear he misses the softening effects of a mother."

Ah Wan frowned, then said, "Perhaps it is youthful enthusiasm. It is easier to rein a man in than it is to instill courage in him."

Kung Lee said, "True."

Again they were silent for a long moment, listening to the subtle sounds of the village as night descended on it.

Ah Wan said, "Things change little from generation to generation."

"The village is much the same as when we were children." Kung Lee turned to look at his brother. "But *you* have changed much. You are a well-to-do businessman, a merchant of great importance."

Ah Wan nodded modestly. "I have made a few *yuan*. But it is a precarious vocation, brother. These are difficult times—more officials than ever to bribe, higher taxes, greater risks . . ." His voice trailed off.

"And?" Kung Lee asked.

Ah Wan caught his gaze and said, "There is much political unrest in the country."

"The War is just barely over," Kung Lee said. "Things will return to normal in time."

Ah Wan shook his head negatively. "I fear not. There is trouble in the southern provinces."

"T'ai P'ing?"

Ah Wan nodded.

Kung Lee uncrossed his arms. "There has always been trouble in the south. As you said, things change little from generation to generation."

"This generation is different, though. These . . . these

young rebels are intent on making a name for themselves and I fear they have the means to do it."

"Revolution?"

Again Ah Wan nodded. "They would overthrow the Manchus if they had their way. They have the support of many peasants, brother. Their numbers mount daily. We hear news that they are building a strong military force with many weapons and great stores of powder." Ah Wan's expression became grave. "The situation grows quite serious." He paused, then said, "I fear war is only a matter of time . . . months, perhaps weeks."

"War?"

"Yes. A revolt."

Kung Lee's hands became animated suddenly. "War, and the great mandarins do nothing to prevent it?"

"There is nothing they can do to prevent it. If they try to intercede they will provide the spark the T'ai P'ing need. All they can do is prepare defenses, and I fear they have grown too lazy and unused to combat to repel these young rebels."

"War," Kung Lee said, feeling suddenly weary. "The memory of a wife butchered by rebels while I was defending the provincial capital, not three years ago, still haunts me like a spirit that will not die."

Ah Wan laid a hand on his brother's shoulder and said, "I had not meant to talk of such things until much later. We shall not dwell on it. There is time after dinner to speak of it."

Kung Lee smiled and said, "You are right, Ah Wan. Now is a time of joy. It fills my home with happiness to have you here once again. It has been too long since your last visit, brother."

"And during that time you have grown thinner, Kung Lee." He shook his head. "It is not good for a man to be without a woman."

"Who has time to select a wife?"

Ah Wan shook a chastising finger at him. "You had better *make* time or you won't have time for anything else. Cooking your own food, tending to household chores, doing the marketing; these are not things for a man to be concerned with."

"You've forgotten your childhood village, brother—the women here are a dog-faced bunch to the last one."

Ah Wan laughed loudly. "My brother is still concerned with a pretty face, then."

Kung Lee joined him in laughter. "Just because one lives in a village does not mean his appreciation for a good-looking woman is lessened."

The dinner had been excellent. Afterwards they all sat around the table having a last cup of tea.

"Tell us more about Hong Kong, Uncle Ah Wan," urged Yang. "Tell us about the British."

"And about the ships," Chin added.

"The ships are as long as thirty houses and as wide as ten." Ah Wan paused as the boys gave a gasp. "Floating villages," he declared, "carrying as many men as live in this village of yours. The great white sails that catch the breath of the Dragon of the Air are as tall as the tallest tree your eyes have ever seen, and wide, twice as wide as the longest throw you have ever made with a stone."

The two boys sat wide-eyed, listening to the story their uncle repeated each time he came to visit.

"And the journey, uncle," Chin prodded. "Tell us about it."

"To the land ruled by the whites—men whose skin is a ghostly pale, as pale as the great sheets that flap above their ships. And the journey to that land and back is as long as the planting season and harvest together."

"And the British?" Yang urged.

"Hong Kong is filled with them—tall, bloodless men who wear suits of white that we would wear for mourning. Long noses," Ah Wan said, stretching his own nose with his fingers and drawing a laugh from Ling, "and eyes split open as though they had seen demons." Ah Wan held his eyes open to reveal the whites.

Now laughter spread around the whole table as he sought to stretch his nose with one hand and hold his eyes open with the other.

"Tell us more of their words," Chin said.

Ah Wan looked around the table, then said, in English, "Chopsticks."

Chin, Yang, and Ling laughed heartily, repeating the word over and over, liking the ring of it, as though it belonged in a verse to be recited by a sing-song girl.

Each of them guessed what the word meant. When none could guess its meaning—and even then, only after they pleaded with him—Ah Wan finally relented.

Ah Wan picked up one of the slender shafts that lay before

him on the table and said, "It means the *fai-tsz* with which you eat."

"No!" Chin declared, unable to believe that the odd-sounding English word could mean an object with which he was so familiar.

"True," Ah Wan said. " 'Chopstick' is the English word."

"Chopstick, chopstick, chopstick," Ling chorused, and everyone laughed at the sound of it.

Yang told of the upcoming martial arts contest in which he would be the defending champion. Chin showed his uncle the set of books he had received from Nanking a month ago—a gift from a cousin there. And Kung Lee discussed the poor crops and harvest of the previous year, offering little confidence that this year's would be much improved.

Finally, Ah Wan said, "And now I have something to tell all of you."

Silence whisked around the table; it was apparent that their relative had important news to impart.

"Word reached Hong Kong four weeks ago that gold has been discovered in the great country of the whites across the sea . . . in a place called California."

He looked at their waiting faces, then continued. "The strike is great and there is much riches. The reports say that there is gold for everyone and that it is lying on the ground in large nuggets, waiting to be picked up."

Now he saw their faces grow wide with excitement and he raced forward.

"The rivers," he said, gesturing with his hands, "are more filled with the precious ore than they are with fish. Like so many pebbles in a stream, they lie on the sand waiting to be scooped up. Fishermen have become men of wealth overnight in this California."

"But what has this to do with us?" Kung Lee asked.

Ah Wan turned to him. "This is the news, brother. These people beckon to us with open arms and open hearts. All over the world, people are making the journey to this California. These travelers are called forty-niners, so as to mark the fact that they make the journey in the year 1849 of the white's calendar. They ask that we come and share in their great wealth."

"Why?" Chin asked.

Yang turned to look at his brother. "Who cares why, Chin? All that is needed to know is that we are invited to come."

Ah Wan considered the question. "Yang, your brother is

right to question their motives and you would profit to learn from his example. Would not a tiger beckon a doe to enter its lair?"

Yang bent his head in respect, accepting the rebuke from his uncle with an air of restrained contrition.

Ah Wan turned to his other nephew. "To answer your question, Chin, the Americans bid us come to their country as part of an accord made between our two nations. They are a people eager to purchase our silks and jades and ivories with their new-gotten riches. They are highly desirous of trade relations with our country, and as a part of a trade pact hewn by the Emperor our people are to be allowed to immigrate there for mining and other commercial endeavors."

Ah Wan paused for a moment, then said, "And that is the purpose of my visit." He glanced at Kung Lee. "I leave in two weeks for those golden hills across the waters; there, I pray, to make my fortune and return a monied man. "I ask you, my relatives, if you would join me in this adventure."

Chin and Yang snapped their heads in the direction of their father, but his face was blank, his eyes deep in thought.

Slowly Kung Lee rose, then looked at his two sons. "I will speak alone with your uncle." He motioned toward Ling, who appeared not to fully grasp what was being said. "Carry your sister outside for some air and occupy yourselves out there until I call for you."

Obediently, their hands shaking with excitement, the two brothers bent and carried their sister from the house. After the door was shut and they were alone Kung Lee looked at Ah Wan.

"I must confess a falsehood to you, brother."

Ah Wan nodded as he took in the grim look on Kung Lee's face. "I sensed that something was troubling you."

Kung Lee looked down at the table for a moment, then back at his brother. "I fear I have misled you. My thinness is not due to lack of proper diet and neither is the absence of a wife a result of my inability to find one."

Ah Wan nodded and bade him continue.

Kung Lee drew a deep breath and said, "I am ill, dear brother."

Ah Wan's face tightened perceptibly. "How ill?"

Kung Lee's eyes lowered to the table and there followed a long silence between the two men.

At length, Ah Wan asked, "How long?"

"A season. Perhaps longer if the gods so order."

14

"Are you in much pain?"

Kung Lee smiled slightly. "It visits me on occasion. But after a hard life one learns to entertain even the harshest visitor."

"You have seen all the doctors? Perhaps a visit to the capital, where a specialist can be found? I can make arrangements for . . ."

"I am certain you can. But I choose not to fight the gods. I accept this as their wishes and ask you to do the same. I shall soon be with Lin Po and the rest of our ancestors and then I shall be happy." He paused, then smiled. "But this news you bring me is the answer to my prayers. For a long time now, I have worried over what will become of my sons after my departure. Now you offer the solution. I want them to go to this place where the gold is, Ah Wan. Let them go and seek out their fortune."

Ah Wan arched an eyebrow in surprise. "To go without their father? You would have them go alone?" He quickly raised his hand and said, "Of course, I would watch over them as much as possible, but in a land where the customs are strange, the tongue foreign, and the tide of life so unlike our own, the task of managing my *own* life will not be an easy one."

Kung Lee said, "I do not ask you to wet-nurse them, Ah Wan. Let them fend for themselves, as would any man. It *is* the answer to my prayers. Soon I won't be here to teach them. Soon they will have to stand on their own. This experience will be a teacher for them. This experience will take my place when I am no longer here." He looked at his brother and said, "It will take my two young sons and mold them into two young dragons."

Chapter 2

Chin had never traveled farther than ten miles beyond the boundaries of his village. But even if he had, even if he had journeyed to all of the cities of China except this one, those journeys would not have prepared him for what unfolded before his eyes, for there was no other city in all of China like Hong Kong.

He regarded with astonishment the maelstrom of humanity—a weave of people running frantically in this direction and that, through streets so crowded that carts moved slower than a man on foot and hence were favored only by those with leisure time, of which there were few.

Time was everything here, Chin reflected. Frenetic activity seemed to abound as messengers, runners, brokers raced through boulevards swollen with humanity, bearing notes, letters of credit, and signed contracts.

Occasionally he would spot a towering Britisher, and both he and Yang would stare open-mouthed for a moment, taking in his snow-white skin and pop-eyes. Once Chin caught sight of a man with blond hair and let out a yelp of amazement. He spoke excitedly to his uncle, asking how it was that the man could have hair of gold. Ah Wan assured him that it was quite common among the white people.

Chin caught the smell of the ocean in his nostrils, felt it tease at him with a fragrance he had never known existed. Ah Wan turned and looked at his nephew, then smiled, remembering the first time he had ever smelled salt air.

"It's the perfume of the Dragon of the Sea, Chin."

Chin looked up at him, surprised to find that his uncle had been watching him. "It . . . it's captivating, uncle."

Ah Wan laughed. "More than one man has been captured by it, I would say."

"Not this man," Yang scoffed.

"Oh," Ah Wan said, turning to look at his older nephew. "And if not the sea, what form would you want your captor to take, Yang?"

"Gold."

"Then you would join a crowded fraternity, nephew."

"Uncle," Chin said, "where do we go first?"

"To the House of the Six Companies so we may register for passage. Your village is in the province which belongs to the Kong Chow Company, while I must register with the Hop Wo Company.

Yang said, "I want to register with the company you register with, Uncle Ah Wan."

"You cannot. Your association is based on your clan heritage, and that is predetermined by your province of birth, Yang. You are a member of the Kong Chow Company, as are all the people from your province. Henceforth you must consider all countrymen from your province to be your cousins."

"But they are *not* my cousins," Yang protested. "There are people in my own village whom I would not consider my cousins—my adversaries," he said, clenching his fist, "people whom I would strike down."

Ah Wan looked at Yang. He was broad, muscled, strong in every way and in every sense a man, except in that sense most important. He turned his gaze to Chin who, though the second-born, was years wiser. Chin, Ah Wan thought, would understand what he was about to say. It was Yang whom he must be especially careful to instruct with his words.

He took both boys by the arm and pulled them out of the traffic, into the proscenium of a jewelry shop. Ah Wan paused for a moment before he spoke, in order to impart a further air of importance to his words.

"Yang, Chin, what I am about to say you must always remember. It will not be repeated to you by any other man because it will be assumed that you, as men, will already understand it."

He looked at each boy, then said, "From this time forth you must forget those petty jealousies and emotions that have ruled your lives. From this time forth you must consider all your countrymen to be your allies. You must consider all men of your province, of your company, to be your cousins.

"We go to a strange land, my nephews; a land where we know not what awaits us. Of what little we do know there is but one certainty—that our people shall be in the minority in this land of the whites. Therefore," he said, straightening, "it is paramount that we stand together, as one. It is paramount that we preserve our heritage, our customs, our traditions that we may retain our identity, the identity that was handed down to us by our ancestors.

"This," he said, turning to Yang, "is why all men of your province are your cousins." He paused, then asked, "Do you both understand?"

The boys nodded solemnly. Finished with his lecture, Ah Wan pulled them both out into the street again and they continued along their way.

Chin and Yang sat in the third-floor Immigration Office of the Kong Chow Company. The affairs of the company, as with each of the Six Companies, were largely concerned with providing services and unity to the members.

That Yang had at first been confused when his uncle had told him to consider all men from his province to be his cousins was not at all unusual. To the British the Six Companies and their function were even more confusing. This confusion was no doubt added to by the translation of the Chinese phrase *Guy Chong* into the English "Six Companies." Most Britishers had believed that the Six Companies were somehow involved in commerce or trade of some type, when they were actually fraternal organizations or clans.

As Ah Wan had stressed, membership was prescribed by a man's place of birth, and loyalty to one's clan was a matter of serious concern if a man was going to have his passage sponsored for him.

As Chin sat in his chair, watching the clerk behind the desk filling out the forms, he speculated about the total amount of money advanced to his fellow countrymen for passage. Surely that sum had to run into millions upon millions of *yuan*—hundreds of millions, perhaps. Yet at the same time he knew that they were secure loans, for he knew that, like himself, few men of China would renege on a loan made in good faith, lest he incur the wrath of both his ancestors and the lender.

"Names?"

"What?" Chin asked, his train of thought broken.

"Names," the clerk repeated.

"Chin," he said at the same time his brother spoke his own name.

The man frowned. "It will be sufficient for one of you to provide the answers."

Yang glared at his younger brother for a moment, irritated that Chin had sought, even if absentmindedly, to provide answers that were supposed to have been given by the older.

Chin folded his hands and lowered his eyes.

Yang looked at the clerk. "Yang and Chin Wong."

The clerk scribbled on the form. "Of what village?"

"T'ai Chow."

He nodded. "For what purpose do you wish to travel?"

"Gold," Yang said.

"And commerce," Chin added.

Yang jerked around to look at him.

The clerk glanced up from the form. "Commerce?"

"Commerce," Chin affirmed with a steady voice.

The man noted down the reply, then asked, "Do you plan paid passage or are you seeking assisted passage?"

18

Yang turned back to the clerk. "Assisted."

"For both?"

He nodded.

"Collateral for two passages comes to 420 *yuan*."

Yang tensed for a moment, impressed by the amount, then leaned forward in his chair. "Sir, we were told that a pledge of servitude by forfeiture may be provided in lieu of the collateral."

Again the clerk looked up. "That is true. You have such a pledge?"

"Yes," Yang said, pulling the papers from his pocket. He handed the documents to the clerk and said, "We pledge our sister."

The clerk unfolded the paper and examined it, noting Kung Lee's signature. "This is the mark of the girl's parent?"

Yang nodded.

The man said, "Very well. This pledge is accepted as collateral. Understand that you will have seven years to repay the funds advanced you for passage. Your salaries shall have a percentage deducted from them monthly for this very purpose.

"Understand, further, that failure on your part to repay these advance monies shall invoke the pledge of servitude and your sister shall become a ward of our company in order to work off your debts."

Both Yang and Chin shuddered, not so much for fear of their sister being thrown into slavery as for fear of the shame it would bring to their name and their father's name should they fail to make good on their debts.

"Do you understand and accept all these things?" the man asked.

Yang nodded. "We do."

The clerk returned his attention to the pledge and stamped it with a *chop* sitting on his desk. He then stamped the passage documents and handed them to Yang, along with a second set of papers. He put the agreement before them and Yang and Chin both signed it.

"When you disembark in San Francisco you shall be met. Present these papers and you shall be attended to." The man looked down and pulled forward another set of papers in preparation for the next applicant. He looked up and saw that the two brothers were still seated.

"That is all," the man said coarsely.

"S—sir," Yang stuttered.

"What is it?"

"Where do we go now?"

The man frowned a tight frown, as though he was a very busy official who didn't have time for needless questions.

"Look on the papers I have given you. They will provide the answers." He returned to his forms.

Chin and Yang stood and began walking toward the door. Yang opened the door, but was halted by the clerk's voice.

"The name of the ship is the *Cornwall*," the man said. "She is at pier sixteen."

Yang and Chin turned to look at him.

"Good fortune and prosperity to you both," the man added quickly.

Chin beamed widely, bowed low with Yang and said, "Thank you, sir; thank you, sir."

"Go on, now," the man said, containing his smile as he returned to his work, "be off with the both of you."

Chapter 3

James Riley snapped the leather rein and the horse pulling his buckboard responded, trotting a few feet through the wagon-congested streets of San Francisco. Then it stopped again. Riley rose from his seat atop the buggy and looked through the dust and fog of mid-afternoon, trying to see if he could make it past the wagon parked on the side of the wood-planked street.

"Come on," he said, slapping the reins again. "Let's get a move on."

He edged his wagon past the one that was parked to his right, just clearing it. He slapped the reins twice more, finally managing to get a respectable trot out of the nag he had bought for fifty dollars in Sacramento.

"Watch where you're going!" a man cried out as Riley cut past his right of way.

"To the devil with you!" Riley replied. He was late and he wasn't of a mind to fancy the needs of pedestrians. He was more than just late. He was a whole week late, and that meant a week's worth of gold had been lost.

It had been the damned wagon train's fault, he reflected. Too many women and children on it, slowing things down, causing it all sorts of minor crises. Women and children had no business coming out West anyway, he thought, cursing the delay.

Still, there had been a sense of peace, of closeness to nature on the open trail. And among the people in the wagon train there was a feeling of boundless hope and faith in what the future would bring. It came, Riley realized, partly from the tales of fortunes to be made in California. But part of it came from the people themselves, from the kind of people who had the courage to cross a savage frontier in pursuit of their dreams.

While the arduous journey had surely been a frustration to him, it had also been curiously uplifting. These people, this country was in marked contrast to the Ireland from which he had come. Even in his youth there had been little joy—he was the sixth son of poor dirt farmers. But with the scourge of the potato famine, James Riley's life, along with those of millions of his countrymen, became a hell.

He looked about at the streets teeming with vitality and greed. If there was a certain feverish look in the eyes of San Franciscans, he thought, it was not one caused by privation or starvation. The memories still haunted him; they probably always would, he reflected. They were the memories of death, of bloated bellies, of his mother and father and three of his brothers dying of hunger, along with three quarters of a million other people.

"The crop's failed," he remembered his father saying, not knowing the horror those three words signaled. He recalled the family discussions about what it would mean—hard times, harder than any they had already known. His father had been confident they would make it through, though. They were toughened by their poverty.

In the beginning, when he still had the luxury of time to reflect, Riley wondered why his family had seemingly been singled out for failure. He knew he and his family labored hard in the fields. He knew his mother—a forty-two-year-old woman who looked twenty years older than her age—had worked from dawn till dusk all her life. The rewards of honest labor, it seemed, were few.

But in the weeks and months that followed, Riley learned

that it was not just his family, but the whole village, the whole countryside, the whole nation that was cursed. Recollections of neighbors meeting at his house, of town meetings or shared stories of grief, welled up in his memories. And then, one day, the meetings stopped and the dying began.

At first it had been the shock of hearing about a neighbor whose child had died in the night. And for a time there was still a sense of community. Those who had something left shared with those who had nothing. But that time was not long, for soon the famine was upon them all and death swept through the country like an avenging warrior, striking randomly at the young and the old. First hundreds died, then thousands, then hundreds of thousands. Disease spread as people died faster than they could be buried, and still more died because of this.

His mother and father gone, his brothers dropping before his eyes, and the specter of a similar fate looming before him, Riley followed the thousands who fled to the cities. Dublin already bursting with the masses who sought refuge there, offered little comfort. Riley scoured the streets, looking for labor at first, begging for crumbs next, and finally turning to crime.

But even among the criminals the competition was fierce. Frequently three or four brigands would stalk the same prey, and a fight would break out among the bandits to determine who would assault the victim. In many cases the prey escaped while the criminals fought each other.

His mettle forged strong by the pain of seeing his family starve, Riley became a fierce street-fighter. And though it went against the quiet upbringing his father had provided, Riley convinced himself it was a matter of survival. It very nearly proved his undoing.

He had killed a man. It hadn't been intentional. In fact, he had regretted it. But the man's death had been the man's own fault, Riley rationalized. The man shouldn't have resisted him. He should have just handed his wallet over and been grateful for his life. That was always the best policy when confronted by a man on a dark street who carries a steel pipe in his hand.

But the fool had resisted and Riley had convinced him with a blow across his head—a blow delivered just a bit too hard. The wallet had netted Riley three pounds, not an inconsiderable sum. He had blessed his luck and thought that was the end of it.

It would have been, had it been an ordinary man Riley had accosted. Certainly crime, even murder, was not an uncommon occurrence in the strife-torn country. What was uncommon was the murder of a police captain. The close-knit criminal community felt the pressure being exerted by the police. A woman had witnessed the murder from her second-story window and a fairly accurate description of Riley was being circulated. While there was no love for the police, the bandits of Dublin had no desire to see an aroused department descend upon them.

All these things Riley overheard in the bars and back rooms where gambling and women were sought to ease the futility of existence. If living in the streets had done anything for James Riley, it had helped to hone his wits. He had the presence of mind to know his peers would turn him over in a minute if it would ease police pressure. When he learned a fifty-pound reward had been offered for the capture of the murderer, Riley made the wisest decision of his life. He gathered every pound he had, spent a fortnight in the alleyways pouncing on hapless citizens to augment his funds, and pulled his belt tighter in a self-imposed fast.

At the end of two weeks' time he had enough money to book steerage class on a cattle boat to America. The wagon trip across America had cleansed the filth of the ocean voyage from his mind. But now, in the noise and commotion of San Francisco, in the great tangle of wheels and dust and people everywhere, Riley's wagon was just one more congestant added to the already tumultuous, swirling frenzy of newcomers.

San Francisco was growing by the hour. Three years ago it had been a sleepy village with a population of four hundred and fifty-nine. When James Riley's wagon rolled down Grant Street on the afternoon of August 3, 1850, the population had grown to more than 25,000.

And although what Riley saw was a dusty city with wooden planks for roads, it was far better than what it had been just months earlier: mud. Mud so deep that it had swallowed up whole horses and wagons when the rains came. And fires, half a dozen of them. San Francisco had been wracked with fire after fire in the year just past. On June 16 there had been a fire that swept through the city, causing over $5 million in damage. And just a month later, on July 17, another fire broke out, razing building after building.

The only benefit of these fires was that they necessitated

the building of a new San Francisco each time. The one James Riley was riding into was a substantial improvement over the ones that had been before.

Everywhere wagons competed for space in the narrow avenues. Even at this late hour he could see men coming from stores carrying camping and mining equipment, provisions and food. Everyone seemed to be loading wagons and rushing to or from the stores that lined Grant Street.

He spit over the side of the wagon in anger. They were all ahead of him. He was half a mind to stock up on provisions, buy his equipment, and make for Sonora or Coloma this very night. But he knew he'd only be putting off the inevitable.

Riley drew a deep sigh. He'd been riding for practically two days straight, without rest except for a few minutes of sleep he'd snatched on the flatlands. He'd wisely bought the buckboard in Sacramento, knowing that prices were already skyrocketing in San Francisco.

He hadn't bothered buying provisions there, though, not wanting any cargo to lessen his speed. He carried a single carpetbag with him. Riley closed his eyes for a moment. Yes; he'd have to get some serious sleep before he went on. One day wasn't going to make that much of a difference at this point, he thought.

Riley fought for a space near the general store. He pulled in on the reins, tied them, and jumped down from the buckboard. As he walked into the dry goods shop, Riley glanced at the regulator clock on the wall and noted that it was past six o'clock. His stomach grumbled a response. He was surprised that the store was open at this hour, but by the looks of the crowd the owner was doing a land-office business and had decided to adapt his hours accordingly.

He spent the next twenty minutes picking out his supplies—a case of beans, three pounds of dried beef jerky, three pounds of bacon, a carton of hardtack, a couple of canteens, and fifty rounds of ammunition. He selected two panning plates and half a dozen pouches for storing nuggets. Riley picked out a horsehair blanket and a mess kit. After he had decided on two wool shirts, the salesclerk sold him on a new brand of canvas work trousers that were being manufactured by a German named Levi Strauss who lived in the city.

The clerk totaled the bill. "That comes to forty-eight sixteen."

Riley stared incredulously at the clerk. "How much?"

The clerk smiled. "You must have just gotten into town. I mean, you haven't been out to the mines or rivers yet, right?"

"How did you know that?" Riley asked.

"It shows." The salesclerk leaned against the counter. "Most folks are pretty shook the first time they find out prices here in the city. Really sets 'em for a loop, all right. You'll change once you get out to the fields, though."

"Oh," Riley said, digging resignedly for his wallet. "Why's that?"

"Listen, mister," the clerk said, wrapping his purchases, "why do you think the prices are so high? You think we'd be able to charge this much if the goldfields didn't support it?" The young man laughed. "Hah! There's so much gold out there it'll take a hundred years to pan it all—and that's just the streams I'm talking about."

"Yeah," Riley said, "well, if there's so much gold out there, how come you're behind this here counter?"

The clerk finished tying the package, then said, "Because my pa owns this store." He laughed again. "Only thing better than panning gold is having panners bring it to you."

Riley nodded, taking the point. "Say, young fella, you don't know where I can get a hotel room by any chance?"

"Ain't no hotel rooms," the young man said. "Ain't a hotel room for fifty miles 'round San Francisco."

"That's what I hear," Riley said, picking up his parcel. "Where the hell's a man supposed to sleep?"

"Tell you what," the clerk said, "my pa's renting out space in the loft out back. If you don't mind sleeping on hay and being a little crowded in by those already sleeping out there, we can accommodate you."

Riley nodded. "Sounds good to me. All I want is someplace to lay my head."

"Cost you five bucks, though." The young man shrugged his shoulders. "It beats sleeping in your wagon or . . ."

Riley dug into his pocket, took out a five-dollar piece, and plunked it on the table. "At this rate I might not even make it to the goldfields."

"You'll make it there," the clerk said, picking up the coin. "They all do."

Chapter 4

His uncle had been right, Chin thought as he walked up the gangplank of the ship with hundreds of his countrymen in front of him and hundreds more behind him. The leviathan *was* as long as thirty houses. The ship *was* as wide as ten. Something about the physical size of the great clipper filled Chin with a surge of excitement, a rushing sense of awe, and he had to impart it before he burst.

As the line of Chinese walking up the gangplank stopped for a moment, Chin tapped Yang on the shoulder. His brother turned to look at him.

Chin smiled. "It is a great ship, is it not, brother?"

"A great ship to take me on a great adventure," Yang answered with little emotion.

"You are angry that I told the clerk I sail to California with interest in commerce?"

"It is your decision to make," Yang huffed.

"You are upset that I will not be in the goldfields with you, Yang?"

"It matters little to me. I shall harvest the riches just as well without you as I would with you."

Chin frowned as Yang turned back around and advanced up the walkway, toward the great ship swallowing up more and more men. Chin followed.

"We are not all of your mold, Yang."

Again Yang turned around. "And what does that mean?"

"It means that not all men are endowed with your physical powers, with your strength, with the stamina so necessary for the rigorous undertaking you seek."

Yang raised an eyebrow in surprise at his younger brother's unexpected praise. "These are strange words coming from you."

"I speak only the truth," Chin said. "A man must do what he can do. For a sparrow to pretend to be an eagle is both foolhardy and dangerous. And yet, if the sparrow accepts his lot, cannot he too flourish and prosper?"

Yang stood on the gangplank, listening hard to his brother's words. He nodded slowly. "You shall make a good merchant," he said, then turned around and continued up the walkway.

Whatever sense of romance Chin and Yang had attached to the voyage and the ship soon vanished as they came up onto the vessel's main deck. At the top of the gangplank, standing off to the side on the deck of the ship, was a dark-skinned snake of a man wearing a filthy short-sleeved shirt and a pair of brown trousers, the odor of which could be clearly discerned from a distance. The man held a foolscap in his hands, making an entry on it as each Chinese filed past him and presented his passage papers.

Chin and Yang presented their papers to the man and walked toward a group of fifty men who had been assembled on the deck.

They stood in the group, apparently, Chin thought, waiting for something or someone. No one seemed to know what to do, but presently Ah Wan appeared by their sides and told them that they were to wait for instructions which would be forthcoming.

Chin made use of the time to examine the deck of the ship which would carry him to California. It consisted of wide wood decking that was at present being mopped by a dozen men who seemed to be in need of mopping themselves.

He looked at the oaken mainmast of the ship, not twenty feet from where he stood. Its circumference was greater than that of any tree Chin had ever seen, and he was amazed that the ship was able to support it, that it would not sink from the sheer weight of the mast.

His eyes traveled up the mighty shaft, looking at the billowy white expanse of the mainsail. It was as though an ivory cloud had descended from the heavens and been harnessed to the mast by these sailors. It flapped loudly in the wind, making a most pleasant sound in Chin's ears, and he said a short prayer to the Dragon of the Air that the god would make his breath abundant so as to fill the sails and thereby make their passage a swift one.

Chin had no sooner finished his prayer than he heard a man loudly clapping his hands. He turned to look in the direction of the noise and saw one of his countrymen standing on a crate. Chin gave this man his attention, as did the other men in his group.

The man bowed, rubbing his hands together in greeting, and the group, en masse, returned the gesture.

He straightened and began speaking quickly. "So, I am Po Kao. I am the Six Companies' liaison for this voyage. I wish you all the best fortune on your adventure."

He paused, then said, "You will be quartered below the main deck, in the area called the hold. You will find the conditions there crowded, but we shall make the most of the situation, bearing in mind the riches that await us in this new land."

Po Kao's eyes jumped, rapidly scanning the group as he spoke. "There will be two meals daily, to be served here on the main deck, providing the weather is kind. At all times each man will be expected to obey the lawful orders of the ship's officers. This is a matter of both safety and etiquette.

"There is to be no cooking of meals in the hold. Nor is there to be any smoking down there. Fire on a ship at sea is a disastrous occurrence, my cousins. Neither will there be thievery or fighting. Violators of these rules shall be harshly dealt with, as they will be endangering the safety of the rest.

"Personal facilities are located on the main deck, at either end of the ship. All persons are to remain in the hold during the voyage except for the two one-hour periods—one in the morning and one in the evening—during which the meals will be served. It is then that you may attend to your personal affairs."

This last pronouncement was met with mild grumblings from some of the older men, and one of them spoke out.

"Po Kao, do you mean to tell us that we must spend the entire voyage confined below?"

The liaison man glared at the man who had asked the question. "It is a matter of safety, cousin. Look about you," he said, motioning with his hands. "Do you not see the massive size of this vessel?" He paused as the men looked at the colossus. "Do you imagine it to be a simple task to navigate such a ship? This is not some single-sailed junk floating down the Yangtze River, cousin. Sailing this vessel is a difficult, complex matter and the men who sail her must not have our problems additionally to deal with. They cannot both sail the ship and watch over us as we romp about the open deck. Surely you can understand this."

He paused again as the men fixed their eyes on him.

"There will be two periods, as I said, where you will come up on the deck. It shall be sufficient."

He turned and spoke briefly to a young Chinese who attended him at his right hand. Then he turned back to the group.

"You will follow Ti Gwei. He shall escort you to your quarters."

The men picked up their satchels, shouldered the poles that held their bags, and followed, single file, as the man named Ti Gwei marched in the direction of a hatchway. Chin looked over his shoulder and saw that another group of fifty men was now being ushered onto the deck space where his group had moments ago stood. Po Kao was still standing on the crate. Another attendant had moved to his side.

Chin bent as they stepped through the hatchway and he followed the line down the stairs. The air was already heavy and thick, not at all like the tantalizing salt air that smacked at one's senses up on the main deck.

As Chin followed his brother down the steps he became conscious of the closeness, the damp, the growing darkness.

The line moved down a second companionway, then a third, and Chin was filled with the knowledge that they were descending deep into the very bowels of the ship.

And finally they came to the hold where they would spend twenty-two hours of each day. It was a long, dank, narrow room—perhaps a hundred feet in length, but only a tenth as wide. It was already crowded with men and Chin kept close to Yang, holding on to his jacket at one point so as not to lose him.

On the bulkheads, every twenty feet, there was fastened a small oil lamp that provided the only illumination in the room. Yang was making his way toward one of those lamps and Chin stayed with him. Upon reaching it they lowered themselves to the floor, which was cold hardwood.

Chin laid his satchel down and rested his back against the wall. He listened and could make out voices on the other side of the wall. He realized that the room they were in was only one of several, perhaps many such rooms in the ship. He wondered how many men were being shipped to California on this trip, how many ships sailed to California each week, each month.

Chin was as sick as he had ever been. It felt as though a demon was clawing at his insides, trying to burrow its way out. He had retched until he thought he could retch no more, and then he had retched still more.

He had been this way for two days, unable to eat more

29

than a handful of rice or to keep down even that for more than an hour.

By the second day Ah Wan had begun to grow concerned. "You must eat something, Chin. It is important that you keep your strength."

He looked up at his uncle, finding it difficult to focus his eyes on him. "If only it would stop rocking so."

"Well, it won't," Yang said, sitting on the deck next to him, "so you'd better get accustomed to it."

"Yang is right," Ah Wan added. "There's nothing you can do about it. You might as well get used to the motion. Try to work your mind against it. Try to think of other things."

If there was any comfort to be taken from the fact, he was not alone in his misery. Fully half the men in the hold had suffered from motion sickness. And although they had tried to keep the hold clean, the stink of bellies emptying now permeated the room so that one's stomach turned even when the sea was relatively calm.

The door of the hold opened and one of Po Kao's assistants came in to announce that the evening meal was being served topside.

"I cannot, uncle."

"You will," Ah Wan said, pulling him to his feet with Yang's assistance. "The air will do you good, as will a mouthful of rice."

"Rice?" Chin moaned. "Don't mention it . . . please."

"He whimpers worse than a woman." Yang laughed. "It's a good thing you're not going to the goldfields with me," he said. "You'd probably run back across the waters with your tail between your legs the first time there's a good storm."

"My older brother offers such warm words of comfort in my time of illness," Chin said as he rose.

"Strength, Chin, not comfort. Comfort is for women—both to give and receive."

Ah Wan was right; the air up on the deck was good for Chin. Even now, as he held his hands tight on the ship's gunwale, Chin could feel his head beginning to clear. He looked out over the water, seeing the tips of the waves shimmering white for a moment beneath the half-horned moon above. Regardless of the tempest that raged in his belly, he had to admit that it was a wonderful sight to behold.

Yang went to get rice for himself and Chin. "Two bowls," he said to the Chinaman dishing the meal out of a large cooking kettle.

"One bowl per man," the server replied.

"One is for my brother," Yang answered. "He is ill."

"He can come and get the rice himself."

"I said he is ill."

"If he is that ill," the man said, thrusting one bowl into Yang's hand, "then he shouldn't be eating."

"Give me a second bowl."

"Move on," the server said. "There are more behind you."

"I said . . ."

The server poked at Yang's chest with his serving spoon. At the first touch of the metal Yang grabbed the spoon and wrested it from the man's hand. He bent the spoon into a useless piece of metal.

The server, not a small man himself, jumped at Yang. But his attack was stopped in midair as Yang's hands moved with speed that was blinding. The other men in line backed away, watching as Yang landed a quick series of blows to the man's chest and neck, drawing screams of pain from him.

Yang advanced on the man, who now lay in pain on the deck of the ship. He was about to kick the man senseless when a voice called out, "What goes on here?"

Yang whirled at the familiar voice and looked at Po Kao standing behind him. In that moment of surprise the fight went out of him.

"How dare you fight?" Po Kao snapped.

"This man would not give me the rice I . . ."

"Two bowls!" the server cried, still nursing his pain. "The swine asked for two bowls!"

Po Kao turned to look at him, waiting.

"I told him one was for my sick brother," Yang explained.

Po Kao leveled a finger at him. "You know the rules. Fighting is expressly forbidden."

"But I . . ."

"You must follow the rules. Punishment is the reward for . . ."

"Honorable Po Kao, if I may interrupt."

The Six Companies' representative turned to look at Ah Wan. "And who are you?"

A large crowd of Chinese had gathered now, drawn by the promise of a break in the monotony.

"I am this boy's uncle."

"He has been fighting. Fighting is expressly forbidden."

"I know that, honorable sir. Please excuse him this time."

"Punishment is the reward for breaking the rules."

"The boy was blinded with concern for his brother, who is truly sick from the motion of this ship. I pray your forgiveness on the promise that it shall not happen again."

Po Kao turned to look at the server. "Are you all right, cousin?"

The man took his place behind the kettle. "It would take more than an attack from this brute to harm me."

The crowd of men laughed at the proclamation.

Po Kao turned back to Ah Wan. "Very well. Keep your nephew in tow. The next time there will be no pardon."

Ah Wan bowed graciously, then turned to Yang. "You must control your temper, Yang."

"I am filled with sorrow that I have embarrassed you, uncle."

"Don't think about it. But do think about minding the rules laid before you. You had better become accustomed to rules, Yang, for there will surely be many of them in California. It is time to learn how to bridle yourself."

Yang bowed.

Ah Wan got two bowls of rice and brought one to Chin, who was at the far end of the ship taking air. "Here," Ah Wan said, "fill your belly."

Chin looked, reluctantly, at the rice. He pulled a pair of *fai-tsz* from his pocket and accepted the bowl. As he raised the bowl toward his lips he caught the aroma of the cooked rice and he was suddenly hungry. He ate ravenously, all thoughts of his illness gone now, and soon the bowl was empty.

"You are feeling better." Ah Wan laughed.

Chin returned the laughter and looked around the main deck of the ship. "Like all strange things, I suppose sea travel takes some getting used to."

Ah Wan nodded. "The measure of a man is his ability to deal with adversity, nephew."

Chapter 5

Riley scooped up a panful of water from the Yuba River, taking a fair amount of sand from the riverbed with it. He deftly swirled the water around in his pan, spilling a small portion of it over the side with each turn. Bit by bit the sand dribbled over the side of the pan. And then he saw it. It was small, no larger than a pea, really. But it glowed as though it had a life of its own.

"Gold," Riley said under his breath. He spoke the sacred word each time he discovered a new nugget, and it never ceased to thrill him to feel the sound of the word tumbling off his lips as he looked at a freshly found nugget.

Riley's lips trembled with excitement as he plucked the small nugget from the pan and held it, rolling it around with his fingertips. Then he reached inside his shirt and pulled out the pouch he had secreted there. He glanced around, instinctively, at the shoreline. But there was nothing to be concerned about. The other men panning were entirely too engrossed in their own efforts to be concerned about another man's good fortune.

He pulled open the rawhide thongs at the top of the pouch and peered inside at the three-score nuggets already resting there. Riley held the nugget over the opening, cradling it between his thumb and forefinger. Then he let go of it and the nugget dropped to join the others. He pulled the thongs together and slipped the pouch back inside his shirt.

He wiped his hand across his brow, then dipped both hands down into the river, splashing water over his face. Riley picked up his pan and rose to his feet, deciding to call it a day.

He walked away from the placer, back toward the encampment where the fifty-four men working on the banks had set up their tents.

Although Riley had been a loner for most of his life, he saw the wisdom in banding together with the other men. A

33

man working alone at a placer would be a sitting duck for bandits. Together, they had the strength of numbers.

Surprisingly, Riley found that he rather liked being a member of the group. His rough manner and tales of adventure had attracted other Irishmen in the camp to him, and he found himself, to his amazement, a popular figure. It was an uncommon role that pleased him in a strange way.

It was hard, lonely work during the day and he was grateful for the company at night. A good number of the prospectors were Irish, and after dinner, beneath the starlit California skies, they would sit around the campfire and swap stories about the old country.

When Riley had first arrived at the site on the banks of the Yuba River, a month earlier, it had been a confused mix of tents spread out over a quarter-mile tract of sand and hills. Each man cooked for himself, kept his own area, and tended to his own chores.

But as more and more men came into the area each day, organization began to come about through necessity. The half a hundred men at the Yuba site made friends with each other over the weeks and the tents drew closer and closer together.

Riley walked over the rise that looked out over the encampment. Tents were set in long rows of ten and fifteen to a group. There were four such groups, each one set apart from the others. Each group represented an ethnic clique. The Irish had banded together, as had the Germans, the French, and the native-born Americans.

It had been a natural phenomenon, an arrangement that was pleasing to all. The rows of tents could be seen as the beginnings of ethnic communities—though all of the men knew that the mini-neighborhoods would dry up as soon as the placer had been worked out.

Riley walked toward what had been dubbed "Irish Row." He pitched down his pan, knelt, and crawled into his tent. Inside he foraged around for his mess kit, feeling the hunger of a full day's work in the hot sun eating at his gut.

He thought he heard something and he stopped for a moment, but it had been nothing. Riley went back to looking for the kit, cursing in the close quarters of the tent.

Again he stopped. He *had* heard something. It was outside. Voices. He turned and crawled out of the tent, then he perked up his ears, listening. It was coming from the flats—a low sand plain about a hundred yards from Irish Row. He looked in that direction. A dozen men had gathered and were talking loudly. More men were joining them and now Riley began running toward them to investigate.

He arrived on the scene, coming up alongside Brian O'Malley, whose tent was next to his.

"What's going on, Brian?"

His red-haired neighbor, a former accountant who had given up his trade when the news of the gold strike came, was cradling a rifle in his arms and he glanced at Riley's holster as he spoke. "Glad to see you're wearing your gun, Jamie. Might be needing it from the looks of things."

"And why's that?"

"We got company," O'Malley said, motioning down the path with his head.

Riley looked past the other men and saw a group of about a dozen Mexicans on horseback. From this distance Riley couldn't see if they were wearing guns. He glanced around at the group he was in. Half the men had rifles and it was obvious that they stood ready to use them. There had been stories about roving Mexican bandits lately.

The Foreign Miner's Tax was aimed at driving the Mexicans, Indians, and Chilejos out of the mines and goldfields so the whites could have them exclusively to themselves. The tax had proved particularly effective. The prohibitive twenty-dollar-a-month tax had forced many dark-skinned prospectors to leave the fields and head home. Still others had taken to the gun.

But as this group approached, Riley saw that they were unarmed. One or two of them had a knife riding on his hip, but there was a noticeable absence of firearms. They stopped twenty feet from Riley's group and a swarthy Mexican, presumably the band's spokesman, stepped forward. A tall Texan named Mead followed suit.

"If you're looking to work this river," Mead said, "you can forget it. And I don't care if you got Mining Tax receipts, either," he quickly added. "We got too many men working here as it is. We let any more in and those what's already here won't be able to pull out enough gold to make a decent living."

The Mexican nodded understandingly, donning his friendliest smile. "*Si, amigo*: I understand what you say. We don't come to mine or pan, anyway. We no can pay the tax." He paused, then added, "We all broke."

"Well, then," Mead said, his hand resting on the butt of his holstered Colt, "what da y'all want?"

The Mexican scratched his stubbly chin for a moment, then looked back at the men behind him. "Me and my *campadres*, we thin' we got somethin' you might be interested in buying."

"What's that?"

"Our services."

Mead arched an eyebrow. "What services?"

"Here it is, *amigo*. We ain' got no money at all. Well, we ain' even got enough money to get back to Guadalajara. We got to do somethin' to make money or we gon' starve pretty soon. We figure maybe we work for you. What you say?"

"Doin' what?"

The Mexican shrugged his shoulders. "Anything. Cook, wash your clothes, chop the wood, keep the place clean." He smiled a broad smile. "What you say, *amigo*? We cook you good food—tacos, tamales, burritos. You won't be sorry."

Mead stood there, eyeing the Mexican for a long moment, thinking back to his youth in Waco. "Tacos and burritos, huh?" His mouth watered with the thought.

The Mexican smiled wider. "Enchiladas and tostadas, too. We do everything, eh? Take care of all problems for you. And at night," he said, pulling the guitar slung over his back around in front and giving it a playful strum, "we even make entertainment."

Several of the panners laughed at the Mexican's showmanship.

The Mexican laughed louder. "What you say, *amigo*? You no be sorry."

Mead cracked a smile. "What's your name, Mexican?"

"Joaquín, señor. Joaquín Murietta."

Mead turned back to the group where Riley stood. "What da y'all think? Sounds pretty good to me. We can pay 'em cheap, get some damned good cookin', and have all the chores took care of. Hell," Mead said, more convinced now that he thought about it, "it'll even give us all some extra time down at the placer."

There was a general nod of approval from the group. Mead turned back to face Murietta.

"Okay, Mexican, you got a deal. We'll pay you and your pals a buck a day. Bein' from Texas I know enough about y'all to know in advance that the food an' music'll be good enough. But if we ever catch one of your men stealing so much as a pinch of gold dust we'll cut your fingers off. You got that?"

Murietta grinned from ear to ear, almost jumping up and down from excitement. *"Si, amigo, si! Gracias, muchas gracias!"*

Then he turned and began talking rapidly to the other Mexicans and they broke out in cheers, waving their sombreros in gratitude toward the panners.

The Mexicans quickly began their task, setting up enormous black kettles and building pit fires to cook with. They had brought sacks of corn and meal with them and in a few hours the smell of cooking mash filled the camp, drawing the men to the fires like moths to a flame.

To Riley the Mexicans seemed happy in their work, shuttling back and forth to the river to draw water, grinding the corn into meal, pounding the thin pancakes. A group of several dozen white men congregated around the fire, smoking cigarettes and watching the Mexicans. It seemed that they were quite skilled in their preparations and several of the white men nodded approvingly.

As darkness fell the meal was served. It was a feast of tortillas, burritos, tamales, rice, and refried beans. It seemed as if the prospectors couldn't get enough; the food was pure heaven after months of beef jerky and hardtack. They filled their bellies with the finest dinner they had had since they had hit the fields, and an open camaraderie broke out between the white and Mexican group as the panners showed their appreciation for the nomads' culinary skills.

After the meal drink was broken out, and the sound of accordian and guitar music filled the air as Murietta and his friends put on a show equaling entertainment offered in the best cantinas south of the border. The panners joined in, dancing, singing, and drinking with their newfound servants, and the festivities cementing the new relationship lasted long into the night. Indeed, it was almost dawn before the last flames of the campfire flickered out and the last panner crawled, both woozily and happily, into his tent.

Mead had a headache—a Texas-sized one. The throbbing started at the base of his neck and traveled over the top of his head. He blinked his eyes open and the pain increased. It was a good thing he'd eaten well, he thought, or else it would have been even worse.

He sat up in his tent and rubbed his closed eyes with the backs of his hands. Outside he could hear the birds chirping. It was late, he thought. Mead smiled, thinking that he wouldn't be the only panner to get down to the placer late this morning—not with the drinking and carousing that had gone on the night before.

He picked up his pan and began crawling out of the tent. Outside the air was fresh, clean, and brisk. It was a beautiful day, Mead was thinking, when Joaquín Murietta grabbed his hair, jerked his head back, and slashed an eight-inch blade across his throat. Mead stumbled to the ground, blood pulsing in spurts from both sliced jugulars. He died seconds later.

Murietta's blood cry echoed long and loud and his band of killers moved in, weapons retrieved from a nearby hiding place thundering a deadly report as they fired into row after row of tents. The Mexicans' rifles and six-guns blazed time and time again at almost point-blank range, drawing cries of pain and death from the prospectors who had been sleeping in the tents.

Occasionally a white man would stumble out, wounded in the arm or the leg, only to be greeted by an expertly thrown knife, embedded to the hilt in his chest. Then the bandits moved in on the remaining panners with their machetes.

In less than ten minutes the carnage was completed, and now the killers moved to take their booty. Tents were ripped open, slashed to pieces. The bandits pulled open the dead men's shirts, searching for the coveted pouches. As each bandit emerged from a tent he gave a loud victory whoop, holding the rawhide pouch over his head, twirling it by the thongs. The pouches were thrown into a pile in the center of the camp.

But it was not only gold that was taken. Anything of value was fair game, and though the gold was to be fairly divided by Murietta, each outlaw knew that he could keep whatever else he could claim. Boots were a prized possession, and Murietta smiled as he watched the grisly spectacle of his men wrestling boots off the feet of men whose faces were contorted in death. Bracelets, watches, belts, even trousers if they appealed to a bandit, were torn from the men.

Two men who worked with Three-Finger Jack, Murietta's second in command, tended to take more grisly treasures. And as fingers and ears were lopped off by these men, they would occasionally discover a prospector who was not really dead, but only playing possum, and then the game would begin in earnest. Some were dragged by lasso behind the Mexicans' horses. Other prospectors were stoned, while still others were taken and tossed in the river with their hands and feet bound together.

Riley lay in his tent, listening as the howls of horror mixed with the Mexicans' laughter outside. His heart pounded wildly against his chest as he waited for the bandits to enter his tent. He had been shot in the arm. It was only a flesh wound and the pain was bearable. Riley had put his hand over the wound until it was covered with blood. He then wiped his hand over his temple so it appeared that he had been shot there.

The flaps of his tent were thrown open and two Mexicans came in laughing. Riley felt them kick him two, three, four times in the ribs. But he lay perfectly still, his eyes shut, knowing that they were watching for any signs of life. Finally he could feel their rough hands ripping at his shirt, reaching inside, feeling for his pouch. They found it and pulled it from him.

He heard their laughter and he could imagine them opening the bag, gloating over the contents that had taken him almost a month to coax from the river. Now he felt them pulling on his boots. They were off in a moment.

He lay there, still, wondering if it was over, wondering if they would go further with him. They were silent, he thought, and wondered why they were still watching him. Riley knew he couldn't stand it much longer, knew he couldn't stand the game they were playing.

Maybe they knew, he thought. Maybe they had seen him breathing and were standing there, just waiting to see how long it would take until he broke. Well, he thought, he'd go out fighting. He'd show them how an Irishman dies, all right.

He slowly felt for the butt of his knife in his waistband, wrapped his hand around it, and then ripped it from its sheath as he jumped to face his tormentors.

But he was alone. He looked down at the knife, saw his knuckles white from the grip he had on it, and drew a deep breath. On all fours he crawled to the flaps of his tent and peered through the crack. The Mexicans were dancing around a pile of pouches—the collective gold of the camp. The man named Murietta was sitting astride a white stallion, *bandeleras* crisscrossing his chest and a Winchester in his arms, his head thrown back in a demonic laugh. There was no resemblance between him and the mild-mannered *peòn* who had come begging for work for himself and his men the day before.

Sitting in his tent, stripped of his gold, his boots, his gun, Riley felt hatred building within him like a bubbling cauldron. Again he gripped the knife and he was seized by an almost overpowering urge to throw back the tent flaps, rush out, grab Murietta off his white horse, and drive the knife into Murietta's heart.

But then Riley heard the screams and he turned to look at a galloping horse ridden by a Mexican who was hopping, acrobatically, off the back of his mount and then up into the saddle. Riley looked at the rope attached to the horse and saw the man being dragged behind. The man's arms and legs were hog-tied, and he bounced over rocks and earth as the Mexican galloped through the camp. Riley watched for a long moment, until the horse and rider were out of sight, until he could no longer hear the tortured man's shrieks.

Then he pulled the tent flaps back together, retreated into his tent, and lay down on the ground, where he waited until the nightmare was over.

Chapter 6

As Chin came up onto the main deck he closed his eyes, squinting in the harshness of the clear morning. The air was sweet, as though the storm had driven all the evil spirits from the sky. A brilliant yellow sun shone overhead and Chin glowed in its warmth.

" 'Sun,' " he said to Ah Wan.

Ah Wan nodded. "You learn the white man's language quickly, nephew."

"It is not a difficult thing to master," he replied, following his uncle to the great kettle where the rice was being cooked. "It is a far simpler language to master than our own——only one-five-hundredth as many characters."

" 'Letters,' " Ah Wan said. "The British do not call their symbols characters."

" 'Letters,' " Chin repeated.

"And in total," Ah Wan continued, "those twenty-six letters comprise the 'alphabet.' "

" 'Alphabet,' " Chin mimicked, taking a bowl from the tall stack on the deck. "It seems inconceivable that they are able to manufacture a full language from such a minimal collection of charac . . ." He caught himself. " 'Letters.' "

Ah Wan smiled as the server dished out a double ladle of rice, filling his bowl. "True," he conceded. "But then they probably think us boastful and gluttonous to possess a language containing eleven thousand characters."

Chin smiled. "I suppose it depends on the way it is viewed, uncle."

"True. The fact is that both languages serve each country well. And although the size of our language may have something to do with the great, long history of our country, that is not to say that the white men have not been sustained adequately by their seemingly poverty-stricken alphabet of twenty-six letters."

Chin turned and looked skyward as he heard a voice call out. Now the other men were looking up and there was a great cheer of excitement among the white sailors.

Chin turned to his uncle. "I know that word."

Ah Wan nodded.

Chin turned and looked up the mast again. " 'Land,' " he said. He turned back to Ah Wan. "We are here, uncle."

Ah Wan looked over the side of the ship. On the horizon he could make out the thin sliver of land. "Yes," he said, "we are at journey's end."

As the ship docked, Chin and all four hundred and sixty-two of his fellow countrymen who had made the journey with him stood on the deck. Chin's bones ached from the three-month passage. Every muscle in his body was contorted, twisted, strained. Sores covered his arms and his legs and a pervading sense of weakness reached from his feet to his neck.

But the voyage was over and that filled him with strength that seemed to spring from some great inner well of energy. Perhaps, he reflected as he turned to look at his brother, Yang had been right after all. Perhaps it was a good thing that the voyage had been a difficult one.

To be sure, he felt stronger for it—if not in a physical sense, then certainly in a spiritual one. Through the suffering, the fear, and the discomfort, Chin felt that he had grown.

He regarded the dock that the *Cornwall* was making for. He could see that there was a large group of people assembled there; a mix, though separate and apart, of white and yellow. Too, there were buggies and horses, and children and women carrying white parasols.

They turn out to greet us, Chin thought; we are an oddity, no doubt. He then reflected, If a trainload of whites were to pull into my native village, would not the entire village turn out to see them?

Chin smiled at the thought, then turned back to look at the pier. I have never thought of myself as being an oddity . . . an attraction, he mused, but perhaps I would do well to begin.

In half an hour's time the ship had pulled to the Pacific Mail Steamship wharf. The gangplank came down and the long rows of blue-jacketed Chinese began filing off the ship.

As Chin followed his brother down the ramp he was struck by the fact that his group must certainly seem odd to the Californians, for the Californians certainly seemed odd to him. Every single man, woman, and child was dressed in a different manner.

Where Chin and the men with him were dressed in the uniform of China—matching blue trousers and jacket, cork-soled shoes worn over white socks—it seemed that every white person on the dock was dressed in a different manner, each wearing clothes of a different cut, each wearing blouses and jackets of a different color. Where Chin and his group looked like a wave of dark blue jackets and yellow faces, the white people waiting to greet them looked like a rainbow.

As soon as they set foot on the dock a smiling Chinese greeted them. When the man spoke it was with a slight accent that was pleasing to the ear. Chin wondered if the accent had been a result of the man's residence in this country, and decided that it probably was.

"Greetings," the man said, bowing toward Yang, "and welcome to California." The man straightened and said, "May I see your papers, please?"

After bowing, Yang presented the man with his traveling papers.

"Very good. Everything is in order. You may join your cousins in the group to the left."

The brothers walked toward a group of a hundred men. Chin looked toward the other groups, watching as the man who had greeted them now greeted other men, examined their papers, and directed them to their clan groups.

"Do you see Uncle Áh Wan?"

Yang shook his head. "No. I lost him after he showed his papers. He will meet us later, after we register at the Six Companies House."

An extremely jovial Chinese now stood in front of the group. Like Po Kao, this man stood on top of a wooden crate. Chin glanced in the direction of the ship and noted that the passengers had completed their debarkation.

The man bowed solicitously. "Greetings, cousins, greetings and welcome to this great land of riches and good fortune. You are smiled on among all men to be at this particular place at this particular time in history. It is a great land with great opportunity and our people are made welcome.

"I am Fan Chr'ye. It is my pleasant duty to escort you to the Meeting Hall of the Middle Kingdom, where you will register and be given temporary shelter. All questions you may have will be answered there."

Again the man bowed. "So, you will please follow me and stay close together."

Fan Chr'ye stepped down from the crate and began walking, at the head of the group, away from the wharf. Chin picked up his satchel, slung his pole over his back, and joined the single-file line that followed the representative. The group walked, almost in chain-step, past the whites who had gathered on the pier to watch them.

As Chin passed by the crowd he caught the astonished looks on the faces of both the men and women, and they no doubt saw a surprised expression on the face of many a Chinese who was as intrigued with them, a new species, as they were with him.

Chin reflected on what it was that each found so curious. To the whites it had to be the sameness of the Chinese, and to Chin it was the endless variety of the whites, their dress, their height, their features. He smiled, amused by the relativity of a world he was just starting to realize existed.

The march from the harbor to Chinatown was an auspicious one. Once within the actual confines of Chinatown the group was exposed to loud clapping and cheering from the people who scurried about the wood-planked streets.

Here things were familiar once again. Signs boasted of fresh poultry and fish for sale; silks, porcelains, and jades were displayed in the windows of shops. Tigers and dragons were suspended over shops, dispelling evil spirits. Other shopkeepers had fastened bright red *Hang Hi* banners of prosperity over their stores.

Everywhere men were shuffling back and forth through the streets, tending to their usual daily routines, and Chin felt a momentary pang of jealousy, wishing that he could be one of them, already ingrained into the system, rather than being a neophyte.

Even before they had reached the company house, Chin had noted the total absence of women in Chinatown. He was satisfied with that, feeling that his uncle was right—that adventure was a man's business and this strange new land was not a place for a woman—at least not a respectable woman.

As the group stopped in front of the Meeting Hall of the Middle Kingdom, Chin thought that if the name sounded pretentious the building certainly lived up to it. This house, in which all of the Six Companies met and in which newcomers and staff members were given residence, was the finest building in all of Chinatown. It took up fully half a block on Stockton Street.

Three stories high, it was bathed in red and gilt. The eaves of the building—arched toward the heavens to reflect back evil spirits should they descend from above—were handcarved by the most skilled artisans. At the second-story level was a great dragon, standing guard against demons.

The group filed through the gold leaf doors and followed Fan Chr'ye down a cool, narrow corridor. The interior of the building was dimly lit by an occasional oil lamp and the succulent smell of cooking rice and fish floated past Chin's nostrils, making his mouth water.

Finally the line stopped. Chin craned his neck and looked past Yang. Ahead he could see a door where the man at the front of the long line stood. Fan Chr'ye had gone inside and, in a moment, the door opened and the first man went in.

Yang turned to face his brother, sensing what questions they would be asked when they registered. "Chin, will you not reconsider?" He paused. "I would like my brother to be at my side when I make my fortune."

Chin drew a deep breath, touched by the fact that his brother was asking him, again, to join him. They had not been the closest of brothers. Their goals and desires had been too dissimilar for them to be compatible, and this was one reason that Chin knew he could not join him.

Surely, he thought, Yang must also realize that. It was a

singularly loving gesture that he should once again ask Chin to join him.

"I would only slow your quest, Yang. I would be both burden and trouble to you, and what love for each other we have would soon diminish, vanish and be replaced by hostility and contempt. This," Chin said, "you must understand."

Yang was silent for a long moment. Finally he said, "I will prosper without you, brother. I hope you will be able to do the same."

"I shall keep my wits about me," Chin replied.

"And I will pray that your wits will be adequate to sustain you in this strange land. Here," Yang said, pushing Chin in front of him. "you go before me in the line. If you are going to be a merchant you will need to get to the marketplace as soon as possible."

Chin turned to look back at his brother, surprised by his actions. "You would let me go before you?"

Yang nodded. "The gold will still be there when I get to the fields."

Chin sat in the straight-backed wooden chair and faced a dour-looking man named Mei Peng, who had identified himself as a "counselor." Mei Peng's face was creased with lines that were downcast, giving the appearance that he was in perpetual mourning.

"And what type of work do you propose to undertake, Chin? Prospecting?"

"No."

Mei Peng looked up from the form. "No?"

Chin smiled amicably. "You seem surprised."

"I am. Most all of our cousins have come for the gold." He regarded Chin for a moment, pleased for an interesting break in the drudgery of registering countless hundreds of his countrymen who came looking for nuggets the size of plums, which they had been told were lying in the streets.

"What type of work do you seek, then?"

"Perhaps commerce."

Mei Peng smiled. "You are a monied man, then?" he asked with amusement. "A man of great riches who comes to trade silks and jades?"

Chin returned the smile. "Were I a monied man I would have hired my own passage and taken a private room so as to avoid the sores that plague my body."

The counselor nodded, the smile easing from his face. "It

45

is a difficult voyage. But it is a voyage we have all made," he quickly added. "You shall recover. It is remarkable how quickly the mind can forget those experiences it chooses not to remember. So," he said, looking back down at the paper, "what is it you are interested in?"

"Perhaps an apprenticeship in an import shop."

"You would stay in the city, then?"

Chin nodded.

Again Mei Peng looked at him. "I am curious. Why would you forego the goldfields for life in the city?"

"Are you a farmer of rice, Mei Peng?"

"No," the man replied, "certainly not."

"And yet you enjoy a bowl of rice at every meal, do you not?"

Mei Peng paused in thought.

"Are you a catcher of fish?" Chin continued. "No, you are not. And yet you take your meal of fine cuttlefish and shark's fin on many an evening. So," Chin said, "I do not see it as necessary for me to dig the earth and sift the streams in order to enjoy the harvest of gold. I will let other men bring it to me."

The counselor said, "You speak the words of a man."

Chin laughed. "The voyage has aged me five cycles."

"It has been said to have that effect." Mei Peng laid his pen down and said, "I made the journey two years ago, before the news of the great strike. I suppose we tend to forget what it was like."

Chin leaned forward. "Why did you come . . . before the strike, I mean."

He regarded Chin's interest as praise and said, "I came as an employee of the Kong Chow Company. I perform several jobs for the Company. But being a counselor is one of the most rewarding. It enables me to help our cousins settle in a new land and, at the same time, maintain a sense of China in this strange country."

Mei Peng looked at Chin for a moment, then returned to his desk. He tore a small slip of paper from a pad in front of him and scribbled a lengthy note, attaching it to the form. He folded the form and placed it in an envelope.

"Take this to Room 316 on the third floor," Mei Peng said, handing the envelope to Chin.

Chin rose and bowed.

Mei Peng returned the bow. "We will talk again, soon."

Chin turned and left the room, pondering the puzzling

farewell offered by the counselor. He passed Yang outside the door.

"Where are you going?" Yang asked.

"I am being sent to another office."

"Why?"

"I do not know."

The door of Mei Peng's office opened and Yang said, "I will see you later, Chin."

"Good luck."

Chin walked down the corridor, past dozens upon dozens of men still waiting in line, and he realized that Mei Peng still had a full day's work ahead of him. At the end of the corridor he walked up two flights of stairs. At the end of another corridor he stood in front of Room 316. He knocked twice.

"Enter," a voice from inside called.

Chin walked into the office. It was considerably larger than Mei Peng's quarters. On one wall was a grand map of China. Windows lined the far wall and bookshelves took up the other two.

The man standing behind the desk had risen and was now returning Chin's greeting.

"Welcome, cousin," he said, as Chin handed him the envelope. "My name is Chang Gwo'jya. Be seated."

Chin sat in the chair across from Chang Gwo'jya's large teakwood desk. He must be a very important man, Chin reflected, to command such an office. There were many fine glass lamps and a painted silk panel that occupied one corner of the room. Also, the chair Chin sat in was not hard and straight like the one he had sat in in Mei Peng's office. This one was stuffed, padded, pleasingly comfortable, and he luxuriated in it after his long ordeal by sea.

"I trust your journey was not too uncomfortable."

Chin smiled slightly. "I have survived."

"More than that," Chang Gwo'jya said, "a man cannot ask for."

Chin regarded the man as he read the contents of the envelope. He was dressed in finery—a light blue jacket of raw silk, fastened by shiny brass shanks. His nails were like rounded almonds and had a sheen to them. Upon two of his fingers he wore large gold rings, one of which carried a sparkling emerald the size of a peach pit.

Chang Gwo'jya's head was cleanly shaven in the most fastidious manner. His queue was tightly braided and extended down across the nape of his neck, splitting his back in half and finishing halfway to his waist. Chang Gwo'jya's hair was of the darkest ebony imaginable, glowing from the application of precious oils.

Chin thought of his own appearance as he sat before this obviously important man. His own clothes were acceptable enough, having been washed, along with all the other men's, shortly before docking. His queue also had been washed, but there was no oil to be had on the ship, so it seemed dull by comparison, and he felt uneasy that his greatest source of pride was in such a poor state.

Worse, however, were the sores that covered his body. Those on his arms were hidden by his long sleeves, and the pockmarks on his legs were covered by his trousers. He moved his arm to cover the ugly festering on his right hand.

Chang Gwo'jya looked up from the note. "Your name is Chin?"

He nodded.

"Very well, Chin. Your registration form says that you are interested in commerce."

Again he nodded.

"I would like you to reconsider this." Chang Gwo'jya held his hand up for a moment. "You needn't answer today. I only ask that you reconsider it."

Chin said, "The fields have no appeal for me."

"It is not the goldfields that I suggest."

"What, then?"

Chang Gwo'jya leaned back in his leather chair. "Service to the Kong Chow Company as an employee."

Chin felt his mouth go dry from the suggestion. He was stunned, unable to speak.

"The counselor you spoke with, Mei Peng, has suggested to me that we approach you on this matter. We try to watch for bright young men who come through our doors. It is natural that we attempt to secure the brightest for employment in the Company. We are in need of astute young men, for it is a large job."

Chang Gwo'jya stood and motioned for Chin to do the same. They walked to a large map of China. Upon closer inspection Chin saw that the name of each of the Six Companies had been stenciled, in tall letters, beneath the provinces they represented.

With his finger, Chang Gwo'jya circled the provinces represented by the Kong Chow Company as he spoke. "This whole great region is the responsibility of the Kong Chow Company. All men from these provinces who immigrate to this land are our"—he turned to look at Chin—"our wards. There is an enormous job to be done in this country, Chin. Someday tens of thousands of our people will pour into the harbor you landed at this morning. It will take strong men, wise men, to make the laws in this land that will best benefit our people. They will need assistance, mediation." He shook his head as he walked back to his desk. "They will not seek out help from the American justice system. They know all too well the corruption of our *own* court system."

He continued, "They will need someone to arbitrate for them, among them, to settle their disputes. Without such an organization, without a seat of authority, chaos will reign for our people in this land.

"This, Chin, is the grand responsibility of the Kong Chow Company and the Six Companies in general—to bring, from China, along with our quest for wealth and our desire for self-fulfillment, a necessary sense of order."

Chang Gwo'jya paused, then said, "You have the opportunity to take part in this." He sat down in his chair. "Consider it, weigh it. In the morning bring your answer to Mei Peng."

Chin bowed and stood up. Chang Gwo'jya tilted his head slightly. Chin walked toward the door.

"Chin," the man said, halting him.

He turned.

"If you decide against working for the company nothing the less will be thought of you. Nothing more will be said of the matter. But if you decide to accept the offer of employment you may well discover a life that offers more challenges and fulfillment than that offered by either gold digging or commerce."

Chapter 7

Yang sat in the straight-backed wooden chair that his younger brother had occupied moments ago. The chair seemed too small for his massive body and he felt uncomfortable in it.

Mei Peng looked up from the form that lay on his desk. "Your name is Yang?"

Yang nodded.

"I see a note here that you engaged in a fight on the ship."

Yang's eyes flashed. "The man instigated it! I had only asked for a bowl of . . ."

Mei Peng raised his hand, clicking his teeth. When Yang fell silent, the counselor said, "I did not lay blame. I only asked if it was true. Your words are too quick and said in anger. Give your mind a moment to think."

Yang drew a deep breath and said, "It is true. I did have a fight."

"Now tell me why."

"I tried to get an extra bowl of rice for my sick brother and the server denied it to me."

"And you struck him?"

"Only after he prodded me with his serving ladle."

"That is all you need to say, then. You should work at harnessing that anger if you want to succeed in this country."

Yang was silent.

"Now what is your purpose in coming to California?"

"I come to harvest gold."

Mei Peng made a notation. "How much currency do you bring with you from China?"

"Twenty-five hundred *yuan*."

"You will need a subsidy to buy provisions, then."

Yang straightened with surprise. "You mean it is not enough to purchase provisions?"

Mei Peng fixed his gaze on Yang. "That sum is adequate to purchase a pan, a blanket, and two days' ration of rice. I suppose it shall take even a man of your magnitude more than two days to make his fortune."

Yang leaned back in the chair as Mei Peng continued.

"We are familiar with gold prospecting. We are more aware of what will be required of you in the fields than you are. You will be issued a standard package that will include such things as you shall need—a canteen, bowls, pouches, headgear, a tent, and other such things. The cost of these supplies shall be charged against your company account."

Yang nodded.

"As you were told in Hong Kong, the cost of your assisted passage is to be repaid from your first year's earnings. There is an additional yearly fee of eighteen American dollars to be paid by those cousins who seek prospecting work in this country. This fee may be paid to the Kong Chow Company on either a yearly or monthly basis."

"What is the purpose of the fee?"

Mei Peng regarded the young man with some measure of irritation. "Were you not taught to allow an elder to finish speaking before you yourself speak?"

Again Yang sank back into the chair.

Mei Peng made a "tsk" sound with his teeth.

Yang slightly lowered his head in supplication. "I apologize, sir. My . . . my excitement caused my tongue to be hasty."

"Very well," Mei Peng said. "The membership fee you pay will help provide the Kong Chow Company with working capital for it to better represent your interests in this country. You may have read glowing reports of the conditions here while you were in China. It may well have sounded as if the gold was being happily handed out on the street corners.

"The truth differs somewhat from this fantasy. The simple fact, cousin, is that we are foreigners, mining a white nation's resources, and someday that fact may find opposition in some quarters. Even now," Mei Peng said, "there has been a Foreign Miner's Tax imposed. Twenty dollars a year, cousin, for all non-Americans who seek to mine in this country."

"Twenty dollars a year!" Yang gasped.

"Yes," Mei Peng confirmed. "However, through the influence of the Kong Chow Company and the other companies of the Six Company union we have convinced the government officials here to look the other way where the Chinese are concerned. As a result the tax has only been imposed on Spanish, Chilean, and Indian people. So you can see that your eighteen-dollar fee has already shown you a profit of two dollars."

Mei Peng paused for a moment, growing solemn. "Additionally, this fee shall provide that if you die while in this country your bones shall be shipped back to the homeland at the Company's expense."

Yang nodded earnestly at this benefit, having no desire to be buried in a foreign land, where his enjoyment of the ever-after would be prevented. There could be no worse fate on heaven and earth, he thought, than to be denied the honor of joining one's ancestors after death.

"Finally," Mei Peng said, "I advise you to keep your personal accounts in order. As all debts between our people are mutually reported to the companies, a record is kept. At the time you wish to return to China you will report first to this house.

"The records will be checked and all debts must be satisfactorily settled before you will be granted passage. For a small fee you will then be issued a card stating that you return to China free of debt and with your dues paid. You may note that without presentation of this card to the ship you travel on you shall be refused passage."

Again Yang nodded, reflecting that the card was an effective way for the Kong Chow Company to get a final few dollars from each departing Chinaman. It amused him that the Company had no doubt made a pact with the shipping lines that the card must be presented. He was certain that the shipping lines enforced the rule because they were getting a cut of the departure tax. But Yang had been accustomed to the oppressive taxes his father paid in China. Legal extortion by the government was common in his homeland; there was no reason for things to be different here.

"Do you have any questions with regard ot these matters?"

"No," Yang answered.

"Good." Mei Peng's features softened a bit as he said, "You will want to rest for a few days after the voyage. Quarters will be provided for you within the house. There is to be no cooking in the rooms, or gambling, or bathing or smoking of opium. Thievery is severely dealt with in this house. Meals are served twice daily. All expenses you incur will be charged to your account. What services you need can be found within the boundaries of the Chinese quarter. You are advised not to venture out into the white section of the city."

Yang nodded deferentially.

"Have you any questions?"

"Where might I find a barber?"

"Two doors to the right of this house," Mei Peng replied, rising. "Remember to conduct yourself with honor and reserve in this new land, as we are all representatives of Mother China. One man's disgrace brings shame upon all his brothers."

Mei Peng paused, then said, "The dinner meal will be served at six. The morning meal is at eight." He made a note on a slip of paper and passed it across the desk to Yang. "This is your room number. Provisions and directions will be issued to you on the day after tomorrow. We expect this week's prospecting group to number around thirty, so you will not be traveling alone."

Yang picked up the piece of paper, rose, bowed, and left the room. He climbed two flights of stairs and walked down a corridor, checking for the room number. At the far end of the hall he found it and knocked on the door before entering.

Yang walked into the room. He guessed it to be ten feet by ten feet. Against one wall of the narrow, windowless room were two oil lamps, which provided the only illumination. On the far wall he saw half a dozen wooden crates containing clothing, burlap sacks, and wrapped packages.

Across the length of the opposite wall ran three tiers of wooden bunks, which provided sleeping quarters for the seven men already living in the room. Four of the men were sleeping, but three others were awake and turned to look at him as he came into the room.

The smell of their bodies was apparent in the cramped quarters of the room, and Yang was once again reminded of the sea voyage he had just completed.

"My name is Yang," he declared, his eyes on the three men, watching them. "I'm assigned to this room," he said, tossing his satchel on one of the two empty bunks in the room.

The three men lay back down on their bunks. Two of them appeared stuporous, and Yang could detect the aroma of opium in the room. The third man went back to reading a newspaper.

Cousins, Yang thought.

He undid his satchel and took out a small pocketbook, which held the money he had brought from China with him. He put the wallet in his jacket and left the room, eager to tend to his grooming needs.

As Yang opened the door of the Company house and stepped out into the San Francisco afternoon he was filled with a sudden rush of excitement. He thought about it as he walked up Stockton Street, and it suddenly struck him that this was the first time in more than three months that his activities were not being supervised by someone else. He was completely free to do as he pleased.

He smiled.

Two doors from the Meeting Hall of the Middle Kingdom he saw a squat green platform standing in front of a store. About three feet high, the four-legged platform had no top. Instead, sitting atop each of its four legs was a cluster of four small green balls, indicating that the business within was a barbershop.

Yang opened the door and entered. Against one wall the Chinese barber stood at a washbasin supported by a platform resembling the one outside. A patron sat in the chair that was provided. Yang took a seat on the long bench that lined the other wall. A wrinkled old man was asleep, snoring on the bench, waiting to be served.

The man stirred as Yang took a seat. The old man nodded a greeting and asked, "How was the passage?"

Yang, startled, said, "How can you tell?"

The old man smiled. "There are ways. Your skin whitens a bit from the confinement."

Yang touched his face.

"The sores on your hands," the old man continued. "Too, you are in need of grooming. And for that reason," he added, "I shall let you be served before me."

"That is kind of you and much appreciated."

"You would do the same for me."

Yang thought for a moment and said, "I don't think I would."

The old man regarded him with an interested expression.

"Not out of callousness," Yang quickly added. "But because I don't think I am as observant as you, old one. I would not have noticed such things as you described."

The old man nodded. "One learns to be perceptive in this land. It is one of the few weapons a wise man can arm himself with."

Yang glanced at the customer in the barber chair and saw that he was almost finished. He turned back to the old man. "How long have you been in California?"

"Almost a year."

"And what is your impression of it?"

The old man pondered the question for a long moment, then replied, "It is a land of danger and opportunity."

"To anything worthwhile there is risk."

"True. But when it is a question of strength or courage that is one matter. Here the dangers are of a different sort and much more sinister."

"Of what do you speak?"

The old man gazed into his eyes and lowered his voice. "I speak of Man. I speak of white and yellow together for the first time. I do not know how they will react—no one does—and that is why there is such danger. It may amount to nothing or it may explode in death and fury. And that is why there is danger . . . because we do not know what will happen.

"It is like taking two greatly different chemicals and mixing them blindly together in a rash experiment." The old man paused for a moment, then said, "You may develop a wondrous drug, or . . . the compound may explode as you put the pestle to the mortar."

"Next," the barber said.

Yang turned to see that the man who had been sitting in the chair had risen. He turned back to the old man, but already he had closed his eyes, drifting back to the embrace of sleep he had been in when Yang first entered the shop.

Yang rose and walked to the barber chair. The barber nodded as Yang sat down in the chair. He wrapped a bright red towel around Yang's neck and examined his scalp for a moment, noting the short black stubble. He critically examined Yang's queue.

"The old man is right," the barber said, "you are in need of grooming."

"Then get on with it, barber. That's why I'm here," Yang snapped.

The barber smiled, realizing that a shoddy appearance could render most any man short of good manners.

Yang glanced toward the old man. "Who is he?"

The barber began washing Yang's naked skull with a mild soap. "An elder of the Sam Yup Company. A very important man."

"He speaks words of fear," Yang said.

"Perhaps words of wisdom," the barber countered. "Sometimes the two are one and the same."

Yang relaxed, enjoying the sensation of the warm water on

his head. "All you men who stay in the city seem to cower behind the walls of its buildings."

The barber rinsed the soap off and then began a fresh application of lather. "You sound like a man who is heading for the goldfields."

"That is what I made that damnable voyage for."

"You would do well to remember the old man's words, then."

"In what regard?"

"About whites and yellows being an untried mixture."

"I intend to have as little to do with the whites as possible."

"That is a wise decision," the barber said. "But it may not be something over which you shall exercise complete control."

Yang suddenly felt tired, too tired to discuss the matter with the barber. This was the first time he had truly relaxed since he had left China and, though he would never have admitted it to Chin, he had found the trip exhausting.

But now, as he felt the barber's hawk-billed razor scraping over his skull, the first truly thorough shaving he'd had in many weeks of growth, he felt himself lulled into that restful state that comes with knowing that one is being revitalized.

The barber made swift, sure strokes, shaving every hair from the top of his head down to his shoulders. He completed the shaving and toweled him dry, noting with satisfaction that Yang had drifted off to sleep.

The barber unbraided Yang's queue and let it fall over the back of the chair. He took a wide-toothed comb from a cabinet and began combing out the hair. Once or twice Yang stirred, but he soon fell back asleep.

When the barber had finished combing out the queue he thoroughly washed it, rinsed it clean, and washed it again. He then towel-dried the queue and applied a generous coating of rich protective oils to it. He expertly braided the queue and worked in a final coat of oil to give it a high, glossy sheen.

The barber gently nudged Yang awake and he sat up in the chair. Now the barber pulled a long, metal rod from his cabinet. The barber inserted the curved end into Yang's ears, probing, scraping them clean of the wax that had accumulated during the months on the ship. He then selected an identical rod and probed each of Yang's nostrils. The barber completed the grooming ministration by clipping Yang's eyelashes.

56

He pulled the towel from him and Yang rose from his chair.

"Half a dollar," the barber said.

Yang dug into his pocket. "I only have *yuan*."

"Best you soon learn to pay in dollars. This is not China. You should change your *yuan* for American currency at your Company house."

Yang paid the barber and turned to leave. He saw the old man stir and nodded.

"I wish you much wealth," the old man said. He paused, then added, "And the wisdom to keep it with."

Yang turned and left the barber shop without a word.

Mei Peng was obviously pleased with Chin's decision. "I am glad you have decided to work for the Company, Chin. I believe it is a wise decision."

"I am honored that you considered me worthy of such a privilege," Chin replied.

Mei Peng leaned back in his chair, relaxed now that he had finished with the grueling task of registering the new arrivals. "My last assistant, Wa Syan Sheng, returned to China only last week, so your coming is a timely one. I trust we shall make a compatible alliance."

Chin smiled. "I am certain of it."

"Good," Mei Peng said. "Your primary duties shall be in the bookkeeping department—at least to begin with. And there is much bookkeeping to do. The Kong Chow Company has over two thousand members in this country and the number grows with each arriving ship. Each member pays dues and many pay a percentage of their earnings to repay assisted passage, as you shall."

Chin waited until he was certain Mei Peng had finished speaking before he asked, "In what manner will my work be of assistance to you, Mei Peng?"

"I am the Company's senior accountant."

Chin was impressed that he was working under a man with such lofty responsibilities.

"During times of arrival," Mei Peng continued, "I also serve as a registration counselor. There are few of us who do not serve double posts in the Company."

"And what of Chang Gwo'jya?" Chin inquired. "What is his position?"

"He sits on the Board of the General Assembly. He is both a delegate and the official interpreter of the Six Companies. It

57

is a position of great responsibility, as he is the voice of the Six Companies to the white government and people."

"I see," Chin said.

Mei Peng rose and the two men walked from the office. As they walked down the corridors of the great house, Mei Peng said, "If you prove yourself useful in bookkeeping you may become an aide to me at the meeting of the Council of the Six Companies."

"What is the Council?"

"The General Assembly," Mei Peng said as they turned a corner of another hallway, "is made up of delegates who represent the members of the Six Companies. These representatives meet in the Meeting Hall of the Middle Kingdom, in this building, there to discuss matters concerning the welfare of all our people. Resolutions are put forth and issues debated. General policies effecting all our people are enacted by the General Assembly."

"And you are one of those representatives?"

"I am privileged to serve as a representative of the Kong Chow Company."

"It is a great honor," Chin said with undisguised admiration.

As they entered a large open foyer, Mei Peng said, "And one which I carry with the utmost humility. Attached to the honor is the awesome responsibility of our people's welfare."

Mei Peng opened a set of double doors and Chin walked into the Meeting Hall of the Middle Kingdom. It was a large, semicircular room, perhaps thirty meters across. The ceiling rushed up two stories. Rows of chairs, whose arms were carved serpents, were arranged in a half-moon facing the raised platform at the front of the chamber. Upon the dais was a long table behind which were five chairs.

"Who sits on the podium?" Chin asked.

"The present directors of the General Assembly—the president, vice-president, secretary, treasurer, and the interpreter."

"How are they elected?" Chin asked, walking down the center aisle with Mei Peng.

"Each year a different Company has its turn at filling the Board of Directors—one year the Sam Yup Company, the next year the Ning Yeung Company, then the Hop Wo, the Yeong Wo, the Yun Wo, and then our company, the Kong Chow.

"The ruling company alternates from year to year so each

organization may have the opportunity to serve. This year the Yeong Wo Company sits in power."

They stopped at the front of the great hall and Chin turned to look out over the rows of chairs. He suddenly realized that he was at the heart of Chinese authority in America, that in all the world only Beijing held stronger influence over his people. He felt the excitement rush through his body like the waves that had ravaged the ship which had provided his passage from China.

"What are you thinking?" Mei Peng asked.

"I am thinking," Chin replied, "that your offer of employment was as providential as my decision to accept it was wise."

Mei Peng smiled.

Yang stood in the small room he had shared with seven other men for two nights. It had been two nights he would prefer to forget. The men were filthy, smoked incessantly, and gambled until all hours of the night. If this was the caliber of men who inhabited the city, then Chin could have them.

He gathered up his satchel and turned for the door, not bothering to bid farewell to his temporary roommates. Yang opened the door to see Chin standing before him.

Chin smiled lightly. "Was my brother going to leave without a good-bye?"

Yang left the room, closed the door and stood out in the hallway with Chin. "I was only now on my way to your room. My group leaves on the hour."

"So I heard."

"We head for Sonora," Yang said, walking down the corridor. "It lies some eighty miles east of the city."

"A considerably shorter journey than the one we made over the waves," Chin remarked.

Yang laughed. "And a more pleasant one, I trust."

"At least you shall be in the outdoors."

They walked down the stairs and reached the ground floor. The two brothers walked in silence to the front door and Yang opened it. They stepped outside and Chin looked over the group of men whom Yang would accompany. Each man wore a blue jacket and trousers. Each man carried an identical pack on his back.

Yang paused at the edge of the group. He turned to his

brother. "I do not know when I shall return to San Francisco, brother."

"I shall wait for word," Chin said. "Did you speak with Uncle Ah Wan?"

Yang nodded. "I spoke with him yesterday, before his group left. He was pleased with the ivory set of *fai-tsz* you gave him. He thanked me as well. That was a fine gesture, Chin. I have always been remiss in matters of etiquette." Yang paused, then added, "And you have always made certain to include your older brother in your thoughtfulness."

Chin said, "I will miss you, Yang."

"And I you," Yang said. He bent slightly toward Chin, rubbing his hands together. Chin returned the gesture. The two brothers looked at each other for a moment, then they both reached out at the same time, clasping each other's forearms.

"Good fortune," Chin said.

"And to you, my brother."

Then the group of men was moving away from the Meeting Hall of the Middle Kingdom, away from Stockton Street, away from Chin.

Chapter 8

"James, me boy," Brian O'Malley said, "you're lucky it's only a slug in the arm you got. Did you see what they did to poor Mead?"

"Aye." Riley nodded, recalling the Texan's bloody scalped skull. "It could have been worse, all right. But they *did* get all my gold. A month's worth of work down the creek."

As Riley walked down the road next to O'Malley he reflected that his fellow Irishman was right; it could have been worse. Riley was one of six men that escaped the carnage alive. Even now, a week after the massacre, he still had nightmares. The memory of the mangled bodies they had found after the holocaust would linger on in Riley's mind for years. Pictures of skin flayed off of arms as if the Mexicans had been skinning coons would haunt him for a long time to come. Perhaps he would always hear the screams of death and agony.

Still, Riley thought, there was the present to be concerned about. No matter how lucky he was to have escaped with his life, he still had to face the fact that he was broke. He thought of the forty-niners' motto, "California or bust." Well, he was in California, all right, but he was busted, too.

Riley shook his head. "Here we are in the middle of the biggest damned gold rush in history and neither one of us got a damned cent to our name."

"Ah," O'Malley said, "you're too much of a pessimist, Jamie. We're ahead of most of the world."

Riley turned to look at him. "And how do you figure that?"

"We're already here," O'Malley said with a smile.

They walked along in silence for a while, the countryside passing slowly by them. Finally O'Malley said, "Don't be worrying so much about it, me boy. We'll hit San Francisco by evening and then we'll see my Cousin Liam. He's a sharp boy. He'll come up with something to get us enough money to get a stake." He laughed shortly. "Before you know it we'll be back in the fields again."

"And Lord help one of them Mexican bastards if I ever see 'em again," Riley said, clenching his fist. "I'd gut 'em like I would a possum."

As it turned out, they were closer to San Francisco than they thought, and by evening they were sitting around the table in Liam Kelly's small house on the outskirts of the city. There was a family resemblance between the two cousins, Riley thought, although Kelly was a bit shorter than O'Malley. Too, they both had the same outgoing personality.

Kelly's wife, a pert red-haired colleen named Katy, rushed around the table serving the dinner of boiled steak and potatoes.

"Your wife's a good cook," Riley said, wolfing down a forkful of meat.

"Aye," Kelly said, giving her a slap on the rear. "She is that."

Riley looked at her and she smiled a sheepish smile, letting her lips part just a bit as she wiped her hands on her bosom, which strained at the seam of the cotton blouse she wore. When Riley returned the smile she dropped her eyes to the floor and returned to the kitchen.

"But cookin' isn't the subject we're all interested in, now is it?"

"Nay," Riley agreed, "you're right about that."

O'Malley shoveled down a forkful of potatoes and turned to his cousin. "Well, Liam, we've told you what happened and you know we'll be wanting to get back to the fields."

"Aye, and I wish I could be going with you. But with the wife and two kids to care for I'll be staying in the city to mind my feed business. And a good business it is, too."

"Then with business being good you'll be able to manage the money to stake us?" O'Malley asked.

"It's not *that* good. You'll be needing full provisions; horses, too, and a couple of guns, no doubt?"

O'Malley had forgotten about their need for horses and guns.

"Clothes and food and equipment, too." Kelly shook his head. "You'll both be startin' from scratch and that means complete outfitting." He paused, then said, "More money's required than I can come up with. More likely you could find someone in the city to stake you . . . for a percentage of what you make."

O'Malley put his fork down and Kelly smiled. "I know, cousin; I know that doesn't suit you." Kelly turned to look at James Riley. "Afraid our family has always been a greedy bunch, Riley. Not much of a mind to share what we make."

"Nothing strange about that," Riley said. "A man works hard, he shouldn't ought to have to share his gain."

"Well," Kelly said, turning back to his cousin, "I suppose before you add it all up it'll come to three, four hundred dollars apiece for you two to get started again."

"All right, Liam," O'Malley said, his patience finally run out. "What is it you're getting around to? I know you got something to tell me or you wouldn't be running on at the mouth like this." He said to Riley, "He's been this way ever since he was a kid."

Kelly laughed out loud. "All right, Brian; you're right as usual. I *do* have a little plan cooking. Have had it brewing for some time now, to tell the truth." He leaned closer over the table and said, "I got a way for us all to make a tidy little sum, I do. Got a way for us to have the bloody money *handed* to us on a platter."

"Well then," O'Malley said, pushing aside his plate, "let's have it, cousin."

Chapter 9

Under Mei Peng's able tutelage Chin soon mastered the principles of bookkeeping. He took to the abacus as a lark would to the air, and his speed on it became so dazzling that it was no longer than a few weeks before several of the elders started coming in at midday to watch him do his calculations. They would nod approvingly as his fingers raced faster than their eyes could follow. Mei Peng soon found that he had a prized protégé.

One autumn afternoon Chin was in the front foyer entrance of the great hall when he heard a knock at the door. He opened it to see half a dozen white faces standing before him. They were big men and their expressions were serious. When they began speaking Chin hushed them with a raised finger that Mei Peng had taught him meant "just a moment" in the white man's sign language. They walked into the hall and stood, waiting.

Chin turned and bolted down the corridor that led to Mei Peng's office.

"Mei Peng!" he said, bursting into his superior's quarters.

Mei Peng stood up from his desk. "What is it, Chin?"

"White men in the hall," he blurted.

Mei Peng walked around his desk. "Calm down. We shall see what it is that they want." As they walked out into the corridor, Mei Peng said, "Go upstairs and tell Chang Gwo'jya there are white men in the lobby. He will interpret their visit for us."

Chin, running ahead of Mei Peng, hurried down the corridor and out into the lobby. Already a group of half a dozen yellow men had formed, regarding the white visitors. Chin pushed past the group and ran upstairs to Chang Gwo'jya's office on the third floor.

Minutes later Chin trailed behind the Six Companies' official interpreter as he walked down the stairs. Chin stood at his side as he spoke the white man's language. Chin listened intently, listened to the jumble of words as they ran together.

Once in a while he could pick out a word he knew: "China-man," "Chinese," "pay," "dollars." But for the most part it was unintelligible, and he stood in awe of Chang Gwo'jya, who perfectly understood this language that was infinitely more complex than Chin had imagined it would be.

At length the white men grew silent and Chang Gwo'jya turned to his cousins. "It seems," he began, "that the California government has enacted an Alien Registration Tax to be paid by all nonresidents of the state. These men are tax collectors."

"How do we know this?" one of the elders asked.

"They have shown me the proper identification. They have government badges of office. They are here to collect the tax today from each member living in this house. It is a one-time tax of five dollars."

There was a rustling among the men at the size of the tax, but Chang Gwo'jya said with a shrug, "There is nothing we can do. It is an act of law and we must comply. Go to your rooms, get the money, and return here. The collectors will enter each of your names in their books and you will be issued a government receipt."

The elders of the house began moving for the stairs, but there was just a moment's hesitation on the part of some of the younger members.

Chang Gwo'jya was quick to chastise. "*Go*," he ordered. "It is better that you pay here than they approach you in the city streets. There your treatment shall not be so mild."

With that all the men moved toward the stairs. In minutes a long line had formed in the foyer and one by one the men who lived in the Meeting Hall of the Middle Kingdom filed past the tax collectors. One of the white men received the money and placed it in a strongbox. The man next to him entered the payee's name in a ledger and issued a receipt. A man stood behind the two seated men, obviously the figure in charge. The three remaining men appeared to be guards, and as Chin filed past and paid his tax he caught a glimpse of short, ugly-looking clubs tucked in each of the three men's waistbands.

By noon the next day Chin had all but forgotten about the incident involving the tax men. While the five dollars he had been obliged to pay would leave a dent in the salary the Kong Chow Company paid him, he realized that it was only a temporary one.

64

Chin was receiving a good wage, twenty dollars a month; his expenses were low and he was able to save a portion of his salary each week. While he knew that it was not the kind of salary that would make him a rich man, he also knew that there were important contacts that he could make through his labors for the Kong Chow Company. He felt they might well pay dividends one day.

He made a final entry in the ledger before him, pushed aside his abacus, and rose from the small desk in the office he shared with four other clerks. He smiled as his belly growled and he walked from the room.

Outside he was greeted by the thousand smells of Chinatown. The air was alternately enticing and repulsive, as aromas of cooking chestnuts and rice and the stench of lodging houses without facilities fought for space in the air.

As he walked down crowded Stockton Street, Chin reflected that if a Chinese was blindfolded in Hong Kong and taken on a voyage and not unblinded until he arrived in Chinatown, he might well guess that he had only been taken to another city along the coast of China. For there was nothing here to tell a man that he was in America. Here the language, signs, and customs were Chinese.

Like Hong Kong, the streets of San Francisco were filled with all manner of squalor and garbage. Fishheads, rags, broken bottles littered Stockton Street. But never would a man see so much as a single piece of paper with Chinese writing on it. It was one of Chin's great moments of shock when he first saw the streets of white San Francisco—during his march from the wharf to Chinatown—littered with American newspapers. To a Chinese, he thought, it was absolute sacrilege to so profane paper with writing on it, for written characters were the sacred vessels of communication which the revered prophets of the past had chosen to transmit their wisdom.

Chin dug his hand into his pocket, feeling the three dollars that jingled there. It was a large sum for him to carry, but he had learned that Mei Peng's birthday was coming soon and he wanted to buy his employer a present.

His thoughts were interrupted by a commotion going on between two Chinese and three whites. Chin looked around and saw that bystanders were scattering in all directions. The two Chinamen talked rapidly between themselves, neither of them understanding a word the whites were saying.

Instinctively, Chin walked toward where the white men

65

were talking. They were tall and muscled, and though they appeared belligerent, they were making a serious effort to explain themselves to the Chinamen through sign language.

Chin stayed near the fringe of the group and listened, trying to pick up a word or two. Finally, he caught it: "Pay money."

He rushed forward, cutting through the two Chinese and standing before the whites, who turned their attention on him. He dug into his pocket and produced a tax receipt he had received the day before. He showed it to the white men and they began nodding wildly.

Chin turned to the two Chinese. "They are tax collectors. There is a five-dollar Alien Registra—"

But before he could finish the sentence one of the Chinese bolted down the street faster than a rabbit. Now Chin could feel rough hands on him, grabbing him about the neck. He turned to see that one of the men was holding the other Chinese.

"Yellow heathen bastards," James Riley said, holding tightly as one man squirmed in his grip. O'Malley and Kelly held on to Chin's arms, but Chin stayed limp, thinking it best not to fight them.

"Tax!" Riley shouted at the man he held in his grip. "Pay tax!"

Still the man squirmed. The man turned to Chin and said, "I have no money. I have no money. Make them understand this, cousin."

Chin gestured with his hands and O'Malley and Kelly loosened their grip, though still not letting go of him altogether. Chin showed them his open palms, shaking his head. He pointed at the man Riley held in a stranglehold and said, "No can pay. No money."

"*You,* then!" Riley declared, pointing his finger at Chin.

Again Chin dug into his pocket and this time he produced the receipt showing that he had already paid the registration tax. O'Malley grabbed the paper and tore it up. It was at this point that Chin began to doubt that they were tax agents. Surely an agent would honor a receipt that had been issued by the government.

He stood there, feeling O'Malley and Kelly's constricting grip on his arms. He struggled, his mind working, trying to remember the English word.

"*Badge!*" he finally blurted. "Badge, badge!"

Riley smiled, looking at Kelly. "We got us a smart little Chink here, don't we, boys?" He turned his gaze back to Chin again. "You pay his tax—you pay!"

Chin shouted louder. "Badge, badge!"

"Turn 'em around," Riley ordered. "We'll show these yellow scum who needs a badge."

The three men spun the two Chinese around so their backs were to each other. Riley glanced up and down the deserted street, seeing if anyone dared watch them. His gaze shot to a second-story window and shutters were quickly slammed shut. He grabbed each Chinaman's queue and tied the long strands of hair together in a thick double knot.

"You pay?" Riley asked once more.

"Badge," Chin replied and now the other Chinese joined him in the bleating, though he didn't know what the word meant.

"Let 'em go," Riley said and O'Malley and Kelly did let the two men go.

They ran in opposite directions, jerked to a halt as the knot of hair pulled tighter. Each man gave out a yelp of pain as the queue pulled taut against his scalp. As the man fell to the ground, Chin tumbled after him, pulled down by the bondage between their hair.

Riley towered over the two men. "You pay his tax," he said to Chin.

O'Malley and Kelly pulled them to their feet and Chin said, "No can pay."

Riley and Kelly answered by winding up and slamming their fists into the two men's mouths, sending them back to the ground again. Chin rose slowly, tasting blood in his mouth. The other man spit out a tooth.

Chin had no sooner risen then he felt a knee jammed into his stomach and he doubled with pain. The blow that followed on the base of his neck felt like a load of bricks and he fell, for the third time, to the ground. This time the knot of hair came undone.

He looked up through teary eyes, rubbing his hand across the crimson river that flowed from the corner of his mouth.

"You pay tax," Riley glared, both his massive hands clenched into fists.

Slowly, pain still lancing through his body, Chin reached into his pocket and gave the men all he had—three dollars. Riley kicked him out of gratitude, pocketed the coins, and then moved down the street with O'Malley and Kelly in search of fresh victims.

Mei Peng looked up from his desk as Chin walked into his office. The senior accountant jumped from his chair as he saw blood covering Chin's mouth.

"What happened, Chin? What has happened to you?"

Chin stumbled to a chair and slumped into it. "I . . . I was beaten," he stammered. "By three white men."

"Beaten?" Mei Peng said, coming to his side. "For what reason were you beaten?"

"Taxes," Chin said, his hands clamping onto the arms of the chair to keep them from shaking.

Mei Peng opened the door of his office and called to one of his assistant bookkeepers. "Shao Kow, bring water, a bowl, and a cloth. Hurry!"

Mei Peng turned back to Chin. "Taxes, you say. But you paid your taxes only yesterday."

Chin nodded. "I know. I tried to explain that to them."

"Tax collectors?"

"So they said. I do not believe they were, though."

Shao Kow, who was one of Chin's roommates, came into the room with the things Mei Peng had sent him for. "Chin," he said, startled, "what has happened to you?"

"A band of whites fell upon me, extorting money from my pockets."

"Slow down," Mei Peng said, taking the bowl from Shao Kow. "What makes you think they were not legitimate tax collectors, Chin?"

"They failed to produce the badges I asked them for."

"They spoke Chinese?" Shao Kow asked.

"No," he said, looking at his roommate. "I speak a little English."

Mei Peng arched an eyebrow, but decided not to pursue the matter at this time. "They approached you on the streets?"

"Actually," Chin said as Mei Peng dabbed at his mouth with the damp cloth, "they were speaking with two other men as I happened by. I understood that they were seeking payment of taxes. When I explained this to my cousins one of them turned and ran. The three whites grabbed and held us." Chin shook his head. "The poor man had no money and could not pay. I tried, as best as I could, to explain this and they said I would have to pay. It was then that I asked them to produce badges."

Mei Peng shook his head, dipping the cloth in the bowl of water to rinse it out. "You asked them to produce badges?"

"Yes. I saw the badges the tax collectors displayed yesterday. These men had none. It was then, Mei Peng, that they became greatly angered and began to beat us unmercifully."

"*Fan quay!*" Shao Kow exclaimed.

Mei Peng turned to his assistant. "White devils, indeed. If Chin had not interfered he would not have been involved in this affair."

Chin straightened in the chair. "But I have been taught to consider men of my Company to be my cousins. This man was—"

"This man was fighting a tiger," Mei Peng interrupted. "Were your real cousin battling a saber-toothed cat would you have jumped in as quickly?"

"No . . . but I did not know the men were . . ."

"And that was where you made your mistake. You compounded it, no doubt, by refusing to pay the money they asked from you?"

"Yes, but they were not . . ."

"All the more reason. You should have given them the money when they first requested it."

"Why?"

Mei Peng finished cleaning Chin's mouth. "Did it profit you to refuse them? Did it profit you to question them?"

Chin bent his head.

"Only to the extent of a split lip. And for what? You ended up giving them the money anyway, didn't you?"

"But they were villains," Shao Kow said, "robbers!"

Mei Peng turned to Shao Kow. "Of what matter is it if they are tax collectors or robbers? They are one and the same and the sooner you and Chin learn this the wiser you shall be."

Chin asked, "Am I to pay every white man who stops me and asks for money?"

"No," Mei Peng said, "that is not the point. The point is that you made the mistake of approaching them. The fool who places his hand in the tiger's mouth deserves the wound he will surely receive." Mei Peng smiled. "I'll make a wager it's a mistake you shall not make a second time."

Chin nodded. "You would win that wager."

"It is good that you are a smart young man," Mei Peng

said. He turned to Shao Kow. "That you are *both* smart young men. Intelligence will serve you in good stead. But to survive in this land you must also develop a pair of swift legs.

"You have learned a valuable lesson, Chin. 'When the white man comes, the yellow man runs.' Prejudice has been a fact of life since earliest times—whether it is class prejudice or national prejudice or race prejudice. We can never hope to overcome it."

Mei Peng looked at Shao Kow. "The most we can ever hope to do is make ourselves tolerable to the white man, to become so meek and submissive that we are allowed to extract our fortune from this country with a minimum of pain and discomfort to ourselves."

Chin frowned at the unavoidable wisdom of Mei Peng's words. Smiling, Mei Peng said, "Learning to accept the inevitabilities of life comes more easily as one grows older."

Chapter 10

James Riley glanced at the candle on the nightstand. It was past midnight. Riley wasn't sleepy. Aside from the fact that he was excited about getting on the road in the morning, there were other things on his mind this night—things he hadn't shared with his friend Brian O'Malley or with Liam Kelly. Least of all Liam Kelly, Riley thought, and smiled in the dimly lit room.

Then, for a moment, his thoughts turned to money matters. Kelly had been right about the scam—he'd had a way to have the money practically handed to them on a platter, all right. Posing as tax collectors was a master stroke, Riley thought. The Chinese were simple fools, scared as yellow as their skin. They were easy pickings and, except for the one Chink they'd encountered this afternoon, most of them forked over the money without so much as a whimper.

He thought about the young Chinaman who'd dared to question them earlier, who'd actually asked them for a badge! Riley laughed. He'd enjoyed the sport, tying up the heathens' braids and then giving them a sound beating. Little yellow bastards had no business being here anyway, Riley thought.

Kelly's ploy had netted them close to a thousand dollars in just a few weeks. Between himself and O'Malley they'd have close to seven hundred—more than enough to stake themselves to equipment and food to go out into the fields again.

Riley's thoughts were interrupted by a tapping at his door. He sat up in bed, naked to the waist.

"Aye?"

He watched the knob slowly turn and then listened as the heavy wooden door creaked open. Katy Kelly stood in the doorway, the light from the candle on Riley's table dancing on her, outlining her long legs that were now visible through the sheer nightgown she wore. She closed the door and stood there, the rise of her full breasts peeking above the deep cut of the bodice of her gown. She smiled, her eyes glowing with excitement as Riley threw back the sheets.

"I was beginning to wonder if you'd make it, lass."

Katy jumped into the bed with him and drew close. "I didn't think he'd ever fall asleep. And after all the ale he drank to celebrate."

Riley turned to her. "He's out now?"

She smiled widely. "Like a light."

Riley mashed his lips against hers and Katy responded by letting her mouth part to his probing tongue. His hands snaked beneath her gown and grabbed roughly for her breasts, kneading them.

She broke the kiss. "Easy, lover, easy. Treat a lady nice." She laughed a short laugh, her voice husky now. "We've got all night. No need to rush."

Again Riley's lips sought hers and he could feel her silky legs as they thrashed against his own, winding about them like two slithery vines. Her hands rushed up and down his flanks, pausing at his loins to squeeze, tease.

Riley brushed his calloused hands over her thighs. She let them part to his explorations and in moments she began to moan as his fingers entered her womanhood. Katy tossed her head back, her mouth open, sounds of ecstasy coming forth as her body undulated with pleasure.

Riley swung over on top of her as the door burst open.

"*Bastard!*" Liam Kelly shouted, standing spread-legged in the doorway, a six-gun in his hand. His eyes were wide with rage as he looked at Katy struggling in the bed sheets. "And you, you whore!" He raised the pistol, pulling back on the hammer.

"Wait a minute," Riley said, sitting tangled in the sheets. "Just a minute, Kelly!"

"There's no more minutes left for you, Riley. You'll both burn in hell," he cried, aiming the weapon. Then the bottle crashed across the back of his skull. Liam Kelly stood there for a moment, the gun still in his hand. Then his knees buckled and he fell to the ground.

Brian O'Malley stepped into the room. He looked at Riley in bed with his cousin's wife. "A fine fix we're in now, Jamie."

"Aye," Riley admitted, sitting up in the bed. "Thinking with me cock has always been me one fault in life." He turned to look at Katy and she smiled sheepishly. He turned back to O'Malley. "Sorry about all this, Brian."

O'Malley bent to look at his cousin. "Nothing wrong with having a romp," he said. "Hell, me an' Katy had that the first night we was here."

Surprised, Riley turned to look at her again and her eyes dropped demurely.

"What you should try to do," O'Malley scolded, "is at least try to keep it quiet enough that all San Francisco doesn't get woke up by it."

Riley tossed the sheets off. "What'll we do now?"

"Get our tails out of here, I suppose."

Riley turned to look at Katy as he gathered up his clothes. "What about you?"

"I'll be all right," she said, pulling the covers up about her neck in a strange sort of sudden modesty. "Sweet of you to ask, love; but it isn't the first time he's caught me."

She laughed, looking at her husband out cold on the floor. "I've caught the old son of a bitch *myself* a couple of times. He'll give me a bit of a spanking, I suppose."

Riley noted what he could swear was a slight curl of anticipation on her lips at the thought of the whipping at her husband's hands.

"But things will be all right in a week or so," she continued. Her voice lowered a bit, growing husky. "I'll make it up to him."

By dawn they were twenty miles from San Francisco. Riley was riding a brown mare and O'Malley was astride a fine palomino. A black pack mule trailed behind them.

"I don't suppose your cousin's going to take too kindly to us borrowing these horses from his barn."

O'Malley laughed. "We left him money for them."

"Yeah." Riley guffawed. "Fifty bucks."

"I reckon he'll get over it. We hit a mother lode and I'll make it right by him, all right."

"Me, too," Riley offered.

O'Malley turned to look at him. "Jamie, I think the best way you can make it up to him is if you take different lodgings if we go back to San Francisco."

It was sundown when Riley and O'Malley made it to the Feather River placer just south of Oroville. Riley didn't know who was more worn out, him or the horses.

Four men stood in the road, blocking their path, shotguns lazily slung over their shoulders or balanced on their knees. This was the second placer they'd come across today. At the first one, the Younger site, they'd been turned away; too many men working the site. But the men had told them to try the Feather River. They'd heard they were charging newcomers to come in, but at least they were still letting them in.

As Riley pulled up on the reins he felt a gnawing worry in the pit of his stomach, brought about by the fear that they wouldn't be allowed in here either. He glanced up at the sky. Storm clouds were gathering fast and he had the feeling that he was going to be wet very soon. Yet he'd happily bear it all if he at least knew that he and O'Malley would have a placer to work.

The man who approached them was an old-timer with a straggly gray beard. He carried his shotgun over his shoulder and smiled as the pair drew close.

"Howdy, gents."

Riley nodded. "We come to do panning, old-timer."

"Well," he said, exposing the gap between his front teeth, "I 'spose you know we're chargin' to get in. Times is tough and good placers are gettin' hard to come by. It's the only way we can limit things." He shrugged his shoulders. "Otherwise we'll have two, three hundred no-'counts here by next week and there won't be 'nuff gold to make it worth it."

"Makes sense, I guess," Riley said.

"Leastwise," the old-timer went on, "this way you know you're in a good camp, with a saloon, a proper barber, and enough protection to guard against the likes of them Mexican devils. Gettin' somethin' for your money, anyway."

"Okay," O'Malley said, "you got us sold. All we want to do now is get some grub and bed down for the night."

"Good enough," the old man said. "That'll be fifty bucks to get in."

Riley dug into his pouch and tossed down an eagle and two double eagles. The old man looked at the coins and then back up at Riley.

"That's fifty a head."

"Fifty a *head*?"

The smile remained on the old man's face, but the three men behind him edged forward, drawn by the tone of Riley's voice.

"That's right, friend; fifty a head."

Riley frowned, then lowered his voice a degree in respect for the four shotguns the men had between them. "We heard tell it was twenty-five a head."

"Where'd you hear that?"

"At Younger," O'Malley offered.

The old man spit expertly. "That's last week's news. News travels kinda slow around here." He gave a short chortle. "No reg'lar mail service up here, ya see. Anyway, the price's gone up. They figure they had to raise it to meet overhead."

"Overhead?"

The old-timer looked to Riley. "Yep. They needed full-time security guards. Used ta have everyone in the camp takin' shifts, but it got so's they'd ruther be down at the placer panning. Gettin' too old for that stuff myself, so I hired out as a full-time guard with the others," he said, pointing over his shoulder at the three men with him.

Riley looked at the other men. As they drew closer he could see that they were all up in years. He turned to O'Malley.

"Well?"

O'Malley shrugged. "Guess this is as good as anyplace. Hell, by the time we get to another placer it's liable to be a hundred dollars a head."

The old man laughed, slapping his thigh. "Probably right about that, friend."

Riley dug into the pouch and tossed down the coins. The old man put them in his pocket, lowered his weapon to his side and said, "Good luck, partner. Hope you strike it rich."

Riley and O'Malley moved past the four men and down the road.

"Say," the old man called, "when you see the cook you tell him to send our supper out. We're hungry as polecats."

Riley nodded.

The two men slowly walked their horses down the road and around a bend, their minds occupied with thoughts of baked beans and fried beef. In the distance Riley could make out the rushing water of the Feather River. They rode up over a small rise and pulled their horses to a stop, looking at the river below.

O'Malley turned to look at his partner. "Riley?"

Riley looked over the site, looked at the banks of the river. "Something's wrong, here."

"Jamie," O'Malley said, a quiver in his voice, "what's going on?"

Riley shook his head, looking at the deserted banks of the Feather River where not a tent stood and not a man was to be seen.

"I don't know," he said, and then he dug his spurs deep into his horse's ribs and was off down the slope toward the river, O'Malley following behind.

Riley pulled his horse to a stop less than twenty yards from the river and jumped to the ground. He looked at the earth. There were footprints, clods of upturned earth, evidence that men had been there not long ago. He looked around, looked in both directions, but there was no sign of life as far as he could see.

"Worked out," Riley finally said.

"Huh?"

Riley kicked the earth with his boots. "The damned placer's been worked out. They milked the Feather dry." He turned to look at O'Malley. "Ain't no more gold to be got from these waters."

"How . . . how do you know that?" O'Malley stammered.

Riley glared at him. "If there was there'd be people around here panning, wouldn't there? You see any panners, O'Malley?"

"No."

"They broke camp . . . moved on."

"But those guards . . . the ones who . . ."

"The ones who took our money?" Riley interrupted. Bunch of old con men who didn't have the guts to call us in a robbery. They worked a con on us, O'Malley."

"Well I'll be damned."

"They're probably halfway to Texas or Nevada or some

other worked-out placer where they can pull the same scam again."

"Bastards!" O'Malley bellowed. "They got our hundred bucks!"

"Aye," Riley said.

O'Malley slumped into a crouch. "Well, what are we going to do now? We ain't got hardly any money left."

Riley shook his head. "Seems to me there just ain't no way to make an honest living out here, Brian. You try to do some honest prospecting and a bunch of Mexican devils like Murietta cut you to ribbons. You try to find a placer to work and some old con men squeeze you for what you got left.

"Looks to me like they're right—the only way to make it out here is with your muscles or your brains." He looked up at O'Malley. "I think it's time we stopped givin', Jamie. I think it's time we started doin' some takin'."

Chapter 11

Chin was working furiously. The meeting of the General Assembly of the Six Companies was called for noon, and if he was to attend he wanted to have the full day's work out of the way so he could show Mei Peng that he could handle this new responsibility without having his regular duties suffer.

His morning's work was interrupted at a few minutes before ten when Mei Peng entered the room where Chin worked with Shao Kow and two other accounting clerks. The young men all stood as the senior accountant walked into the room.

"Chin," Mei Peng said, "may I see you in my office for a moment?"

Chin nodded. "Certainly." He gave a quick glance to Shao Kow as he followed Mei Peng out of the work room.

"Have a seat," Mei Peng said when they were in his office.

Chin did.

"I understand," Mei Peng began, "that you have mastered a number of English words."

"I . . ."

The senior accountant smiled. "Please be at ease, Chin. There is nothing for yout to fear. It is true that you have learned some of the words of the whites, then?"

"Only because I thought it would help me in this land."

"Indeed it may. There is no reason for you to make an excuse for that wise decision. How did you come to learn the English you know?"

"My uncle Ah Wan taught me some of the words on the voyage over. He was a merchant in Hong Kong and thus came in contact with the British. Though I must hasten to add my knowledge of the language is limited to only a dozen or so words."

"Would you like to expand that knowledge?"

Chin was surprised at the question. "Expand?"

"Would you like to learn English?"

"I . . . yes, I would."

"You will have the opportunity."

"How?"

"A class is being taught in this house. It is a new service being offered to us by the Society for Sino-American Relations. This society is a benevolent organization run by the whites."

"You want me to learn English?"

"Yes," Mei Peng said. "It may prove helpful. The more people we have who understand this language, the better our people will be informed of the events swirling about them."

Chin had the feeling Mei Peng had other motives, but decided not to press the issue. If his benefactor wanted him to learn English then he would. It was an added blessing that he was being directed to do something he had always wanted to do.

"It seems it is not an easy language to master," Mei Ping went on. "The size of the classes will be limited so the students will learn quickly. There will only be two young men from each company in the class. With only twelve students you should be able to progress quickly."

Chin bowed. "I am honored that you would think of me in this matter."

"Very well," Mei Peng said, rising from his chair. "Hurry or you shall be late for your first class. It meets on the hour."

"On the hour?" Chin caught himself, embarrassed at having shouted. "I beg your pardon, honorable sir. It is just that I have so much work still to do before the meeting at noon. I wanted to—"

"I know what you wanted to do. Shao Kow will finish your work this day."

Chin's face fell a bit.

The look was not lost on Mei Peng. "Don't worry, it is only this day you shall be excused from your ordinary duties. And I will remember that it is I who so directed you. In the future," Mei Peng joked, "you will be expected to bear all your responsibilities."

Chin smiled in return.

"Now go quickly. Room 208."

"Yes, Honorable Mei Peng," he said, bowing. "Thank you, sir, thank you."

Chin sat in Room 208 with eleven other young Chinese. The room was fairly large and had the luxury of a window that overlooked Stockton Street. Twelve chairs had been provided and the men talked among themselves about what to expect.

Chin turned as he heard the door of the room open and suddenly he forgot about the other men in the room, about everyone and everything except the woman who now stood in the doorway.

She was tall, lithe, and possessed of skin that was like that of the fine porcelains he had seen in the windows of shops on Dupont Street. Her hair was flaxen and piled up on her head like soft mounds of silk. She had lips like gently tied bows, and just to look at them made his heart race.

The woman's eyes were brown and large, larger than any eyes he had ever seen before. He felt that he could get lost in those eyes, that he was lost in them and never wanted to return to the real world; he wanted to dwell in them for all the days of his life.

He loved her in that moment; before he knew her name, before he heard her speak, before she was even aware of his existence. It was a moment of pure love, and for all the years of his life he would cherish it and be grateful for having known it.

Then she smiled and said, "My name is Rebecca Ashley."

Whole minutes passed without his being aware of them. It was as if he was suspended in limbo, totally entranced by this Rebecca Ashley.

He had seen white women before, on the docks and occasionally when they visited a shop in the Chinese quarter. They were very unlike the women he knew of. Their faces were powdered and they wore elaborate contrivances on top of their heads that seemed to serve no useful purpose. But this woman was unlike them . . . incredibly so. She was a creature of such stunning beauty that he reeled from her impact.

"And what is your name?" she asked, and Chin realized that she was speaking to him, sending him into paroxysms of shock all over again. It was as if a dream was molding to his will, that she stood before him, looking into his eyes, actually *talking* to him.

"Your name?" she repeated, smiling, and Chin was thrust back into reality by the fact that she was speaking Chinese. He felt the layers of the dream strip away as he thought about how strange it was to hear this woman speak his tongue.

"Chin," he managed to answer with a tongue that felt as if it had swollen ten times in his mouth.

"Chin?"

"Chin Wong," he finished.

"Why do you want to learn English?"

"You speak such perfect Chinese," he said and drew laughter from the rest of the class. He felt his face flush, growing warm as he remembered that they were not alone. "I'm sorry. I did not mean to . . ."

She laughed with the others and the sound of that laughter was almost too beautiful to bear, like the laughter of angels.

"You don't have to apologize for a compliment, Chin. I thank you for it. And I hope to be able to teach you to speak my language as well as I speak yours."

He fought to regain his bearing, remembering now that Mei Peng had sent him to this class to learn a skill, not to fall in love. He would learn that skill, would make Mei Peng proud of him. Learning from a goddess was something he would have to contend with.

"I shall endeavor to learn it. I will work hard toward that end," he said.

Rebecca paused before his chair. "But you haven't answered my question yet. Why do you want to learn English."

"Be—because I wish to someday own and engage in commerce in this great country. I think knowing your language will help me in that."

"Indeed it shall," she said. "Commerce. You would be a merchant, then?"

He nodded.

" 'Merchant,' " she said in English, the word sounding odd and choppy to him. She drifted back to Chinese. "Do you know what that word means?"

"No."

"It is the English word for the profession you seek. See if you can say it. 'Merchant.' "

"Meer-shant."

"Good," she beamed. "Very good. 'Merchant.' "

"Mer-shant."

"Very good." She turned to the rest of the class. "Today, gentlemen, we are going to concentrate on basic conversation. We want to work toward being able to greet someone, ask how they are, bid them good day. Vital to learning any language are three words—please and thank you. Let's practice these basics, then."

Rebecca walked to the front of the classroom and said, "In English we greet someone with 'Hello.' Let's all try that. 'Hello.' "

The hour was over far too soon to suit Chin. Like a zephyr, she was gone before he knew it, and her departure left a dull ache in the pit of his stomach. He looked down at his notepad and saw that he had written only a few notes, and the meaning of even these was unclear to him.

Concentration had eluded him. He could not go on like this. He would never learn English. He frowned as he sat alone in the classroom. And he was never going to share love with this woman. That had been fantasy, to imagine that anything could be between them. It was childish and he chastised himself for the moment of infatuation he had had when she first entered the room.

He had a job to do and he would do it. He would learn English better than anyone else in the class, better even than Chang Gwo'jya, he thought, amazed at his bravado.

To do this he would have to learn to function with this Rebecca woman. He would have to put aside the foolish notions he had felt for her. And they *were* foolish, nothing but nonsense, and now he was surprised that his logical mind had ever even allowed such thoughts to creep in. Where did such things come from?

And then he felt a pang in his chest as he realized that in just one week he would again spend an hour in this room with her.

He jumped to his feet. "Begone, troublesome thoughts! Begone and do not seek to hinder my path of learning again."

Chin took an early lunch. He was finished by eleven-thirty, leaving himself a full half hour to go to the barber for a proper grooming, pick up his freshly cleaned clothes from the laundry, and have time to dress.

He walked back to the Six Companies' building at twelve o'clock and went to the small room on the second floor that he shared with the three other accounting clerks. Four bunks lined the walls of the room; one chair was the only other furniture. Like the other young men he shared the room with, Chin stored his clothes and personal effects in a long, flat box he kept under his bed.

Shao Kow was in the room when Chin entered it, consuming a large bowl of rice. He watched as Chin laid his clean clothes on his bunk and then said, "You are most fortunate to become Mei Peng's Council aide after so short a time. It is indeed an honor."

"I pray it is one I shall be worthy of."

"If what I hear about you is true then you shall rise to the task."

Chin turned to look at his friend. "What do you hear about me?"

"It is said that you learned the abacus with lightning speed."

"That is a craft, not a skill."

"And yet you impressed Mei Peng during your interview enough to be selected as his assistant."

"Were you not also selected as an accounting clerk?"

Shao Kow nodded. "Yes, but I am no chess master."

"A chess master?" Chin laughed. "I am no master."

"And yet it is said that you are the best of the young men in this house at the game."

"I learned at an early age."

"A master of strategy. A shrewd and cunning player."

Chin felt his face grow hot under the praise. "You talk too much sometimes, Shao Kow."

Shao Kow smiled. "Deserved praise does not satisfy you?"

"Chess is but a game."

"Fortunately for you it is a game that Mei Peng puts great store in."

Chin turned to look at him, waiting for an explanation.

"Mei Peng was the grand chess master of Shanghai when

he attended school in that city. Your prowess apparently has impressed him. He places importance on the ability to play the game. It is said that the General Assembly's business is not all that dissimilar from the game itself. No doubt this helped in making his decision to select you as his Council aide."

"The gods have smiled on me in this."

"Make certain that you take advantage of it," Shao Kow said, and then he went back to his rice.

Chin walked from the room and tramped down the stairs to the main floor. He walked down another narrow corridor and opened a door at the rear of the house which led to the basement. Chin walked down the dimly lit steps, the foul odor assaulting him as he descended.

At the bottom of the stairs he came to the dirt floor and he began to breathe through his mouth. He glanced at the torch on one of the walls as he made his way along the path. At the rear of the expansive cellar he came to the trench dug in the earth.

Chin lowered his trousers, relieved himself, and pulled his pants back up. He turned and picked up the shovel that was stuck into the earth floor of the basement and tossed three spadefuls of dirt down into the trench, which served as the sanitary facilities for the Meeting Hall of the Middle Kingdom.

Then he quickly made for the stairs and went back up to his room so he could dress for the meeting that was now only five minutes away.

Chin knocked on the double doors which were covered with fine green leather. A towering Chinese, the largest Chin had ever seen, opened the door. The man was dressed in light blue trousers and jacket, and about his waist was a red sash. Chin instantly recalled that Yang had once told him that a red sash was an indication that a man had taken the life of an opponent in a martial arts contest.

"What do you want, cousin?" the man asked.

"I am to attend the meeting."

The guard looked skeptically at him. "What is your name?"

"Chin Wong. I am Mei Peng's new Council aide."

The guard picked up a folder and looked down a list of names while Chin prayed that Mei Peng had given word that he had a new Council aide, that his name would be on the list. Chin's eyes fell to the long ceremonial scimitar that rode on the guard's leg, the blade catching the glint from the hundreds of lanterns within the hall.

The guard looked up. "Very well, cousin. You may enter."

As Chin walked into the great hall, the cacophony of scores of different voices competing to be heard assaulted his ears. The conversational tone of the voices allayed his fear that he was late for this, his first meeting.

He looked about at the red lacquered walls rising up two stories, looked at the row after row of chairs in which sat the representatives of the Six Companies. He regarded the delegates—six from each company—and it occurred to him that no mandarin could wear finer garments than these delegates wore. For a moment he was shamed by his poor blue work clothes.

But as he continued to survey the room he saw that the delegates' assistants, young men like himself, also wore humble clothes, and he was consoled by the fact that he fit in with those of his station.

Up on the dais at the front of the great hall, seated behind a long table, were the five directors of the General Assembly. In the middle of the table sat Lao Wen, the current president of the Assembly. To his right was Chang Gwo'jya. The official interpreter was busy at work, his eyes racing over scores of notes spread out before him, as though he was oblivious to all the activity in the hall.

Finally, Chin spotted Mei Peng seated on the main floor. The senior accountant was discreetly waving to attract his attention. Chin smiled and walked toward him.

"Sit here," Mei Peng said, indicating the chair to the right of his own. "You shall find pen and paper in the pocket of your chair. Make notes of everything you think is of importance. That which you consider unimportant and irrelevant you may leave out of your notes. We shall see how perceptive your selections are."

Chin nodded, waiting for further orders.

Mei Peng noted his expression. "You have a question?"

"Is that all I am to do?"

"If you do that much well I shall be both pleased and surprised," Mei Peng said, an edge to his voice.

Chin lowered his eyes, unprepared for the rebuke. As he sat down he heard a gavel in the distance and he looked up to see Lao Wen, at the podium, rapping the Assembly to order.

What impressed Chin immediately was the speed with which silence raced through the auditorium. Where moments earlier half a hundred voices rang together, now there was only the echo of the president's gavel. Chin glanced around at the rows of chairs and saw the total attention the delegates were giving Lao Wen.

"This emergency meeting of the General Assembly of the Six Companies is called to order," the white-bearded president said. His voice carried to every corner of the hall. "I, Lao Wen, chairman of the Yeong Wo Company, preside as the duly appointed president of this Council in this year during which the delegates of the Yeong Wo Company humbly serve their term as directors of the Assembly."

Chin recalled that Mei Peng had told him that each year the ruling officers stepped down and the delegates of another of the Six Companies served as the executive officers for a term of one year. He wondered, with a twinge of excitement, when the company to which he owed allegiance, the Kong Chow, would have its term as executive of the General Assembly.

And then it struck him that Mei Peng, a delegate of the Kong Chow Company, would sit on the dais as one of the ruling officers. He felt a flutter of importance in his chest as he realized that one day he would sit on the right hand of one of the executive officers of the General Assembly of the Six Companies.

He heard a "tsk-tsk" sound and turned to see Mei Peng staring at him. Completely engrossed in his daydreams, Chin had forgotten about the pen in his hand and the paper before him. He snapped to attention and listened to the progress of the meeting. Lao Wen was speaking.

". . . and Chang Gwo'jya will read the news from the pamphlet." Lao Wen turned toward the interpreter.

Chang Gwo'jya rose with great ceremony. He bowed from the waist toward Lao Wen, and the president returned the bow. The interpreter turned otward the Council, bowed, and spoke.

"I shall read the words, cousins, exactly as they are translated."

" 'Know you all men that this day, the 21st of August, 1850, the combined Houses of the Congress of the United States have passed a declaration admitting the territory of California to the United States of America as a sovereign state with all the privileges and responsibilities inherent to such status.' "

As Chang Gwo'jya laid the paper on the table in front of him and turned to look at Lao Wen, Chin put his pen down for a moment. Then, seeing that Lao Wen was about to speak, he picked up the pen again.

As he did, Chin glanced at Mei Peng out of the corner of his eye and saw that his superior was looking appraisingly at him and at the sheet of paper before him. Chin's eyes quickly returned to the paper as Lao Wen began to speak again.

"A sovereign state," Lao Wen said, his crooked finger jutting through the air to emphasize the point. "It is, cousins, perhaps the single most important event in the history of these people's lives."

He paused for a moment, letting the point sink in, before he continued. "We must make it the most important event in our lives as well. I needn't remind you what happened to the Mexicans and Indians because they fell from favor with the whites. The same must not happen with us. This event," Lao Wen said, "shall provide us with a method of proving our esteem for the whites."

Again he turned to Chang Gwo'jya. "Read the delegates the declaration."

Chang Gwo'jya rose. "It is our good fortune, cousins, that the governor of this state happened to be in San Francisco when the news of statehood arrived. Accordingly, we have received this message from the governor, dated October 18.

" 'To the Citizens of San Francisco and all foreigners who call this port home: In honor of the momentous joy of Statehood, I, the Governor of this State, do declare an official period of celebration to exist. I ask you all to turn out our city in bright colors and decorate it with ribbons and bunting. An official Statehood Parade will be held on October 29th, further details to be released through the newspapers. All are invited to attend.' "

Chang Gwo'jya put the notice down.

Lao Wen stood. "We shall use this celebration to endear ourselves to the whites. The magnitude of our tribute shall be great. Here is my plan . . ."

Chapter 12

Throughout the march from San Francisco to the goldfields of Sonora, Yang was constantly reminded of the contrasts between this journey and the one he had made across the sea. Where the ocean voyage had taken three months, this took but three weeks. On the ship he had been confined in the prisonlike quarters of the hold, without fresh air or sunshine; this trip was filled with the beauty of the California outdoors. The sea voyage had been a perilous adventure; this trip had been one of peace and contentment.

As they wound through the hills and the pastures, Yang was impressed with the immense bounty of the land owned by the whites. And though gold was the wealth of the land that he and many others were seeing now, he knew from experience in China that there was equally great riches to be gotten from the crops of the fields.

The march, organized and led by the Chinese, was a model of efficiency. Meals were cooked, served, and eaten twice daily by members of the group. Each took turns at cooking and serving duties.

By the end of the third week they arrived in Sonora and a suitable site along the Stanislaus River was chosen for their encampment. The group immediately set to work.

Tents were raised, a cooking area designated, and a pit dug. A site of worship was set off, a Mon War furnace erected, and a storehouse for rice and other edibles constructed.

By evening of the second day Yang felt his muscles aching, the same aches felt by every other man in the camp. But the fact was that they had succeeded in setting up their entire camp in a space of two days—a camp which was both organized and compact.

On the morning of the third day Yang walked down toward the river with a short, heavyset man named Wan Choi. Yang had befriended him during the march from San Francisco.

The friendship had not been a chance one. During the

march Yang had listened intently as Wan Choi spoke at length and with great knowledge about the construction of the sluice box utilized for extracting gold from the river.

It was by no means a new invention, Wan Choi had explained. Rather, his cousins in Yunnan had used the device twenty years ago when it was rumored that there was gold to be found in the Yangtze. And, Wan Choi continued, though there was no gold to be found at that time, he became intimately familiar with the workings of the device.

Accordingly, Yang had grown friendly with Wan Choi, and the dividend of that friendship was fast in coming. On that third morning, while most of the men were still up at the campsite trying to remember how to construct the sluice box from the instructions they had received back in San Francisco, Yang and Wan Choi were already down at the river, dipping their box, which Wan Choi had made during the night before, into the Stanislaus River.

By noon that day, because of their eagerness to start harvesting the gold, half the men in the camp had given up their efforts to construct the device and had settled for the less productive method of panning.

Before the end of the first month, Yang and Wan Choi had extracted close to fifty ounces of gold and gold dust from the Stanislaus River.

"A good week," Yang said after one Sunday morning meal.

"We are well on our way to our fortune," Wan Choi said. He scratched his lip for a moment and said, "Perhaps it was *too* good of a week."

"What do you mean?"

"The news of our success has spread throughout the camp."

"Let it spread."

Wan Choi frowned. "I do not think it is a good thing, Yang. There are wild rumors as to the amount of gold we have found."

Yang rose and began walking with Wan Choi. "Let them talk all they wish. They are just jealous."

Wan Choi nodded. "Jealousy can be dangerous. I have heard grumblings and I fear that some of our cousins may seek to relieve us of our earnings."

Yang laughed at the man's fears. "Don't worry, Wan Choi. No harm will come to you while Yang is here."

The stout Wan Choi smiled, feeling a little better. He glanced at Yang's massive size and decided that, indeed, he was a good man to have as a friend.

"Perhaps," Yang said, upon reflection, "it would be a wise thing to remind our cousins of whom they would offend by their actions."

Wan Choi stopped to look at him. "What do you mean, Yang?"

Yang stopped walking, focusing on his thoughts. He turned to look at Wan Choi. "I mean that perhaps there is more than a grain of truth to what you say, little cousin. Gold can make mandarins of some men, and yet fools of others. It is possible that, hearing these rumors of our wealth, some fools will attempt the crimes you fear."

Wan Choi said, "That is my greatest concern."

"Then," Yang continued, "to discourage them from such a folly we should let them have a look at the fortress they would lay siege to before they so commit themselves. Such a thing might save both sides needless problems."

Yang began walking again, Wan Choi hurrying a few paces to keep at his side.

"And," Yang continued, "we might well show a profit in the bargain."

Wan Choi shook his head. "Fortress, siege, profit? I confess, Yang, I do not understand a word you have said."

Yang smiled. "Then understand this. Spread the word through the camp that there is to be a martial arts contest this afternoon. It is Sunday," he said. "No one works and all are thirsty for entertainment. We shall provide both entertainment and a lesson for those who would seek to part us from our gold."

Wan Choi turned as he heard the squeal of a chicken. A falling ax, wielded by the camp's butcher, silenced the bird. He turned back to his friend. "But what if you should lose?"

"Lose?" Yang laughed loudly for a moment. Then he grew serious, as though his face had suddenly been cast in stone. "I cannot lose. I am Yang."

Yang had guessed right. The men, weary from a month's worth of panning, were eager for entertainment. It was only necessary for Wan Choi to tell the news of a martial arts contest to four men before word flashed through the encampment. And although not a man besides Wan Choi and Yang knew who had organized the contest, all the men of the camp set about making provisions for it.

Some of the men tended to the construction of the ring. The site chosen, after serious deliberation, was a hundred yards to the north of the campsite, where a small valley dipped. A trough was dug in a circle five meters across. Several of the more enterprising workers rolled huge boulders to the edge of the ring, which they would rent out to spectators who wanted to get a better view of the event.

Another group of entrepreneurs busied themselves with preparing all manner of food for the contest, which had by now taken on major proportions and was being regarded as a festive extravaganza.

Fried dough balls with sesame seeds and bean filling were cooked in black kettles along with thick, round mooncakes stuffed with candied fruit, watermelon seeds, and crushed melon.

The aroma of roasting duck and strips of barbequed pork filled the air, so that soon all the men of the camp were smacking their lips in anticipation of the coming feast. An old man who had been a baker in Tiensin prepared numerous varieties of *dim sum*, some of them covered with fine white sugar, others dotted with silvery white candy dots.

A final group of men, led by Wan Choi—those who had been most prosperous at harvesting the gold—set up a makeshift office near the site of the coming contest. It was here that they established a list of those men who would compete in the games, collected a small fee from each man, and entered into contracts whereby each victor would receive a percentage of the purse.

Lots were drawn and the combatants paired off. Finally, the "bankers" conducted an exhaustive inspection of the contestants—each of whom was stripped to the waist for this purpose—so as to appraise the odds of their emerging victorious. There ensued a lengthy debate among the bankers as to each combatant's relative chances of victory. A chart was erected with the projected odds written next to each man's name.

With the remarkable speed and efficiency peculiar to the Chinese, the games were completely organized by late afternoon. Those men who were not directly engaged in some aspect of the games spent the day in earnest, playing *Fan-tan* or casting the five dice used in the game of *sick*. Still others sought to increase their wealth by playing *Pi-gow*, using pieces from American domino sets as convenient substitutes for the markers used back in China.

All of these gambling endeavors, however, were merely preliminaries, merely a means of increasing the men's purses so they could better compete in the betting that was to transpire at the contest. A clanging gong told them it was about to begin.

It was six o'clock and the area around the arena was thick with men. Behind them stood others on boulders, getting a better view of the pit. At exactly six o'clock Wan Choi stepped across the trough and into the center of the ring. He bowed to the assemblage, quickly adapting to his newfound role of master of ceremonies.

He smiled widely. "Cousins, cousins," Wan Choi said, "welcome to the contest. Welcome all to the contest."

There was a vigorous round of applause from the spectators before Wan Choi continued.

"Tonight eight brave warriors, who come from our own rank's—masters of the ancient martial arts—desire to entertain and provide sport and perhaps profit for their cousins."

Again there was applause, louder this time.

"The initial contest," he explained, "shall pair these combatants off into four matches. The victors shall be matched in semifinal contests and the remaining two men shall fight for the championship of Sonora Camp." Wan Choi paused and then cried out, "And now, the warriors!"

The audience looked about and, at length, a gap separated to allow a single file line of men through. Shoeless, wearing abbreviated cloth britches and sleeveless shirts, their arms shimmering from coats of oil, they paraded into the arena. There was a great show of clapping and cheers from the spectators, who had already begun choosing their favorites.

With much ceremony, Wan Choi introduced each man and each was summarily hailed by the crowd, who now scrutinized the combatants with an eye toward which man to place their money on.

Finally, the eighth man left the arena and Wan Choi spoke once again. "The first contest shall pit Hi Chow of Beijing against Miu Sheng of Chungking. The fighters, please!"

As the two men strutted into the arena a fresh cheer rose up. The fighter from Beijing, Hi Chow, drew off his shirt and the crowd began cheering anew, impressed with his rippling muscles and barrel chest, both the result of a lifetime spent in construction in China's capital city.

But then his opponent, Miu Sheng, unbuttoned and removed his sleeveless jacket and the clamor grew deafening. If Hi Chow was a mighty-looking man, then Miu Sheng was a Goliath. Basking in the acclaim, eager for a great purse so as to increase his winnings, Miu Sheng flexed his massive muscles in a gesture designed to taunt his opponent and instill confidence in his backers. Each arm appeared to be made of steel, the muscles popping forth like rising dough turned to stone. His ribs were wide, like those of a powerful ox, his legs taut and hard, his hands like great hams.

And now, while the two men said prayers of supplication and cast handfuls of salt upon the ground prior to the commencement of the contest, the members of the audiences ran to place their bets with the men who served as the bank.

It was no matter that the odds were fixed at six-to-one in Miu Sheng's favor. It was a bet worth making because it was virtually sure money.

The men of the camp surged and rolled around the bankers, their money held high, clerks recording and issuing receipts for each bet as the money was taken by Wan Choi and the others.

So sure was the bet that only five wagers were placed on Hi Chow, and those were made by men who had also wagered on Miu Sheng and chose to cover part of their bets, unable to pass up the long odds offered on the underdog.

It was a full five minutes before the betting was completed and the spectators returned to their places. As Wan Choi reentered the arena the crowd quieted, its expectations growing with the mounting tension.

There was no need for him to ask for their attention this time.

"The rules of the contest are simple. A victory is claimed," Wan Choi explained, "by either three falls or forcing one's opponent out of the ring."

Wan Choi turned dramatically to look at the contestants, then said, "And now, let the contest begin."

A loud gong sounded and Wan Choi quickly backed from the ring. From the side of the arena, Yang stood with the other contestants. He had placed a quantity of gold on Miu Sheng simply because it had meant easy money. He was more interested, however, in watching the fighting style of the man from Chungking.

It was a rough, lumbering style—that of a brawler rather than a scientist. Miu Sheng stalked his opponent, his massive arms constantly moving like the pistons of a locomotive, reaching and grabbing for Hi Chow.

The crowd roared, egging each man on, shouting both cheers and taunts at them.

The two men were a study in opposites, Yang decided. It was clear that Hi Chow was a student of the martial arts. He had landed three blows on Miu Sheng, each time drawing nothing more than a grunt from his opponent, each time backing away from his grasp.

It appeared to Yang that Hi Chow had received a fairly good education in *aikido* and was incorporating several *tai chi ch'uan* maneuvers as well. A wise choice, Yang decided, against so formidable an opponent.

Hi Chow backed away as Miu Sheng advanced on him, ever circling, the sound of the crowd rising in his ears. Hi Chow feinted to the right, then moved to the left, executing a fine kick with his right leg, catching the giant full in the gut, this time drawing more than just a grunt. He followed with a series of three blows—two to the chest and one to the collarbone of the larger man.

Miu Sheng backed away, nearer to the edge of the circle, out of the smaller man's reach. Hi Chow followed warily, amazed that his blows, which would have rendered a lesser man unconscious if not seriously disabled, had not had a more deleterious effect.

The spectators moaned, shaking their heads in agony, unable to believe that Miu Sheng had yet to lay a hand on his opponent. Clearly the scientific methods of the smaller man were proving more effective than they had imagined.

Again Miu Sheng began to stalk, though this time with a bit more heaviness to his gait. Hi Chow jabbed and lightning-fast blows landed on the giant's face and arms, the air cracking with each one. Another kick, then another. Still Miu Sheng stalked.

Hi Chow landed more and more blows, his confidence growing as the larger man's reflexes slowed, as his guard lowered.

Hi Chow executed a quick series of three blows and the crowd moaned as they saw their favorite weaken, his legs about to give.

Miu Sheng's head lowered; he was stunned from the attack. Confident, Hi Chow screamed a blood cry and flew forward, his feet aimed for the giant's midsection. But then Miu Sheng rose, suddenly alert and prepared. He sidestepped Hi

Chow's leap and his iron grip fastened onto one of his assailant's legs like an eagle's talon.

Hi Chow landed on his hands and looked back at the giant holding on to his leg. With his free leg he kicked at Miu Sheng's face, jabbing fiercely with his foot, but the man from Chungking avoided the foot jabs with as little concern as another man would show a pesky fly. Finally Miu Sheng caught hold of the flailing leg of Hi Chow and then, holding one of his opponent's legs in each hand, began spinning around and around so that his opponent was soon airborne. The world was a dizzying blur speeding by Hi Chow's eyes.

With a last grunt, Miu Sheng let go of his opponent, sailing him through the air, out of the ring, and out of the match.

The man from Chungking raised his arms in victory and the crowd cheered him, then raced to collect their winnings.

The three remaining matches in the first heat were more even, the odds lower and the betting less frenetic. Clearly, however, the bettors were waiting for the semifinals so more money could be placed on Miu Sheng, who, it could now be seen, had merely been toying with his opponent.

Yang had easily won his match, though he made it seem more difficult that it actually was.

By the time the first heat was completed and the combatants were ready for the semifinals, darkness had fallen on the camp and dozens of torches had been lit, as well as two bonfires.

Between each match vendors hawked their goods. Great quantities of pork and duck had been consumed and more than a few men could feel their bellies bloating from too much *dim sum*. Wan Choi was one of them.

He rubbed his stomach. "I haven't eaten this much since I arrived in this country."

Yang smiled. "After tonight you will fill your belly again."

"Ugh," he grunted, "don't talk of eating."

"It is not eating I speak of. Gold, rather."

Wan Choi looked at him. "You are confident of this?"

"As confident as I am that the sun shall rise on the morrow."

Wan Choi lowered his voice with concern. "But how can you be so certain against a man such as this Miu Sheng? He is a giant among men—a giant among giants. His arms are as thick as my chest."

"He is a brawler, not a fighter."

"Not a fighter? You mean like his first opponent?"

"Hi Chow would have beaten him if he had been more proficient. It is merely a question of degree."

"The opponent Miu Sheng faces next, Cheng Li Po, would you call him proficient in the arts?"

Yang nodded. "Yes; but he will still lose. He is no match for this Miu Sheng."

"And you are?"

"I am."

"How can you be so certain?"

"Because to them it is a contest. To me it is not just a battle. It is life itself. It is all."

Wan Choi shivered at the tone of his companion's voice, then turned to watch as Miu Sheng and Cheng Li Po entered the ring.

Cheng Li Po was indeed more proficient than the giant's previous opponent. Too, the ruse had been exposed and Cheng Li Po was not too likely to suffer from the overconfidence that had doomed Hi Chow.

It was more of a tactical match, less one of tricks. Each man landed blows, each man received them. The difference was obviously a question of strength. Where Cheng Li Po's blows landed with a slap or a thud, Miu Sheng's landed like thunderclaps, each time driving his opponent to the ground.

After three falls the match was over and again the crowd roared its approval, satisfied at having gone with the five-to-one favorite.

It was ten o'clock when the semifinal matches had been completed. Yang's match was last. He had purposely drawn it out, letting his opponent get the first fall. He had taken the second fall and then let the match go even at two apiece.

Yang had caught Wan Choi's nervous look and then, assured that his act was convincing, he took his opponent down for the final fall.

Now he stood in the ring facing Miu Sheng. The betting was furious, occupying a full ten minutes between matches, the bettors not caring that they had to bet four dollars on their champion to win one. More than a few looked forward to Yang's defeat at this man's hands, for Wan Choi's suspicions had been right—word had spread through the camp of their success with gold and many of the men envied them for it.

The consensus was that it would be no contest. Both of

Miu Sheng's matches had been one-sided. Both of Yang's had been close contests which could have gone either way.

Wan Choi stepped into the ring, pausing by Yang's side. He lowered his voice to a whisper as he said, "You had better win, my cousin; almost all the fruits of our labors ride on it."

"I shall win more than just a contest, Wan Choi."

Wan Choi stared at him, waiting for an explanation of the cryptic remark. But none came. Yang had already retreated within himself, preparing for the battle.

Wan Choi turned and walked to the center of the arena. The torches burned brightly at the edges. The crowd hung suspended in anticipation, and the night air was charged with excitement.

"And now, cousins, the climax of this night of combat. The two finalists." He pointed to his right and said, "Yang Wong."

There was respectable applause, bearing testimony to the fact that even though they envied his success in the extraction of gold, his cousins still respected him for having advanced this far in the tournament.

"And Miu Sheng."

Now the crowd cheered mightily, many raising their hand over their heads, already celebrating the victory and counting their winnings.

Wan Choi cried, "Let the contest begin."

The gong sounded and he backed away.

Yang advanced toward the center of the ring. He looked at his opponent, at the mass of gleaming, glistening flesh, and he considered it not a man; it was nothing more than a target.

Yang kept his eyes trained on Miu Sheng's ever-moving hands and circling feet. The giant made a lunge and Yang sidestepped him, letting him rumble past.

The crowd milled nervously, and total silence circled the ring in a constricting grasp.

Miu Sheng turned and stalked again, his arms moving, his fists clenching and unclenching. Yang kept low, moving, feinting, circling away from the giant.

Again Miu Sheng lurched for him and again Yang sidestepped him, this time to his left. Miu Sheng stumbled as he passed him this time and he turned quickly, furious that Yang had evaded his grasp.

This time he charged for Yang, his arms in front of him, and Yang, instead of sidestepping, met the attack. He grabbed hold of Miu Sheng's arms and threw him to the ground.

The crowd shook as much as Miu Sheng did from the blow. It was the first time the man had been off his feet, and shock waves rippled through the audience. The air was still and silent as Miu Sheng rose, looking at Yang at the far end of the ring.

Miu Sheng went to the opposite end, a ragged smile coming to his lips. He regarded Yang and Yang stared back at him. For a long moment nothing happened.

Then Miu Sheng's lips pulled back, baring his teeth as he raced toward Yang. Yang charged forward at the same time. Ten feet before they met, Yang leaped through the air. Miu Sheng raised his arms like clubs to meet him. Both men's voices shrieked with death cries that told all the men of the camp that this was no longer merely a contest.

Yang reached the zenith of his flight and descended, his feet arched forward, cutting like daggers, all his weight behind them. He sliced through Miu Sheng's arm's like a sickle would through harvest wheat, ripping through to his throat.

Yang tumbled away after the blow, then stood up and watched. Miu Sheng stood like an oak tree, frozen; the silence was pregnant and waiting. Then slowly, as if the majestic tree had been sawn at its base, he tumbled forward to land on the earth with a great thud, dead.

Yang rose and slowly looked around at the men standing beyond the trough. They were too stunned to speak; even their wagers were forgotten. The only sound was the crackling of the bonfires and the torches.

It was Yang's voice, then, that was heard. "Thus ends the contest," he said. He turned and looked at Miu Sheng's body. "To such an end come all those who would oppose Yang."

From a knoll just above the valley where the contest had taken place, James Riley sat on his horse, surrounded by eight men.

"Looks like easy pickin's," Riley said.

The men nodded, but Brian O'Malley said, "Lot of 'em, though. Let's not get overconfident, lads. Remember what happened last time."

One of the other men, an Irishman named Doyle, looked down at his left hand. It was missing a thumb. "Aye," Doyle agreed.

But Riley shooed O'Malley off with a wave of his hand.

"Ah, them was Mexicans. Whole different story here, Brian. The Mexicans had nothing to lose in the first place; they knew they had no business working a claim. These Chinaboys want to keep working. They'll do what we say. Besides, they don't have guns. They're no match for nine whites with repeaters and pistols."

O'Malley shook his head. "I still say a little care is required when separating a man from his gold—Chinese, Mexican or white."

Riley tossed his cigarette to the ground. "These Chinaboys ain't got no heart for fighting." He looked down at the valley. "Come on, boys."

The nine men rode down into the valley, circled it, and let off several rounds of fire. Riley had no idea why they were gathered around a torch-lit trough in the middle of the night. He didn't care, either. What did matter was that he saw sacks of gold and gold dust lying on makeshift tables.

"Who's in charge here?" Riley spat, cradling his rifle.

The Chinese looked at one another. Finally, one of them stepped forward.

"What wrong, what wrong?"

"We come for your gold," Riley said.

"Gold? Gold?"

"That's right, ya heathen scum. Gold." Riley laughed, looking toward O'Malley. "They understand that word well enough."

"What you mean?" the terrified Chinese asked.

Riley reached into his pocket and pulled out a leather pouch, swinging it in the air for a moment. "Now you understand?"

"No," the man said, his voice quaking. "Our gold. We pan. Is our gold. We . . ."

The man's words were cut short by the lasso that was thrown over him. One of the Irishmen, on horseback, laughed and then spurred his horse.

There was a shriek from the Chinese just before he lurched into the air, bouncing along the ground behind the galloping mount. For a long moment the man's screams echoed into the night.

The Chinese milled about, but Riley kept the circle of rifle-toting men around them. Perhaps it was the shame of losing the martial arts match; perhaps it was something he decided without thought. Whatever the reason, Hi Chow lurched for one of the horsemen.

He Chow was still five feet from the Irishmen when they opened fire. Six bullets slammed into his body, spinning him around like a puppet gone mad. Blood erupted from his face like crimson geysers. He twisted on the ground, his body convulsing in the throes of death.

Not far from where Hi Chow fell, Wan Choi turned to Yang. "What will we do, Yang?"

Yang looked at the body of Hi Chow. "We will give them our gold, Wan Choi." He turned to look at his compatriot and said, "There is a difference between courage and stupidity."

Chapter 13

It was a celebration unlike any that San Francisco had ever witnessed. Throughout the entire day bands and marching groups of every size and variety filled the streets. Schools and fraternal organizations were represented. The army and navy paraded down the streets of the city in full-dress uniforms, passing in review by the grandstand where Governor Peter H. Burnett and Mayor Geary stood waving to the crowd.

Ethnic organizations of Spaniards, Frenchmen, and Hebrews all paraded by, wearing the traditional ethnic garb. Each group was greeted by cheers from the crowd as they paid homage to California. For this day, at least, prejudice was forgotten.

By late afternoon the crowd's enthusiasm for viewing the marching groups was starting to wane, however, and many in the audience began thinking about dinner and the festivities of the night still ahead.

It was well, then, that the Chinese had waited until this momentary lull to begin their march.

From the reviewing stand it appeared as if a cloak of silence had fallen over the entire city, so still was the air. The governor turned to look at Mayor Geary and the mayor turned to look at William Wright, the city's public affairs coordinator.

Wright was baffled and was about to admit it when the air

was filled with the sound of chimes and string instruments and music of a kind never heard before by most San Franciscans.

And then, from the reviewing stand, the Chinese assemblage could be seen snaking its way down the center of the boulevard. Governor Burnett's mouth hung open. Mayor Geary stood transfixed. All watched, practically hypnotized, as the Chinese neared the reviewing stand.

The San Franciscans were accustomed to seeing the Chinese occasionally, although for the most part the Orientals chose to stay within the boundaries of their Chinatown. When the whites had seen them they were used to seeing the loose-fitting blue jackets and trousers that seemed to go so well with the Chinamen's nondescript features.

But today the Chinese presented a rainbow of color. Their jackets were of the finest silk, shimmering bright gold and orange and red. A thousand straw hats seemed to be a thousand different colors. Row after row of musicians carried all manner of instruments never seen before by most Western eyes. A lilting melody, played on moonharps and bamboo fiddles, drifted lightly through the air.

The spectacle seemed to stretch out endlessly. Now the men on the reviewing stand began to crane their necks to see, and finally the great red dragon came into view. Thirty Chinese walked underneath the yards and yards of silk and damask that comprised the good-luck creature. And, as if the dragon was actually endowed with some sort of mystical magic, the crowd broke from its trance and roared its approval.

The boulevard was filled with the sound of thunderous applause and riotous cheering as the citizens of San Francisco acknowledged the spectacle that had been put on for their benefit.

Later, after darkness had fallen, the Chinese capped the evening by putting on the first fireworks display ever seen in America. Lighting the black skies over San Francisco with salvo after salvo of red, white, and blue explosions, the men of the Six Companies had achieved their purpose—they had, for the moment at least, endeared themselves to the populace. Unlike the Mexicans and the Chilenos, they were safe. For the time being, they were safe.

Weeks flowed into months and months into seasons, and

through the passing of the seasons the men who lived in California prospered, each in their own way.

The German named Levi Strauss was quickly amassing a fortune, marketing his canvas work trousers. Others, capitalizing on the need to protect and transport the great riches of the earth, were making their own fortunes. Wells, Fargo & Company began its operations in San Francisco and was soon well established.

In the city itself, a great number of men were reaping the rewards of the gold boom and, as Chin had noted, there were ways other than panning to share in the harvest. Hotel owners realized windfall profits, as did restauranteurs and horse traders.

Chinatown had not been exempted from this period of general prosperity. White men and women flocked to the confines of the Chinese quarter, eager to purchase jade and silks and all manner of herbs and spices from the Orient. For those who had the right connections there were other pleasures, of a more exotic nature, to be tasted.

There was an excitement in Chinatown, a feeling of being in a faraway place—a somewhat wicked one. There was the lottery and the *Fan-tan* parlors and, if you were really adventurous, the opium dens—several of which catered exclusively to whites.

Although the average Chinese did not own an emporium or a gambling parlor, he too shared in the exchange of money. The average Chinese—those without any skill or profession—sought work that was menial, and he attacked the job with a fervor unmatched in California history.

The Chinese would do jobs that no self-respecting white man would do—laundry, ditchdigging, gardening—and he would do it with stunning efficiency and, more importantly, at a price cheaper than anyone else could charge.

So it was that the Chinese became renowned within San Francisco for their cheap, efficient labor, and laundry houses sprang up overnight. All day long men could be seen scurrying back and forth between the city and Chinatown, bamboo poles over their backs supporting wicker baskets of white men's dirty clothes.

And there were cigar vendors and fruit peddlers and cobblers. The streets of Chinatown were pressed full with men hawking their wares, their curious broken English voices calling out the names and virtues of their products; in a good many cases drawing a favorable response from the curiosity-seeking whites who had come day-tripping.

While in many ways the Chinese differed from their white counterparts, in one important way they were similar. Gold had the same deleterious effect upon them, bringing into play all the baser qualities of human nature.

So it was that in the fall of 1853 there came dissent in the house of the Six Companies. While it was still a congress concerned with the welfare of all Chinese, it was rapidly becoming apparent that there was more concern on the part of the respective delegates for the welfare of their own companies than there was for those of the others. In some cases, greed reared its head and concern for individual welfare transcended even that of the Company's good.

On the evening which the elders of the Six Companies would later call the Night of Shame, Chin was sitting at the writing desk in the corner of the small sleeping quarters he shared with the other Kong Chow Company accountants.

He laid his pen down for a moment, his hand cramping, and looked at the candle on his desk. It was just past ten o'clock. He turned and looked at his roommates. Shao Kow was sleeping. Pai Pao was enjoying a smoke of opium before retiring. Chin wished, in that moment, that he could be in either of their places; but the feeling quickly left him.

While there were added responsibilities, and certainly a good deal more work, Chin enjoyed his status as Mei Peng's number-one aide. It afforded him a certain degree of rank among the younger accountants of the Kong Chow Company, not to mention a more sizable salary.

More importantly, Chin realized, it gained him access to the General Assembly, and it was there that he cultivated rich and powerful friends. He was recognized as a bright young man who exhibited the wisdom to offer a sagacious opinion on a wide variety of matters, when it was asked for.

Chin turned back to his work. He had no sooner touched pencil to paper than he was interrupted by a knock at the door.

He glanced at Pai Pao, who was discreetly dousing his opium, for though it was known that everyone from the chairman of the Six Companies down to the lowest transient in the house smoked recreationally, it was something which those of lower status were expected to respectfully conceal from their superiors.

Chin rose, crossed the room, and opened the door. His

101

mouth fell open when he saw Mei Peng standing in the doorway.

His head bowed instantly. "Mei Peng, you do honor to visit the humble quarters of your workers."

Pai Pao had sprung from the bed, suddenly alert, and bowed a greeting, rubbing his hands together.

Mei Peng returned neither man's solicitations. Instead, to Chin he said, "I want you to come with me immediately."

Almost all the delegates were present. Chin listened to the low rumble of whispers being exchanged in the chamber as he and Mei Peng hurriedly walked down the center aisle. He sensed that momentous events were taking place . . . perhaps had already taken place.

Minutes later the meeting was called to order. Wa Shen, a delegate from the Hop Wo Company, which currently sat on the dais, served as the president of the Six Companies' General Assembly. He was an old man, clean-shaven, with soft yellow skin, his brow furrowed with deep dignity.

Chin had watched Wa Shen preside over the meetings of the Assembly with a kind of fatherly authority. His voice had been firm, yet kind. He controlled the delegates with the respect they had for him, respect that was due a man who had worked in service to the Companies for forty years.

But today it was a different voice that came from Wa Shen, a quivering voice that had lost its confidence. And now, as he tried to get order, his voice cracked repeatedly, driving Chin to such distraction that he had to remind himself again and again of the importance of his notetaking.

Wa Shen rapped the gavel and said, "This meeting of the Six Companies is called to order." He paused, put the gavel down and said, "I, Wa Shen, chairman of the Hop Wo Comp—"

From two rows behind him, Chin heard a voice cry, "Chairman of the Liars!"

Wa Shen lowered his eyes.

"Chairman of the Thieves!" another rang out.

The president of the Assembly bowed his head. Stunned, Chin looked back and forth, from one side of the room to the other, as shouts and insults erupted from the gathering. He looked back to Wa Shen. The president of the Assembly stood as if he was made of stone, the gavel of power lying impotently before him on the podium.

Chin realized, in that moment, that Wa Shen could no longer count on the gavel. The president had lost his power.

Chin looked at Mei Peng and in a whisper asked, "What's ha—"

"Hush," Mei Peng said. "Tend to your notes."

For a full minute the reigning president of the General Assembly took the rebukes and insults of his countrymen, and Chin dutifully recorded as much as he could, noting which delegates had hurled which tirades. At length quiet descended on the chamber and Wa Shen raised his eyes.

His voice cracked as he spoke. "It grieves me to be the one to deliver the news of Chang Gwo'jya's deceit."

At the mention of the official interpreter's name a chorus of hisses sprang up from the gathering.

Chin looked up from his papers toward the dais at the front of the meeting hall and for the first time realized that Chang Gwo'jya was not seated at the raised platform. In his shock at the Assembly's treatment of Wa Shen, he had not even noticed the absence of the interpreter.

Wa Shen turned to look down the table, toward his left. "Let the secretary of this Assembly record that it was Chang Gwo'jya who, so greatly abusing the trust and authority granted to him, did enter into agreements with certain whites and did . . ." The old man paused, his voice weak, the words coming with difficulty. "And did make such arrangements as to sell this sacred house, this Meeting Hall of the Middle Kingdom."

Again shouts and catcalls rose from the delegates and Chin felt his fingers numb, so intense was his shock.

"Sold . . ." Chin said aloud.

Mei Peng turned to look at him, saw the expression of disbelief on his face, and nodded slightly.

"Deceit," Mei Peng said, his voice just above a whisper, "deceit most foul and heinous."

Chapter 14

The Six Companies had not always been six companies. At one time there was only one company. In those days there were only clans and the clans were many. But they banded with other clans and eventually associations were formed.

In the beginning there was only one company in the Meeting Hall of the Middle Kingdom. But as fractionalism and special interests grew, division began to occur. The Six Companies emerged because it was an impossible matter for a single company to fairly represent the interests of all Chinese.

For a time they had been able to coexist in the Meeting Hall of the Middle Kingdom. But that coexistence was growing increasingly strained. The treachery of Chang Gwo'jya helped foment the growth of separatism.

Amends were made, after a fashion. The Wong clan, to which Chang Gwo'jya belonged, raised the money to buy back the Meeting Hall of the Middle Kingdom from the whites. But a breach, a rift, had been formed. There was a growing and serious division between the Six Companies. It was becoming apparent that the six different companies could not live forever under the same roof.

The episode was but a portent of further troubles that the Chinese were to experience, both from within and without, during the year.

Governor Bigler, who had waged an anti-Chinese campaign in 1852, once again took up arms against the "yellow horde." Throughout 1855 the governor, eager to capture the American miners' vote, raged against the Chinese, claiming that they were interlopers stealing America's gold from her rivers.

With support behind him the governor was able to secure passage of legislation levying a foreign miners' tax aimed squarely at the Chinese that drove many of them from the mines and rivers. Those who were left behind suffered a worse fate, sometimes at the hands of Joaquín Murietta, sometimes at the hands of white bandits led by the likes of James Riley.

Within the boundaries of Chinatown in San Francisco, however, the Chinese were afforded a certain degree of security. The men of "Little China" had firmly ingrained themselves in the city's way of life. They were depended upon for laundering, cleaning, and other menial tasks which they did well and cheaply.

And though certain lines of division were growing between the Six Companies, Chin could see, from his daily bookkeeping, that the coffers of the Kong Chow Company were growing rapidly.

Each day ships loaded to the bulkheads with Chinese arrived in the harbor. They were received, processed, and sent on their way like so many cattle, each man paying his dues to the Company, each man cheerfully signed into voluntary servitude to pay back the money the Company had advanced him for his passage.

With the flood of "cousins," Chin's hours were long and the days passed with a flowing unity, leading into the next and the next and still the next, until at last, one September afternoon, Mei Peng broke the rhythm.

Chin looked up as his superior walked into his office.

"You have a visitor," Mei Peng said.

"A visitor? Who?"

"Your brother."

Chin laid his pen down. "My brother?" He paused, his mind discarding the numbers as his lips absently said, "Yang?" He looked at Mei Peng. "Here?"

"He waits for you out in the foyer."

Chin straightened the papers on his desk and rose, looking at his superior. "May I take a moment to see him, Mei Peng?"

"Now? During the middle of the workday? With so much work still to be done?"

Chin lowered his eyes. "Of course. How thoughtless of me. I had not thought . . ."

Mei Peng broke into a smile. "Of course you may see him. Go. I have arranged for you to be relieved for the remainder of the day as well."

Chin sprang to his feet and raced past Mei Peng faster than he could exclaim the praises of his employer. As Chin ran down the corridor he called out compliment after compliment, extolling the virtues of Mei Peng so that half a dozen men opened the doors of their offices, laughing, to see what was the matter.

Mei Peng laughed, shaking his head.

Chin walked out into the foyer and looked at Yang, for a moment not certain that this was his brother. Yang was still a massive bull of a man, but there was something in his face that was not there when he and Chin had parted.

Chin drew up to him and bowed. "It pleases me to see my brother after so long a time."

Yang returned the bow. "And I you," was his terse reply. He looked at his younger brother. "How do you fare, Chin?"

"Well." He paused, somehow sensing that Yang was troubled. "And you, brother?"

Yang let the foyer hang in silence for a moment, then said, "Come outside with me, Chin. This hallway is too close. I need air."

They walked from the Meeting Hall of the Middle Kingdom and began strolling down Stockton Street, heading in no particular direction.

"Truly," Yang said, "tell me how you fare. Tell me of your position with the Company."

It seemed to Chin that his brother wanted time before he would speak of himself and Chin decided to give it to him.

"I have received two advances in position since I last saw you. I am now first aide to the senior accountant of the Kong Chow Company."

Yang nodded. "That is good. You were always swift with figures."

They strolled past a storefront from which the smell of roasting pork drifted, and Chin felt his mouth water. He thought about suggesting lunch, but it seemed to him that Yang wasn't in a festive mood, that he sought talk more than he desired food.

"It is my hope," Chin continued, "that by the end of the year I shall be made a full accountant with the Company. Though, of course, I haven't spoken of it to Mei Peng, my superior."

Yang turned to look at him. "And why not?"

"Such boldness might be ill received."

"It is only by boldness that you shall hold what you already have and gain that which you seek, brother."

Chin stopped walking. "You sound bitter, Yang. What is it that troubles you?"

Yang looked up at the thick fog that was beginning to drape over Chinatown, thinking that it aptly suited his gloom.

He turned to his younger brother. "When, five years ago, I left you, it was with barely ten dollars in my pocket. Today I return with half that fortune."

"Yang! No! This cannot be!"

"And yet it is true."

"How? How could such a thing come to pass?"

"By degrees, brother."

"But the gold . . . We heard there was so much gold being . . ."

Yang nodded. "There was. For a while there was nothing *but* gold. My partner, Wan Choi—"

"You have taken a partner?"

"Yes."

"You have changed."

"In many ways." Yang began walking again, Chin falling into step beside him. "When Wan Choi and I began working the river it was as though the gold drew to us as baby chicks to their mother, and for a while it was all we could do to keep up with the harvest."

"Was this so for all the men of your camp?"

"Of some," Yang said. "But particularly for us. Wan Choi is a master in the art of extracting gold from the waters. This very fact caused great jealousy in our camp. Although I managed to stifle any foolishness on the part of those who might have sought to relieve us of the fruits of our labors."

Chin nodded. "I heard the news."

Yang looked at him. "What news?"

"That you killed a man."

"How could you have heard of this?"

"It was reported in the *Golden Hills*." I read of the man's death."

"How was it reported?"

"As an accident in a martial arts contest."

"The *Golden Hills* would do well to find reporters who can more accurately convey the news."

Chin regarded him as he would a stranger. "Then you freely admit that the man's death was no accident?"

"As a tiger would slay a leopard, it was no accident."

"I cannot believe my brother would take another man's life."

"Believe it, Chin."

Chin shook his head. "I cannot."

Yang looked away. "Perhaps it is true that you cannot. City living exacts its toll."

"*City* living exacts its toll? What toll have the goldfields exacted from you, brother, that you would kill another man?"

Yang's eyes blazed. "It is by this method that one insures what gain he has already made and so increases it."

"Increases it to a five-dollar fortune such as you possess?"

"Yes!" Yang said. "Precisely so. The white bandits who profited from my labor did so because they were better armed and more ruthless than those I was surrounded by. And do not think for a moment that I begrudge them their gain. Rather, I respect them as one warrior respects another, as one combatant respects a superior adversary."

"And what of our family?" Chin asked, his eyes narrowing. "While you so nobly pay homage to the white bandits, do you think of our family?"

"Say what you mean, Chin."

"Our sister Ling. That is what I mean. With your fortunes at this low ebb have you continued your payment for the passage we received?"

"I . . ." Yang hesitated.

"You have not, have you, brother? You have defaulted in your obligation. And because of it our sister has gone into servitude." Chin turned his back on Yang, closed his eyes. "What shame this is. Double shame. You have failed to live up to your obligation and sent our sister to slavery in one swoop."

"You must have known of this," Yang accused. "You sit here in your office, prospering well enough. *You* could have taken up my portion of the debt. If you were an honorable brother you would have aided me in my time of difficulty."

Chin turned to look at Yang. "And how would I know of your troubles? I have never received a letter from you."

"Didn't our father write to tell you the payments had stopped? Didn't he write to tell you Ling was being placed in servitude? It was always the two of you who corresponded; never him and I. Didn't he—"

"Our father is dead," Chin said.

Yang fell silent, staring at him for a long moment. His lips quivered for a moment and when he finally spoke there was a flutter to his voice. "Dead? Our father, dead?"

Chin nodded.

"When did you learn of this?"

"Only last year. A letter came." Chin drew a deep breath. "He died peacefully, in his sleep. It had been a long, lingering illness." With a hint of rebuke in his voice, Chin added, "For a time I sent him money for medicine and the doctors."

"And did he speak of Ling?"

"Only to say she was growing, that she was becoming a young woman." Chin's voice softened. "I had written many times, bemoaning the fact that he could not sell her because she was the collateral for our passage and thus had to remain his property. But each time he answered that it was a wise investment, that his time was short and that our future was what mattered."

"So she was not sold while he lived?" Yang asked.

"No. At least he was spared that indignity." Chin glared at Yang. "An indignity you have not spared me. Let me assure you, had I known of your insolvency I would have taken it upon myself to guarantee our sister's freedom. Why didn't you at least advise me of what—"

"Because I was too busy trying to survive!"

"And what of our sister's survival? What of her life?"

"I have trouble enough with my own existence."

"I cannot believe it is my brother speaking these words."

"Perhaps if you had gone to the countryside with me you would understand. It is hard and brutal, but it is what life is about; not this comfortable existence you lead here."

"You haven't changed," Chin said. "You've only grown. You've expanded the kicks and punches of the arena into your life."

"If that is so, it is because kicks and punches are necessary in my life."

"Are they?"

"Yes, Chin, they are. In *my* life they are. Would you have me be a shopkeeper or a laundryman or a . . . a bookkeeper?"

"Is that so terrible a fate?"

"For you, no. For me, yes. You are what you are, brother, and I am what I am. I will be what I must be."

"And what is that, Yang?"

"Unfettered."

They walked along in silence for a moment. Then Chin said, "Won't you consider living in the city for a while? You may yet find it to your liking. I can obtain a position for you with—"

"No, Chin. I will go my own way."

"And where is that? Back to the goldfields?"

"No, I think not. It is no longer safe for our people in the goldfields. The whites let us mine only until we have enough gold to make it worthwhile for them to steal from us."

"What will you do, then?"

"Work the land for a while, perhaps."

Chin clicked his teeth. "You journeyed across the sea to become a farmer?"

"I will bide my time. I will do what I must until my fate presents itself."

"Farming," Chin said with disdain.

"I find it preferable to being caged in an office as you are."

"Perhaps," Chin said, "your fate is to be a farmer."

Yang turned abruptly. "Be careful of your words, brother."

"The great and powerful Yang, master of the martial arts, to spend the rest of his life wallowing in the fields . . ."

Yang stopped walking and stood before Chin, his legs spread in a stance of anger. "I warn you, Chin—"

"What happened to all those grand plans of yours, my powerful brother? What happened to all your dreams of wealth? You were going to return to China richer than a mandarin. Now what? You will spend your days growing old, your hands digging up mud like a turtle?"

Yang lashed out, catching Chin full across the face, sending him to the ground with a single angry blow. Chin lay there for a moment, then looked up at his brother, wiping at the blood that trickled from the corner of his mouth.

Yang looked down at him, looked at the blood, then turned and walked down Stockton Street, leaving Chin on the ground.

"I acted like a fool," Chin said. "I taunted him."

"Why did you do such a thing?" Mei Peng asked.

"I wanted him to stay in the city for a while. I think he's had a difficult time of it in the fields, Mei Peng."

Mei Peng nodded. "Many Chinese have had a difficult time in the goldfields. More than a few have been beaten for their efforts."

Chin felt the wound at the corner of his mouth split as he spoke. "I thought if I made him angry enough he might seek another means of making his fortune, perhaps here in the city."

"Instead it only served to drive him away."

"He has become bitter, Mei Peng."

"Hardened. It happens, Chin."

Chin sighed. "He was always a hard man, my brother. Determined, purposeful. But never bitter."

"Perhaps he will return after he has had time to think."

Chin shook his head. "I don't think so."

"Where do you think he will go?"

"Somewhere where he can wait."

"Wait? For what?"

"For his time."

Mei Peng cocked his head. "His time?"

"Yes." Chin paused, then said, "There is always a time for men like my brother."

Chapter 15

During the second week of January in 1856, Chin was sitting in the room where he had learned to master English. His fluency was a matter of personal pride to Rebecca Ashley, who now stood at the front of the classroom watching it empty of students.

Chin Wong was her prized student and she regarded him now, sitting at the rear of the class.

"Chin?"

He looked up from his desk, hardly realizing that the room was empty. "Yes? Oh . . ." he said, looking around.

She walked up the center aisle. "Are you all right, Chin?"

"Oh, yes, Rebecca," he said, their years of association granting him the right to address her by her Christian name.

She sat on the edge of the desk before his own. "You seem preoccupied today."

"I'm sorry. I guess I am."

She smiled. "Anything I can help with?"

"No," he said. "No, I don't think so."

"Why don't you give me a try?"

He looked into her eyes. They were kind eyes. He remembered the infatuation he had had when he first saw them. To some degree it had dissipated. Familiarity had cooled the fires, and as the student-teacher relationship grew he suppressed his romantic feelings.

But now, sitting alone in the room with her, listening to her ask personal questions, he felt it nip at his chest again.

"I will answer your question if you will answer one for me."

She smiled. "Of course. What do you want to know?"

"How old are you?"

Rebecca was caught completely off guard by the question. "Wh—why ever do you want to know?"

"Curious," he said.

She stood up from the desk, smiling. "I'm twenty-six."

She was three years older than he, then. Not so much older.

"That is good," he said.

She stared at him for a moment. The Chinese were a mysterious people in some ways. They had strange reasons for asking the questions they asked. She would not pry at his motivations. He would only lie if he didn't want her to know the truth. They harbored no guilt feelings about lying. If he didn't want her to know his reason for asking the question then he simply would not tell her.

"Now that I have answered your question, answer mine. What's bothering you?"

It was a fair exchange, Chin thought, because he had truly wanted to know her age.

He leaned back in his chair, sighing. "I fear many bad things are on the horizon, Rebecca, for my people. The whites of this city are less and less sympathetic toward us."

She frowned, then said, "Chin, that's only politics. The governor keeps the people worked up because . . ."

He nodded. "I know, I know. But it is not good. It is the sort of thing which can get out of control." He closed his eyes for a moment. "Too, there is discord from within."

"From within?"

He opened his eyes and looked at her and saw that she was genuinely interested. "The Six Companies are growing farther and farther apart. They are no longer the unified force they once were."

"Things change, Chin. Where once your people needed unity, they now need representation." Again she sat on the edge of the desk. "More and more of your countrymen come to California. It's impossible for a congress to represent the same view and still fairly represent the views of all of those people."

He nodded. "What you say is true. But I fear that without unity we will fall prey to weakness. We do not have much in this land, Rebecca. We have little protection from white courts, few legal rights. The unity of the Six Companies offers us our only shield. Without it I fear for the well-being of my people."

"Sometimes," Rebecca said, "sometimes a people must go through trouble before they can know serenity."

As to her prediction about serenity, Chin would have to wait and see. The forecast of trouble was right on target. With the passing of time, the temples of Chinatown began to fill daily with hundreds of Chinamen who went to pray for relief from the curse that had been visited on them. They made offerings to the gods, burned money, and issued prayers of supplication. Nothing seemed to work.

It was the curse of discord and it worked from both inside and outside their ranks. As the mines and goldfields became worked out and the realization came that the great gold strike was waning, the city of San Francisco began to swell up with an unemployed hoodlum element that made the journey outside the confines of Chinatown a danger to any yellow man.

The gold rush had attracted the dregs of the world—criminals from Australia and New Zealand, bandits from Great Britain, ruthless and greedy men from throughout the United States. Now, with the gold supply dwindling, these unskilled men flocked to San Francisco, where they thought they would get work at high wages.

They were wrong. The labor force was bloated and, accordingly, the price of labor fell. Seeing the Chinese charging so little for their labor, many whites felt that this was part of the cause for low wages. Politicians who wanted their votes eagerly encouraged this type of thinking, and a wave of anti-Chinese sentiment broke out.

But even worse was the dissension which had sprung up within the Six Companies, at a time when unity was most needed. It was as though the initial seed planted by Chang Gwo'jya had blossomed and grown like some sort of killer weed, grasping and strangling everything in its path.

In that January Chin sat through eight meetings of the Council, in which he heard dozens of arguments and allegations of misconduct debated. The worst of these allegations was that the Sam Yup Company had tried to bring the tongs of Chinatown into their own Company on an exclusive basis.

The tongs were trade guilds which drew their membership from the different labor sectors that existed in Chinatown. There were laundry tongs and cigar-vending tongs and business-operator tongs. As men joined these guilds they found themselves in organizations that included members of many Companies. Thus cigar vendors who were members of the Ning Yeung Company found themselves in a union where there were members of the Sam Yup Company.

The ruling body of the Six Companies feared that this intermingling would dilute Company allegiances, and it was the Sam Yup Company which first tried to capitalize upon this.

Certain members of the Sam Yup Company tried to persuade various tongs that they should join the Sam Yup. This went totally against the principle that Company membership was solely determined by place of birth. The plan was to form a unified, strong new Company, based upon members of the Sam Yup Company and the new recruits from the tongs.

With such a combined force they felt they could influence legislation passed at the Meeting Hall of the Middle Kingdom and pass laws that would benefit themselves.

The plan was discovered, however, and exposed before the entire Assembly. A vote was taken and the leaders of the ruling board of the Council—all members of the Sam Yup Company—were ordered to resign their posts. As members of the ruling board of the General Assembly, however, they refused to step down.

For a full week verbal battles raged in the meeting hall. These meetings were presided over by the very delegates who were being ordered to resign, and they used every trick they could think of to confuse the meetings.

During those debates, many of which lasted long into the night, Chin took detailed notes. Afterwards he spent many hours transcribing these notes for Mei Peng to read.

At the end of the week it was apparent to each of the Six Companies that they could no longer expect to function as a unified body. Each was too involved with its own interests and suspected the others of deceit.

It was decided that the Companies would leave the Meeting Hall of the Middle Kingdom, each to establish their own hall, only to meet in the great chamber when questions of mutual interest arose.

Ironically, the plan of the Sam Yup Company to recruit

tong members failed. When it was learned that the Six Companies were splintering, the tong members decided that they would remain independent of any Company allegiance, hoping for a future time when their strength could eclipse that of the organization that now held the scepter of political power in Chinese America.

Almost a full three years had passed between the time of Chang Gwo'jya's deceit and the day that the Six Companies decided they would go their separate ways.

The events of those years met with mixed reactions by Chin. On the one hand, he was saddened to see the dissension among his countrymen. On the other hand, the split had solidified his own position and increased his importance within the Kong Chow Company.

During the years of turmoil his stature had risen within the company. He had been appointed full accountant. But, more importantly, his opinions on several important matters had been borne out and he was respected by many of the older members as a young man who exercised good judgment.

One of his major coups had been with regard to Rebecca Ashley. It was the day before the Kong Chow Company was to move out of the Meeting Hall of the Middle Kingdom and to its new headquarters on Clay Street.

Chin purposely waited until the class was over to approach her on the matter. When they were alone he stood before her.

"We move to our new house tomorrow," he began.

She nodded, gathering up her English books. "I am sad to hear that, Chin. I am sad for the problems the Six Companies has had."

"Perhaps it is for the best," he said. "We have all grown. We must move on to a new period in our lives."

"You sound like a politician."

He laughed. "I would not mind that profession."

"Perhaps you ought to pursue it."

"Perhaps I shall." He paused, then said, "If you will help me."

She looked up from her books. "I? How could I help you?"

"By agreeing to move with us to the new Kong Chow House. We will have need of a skilled teacher to instruct our young men."

She stifled a smile at the way he tried to sound like an elder. "Well, I don't know, Chin. I mean, I was working for the Six Companies and . . ."

"But there is no longer the union between us that there was. This house will not be occupied, except for administrative workers. You will have to work for one Company and I want it to be the Kong Chow Company."

"Why?"

"Because I want it to benefit my cousins. You are a good teacher."

"But all of your people should have the opportunity to . . ."

"We will pay you well."

She fell silent.

"Fifty dollars a month."

She smiled at his offer, then grew serious at its implication. "Chin, do you have the authority to make such an offer?"

"I do," he lied.

She thought about it. She had known him for a long time now. Perhaps she was wrong in still thinking of him as just a young student. He had worked hard for the Company and apparently he was being advanced in rank. She looked at him with new respect.

"Chin, I appreciate your offer. But money isn't . . ."

"Rebecca," he said, interrupting her again, "I have another reason I want you to teach my people."

"What is that?"

"Because . . . because I don't want to lose your friendship. I . . ." He lowered his eyes. "I would miss you."

Rebecca felt her heart jump, deeply touched by this admission, which she knew was very difficult for him to make. Chin watched as lines formed at the corners of her eyes and for a moment he thought she was thinking, but then he knew it was something else.

"What's wrong, Rebecca?"

"Nothing."

"Something, I think. Sometimes you are so . . . so puzzling."

Then she smiled, "Do you think only the Chinese can be inscrutable?"

Chin laughed. Whatever had been bothering her receded and she said, "Chin . . . Chin, look at me."

He did.

"You are a dear friend; more than the student you once were. We shall always be friends."

"But if you don't . . ."

"The problem is solved," she declared. "I will work for the Kong Chow Company."

116

"Rebecca!" he said, grabbing her hands in excitement. "You will?" Then he realized what he had done and he quickly withdrew his hands.

"What's the matter, Chin?"

"I'm sorry. I didn't mean to . . ."

"You don't have to apologize," she said, reaching out and taking his hand in her own. "I'm moved that we have a friendship and it is out of that friendship that I will work for your company." She smiled. "You can forget about the fifty dollars a month. This is a friend doing a favor for a friend."

Chin smiled, daring to look at her. He looked down at her hand holding his. Then he looked at her eyes. He loved her. He had always loved her. His throat tightened, choking off his voice from saying those words. He worked at shaping his mouth and instead the words came out as, "Thank you, Rebecca. Thank you very much."

One evening during the spring, Chin followed Mei Peng into the Meeting Hall of the Kong Chow Company. As usual, he took his place by Mei Peng's right hand.

The chamber was, of course, smaller and less elaborate than the chamber of the Meeting Hall of the Middle Kingdom; and yet it was not that much smaller, for in the years since the Kong Chow Company had begun in California, the number of its delegates had increased fivefold. Now the company was represented by thirty men, where before six had sufficed.

Lo Chi, the president of the Kong Chow Company, began by expressing the Company's regret at losing the services of its respected treasurer, Tang Chao. After announcing the banquet to be held in the treasurer's honor before he returned to China as a monied man, Lo Chi approached the main business of the meeting: the appointment of Tang Chao's successor. In five minutes' time, Mei Peng had been elevated to the position of treasurer of the Kong Chow Company.

It was Mei Peng who nominated Chin for the delegate seat being vacated by his appointment. To his great surprise and pleasure, Chin won the seat.

Sitting in Mei Peng's office after the meeting, Chin began to realize the responsibility that had been given him. Shao Kow, he decided, would be his own assistant. He, Chin, was now the personal representative of three hundred of his cousins! In addition, Mei Peng's elevation meant that Chin would now become senior accountant of the Company. His salary would be almost doubled; he would have new, private living quarters. When Chin rose to leave, Mei Peng had to remind him that the office which the new delegate was about to respectfully remove himself from was now his own.

Chapter 16

Chin opened his eyes. He lay still in his bed for a long moment, not wanting to get up quite yet. He preferred to luxuriate beneath the fresh sheets. He had been in his new living quarters, on the third floor of the Kong Chow Company, for a month now, and it still had a dreamlike quality to it, as if he could awake at any second and find himself back in the small room he shared with three other accountants.

But it was not a dream.

Chin pushed back the covers and swung his legs over the side of the bed. Morning light was flooding in through the window and he sat on the bed looking at it.

A window, he thought; a *window*.

He shook his head for a moment, then rose, slipping his feet into the clogs beside his bed. He crossed the wood floor and threw a match into the stove in the corner of the large room. Good-luck banners dominated the wall by the stove.

He turned and went to his dresser—this a present from Mei Peng to celebrate his new apartment. He took out his trousers and began dressing.

Chin liked this time of day most; when it was quiet, when he was alone, when he could reflect upon his good fortune.

He ate his morning meal of rice and then left the room. He took the stairs down to the second floor, opened the door of the office where he had previously labored and saw that Shao Kow was already hard at work.

His former roommate looked up as Chin opened the door. He bowed his head slightly. "Good morning, Chin."

Chin bowed in return. "Will you have the work I gave you yesterday finished by noontime?"

"By ten o'clock, Chin."

118

Chin smiled. "That is very good, Shao Kow. I will be in my office if you need me."

Shao Kow bowed again as Chin left. Chin walked down the hallway, thinking that he had made a wise choice in selecting Shao Kow to be his assistant. In the years they had roomed together he and Chin had forged a strong friendship. Now there was a subtle change in their relationship, yet not one which changed its quality.

Clearly, Shao Kow regarded Chin as a superior and that filled Chin with a strange feeling. It was a queer thing for him to think of himself as a leader. He had always felt that he was an employee of the Kong Chow Company; but a leader?

He opened the door of his office and walked inside. It was a large office. It seemed much larger to him than it had when it was Mei Peng's office. He sat down behind his oak desk, leaned back in the chair, and smiled. Then he shook himself out of it.

But by noon his mood had swung from elation to depression. He had seen a long stream of his constituents. Each had complained of beatings, robberies, brutalities at the hands of whites. His final visitor had been an old woman who had been robbed and beaten by a gang of white hoodlums.

Chin paused during lunch and said, "I tell you, Rebecca, it was one of the saddest mornings of my life listening to that old woman's tale of woe."

Rebecca sat across the table from Chin in the restaurant. She had felt honored that she was one of the first people with whom he had shared the news of his appointment as a representative.

But Chin saw the tides running against the Chinese and though he felt warmth toward Rebecca, he knew their friendship would be sorely tested. To Chin she seemed a woman reluctant to change. She sought to keep things as they were and improve upon them as best she could, rather than risk the danger of bold action. Accordingly, their meetings had grown increasingly morose. Lately an air of tension had forced its way between them as well.

"There must be an end to it, Rebecca. It isn't right for old people to suffer so."

Rebecca nodded, sipping her tea. "And you were right to tell her you are doing all you can do."

"Perhaps. But, as she pointed out, that will not fill her belly. No, Rebecca, it's just not enough."

"You can't very well be her personal bodyguard."

"No, I can't." He picked up a water chestnut and popped it into his mouth. "Were it that simple I would offer her my services. But she is just one in a long line that files through my office each day with complaints of abuse."

"You can't assign a protector to each person living in San Francisco."

Chin nodded. "You're right. And even if I could it wouldn't accomplish anything. The power to bring about change lies with the whites. And still, I must be realistic; those San Franciscans who are pro-Chinese are only a small minority." Chin glanced toward the window. "Anti-Chinese sentiment will garner votes at the polls for the present and it is a fact of life that my people must live with. And yet, the whites are our hope."

The waiter came to their table and poured more tea. When he left, Rebecca said, "What do you mean, the whites are your hope?"

Chin glanced around the restaurant, then lowered his voice a degree. "Rebecca, what I tell you is in utmost secrecy and only because you are a dear friend. You must swear never to repeat it to anyone. Do you swear?"

"I swear."

"Tonight, Mei Peng takes me with him to a secret meeting of the Vigilantes. It is there that we hope to find the solution to the problems of violence in our streets."

Her hands went to her mouth. "Oh, no, Chin. You mustn't. The Vigilantes operate outside the law, above the law."

"Sometimes it is necessary to operate in such a manner."

"Never. Laws are the only things that keep us civilized."

"But when the laws are not complete enough, when the ordinary police are not compassionate enough to—"

"Civil obedience is what keeps society together, Chin."

"When the laws and elected officials do not do their job, then other methods must be resorted to. These are difficult times, Rebecca. My people bear the brunt of it. We must seek justice and protection where they can be found."

Riley and O'Malley walked at the head of the gang of eight Irishmen. They'd spent the better part of the afternoon drinking and now, as dusk fell on the city, they were heading for Chinatown and an evening's entertainment.

The ragtag bunch crossed into the Chinese quarter, their laughter growing louder now. As they ambled down the

120

middle of DuPont Street the crowd seemed to scatter before them. Men quickly ducked indoors and into shops. Others froze as they rounded a corner and, seeing the gang, turned back in the direction they had come from.

Tim and Colin Shaughnessy lagged behind the rest of the gang, their pace slowed as they stooped to scoop up some stones. These they began throwing at whatever Chinese happened to be in the area, sending them running, to laughter and cheers from the rest of their group.

The men rounded the corner of DuPont and Clay. Riley's eyes narrowed as he looked at a man carrying two wicker baskets of laundry suspended over his shoulders by a pole.

"Hey," Riley said, grabbing the man by his blue jacket, "lookie what we got here."

The yellow man struggled, trying to get free from Riley's grip and balance the load at the same time.

Riley laughed harder than all the rest of his gang and tightened his hold on the man. "Look at this little yellow worm squirm!"

Then Riley stopped laughing and shook the man hard. "Where you think you're goin' to, boy?"

The man's eyes went wide with fear. "No sabbie, no sabbie!"

" 'No sabbie,' huh? Maybe you'll sabbie this," Riley said, slapping him across the face with his open hand.

Behind him, Brian O'Malley glanced over his shoulder, then back to Riley. "Come on, Jamie. Let's be done with it."

"Ah, what's your hurry, Brian?"

"Coppers are liable to come down on us if we aren't careful."

"Coppers, hell. You think they care about this little yellow scum?"

Tim Shaughnessy slid behind the laundryman and pulled the wicker baskets from the poles. The laundryman turned frantically, struggling against Riley as the load tipped.

"No! No! No take laundry! Not mine!"

Tim kicked the laundryman viciously in the kneecap, simultaneously drawing a yelp of pain from the man and laughter from the gang.

"Tell me what to do, will you?" Shaughnessy pulled the lid off the wicker basket and tossed it away, watching for a moment as it sailed through the air.

Then he turned back to the terrified man. "We have to

scrounge for work and you bastards get all the business you can stand!"

"No, no," the man said, shaking his head hysterically. "White man's laundry! White man's laundry!"

Tim Shaughnessy turned the basket upside down and dumped the contents into the dirty street. The gang laughed raucously as the laundryman began to scream a high shriek.

Now the men in the gang moved in and kicked the freshly washed sheets and shirts around on the ground.

O'Malley edged closer to Riley. "Come on, Jamie."

But Riley, with the man in his grasp, turned to eye O'Malley. "You must be gettin' old or somethin'," Riley said. "Don't you like to have fun anymore?"

"Not when it could land us all in the calaboose."

"All right, all right." Riley turned back to his victim. "Let's have your money, Chink."

"No sabbie, no sabbie."

"You sabbie, all right. The game's over, you runt." Riley stuck out his open palm. "Come on; let's have it."

"No sabbie, no sa—"

Riley interrupted the man's words with a well-placed knee driven in the groin. The man screamed with pain, clutching at his loins.

Riley jerked him back up. "Well?"

"No sab—"

Riley rammed his knee home again, doubling the hapless man anew. This time when the man opened his mouth to scream he was unable to. Tears trickled down from his eyes.

Again Riley pulled him up straight. "The money, you little yellow cockroach!"

"No . . . no sabbie . . ."

Riley frowned. "Little weasels don't know how to cooperate." He slammed the man down to the ground, watching as he crumbled to a heap, not unlike the laundry which lay scattered about him. "All right, boys, let's get moving."

Two of the gang members bent down on either side of the man and began ripping at the pockets of his trousers. The man began to yell, but his shouts were silenced when Colin Shaughnessy lashed a pistol butt across his jaw. One of the men found money stuffed deep in the man's pocket.

O'Malley kept glancing around the street, which by now was as empty as a ghost town. Every few minutes a Chinese would round the corner. Sometimes he would stare for a moment. But he'd take off running as soon as one of the gang looked in his direction.

In another moment it was over. One of the men tossed the money up to Riley, while the Shaughnessy brothers each gave the battered laundryman a last set of kicks in the ribs to remember them by.

Then the gang moved up the street, rolling through Chinatown, looking for fresh prey.

"I'd like everyone to settle down, please." The speaker pounded a gavel on the table in front of him. "If we could all just settle down, please."

Chin looked about the warehouse. Boxes were stacked behind them. Of the perhaps half a hundred men in the room, all but a few were white. There were a dozen Chinese present, two delegates from each of the Six Companies.

"All right," the speaker said once again, "let's quiet down."

Chin looked back to the table at the front of the room. Four whites were sitting along its length. Standing in the middle was the tall man who was speaking at present. He seemed to be little more than an introducer, since he was having a difficult time getting order. Finally the room grew quiet.

"All right," the man continued, "now you all know why we're here." He paused, making certain he had their attention before he continued. He shook his head sadly. "Things have just started getting way out of hand. We got to deal with this riffraff element."

There were hardy choruses of agreement from the men, and Chin, too, nodded.

"Bad enough they were picking on these poor Chinese fellows," the man said, gesturing toward the delegation from the Six Companies, "but now they've taken to beating up decent white folks."

"We have to stop 'em," someone shouted.

"Getting so my wife's afraid to go to the store," echoed another.

"Right, right," the man said, quieting them with his hands. "That's what we're here for. Don't seem like the police can do much, or care to, for that matter."

"Damn right!" a voice called.

"All right. So it looks like it's up to us." He lowered his voice a degree. "Some of us have already been . . ." He paused as he searched for the words. "Have been taking action on our own. But we're working against a large number

123

of hoodlums in this city and it's going to take a combined effort to overcome them." The man looked up and down the length of the table, at the four men who flanked him. Then he turned back to the crowd. "Now I'm going to introduce a man who some of you know. Those of you who don't know him personally probably know *of* him. I'm talking about William T. Coleman."

A cheer rose up from the men in the warehouse, with the delegates from the Six Companies politely joining in. Coleman, seated to the speaker's left, rose. Six foot four, with great curls of hair covering his mouth and chin, he looked like a burly bear. Coleman strode to the speaker's position. He looked out over the audience and waited until the man who had introduced him sat down.

Finally, Coleman said, "Thanks for the introduction, Jess." He turned to the men and began. "I'm a law-abiding man."

His tone was soft, almost reverent, and the men in the room grew deathly silent, listening.

"I think we're *all* law-abiding men," he said, spreading his arms outwards toward his audience. He paused a moment, letting the point sink in before continuing.

Coleman's eyes ranged over the men. "Like Jess said, a lot of you know me. And I know a lot of you pretty well, too." He nodded at several of the men as he spoke. "Pete, Ted, Clint Morgan. Our young'uns go to school together, don't they, Clint?"

The man in the audience nodded in response.

"We're just regular folks. But this isn't a regular situation we're in. Now I don't hold with people taking the law into their own hands, any more than I hold with breaking the law in the first place. But it seems to me that when the police don't or can't do much of anything about it, then it's time someone *did* do something about it."

Hearty shouts of approval testified to the fact that he was telling the crowd what they wanted to hear.

When they had quieted again, he said, "Any man who wants out now, no one will think the less of him and he won't be afforded any less protection than any other citizen. We're looking for law enforcement officers at this meeting tonight. Any man who doesn't think he's got the gumption or the strength for it, then he'd better say so now than later."

Coleman paused, looking around the room at the frozen audience.

He nodded. "Good. Then we're together on this thing." He

pulled a sheet of paper out of his jacket. "All right, we're going to break up into groups. In a minute I'll read the names of your captains and which group of enforcement areas you're assigned to. We've tried to keep it as close as possible to the neighborhoods you come from.

"Your captains will brief you on enforcement procedures and our operating plans for the next few months. I'm sure that if we all pull together we can make quick work of these hoodlum gangs and get our city back in working order in short time. I want to thank all of you men for coming tonight."

Coleman read the names of the district captains and then the names of the men assigned to them. The audience split into different corners of the warehouse to be briefed by their captains. The Vigilance Committee of 1856 had been formed.

William T. Coleman stepped down from the platform and walked across the cracked concrete floor of the warehouse to the delegation of the Six Companies.

He nodded. "Well, that's about the size of it. You boys got any suggestions?"

Mei Peng, the official spokesman of the group, stepped forward. "Our concern, Mr. Coleman, is the extent of protection which will be offered to the Chinese community here in San Francisco."

Coleman frowned. "I can't make any guarantees. We got a big city to cover and while I can sympathize with your situation, you have to understand that our first obligation goes to our own citizens."

Mei Peng nodded. "We understand this. However, *you* must understand that *our* first obligation goes to *our* own people."

Coleman stiffened. "Then maybe you ought to form your own vigilance committee."

Mei Peng smiled, lowered his eyes for a moment, and then leveled his gaze at the towering man. "It seems you have misunderstood our purpose in coming to this meeting tonight. It is, of course, quite impossible for us to do what you suggest. The thought of a band of Chinese punishing a gang of white hoodlums can only be followed with immediate thoughts of that same Chinese band escorted to jail by white police officers."

"I don't know what you—"

Mei Peng silenced the man with a graciously outstretched hand. "As I said, I fear you have misunderstood our presence

125

here tonight. We have not come here to beg protection of you. Our purpose was to observe the sincerity of your desire to contend with the hoodlums and analyze your ability to achieve those goals. It seems that both of these things are at a commendably high level." Mei Peng paused, then said, "What we propose to do, Mr. Coleman, is purchase the services of your organization."

Coleman stared incredulously at the diminutive man standing before him. "Purchase?"

Mei Peng nodded slightly. "Exactly, sir."

"We're not professional police officers."

"Thankfully so," Mei Peng remarked with a wry smile.

Coleman laughed heartily at the remark. He placed his massive hands on his hips. "I like you, Chinaman. Go on. Let's hear what you have to say."

"We fully realize, as you have said, that your first obligation is to your own citizens. What we suggest is to put in your hands a certain sum of money with which you shall recruit and administer a subdivision. This group shall be trained by your men and responsible directly to you. They shall operate within the boundaries of Little China. Their sole duty shall be to make that area safe for our people."

Coleman puckered a lip. "I don't know. If we were talking about white areas it'd be another story. Folks got a vested interest in their own community. But Chinatown—you'd have to pay a man a pretty fair wage to convince him to police that area, even with jobs as scarce as they are."

Mei Peng turned to Chin, who handed him a slip of paper. "We are so prepared," the treasurer said. Mei Peng handed the slip to Coleman.

Coleman took it and looked at it. It was a check from Wells, Fargo for $10,000. Coleman whistled a long, slow whistle.

Mei Peng said, "That shall be the first installment. We shall provide additional money as you require it."

The tall vigilante chief looked down at the treasurer of the Kong Chow Company. "How do you know I won't cheat you? How do you know I won't ask you for more money when I don't need it?"

"There is a bond between honorable men, Mr. Coleman. It is invisible; but it is as apparent as a badge of gold pinned to one's shirt. The mere fact that you and your men are taking the risk of vigilance upon yourselves is proof that you are honorable men.

"You will not cheat me, sir. It is not in your nature to cheat a man who solicits your help."

"Chinaman," Coleman said, holding his hand out, "you've just made yourself a deal."

Mei Peng looked at the white man's outstretched hand. His stomach tightened, thinking about the repulsive Occidental habit of pressing palms to seal a bargain.

He fought against the feeling, and reached out and clasped Coleman's hand, his own small yellow fist all but enveloped. Coleman shook his hand and then Mei Peng picked up the tempo, shaking Coleman's hand harder and harder, up and down, smiling widely as the delegation from the Six Companies began cheering around them, clapping their hands together and nodding with great enthusiasm and excitement.

The pact had been made.

The following Saturday found James Riley and his men at Gallagher's Saloon. Riley downed his fourth stein of ale and pushed away from the bar. He slapped O'Malley on the shoulder.

"Pay Gallagher and let's be going," he said.

O'Malley was the gang's unofficial treasurer, by virtue of his experience in an accounting job he'd held some years back. He dug deep into his pocket and produced a wad of bills. O'Malley peeled off a five and paid for the gang's drinks.

Out in the streets in front of Gallagher's, Tim Shaughnessy was engaged in a playful fight with Billy McNamara. They kept up the banter, slapping at each other with open hands, as Riley walked out of the bar with the others.

"Come on, boys; save that stuff for the Chinks." McNamara and Shaughnessy fell in with the others as the gang began its march toward Little China.

The streets were quiet and Riley didn't really hope for much of a take this evening—just enough to pay for next week's drinks and board, with a little pocket money left over.

Shadows were beginning to fall as they crossed into Chinatown. They'd gotten a late start, having slept till noon after the previous night's revelry.

They started the evening off by strong-arming a couple of young men who were unfortunate enough to be caught in their net. But the take was meager—a few dollars. Half an hour later a laundryman fell prey to them and they were ten dollars richer.

It was starting to get dark and Riley was more than a little tired. Saturday wasn't even worth the effort, he reflected. In the future, he decided, they'd take a break on the weekends. There was enough to be made during the week.

They rounded the corner of Stouts Alley. Riley was about to call it a day when they spied a Chinese selling cigars on the corner.

"Cigars," Riley said to O'Malley. "I could do with a smoke."

O'Malley nodded, glancing about. "Let's be fast about it."

Riley glanced at him out of the corner of his eye. "Takes time to enjoy a good smoke." He looked back to the rest of the gang. "Anyone for a smoke?"

There was a rumble of affirmation from the hoodlums. They advanced up the street on the cigar vendor. The vendor turned and saw them too late. The box on which his wares were displayed was slung over his shoulder by a leather strap and he knew he would never have time to get it off and run. The hounds would overtake him before he got a block. He decided to try and bluff it out.

He smiled affably as the gang of hoodlums approached. "Evening, evening, boss."

"Hi, Chink," Riley spat.

The Chinese smiled wider. "Evening, boss. Want a smoke? Good cigar," he said, drawing on all his English, hoping they would be pleased. "Very best, boss."

Riley leaned against the brick facade of the building on the corner. "Sure, scum; you can sell me a cigar." He paused. "Make it two cigars."

The Chinese nodded, eyeing the other men in the gang. "Sure, boss," he said, pulling the cigars from the tray. "Two good smokes." He handed the stogies to Riley and Riley grabbed them.

The vendor was still smiling, but now a trace of fear crossed the corner of his mouth. "That be a quarter, Boss."

Riley bit off the tip of one of the cigars and spit it out, missing the vendor's feet by a hair. He pulled a match from his pocket and ran it along the face of the brick wall. The match flamed to life and Riley touched it to the tip of the cigar, puffing.

"A quarter? For this shit?" Riley puffed harder, billows of smoke rising now. "This stuff tastes like it was made from cow chips."

"Good cigar, good cigar," the vendor said, his mouth starting to quiver now.

"You got a license to sell this crap?" Riley asked.

"License?"

"Yeah. You got a peddler's license?"

"Good cigar."

"You ain't got a license we have to confiscate this as evidence." Riley grabbed at the cigar tray and the vendor started shouting in Chinese, drawing gales of laughter from the rest of the men.

Riley easily pinned the little man's arms and pulled the cigar tray off of him. He tossed the cigars around to the rest of his men, while half the tray's contents spilled to the ground.

The vendor bent, frantically trying to pick up what was left of his cigars. Riley kicked his knee into the side of the man's head, sending him crashing against the brick wall. The man crumbled, unconscious, to the ground.

Riley frowned. "Looks like we ain't gonna get much of a fight outta this fish." He nodded toward the Shaughnessy brothers and they moved in, frisking the man's pockets with their hands. In a moment they found the roll of bills and a change purse. Colin tossed the bills to Riley. Tim did the same with the change purse. Riley looked at the unconscious man and spit on him.

He laughed. "That'll teach him to sell lousy cigars." They moved down Stouts Alley, smoking the cigars and laughing.

McNamara was the first to see them. He froze in his tracks. Riley was still laughing when he looked up.

"What's wrong?" He craned his neck, looking past his men, who'd stopped walking. "What is it?" Riley spat on the alley, pushing them aside.

As they moved out of his way, Riley looked down the alley. Blocking their way, at the mouth of the street, were eight men. The men were big, each as big as Riley himself. Each man wore a hood, which was fastened about his neck so it couldn't be pulled off.

"Hey," Riley said, "what is this?"

One of them raised a club in his hand and began smacking it into the palm of his other hand, with a sound like that of a razor slapping a strop. Riley's eyes focused on the weapon. It was an ax handle.

Instinctively, Riley turned. At the other end of the alley,

cutting them off, was an identical group of men. The two groups of men began closing in on Riley's gang.

In the narrow alleyway half of Riley's gang turned in one direction and the other half headed up the alley. The masked vigilantes cut through Riley's group like a lance through straw. The sound of ax handles thudding against shins and collarbones reverberated back and forth against the walls, blending with the screams of pain that came from Riley's men.

Somehow the Shaughnessy brothers managed to make it past the vigilantes. McNamara was grabbed by two of them and struck four times with ax handles. When the men holding him were certain that both his arms had been broken they turned him loose to run screaming down the alleyway.

It was over in a matter of minutes. Riley's men lay broken and bleeding in Stout's Alley. Of the men caught in the trap, there was not one who hadn't suffered a broken bone, and more than one of them had multiple fractures.

Moans and whimpers of pain were all that Riley heard as four of the vigilantes dragged his beaten body away from the scene.

The rough burlap cloth chafed against James Riley's face as he struggled to get into a more comfortable positon. He'd long since given up trying to get free. There wasn't any sense to that, he reasoned. He was vastly outnumbered and he'd been badly beaten. He wasn't in any kind of shape to fight them even if he did get free.

Besides, he thought, there wasn't much chance of getting loose. They'd firmly bound his hands behind his back with heavy hemp rope that chewed painfully into his wrists when he tried to loosen it.

Someone pushed him forward and he stumbled, unsure of himself.

"Move it along," a voice ordered from behind him.

He walked along another two paces and the ground fell out from under him. He fell, pitching forward, down three stairs, trying to catch his balance. He tumbled to the ground, banging his knee, then slamming his chest into the hard ground. He lay on the ground, fighting the pain.

He felt the ax handle prod at him. "On your feet," a different voice said.

"Give a man a chance," Riley pleaded.

"Like you gave those Chinaboys a chance?"

130

"They're only Chinks!" he snapped angrily. "What the hell do you care about some goddamned Chinks?!"

The pain that exploded when the blow landed was awesome. Riley hadn't known that anything could hurt so completely, that anything could control so terribly. It had struck in his back, and the force of the ax handle lashing into his kidney drew a mute scream from him. He rolled on the floor inside the burlap potato sack roped over his head.

Hands grabbed him roughly and pulled him to his feet, then shoved him on his way again. Riley wrestled with the gripping pain, not wanting to let it show. He was totally at their mercy, but he didn't want to give them the satisfaction of knowing they'd hurt him.

He listened to a heavy door sliding open. A livery stable, he thought. No, not with a heavy door like that. It was a steel door. A warehouse. Yes, he thought, a warehouse.

Someone pushed him inside and it was suddenly cooler. He felt a little fresher as the cool air wafted over him, the pain receding a bit. Then he was pushed forward again. He walked with the halting steps of a man who was unsure of his footing. Ten steps, twenty steps, twenty-five. Then, for the first time, he felt someone slow him down, stop him.

He halted. He was there, he thought, wherever "there" was.

Again Riley felt hands, this time rudely pushing him down into a stiff-backed chair. He could hear men milling about him, and others in front of him. He felt a man at his side, untying the ropes. There was a tremendous release as the ropes came undone, and Riley's hands tingled as the blood began to circulate once again.

Suddenly the burlap sack was pulled off his head and light pierced his eyes, forcing them shut.

"Open your eyes," a voice commanded, and Riley struggled to do so.

He squinted, the harsh light making him tear, and he felt a pang of shame because he feared the men might think he was bawling.

"What's your name?" the voice in front of him asked.

"What's yours?" Riley answered.

From his left a man walked up to him and swung forward hard, cracking Riley across his left shin with an oak ax handle.

"Oh JEEESUSSS!!" he screamed, the pain wrenching the cry from him. He clenched his eyes tightly, seeing only red on the backs of his lids as the hurt lanced through every part of his body.

"We'll not have any of your smart gutter talk here, you trash. And none of your blasphemies, either. When you're asked a question you'll answer it; do you understand?"

Riley nodded his head, still unable to speak after the blow.

"All right. Your name, then."

"Riley. James Thomas Riley."

He opened his eyes, becoming more accustomed to the stark beam in his face. He tried to look past it, and he could just make out the shape of four men sitting behind a long table. Each of them wore hoods identical to those of the men who'd attacked them.

"Sit up straight!" one of the men at the table barked. "And don't try to make out anything. You'd do better to worry about yourself than us."

Riley obeyed, sitting upright, the beam of light more directly in his face now.

"So it's Riley, is it?" the first voice said.

"Aye. Riley."

"We've just about had it with scum like you, Riley. People like you make it so decent folks are afraid to walk the streets."

"I ain't—"

"Shut up, boy!" the second voice said.

"Say, listen," Riley barked, "you take me to the coppers if you—"

"Forget about the coppers," another voice called. "Coppers are part of the reason you're here. Half of them aren't much better than you and that isn't saying much."

The first vigilante began speaking again. "You give this city a bad name, Riley. You give the Irish a bad name."

Riley bristled. "Now wait a minute. Don't start talking about the Irish, I don't care what—"

"I'm Irish," the man said, cutting him off. "Don't give me any false pride, Riley. If you cared at all about Ireland you wouldn't act in a way to bring shame on it."

Riley fell silent again.

The man continued. "Bands of young punks ringled by bigger punks like you. Terrorizing decent folks, persecuting the Chinese. You make it bad for everyone. We're not going to put up with it anymore. You understand that?"

The man's voice was louder now, more angry. "There's no place in this city for the likes of you and your kind. We're

132

going to run you out if we have to round up every last one of you. We want you out of here, out of our city. If you know what's good for you, you and your men will get out while you're still in one piece. Tonight's only a sample of what you'll be getting if you stay."

"To—tonight?"

"That's right," the voice said, "tonight. You've committed crimes, Riley. You've got to pay for them. You've got to pay in full."

"What crimes?" Riley demanded, a nervous edge to his voice.

"Assault and battery, theft . . . God knows what else you've done that we don't know about."

Riley leaned forward, his heart pounding. "But them was only Chinese . . . just yellow scum . . ."

"They're people, Riley . . . people. Maybe you'll remember that next time." The man paused for a moment, punctuating his remarks. Then he said, "Let the punishment be administered."

"Punishment?" Riley said. "What punishment?"

Four men moved into his field of vision, two on either side of him. Two of them fastened his arms and legs to the chair, while another slipped a hood over his jerking head.

Riley shouted as they readied him. "What *right* do you have to do this?"

"The right that decent people have to protect themselves when their elected officials fail in that job."

Riley jerked back and forth on the chair. "You have no right, you have no right, you have—"

His words were cut short as he felt the cold steel hammer slam down onto the fingers of his right hand, crushing bone, tearing skin in the process.

Riley's shrieks rose in a horrible cacophony of pain as the iron tool hit again and again, breaking bone after bone, smashing knuckle after knuckle, splitting nail after nail until his hand was a throbbing ball of meat and agony made wet and sticky by the pulsing flow of blood. Still he screamed, on and on, until at last blessed unconsciousness mercifully cloaked him.

BOOK TWO

BOOK TWO

Chapter 17

The gold with which the Six Companies had bought the aid of the Vigilance Committee of 1856 helped halt the growth of violence against the Chinese. But it did not wipe it out. The Chinese were too convenient a target for either the unemployed or the politicians to ignore.

By 1857 the gold mines and the streams were all but worked out, and new hordes of unemployed flooded into San Francisco, reenforcing the already sizable hoodlum element. The vigilantes grew in size too, and more than three hundred men wore the white hood.

The Six Companies put aside some of the dissension which had ripped them apart and pooled their resources during this time of crisis. They raised large sums of money and donated it to Coleman's men. Violence flared in 1857, though, as throngs of unemployed demonstrated during the winter months.

The politicians played on the emotions of the masses, and none was more successful than John Bigler, incumbent governor of the state. Bigler had remained in office since 1852 by capitalizing on racist issues.

Curiously, once he was reelected the outcry against the Chinese began to wane. Perhaps it was because the unemployed felt the election of Bigler was a victory for them; but more likely it was because Californians had more important events in other parts of the country to concentrate on. By mid-1860 it appeared that there would be a civil war.

Steamers brought news daily. Transcripts of speeches by Lincoln, by Lee, by Grant arrived. Jefferson Davis was a household word. Still, it appeared that California would ally itself with the North, and because of this some measure of racism began to subside.

In late 1860 there was a flurry of excitement over the news of a small gold strike not far from the original 1849 strike at Sutter's Mill. At first there had been wild rumors as to the size of the strike. But later it became apparent that it wouldn't be anything approaching that of the Mother Lode.

It was on the last night of 1860 that Chin, who had labored diligently throughout these years, knocked gently on the door of Mei Peng's living quarters on the third floor of the Kong Chow Company house.

Mei Peng opened the door. "Chin," he said, surprised. "I had not expected you."

Chin remained in the hallway. "If the hour is late I shall go. I didn't mean to disturb you . . ."

"No, no. By all means, come in." Mei Peng stepped back. "I welcome the visit."

Chin stepped into the large living room of Mei Peng's apartment and closed the door.

"Be seated. I'll bring some tea," Mei Peng said, walking toward the couch he had been sitting on when Chin first knocked. Mei Peng sat and picked up a silver bell. This he rang, and shortly a servant appeared at the doorway of the kitchen.

"Some tea for Chin and myself," he said, and the servant disappeared.

Chin sat on the low divan and glanced about the apartment, marveling. No matter that he had been in the treasurer's apartment five score times; each visit held a new delight. Its size was worthy of a mandarin, Chin thought.

The walls were washed in white. Red banners covered many of them. Chin read the symbols on the banners, taking in their meaning.

"Old and Young in Peace and Health." Another read "May the Five Blessings Enter." Still another, "May Health and Prosperity Prevail."

Bamboo mats and silk scrolls hung on the walls, with fierce lions and tigers in yellow and black painted on them to drive away evil spirits and keep the apartment pure. A great bronze statue of a dragon stood at the far end of the room and Chin marveled at its beauty and power until Mei Peng broke into his thoughts.

"You have often regarded the dragon, Chin."

Chin nodded. "It is a thing of rare beauty."

The servant entered and served the tea.

"It was my father's," Mei Peng said, sipping his tea. "He shipped it all the way across the sea."

"How wonderful."

"Not so. It was a signal of his death." Mei Peng paused.

138

"And yet he is truly happy now, for he is with our ancestors in the heavens."

Chin sipped silently at his tea.

Mei Peng turned to him. "And now, what is the purpose of your visit? Surely not a social call? You would not waste your evening with an old man."

Chin clicked his teeth in protest. "Time spent with you, noble teacher, could never be wasted."

Mei Peng laughed. "You are as swift with answers as you are with figures."

But as Mei Peng sipped at his tea Chin watched him, and for the first time he realized that Mei Peng *had* grown old, almost without his noticing it. He had been too occupied with his own efforts to watch his master closely.

How many years had he been in this strange land, he thought. He tried to remember the year he had come. Ten years, more than ten years. He was stunned by the weight of this realization.

And then he looked back to Mei Peng. He had aged; the fringe of hair about his jaw was starting to show traces of white.

"Come," Mei Peng said, leaning forward, "what is on your mind this night that you are so ponderous?"

With the diplomacy which he had learned from the man he was sitting with, Chin raised the teacup to his lips and sipped it, slowing the conversation. Mei Peng smiled faintly.

Chin set the cup down. "In the course of my life in this country I have sought to set aside savings so I might invest and make my fortune."

"That is the wish of every man who comes to this land; to make his wealth and then journey home."

Chin straightened slightly. With a measure of pride in his voice he said, "I have managed to save a somewhat sizable amount. It has come to the point, Mei Peng, that I need advice concerning how to best invest this money, and that is the reason for my visit tonight."

Mei Peng poured more tea from the pot his servant had left. "How much money have you saved?"

Without a moment's hesitation, Chin answered, "Nearly four thousand dollars."

The treasurer's usually expressionless face registered rare surprise. He regained control, setting the teacup down on the teak table before the divan. "You have done well, Chin, to have saved such an amount. It is no mean task."

"I have deprived myself of luxuries which others partake in, that my future might be golden."

Mei Peng nodded. "A wise path, for now while your contemporaries find their pockets filled with but a few dollars you are prepared to venture forth into business."

Chin smiled proudly.

"But let me make certain I am clear on your meaning," Mei Peng quickly added. "Is this to say you propose to step down from your position with the Kong Chow Company? That you would forsake your post?"

A frown crossed Chin's lips. "That is the great dilemma with which I am faced. On the one hand I deeply respect my responsibilities toward this company which has afforded me the opportunity I now have. Yet I realize that it is the desire to make my fortune which brought me to this land to begin with."

"Perhaps you can achieve both purposes."

Chin leaned forward eagerly. "How?"

"There are more than a few representatives in the company's delegation who are private merchants. You can serve both yourself and the Company."

"That would be my dream," Chin said excitedly.

"Then it shall be done," Mei Peng said, slapping his knees with his palms. "Of course," he added, "it shall mean you will have to step down as senior accountant of the Kong Chow Company. You cannot hold the position of merchant and company bookkeeper at the same time and expect to do either job well."

Chin nodded. "I understand and accept this."

"Then, if you do, it shall be done. Your abilities will be sorely missed, but your wisdom shall still be available to the company delegation."

"I shall make myself available to the Council for as long as my services are required, until the end of my days; so great is my gratitude for what it, and you, have done."

Mei Peng clicked his teeth, turning partially away. "Do not include me in such lavish praise. I gave you no special gift. I would have treated any talented young man the same."

But when Mei Peng turned back to look at him, Chin saw that the treasurer was unable to hide the trace of a smile, which showed at the corner of his mouth.

"Very well, then," Mei Peng continued, "when shall you divest yourself of your office?"

Chin checked his own enthusiasm. Things were moving

forward too rapidly. "I . . . I have not decided. I have no idea what business endeavor I shall go into. I only came here to discuss the matter with you."

"You shall be my business partner, of course."

"*Yours?*"

Mei Peng finished his tea and poured yet another cup. "Of course." He looked at Chin's astonishment. "It is the natural course of things."

"But . . . but . . ."

Mei Peng poured more tea into Chin's cup. "I have taught you all I could about the business of the Six Companies, about the business of the Kong Chow Company. You are prepared for the next step in your life. I have been waiting for you to reach this plateau, to step beyond the bounds of the Company. I knew this day would come and now it has."

"But what business do you speak of? In what commerce do you practice?"

Mei Peng stiffened, a wrinkle appearing where a moment ago a smile line had been. "Perhaps I have spoken too quickly. Perhaps I have assumed too much." His voice had changed, had gone blank, masked, void of inflection. "If you are reluctant . . ."

A look of greater astonishment replaced the one which had just been on Chin's face. "No, no; you misunderstand, noble one. Nothing could please me more than to continue to be under your guidance. Indeed, that was one of the things which kept me from making this decision sooner. But now, now to learn that it is possible . . . to learn that such a thing can be . . ." Chin searched for the words. "I had no idea you were in commerce. It is only amazement you see in my face, Mei Peng, not reluctance."

Mei Peng smiled, reading the honesty of Chin's words. "Previously there was no need for you to know of my commercial endeavors. It is best if a man keeps private the affairs of his life which should be kept private. With some men a desire for self-importance makes their tongues loose. But this is not a shortcoming of yours, so there is no need to lecture on it."

Mei Peng crossed one leg over the other, then said, "Now to the point at hand. You desire entrance into the world of commerce and I am in need of a partner."

"Why?"

"I have needed one for quite sometime. The scope of my holdings has multiplied in recent years. It is difficult to find men who are capable of honorably running your business for you unless they, too, are a part of it."

"And what business is that?"

"Import."

Chin's features came alive. "Import! It is an omen of great fortune!" he declared, leaping from his chair. "That is precisely the business I so wanted to become a part of!"

"Sit, sit," Mei Peng ordered with a laugh. "Before long you'll wake all the elders of this house."

Chin sat and said, "Tell me about your business, honorable one."

"A chain of four shops in Little China. Each carries a wide variety of goods—porcelains, silks, jade, ivory carvings." Mei Peng shook his head. "The whites cannot seem to get enough of our homeland's treasures, as we cannot seem to get enough of their gold."

"It is primarily to whites that you cater?"

Mei Peng nodded. "Almost exclusively. I must admit to you that lately business has been off. With the mining out of the goldfields there has been a gradual downturn. But I expect business to pick up again soon; this latest gold strike in Sonora will have a positive effect. More gold will flow through the city. Additionally, I am all but certain there shall be civil war soon, and where there is war there is also profit. All indicators show we are about to move into an era of new prosperity."

"Then I should like to ally myself with you, Mei Peng, if you would so graciously accept me."

"I have already said as much. You shall be a full partner," Mei Peng said, "with an equal share."

Chin stiffened with shock. "An equal partner! But . . . that is not . . ."

Mei Peng silenced him with a raised hand. "There is nothing more to speak of."

"But there is," Chin protested. "I cannot allow you to—"

"I shall do what I want to do."

Chin fell silent.

Mei Peng's tone softened. "Chin, I am growing old."

"You are not . . ."

Mei Peng lowered his eyes and Chin was silent again. Mei Peng continued. "I am at that point in my journey where I am closer to the end than I am to the beginning." He drew a short sigh. "Little things. My sight is not what it used to be. I tire more easily."

He leveled his gaze at Chin. "You will be as much a boon to me as I shall be to you. You will relieve a great burden of the work from me. And do not think you shall get an easy ride, my friend. You shall work as you never worked before. You shall earn every dollar you make. You will rise before the robins and still be awake long after they have bedded down. You will learn how to work the dockfront to find the best bargains and the newest merchandise."

Chin smiled.

Then Mei Peng's voice grew softer. "I have no son. You have been my student. You have learned well. You have washed praise over me by your actions. My peers hold me in high esteem because I have given our company a wise and able leader. It is only fitting that I do something for you in return."

"But a full share, Mei Peng . . ."

"Let's have no more talk of this. It is fitting, young one. Don't worry," Mei Peng said, leaning back on the divan, "I have all that I need." He smiled slightly. "I am a man who is accustomed to luxury. Don't think that I would deprive myself of it in my old age. The golden years are only golden to those who possess the gold."

Chin gave a short laugh.

Mei Peng lowered his voice. "I have all that I need, Chin. More than I need. The years have been very good to me. Importing is not the only business I have engaged in and someday I shall expose you to the full breadth of my interests."

He paused, then said, "But you must master one field at a time. If you listen to me, as you have in the past, you shall prosper."

Chin bowed his head. "My gratitude fills me so completely that it overflows."

And then, in a rare physical expression of his feelings, Mei Peng leaned forward and patted the back of Chin's hand. "You have been a good student, Chin. You have made this old man proud. Now rise to this new adventure and fulfill your destiny."

The carriage rolled through the streets of white San Francisco. It was a foreign world to Chin, one which was at once frightening and exciting. He peered out the window of the carriage, watching white couples strolling down the wide, clean avenues of the city.

Magnificent wood houses, painted every color of the rainbow, lined the blocks. They were set back, with neat, green lawns stretching out before them like a carpet. He wondered what Rebecca Ashley's house would look like.

Good sense told him to wait until he saw her to tell her the news. But the news was too good to bear. He had to share his good fortune with her. He had gone to the hospital where she had said she did volunteer work. Chin had convinced the old white doctor that he had to see her on an urgent matter concerning the Six Companies.

The physician had finally relented, after Chin had assured him that they were friends, and given him her address. He clutched it in his hand now as the carriage pulled over to the curb.

Chin got out, paid the driver and turned to look at a beautiful house, tall, white, stately. He realized how foolish he had been when he had tried to convince her to work for the Kong Chow Company, teaching English; the fifty dollars a month he had offered her meant nothing to a person living in such a mansion.

Chin walked boldly to the door, buoyed by his success with Mei Peng. He rapped the brass lion's-head knocker against the plate and waited. In a moment the door opened and a black manservant looked at him.

"Yes?"

"I am Chin Wong," he paused, then added, "delegate of the Kong Chow Company."

The servant looked unimpressed. He was still blocking the doorway.

"I am here to see Rebecca Ashley."

"Is she expecting you?"

"She . . . no . . ." He drew himself together, reminded himself that he was speaking to a servant. "She will see me. Tell her I am here."

"Very well," the man said, moving aside. "Have a seat in the foyer while I tell her you are here."

Chin stepped inside her house. The entrance foyer was a large, circular room with shining wood floors. He looked at the tall oil paintings hanging on the walls, the cherrywood hall tree, a library table against the far wall. Chin caught his reflection in a mirror over the table as the door closed behind him.

He turned with a start.

"Have a seat," the servant said, indicating one of the chairs in the room.

Chin sat, looking at the winding stairway that led to the second floor. A red carpet runner flowed down the center of the oaken stairs. When Chin turned, the servant was gone.

He busied himself thinking about how to tell Rebecca the news. It was still difficult to believe that she lived in a place of such splendor. As he gradually came to accept it, he felt a tightness grow in his chest. This was her house, the place where she lived, and there was something intimate about the fact that he was here.

"Chin."

He turned at the sound of her voice. She was wearing a long pale blue dress. Her hair was down; it dawned on him that he had never seen it that way. Rebecca's hair was long and glistening and exciting in a way that made him dizzy as he rose.

But as he looked into her eyes he saw that something was wrong.

"What are you doing here?" she asked evenly.

"I . . . I came to tell you some news."

"Come into the den," she said, leading the way.

He followed her, feeling that he was a student again. She wasn't pleased to see him; he could sense that. He had made a mistake in coming. He was an uninvited guest and his presence had put her terribly on edge. He had presumed too much on their friendship.

The den was equal in size to the entrance foyer. Its walls were paneled and warm. Chin didn't bother to look at the furnishings. He couldn't focus on them. All he could feel were the walls, warm and dark and closing in on him. He had made a mistake in coming.

She turned to look at him, for a moment saying nothing, her teeth biting gently into her lower lip as she reached for words. Finally, she said, "Now, what is it you have to tell me?"

"I . . . I shouldn't have come."

She frowned, sensing that her mood was too harsh, knowing that it was wrong to make him uncomfortable just because she was. "I had no idea you knew where I lived."

"I called on the hospital and convinced them to give me your address."

"Whatever for?"

Perhaps the news would salvage the situation, he thought, and he smiled at the possibility. "I have the most marvelous news, Rebecca. I have been offered a position with Mei Peng.

I am to be his partner in his import shops. A *full* partner, Rebecca."

She smiled slightly. "That *is* marvelous news. Congratulations, Chin. I am very happy for you."

"But I should have waited until you came to the Company house to tell you the news?" he asked. "Is that what you mean to say?"

She turned slightly from him, resting her eyes on a pedestal and a bronze statue that sat on it. "Yes," Rebecca said. "Yes, you should have waited."

"I . . . I'm sorry. I thought we were friends and I could . . ."

She turned to look back at Chin. "We are friends. You know that, Chin."

"But not that good friends? Not so good that I could call on you at your home?"

"You don't understand."

"I understand."

"No, you don't," she said firmly and took a step toward him. "Not at all. You have some idea in your head that I'm ashamed to have you call on me because you are Chinese."

He was silent.

"That isn't true. I think you know how I feel about your people by now. I have proven myself."

Chin nodded at the truth of her statement, then said, "Then why are you upset with my visit?"

For a long moment she didn't say anything, thinking. At last she drew a deep breath and said, "Chin, I dedicate a part of my life to you and your people and the poor and the sick. This has not been an easy thing for me to do. As you can see I come from a . . . a comfortable background."

Chin relaxed a bit, sensing that she was speaking from her heart.

"I do what I do because I have a need in me to help those less fortunate than myself. My friendship with you is because . . . I find you an interesting and kind person."

Chin smiled, feeling more uneasy about his previous attitude.

"But it isn't easy for me to give all of this up," she continued. "You must understand that this house is a part of my life, too. I need it. I need the solitude that it gives me. I need the fact that it gives me a separation, a respite from the problems of the people I help."

She frowned. "Call it weakness if you want. Someday perhaps I will be able to do without this. Someday I may be able to . . ."

"Why should you?" Chin asked. "You shouldn't apologize for having comfort. You should enjoy it."

She looked into his eyes. "Can you understand what I'm trying to say? For now I need to keep a part of my life private. This house is like a sanctuary to me."

Chin nodded. "I understand, Rebecca. It was thoughtless of me to have come. It won't happen again. I promise you."

Rebecca stood before him. "I hope this doesn't hurt our friendship. I wouldn't want that."

He smiled widely. "Nothing could ever injure our friendship."

Rebecca's eyes danced in the light from the lamps about the room. "I'm relieved. And I am happy for you and your good fortune."

On impulse, Rebecca reached out and kissed him lightly on the cheek. It would linger with Chin for weeks, that kiss. He would recall how sweet she had smelled, how her hair had glowed. But he would also remember how cold her lips had felt and the tremble he had seen in her hands, and that would trouble him and make him wonder.

Chapter 18

Mei Peng's words had been prophetic, for a little more than three months later, on April 12, 1861, a white-haired Virginian named Edmund Ruffin touched fire to a Confederate cannon and fired the first shot on Fort Sumter, beginning the Civil War.

But Californians didn't have much time to think about the war. One night in the fall before the Civil War began a meeting had taken place over a hardware store in Sacramento which was to change California for all time.

A dozen men had come to Huntington, Hopkins & Company's hardware store to listen to a young civil engineer named Theodore Judah. Judah was trying to drum up investors for a brash undertaking—the construction of a railroad which would link the eastern and western United States.

Four men agreed to give support to the project. They were Charley Crocker, Leland Stanford, Mark Hopkins, and Colli P. Huntington. The latter two were the owners of the establishment the meeting had taken place in. Charley Crocker was a dry goods dealer. Leland Stanford was the only one of the four who had any degree of reknown. He was the founder of the Republican party in California and an aspiring politician. His occupation was wholesale groceries. Stanford would go on to become governor of California.

That night these four men formed the Central Pacific Railroad Company, with each of them assuming offices of responsibility. Leland Stanford became its president. Huntington was vice-president and Hopkins became treasurer.

Theodore Judah went back to Washington, confident of financial backing, and began hammering away at Congress. His strategy was to convince Congress that the railroad was a military necessity. It would serve to link California to the rest of the Union.

He was successful, and on June 1, 1861, Congress voted to approve construction of the railroad. More than $25 million in federal loans and massive land grants followed. The responsibility for constructing the railroad fell squarely to Charley Crocker. Actually, it became Crocker's job by default. By January 1862 Leland Stanford was governor of California and he couldn't very well spend his time walking the tracks. And Huntington and Hopkins were really numbers men, investors.

Charley Crocker knew how to deal with people and it was natural, then, that he should be put in charge of the actual construction.

With much fanfare, construction began in January 1863. There were eight hundred miles of track to be laid, through rugged mountain passes. Crocker told an excited world that his men would do the job.

But what had begun as a spurt of excitement soon turned into a sputter. A year after construction had begun, only nineteen miles of track had been put down, and blame fell, now, to Charley Crocker.

Crocker was a man of determination, though, a man to be reckoned with. So on a hot August morning in 1864 Crocker sat in the elegantly appointed conference room of the Central

Pacific Railroad. He granted, to the board, that there were problems. But he had come to present a solution.

It was a radical solution and one which his chief foreman, James Strobridge, also in attendance, was firmly against. Crocker spent the better part of an hour restating the problems already incurred. Then, when he had dragged the board into the deepest valley of depression, he sprang the idea on them.

Crocker saw the Chinese as a vast, cheap labor pool. And though his chief foreman vehemently protested, Crocker pointed out that nothing could be worse than the lazy, shiftless white men already working on the tracks.

Several of the board members were skeptical. But Crocker pointed out what the future held for them if they failed to complete the railroad. Not the least of those concerned was Governor Leland Stanford, who knew the stakes included his reelection.

Strobridge, who had worked as a foreman on four different continents, was adamantly against the idea of using Chinese on the railroad. He pointed to their small stature, their diet, and the arduous nature of the work. Strobridge refused to take responsibility for their failure, knowing it would reflect on him as well.

Crocker was intelligent enough to know that James Strobridge was the best railroad foreman money could buy. Rather than force the issue, Crocker suggested a test team of fifty Chinese workers.

Strobridge still refused, and words between the two were becoming heated when a secretary entered the conference room with an urgent message. It was a mixed blessing for Charley Crocker—the railroad workers were threatening to strike for higher wages. Crocker made the most of the threat, forcing Strobridge to admit that the men hardly deserved what they were making, let alone a raise.

With only a few miles of track laid and now the men striking for higher wages, the board members began to sway in Crocker's direction. Even Strobridge was incensed by this latest affront. And so, with some reluctance, the men decided to try an experiment with a team of fifty Chinese workers.

Yang was always tired, dog tired. Knowing that he was stronger than most men, he wondered how the others, who had worked at his side in the mud, felt. There was no harder work in the world, he decided, than clearing and reclaiming swampland.

He labored twelve hours a day, knee deep in bog and muck that smelled so foul it turned his stomach in the beginning. It was back-breaking work. There were swarms of ravenous mosquitoes to deal with. Leeches would have to be burned from the men's legs. Nausea and illness broke other men. Once in a while a man would simply collapse forward into the water and have to be dragged from the swamp.

It was the worst kind of work, for the most meager of wages. But at least it was out-of-doors work and that was a consolation to him. He'd not have the padded prison his brother worked in, no matter what the wages.

But at the end of the month's work the men were given a two-day respite and Yang felt himself drawn to the city for relaxation and a change of scenery.

With Wan Choi at his side, he walked through the streets of Chinatown, watching men and boys bustling back and forth, carrying messages, depositing checks and letters of credit at banks. He watched the business of the city and, though he would never admit it to anybody, he felt a small measure of envy. They were caught up in the business of business, and there was a certain importance attached to it.

"It is good to be in the city," Wan Choi said.

"It is a change," Yang agreed.

"And change is good."

"For a time, perhaps." Yang glanced at the sign above a restaurant as the scent of cuttlefish caught his nostrils. "I couldn't live here all the time, Wan Choi."

The two men had dinner. After they left the restaurant Yang noticed that foot traffic had begun to ebb. The business day was finished. Yang felt his mind begin to unwind along with it. His muscles still ached, but he was free of the burdensome work for a few days, free from the sweltering, oppressive heat of the swamp, and he meant to make the most of it.

An ache of another sort slowly replaced the one that had been in his muscles.

As the evening fog began to cloak the city, the two men found themselves in Barlett's Alley. It was exactly where Yang wanted to be. Dim street lamps cast their flickering gas flames on the ground. On either side of the street there was a long series of open doors at street level.

Wan Choi crossed to the opposite side to investigate on his

own. Yang stared in through one of the doorways as he passed by it and saw a young woman inside the bagnio, sitting on a wooden bunk covered by a mattress. He stopped and looked at her.

She was an attractive yellow girl, not more than seventeen or eighteen. His eyes focused on the girl. She was pretty, her hair long and jet-black, well oiled and straight. Her eyes were narrow almonds, barely more than slits that glistened at him. The girl's lips bore a thick coat of lipstick and she wore a checkered handkerchief in her hair—the badge of her profession.

"You like her?" A woman's voice asked.

Yang turned to look at the crouched-over hag standing behind him. She wore a full skirt and a black blouse. Her skin was wrinkled with the fullness of her three-score years. About her girth was a wide belt, to which was hooked a huge ring bearing the forty-three keys which she used to lock the prostitutes in at night.

"I like her better than I like you, old witch," he replied.

The woman laughed heartily. "Well that you do, son. Otherwise I'd have to call for the hospital to have you put in chains with the rest of the loonies there."

Yang returned the woman's laughter. "You're a shrewd old hag."

"When one reaches my age one is either shrewd or dead."

Yang nodded. "How much is the whore?"

"An hour or a full night?"

"I could not bear a full night in the filth-pen she lives in."

"An hour is three dollars."

Yang puckered a lip. "Expensive."

"She's worth it, that one. She's a tiger. Able to please the most demanding man."

Yang looked through the door to the prostitute. The girl looked for a moment to the whore-keeper, then quickly smiled, turning back to Yang.

Yang returned his attention to the old woman. "And how much do you make, withered one?"

"A fair percentage." She sighed a deep sigh. "Less than fair, really, for the amount of work I do."

Yang nodded. "I imagine you find it taxing to lock all those doors at night."

"Hah! Would that that was all there was to it. Keeping them clean, in good spirits, training them in pleasing a man; it is endless."

"Pleasing a man? You? Can you remember back that far?"

The woman spread her feet and perched a hand on each of her hips. "I was pleasing mandarins before you were being weaned, young sprout. Before you were even a thought! Up here," she said, tapping her temple, "up here there's more knowledge about men than a legion of whores could learn in ten lifetimes."

She cackled, then said, "The body may have lost its glow, but the memory still remains—as I'm sure it does in the minds of thousands of grateful men in this world and the next."

Yang laughed loudly, looking at the defiant ex-prostitute standing before him. "All right, old woman." He dug into his pocket and handed her the coins. "I'll take your whore."

The woman pocketed the money and swept her hand toward the open door. "Take your pleasure, young one."

Yang walked toward the door. The girl inside smiled up at him, but as he drew closer and walked into the confines of the cell he noted that the smile was on her lips but not in her eyes.

Yang looked about the cell. The floor was covered with sawdust and straw. The walls were brick. The whole room measured no more than eight by four feet. There was a closeness to the room that was compounded by the smell of the countless bodies which had perspired in it.

Yang closed the heavy door behind him. A single peanut oil lamp on one wall illuminated the bagnio.

"What is your name?" he asked.

"San Mei Dung."

He unbuttoned his shirt and pulled it off. "You are fortunate to be made love to by Yang this night."

She looked fearfully at his massive dimensions.

"Prepare yourself," he said, unbuckling his belt.

The woman rose, still a full six inches below the top of Yang's shoulder. Her hands trembling, she began unbuttoning her blouse.

Yang removed his trousers and the woman's gaze fixed on his massive phallus, stiff and throbbing with excitement from weeks of deprivation.

"What's wrong?" Yang asked. "Have you never seen a cock before?"

Her eyes were frozen on him. "You . . . you will be gentle with me, kind sir? You will be gentle?"

Yang's arm shot out and wrapped about the woman as

152

would a boa constrictor. He pulled her brutally to him, crushing the breath from her as he held her in his grasp.

"I shall be any way I wish with you, whore. I've paid for you and I shall take my pleasure as I choose. No one dictates to Yang."

He pulled her up off the ground and mashed his lips against hers, shooting his probing tongue into her mouth. Yang ripped her away from him suddenly and thrust her back down on the bed.

"Now please me first, whore, in the manner of those in your profession."

Her eyes pleading, she looked up at him. "Please have compassion, great one. Please have—"

The slap of Yang's hand rang as it cracked against the girl's face. "Do not anger me, woman. Now."

Resignedly, she leaned forward, parted her lips and received Yang's pulsing member. For a full minute she worked at him, felt his hands pulling at her hair, felt them kneading and pinching and twisting at her breasts.

And when she felt he was close to completion he pushed her away, forcing her back on the bed. Yang moved his massive body on top of her, crushing the prostitute with his weight, driving the full length of his engorged penis into her with such pain and suddenness that it ripped a cry from her.

She did not have to bear it for long, because in a moment he had reached completion, shooting hot come into her. Her humiliation was complete. He rolled off her and looked down at the whimpering woman-child.

"A fine whore you make," he spat. "The old woman was not so good a teacher as she claimed."

A new fear surfaced in the girl's eyes. "You—you will not tell her this."

"I shall. I shall tell her you still have lessons to learn in pleasing a man."

"But I—"

He smiled. "I will tell her that you were uncooperative."

"You don't understand—you don't—"

"What is there to understand?" he asked, buckling his belt.

"The hag will beat me if you tell her that."

He turned and opened the door. "So much the better. Next time you will learn to do your master's bidding without having to be asked."

Yang left the bagnio and slammed the door shut.

Having satisfied their bodies, Yang and Wan Choi next decided to sate their minds, and so they walked up Dupont toward the Palace Hotel, where they knew an opium den to be located.

But Yang stopped as he crossed Pacific Street. A crowd of Chinese had gathered and he walked toward them. As he and Wan Choi reached the group, they saw that four white men were speaking to them.

For a moment Yang thought about turning and leaving, worried that perhaps they were police. But something about the crowd told him that they were not.

He tapped an old man on the shoulder and the man turned to look up at him.

"What is happening?" Yang asked.

"These white men come from Sacramento. They're hiring men to work on the railroad."

"Railroad," Yang repeated. He listened to the whites, picking up a few of their words which he had learned.

He listened in silence for a while. Apparently they weren't having much success in recruiting. One of the men appeared well mannered. But the one standing next to him looked like a laborer. Yang quickly deduced that the other two men were merely along to insure security.

Strobridge waved a hand toward the crowd of Chinese who had gathered to listen to them and then turned to Crocker.

"I told you it was a crazy idea, Mr. Crocker. These yellow boys don't want to do a man's work. They're not capable. Even if they were, they couldn't figure out what we were talking about."

"I think they understand more than they let on," Crocker said.

Strobridge spit at the ground. "Been here twenty minutes and they still don't know what we've been saying."

Something in the foreman's tone and manner told Yang that he was talking about his countrymen. He didn't need a command of English to get the general idea of what he was saying.

"Railroad," Yang said again to himself. He thought about the swamps, the heat, working in the mud day in and day out.

Yang pushed his way through the crowd and stood before Strobridge and Charley Crocker. "What pay?" he asked.

Crocker came alive. "An honest wage," he said. "A guarantee of thirty dollars a month and all the rice you can eat."

154

"I work," Yang said. "I work railroad." He turned and looked at Strobridge for a moment, their eyes level.

The foreman turned to Crocker. "If they all looked like this one we might have half a chance."

"All right," Crocker said, raising his voice. "Who else? Who else wants to work?"

Wan Choi stepped forward, standing next to Yang, and said, "I work."

"Good," Crocker said, "good." He looked out over the rest of the Chinamen. "Who else? Who else? We're going to build a railroad, damn it! We're going to build it together! Who else will work?"

The other Chinese looked at Yang standing inch for inch with Strobridge. The burly foreman was no longer sniping at them, no longer spitting impatiently on the ground.

Something about the sight of Yang's muscled body being equal to that of the white man inspired them, and one by one the Chinese began stepping forward.

Charley Crocker was to have his Chinese test crew.

Chapter 19

Riley swished some water around in his mouth and spit it out on the ground. He looked up and then turned to Brian O'Malley.

"Another scorcher," Riley said.

"Looks like it," O'Malley agreed.

They had a leisurely breakfast and got to the track site by ten o'clock, slightly over an hour late for work.

Riley and O'Malley were working with a crew of sixty-three men, half of them Irish, half of them French. They were working at Iron's End, the furthermost point of track laid by the Central Pacific Railroad.

It was nothing to brag about, but Riley didn't particularly care. Few of the men on the crew cared about the progress—or lack of it—made by the railroads. The wages, while they weren't spectacular, were enough to keep them in gambling money and buy an occasional whore from the traveling brothels that floated through the camps on weekends.

The food was good and the work was light. If they laid a couple hundred feet of track a day that was exceptional. It was steady work, and while Riley didn't want it as a lifetime profession it sure beat having the vigilantes running after him.

With the vigilantes riding herd over the lawless element in San Francisco, unemployed men had flocked to the railroad in droves, and Riley was one of them. His mauled and twisted right hand was a constant reminder. It was only through the blessing of fate—he had been born left-handed—that he was not too severely inconvenienced by the "lesson" of the vigilantes.

Still, it was a remembrance. When it was about to rain his knuckles would ache painfully. Riley decided he'd wait until the aching stopped before he'd go back to San Francisco. He counted himself fortunate that he'd mended well enough to have use of the fingers on that hand.

Riley was standing with a group of a dozen Irishmen, talking about the Emerald Isle, when he heard the sound in the distance.

"Listen," he said.

The men stopped talking for a moment. One of them, a man named Groggin, said, "I don't hear nothin'."

"No," Riley said, waving at him to be quiet. "Listen."

They listened again and now, in the distance, they could hear the sound of the approaching locomotive.

O'Malley frowned. "Can't be the pay train. Not due until Friday."

"Maybe they're giving us a bonus," one of the men cracked, drawing a laugh.

They leaned against the tools they used for grading and laying rails—shovels, picks, sledgehammers—and waited for the approaching train. It was a diversion and the men welcomed any excuse to stop work.

The black locomotive rose over a ridge half a mile down the tracks and came into view. It was pulling two passenger cars.

O'Malley looked at the approaching black monster, listened to it screaming like a banshee, watched as it spewed thick puffs of gray smoke into the clean California air.

"What do you reckon it is, Jamie?"

Riley scratched his head. "Beats me. Guess we'll see soon enough."

The men moved to either side of the tracks as the Central Pacific locomotive approached. At length it slowed, coming to a huffing, wheezing stop not a hundred yards down the track from them.

The locomotive had no sooner stopped when hordes of dark-blue-suited Chinese began pouring off the passenger car at the rear.

"Well I'll be damned," Riley said.

"Chinamen!" O'Malley exclaimed.

"What the hell are they doing here?"

The Chinese lined up alongside the railroad car and stood at attention. Then, from the first car, Charley Crocker and James Strobridge emerged. The gang of Irishmen scrambled about, the Frenchies joining them, suddenly alive, each of them reaching for a pick or shovel so as to look busy.

Crocker hadn't even looked in the gang's direction. He had other things to think about.

"All right, you men," Crocker began, "we expect an honest day's labor out of you."

Standing next to Charley Crocker and James Strobridge was a stout Chinaman named Wo Ti. As Crocker spoke, Wo Ti's high-pitched voice translated their words into Chinese.

"You've signed on with the Central Pacific for a one-month trial employment. You'll find that if you work hard and well you'll have a steady job with a good wage and all you can eat."

The Chinese nodded enthusiastically as they listened to Wo Ti's interpretation.

"Now, are there any of you who have any questions about what Mr. Strobridge explained in the train on the way out here?"

Crocker waited. There were no questions, only staring slanted eyes.

"You're all sure you understand what's expected of you and how to do the work?"

A sea of straw-hatted heads bobbed in unison. Crocker drew a deep breath and said, "All right, then; let's get to work."

Twenty-five yards up the track James Riley said, "Well, I'll be a blue-eyed son of a bitch. Old Crocker's puttin' Chinks to work on the railroad."

157

Riley laughed a short laugh. Then he laughed again. The men in the group turned to look at him.

"Can you believe it?" he said. "Them little fellas workin' on the railroad? Crocker must have been smokin' locoweed when he came up with this one."

One by one the men in the gang began laughing as they imagined the Chinese lifting sledgehammers that were almost as big as they were, and before long the whole group was laughing hysterically.

The Chinese team didn't hear the men laughing or, if they did, didn't take note of them. Instead, they set about their task. They split into several groups.

One group picked up shovels and began working on the grade. Another group walked toward where the ties lay and paired off to lift the timber. Two other larger groups walked with Strobridge toward where the iron tracks lay.

By noon seventy feet of track had been laid, and James Strobridge stood between the rails with Charley Crocker at his side. Strobridge watched the Chinese moving, swarming, masters of the art of imitation.

"Like a damned swarm of ants," Strobridge said, scratching his head.

Crocker smiled, then clamped a hand on his foreman's shoulder. "Jim, those ants are going to build your railroad for you."

By nightfall the Chinese crew had laid over a thousand feet of Central Pacific railroad track.

The more the Chinese worked, the faster they became. By the end of the week more than two miles of track had been laid. Charley Crocker sent to San Francisco for more Chinese teams, and by the end of the month three hundred Chinese were working on the railroad, with provisions for double that amount in the works—this time with James Strobridge's blessing.

The Chinese quickly adapted to railroad life. They set up their own camps, separate from the French and the Irish. Each evening they dug a pit, filled an enormous cauldron with water, and cooked pot after pot of rice.

Once in a while a group of Frenchmen would stroll by the Chinese camp to watch them eat, unable to believe the Chinamen were not including meat in their diet. The Irish workers were no less amazed that the Chinese didn't include potatoes in their daily rations.

Crocker moved the French and Irish crews out to the point, having them clear the way and build the grade for the Chinese. The Chinese pressed forward, working at a steadily increasing pace, and soon they were pressing the Irish and French, making them move faster so they could lay track.

By late August the heat had become almost unbearable. For eight days in a row the mercury rose over a hundred and tempers flared accordingly. Fistfights broke out among the Irish. The French cursed the heat. The Chinese continued working.

Night was little better. The men sweltered, drinking warm beer, winning and losing their wages in dice and card games. But on August 29 the white men put aside the cards, called a peace in the camp, and had a meeting.

Management was not invited.

Riley stood before them. His rough nature and ready fists had established him as a leader in the camp, and many of the men respected him. He felt himself rising to the role, welcoming it.

"I say if we're gonna have to work harder in this damned heat then we'd damned well better be paid for it!" Riley shouted.

The men cheered his proclamation.

"We told them a month ago we wanted better wages and they've been putting us off and putting us off. Now it's time we did something about it!"

Wild applause swept through the camp as Riley spoke.

"I'm gonna meet with Crocker and Strobridge tomorrow and I want to know if you men are with me. If they turn us down, are you willing to strike?"

Cries of affirmation rang from the crowd, and a spontaneous celebration began.

"There's no way we can justify giving you and the men a raise, Riley." Charley Crocker puffed on his cigar. It was hot in the work shack and he wanted the meeting to be brief.

"Besides," Strobridge said, "you men aren't working any harder than you're supposed to."

"The *hell* we aren't!"

"The hell you are!" the foreman countered. "It's just that you haven't been doing the damned job right since you men started and now all of a sudden you've got to do some work."

"We're working like the bloody devil out there, Strobridge!"

159

Strobridge leveled a finger at Riley. "You're doing the job you're being paid to do for a change!"

Riley stood up. "We'll strike if we don't get a raise." He turned to Crocker. "We mean it, Mr. Crocker."

Crocker tapped a cigar ash into the ashtray on the desk in front of him. "You won't leave me any choice then, Riley. I'll just have to import more Chinese to take your place."

"They'll strike along with us."

Crocker raised an eyebrow in question. "You sure about that? You talked to them yet?"

"Don't have to. They'll do whatever the hell we tell 'em to."

"I wouldn't be so sure."

"You think about it," Riley said. "You think about it and give me an answer."

"Don't have to think about it," Crocker said. "The answer is no. The railroad can't afford to give a raise. You go out there and lay me a couple hundred miles of track and maybe we'll talk about it. Until then just do the work you're being paid to do."

Riley turned on his heel and stormed from the office. He crossed the clearing to where ten men, who were camp representatives, were waiting for him.

"Well," a Frenchman named Le Beau asked. "What did Crocker say?"

"He said no raise."

"*Quel con!*" Le Beau exclaimed. "I am not surprised."

"What did you tell him," O'Malley asked.

"I told him we'd strike."

"What did he say to that?"

"He said they'd just hire more Chinese to do the job."

A murmur swept through the men.

"If we're going to strike," Riley said, "we'd better make damned sure those Chinks go along with us."

"We'll have trouble with them," Le Beau said. "Those little fellows would be happy digging cow manure for half the wages the railroad's paying them now."

"They'll come around," Riley answered. "They'd better, or we'll wise 'em up real fast. I know how to deal with Chinks."

At midday Riley and the same group of men, this time bolstered by another twenty-five white crewmen, walked back from the point to interrupt the Chinese meal. Riley sought out Wo Ti, the stout Chinese interpreter.

When he found him, Riley said, "We have to talk."

Wo Ti looked at the group of white men standing behind Riley. He disregarded the rudeness of the interruption and put aside his plate.

The two men walked to the shade of a tall tree and Wo Ti sat. Riley preferred to stand. The rest of the white men fanned out, just beyond hearing range.

"Look," Riley began, making an effort to disguise his hostility, "these railroad people are paying us slave wages to work out in the sun. Now I'm as able as the next man, but if we're gonna have to work in this kind of heat it seems to me that we should get paid better."

Riley watched the inscrutable Chinese. He was clearly listening to him, but his face registered no expression.

"You understand what I'm talking about?"

Wo Ti nodded.

"Good." Riley rubbed the back of his hand across his sweating forehead. "This sun can wilt a normal man. Must be hell on you little fellas."

"It is warm," Wo Ti agreed.

"You bet it is. Now we had a meeting the other night and we decided we're gonna lay down the law to Crocker and Strobridge."

"Lay down the law?"

"Yeah. We told 'em a month ago we wanted higher wages and they stalled us. Said they'd think about it. Well, they've had long enough to think. So this morning we went in and told them either we get a raise or no work."

"No work?"

"That's right. A strike."

"How will you be paid, then?"

"Paid? We won't be paid. But they won't get their railroad built either. Don't worry, Chinaman; they'll come around. Soon as they see we ain't gonna work for slave wages they'll come up with a nice fat raise." Riley paused, then added, "For all of us. You fellas included. Now what we need to know is that you're with us."

Wo Ti sat for a moment, thinking.

"Well?" Riley pushed.

"I have heard what you say. There is a problem. We are not as angry as you about the wages being paid. My people are content for the salary we receive. We have no complaint."

"You're content with slave wages?"

"We are not accustomed to the salaries of whites. For us it is a boon."

Riley shook his head. "Thirty bucks a month and a few bowls of rice is a boon, huh? Do you know you fellas get paid a little over half of what we get?"

Wo Ti nodded. "We are aware of that, too. Perhaps our needs are not as great as yours. Too, it would be unfair to pay us as much as you. It is, after all, your country."

"You're damned right it is. And what we say goes. We need to all be in on this thing. It ain't gonna work otherwise."

"Why not?"

"If Crocker sees that you and your boys will still work then he'll just hire more Chinese. You have to go along with us on this thing."

"I have to talk with the rest of the men."

"Do it, then."

"Can I give you an answer tomorrow?"

"No," Riley said, glaring at him. "Today. Right now. You talk to them right now. We want an answer. We're gonna strike this afternoon and you'd better be with us."

"Very well," Wo Ti said, rising. "I shall speak with my countrymen now."

He walked back to where the rest of the Chinese work gang was eating lunch. He called out and the men gathered about him. At the outskirts of the Chinese group the whites stood, waiting. They listened for five minutes as Wo Ti spoke in the foreign tongue. They listened to dozens of voices raised excitedly in answer.

Finally, Wo Ti walked from the group to where Riley and the rest of his men were waiting. "I have spoken to them. They want to work. They are happy in their work and satisfied with their wages. They will not strike with you."

"The hell they won't," Riley said, grabbing Wo Ti by the shirt and pulling him toward him.

"No strike, no strike," Wo Ti cried.

Riley rammed his fist into Wo Ti's mouth, cracking a tooth and drawing a scream as blood burst from his split lip.

"We'll teach you little heathens to make trouble for us," Riley said. He pushed the translator to the ground, then turned to his men.

"Come on, boys; let's show 'em we mean business."

Incensed by the heat, aroused by Riley, filled with the frustration of back-breaking labor, the white men surged forward

162

and tore into the Chinese camp. They kicked, pushed and beat the Chinese. The Chinese shouted terribly as the whites lifted them off the ground and hurled them through the air.

The giant cauldron of cooking rice was turned over and spilled on the ground. The tents of the Chinese were ripped apart; their belongings were strewn through the camp. Riley picked up a smoldering piece of wood and used it as a club, cracking it against head after head. Spotting a fallen Chinese man on the ground, he raised the club over his head to strike.

But when he swung down he found the club would not move and he turned around to see Yang holding the burned-out end of the club in his hand. Riley spun to face him.

"Let go of the club, Chink!"

Yang obeyed. "Don't use it on a fallen old man," Yang ordered.

"Tell me what to do, will you? I'll use it on you instead."

Riley pulled back and swung the weapon forward, toward Yang's skull. At the same time Yang's hands slashed through the air, meeting the club and cracking it in two.

Riley looked at the useless piece of wood and threw it to the ground. He glared at Yang amid the fighting that surrounded them. "I'll tear you to pieces with my hands, Chinaman!"

And with that Riley charged toward him. Yang sidestepped the hulking Riley easily and, grabbing him by his collar, tossed him to the ground with little effort.

The Irishman was on his feet in an instant. He stalked Yang, swinging at him, missing him each time. Yang lashed out, landing a blow to Riley's rib cage, and Riley grunted. Then the lumbering Irishman swung a roundhouse and caught Yang square in the jaw. Taken by surprise, Yang tumbled backward and fell to the ground, amazed at the force of the white man's blow.

Yang leaped to his feet, anger coursing through him, and pulled his hands into an offensive position. He readied himself for the death blow and closed ground on Riley as the Irishman rushed toward him.

They were five feet apart when the shotgun blast rang out. Instantly, the Chinese, the Irish, and the French stopped fighting. They turned to see Charley Crocker, James Strobridge, and a dozen other railroad employees sitting on horses behind them. Each had a weapon. Crocker had a double-barreled shotgun in his hands.

"Next man who throws a fist will lose it," Crocker said.

"And I mean it, damn it. If there's any more fighting I'll order my men to open fire and we'll be within the law. We've got the federal government on our side."

The men backed away from each other. Riley and Yang, alone, still faced each other.

Crocker looked at the pair. "I mean it! I'll blow you both to kingdom come."

Riley didn't budge. Neither did Yang. Crocker moved his mount forward at a slow walk and the rest of the workers parted for him. He stopped his horse in front of Riley and Yang.

"You think I'm bluffing?" Crocker asked.

Riley turned slightly to look at him. "You'd shoot a man for beating up on a Chink?"

"I've got a railroad to build, Riley." Crocker pulled back on the hammer of the shotgun. "I mean to build it."

Riley looked at him for a moment, then straightened out of his crouch. Yang did likewise.

"By rights I should throw the lot of you in jail," Crocker barked. He eased off the hammer and said, "Riley, I want you in my office inside five minutes; you understand?"

Riley bent and picked up his hat.

"I asked you a question, mister."

He dusted the hat against his pants and put it back on his head. "I understand, I understand."

Riley felt a dull ache in his rib cage as he sat in the shack listening to Charley Crocker and James Strobridge.

"For better or for worse, Riley, these men have confidence in you." Crocker leveled a finger at him as he spoke. "They listen to you. You've got their respect as a leader."

"Don't try to soft-soap me, Mr. Crocker. No sweet talk is going to change our minds. We want—"

"Why don't you shut up a second and listen to what the man has to say," Strobridge interrupted. "I swear, Riley, you're the most thick-skulled man I ever met."

Riley shot Strobridge a scowling glance, then sat back in his chair. "Well, then, go on. Won't make no difference, though."

Crocker leaned forward. 'Now you listen to me, Riley. We've got a railroad to build out here and we're going to do it; with or without your help. I meant what I said about the Chinese. I'll pull five thousand of them out here if I have to and fire everyone of you men. And if there's any more rioting I'll call out the militia."

164

Riley laughed. "You think anyone gives a damn about the Chi—"

"And if the militia isn't enough I'll get federal troops. This railroad is a military necessity, Riley. I don't think I have to remind you there's a war going on."

The smile left Riley's face. Crocker probably could get federal troops, now that he thought about it.

"Come hell or high water this railroad's going to be built, man." Crocker shook his head. "If you'd just think with your brains for a change, instead of your fists."

"What do you mean?"

"I mean if you and your men would only work as hard at building this railroad as you do at loafing maybe we'd all be a lot better off."

"We'll be better off when we get a raise and not until . . ."

"Damn it," Strobridge said, slamming a fist on the table, "you men don't deserve a raise!"

Riley turned toward the foreman.

"You know it's true," Strobridge continued. "Listen, Riley, I was as much opposed to bringing these Chinese in as anyone. But the fact is the job just wasn't getting done. How can we justify giving raises if we're so far behind on production? If you want something you've got to give something for it."

"It's hotter than hell out there!" Riley said. He turned back to Crocker. "You and them directors don't know what it's like because you're not out in the field. But I know," Riley said, slapping his fist on his chest. "The men know."

"We're not talking about heat, Riley. We're talking about work. We're talking about the amount of work getting done, and until we're at least up to schedule I won't even talk about a raise."

Crocker let the point sink in before continuing. "On the other hand, if you'd think with your head, like I said, maybe you'd all get that raise a lot sooner."

"Meaning what?"

"Meaning these Chinese are good workers. Meaning if you'd work with them and alongside them we'd start making some real headway."

"I still don't get your meaning."

"I talked to the board of directors yesterday. They're impressed with the progress we've made since we brought the Chinese in. They've agreed that we can bring in more, a *lot* more Chinese. You know what that means?"

"More fights."

165

Crocker shook his head. "No. It means progress. It means we can start this thing moving. Look, these yellow men are only interested in earning thirty bucks a month and some rice. They aren't leaders, they're workers. They're content just to work."

Crocker fished for a cigar and lit it. "But if we can get five hundred, a thousand, maybe even five thousand of them working on the railroad then we can really start laying some track."

"I still don't see what that has to do with me and the men."

"Figure it out. Riley. Are we going to hire yellow men at thirty bucks a head or more whites at almost double that price."

"Chinks, of course."

"Okay. So you and your men will be just about the only whites around here."

"Yeah, if you don't fire us altogether."

"Fire you?" Crocker laughed. "We *need* you. We're going to need leadership. Strobridge can't manage thousands of Chinamen by himself. He's going to need teams of foremen and powdermen. And that means your boys. You play your cards right and you fellas will all end up foremen, and that means a damned sight better wage raise than you ever thought you'd get."

Riley scratched his chin. "Foremen, huh?"

Strobridge leaned forward. "That's right, Riley."

Riley turned to look at the chief foreman.

"I can only be at one place at a time," Strobridge said. "If the rest of the Chinamen are anything like these ones, we can split them into a dozen separate teams and scatter them all the way down the line ahead of us. That'll mean foremen and supervisors for every team."

"And a higher wage for most of your men," Crocker said. "Well, Riley, what do you say?"

"And what about those who don't get appointed foremen?"

"They'll be made into assistants."

Riley nodded. "All right. We'll give it a try. You go ahead and hire your Chinamen, Mr. Crocker."

Chapter 20

As the summer of 1864 blended into the fall of 1864 California breathed a sigh of relief. It had been a scorching, searing summer and many crops had failed to live up to the expected yield. But at least the heat was gone and the air was breathable again.

San Francisco had not faired as poorly as her neighbors to the south. The breezes off the bay had kept the city livable. Throughout the summer most San Franciscans found themselves kept busy by the whirl of important, unfolding events. With the war-time economy, the stock market was soaring and everyone was speculating.

The daily war dispatches from the East were cause for much debate, both in the streets and the newspapers. The progress of the railroad, which had once been ridiculed, was now beginning to register some positive reactions as word of the surprising work being done by Chinese crews reached the city.

There was a growing feeling of respect for the Chinese. Contributing to it, of course, was the fact that many of the white unemployed had been absorbed into the war-time prosperity and the work of building the railroad.

But beyond that, many San Franciscans were beginning to realize that the Chinese were hard workers and a worthy addition to the community. The city became more and more dependent upon the Chinese for all manner of services, from laundering to fruit and vegetable vending. More than a few San Francisco houses had live-in Chinese cooks who were jealously guarded by their employers.

Chinatown once again became a tourist mecca, and the citizens of San Francisco flocked there to taste the strange and unusual, the foreign and the forbidden. And many of the Chinese prospered because of it. Chin was among them.

Mei Peng had made good on his word. Chin did work long and hard in return for the partnership which Mei Peng had offered him. There were many nights in which he got only a few hours sleep—up late doing inventory and then up early to meet incoming ships at the dock.

But the profits were spectacular and by the fall of 1864 Chin was recognized as a monied man in the community. In addition, his countrymen regarded him as an increasingly powerful political figure in the Chinese community.

In a very short time—just three and a half years since the night he had visited Mei Peng seeking financial advice—Chin had doubled to eight the number of import shops that Mei Peng owned when their partnership began. Mei Peng had spent long hours schooling Chin in the methods of selecting and buying merchandise from sea captains and traders. Their shops became known throughout San Francisco as emporiums which offered the most beautiful silks, the most delicate porcelains, the most unusual wares.

Rebecca Ashley had helped spread the word throughout the city's elite, and many society women flocked to their shops. Additionally, the *nouveaux riches*, the overnight gold and stock millionaires, sought out their shops, looking for instant chic. As time passed it became a symbol of status to have purchased an item at one of the stores.

So it was when the chilly and damp winds began to blow that fall that Chin's lot in life was a pleasant one, and when Mei Peng visited him on the first day of October he found him in the rear of one of the shops unpacking a carton which had just arrived.

"You look like a child opening presents on his birthday," Mei Peng said.

Chin looked up from the crate. "I feel that way."

He reached into the crate, pushing aside shredded paper, and gently lifted out the carved jade figurine of the God of Wealth. Chin luxuriated in the cool touch of the precious stone. His eyes lingered on it, absorbing the deep, green. For a moment he was lost in it.

Then he turned to Mei Peng. "It is beautiful, is it not?"

Mei Peng smiled, equally impressed by the piece as he crossed the room. "Magnificent. A beautiful piece." Then Mei Peng began to laugh.

Chin turned sharply. "What is it?"

The treasurer of the Kong Chow Company stifled his outburst. "Excuse my laughter, Chin." But then he began to laugh again. "I can't help remembering when that French sea dog brought in that piece of carved soapstone that he'd dipped in green dye and told you it was jade."

168

Chin smiled wryly. "Am I never to hear the end of this tale?"

"Probably not. Oh, how excited you were. You practically burst into my apartment with the news. The purchase of a lifetime! An unbelieveable price!"

Chin shook his head. "That seems like so long ago. As if it was a lifetime ago."

Mei Peng replied, "It was. You have learned much since your early days in commerce." He took the jade piece from Chin and examined it. "You have lived up to my expectations. You are as quick a learner in business as you were in bookkeeping."

"I have had a good teacher."

Mei Peng smiled, but then began to cough. He sought to catch his breath, but was unable to for a long moment. He reached into his pocket, pulled out a handkerchief, and finally spat into it.

"I do not like that cough," Chin said. "It is too frequent a visitor."

Mei Peng put the handkerchief back into his pocket. "One learns to accept minor discomfort as one grows older."

"Still," Chin said, opening another crate, "perhaps it requires an examination."

"Now the student is teaching the instructor?"

Chin laughed. "Only a suggestion."

"I am able to take care of myself. And how were the receipts for this week?"

"Over fifteen thousand."

Mei Peng nodded. "Good. Very good. I'll make a wealthy man of you yet."

Chin looked up from the crate he was unpacking. "You have already done that. You have given me wealth beyond what I had dreamt of."

"And still you do not know wealth at all."

"Perhaps I do. Perhaps I know more about wealth than you suspect, Mei Peng."

The treasurer of the Kong Chow Company raised an eyebrow in question. "How so?"

"I know the wealth of friendship. I know the wealth of knowledge imparted by one man to another, unselfishly, without thought for himself."

Mei Peng waved a hand at Chin, dismissing him. "You know nothing. Have you not increased my wealth through your labors?"

"A wealth that did not need to be increased." Chin leveled a finger at him. "You do not fool me, old friend. You give unselfishly, as a father would to a son."

Mei Peng stood. "Enough! You waste too much of my time." He turned, smiling, from Chin. "And too much of yours, too, if you are my partner. To work! Before I find some other young man to work for me."

Chin nodded after him, smiling. "Yes, honorable teacher."

Mei Peng walked out into the afternoon, letting the air wash over him. He breathed it deeply, but was caught in mid-breath. He began to cough. For a moment he fought to control himself. But he could not and he let it take him.

For long moments he coughed, finally backing to the wall of the shop, leaning against it for support. When he finally stopped he reached into his pocket, pulled out his handkerchief, and spat into it. As his eyes cleared he looked into the handkerchief. It was stained with blood.

It was February, and it was very cold.

Chin passed Powell, heading down Jackson Street toward the house of the Kong Chow Company. From a full block away he saw the crowd of mourners who filled the street.

They were ordinary people, Chin thought. Not Mei Peng's close friends. Just ordinary people who respected him, grieved for him. They were several hundred strong, and the great mass of white-clothed mourners surged and flowed about the entrance of the Kong Chow House, waiting for the procession to begin.

Chin inspected himself automatically, smoothing the front of the crisp white trousers and jacket he wore. Instinctively he looked at his hands, which were scrubbed clean.

He threaded his way through the mourners and nodded to one of the guards standing at the entrance of the company house. The guard let him pass.

As he came into Mei Peng's apartment, Chin exchanged greetings with several of the ranking members of the Kong Chow Company—Lo Chi, the company president and Tang Chao, the vice-president.

The apartment was filled with the most powerful Chinese in America—politicians, men of trade and commerce, gambling and opium emperors. All had come to pay their respects to Mei Peng, and Chin felt that it was a fitting farewell.

He drifted into the bedroom and pushed through a group

of men standing about the coffin. It was a fine coffin, Chin thought. It bore many coats of lacquer, painted over the most exquisite teak money could buy.

Chin paused at the foot of the casket. Inside, resting on a bed of down covered by a white silk sheet, Mei Peng reposed, looking as alive and vibrant as Chin had known him to be in life.

"He would be pleased to see a tribute such as this," a voice said from behind.

Chin turned and looked at Shao Kow, his one-time roommate and, later, assistant.

"Shao," Chin said, a smile breaking on his face. "It has been a long time since I have seen you."

Shao Kow bowed. "But you knew where I was. You only had to call an old friend."

The smile eased from Chin's face. "You are right. I have been neglectful of our friendship."

Now it was Shao Kow who smiled. "I only jest. I know how hard you have been working. Mei Peng spoke often of your labor in the import shops."

Chin turned back to look at him. "It . . . it's so hard to believe that he's actually . . ."

"I know. It is a tragic loss to all Chinese. He was a great person. He will be sorely missed."

Chin looked at the rows of food on either side of the coffin, set on tables. The required five different animal foods were present—a large roast duck, a suckling pig, a roast rabbit, a large cut of beef, and a pressed pheasant. In addition there were cakes and generous amounts of *bok choy*, bean sprouts and pods, as well as an assortment of fresh fruits, a selection of wines, and large quantities of tea in polished brass kettles.

On a separate table delicately prepared *dim sum* were arranged, decorated by the finest baker in Chinatown.

Mei Peng's soul would not be hungry, Chin reflected, and those spirits who hovered about during the feast, too, would be appeased.

Consuming the feast was a blur to Chin, a ritual he went through as though he were a marionette on strings. When the feast was all but completed, Lo Chi approached him.

"Chin, it is felt that you should make the food offering to Mei Peng."

Chin turned to the Company president. "I? Surely an elder should . . ."

"No," Lo Chi said, "it should be you. We all know of Mei Peng's love for you. You brought him great happiness as the son he never had and it is proper that you should have this final honor."

Chin bowed. "I accept this great privilege with humility."

Chin crossed to one of the tables and picked up a small piece of duck. He carried it to the coffin, conscious of the stillness in the room. Gently, he placed it to Mei Peng's lips and held it there for a moment so that his spirit might partake of the feast.

Chin felt his stomach tighten, his eyes close, his soul ache. Then, finally, he opened his eyes and looked down at Mei Peng. It was over, he thought, and he could cry no more.

After the funeral feast the coffin bearing Mei Peng was closed and sealed. Chin, along with five other pallbearers, carried the lacquered box down the stairs and out into the evening air of San Francisco.

As soon as the pallbearers appeared the air was filled with a jarring cacophony of crashing cymbals, stringed instruments, and gongs so as to frighten away imps who might be hovering about in the heavens.

Chin and the other men carried the coffin to a large, snow-white funeral wagon waiting by the curb and laid it gently on the flatbed. Slowly the mourners who had gathered filed by the coffin of Mei Peng and touched it as a final tribute.

Chin watched them—old and young, rich and poor, the people whom Mei Peng had fairly and honestly represented in his lifetime, and he thought that the multitude who had gathered was a fine tribute to this teacher. He knew that Mei Peng, even now watching, would be pleased, and he smiled softly.

When at last, nearly an hour later, the final mourner had passed by the coffin, the driver snapped the reins and the white stallion moved away from the curb. The great line of mourners followed the wagon, threading through the streets of Little China like a creeping white snake.

In front of the funeral wagon, Mei Peng's old friends led the way, tossing strips of brown paper, pierced in the middle so as to resemble Chinese bronze money; this was to assure purchase of the right of way from evil spirits and to appease the imps lurking about who might interfere with Mei Peng's spirit as it proceeded on the journey to China Heaven.

The funeral cortege wound its way past shops and lodging

houses and finally out of Little China itself. The group made its way through the streets of white San Francisco, marching to the dockfront. And it was here that they drew curious stares from the citizens of the city.

Most of the whites, however, bowed their heads and removed their hats when they realized that the music and ceremonies preceding Mei Peng's coffin were part of a funeral march. Chin was pleased to see their regard for Chinese customs.

At length the Pacific Mail Steamship wharf came into view and those Chinese who had been waiting there now began their duties. A great battery of firecrackers, like volleys of bullets, filled the air; these, too, were to frighten spirits away. The sound of gongs and cymbals from the dock joined with those of the band which walked in front of the cortege and blended with them.

Now Chin caught the faint aroma of incense and burning candles carried by the breeze coming in off the bay, and he felt himself becoming light-headed, as though he were taking part in some sort of fantasy. Presently, he felt himself growing drowsy, dreamlike.

He snapped himself out of it, remembering the seriousness of the proceeding and accepting the reality of it.

Chin looked toward the pier, at the ship that would carry Mei Peng back to Mother China, where he would rest with his ancestors and his ancestors' ancestors; back to Mother China, where he would be able to gain entrance to China Heaven.

As they neared the dockside Chin could see the long tables, elaborately laid out with more foods and rice and rice-wine and tea, there so the feasts' essence could be inhaled by spirits which were surely in attendance.

Now, as they drew up to the dock, Chin looked at the small furnace which stood on the wood planking of the boardwalk. He left the wagon for a moment to inspect the paperworks exhibited on a long table which was covered by a white silk cloth.

There were paper servants and paper horses and paper cows; paper clothing, tobacco pipes, spectacles. There were clever paper counterfeits of great sums of money. And now the artisans who had painstakingly labored to create these totems began to gather them up and place them in the small furnace, which was alive, inside, with embers waiting to consume the symbols and so transmit them to the spirit land where they would wait for Mei Peng's arrival and future use.

Chin watched as the white smoke curled up from the furnace, drifting in the same air that was now filled with prayers, supplications, and the sound of friends and elders testifying to Mei Peng's life and good deeds.

Finally, the dockfront was shattered by the piercing explosions of volley after volley of fireworks, and Chin joined the other pallbearers in lifting the coffin from the wagon.

Gently, softly, without conscious effort, the pallbearers moved up the ship's gangplank. When they came up onto the main deck Chin saw that most of the crew had gathered, curious to watch the proceedings. He noted that they too removed their caps and bowed their heads, and he was pleased.

They moved slowly down the companionway and came into the hold—the room in which the coffin containing Mei Peng's essence would be secure for the voyage which would take him to his final resting place.

One by one, the men took a last look and left the hold of the ship, until only Chin remained. He paused, looking and yet not looking at the coffin, and realizing that it was in his memories of the man and not the box that Mei Peng's true essence was. And then, though he had thought that he could cry no more, Chin felt a single tear track warmly down his cheek.

He turned and left the hold.

Chapter 21

The number of Chinese working on the Central Pacific Railroad rose from the first fifty-man experiment in the summer of 1864 to more than five thousand by the fall of 1866.

The progress had exceeded everyone's wildest dreams— even Charley Crocker's. It was one of the engineering miracles of the century, and no less miraculous was the industry which the Chinese brought to their work. Mile after mile of track was laid and journalists were sent from San Francisco and Sacramento and Los Angeles to chronicle the event.

As the work progressed Charley Crocker, true to his word, saw to it that the Irish and French who worked on the railroad were promoted.

In point of fact, it was the only course of action open to Crocker. He followed a plan of hiring fifty Chinese for every white worker, and though the Chinese were good and honest workers they did, as he foresaw, need guidance and supervision.

But as the work progressed and the altitude increased, Nature conspired to fight against Charley Crocker and the Central Pacific Railroad Company. It was as if she knew that the railroad they were building was being built to conquer her. She was not quite ready to be conquered.

It had snowed all through October—an early, hard snow. In November the temperature had plummeted to the point that coffee was all that kept the white men from freezing to death. Scores of Chinese lost their fingers from frostbite. A demon wind cut their progress to a few feet a day.

But the cold wasn't the only thing slowing them down. They had reached the very spine of the Sierras, as fortune would have it, at the very worst time of the year. There was no going over the summit—the grade would be too steep for tracks. There was only one solution: a tunnel.

It would be called Summit Tunnel. This was some of the hardest rock on earth, and men who worked for eight hours in the frozen tunnel came out with the tips of their steel chisels blunt and with inches of progress to show for their efforts.

They tried blasting, but had little success with dynamite. The explosions caused avalanches that made the uneven progress not worth the effort. The dynamite exploded in all directions and there was always the chance they'd blow out the side of the mountain.

The men worked wearily, not knowing that even as they did, the solution to their problem was forthcoming. Charley Crocker, willing to try anything at that bleak point, had paid to have a Swedish chemist named Swanson brought to the worksite. Swanson had corresponded with Crocker, telling him of his success in synthesizing a powerful new explosive. It was called nitroglycerin.

But when Summit Tunnel was completed, another problem awaited them on the other side. The slope of the mountain was almost a sheer face. There was no ledge to lay track on. Crocker had a solution for that, too. They would simply *create* a ledge.

Yang pounded his gloved hands together to keep the blood circulating as two Frenchmen hitched ropes about his chest. The big Frenchman watching, the one named Fontaine, walked to Yang and checked the ropes himself.

"*La corde n'est pas assez serrée*," Fontaine barked. The two workers examined the ropes closely, tying another knot at the foreman's order.

Yang could not understand a word of French. He was only now mastering a moderate amount of English. But it was not necessary to understand Fontaine's tongue to know the foreman had reprimanded his workers for not securing the ropes properly.

Yang looked at the hulking Frenchman standing in front of him. Fontaine was as tall as he, and his eyes critically watched as the workers readjusted the ropes.

Then, for a brief moment, Yang's eyes locked with Fontaine's. "Thank you," Yang said.

Fontaine's mouth fell open, surprised for a moment. Then he smiled, slapped Yang on the shoulder and said, "*Ne rien, mon ami.*"

Fontaine moved to the next Chinaman and checked the ropes harnessed about his body. Yang looked down the line of his countrymen—twenty-five of them—standing with their backs to the edge of the mountain's ridge.

Standing next to him, Wan Choi said, "I wish we were back in the swamps."

Yang laughed. "When we were in the swamps you wished we were in the mountains. You're never satisfied."

Wan Choi looked skyward and drew laughter from several of his countrymen as he cried, "Is there no middle ground?"

Yang shifted, moving the pack on his back into a more comfortable position. A few moments later Fontaine stood before them and signaled to the French workers, who began letting out slack on the rope.

Yang held the rope between his gloved hands and backed over the edge of the mountain, his feet digging against the rock as he rappelled down the side of the mountain. Yang jumped away from the mountainside, getting slack from above, and dropped another ten feet.

The Frenchmen had been good teachers, Yang thought. In the short space of a few weeks they had taught five hundred Chinese the rudiments of mountain climbing.

The wind whipping at him, the air making the skin on his

cheeks pull tight, Yang kicked away from the mountain again and lowered further. He glanced at Wan Choi.

"Wan-Choi," he called, "watch your pick."

Alongside him, Wan Choi reached over his shoulder and pushed down on the pick strapped to his back.

He turned to Yang. "Thank you."

Yang nodded, then returned to his ropes.

In less than five minutes the team of twenty-five Chinese had been lowered over a hundred feet to the work level. There, suspended by the ropes that rose up to the top of the mountain, they would work for two hours in the freezing cold before they would be pulled back up to safety.

They had been working on chiseling out a ledge to lay the tracks for more than two weeks, and the proof of their labors was a narrow flat ledge carved less than a foot into the mountainside.

Yang rested his feet on the ledge, pressing his body up against the cold stone. Like puppets, the twenty-five men in the team danced on the strings just ten feet apart from each other.

"My destiny," Wan Choi said. "For this I journeyed from our homeland."

Yang laughed. "We came for gold and end up as goats. The gods have a plan."

Wan Choi pulled the pick over his shoulder. "If they have a plan I should like to know what it is."

The man on Yang's other side, Peng Ku, said, "You should not question the gods." He paused, then added, "Certainly not at a time such as this."

Wan Choi glanced down the slope, looking at the sheer, ragged rock as it dove three thousand feet into the white abyss below. "Perhaps you are right, Peng Ku."

"I am right. There is no question of it." Peng Ku swung his pick, driving the point into the adamantine rock, barely making a chip. "Perhaps this is not so bad a destiny after all."

"How so?" Wan Choi asked.

"Sometimes," he said, swinging the pick again as he slipped into the rhythm of his work, "sometimes when I am on the ledge like this, suspended between life and death, fighting against the rock, sometimes I feel that this is the kind of work the gods do—great tasks with little but the will to see them through."

"Foolishness," Yang called, striking his pick into the mountain. "Philosophical foolishness. You sound like my brother, Peng Ku."

"Oh, and how do you see this work?"

"It is work not even fit for animals."

"Does the noble Yang consider himself less than an animal?"

Wan Choi laughed coldly. "Watch your tongue, Peng Ku, or you're liable to end up with your rope severed."

"No," Yang said, "I do not consider myself less than an animal. That is merely the caliber of the work that I do."

"Then why do you do it?"

"Because that is all there is for me to do now."

Peng Ku grimaced as a blistering wind whipped at them. He drew his peacoat tighter about him. "You sound as if you do not intend to make labor your life's work."

"Do you?"

"Not at all."

"Then we are agreed on that score."

"True," Peng Ku granted. "It is but a passing thing, thank the gods. And I suppose you are right, Yang; it is work not befitting animals." He struck his pick against the mountain again. "Maybe that is why I try to make more of it than it is."

"I think that is unwise."

Peng Ku glanced at him "Why?"

"Because it is best to realize a thing for what it is. Then one is not deceived by it. It is acceptable to deceive others—enemies, even friends—but one ought never to deceive oneself."

Wan Choi called, "Now who sings of philosophy?"

Peng Ku said, "Perhaps there is some small measure of your philosophical brother in you."

"Never tell my brother this." Yang laughed.

The men's talk was suddenly interrupted by the report of a rifle in the distance. Their picks froze in mid-stroke.

Wan Choi's lips trembled. "Gods in heaven, are they mad?"

"Be still!" Yang barked.

The rifle cracked again. Yang leaned back, looked up the slope. "Be still, all of you. Not a word."

But it was already too late. Yang felt pieces of snow falling, slapping him in the face. Up above he could see

178

larger chunks of snow, like clouds, as they separated and drifted away from the mountain.

Now clumps of snow and ice, the size of melons, were falling about them.

"Grab for the wall!" Yang shouted. "Avalanche!"

And then it was upon them, like an angry white sea. The shower of snow and ice fell down on them and Yang clutched tight to his rope, his body pressed against the cold, unfeeling face of the mountain.

To his left he could see Peng Ku grasping his lifeline with his gloved hands. "Hold tight," Yang yelled, but he was uncertain if the man heard him.

A large chunk of ice slammed into his shoulder and he turned his head, in pain, to the opposite direction. The snow beat down on him, pounding at him and then growing less violent. In those moments when the torrent abated he could make out the shadowy figure of Wan Choi not five feet from him.

For one moment the avalanche slackened in intensity and Yang almost thought that it was over. In that moment he could clearly see Wan Choi, could make out the fear in his friend's clenched eyes, could see the stark terror in the face that started out from behind the scarf wrapped around his head.

Then the snow and ice thundered down again and Yang saw his friend pushed away from the side of the mountain, grasping at the slick rope, his legs kicking in thin air. Yang saw him slipping, losing his grip on the lifeline.

Suddenly there was a great sheet of white and Yang closed his eyes for a moment against it. When he opened his eyes Wan Choi was no more. There was only a loose rope flapping in the wind where the man had been. Yang closed his eyes once more.

It was one of the rare quiet days in the forward camp of the Central Pacific Railroad, thought Doctor Ma Ti Fu as he worked in his small shack of an office. Few whites in the camp were working. Most were celebrating their Christmas Day.

Occasionally the air would smack of a hint of the roast turkey which had been brought up from Sacramento for the feast.

Nevertheless, some of the Chinese had worked, with a

small crew of whites to oversee them. So Ma Ti Fu had seen a few patients this day.

He looked at the young man's fingers. They were without color, ashen. Ma Ti Fu had seen many dozens of cases of frostbite in the past months. There was nothing unusual about this case.

He dipped the Chinaman's hand in a solution of lukewarm water and looked at him. "How long were you exposed?"

"Six hours."

"Six hours?"

"But I was working in the tunnel," he added quickly. "Not outside."

Ma Ti Fu looked back at the fingers in the bowl. "Still, that is far too long. When it is this cold you must not be in the elements for more than two hours at the most. After that you must pause to warm yourself."

The young man was silent.

"I have told the foremen that they must take breaks more often." Ma Ti Fu stood. "Let your fingers soak in the water. Perhaps we shall be lucky; I may not have to cut them off."

The man's face tightened and Ma Ti Fu was pleased that he had succeeded in throwing a scare into him. Next time, the physician thought, he would take a break when he started getting cold.

After a moment he asked, "Is there any feeling in the hand?"

The man nodded. "Yes. The feeling is pain."

"Welcome it. It means you'll keep those fingers."

The doctor turned as the door of the shack opened and Yang walked in. The cast which Ma Ti Fu had applied to Yang's arm more than a month ago was ready to come off.

The doctor nodded. "Sit down. I will attend to you presently."

Yang did so without a word.

"Doctor," the frostbite victim said, "my hand feels better now."

Ma Ti Fu looked at him. "Good. Then you may go." He raised a finger toward the man. "And next time take a break to warm your fingers or you may not have fingers left to warm."

"Thank you, doctor, thank you." The man removed his hand from the solution, dried himself, and got up to leave. He nodded to Yang as he passed and Yang, sitting on the log, nodded only slightly in return.

"You are ready?" Ma Ti Fu said to Yang.

"Yes."

Ma Ti Fu led him to the chair where the frostbite victim had been sitting. The doctor pulled a small saw out of a cabinet. He carefully sawed into the clay cast that had held Yang's arm in place so the bones could knit. Yang was fascinated by the fact that the doctor knew exactly how deep to saw so that he did not cut into Yang's skin with the blade.

Ma Ti Fu placed the saw on the table beside Yang's arm and picked up a cast spreader. He inserted the tip of the spreader into the incision he had sawn in the cast and squeezed the handle.

Yang felt the cast begin to separate, felt the pressure of the month-long imprisonment begin to ease. Abruptly the clay cracked and fell away from his arm. Ma Ti Fu removed what remained of the cast and dusted away the debris. He picked up a damp cloth and washed away the clay dust.

After he felt Yang's arm where the break had been he said, "It has mended well. Do not use it too strenuously for a week or so. If you have any pain—"

"If I have any pain I shall bear it," Yang said.

The doctor looked at him for a moment, then said, "Very well."

Yang stood, walked to the door, and opened it. He was about to leave when he turned to look at Ma Ti Fu. "Thank you."

Ma Ti Fu bent his head just slightly and then Yang walked outside, closing the door after himself.

Chapter 22

Chin sat in the long, narrow office which occupied the second floor of his import shop on Dupont Street. He was listening to Chang Mai Mai, the gaunt general manager of Chin's chain of eleven shops.

Directly across from Chang Mai Mai was Tai Pien Sing, who managed Chin's other business enterprises. At the far end of the conference table sat Shao Kow, to whom Chin had made a junior partnership offer. Wisely, Shao Kow had accepted.

Chin turned his gaze to Tai Pien Sing for a moment. He was a formidable man, from Manchuria. Muscled, thickset, he reminded Chin of his brother Yang in some ways. But for all the power Tai Pien Sing exuded, he also possessed a head for business and, Chin reflected, were that not so he would not be sitting in the room with the other men.

It was not the man's brute strength which made Chin feel slightly uneasy in Tai Pien Sing's presence. Rather, it was the nature of those other business interests of Mei Peng's which only came to light after the death of the Kong Chow Company's treasurer.

Chin was the one who was most surprised at the reading of Mei Peng's will, when he heard that Mei Peng's vast interests were left—with the exception of a sizable cash bequest to the Kong Chow Company—entirely to Chin.

Upon dismissing the others who had attended the reading of the will, Mei Peng's personal lawyer had a lengthy conference with Chin to explain the nature of Mei Peng's holdings, assets, and business interests.

In his particular area—that of import shops—Chin had done a wondrous job, the lawyer had said. So wondrous that it was necessary to employ more than a hundred men in the chain of stores, which was grossing close to a million American dollars a year.

But this enterprise, the lawyer explained, was but the tip of Mei Peng's empire, and for the better part of two hours the lawyer proceeded to outline, in detail, precisely what comprised that empire.

Tai Pien, the governor of that part of Mei Peng's empire which was kept secret, turned to look at Chin and Chin turned his attention back to Chang Mai Mai.

"What do you think?" Chang Mai Mai asked.

"What?"

He looked at Chin. "About the new building available. It will be our first location outside of Little China. Our first location in white San Francisco. Should we take it?"

"By all means." Chin nodded. "The white section of the city is ready for us. It is time we expand our scope. Take the store." Chin paused. "By next year we may expand to Los Angeles. Who can say."

Chang Mai Mai made a note. "Good. I shall make arrangements to secure the store, then. That is all I have for this meeting."

Chin turned to Tai Pien Sing. "Tai Pien?"

The man bowed his melon of a head and looked first to Chang Mai Mai, then to Shao Kow, and finally to Chin. "We have recorded an eighteen percent increase in our division for the last quarter. We would have shown a greater profit, but an old man actually hit an eight-number lottery bet, so it meant a payout of ten thousand dollars."

Tai Pien smiled. "That's the first time we've had an eight-number winner since the operation began. We're not likely to have one again for many years. At any rate, the payout is the best form of advertising we could possibly have. Lottery ticket sales increased thirty-two percent the week after the big winner was paid."

Chin said, "I would like a breakdown of income from the different areas."

Tai Pien nodded and began passing duplicate copies of a report which lay on the conference table in front of him. The men passed the reports around the table.

"As you can see, the lottery is still our number-one source of income, with net receipts of $380,000 for the quarter. Close behind are the *Fan-tan* parlors, with $310,000 for the same period."

He paused for a moment, watching the men digest the figures. "On the other hand, our opium dens lag seriously behind. For this quarter we saw only $105,000."

Chin frowned.

"What is the reason for this?" Shao Kow asked.

"As I reported at our last meeting, a good deal of the opium business is being run by the tongs which have sprung up around the city."

Shao Kow turned to Chin. "They are bad news, these tongs. I knew this when they were first formed, Chin."

Chin nodded. "I recall your saying so."

"They go under the guise of trade guilds," Shao Kow continued, "when in reality they are little more than hoodlum gangs."

"We are all familiar with your point of view," Chin said sharply.

Shao Kow fell silent.

Tai Pien picked up the argument, though. "Shao Kow is correct to show concern. Were it not for these tongs we could capture a much larger share of the opium business. It is a large market and we are not getting a big enough—"

"How would you deal with them?" Chin asked, cutting him off.

"Why not offer to buy them out?" Chang Mai Mai offered. "In much the same manner we bought out the Lee group when they began opening rival import shops. We acquired three more shops by that method. Perhaps we can acquire the tong opium parlors in the same way."

"It will not work," Chin said. "The Lee group was a single consortium of businessmen who were operating a chain of stores. There are at least half a dozen different tongs in Chinatown, each with its own interests. Besides, there is a question of pride."

"Pride?"

"Yes. These young gangs are boastful and proud like peacocks. They fancy themselves a mix of entrepreneur and warrior. For them to sell out to us would be an admission to rival tongs that they are weak and unable to remain in business." Chin shook his head. "They will not deal with us."

Tai Pien said, "Then we should pursue opening more opium dens of our own."

"No."

"Why not?"

Chin glanced around the table, knowing full well where Tai Pien was leading him. "There are already half a hundred opium parlors in the city. We would be in competition with all of them."

"I think that is not the true reason," Tai Pien said.

Silence swept around the conference table. Then Tai Pien said, "I think you are concerned that these hoodlum gangs would oppose your efforts.

Chin laughed. "You speak of them as though they were whites. Are they not Chinese? Are they not our cousins?"

"No," Tai Pien said, "these tong members are not our cousins. They are their own cousins only. They are true to themselves alone. They care not about the Six Companies or any other Chinese, for that matter, except members of their own tong."

Chin was silent as Tai Pien continued.

"You *are* worried that they will physically oppose us if we attempt to open competing opium dens. And, what's more," Tai Pien said, "it is wise that you are worried. They may well oppose us. But if that is so then we must make our efforts now. The longer we wait the more powerful they grow."

Shao Kow said, "You sound like a general, Tai Pien."

"You are perceptive, Shao Kow. For war may be in the offing."

"You exaggerate," Chin said.

"Then why not open the parlors?"

"I am content with out business holdings at present."

"You worry about the tongs," Tai Pien said, leveling a finger at Chin.

"I have not time to worry about every gang of young rascals which comes along."

"Then give me permission to open more parlors."

Chin leaned forward. "Neither do I have time to concern myself with risky endeavors."

"Risky! The profit potential for opium is—"

"Provided there is not strong competition to drive the price down; not to mention the bribes necessary to operate the dens. Why should I bother devoting my efforts to a business in which there are already established shops? My other businesses show more promise."

"You must bother because the tongs have to be dealt with. One day they may decide to open import shops and then what will you do?"

"That day will not come," Chin said. "For the same reason that I do not seriously infringe on their main interests. They know full well that I am the established leader in importing in this city."

"Already they probe into legitimate businesses. They have employees working in vending and laundry houses. These are not hoodlums, but a legitimate branch of—"

"We dwell too long on this matter."

"You must deal with them," Tai Pien said.

"I am pleased with the profits your report shows," Chin said, ending the discussion. "Have you anything to add?"

Tai Pien looked at the report. "Income from miscellaneous sources totals $20,000." He looked up from his notes. "I have one other piece of business."

Chin waited.

"I would like to reopen the discussion of prostitution."

"No," Chin said.

"I think it's a matter of—"

"I said *no*. I will not hear of it. I will not discuss slavery at this table."

Tai Pien's eyes fell.

Shao Kow said, "It is getting late, Chin. Remember, there is a noon meeting at the Kong Chow House."

Chin stood, and the three men who were his top advisers took the signal and also stood. "I am pleased with your reports," he said, looking at each of them. "Tai Pien, I would speak with you alone for a moment."

Shao Kow and Chang Mai Mai left the meeting room, leaving Chin alone with Tai Pien. The two men sat down at opposite ends of the table.

Chin was silent for a long moment, then said, "You know that when Mei Peng was alive I had no idea what his other business endeavors were. It was my business only to run the import end for him."

Tai Pien sat unmoving, listening.

"After his death, when I learned the nature of his other holdings, I must admit that I was surprised that they were in your particular area of expertise. I confess to you, Tai Pien, that I have no taste for vice. It is not in my nature."

"And yet," Tai Pien said, "you continue to run Mei Peng's businesses for him—the opium parlors, the gambling concerns."

"They are no longer Mei Peng's businesses," Chin said. "They are mine. I am the proprietor." He paused for a moment, letting Tai Pien think about his words. "But what you say is true. I continue to run these enterprises because I have an obligation to continue operating them. They were a legacy."

"But there is no obligation to expand them?"

"That is correct."

"That is why you have opened no more opium parlors? Because you oppose vice?"

"That is also correct." Chin paused, thinking. "Gambling and opium and prostitution are all vices and, as such, are dangerous only when taken in excess. In China they were controllable, to a degree. But here such is not the case."

Chin folded his hands. "Our people do not have the golden path they were led to believe they would have in this land. Men such as you and I are the exception, Tai Pien, not the rule."

Tai Pien nodded, accepting this point.

Chin continued. "So most of our cousins seek escape in vice. But it is a trap. The poor man spends the bulk of his wages on the dream of winning a lottery or the dreams brought on by the opium pipe or the whisperings of a paid whore. These things have been taken to excess by our people."

Tai Pien said, "If we do not provide them they will find others who shall."

"Let it be on their conscience, then."

"And what of me?" Tai Pien asked. "Am I to be the manager of businesses which shall never bloom beyond the point they now occupy? Am I to be nothing more than the caretaker of the legacy left you by Mei Peng?"

"No," Chin said. "It is true that I shall not expand those businesses any further. But I will always have need for a man like you, Tai Pien—a strong adviser whom I can trust."

"For what purpose?"

Chin paused, then said, "I fear your predictions about the growing strength of the tongs may come to fruition before very long."

Tai Peng looked at Chin and said, "You are a wiser man than I had thought."

Chapter 23

Sitting in the meeting chamber, Chin recalled the sessions he had attended years ago in the Meeting Hall of the Middle Kingdom. Occasionally there would be great excitement. But for the most part the meetings in those days dealt with the collection of dues and the refinement of the Six Companies' laws as they applied in this new land.

How different, he thought, from the meetings of the present. Each gathering bemoaned a new crisis. The main order of business, on this day, was a familiar one—how to combat the vicious, anti-Chinese campaign of Henry H. Haight. The consensus was that this could best be accomplished by supporting Haight's strongest opponent, George Gorham.

Rebecca Ashley, who was the secretary of the Society for Sino-American Relations, attended the meeting. It had been decided that donations from the Kong Chow Company would be funneled through the Society so that it did not appear to be Chinese money.

Rebecca delivered an impassioned speech, calling for support and donations. Chin was the first to speak after her, and his donation of five thousand dollars set the tone for the other representatives.

A motion was made and passed recommending that all Chinese in America donate ten percent of their earnings until the election campaign was over.

After the meeting Chin had asked Rebecca to join him for lunch. At a nearby restaurant, sipping from two glasses of *Ng-ka-py*, the two friends rehashed the events of the day.

"You succeeded admirably in raising funds today," Chin said. "You have much to be proud of, Rebecca."

She smiled, sipping the gin. "The pride is only in what we can accomplish, not in what has already been done."

"I don't know if that's true," Chin argued. "Your Society has accomplished many good things already."

"I know, Chin. But there is so much still to be done. This election is so very important. You don't know Henry Haight. If he wins the—"

"He won't."

"We can't be sure."

"With people like you on his side, George Gorham will emerge victorious."

"A great many people support Haight."

"He won't win."

"It is a generous donation you made."

"For a worthy cause."

"Would you have donated as much if it was someone else asking for the money?"

Chin nodded. "Yes." Rebecca seemed suprised. Then he added, "But not as quickly."

She smiled. "I'm flattered."

The waiter returned to their table carrying a silver platter on which rested the Beijing duck Chin had ordered. His eyes smiled as he looked at the clay-bound fowl, and he nodded appreciatively to the waiter.

The waiter took the platter to a serving station and began to crack the clay in which the duck had been baked. The waiter snapped his fingers and an assistant appeared at his side, bearing two delicate English bone China dishes. Onto these he placed pieces of the duck as he sliced it away from the bone.

"You have been working hard lately," Chin commented.

"How can you tell?"

"From your eyes." He paused. "They are tired."

She blinked them shut, then opened them. "Do they really look tired?"

"Yes."

She sighed deeply. "And I wanted to look nice today."

"You do. But you also look tired, and that worries me. You *have* been working too hard, Rebecca."

"There is a great deal of work to be done. Conditions are so bad." She shook her head. "The hospitals are so bad. Healthy people shouldn't have to endure the conditions in some lodging houses in this quarter, let alone people who are ill."

Chin smiled slightly. "You are a good woman, Rebecca, to care so deeply for my people."

"They are my people, too."

Chin narrowed his eyes in question. "They are Chinese."

"They are people," she said. "White, yellow, red, it doesn't matter. We're all people, Chin. Until everyone gets over the idea of Chinese and Indians being different from whites we'll always have problems."

"Then it is a serious obstacle that lies in your path."

"How do you feel? Do you think you're any different from me?"

"Oh yes," Chin said, nodding his head. "Very different. Were I not different from you it would be an odd thing for me to take you to this restaurant tonight."

She laughed for a moment and Chin watched her laugh, caught the marvelous sparkle in her eyes, heard the lilt of her voice as it rolled from her lips. He liked what he saw and heard.

"I'm trying to be serious," she said.

"I'm sorry." He paused as the waiter brought their plates. Another waiter brought more *Ng-ka-py*, bid them a good dinner, and then left.

"But I really am serious," Chin said. "There is a difference between you and me and it is more than just the difference between a man and a woman. Surely you must see that."

"There is no difference between white and yellow, as there is no difference between a gray cat and a black one."

Chin smiled, tasting the duck which gently dissolved once inside his mouth even before he could chew.

"But you are wrong, Rebecca. There is a great difference."

"The duck is excellent," she said.

"Superb," he agreed.

"What is the difference you see, Chin?"

"A difference in cultures. Occidental and Oriental are as different as two cultures can be. My people are generally reserved in their deportment, whereas the white man is gregarious and aggressive. We tend to be structured and formal in our mannerisms, whereas your people are casual and matter-of-fact about their affairs."

"That doesn't mean we can't get along."

"I didn't say that it did. The only thing I said is that there are differences and it is unwise not to recognize them as such."

"You're supposed to be on my side."

Chin smiled. "I am."

"I know you are. And I *am* grateful for the donation."

"I want to know what else I can do to help."

"You've already done more than enough."

"I have done nothing. Merely giving you a check is hardly an effort on my part. I want to do more." He took a sip of the gin and said, "After all, it is for the benefit of my people."

Rebecca eyed him questioningly. "You're sure that's why you're involved in this?"

"I'm sure," he said. But he was unable to stop the corner of his mouth from curling into a slight smile, and Rebecca saw it.

The next weeks were a blur of activity for Chin as Rebecca Ashley thrust him into a whirl of meetings and lectures. She used him as a chef would use a fine herb—lightly and for seasoning at just the right times. Chin found himself amazed at her capacity for work. He had a growing respect for her ability to function in the world of politics.

Rebecca Ashley was as comfortable extracting a donation from a powerful banker as she was visiting a hospital filled with wounded war veterans. She worked twelve, fourteen, sixteen hours a day. And when she returned to work the next day she was fresh and eager to tackle new challenges.

Two weeks before the election she took a much-needed break before the final push. One October evening she found herself finishing the last of a succulent lobster prepared by Chin's houseboy. She had come to his house for dinner so they could discuss their plans for the week.

They rose from the table and walked to the library of Chin's house.

"When Mei Peng died I moved from the Kong Chow Company house. I wanted to have as little as possible to do with the Company."

"Memories?"

"Yes."

She looked around at the walnut-paneled library, at the floor-to-ceiling bookshelves lined with hundreds of leather-bound volumes. She took in the cherrywood desk, imported from England, the Axminster carpeting, the Louis XIV divan they were sitting on.

Rebecca smiled. "Your Elba is most well appointed."

Chin laughed. "Oh, no. I didn't move here first."

"You didn't? Where, then?"

"A small apartment over one of my import shops."

Now Rebecca laughed. "You! Living over an import shop?"

"The idea seems incredible to you?"

"Yes, it certainly does."

Chin crossed a leg, feeling the delicate silk of his trousers as it brushed against his leg. "It seems so to me, now, as well. But then, not too long ago all this seemed incredible to me." He paused, then said, "And most incredible of all was the dream of having you dine here with me some day."

Rebecca looked into Chin's eyes. She broke the stare when a knock came softly on the library door.

He turned and said, "Come in."

Chin's houseboy brought two glasses of brandy on a silver tray. He held out one to each of them and then left the room.

Rebecca sipped her brandy. "Excellent. So smooth."

"Thank you. It's a very special bottle, for a very special occasion." Then he looked at the glass in her hands, looked at it shaking. "Why do you tremble, Rebecca?"

She set the glass down. "I'm not trembling!" she lied and she sucked her lower lip up over her teeth, biting it for a moment to control herself. "I'm sorry, I'm sorry." Then she smiled. "Let's talk about you . . . please. You were already running Mei Peng's import shops at the time of his death. You were a man of means, a full partner. Why did you choose to move into a small apartment? Surely you could have afforded a house?"

"True. I could have afforded it. But you don't understand, Rebecca."

"Understand what?"

He thought about how to phrase the explanation. "You . . . you've never known privation, have you?"

"Well . . . no, I really haven't." She sipped more of the brandy, feeling its warmth as it calmed her.

He smiled slightly. "It isn't a thing to be ashamed of."

She straightened. "I'm not."

"You needn't be. But you've always known money. I mean, you've always been comfortable, haven't you?"

"Yes," she said, "yes, that's correct."

"You are fortunate. I was not so fortunate, I and my brother Yang. We were very poor, with my father Kung Lee and my sister Ling in China."

He sipped his brandy. "We were rice farmers. We spent most of our working hours in water up to our knees trying to coax the rice into growing. We were poor, Rebecca—poor beyond description—and yet we did not know that we were poor."

She set her drink on the English tea table and waited for him to continue, engrossed in his tale.

"I was always hungry. But it did not bother me greatly because I grew up thinking that hunger was a natural state. These things must sound very odd to you."

"They're fascinating," she said unabashedly. "Go on."

Chin leaned back on the sofa. "We lived, the four of us, in a hut about half the size of this room. We had nothing, but in a very strange way we had everything. There was a sense of continuity, Rebecca. We knew that what had always been would always be."

"And then?"

"And then my Uncle Ah Wan came along with the news of the gold strike in a strange land called California and my world was turned upside down."

"But what does all that have to do with moving into a small apartment over one of your shops?"

"Even after I made the money I nursed a sense of fear for a long time."

"Fear?"

"Insecurity. I had made a great deal of money. I had found out what money could bring. I tasted the quality of life, and for the first time I realized that there was a better life than the one I had led."

192

"But then why . . ."

"Because now that I knew what it could be like, I realized, also, how miserable I had been. I could never bear to go back to that again. And even though I had amassed a considerable sum at that time, I had also amassed a towering sense of insecurity."

"Fascinating," she said, "positively fascinating."

"It took me a long time to stop being afraid."

She glanced about the room and said, "It looks like you've gotten over it."

"I have," Chin said. "I've learned to live with it." His voice dropped. "I've learned many things in this land."

"What things?" she asked softly.

"That there are ways other than those I knew of, and that they are not bad just because they are not my ways."

"And what else?"

"That a people different from my own can hold as much interest for me as I find in my own countrymen."

"And countrywomen?"

"Yes." He reached out his hand and felt the silk that was her hair. "Yes. Your people are strangely attractive to me, attractive in a way I have never known before."

Chin watched his prayers being answered, as she closed her eyes. And as she said, "How odd that I find my feelings the same for you."

He drew closer, letting his fingertips gently stroke the nape of her neck. "You are very beautiful, Rebecca."

Her eyes opened for a moment, only to flutter closed again. Her voice whispered, "Kiss me, Chin."

He brushed his lips against hers, softly, barely touching them, as a hummingbird in flight draws pollen from a flower almost without disturbing it. As he pressed his body against hers, he could feel her heart, deep within her bosom, shudder in response.

Her lips were parted then, and he could feel their tongues swirling, wonderfully, about each other, the world below quickly falling away. He could hear his own heart pound as his fingers first grazed, then closed on her breasts.

For a moment they seemed to surface and suddenly he was looking into her open eyes. She smiled lightly and closed her eyes again, giving herself over to him.

He kissed her neck once, twice, uncountable times as his fingers undid the buttons of her blouse. Then, she as naked as he, Chin lowered her back on the divan, feeling the creamy press of her body next to his. They explored each other for long, languid moments; for how long he knew not. He traced her body with great tenderness, following each curve, each valley, caressing her, teasing her, squeezing her, until at last his fingers slipped into the damp crevice of her intimacy, drawing a soft cry of pleasure from her throat.

Chin marveled at her abandon, aroused almost unbearably as he watched her undulate, seeming to draw his fingers into her. He clenched his eyes tightly as Rebecca's cool and damp hand closed around the proof of his own anticipation. And through her attentions it was apparent that she was ready for him, wanted him now.

He moved over her, pressed against her, parting those swollen and moist lips that so longed for him. And as he entered her, Rebecca gave out a low moan, a mixture of both pleasure and pain. Then they were moving together, Chin thrusting deeply within her, feeling the heat as it enveloped him, then reluctantly let him slide out, knowing he would return.

They moved as one, thrusts met with counterthrusts, flesh and bone grinding against each other with a unity and singleness of purpose that was inexorable.

He moved faster, faster still—the ecstasy rocketing almost past him, soaring out of control. Rebecca's short, desperate cries told him she was by his side, approaching that same summit.

It was a divine crescendo of mutuality, thundering in its force. He could feel his manhood throbbing within her, pulsing, pouring, erupting with great hot rivers, and she answered perfectly, their bodies and spirits blending at that dizzying zenith of culmination. They shuddered together, both of them crying out, knowing for a brief moment the bliss of the gods.

Chapter 24

Ling sat on the floor of the ship's hold, her back resting against the bulkhead. Her eyes were open, but they might as well have been closed. In the pitched black of the hold she could smell the stench of bodies that could hold their waste no longer. She could hear the weeping of the two hundred and eleven women crammed into the prison that was the hold of the ship *Majestic*.

She wondered how many hours she would have to wait until feeding time. Food was all she thought about lately. It was the only way she could mark the passage of time. There was no light, no window for light to come through. Occasionally she could feel a bilge rat's paws as it scampered over her legs, but she was too weak to care. So long as it didn't bite she would let it use her as a path.

Ah Toy Yee, sitting next to her in the darkness, had been the only person she had spoken to during the passage. Ah Toy was from Pachung in Szechwan province. Like Ling, she had been claimed by the Six Companies and sold into slavery because of a forfeited passage pledge. The pledge had been made by her father, who regarded his obligation to his daughter as ended the moment he landed in California.

The two women had been exceedingly fortunate—bought by a wealthy merchant from Tientsin, whom they served honorably for eight years. He was a kind master, asking little more than to be served and cooked for. He was rarely home, so for Ling and Ah Toy it was an easy life.

A month earlier the merchant had died. Ling had never learned how he died. A distant nephew from Chengtu had claimed his estate and promptly converted all his assets into cash. As Ling and Ah Toy were part of those assets, they were sold.

The buyer was a slaver who never spoke a word to her. She and Ah Toy were bought as a single lot. They were transported, in a cart, to a waiting-hall near the sea, which they occupied with a multitude of other women.

Ling listened to predictions about their future, but she dismissed them as nonsense. They would probably be individually auctioned to new masters, she told the rest of the women. And if they were half as kind as the master she had just finished serving, then their fate would not be so bad.

She was wrong.

"My wrists are bleeding again," Ah Toy said.

"How can you tell in this darkness?" Ling asked.

"I can feel the blood oozing."

Ling was suddenly conscious of the shackles on her own wrists. She twisted her hands slightly, feeling the cruel metal as it bit into them.

"I wonder why they have us in chains."

Ah Toy moved closer to her. "So we won't try to escape."

Ling laughed bitterly. "Escape? Escape to where? Are they afraid we'll jump overboard and swim back to China?"

"I don't know."

"Or maybe they're afraid we'll overpower the sailors and take the ship away from them."

Ah Toy laughed. Then she asked, "Where do you think they are taking us, Ling?"

"To the land of the white men."

"How do you know this?"

"It is the only place I can think of that is this far away from Mother China."

"Is it a horrible place?"

"Wondrous, from what I've heard of it."

"Then perhaps we shall get a kind master after all."

"Perhaps," Ling said. "If we survive this passage." She sighed for a moment, then turned in the darkness to Ah Toy. "We should not deceive ourselves."

"What do you mean?"

"I mean I fear difficult times are to come for us."

"Why?" Ah Toy asked, a tremble in her voice. "Back in China you said you believed we would—"

"That was a different time. The way they handle us speaks of trouble. Were we to go to well-to-do masters they would not bind us in such a damaging way." She lifted the heavy links around her hands and then let them drop to the floor. "It is better that we prepare ourselves for what awaits us."

"I think you worry too much," Ah Toy said, her voice revealing her own fears. "I think—"

"Shhh!" Ling said. "Be quiet. Listen!"

"Listen to what?"

"Be still!" Ling listened for a moment, the shouted, "Be still, all of you!"

Silence fell on the hold and Ling strained to hear. "Don't you hear that?"

Ah Toy listened, too, but all she could make out was the creak and groan of the ship's timbers. "I hear nothing."

"There! There, listen."

Ah Toy listened again. "I *do* hear it. Voices; many voices."

There was a loud sound from above and Ling could feel the speed of the ship drop in response. "We have arrived!" she shouted, and the women in the hold began cheering.

196

When they had first come out onto the deck Ah Toy and Ling had cried, so horrified had they been at each other's appearance after the long trip. But worse things than that awaited them. The "search" by customs inspectors was a study in humiliation. No part of their bodies was free from the probing, grasping, pinching hands of the inspectors.

After the inspectors had finished, they had turned them over to an old hag of a Chinese woman named Chou Bai Tsai. Swathed in black, attended by four muscled young Chinese guards, the old woman moved the girls into a march toward Chinatown.

Ling looked down at the shackles still about her hands as they passed into the Chinese quarter. "These cuffs weigh me down like an anchor."

Ah Toy said nothing.

"Ah Toy, are you all right?"

"Those men . . . ," she murmured, "their hands all over us . . ."

"It's over. Forget about it. We must go on from here."

They walked along in silence for a moment. Ling looked at the buildings of the Chinese quarter. She felt considerably more at ease. There were signs with Chinese characters written on them. There were the smells of China—cooking rice, steaming cuttlefish. But most of all there were the familiar Chinese faces up and down the streets.

"It is much better here than at the pier," she said.

"Anything would be better than at the pier. *Fan quay.*"

"With luck that shall be the last we'll see of the white devils," Ling said. "We will be sold to a rich old Chinaman with a long beard and failing vision, who possesses a kind nature."

Ah Toy smiled at the thought.

"He will only want us to cook for him and when he dies he will leave us all his money and we will return to China with his riches," Ling continued.

"You're dreaming," Ah Toy said.

"Yes, I suppose I am. But at least if we can stay in this quarter it will not be so bad. At least we shall be with our own people."

The woman in front began to slow down and Ling heard a shouted order. The young men formed the women into a line of twos and they slowly began filing into a building on the corner of Dupont and St. Louis Alley.

As Ling passed through the portals of the house she turned

to Ah Toy. "At last. Now we will get some good food in us, instead of the slop they served on the ship."

In the entry foyer of this house there were more men. One of them counted the shackled women as they entered. Others moved them along, down a narrow corridor. At the end of the corridor was another door.

As Ling approached the door she saw that steps led down to a lower level. She felt a sharp point prod her in the back and she turned to see a man, his face glistening with sweat, holding a pointed rod in his hand.

"Move," he snapped. "Downstairs."

Ling turned and headed down the stairs. She looked over her shoulder to see that Ah Toy was still behind her.

In the growing darkness, Ah Toy reached out for her. "Stay close, Ling."

Ling waited a moment for her, then continued down the stairs. At the bottom of the staircase were two more men, these two also moving the women along. Ling moved past them and into a large barracoon some eighty feet by eight feet.

Four torches, one on each wall of the barracoon, dimly illuminated the subterranean refuge. Ling shivered, feeling the dampness in the air. She made for one of the walls, Ah Toy right behind her.

Moments later she heard the clap of hands and turned to see Chou Bai Tsai standing at the entrance of the large cellar.

"Very well," Chou Bai Tsai said. "Soon the doctor will be here to tend to those who require medical attention. Dinner will be served shortly thereafter. I shall return tomorrow."

And with her short address ended, the old hag turned and left the room. The men followed after her and closed the heavy oak door. Ling heard a bolt slide across it on the other side.

Immediately the confinement room was filled with a chorus of jabbering voices. A hundred different conversations filled the air as wild speculation sprang free.

"What do you think?" Ah Toy asked.

"I think we shall have to wait and see."

The medical examination was a cursory one, the food served for dinner worse than the slop served on the ship, and the floor a cold and cruel bed. Ling woke to her first morning in California with a sharp pain in her back.

198

She rolled over and looked at Ah Toy. "How long have you been awake?"

Ah Toy was looking straight ahead. "An hour. Maybe two."

Ling looked around the barracoon. Half of the women were still sleeping. Others lay still, each with their own thoughts. Still others were stirring, up and walking quietly about.

"What are you thinking about?" Ling asked.

"I do not think it will go well for us in this new land."

Ling laughed. "You have finally reached that conclusion?"

Ah Toy turned and looked at her, her eyes filled with sadness. "Yes."

Ling stretched. "Perhaps you worry too greatly. It may not be all that bad. We may get lucky, as we did with our master in Hong Kong."

Ah Toy shook her head. "No. We will not be lucky. We will be sold to a cruel master."

"You overreact."

"This is a terrible place."

Ling looked at her friend. Ah Toy was on the verge of tears. "If you cry your face will be streaked and you will look unattractive except to the most lowly of men. You should concern yourself with looking as good as you can this day."

Ah Toy fought back the tears.

"All right," Ling granted, "it is true that this place is horrible. But we know for certain that this is not to be our final residence. That alone should bring you joy."

Ah Toy laughed a short laugh. "That is true enough."

"See, it could be worse. What if you had to stay in this horrible room forever?"

"Yes," Ah Toy smiled, "yes, that would be horrible."

"Then rejoice that when we leave this place we shall never have to see it again."

"That is cause for rejoicing."

Ling stood, stretching her legs. "I wonder what time it is? Without windows we have no way of knowing."

"Past breakfast time, that much is for certain."

Ling looked at Ah Toy. "Hungry?"

"I could eat a dozen bowls of rice in a single sitting."

"Even the garbage they served us on the ship would taste good now."

And then, as if they had heard the women talking, the

doors at the front of the barracoon opened and four men came in with large pots of rice carried between them. The smell quickly filled the air and the women who moments earlier had been sleeping were awake and on their feet now.

Ling and Ah Toy fought their way through some of the women and stood in line for the rice. When they passed by the large cauldron Ling's eyes went wide with surprise. In with the steaming white rice she could see generous chunks of fish and chicken. She blinked, not believing what she saw. But when she got closer and saw that it was real she smacked her lips, feeling her mouth fill with anticipatory juices.

"Chicken," Ah Toy said, looking over her shoulder.

Ling felt her mouth ache as she smiled widely. "And fish, too." She looked at her friend, not wanting to take her eyes off the rice for more than a moment. "It will be a good day after all."

After the meal the women were herded up to the first floor of the building. There they were taken, in groups of ten, into a large room with a concrete floor and bare walls.

"Strip," said one of the five men in the room.

Ling turned to Ah Toy. Fear showed in her friend's eyes.

The man looked at the women, seeing their hesitancy. He pulled back his jacket and removed a large, ivory-handled knife from the waistband of his trousers.

"The next woman who fails to instantly obey my orders, I shall cut her breast off and she shall have it for her noonday meal."

Within moments the ten women in the room stood naked before the guards. Ah Toy concealed her womanhood, her eyes downcast. Ling watched as more men, guards carrying buckets of steaming water, came into the room.

The guards set the water on the floor and took long-handled brushes from a set of cabinets against the far wall of the room. The men set to work, dipping the brushes in the water and then scrubbing the women clean.

After a few moments the women were at ease, forgetting their modesty as they luxuriated in their first bath in months. Even Ah Toy seemed less afraid.

"It feels so good to finally be cleaned," she said to Ling.

Ling turned around so the man washing her could bathe her back. These men, she reflected, were unlike the whites at the dockfront. There was no lewd remarks, no grasping hands, no leering gazes.

Instead they simply performed their tasks. Perhaps, she thought, it was because they saw so many women that it no longer mattered. But Ling preferred to think that it was because they were Chinese and the women were Chinese and that, therefore, a common bond existed.

There were even bursts of laughter now as the wash-men emptied the remains of the buckets over their heads and began to massage in soap.

Ling moaned gleefully as dust and dirt accumulated from the many weeks of passage from China were washed clean.

Afterwards, Ling's group was handed clean smocks and towels. They followed the guards from the room to be replaced, Ling assumed, by another group of ten women, who did not imagine the joyous surprise they had in store for them.

On the second floor of the house Ling and Ah Toy sat, with the other women, in straight-backed chairs while attendants went about oiling and braiding their hair.

"Perhaps I am still asleep," Ling mused, her eyes closed.

"Or dead," Ah Toy countered, "dead and gone to heaven."

The remark drew laughter from the other women as well.

An hour later, feeling like new women, Ling and Ah Toy stood in front of the building. Ling watched as the last group of ten filed from the house and joined them. The two hundred and eleven women stood again in rows of twos, waiting for Chou Bai Tsai.

Ling smelled the air and picked out familiar scents—incense, the smell of roasting pork and duck. She looked at passersby—messengers scurrying with morning missives, businessmen on their way to work. She looked at the buildings—pagodas with their eaves slanted upward so as to dispell and send back skyward whatever evil might fall from above.

It could easily be Beijing, she thought—almost. But she sensed that something was not quite right. For a moment she tried to decide what it was, and then it dawned on her. None of the people passing by them on the streets—the messengers and businessmen and young boys carrying baskets of laundry suspended on poles—were looking at them.

Ling thought that perhaps she was mistaken and she tried to catch someone's eyes, exchange a glance. But it didn't work. She wondered if it was just that they were in a hurry to get to work or if there was some other reason.

It was a peculiar feeling and she felt herself shudder in response to it. It was as if she didn't exist. She turned suddenly as the women about her grew quiet. Ling saw Chou Bai Tsai striding out of the building and she tensed.

The old woman's garb was identical to what she had worn the day before. But today there was a white belt fastened around her girth, and to the belt was fixed a large chain. On the chain were dozens of iron keys. With her four ever-present guards flanking her, she walked up the long rows of women, looking at each of them with an approving eye.

When at last she was finished, she turned and walked half-way down the line, stopped, and turned again to face the women.

She stood before them, her legs spread wide, her hands on her hips.

"So," Chou Bai Tsai began, "the doctor has examined you all. You have been fed, scrubbed, and tended to."

She cackled for a moment, then said, "I know the accommodations were not the finest, but I trust you all managed to get some rest."

A few of the women giggled nervously, not sure whether or not they were supposed to laugh.

Chou Bai Tsai grew serious. "Today is a very important day for each of you. You are to be auctioned on the block today."

As she spoke the old woman walked up the line a few paces, turned and walked back down the line. She repeated this stroll over and over again as she spoke.

"Today is a very important day for you. Today is the most important day of your life, because today will determine your fate for the rest of your life. I want you all to think about this."

Ling felt as though her body had gone rigid, as though everything else except Chou Bai Tsai's words had ceased to be.

"You have all been cleaned and groomed and made to look attractive so as to fetch a better price on the auction block. This will benefit the man who is selling you."

The old woman stopped suddenly to emphasize her words. "*But* remember that it will also benefit you. The finest of you, the best looking, the most alluring will attract the best buyers—men of incredible wealth, with great houses and many servants."

The women broke into purrs of pleasure at Chou Bai Tsai's words.

The old hag smiled, showing spaces where time had rotted her teeth away. She nodded. "Yes, many of you will find more than you ever dreamt of. These men bidding on you today have worked the gold mines, ripped forth the harvest of gold, and live like mandarins—like *mandarins!*"

The women turned to each other, excitedly exchanging clips of conversation.

"Remember these things when you step up to the auction block. Display your charms and act comely and you shall attract heavy bidding. Appear exotic with the promise of consummate skills in the art of pleasure and you will draw a good and kind and wealthy master."

Chou Bai Tsai looked over the women, sensed their excitement, and was satisfied that she had infused them with the proper spirit.

"Very well," she concluded. "And now to the auction block."

It was a short walk up Dupont Street to the site of the auction. The women were practically skipping along the streets in anticipation, speculating about their wealthy masters-to-be.

Walking alongside Ling, Ah Toy asked, "Do you think it will be possible for us to be sold together?"

"We could ask," Ling said.

"I would not want to be separated from you, Ling."

"Nor I. I think if we stand close together and insure that one is sold after the other, then perhaps the same man will buy us both."

Ling turned, hearing voices ahead of them. She could make out their faces.

The men were smiling, laughing, sharing jokes with each other. They wore fine jackets of dark blue and black silk. They wore matching skullcaps. Their queues glistened in the morning sun from many applications of rare oils, and Ling thought that Chou Bai Tsai was right when she said that these men were richer than the mandarins.

The men looked at the women as they approached and Ling felt a strange sense of relief. At least, *they* acknowledged their existence. She felt a sudden pride, from the realization that she was wanted by these men, even if it was only as a commodity, a servant.

Along with the other women, she was led to a shady spot by the wall of a building. From her vantage point she could see a small raised platform in the middle of the street's intersection. On the platform, which looked to be about six feet by six feet, an always-smiling snake of a man stood with a thick sheath of papers in his hand. He was busy talking with two of his assistants.

About the platform, forming a semicircle, stood the men who had come to take part in or just watch the auction. It was considered good sport and a pleasant way to pass the morning hours.

Ling now saw Chou Bai Tsai as she trudged up the steps of the platform and began talking with the auctioneer. They exchanged a few words and then she left. Finally, the auctioneer turned to the gathering.

"The auction is about to begin," he cried urgently, "the auction is about to begin."

And in response the men grew more quiet and attentive.

Certain that he had their attention, the auctioneer continued. "And today we have as fine a shipment of young women as has ever touched these shores."

Scattered applause broke from the men and the auctioneer acknowledged them.

"Thank you, cousins. But wait until you see them. Then I will need a weapon with which to fight you off, because you will be so eager to express your gratitude for the offering I bring you this morning."

Now hearty laughter replaced the applause and the man smiled, basking in the attention. He gestured gracefully with his hand toward the women lining the wall.

"Truly, has there ever been a finer lot of women than these?" He turned back to the men. "And you shall see each of them individually. Each is a charmer, selected for her beauty and—" he paused while his face twisted into a knowing leer—"selected for their skills."

Again there was laughter from the men, and it turned into appreciative clapping.

"Each pearl has been carefully selected for her docile nature and her intricate training. They will please you and bring their owners great wealth and prosperity if properly employed."

One of the auctioneers handed him a sheet of paper, which he held up. "With each woman comes a certificate of health attested to by a physician. We do not deliver questionable merchandise. Each of them is fit and ready to serve, delivered in top condition."

He handed the slip back to his assistant, clapped his hands, and said, "Let the auction begin!"

Cheers broke forth as the men responded to the auctioneer's enthusiasm.

One of the assistants walked to the wall of the building where Ling stood with the others and selected the first woman. She walked five paces behind the man, smiling demurely as she did so.

As she walked up the steps of the platform the auctioneer gasped with astonishment.

"Look at this beauty! Look at this pearl of Mother China! Descended from the heavens to serve some lucky owner!"

He turned back to the men. "I am sorely tempted not to sell her at all. Maybe I should keep her for myself. Yes!" He turned to his assistant. "Take her away! I will not sell her! Take her to my home!"

These words were greeted by shouts and calls from the men, who objected strongly. Finally, affecting a downcast look, the auctioneer said, "Very well, very well. You win." He turned to the assistant. "She stays. We'll sell her."

He turned like a vulture on the audience. "Who will start the bidding on this gem? Who will give me a thousand dollars? Who?"

A man at the rear of the audience shouted out a bid of five hundred dollars.

"An insult!" the auctioneer declared. But the bid was immediately topped with one of six hundred dollars, then seven. In turn came a bid of seven hundred and fifty.

Minutes later, when the flurry of excitement had ended, the auctioneer slapped his hands together for the third time and shouted, "Sold for one thousand one hundred dollars. And a steal at that price!"

By the time half a dozen women had been auctioned, the excitement began to simmer down a bit and more serious buyers started to do their bidding. The men who came to the auction to do business knew not to think about buying women until the first five or six had been sold. During that time the auctioneer would pull in bids well over the going rate from newcomers who were infected by his excitement.

But now, with things getting serious, the bidding hovered closer to the going market price of seven to eight hundred dollars. And as the acquisitions began in earnest, scrutiny of the merchandise became more careful.

During the next hour Ling watched as one man purchased

eight different women and another man purchased six, and she shuddered to think of the appetite these men must have to need so many women to please them.

The buying had taken on a different tone—more businesslike and clinical. As each woman ascended the platform she stood before the auctioneer. He drew up her robes, displaying her for a moment to the men before the bidding began.

Ling's thoughts were interrupted as one of the auctioneer's assistants appeared at her side. She went with the man and climbed the platform.

The auctioneer quickly glanced at her, then said, "A fine young beauty, fresh from eight years of service with a wealthy merchant." He winked his eye at the audience. "She'll be wise in the ways of love. Eager to please, this one."

The auctioneer turned back to Ling, grasping the hem of her dress. "Now let's see what we've got under here."

He lifted the dress hem over Ling's head, exposing her supple young body to the view of the men below the platform. She felt the blood rush to her face with shame as the auctioneer spoke.

"Fine body," he said. "Nice round titties that I'd pay for myself." He leaned closer and squeezed Ling's left breast. "Don't mind if I do," the auctioneer proclaimed, drawing a laugh from the men.

He let the hem drop and continued his banter. "She'll make a real pleaser, this one. She knows all the special tricks." The man turned to Ling. "Don't you, dear?"

She tried her best to raise a smile to her lips, remembering Chou Bai Tsai's admonition about securing a good master by appearing attractive.

The auctioneer turned back to the men. "There, you see? Ready and willing to please. A good worker, this one. What am I bid?"

The bidding was a blur to Ling. She was numb, unfeeling. Her next recollection was the feel of a hand on her arm and she turned to face one of the auctioneer's assistants who was leading her down the steps of the platform.

The assistant took her to the small station at the rear of the crowd where a man sat at a table on the sidewalk, making entries into a ledger. Ling stood before him and waited. The man at the table looked up.

"Your name is Ling Wong?"

She nodded. "Yes."

"You have been sold, this day, for the price of $825. Put out your hand."

Ling put her hand out and the man behind the table placed a pouch containing the sum in her hand. "You have now received the said $825. Give me your other hand."

She obeyed.

The man took her thumb and rolled it on an inked pad. He then transferred her thumbprint onto a document attesting to the fact that she had willingly sold herself and that she had received $825 in return for her servitude.

The man folded the document and placed it in a file. He then took the pouch containing the money from her hand and placed it back in his strongbox.

He looked to the attendant. "Take her away."

As the attendant again took her by the arm she turned, suddenly remembering Ah Toy. Ling caught a glimpse of her as she rounded the corner of Dupont Street. Ah Toy was standing on the platform, being bid upon. It seemed to Ling that her friend looked very small.

Chapter 25

Yang was bone tired. Even a grooming did little to lessen his fatigue. He had been on the train for two days, packed with seventy other men in a passenger car designed to carry twenty. He arrived in San Francisco exhausted and dirty.

Peng Ku was his usual philosophical self. "At least they supplied us with free transportation back to the city. They could have charged us."

Yang nodded in agreement as they walked through the streets of the Chinese quarter. "That would have been more in keeping—charging us for passage on a railroad we had built."

"I'm glad it's over."

"I as well. Now we can get on with the business of life."

"And what business is that?" Peng Ku asked.

"The business of wealth."

"Why are so determined to be a mandarin?"

"Why are you so determined to remain a pauper?"

Peng Ku smiled. "You are driven by something within, aren't you?"

"We all are." He sniffed the air, and the aroma of roasting chicken caught him, stopping him in his tracks. "Are you as hungry as I?"

"Probably more so," his companion chided.

Yang turned toward the restaurant. "Then let's eat."

An hour later they emerged from the restaurant, glutted with roast chicken, rice, and wine.

Yang shook his head. "Eight dollars for a meal. The prices have soared to the heavens."

"The prosperity of the railroad has not been lost on our people. Too," Peng Ku said, "we are accustomed to the free meals we've had."

"I don't think our savings will take us too far in this new economy," Yang speculated.

"It's a good thing we had the foresight to save something."

They began walking down the cobblestoned streets of Chinatown, heading in no particular direction, merely reacquainting themselves with the quarter. Flames from the gas burners of the street lamps flickered and cast shadows on the ground as they walked, and Yang was surprised to find himself happy to be in the city, happy for the change after so many years in the wilderness and the ice and cold.

The San Francisco air was crisp and carried with it smells and scents that were familiar. He listened to the sound of men talking, laughing, arguing, and he was glad, for the moment, that he was back in civilization.

"Your brother lives in this city, does he not?" asked Peng Ku.

"Yes."

"I imagine you would want to visit him."

"There is time."

"You do not wish to speak of him?"

"No."

"Why not?"

Yang turned to look at him. "Did you not hear the answer to your previous question? I do not wish to speak of him."

Peng Ku turned away. "Very well."

They walked along in silence for a moment. Yang could feel the hurt he had done to Peng Ku. He glanced sidelong at his friend. The man was small, compact of build but strong of brain. It was wise to have such a man as a friend, Yang realized.

"I did not mean to be short with you."

"It is of no importance."

"It is," he insisted. He paused, then said, "I apologize."

"Unnecessary, but accepted."

Again they walked in silence. Finally, Yang said, "All my life I have been resentful of my brother."

Peng Ku was silent, waiting for Yang to continue.

"I don't know why that is," Yang said. "I've tried to understand it often."

"Was he unkind to you?"

"No. Certainly not."

They turned a corner and walked down a side street. Yang thought for a moment before continuing.

"We never seemed to agree on anything."

"You argued often?"

Yang turned to look at Peng Ku. "No. That's the curious thing, Peng Ku. We did not have many arguments. Not even a great many discussions. Chin was not of an argumentative nature."

"Then how can you say that you never agreed on anything?"

"I think it was largely a question of different philosophies."

Peng Ku nodded.

"My brother was always a gentle man. Cerebral; in many ways like you."

"I see."

"Where I would stand and fight an enemy with my fists, Chin would outsmart him with his wits." Yang smiled.

"Happy memories?" Peng Ku asked.

"Some." Then Yang nodded. "Yes, many. He was a smart rascal, my brother." He laughed. "He could talk a rabbit out of its fur."

"A chess player?"

Yang turned sharply. "How did you know?"

"It was not difficult to guess."

"Yes. Yes, Chin was always good at chess. My uncle said that he never played a man who was better. But you see, Peng Ku, that was the crux of our problem. I was a *tai chi ch'uan* master and Chin was a chess expert."

Peng Ku turned slightly toward him as they passed a flickering street lamp. "And the two do not mix?"

"No."

"Why not?"

"Chin thinks with his brains. I think with my hands."

"Perhaps you demean yourself. I think you are more intelligent than you give yourself credit for."

"Then you do not know me as well as you think you do. I know what I am. I accept my limitations along with my capabilities."

"I think not, Yang. I think there is something in you that is afraid to admit your intellect, as if that would make you less a man."

"Careful," Yang warned, an edge to his voice. "You begin to sound too much like my brother."

Again the two men fell silent. They had not walked far when a particular aroma caught Yang's attention. He looked at the large red sign hanging over a shop on the corner of Kearny Street.

Yang read the large, neatly drawn characters on the sign. "*Kung in san tiu.*" He turned to Peng Ku, who was also looking at the sign. "Panta opium," he said, his senses already reeling in anticipation, whetted by the fragrant scent of the drug in the air.

Peng Ku closed his eyes and inhaled. "I had almost forgotten what really good opium smells like. That cow dung that passed for opium in the wilderness was fit for little else but fertilizer."

"How many years has it been since we've smoked Panta?" Yang asked. "Eight, nine years?"

They walked toward the brick building on the corner. It was not an unattractive building, Yang thought. It was three stories high and most solid looking. On the upper floors he saw many fine stained-glass windows and now, as he and Peng Ku drew closer, he could make out the sound of laughter coming from inside.

As he heard the cry of a woman's laughter, Yang turned to his companion. "Women, too. This promises to be a night to remember."

They walked up a short flight of stairs and Yang rapped on the door. A small porthole in the door opened and a face said, "Yes? What do you want?"

"That which is advertised," Yang answered.

"It is not intended for you."

Yang straightened belligerently. "Who then?"

"This place is for whites," the gatekeeper said, and before Yang could issue a protest the tiny porthole slammed shut.

210

Yang could feel his body tense, his muscles tighten, as he turned and walked down the stairs with Peng Ku at his side. He could still hear the laughter coming from within the building, and as it grew louder he felt that it was somehow directed at him. His anger rose even higher.

"It is not enough that we slave for the whites; now they even take over our own quarter."

"Don't look at it that way," Peng Ku said.

He turned angrily. "How should I look at it?"

"That this is simply a place where the white man gives his money to our people. It probably isn't even Panta opium."

Now Yang laughed, pleased with the idea that the rich white people who favored the house were being cheated.

"Come," Yang said, "let us find a place which caters to us."

It was not a long search. Three streets away, in Beckett Alley, they caught scent of the pungent drug again. Yang turned into the alleyway with Peng Ku.

They walked into the darkness, pulled along by the sickly-sweet aroma. Finally they stopped in front of a building that advertised itself as a lodging house. Standing in front of the door was a man as large as Yang. He turned, unsmiling, and looked at the pair.

"What is it you seek?" the man asked.

"Dreams," Peng Ku replied.

He stared at them for a long moment, then stepped aside. As Yang passed alongside the man he caught the glint of a knife handle in the waistband of the guard's trousers.

As Peng Ku opened the heavy wooden door of the lodging house they were assaulted by the odor of burning opium. It was thick in the air, causing a haze in front of the oil lamps that flickered on the walls of the narrow hallway.

At the end of the corridor stood another man, of no less impressive dimensions than the first they had encountered.

"Raise your arms," the man ordered.

Yang and Peng Ku obeyed and were rewarded with a rude body search. Afterwards, the man pointed to the left and Yang turned to see another door.

Yang opened the door and looked down into the cavern that was the basement of the lodging house. He began to feel his head become light from inhaling the fumes, which were by now so thick that Yang had to squint in order to see clearly.

They began walking down the rickety wooden steps, which creaked with each footfall, threatening to give way at each step.

As soon as they reached the bottom of the stairs a squat, round Chinese appeared out of the shadows.

"Opium?" he said, not mincing words. "You come for Panta?"

Yang nodded.

The man smiled widely, bowing. "You have come to the right establishment, cousins. There is no better opium to be had in all of Little China. Your wishes will be granted and your dreams shall be many."

"How much?" Yang asked.

The man's smile lessened a degree. "Twenty dollars will guarantee both of you a night of dreams you shall not soon forget."

"Twenty dollars?"

"For both," the man noted. "No fairer price will you find in the city."

Yang turned to Peng Ku. "They have learned well from the whites how to take advantage of their own people."

Now the smile vanished completely from the man's face. "You wound me, cousin, to say such a thing. It is apparent that you have been gone from the city for a long time. The railroad, perhaps?"

"It does not take a temple priest to divine that," Peng Ku said.

The man turned to Peng Ku. "Why are you both so saber-tongued? Is it because you have been so long away from civilization?"

"No. It is because your prices are so outrageous."

"They are in keeping with the market." The man's voice became clipped as he said, "Perhaps you would like to try elsewhere?"

"This will do," Yang said as he reached into the pocket of his trousers. He paid for himself and Peng Ku. When Peng Ku tried to pay him for his portion, Yang said, "I insist."

"Why?"

"Because I do," Yang said.

"Why?" Peng Ku tried again.

Yang sighed and turned to him. "Because you are my friend."

The smaller man brought his hands to his mouth in mock astonishment. "A monumental confession."

212

Yang looked at him for a moment, then laughed.

The opium den operator said, "Are you two here to smoke or converse?"

"You're right, weasel," Yang said, turning his attention to the man. "Lead the way."

Yang looked about as he followed the man through the drifting smoke. Now, as his eyes began to grow more accustomed to the dark, he could see the dull, hazy glow of a spot of amber light here and there. And, emanating from the balls of light, he could make out the sound of the sputtering pipes which were attached to the opium lamps.

The air was close, fetid, and oppressive. It was as if they were moving through layer after layer of wispy clouds and Yang had to strain to see the keeper as he made his way through the den of iniquity.

At length the three of them stood before the far wall of the den, against which was fixed a long double tier of bunks, one above the other.

"Enjoy yourselves," the man said, and then he vanished into the clouds.

Yang bent over and saw that the lower bunk was occupied. He turned to see Peng Ku already climbing onto one of the bunks on the top row.

"Can't wait, eh?"

"The sooner the better," Peng Ku said, settling himself on the straw mat. "I've waited a long time for this."

Yang grabbed hold of the edge of the bunk frame and hoisted himself up. Through the smoke he could barely make out Peng Ku's features as he sat on the adjoining bunk.

Yang looked at the wall and saw that it was blackened from years of exposure to the continuous smoke. He drew back the thin blanket that covered the straw mat and rolled it, placing it at the other end of the bunk.

He was feeling quite light-headed by now; the exhaled smoke in the room was having its effect. Yang looked at the yellowish glow of the smoking lamp on his bed and picked up the plate it rested on. He located the smoking paraphernalia and set to work.

He picked up the small buffalo-horn box and pried open its top. Inside Yang found a black lump almost the size of a prune. Next he found the earthernware plate over which the opium would be placed.

Yang took the sponge that had been provided and dipped it in a cup of water. He cleaned the plate and then set it aside. Next he picked up the short, ivory-mouthpieced opium pipe and held it between his fingers, feeling a tremble of anticipation.

With the sound of sputtering pipes urging him on, Yang held his own pipe over the flickering flame of the opium lamp, heating it for a moment. Then he picked up the wire pincers and aligned them with the tip of the pipe over the flame. These two elements he now dipped into the buffalo-horn box containing the opium.

The opium softened from the heat and adhered to the end of the pipe and the pincers. He held the bottom of the pipe bowl over the flame and watched as the heat conducted through the smoking tool inflated the pill of opium which was like a bubble filling up with steam.

The opium ball got larger and larger, growing like a balloon until it was the size of a grapefruit.

Next Yang placed the ball on the earthenware plate which had a single small hole in its middle. He drew the wire pincers out from the bottom of the ball so that now the balloon of opium rested on top of the plate, with the pipe extending out at a perpendicular angle on top of the ball.

Carefully, Yang lifted the plate over the point of the flame coming from the lamp. As the ball continued to grow in size Yang put his lips to the ivory mouthpiece of the pipe and sucked in.

Moments later he felt his head begin to swell; the rush was upon him. Pleasure—exquisite, all-consuming pleasure—coursed through his body, filling every nerve, every inch of his being with a sweet tingle of joy that was all but unbearable.

He could no longer smell the stale air, hear the sputter of pipes about him, or see the black smoke smudges on the walls. There was only his pipe, his smoke, his pleasure. All was Yang.

He brought his lips back to the ivory tip of the pipe.

Chapter 26

In the early part of the fall of 1869, Chin moved his business headquarters out of the cramped quarters over his import shop on Dupont Street and into a large suite of offices on the second floor of a brick building kitty-corner to the Wells Fargo Bank at the intersection of Montgomery and California streets.

The move was looked upon by his associates and his competitors alike as an act of faith and a testament of his organization's strength. There had been murmurs throughout the business community of the quarter that Chin had not been exercising the soundest business sense during the last few years, particularly with regard to the lucrative gambling concerns he had inherited from his benefactor Mei Peng.

Why these and his opium interests were not both expanded was a matter of considerable debate among his peers in Chinatown. Tai Pien, Chin's powerful head of vice, had told his subordinates that Chin simply wanted to consolidate his holdings before he began a plan of expansion.

But after years of waiting for the expansion, several managers of Chin's *Fan-tan* parlors and one of his best lottery operators defected and joined other, more ambitious gambling concerns.

It became apparent, eventually, that Chin had no stomach for gambling and vice, and it was not long before that realization set certain forces into motion against him.

As his gambling enterprises dwindled more and more, Chin began to feel resistance on the part of certain creditors and suppliers of goods to his import shops. It was no matter that he was eminently solvent. Weakness in one area was viewed as weakness in all areas, and rumors spread that he might be thinking of returning to China.

So the move to the new headquarters on California Street was a deliberate attempt to show them all that Chin Wong meant business and intended to stay in business in this country for some time to come.

But as Chin, Shao Kow, and Tai Pien sat in the plushly decorated conference chamber of the new headquarters, listening to an old man's story, Chin was not at all certain that all was well with his company.

"I do not know where they came from," the old man said, his eyes a mixture of fear and sadness. "They were all upon me at once."

Chin watched carefully as the man spoke. There was no question in his mind but that the man was speaking the truth. Chin had dealt with dishonest runners before. There were always signs, ways of telling when a man had secreted lottery receipts somewhere and was faking a holdup—a furtive look, a nervous twitch, a telltale clearing of the throat. Not so with this old man, Chin thought. He was more frightened than nervous. He could not clear his throat because it was still clenched with fear.

The man hung his head abjectly. "I am so ashamed, honorable Chin."

"There is nothing to be ashamed of."

The runner looked up at him. "I should have opposed them, fought them off. Twenty, even ten years ago I would have . . ." His voice trailed off. "But I am old now. Just an old, useless man."

"There is no shame in surrendering to a superior force."

Tai Pien's voice was emotionless as he asked, "How many were there?"

"Four."

"How old?"

"Young."

"How young?"

"Young," the old man said. "When I was that young I would not have thought of—"

"How were they dressed?" Tai Pien asked, cutting him off.

The runner gave him a peculiar look. "Dressed? They were dressed as any other young men dress."

"Was there anything unusual about their manner of dress? Anything out of the ordinary?"

"What do you mean?"

"A scarf, perhaps a colored sash?"

"No, no there was nothing."

"Think harder, old man."

"There was nothing out of the ordinary about them. Just a gang of young hoodlums."

"Think!" Tai Pien shouted.

216

Chin shot him a disapproving look. Tai Pien lowered his voice when he spoke again.

"You have lost a great deal of money. Through no fault of your own," he added quickly. "But it is money lost all the same. Now you must try to remember something which can help us recover it."

The old man retreated within himself, his mind working, reconstructing. He sat forward with a bolt. "They all wore a certain gold ring."

"Good!" Tai Pien exclaimed. "Tell me about it."

"I cannot remember it too clearly. It all happened so quickly."

"Tell me what you can."

"Gold rings . . . worn on the first finger," he said, pointing to his own. "Each ring with a single emerald in it. That's all."

Chin said, "You may go now."

The man rose, his voice quivering. "Am . . . am I still in your employ?"

Chin smiled. "Of course you are. Return to your job, old father."

The man bowed as he backed out of Chin's office, expressing his gratitude.

After he closed the door Tai Pien turned to Chin. "It is the Yee tong. I'm certain of it."

"How can you be so certain?" Chin asked.

"Members of that tong wear a gold ring with a single emerald in it as part of their identification."

"Such a ring is quite common," Chin said. "Lo Chi himself possesses such a ring."

"But he does not wear it on the index finger as these hoodlums did. Such a thing is done by the Yee tong. We must confront them and demand a return of the lottery money."

"I will not make such an accusation."

"It shows weakness," Tai Pien said.

"I will not hurl accusations about like an old woman gossiping."

Shao Kow, who had been listening silently up until now, said, "I fear Tai Pien is right, Chin."

Tai Pien turned quickly to look at Shao Kow, surprised that he was receiving support from this man.

Shao Kow continued, "I am not as certain as Tai Pien as to the Yee tong's involvement in this particular affair. That is not the point. The point is, we must do something about the tongs."

Chin folded his arms, his eyes locking with those of his chief adviser. "Are you advocating force?"

"No. I am simply saying that something must be done. We must oppose the growing strength of the tongs. They are no longer simply a group of trade guilds. They are a growing force in the community and this warrior branch is causing much disorder."

"They are a force of violence," Tai Pien added. "And it is with violence that we must oppose them, for it is all they will understand."

"I cannot accept that," Chin said.

Tai Pien felt his frustration surface. "Then we shall continue to have our lottery runners assaulted, we shall continue to have our *Fan-tan* parlors robbed, we shall continue to see our entire operation disrupted."

"Our entire operation is not being disrupted."

"It isn't? Last month three of our opium dens had to be evacuated because hooligans raided them, tipped over bunks and made off with eighty tins of opium. The patrons, who were stuporous at the time, had to leave the dens, and you can rest assured that they will never return."

"These are isolated incidents you speak of."

Tai Pien shook his head angrily. "They are not! They are connected, planned, and premeditated, and I cannot understand why you fail to see this."

Shao Kow leaned closer to Chin. "Tai Pien is correct. There can be little doubt but that all these attacks are the work of the tongs, which are growing more bold in our streets every day. It is rumored that they have taken to blackmail and assassination to gain revenue."

"They shall not blackmail me," Chin said.

"They already do," Tai Pien insisted. "They continue to make demands through force and you continue to acquiesce."

Shao Kow said, "It must be clear to you that they are testing you, Chin, trying to see how far they can go."

Chin angrily stood up from the conference table. "I will not start a war because of a few difficulties in one area of my business affairs. And certainly not over vice!"

"Then would you give up these interests which you inherited from Mei Peng?"

Chin turned to look at the man. Mixed with his anger was a grudging respect for Tai Pien for being shrewd enough to mention that Mei Peng had willed the gambling interests to him. Tai Pien knew that Chin would never completely forsake that responsibility.

Chin smiled through his anger. "You are a wise man, Tai Pien. Perhaps you should have sat on the Council of the Kong Chow Company."

"I prefer the challenge of building an empire for you," he said, adding, "if only you will let me."

Chin's voice softened. "An empire built on wages lost in card games and fleeting dreams of drugs?"

Tai Pien was silent.

"Very well," Chin said. "As you say, I have an obligation to Mei Peng's memory. Too, I suppose you are both right. If we do nothing it will be interpreted as weakness." He looked at Tai Pien. "Do that which is necessary to protect our interests. But let me warn you, Tai Pien, I will not take lightly to offensive measures. I merely want protection . . . not conquest. Do you understand this fully?"

"Fully," Tai Pien said.

Rebecca lay next to Chin, beneath the sheets. She could feel his naked thigh, warm and soft, against her own. But his mood was distant tonight, and when they had made love it seemed to her that his thoughts were elsewhere.

Finally she said, "You're preoccupied tonight."

Chin stared up at the ceiling in the darkness of his bedroom. He smelled the faint aroma of burning incense. He heard Rebecca speaking, as much a question as a statement.

"You're right," he answered.

"Do you want to talk to me about it?"

He was silent for a moment, then said, "There is no need."

"There is."

He turned slightly toward her. "Why?"

"Because what concerns you concerns me."

He kissed her gently on the cheek and turned to stare up at the ceiling again. "You are a good woman."

"That doesn't answer my question."

"There is no need to discuss it," he repeated.

"Why not?"

"Because I already know your views on the matter."

"What matter?"

He sighed, growing edgy. "You ask too many questions tonight."

Rebecca withdrew, felt his leg as it moved away from hers. For a long time they were silent.

"Is it me?" she finally asked.

Chin turned sharply, a smile on his lips. "You?"

"Yes. Don't I please you anymore?"

He tried to conceal his amusement, but when he no longer could he let out a long laugh.

"There's nothing funny about it," she said.

"It isn't you," he said, reaching out a hand so he could stroke her luxurious hair, which was now unplaited and spread like a great fan on the silken sheets of Chin's bed.

"Everything about you is good and right," he said. "You bring me more pleasure, both intellectually and physically, than I have ever known from any woman."

She half sat up in the bed. "Then what's bothering you? I have a right to know when it affects me as well."

He sighed, giving in. "An old man was robbed today; a runner."

"A runner?"

"A man who works for me, who takes bets on the lottery."

She frowned in the dark and Chin could feel the frown, could feel her disapproval. He waited for her to ask another question and when she didn't he decided that he would tell her anyway, inasmuch as she had pried it loose from him.

"Each day, after he had collected his bets and recorded the numbers, he brings all the receipts and money to our offices."

"You must have many men like him."

"Yes, many. There must be many runners in order for the lottery to pay handsomely. It is a volume business—many small bets."

"And he was robbed?"

"Yes."

"By whom?"

"A group of men."

"What will happen to the old man?"

"Nothing."

"You won't hold him responsible for the money that he lost?"

"No. He didn't lose it. It was taken from him."

She nodded. But then she asked, "How do you know he didn't fake the robbery?"

"The same way I know you do not fake your feelings for me."

She laughed at his answer. "Was much money taken?"

"A thousand dollars, more or less."

"You'll make the money back."

220

"It is not the money so much that bothers me. It is the loss of prestige."

Rebecca rested on one elbow, looking at Chin. In the darkness she could partially make out his features, could see that he was staring up at the ceiling, not really talking to her—talking more to himself.

"What do you mean?" she asked.

"This is not the first such incident."

"Robbery?"

He nodded.

"Maybe you should get out of gambling."

"I cannot."

"Why can't you?"

"It's a long story."

"Tell it to me."

"Not now, you wouldn't understand, Rebecca." He thought about it and added, "At least not yet, anyway."

"Why don't you think I'd understand?"

"Because you don't know the Chinese mentality well enough. You don't even know *me* well enough." He shook his head. "It takes years to—"

"I've worked with the Chinese for—"

"It means nothing." He waited for her to say something, but when she did not he realized that he had cut too deeply, that he had denigrated the good and honest work she had done helping. He was sorry that he had done that, because it was not his intention to wound her.

"It means little," he amended, "in helping you to understand the Chinese." He softened his tone. "I am not speaking of the importance of the work you have done, Rebecca. I want you to understand that. The work you have done is a great and important thing which has brought happiness to many of my people and pride to me."

She shifted slightly on the bed, drawing closer to him now.

He looked back up at the ceiling. "But the work you have done with my people, the few scant years of exposure to them, will do little to help you understand our nature; that is what I meant by what I said."

"I feel I understand some things," she said.

He nodded. "Some things, yes. But these things are only on the surface. It is like geese who glide on a lake's top not knowing the world that teems beneath it."

"What does this have to do with your being in gambling?"

"It is an obligation."

"Why?"

"Because it was inherited by me, willed to me."

"From Mei Peng?"

"Yes."

"That was a gift, to do with as you please."

"That is how you see it. To me it is an obligation. To discard Mei Peng's business interests would be to defame his name."

"I don't think Mei Peng would feel that way."

"Then you do not know Mei Peng and, as I have already said, you do not know the Chinese mentality."

"What if Mei Peng had willed you a brothel?"

"But he did not."

"All right, if you're afraid to answer the—"

"I am not afraid to answer the question. If Mei Peng had willed me a brothel then I would become a whoremaster."

"I cannot believe that you would."

"I would. Reluctantly, but I would."

"And it is with the same reluctance that you run your gambling houses?"

"Yes."

"And is that why you're upset? Because you're trapped into doing something you find morally offensive?"

"No." He paused. "Yes, partially." He turned toward Rebecca and said, "You must understand that I do not find this as objectionable as you do. Gambling has been a part of Chinese life for thousands of years. It is indigenous to China."

Now Rebecca sat up in the bed. "Chin, you must realize the true effect of these things on your people. You aren't blind."

Chin felt his head ache, knowing that Rebecca was speaking words that he felt, that he was defending a position he didn't want to defend.

She went on. "The wealthy Chinese know how to indulge these vices with moderation. But the poor, the ones who can least afford luxuries, are the ones who are spending the most money on vice. They're the ones who squander their wages on dreams that *Fan-tan* and opium offer them."

"Rebecca, I know your opinion on these matters."

Again she fell silent. At length she asked, "Well, if it isn't the moral question, then what's bothering you?"

Now it was Chin who sat up in the bed and turned to face her. "It is *because* of the moral question that I have a problem. In fact, Rebecca, it is partially because of *your* continued expression of displeasure about certain of my holdings that I have a problem."

"Because of *me*?" she asked.

"Yes. For a long time my advisers have told me to expand my operations, to make them more secure. But I have not done so, mostly because I know of your objections."

"Well, if my feelings have stopped you from opening more *Fan-tan* parlors and more opium dens then I'm proud to claim the credit. Though I can't remember forbidding you to do so. I don't even remember discussing—"

"Oh, not in so many words. But I know of your high standards. I know how you feel about gambling and . . ."

"I'm sorry that my high standards offend you. I had thought that they were one of the things that attracted you to me."

"They are, but—"

"I'm pleased to claim credit for stopping your expansion of vice, if you throw the blame to me."

Chin threw the sheets off and swung his legs over the side of the bed. He pulled his robe on. "Very well. Then you can also claim the credit for my diminished prestige in my community."

"Diminished prestige?" She gave a short laugh as she got out of the bed and wrapped her robe around herself. "I can't believe what you're saying. You mean because you won't expand an empire of vice, an empire that takes money from the poor, that you've lost the respect of your peers? Maybe their respect isn't worth that much, then."

"Not the respect of my peers, Rebecca. I have lost the respect of my adversaries, and that is a much more serious matter. Because I have been weak, because I have failed to expand my holdings, the tongs have taken to testing my strength. Many of these young gangs think of my organization as a bunch of old women who are afraid to stand up and protect their holdings."

"The tongs? They're just trade guilds."

He smiled. "How little you really know. The tongs are no longer just trade guilds. They have warrior branches, gangs of thugs who roam the streets." He paced about the room. "They've robbed my people on half a dozen different occasions. I'm losing business and workers."

"Let me ask you something. Have they robbed any of your

import shops? Have they attacked any of your legitimate businesses?"

"No."

Rebecca stood before him. "Then why don't you let them *have* the gambling? Why don't you let *them* have the tainted conscience?"

"I told you. There is an obligation." He looked at her. "More than that. It is only good business sense. If I were to withdraw from gambling and opium I would lose face. How long do you think it would be before they began robbing my import shops and terrorizing my warehouses?"

"I cannot believe that they would do that."

"Why not?"

"Because you cannot rob an honest business and get away with it for long. Wouldn't the Six Companies exert their influence if they found the tongs robbing honest businessmen?"

"Perhaps," he said, turning away.

"The mere fact that these gangs have only sought to strike against vice operators shows that they realize they are safe so long as they stay within the boundaries of filth."

"Perhaps you are right. But I cannot allow them to continue to pillage my operators. The word gets around. People will become reticent to deal with me in other areas if I show weakness in this matter."

"What will you do, then? Open a hundred more opium dens?"

He turned back to her. "No. I will merely consolidate what I have. I will protect that which I already own."

"With force?"

"Only that which is required to protect my workers."

"It means that people will be injured, maybe innocent people."

Chin sat on a sofa at the far end of the room. "You do not approve."

"I will never approve of violence."

"A man must protect that which is already his. I would fight to protect you."

"There's a difference, Chin, and you know there is. You're talking about protecting a business which is built on false hopes and dreams."

He turned away from her and walked toward the door. "I have no recourse. It must be this way."

Rebecca shook her head and turned to look out the window. "No good will come of it."

Chapter 27

Chin raced through column after column of figures. On his desk lay piles of ledgers still to be checked. He had not personally checked his company books in years. That work was ordinarily assigned to the bookkeepers who worked for him.

Chang Mai Mai, the general manager of Chin's import shops, was surprised earlier in the week when a message came stating that Chin wanted all company books delivered to his office. Chang Mai Mai first feared that there was an embezzler in their midst and that Chin had found him out.

But the general manager dismissed that notion. A complete audit had been done only a month earlier by an independent accounting company and everything had been found to be in order.

Shao Kow alone knew the reason for Chin's behavior, for it had been he who delivered the message to Chin's house. He alone, through his many years of association with Chin, knew that this was his employer's way of retreating from bad news. By burying himself in figures, Chin would occupy his mind until that time when he chose to face the reality of what confronted him.

There was a knock at the door of his office and Chin turned from the books. "Come in."

The door opened and Chin's private secretary walked in. "There is a man to see you, sir."

"I told you I want no visitors today. I told—"

"But—"

"No one," he repeated.

"The man says he is your brother."

Chin felt as if a river of ice had suddenly replaced the blood that ran through his body. There was a sharp tingle in his fingers and his lips grew numb.

"My . . . my brother?"

"He says his name is Yang."

Chin's lips moved without his full knowledge, practically without effort. "Send him in. Send my brother in."

The door closed and in too short a moment it opened again, and in the doorway stood Yang.

"My brother," Chin said, rising on shaky legs from his chair.

Yang closed the door behind himself and walked into Chin's large private office. He slowly took in the regal surroundings—the silks and lamps and fine furnishings.

Then Yang looked at Chin. It was hard to believe that the man standing behind the desk was his younger brother. Yang could accept that the man was a wealthy merchant, a man of power. But it was difficult for him to accept that it was Chin.

"Chin?"

Chin smiled. "Yes, brother, yes." He came from behind the desk, nodding, bowing, rubbing his hands together with great vigor.

Yang returned the bow, still stunned by the opulence before him. Chin led him to the settees against one of the walls of the office and they sat.

"You have changed greatly," Yang said, his eyes trying to take in everything at once.

"I have." He paused. "And so have you, brother."

Yang looked down at his hands, suddenly conscious of his appearance, of his too-large hands with their split nails, his workman's blue trousers and jacket. At least his hair was well oiled.

"I have changed little," Yang said.

Chin stood. He was physically unable to sit any longer. He was too excited to see his brother again. His voice was animated. "Tell me what you have been doing. Tell me of your travels, your combat. I have tried to contact you so many times, but it was as if the earth had swallowed you up."

Yang laughed. "The earth very nearly did swallow me up on one occasion, and I shall tell you of it later." But now he raised an eyebrow in question. "You tried to contact me?"

"Many times. I tried to trace you . . . through company work records, through newspapers. I waited, many days and weeks and years, for a letter telling of your well-being. But none came."

Suddenly Yang felt ashamed. He felt it well up inside of him. He remembered that he and Chin had parted with harsh words, and that for a long time he had carried that feeling with him.

But he had long since forgotten the cause of the argument,

the details of it. Rather, it had evolved in his mind into a fundamental conflict of their personalities, their philosophies.

But now, sitting in Chin's office, Yang saw that his brother had not carried that feeling with him. Instead, concern was his companion, and Yang felt sad that he had let Chin worry for so many years.

"I . . ." Yang felt his throat tighten. "I didn't think . . ." His voice trailed off.

Chin shifted uneasily for a moment, then he said, "It is of no importance. You are back now and you are well and that is all that matters, Yang. There's going to be trouble with this devil Haight as governor, and I'm glad you're here and close."

For a moment they were silent and warmth flowed between them.

Then Chin said, "Now tell me. Tell me everything. What have you been doing for these fifteen years, my brother?"

And Yang began his tale.

They talked for hours, each recounting stories for the other, and Chin felt closer to his brother than he ever had in his life. They talked on into the night, past the dinner hour, and when it grew very late and their stomachs began to loudly protest, Chin had food brought in.

He sent Shao Kow to take care of the food, knowing that his trusted friend would handle the occasion of his brother's visit properly.

Chin was not disappointed.

Yang sat on a huge stuffed pillow, watching as servant after servant brought in endless gleaming silver trays bearing endless varieties of food. There was bird's-nest soup made from a rare sea moss gathered from the cliffs of Sumatra and literally worth its weight in gold. Deep bowls of fine bitter melons were served, surrounded by bean curd and mounds of bamboo shoots, water chestnuts, and *bok choy*. A platter bearing a shark's fin flanked by snow peas and rice was laid before Yang, and Yang responded, licking his chops. Roast duck, goose, pork, and rice cakes filled with meat were presented to the honored guest.

Then the servant retreated, Chin winking his eyes in appreciation to Shao Kow, and the brothers gorged themselves. When they could eat no more, when there was little but bones and gristle left, Chin clapped his hands and the trays were removed.

"My only wish," Yang said, "is that Uncle Ah Wan could be with us to enjoy this feast."

Chin's eyes fell to the floor, joy fleeing from him at the mention of his uncle's name. Yang saw his reaction and said, "What's wrong, Chin?"

"I . . . I had not wanted to mention this. Our uncle is dead."

"Dead? Ah Wan?"

Chin nodded.

"How?"

"He died at sea. He was returning to China. He knew his time was near and that was his wish. I will not grieve his death, only celebrate his life."

"He was fortunate indeed," Yang agreed, "to have lived the life he did. How unlike most of our people he was. My thanks to the heavens that our uncle never had to labor on the railroad or in the swamps, as I did. The whites cared little about us," Yang reminisced. "They are a hateful race, to the last one."

Chin stiffened, thinking of Rebecca. "Perhaps not to the last one."

Yang turned to him. "To the *last one!*"

Chin frowned, then said, "There is nothing we should argue about this night." Chin raised a glass of brandy which had been brought in and said, "I drink a toast with you, my brother, to the memory of our honourable uncle Ah Wan."

Yang raised his glass. "To Uncle Ah Wan. May he find peace." He drank the brandy in a single gulp, then set the glass down and looked at Chin. "Good brandy. You have done well for yourself, brother."

"I have been fortunate."

"That is only part of it. You are a shrewd businessman, I would guess."

Chin laughed. "I have heard that said. But I had a good teacher."

Yang nodded. "Too bad he, too, is gone. I would have liked to have known him better."

"He was not unlike our father," Chin said, and felt a thin shaft of pain lance through him. He reflected that the wise men who meant the most to him—his father, Ah Wan, and Mei Peng—were all dead. He was alone, he thought, to carry on in the world, with only the knowledge they had imparted to him.

Only knowledge? He smiled at the thought. What a fine

legacy they had left him. And as for seeing their passing and being alone—that was what life and growth and strength were about.

"Mei Peng was a wise and understanding man," Chin continued. "Firm, but understanding."

"You were fortunate, indeed, to have such a man as a teacher." Yang sipped his wine. "But not every student would have learned his lessons so well," he added, gesturing about the office.

Chin bowed, graciously accepting his brother's praise. "I give myself some small measure of the credit. A large part of it, though, is being in the right place with the right business at the right time."

"Importing is prospering?" Yang asked.

"Assuredly so. Even during the occasional slumps in the economy. It seems Americans cannot get enough of our goods. Too, our own people frequent the shops, eager to buy remembrances of our homeland."

"I should like to visit one of your shops, brother."

Chin smiled widely, pleased. "I insist on it."

Yang set his glass down. "I, too, would remember our homeland."

"I confess I can hardly remember it myself."

"The details are obscured by time," Yang agreed. "But sometimes, late at night, I can still remember snatches of it—the smell of the paddies, the feel of mud cool against my feet, the sound of the workers marching home from the fields after a full day's work."

"My brother waxes sentimental."

Yang stiffened, checking himself. Then he looked at Chin. "Sometimes I wonder if I ought to have come to this land at all," he said, tracing his finger down the scar on his cheek.

Chin frowned.

"Perhaps it is meant for men like you—men with a head for figures and smart business sense."

"These are strange words coming from you, Yang."

Yang spoke more to himself than Chin. "I have seen many things these past years, Chin. I have seen cruelties and brutalities that I did not know. I've watched whole scores of men die at a time. I've watched men frozen, crying from pain, limbs sawn from their bodies."

He turned to look at Chin now. "And I've watched the whites look on, only concerned about building their railroads. Perhaps I saw something of myself in them and I did not like what I saw." He paused for a moment, thinking. "My fear is that I will have to become like them if I am to survive in this land."

"That is not so," Chin interrupted. "It need not be."

"For you it is true. You are a businessman with a sharp wit. I am not. I am . . . I am only strong."

"Yang, this is true. But you have never given your brain a chance. It has always been as though you are afraid to admit that it exists."

Yang picked up his glass and filled it with more brandy. "And what will I do? Become a merchant? An importer?"

"There are worse lives."

Yang laughed loudly. "True," he said, looking about the office. "There can be no argument about that. But one needs to be equipped for such a profession."

"Ah," Chin said, dismissing him with a wave. "There is nothing to it. I will instruct you in the ways of the business."

"I would be a poor student."

"I mean it. I do, Yang. I will teach you all that I know. We'll begin tomorrow."

"This is madness. It can't work. You can't be serious. Me, a businessman?"

"And why not?"

"Because . . . ah, it just won't work."

"Give it a try, Yang. At least you can do that much. It will cost you nothing. A week, two weeks. Come with me to one of my shops. See how the business is conducted. See the profits to be made," Chin said, flashing a large diamond ring before his brother's eyes.

Both of them laughed.

"You see," Chin said, "you can be persuaded."

"There is a problem."

"There is no problem we cannot solve."

"I have a friend who accompanied me to this city. I worked with him on the railroad. A very sharp fellow named Peng Ku."

"That is no problem. He shall also work in my employ. See, already you are becoming a trader."

Yang gave in. "All right, all right. You win. You always were a better debater than I. One week. But that's all. After that I buy passage back to Mother China." Yang drained his glass, set it down on the table and sighed. "At least there I can earn a living as a *tai chi ch'uan* instructor."

Chapter 28

Ling had never even seen the man who had bought her. Chou Bai Tsai, the old hag who had marched them to the auction block, still appeared to be in command as Ling walked along the streets of Chinatown with twenty-two other women, who had been bought in a single lot at the auction.

They had spoken among themselves for a few moments, speculating as to where their new house would be. But Chou Bai Tsai quickly quieted them. Her tone was different now, Ling decided. More stern.

When before the old woman had told them to make themselves attractive so as to command a good price and a kind master, her tone had been friendly and instructive. But now, with the sale over, she was short and curt.

Ling glanced ahead and saw four guards walking by Chou Bai Tsai's side. She looked back and saw another guard taking up the rear.

"I wonder why these men guard us," Ling whispered to the girl next to her.

The girl shook her head.

The group walked along in silence for another ten minutes. Then they rounded the corner of Bartlett's Alley. Ling felt herself shudder as the chill air nipped at her.

She stared down the narrow alleyway, where gray brick walls rose up on either side. She looked around and saw that all the women in the group had stopped walking, as if frozen by a communal, instinctual fear.

"Move!" Chou Bai Tsai's voice slapped at them. And Ling saw that the two guards began moving toward them, their hands poised now on the truncheons that rested on their hips.

The women began walking again, down the narrow alley. Ling felt the impenetrable walls of the building closing in on her. She looked at the gray lid of fog that was moving in over the city. She could feel her heart beginning to flutter beneath her breast.

One of the guards stood off to the side, letting the women

walk past him so that two men now brought up the rear. Ling could see Chou Bai Tsai striding ahead of them, leading the way.

Then, on either side of the alley, Ling could see a long row of wooden doors, spaced no more than six feet apart. Each door had a small window in it at eye level.

Chou Bai Tsai stopped in front of the third door and reached for the great iron ring hooked to the sash about her waist. Out of the fifty-three keys she selected the correct one and fitted it into the keyhole. She twisted the key rudely, jerked down on the handle and pushed the door in.

Ling heard the door creak inward, heard the groan of the wood, the reluctant whine of the hinges that had never seen oil. She watched as a guard took the first woman in their group and pulled her along with a viselike grip on her arm.

Chou Bai Tsai stood watching dispassionately as the guard pushed the woman in through the doorway and slammed the door shut. The old hag stuck the key into the door and locked it.

The woman moved on to the second door.

The door clanged shut and darkness fell over Ling like a cloak. She listened as the door was locked, and heard Chou Bai Tsai's shoes as they scraped along the gravel of the alley. The next door opened and then closed.

Ling stood in the darkness and closed her eyes. There was no measurable difference when they were open. She felt her body begin to shake, felt her teeth begin to chatter.

She dug her hands into her thighs, felt them ache as her fingernails dug into her skin, and she was grateful because it gave her something to concentrate on.

Then it passed.

She breathed deeply, calming herself, trying to adjust to the situation. There was no way out of it, she reasoned, and getting hysterical wasn't going to solve a thing.

The first thing that was necessary, she decided, was to determine the size of the room she was in. Ling took a step forward, then another. With her third step she felt her shin knock into something. She bent, feeling about in the dark. Her hand touched the wooden slat and she felt along it. It was long, a foot or two off the ground. A bench? No. She felt the straw on top of the platform. It was a bed.

She ran her hand across the top of it until she touched the

232

wall. She stood partially up, at least having a point of reference now.

Ling walked sideways, her hand running along the wall. In this manner she walked around the entire perimeter of the room. She guessed, correctly, that it measured seven feet by four feet.

When she came back to the point she had started from she bent again, this time sitting on the edge of the bunk. The straw mattress offered little comfort. She prayed that this was some sort of waiting room where she would stay only until her master could come and claim her. But there was an emptiness welling in her chest that would not subside.

She felt on the verge of tears when her hand brushed against something on the bunk. She turned, feeling it with both hands. It was a box and, automatically, she felt inside it.

Something was in the box—something long and smooth. She took it out and felt it. Ling's pulse began to race as she realized that she was holding a candle. She felt in the box again and pulled out what she knew were stick matches.

Excitedly, she ran the match along the wall and it flared to life. Without looking around she touched the tip of the flame to the candle's wick. In a moment it caught and the room grew light.

Ling dripped a few drops of wax on the bunk and set the candle carefully down on it. Then she looked about. The cell was pitifully cramped—smaller even than she had imagined it to be. Rough, cruel, raw brick lined each of the four walls that crushed in on her. The ceiling was low and suffocating.

Everywhere there was straw; on the bunk, strewn across the floor. The bed was the only piece of furniture in the room. Her eyes gradually became accustomed to the candlelight and she made out a shape beside the door. She got up and walked toward it.

Ling bent and looked at the bucket. There was a towel covering it and she removed it to look inside. She immediately felt sick as the odor of feces made her retch. She threw the towel back on the bucket and went back to the bunk.

Ling looked at the weathered door against the opposite wall of the room. She wondered how long she would have to spend in the room, and it struck her that since the bucket was provided for her personal needs it would probably be at least for a day.

Exhausted from the day's events, she decided to get some

rest and laid down on the straw. As soon as she had closed her eyes she heard a key being fitted into the door.

Ling sat bolt upright as the door was pushed inward. The cold air rushed inward, freshening her. It was dark outside now, and she had trouble seing who was standing outside the doorway.

Chou Bai Tsai took half a step into the room, her face growing more discernible in the candlelight.

"So," Chou Bai Tsai said, "you are comfortable?"

Ling stood. "When am I to meet my new master?"

"You do not understand, child. You will not go to your new master. You will work for him."

"But how can I work for him if I am not at his home?"

Chou Bai Tsai smiled. "You shall learn the ways." She pulled a checkered bandana from the mass of clothes that made up her garments and tossed it to Ling. "Wear this always in your hair."

"To what end?"

"As a badge of your profession. You are a prostitute in the brothel."

Ling's eyes went wide with horror. "Br—brothel?"

"You heard me," Chou Bai Tsai snapped. "Now put the bandana in your hair."

"But . . . but I was trained to . . ."

The old woman leveled a crooked finger at her. "You were bought and paid for and you shall do the bidding your master sees fit."

Ling crumpled onto the bunk; her knees were no longer able to hold her weight. The bandana fluttered to the dirt ground of the bagnio. Her lips quivered, but words would not come.

Chou Bai Tsai took another step inside the room, her voice growing a bit softer. "You can make what you will of the work. It can be an easy job or a difficult one. If you try to fight it then every lover will be a rapist, for we have a good many men who enjoy their loving in this way."

The madame bent and picked up the bandana. "If, however, you do your work well and learn to bring a skill to it you shall be rewarded." Chou Bai Tsai motioned about the room. "Not all women remain in bagnios such as this that you now occupy."

Her voice grew stern again. "But they all start out here. Whether or not you remain in such surroundings is a matter of your own choice." Chou Bai Tsai thrust out her hand toward Ling.

Ling looked up at the old woman, looked at the gnarled yellow hand holding the red and white checkered bandana. Tears obscured her vision, but still the image of the bandana and all that it meant remained.

Her hand shaking, she reached out and took the cloth. Chou Bai Tsai nodded.

Ling began fixing the cloth in her hair. Finally she asked the old woman, "I . . . I know little of these things. I was trained as a house servant. I worked for an old man whose amorous demands were few. Wouldn't I be better suited for . . ."

But Chou Bai Tsai had already turned toward the portal. Over her shoulder she said, "Don't worry, little one. You'll learn fast. Tung Chai will see to your education."

And with that the old madame left. Ling sat on the bed, trying to decipher the meaning of Chou Bai Tsai's enigmatic parting comment. Then it struck her that the old woman had left the door open.

In her excitement, Ling thought that perhaps she had forgotten to close and lock it. It was a chance, she thought, perhaps her only chance to escape a life filled with degradation and forced indignities.

With no idea where she would run, with no idea how she would live, Ling stood and started for the door.

She had gotten two paces when a man stepped in front of the door. She had never seen such a man. So great were his proportions that the width of his body completely obscured her view of what lay beyond him. Instinctively, she backed up.

The man bent, lowering his head, to make it through the doorway. As he came into the room the candlelight cast dancing shadows on a face rough with exposure to the elements. Aside from his queue, there was not a trace of hair on his body—no eyebrows, no beard. His eyes were the only telling feature. They gleamed like two glistening chunks of black jade. Deep-set, afire, they bore into Ling, filling her with dread.

She backed up more and tripped, falling to the bed. The man slammed the door shut behind himself and began unbuttoning his shirt. All the while his eyes focused on Ling. He pulled off his jacket, the candlelight dancing on his muscled frame.

Unable to stop herself, Ling's eyes fell to the man's trousers, and she could see the massive swell of his manhood as it fought for freedom. Like a throbbing branch, it pulled, gnashing at the material, thrusting out from his thigh.

"Wh—what do you want? Who are you?"

The creature in the cell smiled coldly and said, "I am Tung Chai . . . your instructor."

He undid the buckle on his belt.

Chapter 29

Yang wondered if he had made the right decision, if he was cut out for this sort of life.

On the one hand it certainly was preferable to clearing marshes and chipping away at the sides of mountains. Still, as he stood behind the counter of the import shop on Commercial Street, he felt confined. He had worked and played in the outdoors all his life.

Certainly it was easy enough work for him. And, too, Chin had placed Peng Ku in the same shop, so he would have his friend to keep him company. Yang was still amazed at the prices people would pay for silks and porcelains. And while Chin carried only the finest goods, there was still a more than ample markup and profit.

This was particularly appealing to Yang, since a large portion of the customers who patronized the shop were white. That was the one part of his job that bothered him the most. It took him to the brink of revulsion to have to wait on white customers. That he had learned English only made it worse, because now he knew what they were saying, could sense their arrogance and condescension more easily.

It was a singular delight to him when he sold an item to a white which he knew was overpriced and meant a huge profit.

Yet even with this consolation it was difficult to work with the continuous flow of whites seeking Chinese goods. Yang knew the whites' nature all too well—their callousness, their hatred for the Chinese, for anything unlike themselves. He returned these feelings in kind.

To amuse himself he would swear at them in Chinese, while maintaining a polite smile. He would return their change in *yuan*, shortchanging them in the process. Sometimes he would twist the truth about an antique.

These things he was careful not to do in front of Chin, although he made no secret of his feelings toward whites. What puzzled him was that Chin seemed to be disturbed by his attitude—almost as if he felt nothing against them. Yang decided that it was because his younger brother had had close contact with the whites for so many years as customers.

Chin had decided that it would be best if Yang would learn the business of import from the retail side first, to see if it suited him. Accordingly, Chin had placed him as a clerk, with Peng Ku, in one of the stores. Because he was Chin's brother Yang was in a position of authority.

Chin had instructed Yang in how to record sales, how to receive and check in shipments, and how to deposit money. This final task was an important one, since large sums of money came into the store because of the price of the goods. Many of Chin's customers ranked among the San Francisco's wealthiest, and were able to afford the finest vases and statuary.

Large amounts of money, Chin had said, should never remain in the store. Rather, he had told Yang, they should be deposited at the Wells Fargo Bank less than two blocks away from the shop. Yang was so directing Peng Ku this morning.

The wife of a prominent banker had visited the shop and bought a tapestry for two hundred dollars. While it was not a monumental sum, Yang nonetheless decided he would feel better if it was in the bank. Added to that were the rest of the day's receipts—another three hundred dollars.

"Take the money to the bank and deposit it in our account, Peng Ku."

Peng Ku nodded.

"Afterwards, go to Pier Four and receive our shipment of chessboards. They are due this morning. You have the order?"

"Yes," Peng Ku said, producing the papers.

"Good. Make certain you count the number of sets before you sign for the goods."

"Of course."

"Be on your way," Yang said.

Peng Ku left the shop with the money and deposit slip in the front pocket of his blue pants. He was glad for the excuse to get some air. It was an unusually clear day, the fog far out in the bay.

He walked along the street, which was crowded with morning foot traffic. He rounded Montgomery Street and could see the Wells Fargo Bank sign on the corner. He quickened his pace.

Peng Ku was within fifty steps of the bank when he felt a viselike grip on his arm. He turned and looked into the face of a Chinese who said, "You will move into the alleyway. If you make a sound or resist you shall die where you stand."

Giving force to this threat was the press of a blade into his ribs.

Peng Ku obeyed.

Once in the alleyway, three more Chinese appeared from out of nowhere. Sensing mortal danger, Peng Ku opened his mouth to scream. But lashing blows to his neck and belly silenced any scream that might have come.

He slumped against the wall, feeling hands on him, grabbing, searching him. He wanted to fight, but it was all he could do to keep from blacking out.

The four men stood, one of them pocketing the money. Three of them walked away. The fourth lingered long enough to deliver a body kick that sent Peng Ku crashing to the hard earth of the alley.

And then they were gone. Peng Ku lay in the alley, pain still lancing through his body. As it gradually subsided he became aware of other pains—in his ribs, in his chest.

He lay there for many moments, thinking how there was no great rush now that he had lost the receipts. And then he remembered the shipment he was supposed to receive at the pier.

He rose to his knees, then to his feet, the pain in his side sharp as he moved. He knew that he was in enough trouble for having lost the day's receipts. If he was not at the pier at the appointed time he would fail to receive the consignment of chess sets. The ship's captain would sell them to jobbers who frequented the pier looking for just such an opportunity.

Peng Ku would return without cash and without the merchandise. He would be fortunate to escape without being skinned alive. He stumbled out of the alley, drawing momentary stares from passersby.

238

Then he turned up Commercial and made for the water-front.

"Two dozen chess sets delivered and received," the captain of the *Caledonia* said. "Bill's been forwarded."

Peng Ku hoisted the crate on his shoulders, wincing as he did so.

"Here, now, mate, you all right?"

He looked at the captain, seeing that his concern was genuine. He nodded.

The ship's captain was skeptical. "You sure? You want to come on the ship and rest for a bit?"

"No, no. Have to get back."

The captain frowned. "Should have sent two fellows for a crate like that."

"Have to get back," he repeated.

"Very well," the captain said, slapping the crate, "be off with you."

Peng Ku turned and walked away from the ship, braced up by the breeze coming in off the bay. The breeze brought the thick afternoon fog with it, and soon it was difficult to see more than a few yards ahead.

More than once a cart or buggy had nearly rammed him. But he hurried along the streets and soon he was in the Chinese quarter again.

He could feel his ribs throbbing, both from the kicks and from the weight of the shipping carton the chess sets were packed in. With each new step Peng Ku thought about how he would explain the stolen money to Yang.

Would he believe him? Even if he did, would Chin believe him? Would he be fired on the spot?"

The fog was rolling in, heavy now, so thick that he could barely see his footsteps. He practically bumped into the man standing in his way.

"Pardon me," Peng Ku said.

James Riley turned slowly to look at him. "I'll have what you got in that crate, Chink."

"Please . . ."

From his other side he saw another white man moving toward him. There was a glint of steel in the second man's hand. For Peng Ku it was just too much. The thought of explaining the stolen money and then having the shipment taken on top of it was too awful to contemplate.

He whirled to face his second attacker and thrust the crate over his shoulders down across Colin Shaughnessy's skull.

"*Colin*!!" Tim Shaughnessy cried from the shadows.

Riley pinned Peng Ku against the wall as Tim ran to his fallen brother. "Colin, Colin!" he cried, kneeling at his side.

What he saw was horrible. Colin's head had been split open by the crate containing the heavy chess sets. Colin Shaughnessy had been dead before he hit the ground.

Tim Shaughnessy was like a madman. Springing to his feet, he lunged for the man Riley held in his grip. Riley backed away. He'd seen dogfights and he knew it was best to stay out of such affairs.

Shaughnessy was merciless with the man who had killed his brother. He beat him over and over again. When Peng Ku slumped to the ground, Riley said, "Come on, Colin. There's coppers about."

"Fuck the coppers," Shaughnessy said and fell on the man, working at him with his knife as a butcher would attack a side of beef.

After a full minute Riley's stomach could stand no more of it. He grabbed Shaughnessy and shook him. "Enough, man! That's enough! He's dead." He glanced at the grisly job Shaughnessy had done on the man and said, "Let's get your brother's body out of here so he can have a Christian burial."

"I warned you," Tai Pien said. "I told you it would come to this."

Chin sat at the end of the conference table, listening to Tai Pien's words, knowing that he was right.

Tai Pien pressed on. "You would not listen to me when I said the tongs must be dealt with. Now you must pay the price."

Chang Mai Mai regarded Tai Pien. "There was no need to deal with the tong up until now. Their interests were only in gambling."

"Ah," Tai Pien said, rising in anger, "but now that they infringe on your domain, Chang Mai Mai, now that they seek to expand their influence to commerce, suddenly you are aroused? When I alone had to worry about them it wasn't important to concern ourselves. After all, it was only gambling and drugs, correct?"

Chang Mai Mai averted his eyes.

Tai Pien turned back to Chin. "But as I predicted, if we allowed the tongs to grow strong in one area it would not be long before they seeped into others. Like rats and vermin, once they have exhausted a supply of food they shall seek another."

"I wanted to avoid violence," Chin said.

Tai Pien nodded. "A noble desire, honorable Chin. But a desire for peace can be misinterpreted as a distaste for strength. Kindness and benevolence can be mistaken for weakness." Tai Pien clenched his fist. "We must arm ourselves against these bold hoodlum cousins of ours and teach them a lesson that they will understand."

Finally Shao Kow folded his hands at the far end of the table. "It is true what Tai Pien says, Chin. But it is even more than that. I fear we are fighting a battle on two fronts." He paused, then began again. "According to reliable witnesses, the deceased suffered two attacks. Of course the fatal one occurred after he had visited the wharf. But it appears that the money was stolen earlier."

"How do we know this?"

"For one thing, he had no deposit slip from the bank for the funds. We checked with Wells Fargo and they said Peng Ku never came into the bank."

"Perhaps he was going to deposit the money on the way back from the pier."

Shao Kow shook his head negatively. "Highly doubtful. He would have stopped at the bank on the way to the pier. The bank closes at noon on Wednesdays. Moreover, he would have wanted to come directly back from the pier with the shipment, rather than lugging it back to the bank. Finally, just having the money on his person would have made the clerk nervous. He would have wanted to be rid of it as soon as possible."

Chin leaned slightly forward. "What do you mean by 'two fronts'?"

"It is my belief that the second attack was by white villains," Shao Kow said. "Were he attacked and killed by tong highbinders, the method of killing would have been different. The marks of death were administered by a knife, not the instrument of the tongs. The tongs, as you may know, use battle hatchets."

Chin turned to see Tai Pien nodding; the man who ran his vice interests would know of such things. He turned back to Shao Kow and said, "Go on."

"The final thing. Police at the scene of the death said that it appeared that Peng Ku put up a fight, apparently smashing the crate containing the chess sets over the skull of one of his assailants."

"What does this prove?"

"I viewed the crate when it was finally delivered to the shop. Its corner was covered with blood . . . blood and one more thing."

"What's that?"

"Red hair," Shao Kow said. "The blow tore loose part of his attacker's scalp, and on that scalp was red hair." He looked around the table. "Has any of you ever seen a Chinese with red hair?"

After a moment, Shao Kow said, "What it amounts to is the resurgence of the white hoodlums. Thus we find ourselves fighting a war on two fronts—one without, against the white brigands who once again raise their ugly heads; the other within, against these hoodlum tongs who are related to us in blood and skin color alone."

"A profound analysis," Tai Pien said. "What do you propose we do about it?"

Chang Mai Mai could bear the tension no longer. He rose, his voice quivering. "We must do something! We must protect ourselves! Today these bandits murder our clerks on the streets; tomorrow they will be robbing our stores, setting fire to—"

Tai Pien began laughing.

Chang Mai Mai wheeled to look at him. "I fail to see any humor in this crisis."

Tai Pien's laughter turned to a cold smile. "What amuses me, my mercantile friend, is that you so complacently sat by when I spoke of the threat months ago. You are so typical. You think that crime and violence are tolerable so long as they visit only those enterprises you consider disreputable. But let the vandals reach into the import shops you manage and you begin to squeal like a piglet."

Chang Mai Mai raised his palms up in supplication. "All right, all right, Tai Pien. I confess you were right!"

Chin raised a hand to silence them all. "Sit down, Chang Mai Mai. This is not a time for hysterics." He turned his gaze to the man who ran his vice business. "And you may cease your chiding, Tai Pien. We have all acknowledged that you were right in your predictions. Out interests would be better served if you would now devote your time to thinking of a solution to this problem."

"Problems," Shao Kow corrected.

Chin dismissed him with a wave of his hand. "The whites I am not worried about. They will hang themselves. We have dealt with them before and we shall deal with them again if need be.

"If they become too violent then the decent citizens will rise up. Besides, we can always buy protection from vigilantes." He shook his head. "No, it's the tongs that bother me. I underestimated their strength."

"Vigilantes?" Shao Kow said. "There are none. They are disbanded."

"They will reband if they are needed. No, we must focus on the tongs."

"Perhaps it is time we strengthened ourselves," Tai Pien said.

Chin turned to look at him. "A private army?"

Tai Pien nodded.

"I don't think we're ready for that."

"You said that before."

Chin leveled a finger at him. "No, I did not say that. Before I said I didn't think we needed that. Now I *do* think we need one. I just don't think we're ready for it."

"I fail to see the distinction."

"We are a private enterprise, Tai Pien. If we were to suddenly enlist an army of soldiers, our people and the Six Companies would fear that we were like the tongs themselves."

"Then how will we—"

"By growing slowly. We must undertake a program of slow martial growth, only adding to our ranks as it is necessary. The murder of Peng Ku will give us an adequate reason for adding to our protective forces. No one in Chinatown can argue with us about hiring men to guard our runners and gambling parlors. Each foray by the tongs will provide reason for more troops."

Chin paused for a moment, thinking. "The people who frequent those parlors and buy from our import shops are dignified, honest people. They will see the additional guards only as a measure toward their own security."

"And if that alone is not sufficient?"

"Then we will increase our protection as it is needed."

"Up to what point?"

"Up to the point necessary to ensure our safety from these tongs."

"And what of countermeasures?" Tai Pien asked. The room grew hushed, the three men waiting for Chin's reply.

243

"No," he said firmly. "I will not sanction those kinds of actions. Then indeed we would be nothing more than a tong ourselves."

Chapter 30

Billy McNamara and Tim Shaughnessy made a perfect team. They were well suited to the job of terrorizing the Chinese. James Riley realized this when he assigned the job to them.

McNamara was a man of muscle who took delight in beating any man, just to prove his manhood to himself. For McNamara it might just as easily have been Mexicans or Indians he was beating.

Tim Shaughnessy was a different case. When his brother Colin had been killed when they tried to rob a Chinese, James Riley realized that he had been given a gift of hatred.

It was time to use that gift, Riley felt. So he turned the two men loose on the Chinese. He had been tempted to let Brian O'Malley and a few of his other cronies join them, but he decided against it for several reasons.

He decided that O'Malley was too softhearted for the job, for one thing. But more importantly, he wanted O'Malley close to him. This for two reasons. First, he didn't want either O'Malley or himself associated with the campaign of terror against the Chinese. A time would come when he'd want clean records for both O'Malley and himself. Second, O'Malley had a brain and Riley wanted to use it.

So McNamara and Shaughnessy worked independently of Riley, forming their own gang of hoodlums. The booty they took was delivered, however, to Riley. O'Malley, accountant that he was, would figure up the take and divide it among the men.

Riley sensed the mood of the times. He had been right—all that was needed was a spark. McNamara and Shaughnessy were successful at providing it. The reports in the San Francisco newspapers of violence against the Chinese seemed to have an incendiary effect.

Beatings became commonplace. A glut of labor was on the

market now that the work of the railroad was done, and unemployment soared again. The Chinese, a huge labor force, appeared to be taking jobs from the whites—even though they were menial jobs the whites wouldn't bend to doing.

The gang leaders attracted many of these disheartened men to their ranks. Robbing Chinese street vendors once again became the order of the day. Dozens of gangs of thugs sprang up, roaming the streets of Chinatown, preying on the innocent. There was talk of another vigilance committee being formed, but as yet the violence had only been directed against the Chinese. Many whites felt it was best to leave things alone, so as not to incur the hoodlums' wrath.

By February 1871 McNamara and Shaughnessy had a gang of almost two hundred men under their control, with direct ties to nine other gangs, each of which contained almost as many men. Beyond that, thousands of other unemployed men who filled the city had come to regard the two Irishmen as folk heroes.

It was by no means only money that formed the booty the two extracted from the Chinese quarter, and it was with thoughts of other pleasures that they walked through the bone-chilling cold of the quarter one winter night.

"Good night for whoring," McNamara said, pulling tighter the collar on his coat.

Shaughnessy grunted a neutral reply.

McNamara turned to look at him as they walked. "Sometimes I wonder about you, Tim."

"What about?"

"I mean with the ladies."

"I don't get as much satisfaction as you do out of romping with Chinese women, if that's what you mean."

McNamara shook his head. "Don't see why. Some of them are downright artists when it comes to romping. They got muscles inside them that—"

"Your brother wasn't killed by a Chinaman."

The bigger man fell silent for a moment. Then he said, "Doesn't have anything to do with enjoying yourself with one of them."

"I didn't say I don't enjoy myself with them."

"But you ain't never yet told me how you laid a—"

"There're different kinds of enjoyment," Shaughnessy said.

The two men rounded the corner of Bartlett's Alley. McNamara saw the old whore-mistress and nodded.

Chou Bai Tsai felt her heart quicken. She knew the two

245

Irishmen. Good customers. Never argued about the price. And the shorter one with the angry eyes was a "special." Always double price, and that increased her percentage for the night.

She smiled a toothless smile, nodding as they approached. "Evening, gentlemen, evening. Fine night for a woman."

McNamara laughed. "We was just sayin' that."

Shaughnessy looked around the alley, his eyes taking in the strolling men who looked into the open bagnios to peruse the women. At the far end of the alley Shaughnessy could see three Chinese huddled together.

Shaughnessy knew they were guarding the brothel. He turned to Chou Bai Tsai. "You know what I want, old woman?"

She nodded, watching as McNamara made for one of the open bagnios. She turned back to Shaughnessy. "Special?"

He nodded in answer.

Chou Bai Tsai looked at his money for a moment before she dropped it into her pocket. Shaughnessy heard it click as the coin joined others she had collected this night.

The old woman was silent now as she turned and pointed to the door of one of the cells in the alley. Shaughnessy began walking in the direction she had pointed. He put the whore-mistress out of his mind; the tightness began to grow in his trousers.

He stood in front of the door, turned the knob, and pushed in. The small cell was like any of a dozen others he had visited—small, with a mattress and a pail and straw everywhere.

Shaughnessy came into the cell and closed the door behind him. He looked at the young woman sitting on the bed. Her features were illuminated by the flickering candle that had begun dancing when he opened the door.

The woman looked up at him, not really seeing him, looking through him. Shaughnessy was familiar with the gaze. Once, a long time ago, in Wichita, he had asked a young prostitute why she didn't look at him. The woman had told him that if he wanted her to look at him then she would comply. But when she had turned her gaze directly into Shaughnessy's eyes she still wasn't looking.

"Get up," Shaughnessy said.

Ling obeyed. She let her body go limp in preparation for the assault. She had been taken so many times she was beginning to grow numb from it. But still, each time, her stomach tightened. Somehow she felt that this was a good sign, that when her insides ceased to convulse at the thought then she would be completely lost.

Shaughnessy crossed the cell and turned her around. Ling stood facing the wall, agreeable to whatever the man would want.

Then she felt his hands slip over her head, felt a cloth pulling into her mouth. She opened her mouth to call out, but the gag pulled tighter as Shaughnessy knotted it.

He pulled her hands behind her back and in an instant bound them. That done, he pushed her down on the bed. He stood, legs spread, looking down at her. Ling looked up at him, terror in her eyes.

Shaughnessy pulled his coat off, reached into the waistband of his trousers, and pulled out a long switch. Ling's eyes went wide, her cries muffled by the gag. She twisted her hands against the rough hemp, cutting the skin on her wrists, as Shaughnessy brought the thin stick down for the first blow.

The smooth birch rod caught her across the thighs and her world went red with pain. Ling's eyes clenched tightly. Shaughnessy raised the switch up over his head and brought it down hard, the wind whipping as he did. This time the rod slashed across Ling's soft belly, and her legs shot out in a convulsive reaction, her face contorted with pain.

"Bitch," Shaughnessy declared. "Yellow scum!" He reached down and ripped her clothing from her, exposing her naked body. He looked to the ceiling and actually *saw* his dead brother's face staring down at him, and he cried, "I'll whip her, Colin, I'll whip her! For your memory, I'll whip this bitch!"

Then he turned back to Ling, raised the switch, and slashed it down across her bare breasts, drawing a stifled scream of agony. Shaughnessy looked at the welt that formed below her left breast and he ripped at her with the switch again, aiming for the same spot.

Again and again he struck Ling with the rod, each time raising ugly red streaks from the blows. Finally he paused, wiping his forearm across his brow. Shaughnessy could feel his heart pounding as though it would burst from his chest. His excitement was apparent to him by the swelling between his legs; at the same time he hated and loved the pleasure he was getting from the woman.

He glared down at her. "You love it, don't you, whore?" He slapped the rod in his hand in anticipation. "You love this, don't you!"

Ling shook her head wildly, her eyes pleading with him to stop. But there was no stopping Shaughnessy.

"You lying bitch! You know you love it!"

And with that he bent down and grabbed her, rolling her over onto her stomach. The lust took over again and he raised the switch over his head.

He brought it down across her buttocks, over and over again. He beat her with the rod until his arm ached and then he beat her some more. He could hear her muffled screams and knew that her throat was raw from screaming, and that pleased him.

Red streaks covered Ling's body from her calves up to the small of her back. Still the beating continued, and Shaughnessy felt his arousal growing, getting past him, getting away from him.

"No, no, *noooo!*" he screamed, and he threw down the switch, ripped open his trousers, and held his phallus toward her as he erupted, spraying Ling with his climax.

Outside Billy McNamara had finished and was standing around with three white men who had patronized the brothel.

"Those Chinks." One of them laughed. "They can lay there and make you come without even moving. They got muscles inside of them that ain't like normal women's."

One of the men nodded enthusiastically. "You're right about that, mate. I had one last week, I swear she must have had a hundred tongues in her pussy."

The men laughed heartily.

"And all the time she was just laying there, not even moving." The man shook his head. "I swear it was the damndest thing ever happened to me. Kind of creepy, if you know what I mean."

"Creepy," McNamara said. "Did it stop you from coming?"

"Hah!" the man exclaimed. "I came like a fire hose."

Again the men broke into laughter. McNamara turned as he saw Shaughnessy approaching. "Tim, boyo, how did it go? A good romp, I trust?"

He nodded, joining the rest of the men in the circle. After a few moments one of them would drift away from the conversation, either to disappear into a bagnio or make his way home. But then another man would join them. There was a mood of camaraderie, of shared, communal lust among the men.

"I get pleasure out of fucking these Chinese," a Frenchman named Jacques said matter-of-factly. "They've been fucking us for long enough, what with the low wages they'll take and the jobs they steal from us."

Shaughnessy perked his ears up at the comment. "How do you mean, Jacques?" he asked, playing it dumb.

Jacques turned to look at him. "Who do you think is responsible for all this unemployment? Who do you think is responsible for us practically having to beg for work? The Chinese, of course."

The other men nodded in assent as Shaughnessy shot McNamara a quick look.

"That's why I enjoy giving it to these little Chinese whores." He pounded his chest. "It's my way of getting back."

Shaughnessy looked around at the four men in the circle, appraising them. He quickly reached the decision that they were all either out of work or working for low wages. It wasn't a difficult assessment to make—there was a certain tattered, desperate, angry look he had come to recognize.

Finally, Shaughnessy said, "How'd you like to do more than just fuck the whores, Jacques?"

The Frenchman laughed. "Don't see what else you can do with a whore."

"I'm talking about taking care of other Chinese."

Jacques gave Shaughnessy a peculiar look. "If you mean men you can count me out. My tastes aren't—"

McNamara interrupted the Frenchman with a laugh. "He ain't talkin' about that." McNamara looked at the other men. "That's the whole trouble with Frenchies; all they can think about is fucking."

The men laughed in agreement and McNamara returned to Jacques. "He means taking care of them," McNamara said, driving his fist into the palm of his hand in explanation.

"Mmm," Jacques said, nodding.

McNamara lowered his voice conspiratorially. "See, me and Tim got a group of boys who take care of these Chinese; kind of keep 'em in line, if you know what I mean."

The Frenchman scratched his lip, listening intently.

Shaughnessy picked up the conversation. "And we pick up plenty of bucks in the process."

The men drew closer at the mention of money. One of them, a short man named Paulson, asked, "You mean robbin'?"

Shaughnessy turned to look at him. "You call taking money from the Chinks robbin'?"

Paulson was silent.

"It ain't robbin' to take back what's rightfully ours. Them yellow scum came over here and mined half our gold out from under us and then when they'd done with that they started workin' cheaper so they could rob us of our jobs."

McNamara continued. "Tim's right. Ain't robbin' at all. It's just taking what's rightfully ours."

One of the men drifted from the group, leaving Shaughnessy and McNamara with an audience of three. The third man, a Swede named Jorgenson, voiced his approval.

"Well, I'm with you if it's recruiting that you're doing. I'm sick of living in a hellhole of a room. Before these Chinamen came along I could get all the work I needed chopping wood and building houses. Now them little buggers do the work for less than half what I used to charge and I can't get any jobs at all."

McNamara slapped him on the shoulder. "Good, Jorgenson. We'll be glad to have you." He looked at the others. "What about you two?"

But before Jacques and Paulson could answer the air was shattered by a horrible scream. The men turned to see one of the Chinese guards at the end of the alley running toward them. The man stopped not more than ten feet from them and fell forward, a hatchet embedded in his back.

McNamara looked to the end of the alley and saw half a dozen Chinese blocking it. The two remaining guards lay unmoving on the cobblestones. He whirled around and saw five more men at the other end of the alley.

McNamara saw Shaughnessy's hand slip inside his coat, but he grabbed it, whispered to him, "Stay calm, Tim. We don't know that their quarrel is with us."

Shaughnessy tugged under McNamara's grip. "Don't think we should wait to find out."

"Forget it. There's too many of them, and besides, they're too far away. You might get off a couple of shots, but from what I hear them Chinks can throw hatchets like lumberjacks. Reckon they're these tong boys we've been hearing about."

"I don't care who they are. Let's take 'em."

"Steady," McNamara said. "I hear these tongs are pretty good-sized gangs in their own right." McNamara looked at the other men—Jacques, Paulson, and the Swede. "Ain't no telling how many more of them are waiting around the corner. We take a couple of shots and could be half a hundred of 'em down on us."

"Makes sense to me," Jacques said.

"Let's just wait and see what happens," McNamara said. He looked at each of the men and said, "Push comes to shove, though, you boys all ready to fight?"

Jorgenson said, "I'll be damned if I'll let some Chinaman get rough with me without a fight."

"Okay, then. Let's just see what they want."

From each end of the alley three tong highbinders approached. McNamara watched the warriors walking toward them. Each man carried either a hatchet or an iron cudgel. The hatchets were ugly affairs, with short handles so they could be concealed beneath a jacket. The double-edged blades of the axes glistened in the night, occasionally catching the glint of the gaslights at the end of the alley.

The highbinders didn't look particularly well built to McNamara, but then the Chinese never did. He saw something in them, though, that he had never seen before in Chinese. It was a fierceness, a look of blood in their slitted eyes.

McNamara had always known them to be a docile people, easily scared out of their money, easy prey to beatings. These men were different.

The hatchetmen stopped twenty feet on either side of the brothel. Some of the customers wisely ran to the bagnios and slammed the doors shut.

McNamara knew that the highbinders had set up an effective double buffer, hemming them in on either end of the alley. Even if they could fight their way past the first flank, there were still others at the other end. It was a technique he and Shaughnessy had used in trapping large groups of Chinese at night, and it crossed his mind that maybe one of these men had heard of it and adapted it for the tong. He smiled wryly at the thought.

Sitll, he reminded himself, they didn't know about Betsy. McNamara let his hand drop to his jacket and unbuttoned it.

One of the hatchetmen walked forward. During all this time Chou Bai Tsai had been running in short circles, her hand appealing to the heavens. The old hag was without protection now, her guards either beaten senseless or slain. Others could not be summoned, and she knew that she was at the mercy of the tong's warriors.

"Be still," the hatchetman said, standing before Chou Bai Tsai.

"Please," she said, her hands quivering. "Please have mercy on an old woman."

The man glared down at her. "I have no quarrel with you, old woman. Only the money."

She fell to her knees. "Do not rob an old woman."

"The money."

"If you take the money my master will beat me. He'll make me pay from my earnings for the rest of my life. I'm an old woman. I—"

The man raised his hatchet quickly over his head. McNamara felt himself gasp involuntarily. The night air was split by the woman's cry.

The ax paused in midair.

"Take the money! Take the money!" Chou Bai Tsai bellowed. "To hell with my devil of a master!"

In spite of themselves, the hatchetmen laughed. The woman pulled the coins from her pocket and dropped them into a bag the man held open before her.

The highbinder closed the pouch and stuck it inside his jacket. He turned and regarded the group of whites.

"*Fan quay*," he said, walking toward the men. He mustered his best English for the meeting. "What riches do you gentlemen have to contribute tonight?"

McNamara caught his stare. "Don't be foolish, boyo. It's one thing to rob an old yellow hag, quite another to assault a white man."

The Chinaman's hand dropped to the handle of the hatchet he had put back in his waistband at the same moment McNamara whipped his hand inside his own jacket. The Irishman drew the sawed-off shotgun from his pants as the rest of the men scattered.

The warrior pulled his ax, swinging it in the same motion toward McNamara. McNamara raised the barrel of his shotgun, deflecting the arcing blade. He could hear others of the tong screaming their charge as they descended on the bordello's customers, wielding their axes.

McNamara heard the screams from some of the men as the hatchets did their work. Shots sounded as Shaughnessy pulled his weapon.

But McNamara's eyes were on the hatchetman in front of him, and as the man raised his blade again McNamara squeezed the trigger of his weapon. The shotgun blast caught the man square in the belly, lifted him from the ground, and rammed him back through the air.

At the sound and sight of the man's grisly death the other tong warriors retreated. McNamara looked around the narrow alley. Two white men lay bleeding, and crimson rivers streaked the cobblestones. Three Chinese lay unmoving in Bartlett's Alley.

McNamara turned to Shaughnessy, Jacques, and Jorgenson. "Come on. Let's beat it. The coppers will be here soon."

McNamara began walking, then stopped, looking at the dead hatchetman on the ground. He bent and rummaged through the man's pocket, pulling the purse from it. McNamara stuffed the pouch into his pocket. "At least the night's not a total loss."

Then he disappeared into the fog with Shaughnessy and their two new recruits.

Chapter 31

The two brothers sat in the San Gwo'Jya Restaurant eating a lunch of goose.

Chin said, "There is nothing more I can say about Peng Ku's death."

Yang nodded. "I appreciate the funeral provided by you for my friend. It was an act of great kindness."

"As you say, he was a friend of yours. What hurts you hurts me."

"I have heard," Yang said, "that Peng Ku's death is not an isolated act?"

Chin nodded soberly. "It is the fifth killing this month."

"Were all the deaths, like his, attributable to the whites?"

"No," Chin said. "All of the others were done by our own people. The tongs claim responsibility for them. They were mostly assassinations." He chewed on a piece of fowl. "That disturbs me more than anything else."

"The assassinations?"

"No. The death of Peng Ku. It means the whites are once

253

again a problem to be dealt with." He shook his head. "But they are an added problem to that of the tongs."

"These tongs worry you greatly, Chin."

"Especially now. The attack on Peng Ku means they are branching out into other directions. Before they kept to vice. Now they rob messengers."

Yang speared a piece of meat and asked, "How powerful are the tongs?"

"They grow more powerful with each passing day. The Kwong Dock is the most powerful of these young rebel bands."

"Rebels? Why do you call them that?"

"They have broken from the Six Companies, declared their independence from us."

"Why?"

"For their own thirst for power, I imagine."

Yang wasn't so sure. "Could there not be another reason?"

Chin looked at him for a moment. "My brother is learning to think with his head."

Yang smiled.

"Very well," Chin admitted. "I must confess that the power of the Six Companies has, shall we say, remained somewhat stagnant." Chin made an offhand gesture. "These things happen when a bureaucracy becomes top-heavy."

"Stagnant in what ways?"

"Slow to act. There has been a great deal of persecution by the whites."

Yang nodded. "I am no stranger to that. If I had my way I'd slit every white devil's throat."

Chin stiffened, thinking about Rebecca again. "There are *some* good whites, brother."

"Not a one."

"You make too broad a generalization. You do not know them all."

"You are soft because you deal with them. I know them for what they are. Devils to the last."

"At any rate," Chin continued, "many of the younger members are tired of being pushed around. They want quick action."

"And the tongs promise them this?"

"Yes," Chin said, adding, "but for a heavy toll—descent into the depths of blackmail, murder, assassination, drugs, and perversions we can only guess at. Their society is a secret one and we know little of it."

254

"And now they grow stronger?"

Chin nodded. "There are half a dozen tongs in San Francisco, with brother chapters in Los Angeles and other cities. They promise their members protection from the whites and they seek to fill their coffers through ill-gotten gain."

"In what manner?"

"As I said, assassination and blackmail. And now robbery." Chin frowned. "Before it was not so bad. In the beginning, they only provided services of vice to those who bought them. The blackmailing, even the assassinations, were against others of their underworld. But now, with the death of Peng Ku, I fear they are extending their devil's hand into legitimate business."

"Can they be that powerful that they can rob honest businessmen and get away with it?"

"Possibly. At the same time, though, they are divided. The half-dozen tongs are rivals against each other. They constantly seek to expand their territories, to take over those of their rivals. Perhaps they will turn upon themselves and so destroy each other."

"They may turn upon each other," Yang said, "but I doubt they will completely destroy each other." He paused, then added, "The strongest will prevail."

They finished their meal and returned to the shop where Yang was working. A new clerk was behind the counter—Peng Ku's replacement—and he straightened as the brothers walked in. He bowed and Chin returned it.

The woman the clerk was waiting on turned and said, "Hello, Chin."

He smiled widely. "Rebecca."

Yang, thinking that she was a valued customer, assumed a respectful air, although he was surprised that his brother had addressed the woman by her first name.

Chin was pleased beyond words that she had decided to come to his shop. He knew that Rebecca had not agreed with his philosophy regarding his obligation to Mei Peng's memory. And he knew that she would never apologize for the views she held. But the fact that she had come to him, after so long an absence, was a concession on her part and he was grateful for it.

Now, in retrospect, he realized that he was wrong to blame her for his diminished prestige among his peers. It had been *his* fault that he had allowed her to influence him. It was her

255

nature to strongly espouse those opinions she truly felt. That was part of what he loved about her.

If she had been successful in her attempts to persuade him, then it was to her credit as a diplomat.

He came from behind the counter and bowed to her. "How good of you to come this day."

She lowered her voice slightly. "I missed you."

Chin straightened. "And I you." Then he turned. "Come and meet my older brother."

Chin led Rebecca to the counter where Yang was standing.

"Yang, I want you to meet Rebecca Ashley."

Yang bowed graciously. "A pleasure to meet you, lady."

"The pleasure is mine," Rebecca said. "Chin has told me so much about you."

Yang stiffened, surprised at her words, surprised at her great informality.

"He has?"

"Of course. Of your childhood together. Of your triumphs in martial arts. Of—"

"Why?" Yang asked, interrupting her. "Why has he told you these things?"

Rebecca stopped talking, the smile still on her face. She looked at Chin for a moment, uncomfortable, not knowing how to proceed.

Yang turned and looked to his brother for an explanation.

Chin said, "Rebecca is a dear friend of mine, Yang."

Yang's eyes bore into him. "How dear?"

"Very dear."

For a long moment the two brothers held each other's gaze; then, fully understanding, Yang undid his clerk's apron, dropped it on the countertop, and walked from behind the counter and out of the store.

Rebecca and Chin stood for a moment, listening to the jangle of the bell above the door. Finally, Rebecca turned to him. "What did I say? Did I offend him?"

Chin looked into her eyes, unable to say the words which would explain. "It is nothing."

"It's anything in the world except nothing, Chin. I was just standing here. What was it?"

"He is too new to the city."

"It is because I'm white?"

Chin averted his eyes. "That has nothing to do with my brother's actions."

"Look at me when you answer my question."

Chin brought his eyes back to hers. They were silent for a moment, then he said, "I must go and speak with him."

The door of the small apartment in the lodging house on Pine Street was ajar. Chin pushed it open and walked in. Yang was packing.

"Where will you go?"

"I do not know."

"You are angry with me," Chin said.

"Please," Yang replied, laying several pairs of trousers in his carpetbag, "none of your politics with me, brother. I never was one to match intellects with you."

Chin closed the door. "Is it because the woman is white?"

Yang turned to the dresser and pulled a set of trousers from one of the drawers. "No. Yes." He looked up at Chin for a brief moment. "Yes, I think that is partly it. Perhaps finding you are intimate with a white woman so short a time after my friend Peng Ku was killed by a white man does not sit well with me."

"The woman did not kill him."

"I have never known a white man I liked."

"I have," Chin said.

Yang nodded. "That's why I'm leaving. I'm not ready for this life of yours. I don't want any part of it." He closed the bag and looked at his brother. "You live in two worlds, Chin. I won't have it."

"Why do you hate the whites so much?"

"I have enough treachery to deal with from my own people. I don't want to have to worry about whites as well."

"What treachery?"

Yang sighed. He pulled the suitcase from the bed and set it on the floor. "Do you remember hearing of my killing that man at the gold camps years ago?"

Chin nodded.

"Did you ever learn why I killed him?"

"No."

"It was because a number of my 'cousins' were jealous of the success Wan Choi and I were having in our search for gold. They were thinking of banding together and robbing us. I had to kill that man to set an example—to throw fear into the others."

Chin said, "You could have reported the threat to the Six Companies."

"Hah! The Six Companies? They have no authority,

brother. You just think they do." Yang glared at Chin, and his words slapped at him. "The boundaries of the Six Companies' authority can be clearly measured—they are the limits of this city. Even smaller, because you have become fractionalized so that each company controls less and less."

"We have authority over all of—"

"Over nothing but this city," Yang said. "And even that diminishes as these tongs you spoke of grow stronger." He turned and emptied some coins from the top drawer of the dresser.

"I tell you, Chin, there is enough hate to worry about from Chinese; I don't want to have to concern myself with whites as well."

"How little you know of the whites."

Yang looked at him. "I know enough. I've seen them use and exploit our people."

"Haven't we used and exploited their land, their gold?"

Yang crossed the room, standing before him, his words filled with venom. "I'm not talking about gold or land. I'm talking about flesh and blood. About breaking our backs for thirty dollars a month and a few bowls of rice. About Wan Choi and Peng Ku and the thousands of other poor Chinese who have died and suffered in this godforsaken country of white demons."

"No one forced you to come to America. No one forced you to build a railroad."

"You're right. But I'm glad that I took part in that work. I learned from it. I saw the strength and brute force of white might," Yang said, clenching his fist. "I saw that I was right, that all that matters is how powerful a man is." He smiled bitterly. "I had almost forgotten that. Working in the city almost made me forget that . . . working for you."

"You are angry because the woman is white. You would not react this way if she were Chinese."

"I am angry because you talk of our people exploiting their gold. At least the whites I knew were cruel and vicious enough to watch men swept to their deaths and order us back to work minutes later. You listen to a different white," Yang accused, "to a more sophisticated white. You put forth the lie that we owe the whites something because they let us scavenge for what flakes of gold dust remained.

"You speak like a woman, Chin, and I think you have become one yourself because you sleep so much with her."

Chin raised his hand and slapped Yang hard across the

mouth. Yang stood, immobile, the sting of the blow like that of a hornet on his cheek.

"Because you are my brother," Yang said, "I shall forgive you this one time for being a fool." He paused, then said, "If our paths ever cross again and you ever attempt to strike me again, I shall kill you. I promise you that, Chin. On our father's grave I swear I shall kill you."

Yang grabbed his suitcase from the floor, turned, and left the room.

Chin let his head hang down as he sat on the bed in the lodging house.

Chapter 32

Ling had heard the shouts and cries, the sound of gunfire, the curses both in Chinese and English. It meant nothing to her. It was her deepest wish that all outside her cell were killed in whatever fight was going on out there.

It felt as if every inch of her body was bruised and beaten. The feeling wasn't far from right. Even now, almost a full day after the white man had left the room, she still felt waves of pain sweep over her body, felt her stomach convulse with memories of the man.

She stirred. Slowly, she lowered one leg over the side of the bed and opened her eyes. The candle was still lit. Intentionally she turned her eyes from her body, looking at the walls of her cell, the ceiling, anything.

Ling heard a key as it was inserted into the lock. As the door opened she turned her eyes toward it and saw Chou Bai Tsai come into the room. Even through her pain it occurred to her that the old woman looked distressed. Ling wondered for a moment if the whore-mistress was worried that the white man had beaten her too severely. To fuel this, for sympathy, she moaned a low groan.

That thought quickly fled as she remembered the gunshots. It had been a robbery, of course. Had they stolen Chou Bai Tsai's money? She hoped so.

Chou Bai Tsai reached behind her and grabbed a handful

of material. She pulled Ah Toy into the cell. Ling hadn't seen her friend since they had been sold on the auction block, and the shock registered even through her pain.

"Tend to her," Chou Bai Tsai said, giving Ah Toy a long stare. Then she slammed the door and was gone.

Ah Toy, holding a bucket in one hand, went to Ling's side, weeping. "I thought I'd never see you again, Ling."

Ling tried to sit up in the bed. "Nor I."

Then Ah Toy's eyes swept over Ling's body, taking in the row after row of whip marks, the trickles of dried blood and semen mixed together, the bruises and welts.

Ah Toy closed her eyes.

Ling tried to force the pain from her mind and after a moment said, "I didn't even know if we'd been sold to the same master."

Ah Toy dipped a sponge into the bucket Chou Bai Tsai had given her. "Neither did I, until last week."

"Last week?"

Ah Toy dabbed at the bloodstains on Ling's stomach, stopped the instant Ling winced. "I'm sorry."

"No," Ling said, her eyes closed. "Go on. Please, please get me clean. I feel so . . ." Her voice trailed off as Ah Toy continued to sponge her. "You were saying?"

"Yes," Ah Toy continued. "I learned last week that you were working Bartlett's Alley; the place we are now."

Ling nodded in understanding. Then she was filled with a sense of helplessness as she realized that she had not even known the name of the street she was imprisoned on. She felt a hollow void in the pit of her stomach as she grasped how little control she had over her own life.

"I learned that you were here from Chou Bai Tsai."

Ling opened her eyes and looked up at Ah Toy. "You have learned much more than I. How did you pry this information from the old hag?"

"I made peace with her."

"How?"

Ah Toy dipped the sponge back in the bucket. "It was not difficult; it was by comparison, really. Most of the other women gave her an awful time—screaming, protesting, not cooperating at all."

"And you?"

Ah Toy ran the sponge over the reddened streaks on Ling's shoulder. "I cooperated." She paused a moment. "There was really nothing else to do. You told me that. We have to accept what has happened and make the best of it. Wasn't that what you said?"

"Don't you see the marks on my body?" Ling snapped. "Will you accept this when it happens to you?"

"It already has. The first week."

"And you 'accepted' it?"

Ah Toy stopped sponging. "What was I to do? What would be gained by bitterness? Nothing. But I will tell you a secret, Ling. If you do not make much of a fuss the old woman will be pleased and not single you out for that type of man in the future. She only gives the beaters to the women who are uncooperative."

Ling couldn't believe what she was hearing. She couldn't believe that it was the same girl who had been so fearful in the ship's hold, whom she had comforted and consoled.

"But by cooperating," Ah Toy went on, "there are many other benefits and privileges to be enjoyed . . ." She brushed the sponge over Ling's arms. "Better food and more of it. Last night I had half a fish for dinner."

"Fish?" Ling exclaimed. "You had *fish*?"

"Mmmm," Ah Toy said, smiling. "A fine whitefish. With rice and a bit of melon."

"You tease," Ling accused.

"I do not. As I said, there are rewards."

"Just for cooperating?"

"The old woman has many troubles. When she finds someone who makes her job easier, who doesn't raise a fuss, she likes to keep them happy. Things can be . . ." She searched for the word, then found it: "tolerable."

Ling looked at the bruises and switch marks on her breasts. "I could never find this tolerable."

"It appears the white man went too far. Chou Bai Tsai was upset when she saw you through the window door."

Ling turned and looked at the door, at the small peep window at eye level. She hadn't known that Chou Bai Tsai had opened it. She must have done it when Ling's eyes were closed, during the time she was recovering.

She looked back to Ah Toy. "She was upset?"

"She's going to talk to the white man, and warn him not to go that far again. He's a regular, who enjoys the pleasures of striking women." Ah Toy shrugged. "That's his pleasure and he pays dearly for it. But Chou Bai Tsai can ill afford to have her women beaten to the point of incapacitation."

"What if the man wants to use me in this way each time he visits? What if I become his steady woman? I could not bear that, Ah Toy."

Ah Toy smiled. "Do not worry, dear friend. I have spoken to Chou Bai Tsai on this matter. You will not be troubled with beaters again."

Ling sighed a sigh of relief.

Ah Toy moved the sponge to Ling's legs. "But Chou Bai Tsai has worse problems to worry about this night."

Ling closed her eyes, enjoying the feel of the damp sponge. "What problems?"

"You heard the shots?"

Ling nodded.

"An attack by the Kwong Dock tong. Very bad. Three men killed. Several others injured. And Chou Bai Tsai's purse stolen from her by the tong. She will be in big trouble with the master. The whole night's receipts gone."

"It's too bad she wasn't taken with it."

Ah Toy frowned, rubbing the sponge over Ling's bruised thighs. "You shouldn't say such things. Chou Bai Tsai has a job to do. If we can make it easier for her then we will live that much better."

Ling sighed, relaxed by Ah Toy's gentle ministrations. Perhaps her friend was right, Ling reflected, as her thoughts turned to the fish and melon dinner Ah Toy had described. After all, hadn't she told the girl as much when they had been in the cargo hold of the ship? Now that it was time to stand by those words it appeared that Ah Toy was doing a better job of it than Ling herself.

"You may be right," Ling said.

"I am," Ah Toy replied. "If we don't give Chou Bai Tsai any trouble, if we are well mannered and produce, then there are all manner of privileges she can extend to us."

"Such as?"

"Aren't you lonely in this cell?"

"Of course."

"Well, if we cooperate and do our work well, Chou Bai Tsai will let us visit each other from time to time."

Ling smiled. "That would be wonderful; to have you here, to be able to talk to you. I have missed you, Ah Toy."

"And I you," Ah Toy said, slowly moving the sponge up the side of Ling's thigh and across the flare of her hip. "I have missed you more than you know."

Ah Toy stroked the sponge across the lower part of Ling's stomach, just touching the fringe of dark woman-hair.

"Ah Toy . . ." Ling began to say, trying to flutter her eyes open. But then she felt Ah Toy gently touch her arm and press her back down on the straw mattress.

"Don't talk," Ah Toy said. "You need to rest."

Ling eased back down and felt Ah Toy's hands where the sponge had been. She closed her eyes as Ah Toy's fingers twined through the locks of her pubic hair, pausing there for just a moment before they traversed lower.

Ling opened her mouth to protest but a moan escaped instead. Gently, Ah Toy laced her fingers through the silky foliage, seeking her friend's womanhood, spreading back the hood that covered it. Ah Toy stroked softly, rubbing her fingers back and forth across Ling's pulsing vulva, drawing moan after moan from her.

Ling felt her legs spread involuntarily as sweet pleasure swept across her. She felt her fingers tighten and then loosen and her legs spread wider in response. Then she called out in ecstasy as she felt the exquisite sensation of Ah Toy's tongue beginning to lap at her, across, up and down, around, flicking at her over and over again, sending shafts of pleasure through her.

Ling thrashed her head back and forth on the straw, her hip undulating in response, conscious of Ah Toy's fingernails digging gently into her uplifted buttocks, conscious of Ah Toy's hands caressing her thighs, touching the underside of her knees, stroking her heaving belly.

"Oh . . . oh no . . . ," Ling moaned, suddenly awakened to the tingling thrill of her erect nipples as Ah Toy's hands began to massage her breasts, passing her palms across the dusky tips, exciting them into distension. Then her mouth replaced her fingers and she was gently sucking, biting at Ling's nipples.

Ling's hips ground quicker and quicker as she felt the impending approach of climax. "Please . . . please, *please!*" she cried.

And then Ah Toy moved her head down Ling's body, tracking a long track across her belly with her moist tongue. Now Ah Toy slurped greedily at her, and Ling felt her friend's moist fingers as they kneaded and scratched at her buttocks and then spread and penetrated the orifice there.

Ling arched her hips violently, coming in jolt after jolt as

263

Ah Toy's darting tongue drove her to completion, all parts of her body galvanized by the crash of supreme fulfillment.

She was not, could not be, aware of Chou Bai Tsai's face looking through the peep window of the door. The old woman was smiling.

Chapter 33

"Then why don't you go to the police?" Rebecca asked.

Chin paced the bedroom like a caged tiger. "Because the police are of no help to us." He stopped and looked at her. "In many cases they're *worse* than no help."

"The police are—"

"The police are vandals themselves," he said, cutting her off. "Last week one of my shop managers arrived after a burglary to see that the police had already beaten him to the scene. Do you know what these law officers were doing, Rebecca? Your noble defenders of the law were pulling goods from my shop window and loading them into a police wagon."

"Did you report it?"

"To whom?"

"To their commander."

"Hah!" Chin laughed. "They probably split their take with him."

"You don't know that."

"I know all I need to know. Chinese people will never get justice from the whites."

"Thank you for that," she snapped.

Chin softened his tone. "You know I don't mean you, Rebecca."

"And what about the Society and organizations like it?"

"Good, honest white people working for better Chinese-American relations. Yet they are but a drop of water in a sea of discontent." He sighed. "I fear we have overstayed our welcome in this land. The time is coming when white will blame yellow for all problems. We are a convenient scapegoat."

"Taking the law into your own hands isn't the answer, Chin, and you know it."

"A vigilance committee worked before. It shall work again."

"It will only enflame things more."

"Better that than to be engulfed by the flames already licking at us." Chin sat on the settee by the window and gazed outside. "But I know the whites will not institute such a committee yet. They are not aroused enough."

Rebecca sat on the edge of the bed, frustration welling in her. "You say that as if you're disappointed."

He turned to look at her. "I am, Rebecca. Would that your people were as aroused as mine; then they would form protective societies again."

Chin looked back out the window, pondering the problem. "But it isn't the same now as when the first vigilance committee was formed. The whites are more selective in their violence—directing it primarily against Chinese. It's . . . almost as though it was orchestrated."

Rebecca stood. "You mean a conspiracy?"

He nodded. "Possibly."

"I think you're jumping to conclusions."

"Perhaps. But why are they only attacking Chinese?"

"Maybe they learned their lesson the first time."

"A marvelous thought," Chin said sarcastically. "Yet it seems you are right. They've learned that it is permissible to beat people so long as they are Chinese."

"I'm sorry to say it, Chin, but that looks like the truth. These thugs have discovered that they can get away with vandalism and beatings and robberies as long as they don't anger or threaten whites."

Chin shook his head negatively. "But I can't accept that they have the individual wisdom to make that decision. There must be a controlling force doing their collective thinking for them." He thought about it for a moment, then said, "But that doesn't matter. What matters is that it is a Chinese problem and it must be solved by Chinese."

He looked at Rebecca. "Besides, the violence isn't just committed by whites any longer. There is violence committed by Chinese against other Chinese."

"The tongs?"

Chin nodded. "They grow bolder by the day. The night before last they attacked a brothel in Bartlett's Alley. Three Chinese were killed in the assault."

Rebecca's gaze fell to the floor. "It's the beginning."

"Perhaps it could have been avoided," Chin said coolly, "if action had been taken sooner."

"I don't like the sound of that."

"It is only speculation."

Rebecca crossed the room, standing before him. "I know what you're saying, Chin. You're saying that I influenced you not to take any action."

"Isn't that true?"

"Why . . . why, yes, it is. But the only thing it accomplished was delaying this violence."

"We don't know that," he said. "It is possible that if we had acted sooner we could have stopped the growth and power of the tongs."

"We don't know that, either," she said, advancing on him.

He nodded. "That is true. All that we know is that action must be taken now. Because of the deaths in the bordello raid, a special meeting of the entire Six Companies Council has been called for tomorrow night."

"And what will you say at that meeting?"

"I have not yet fully decided, Rebecca. But you can be certain that I won't suggest that we stand still for the violence perpetrated by both white and Chinese bandits against my people."

"The hospitals will fill with innocents and blood will run in the gutters of the quarter, Chin."

"That will happen regardless. What is important is that my people defend themselves."

She turned away. After a moment she said, "I sense resentment in your words."

Chin was silent.

She turned to face him. "Toward me?"

Again he was silent. But he could not hold it. "It hurt me to lose my brother, Rebecca. I cannot lie to you about this."

"And you lost him because of me?"

"Partially. He is of the old ways in some respects. You must understand how he feels."

"And how do you feel?"

"I am not sure." He paused. "Much has happened. We have differing views on so many things, Rebecca."

"We didn't always. You've changed, Chin."

"Sometimes a man must change." He paused, then said, "I think things will become more strained between us. You will not agree with the decisions I must make in the coming weeks."

She turned away from him for a moment. "In a way I'm glad that you feel this way. It makes what I have to say a little easier."

"What you have to say?" he asked, alarmed.

With her back still to him, Rebecca said, "I have to go away for a while, Chin."

"What are you talking about?"

"I won't be able to see you for a time."

"A time? How long a time?"

"A long time."

"Rebecca, I want to know what you're talking about."

When she turned around the pretense of a smile cloaked her face. "I'm going on a trip. To Europe."

"You're not making any sense."

"But I'm making perfect sense. I'm taking a long holiday. I need some time by myself. I need some time to think."

"You never spoke of this trip."

"I decided rather suddenly."

"That's not like you at all."

"I'm a free woman. We've always had that understanding."

"Yes, but . . ."

"Then I will go where I want to go," she snapped.

Chin crossed the room, angered by her tone. He grabbed her by the arms. "Make sense, woman! What are you talking about?"

"You're hurting my arms. Let go of me, damn you!"

"Not until you tell me what you're talking about!"

She struggled in his grip, crying out, "Let go!"

Chin shook her, hard.

"Let go of me, let go! I'm *pregnant!*"

Chin's hands froze and he stopped shaking her abruptly, reading the fear and the truth in her eyes. "Pregnant," he gasped. "You know this for certain?"

"Yes."

His hands were still wrapped around her arms, but he had loosened his grip and she pulled away from him. Again she turned her back on him.

"Why didn't you tell me of this sooner?"

"It's none of your affair."

Angrily, Chin walked around her. "None of my affair? Is it not my child?"

Rebecca's eyes bore into Chin's. "Of course it's your child."

"Then it's my affair."

"It is *not*! I'll handle this in my own way."

"By putting the child up for adoption? No! Never!" Chin drew a deep breath and said, "We'll be married."

For a moment there was nothing but silence between them, then Rebecca answered, "No."

"Why not? I love you and you love me."

"A moment ago you were just about to tell me that we should not see each other."

"I was not."

"You were, Chin. You know you were."

"I want us to be married."

"No."

"Look at me. Tell me that you don't want to be my wife."

But she couldn't look at him. Again he held her arms. "Rebecca, marry me."

"NO!" she screamed, breaking from his embrace. "Leave me *alone*!"

"Control yourself," Chin said, watching her as she moved about the room. There was a look of fear on her face that he had never seen before. He thought back to all the times he had seen a troubled expression, all the times he had seen her bite her lip in contemplation, and he realized that this fear was what she had been hiding.

"Rebecca," he said softly, "I only want to make you happy."

"Then leave me alone!"

"I want you for my wife."

She lifted her head toward the ceiling and cried out, "NO!"

And then she stopped screaming, she stopped pacing, she stopped breathing. Her hands gripped her stomach, and a look of stunned pain came over her face.

"What . . . what is it?"

She blinked her eyes, tears welling in them, and looked at him. "Chin . . . take me to the hospital."

Morning light filtered through the tall windows of the hospital waiting room, unnoticed by Chin. The night had been an eternity. He had jumped up each time a nurse pushed through the operating room doors. When at last Doctor Feist, the chief of staff, came into the waiting room Chin felt as though he no longer had the strength to stand. But he did.

The gray-haired doctor looked haggard and weary. He looked at Chin and said, "She's had a difficult ordeal."

Chin waited.

"I'm afraid she's lost the baby."

Chin's eyes dropped to the floor, thinking of the child he would never know. When he looked at the doctor again he asked, "How is she?"

"As I said, it was a difficult ordeal."

"When may I see her?"

Feist looked away from him, closing his eyes from the strain. He opened them and said, "I'm afraid you can't see her."

Chin nodded. "Tomorrow?"

"No. You don't understand. You can't see her."

"But you said she—"

"She has survived. But you must not see her."

"You know that it was my child, don't you, doctor?"

"I do. She's had—"

"Other women have lost children. I insist on seeing her."

"And I insist that you don't. To begin with, she does not want to see you. As her doctor, I must say that I agree with her decision. She's in an extremely delicate emotional state. If you force yourself on her . . . well, I wouldn't want to take that responsibility."

"I love this woman, doctor."

He nodded. "I believe you." He reached out and touched Chin's arm. "If you really love her then you won't press the issue."

"But when—"

"I don't know. Not for a long time, I believe. You must wait until she sends for you, and I must warn you that it will be a long time."

"Why?"

"Because . . . You can ask her when you see her again. There are . . ." Doctor Feist tried to find the right words. "There are things about Rebecca Ashley that you cannot understand. You must give her time to recover from this thing. To her it is much more than losing a child."

"You speak in riddles."

Doctor Feist said, "I know. And only she can provide the answers to them. If you love her then you must be patient; you must believe me. When you see her again I'm certain she will explain. But for now . . . for now, you must put her out of your mind. If you truly love her, then you must do this."

Chin turned and left the hospital. He could accept what had happened if he believed that it was the will of the gods. And because it was their will that she be out of his life, then his path was clear.

BOOK THREE

Chapter 34

The Los Angeles headquarters of the Kwong Dock tong was located in the basement of a dilapidated frame building on Fort Street in the city's Chinese quarter. As soon as he had arrived in the city Yang realized that it did not have a Chinese population as large as that of San Francisco.

The quarter itself was smaller and more compact. The shops, while varied, did not have the richness of those he had seen in San Francisco. Still, the climate was more to his liking. There was something in the San Francisco air that chilled him to the bone—a pervading, ever-present dampness. And he had always hated the fog which seemed to eternally cloak the Chinese quarter in that city to the north.

Rarely did Yang admit to himself that placing distance between himself and his brother was one of the two real reasons he had left. It was far too soon after their rift for him to think about that. But the other reason, though it grew out of the first, was something he thought about constantly.

The frame building of the secret society had once been painted a sad mustard-yellow. But the color had long since faded, and only streaks and chips of it remained. It was suitable for the purposes of the tong, for at this point the chiefs of the Kwong Dock wished as few people as possible to know of their headquarters. The drab building blended with the rest of the quarter so well that few of the neighboring residents even realized that the tong met and conducted business in it.

As Yang sat in one of the chambers, waiting for the council of the warlords to begin its meeting, he thought about how fate had acted to bring him here.

The night he had argued with Chin, Yang had sought diversion in a *Fan-tan* parlor on Jackson Street. He knew the parlor was owned by Chin and he wanted, badly, to win—feeling that in some way this would strike a blow against his brother.

Yang hated the whites. He had seen enough of their brutality. When Chin had spoken of how the whites were not so bad, Yang knew too much of the city had rubbed off on his brother. But that Chin had taken a white woman as his mate was more than Yang could bear. Chin had become almost one of them.

And yet Yang admitted—to himself alone—that he saw more than a little of the white man's influence on himself. He secretly admired their passion for success, their emphasis on strength and might. The difference was, he felt, that Chin reflected the weakness in their race while he reflected their strengths.

The trip to the *Fan-tan* parlor had been ill advised. Filled with anger and jealousy at Chin's success, Yang could not concentrate on the game. And because the "house" didn't participate, but only drew a ten percent take from each pot, Yang found his frustrations further agitated. When he lost a game, he simply lost. But even when he won, the house, and Chin, still got their take off the top.

When he had drunk enough wine, and the hatred against his brother had fulminated to its limit, Yang had exploded. He erupted like a madman, for no apparent purpose, grabbing the croupier and tossing him through the air like a doll. The players scrambled for safety as Yang toppled tables, sending the chips, *peks*, and game pieces flying. Money rolled across the floor as Yang lashed out at whoever was in striking distance.

It was when that anger was fully spent, when he was certain he was alone in the gaming room, that Yang heard the voice call to him. He turned to see the cadaverous man whose name, he would learn, was Po Dung.

"You and I must talk," Po Dung had said softly.

Surprised that the man was brave enough to confront him after his rage, and curious as to what he wanted to talk about, Yang allowed Po Dung to lead him to a restaurant across the street.

He was a singularly odd-looking man—his cheeks sunken and hard, his skin glistening, his oiled queue as black as his eyes. Over dinner, Yang learned that Po Dung was a member of the Kwong Dock tong, headquartered in Los Angeles. Inwardly Yang smiled at the ways of the gods—how they had brought him face to face with the force his brother both feared and loathed.

Po Dung was a skillful interviewer, extracting the story of Yang's work on the railroads, his hatred of the whites, and,

274

eventually, his failed business relationship with Chin. When the man asked him if he ever killed anyone, Yang raised an eyebrow. He thought to ask a question in return, but somehow sensed that this was a man of importance and someone upon whom his future might well turn.

Instead, he recounted the story of the man he had killed in the goldfields. Once he had confessed this, the details of the killing spilled forth, and Po Dung nodded in satisfaction as they did. When Yang finished telling of the martial arts contest he had staged to teach his fellow prospectors a lesson, Po Dung said, "That is good. It shows not only forethought, but creativity."

Yang regarded Po Dung for a moment, his *fai-tze* poised in midair above his rice. Yang had never considered the act to be creative. But the more he had thought about it, the more he realized Po Dung was right. He had devised the plan for dramatic effect and carried it out to its successful end.

When Yang explained how they had profited by running a bank for the bettors, when he explained how he had sought to raise the odds against himself so he could profit from the betting, Po Dung commented, "You are truly an artist."

Wisely, Yang neglected to mention the untimely attack of the white men after the contest had ended.

It was then that Po Dung suggested the possibility of Yang joining the Kwong Dock tong. He confessed that the society was a ruthless bunch, involved in many illicit businesses. At the same time, he explained that the tong ran many legitimate businesses, and that these needed protection from rival tongs. This job fell to the highbinders—the elite band of tong warriors.

Po Dung was careful to explain the complete obedience that would be required of Yang, making it clear that Yang must be willing to kill if necessary. In return, Po Dung said, he would be well paid, respected within the tong, and supplied with women and other pleasures.

When Yang expressed his interest, Po Dung told him of the ritual of admission he would have to endure. The other question he asked was whether Yang would object to moving to a new city.

Neither the ritual nor the move, Yang had felt, posed a problem.

Entrance into the tong included a probationary period and the ritual of admission. The former Yang had undergone for the last month. Now, sitting in the chamber in the tong head-quarters in Los Angeles, Yang paid close attention.

Po Dung, whom Yang had learned was the *Hung kwang shan*—chief swordsman—of the Los Angeles chapter of the Kwong Dock tong, was seated behind a long table. Also behind the table were two of the tong's warlords.

"Your probationary period is coming to an end," Po Dung began. "It is the opinion of the War Council that you have performed admirably so far."

Yang sat attentively in the straight-backed chair, listening to the men who would decide if he would be allowed entrance to the rituals of admission to the tong.

Po Dung said, "There is a final duty you must perform before judgment is made in the case of your admission to the rituals." Here Po Dung paused for effect. The dark room bore in on him as if to emphasize the importance of the chief swordsman's next words.

"There is a man. His name is Bei Ting Hwa. He is an enemy of the Kwong Dock tong."

Po Dung hesitated, waiting to see if Yang would question what the man's crimes had been. To his credit, he did not. Po Dung was pleased.

Proud that his protégé had exercised restraint, he became expansive and decided to privilege him with the knowledge. "The man's crime was taking a woman who belonged to a member of our tong."

Yang bowed his head slightly, to register both his understanding and his appreciation of the fact that Po Dung was giving him this additional information.

"He is to meet the fate of all who would act against the Kwong Dock tong." Po Dung paused, then said, "Wash his body."

Yang nodded, then asked, "By what method?"

"I shall leave that to you. Our only instruction is to make his death a grisly one so as to make harsher the lesson to those who would oppose us. But make no mistake about this, Yang. Bei Ting Hwa is a powerful member of the Suey Sing tong. As such he is guarded and attended by protectors. Your job will not be an easy one."

"I shall do that which you order. I shall lay waste to the enemies of the Kwong Dock tong."

And he did. Yang took Bei Ting Hwa while he was being groomed. Assisted by two novices named Ho Huan and Yin

Yip, Yang overcame three bodyguards in order to get to his target. Once inside the barber shop Yang had silently approached his prey, whose face was swathed in warm towels. He had taken the razor from the trembling hands of a barber who was grateful just to survive.

In a single swoop, Yang had slit the Suey Sing highbinder's throat from ear to ear, and thus assured his ascendency to full membership in the Kwong Dock tong—an ascendency heralded by the heroic deed he had done for the tong.

That night was a night given to celebration. The novices of the tong held a party in honor of Yang and his accomplishment. As Yang sat chewing a large piece of pork, the fragrance of fried rice, tea, and incense filled his nostrils. A half-dozen sing-song girls danced before him, their moon-harps playing softly as they sang words of love, tribute, and adulation.

All about the room dozens of novices raised their glasses and cups to him, uttering words of praise to the assassin of Bei Ting, enemy of the tong. Yang bathed in the homage.

He looked at Yip Yin sitting to his right. The young novice who had helped in the assassination had a glazed look to his eyes—the result of pipe after pipe of opium. Ho Huan, Yang's other accomplice, sat on the other side drinking rice wine.

Ho Huan caught Yang looking at him and raised his cup toward him. "To you, honorable Yang, master of the hatchet, avenger of the tong."

Yang smiled and lifted his cup to his lips.

"You have become a legend to the novices," he heard a voice say, and for a moment he thought it was the whisper of Kwan Kung, the god of war himself.

But then he turned to see Po Dung kneeling at his side and he brushed away the haze of opium that lay over his brain. He instantly bent his head to the chief swordsman. "We are honored by your presence, Po Dung."

The swordsman took his position on a pillow next to Yang. For a moment he listened to the sing-song girls, then he returned his attention to Yang.

"Usually I do not disturb the novices' parties. But tonight I felt it only proper to pay a brief visit so you would know that the tong's regular members join in this celebration in spirit and that they are, at this moment, toasting your name and that of your able assistants."

Yang looked at Po Dung. "The expression you make overwhelms me, Po Dung. I am pleased beyond description that you have visited our celebration this evening."

"It is one you well deserve."

"No," Yang said. "It is not for me. It is a joy we express that Bei Ting, enemy of the Kwong Dock tong, is passed."

"But it was you who brought this about," Po Dung reminded him, "and the tong will not forget it." He paused, then said, "You have distinguished yourself as a novice. Soon you will be inducted into the rites of the tong."

Again Yang bent his head. "My joy this night is complete with this news."

The fete was one of many the Kwong Dock tong had put on since the assassination of Bei Ting, one of the warlords of the Suey Sing tong. The streets surrounding the Kwong Dock headquarters were filled with the explosions of firecrackers and the music of the sing-song girls late into the night. With the death of Bei Ting the Kwong Dock tong had been avenged. But more, they had thrown down the gauntlet.

The continuing parties and celebrations took the victory beyond the point of a military triumph. For the Suey Sing it was a matter of disgrace. Each party, each feast, each festival celebrating the murder of Bei Ting by a handful of Kwong Dock novices was a further affront to the strength and power of the Suey Sing tong.

Finally, when they could bear it no longer, the Suey Sing retaliated.

On the morning of October 22, Yang was awakened at dawn. He was led through the corridors of the tong building to the apartment of Po Dung.

Yang had never been inside the warlord's apartment and he was impressed with what he saw. The decor was austere, spartan, the walls adorned only with axes, hatchets, and swords. In one corner of the living room stood a three-foot-high statue of Kwan Kung, the god of war. A *mon war* stood next to it, a fire raging within.

Po Dung stood erect, alert, his hands on his hips as he spoke to Yang. "You are to ready your novices for battle."

Yang felt stunned by the swordsman's words—not so much because of the talk of battle but because he had never considered the novices his, had never considered himself in charge of them. Evidently Po Dung did . . . at least from this time forward.

Po Dung continued. "Only this morning we have received

word that the Suey Sing tong has secured one side of Nigger Alley. It is a challenge of war and one that cannot be ignored. They are fools to make such a move at this time, when they are short a warlord. We shall crush them," Po Dung said, clenching his fist. "Our soldiers, warriors, and novices will drive them into extinction."

He looked at Yang. "It is the best possible thing which could happen. We shall emerge as the most powerful tong in Los Angeles," Po Dung said.

Then the swordsman fell silent, his eyes locking with Yang's. When he spoke again his words were like beams of piercing light, searching out the truth.

"Are your men ready? Will they commit themselves fully to this effort? Do you feel confident to lead them?"

Yang's answer rang with iron conviction. "My men are prepared. They are honed as sharp as the razor with which I slit Bei Ting's throat. They will charge into the fires of hell if need be, and I will lead that charge."

Po Dung nodded. "Good. Go prepare them for combat." The swordsman turned and walked to his worktable, the matter settled, and began working on other details and strategies for the coming war.

Chapter 35

During the years that James Riley had worked on the railroad he had made more than a few friends. He had sensed an ability within himself to attract men and mold them to his way of thinking. Still, he was realistic enough to know that the only men who would be attracted to him were common men. This did not bother his pride. Rather, he accepted his station in life, and thus was able to capitalize on it.

As a foreman he had extended favors to many of his fellow workers, and during fights with management he became known as a man who looked out for his coworkers.

In the years after the railroad was completed San Francisco filled up with many men who had worked on the Central Pacific. Many of whom knew Riley or at least knew of him. In February 1871 Riley decided that it was time to start calling old favors in.

He had formed a close-knit clique, an inner circle of friends, that included Brian O'Malley and Michael Gallagher, the owner of the bar he frequented. Riley himself no longer roamed the streets. This he left to Tim Shaughnessy and Billy McNamara. The Shaughnessy-McNamara gang was the largest of the Irish gangs in San Francisco.

It had become the largest because it had more protection than any other gang. Riley managed this by setting up a split of the booty that enabled him to buy off certain lawyers and bribe many foot-patrol officers. Sixty percent of the take was divided among the gang's members. Five percent was split between Shaughnessy and McNamara. The remaining thirty-five percent went to Riley and O'Malley.

Out of their percentage Riley had to pay for the gang's overhead, which included bribes, bail money, and general operating expenses. But the income was tremendous. The gang's money was able to furnish bribes that coaxed police into turning their heads when warehouses and stores were burglarized.

Riley knew that if he and his cohorts were to reach a position of power—one higher than just that of a street gang—then Riley himself had to assume an air of semirespectability.

Riley had his sights set on high goals, and he knew they could not be achieved if he spent his time running about the streets with the gangs, preying on the Chinese, and running the risk of being arrested by the coppers.

Still, he realized that it was essential to his plans that he control the streets—because of the money and the potential manpower it meant he could call upon.

Having Shaughnessy and McNamara as figurehead leaders suited him well. Too, they did their job thoroughly and were intensely loyal to him, sensing that he was a man of purpose.

For Riley to achieve the respectability he wanted he knew that his first goal was to get a job. But Brian O'Malley had advised him that getting a job was not enough.

It would be much better for his image if he was a small but independent businessman. Riley agreed, knowing that owning a business would give him the freedom to make his own hours and devote whatever time he needed to his other enterprises.

After much consideration, they decided on a livery stable. O'Malley made the inquiries, got in touch with some old friends, and found a building on Fremont Street that they could pick up for a reasonable price. They bought the necessary provisions—hay, feed, grooming supplies. O'Malley hired two black boys and bought a used dray that could be rented out. In April 1871 Riley & O'Malley's Livery opened for business.

The structure was frame and two stories. It was on the second floor of the building where most of Riley's business was conducted. There Riley had had offices built. It was a suite of three offices—one each for Riley and O'Malley and a common room as well. Off the offices were a bedroom each for the partners. In these comfortable quarters Riley and O'Malley both lived and worked.

On the last day of April Riley was sitting in his office with Brian O'Malley, behind a large oak desk that had been bought with money robbed from Chinese vegetable vendors.

"Total in our account," O'Malley said, "is $26,054."

"Good," Riley answered. "That gives us a nice cushion."

"We're doing a nice business here, too," O'Malley continued. "The livery took in two hundred and eighty dollars the first week we were open."

Riley was surprised. He hadn't expected the livery to really do much business. He had planned it as little more than a convenient front. But a good number of his acquaintances had showed up out of loyalty and saw to it that their horses were boarded at Riley & O'Malley's Livery.

"Guess we got a lot of friends," he said.

O'Malley nodded in agreement. "Best be careful about who we say our friends are, though."

"Aye," Riley agreed.

"It's a thin rope you're walking, Jamie."

"I heard you the first time, Brian. I know what I'm doing."

"I hope so."

"Have you ever gone wrong with me yet?"

"No, no, I haven't. But before it was just you and me and a couple of the boys. It's getting big now. I just hope it's not getting too big."

"Brian, that's the only way we'll ever see the really big money. When we were small-time Chink beaters what were we pulling in—a couple of hundred dollars between the lot of us? Barely enough to pay for room and board and a few beers."

Riley leaned across his desk. "Now what are we doing? Why, Shaughnessy and McNamara's boys are bringing in close to ten thousand a week. We all live nice. The boys are happy and we're building for the future." He leaned back in his chair. "I tell you, Brian, if things go the way I think they will, that three grand a week will look like chicken feed before long."

"It's getting dangerous, though," O'Malley pointed out. "It was one thing to rob Chinks. But breaking into warehouses and burglarizing . . ."

Riley smiled. "One day it may be different. One day we may be able to just walk in and help ourselves." He didn't bother to explain, but instead said, "Of course there's risks. There's always risks when you play big. But we can take care of the coppers. We got plenty of them on the payroll."

Riley turned as he heard a knock at the door. "Yeah?"

The door opened and the two gang leaders came in.

"We were just talking about you two," Riley said.

McNamara slapped O'Malley on the shoulder as he sat down. "Good things, I trust?"

"How could they be anything but?" Riley asked.

Tim Shaughnessy slid a canvas bag across the desk to Riley. He said, "Here's the week's take. Twenty-four hundred after expenses."

"Not bad," Riley said. He dropped the money bag in a drawer of his desk and looked at the two gang leaders. "Boys, it's time for us to move to the next step."

Shaughnessy and McNamara centered their attention on James Riley, while Brian O'Malley pulled some glasses and a bottle of Irish whiskey from the cabinet by the door.

"It's time for us to start going public," Riley continued. "I want you to spread the word to your men. Tell them to spread the word to every other gang in the city that there's going to be a big meeting next Saturday night down on the sandlot near Spear and Market Streets."

The two men nodded.

"I want as many men there as you can muster. A thousand, two thousand if you can manage it. The more the better."

Shaughnessy sipped at his drink. "What's going on, Jamie?"

"What's going on is that it's time for us to flex our muscles a little." He paused, then turned to McNamara. "Billy, this is going to be a big meeting and I'm going to do a lot of talking. If I've called it right we're going to get these boys plenty worked up."

Riley emphasized his next words with his left hand. "But

it's important that we don't have any violence. That's real important, do you understand?"

"I gitcha, James. We'll tell 'em."

"I want you to make sure everybody understands that. I don't want any rioting. I don't want any damage done. Lots of noise and yelling, but no damage."

Riley motioned to O'Malley. "Brian's going to notify the press. They're going to be there. I want them to see a powerful mob. But I want them to see that power under control."

Shaughnessy sipped at his whiskey. "But the press has been bad-mouthing us for months. Who cares what they think about us?"

"I care, damn it! Look, Tim, the time's coming when we're going to need the press on our side. If things are going to happen the way I picture them, we've got to have their cooperation. I want them to be scared of the gangs, but I don't want them to be angry."

"What's the difference?"

O'Malley said, "Believe him, Tim, there's a difference."

Shaughnessy finished the whiskey and poured another. "Don't see why we need them, anyway. We're doing all right now."

"We're doing horseshit," Riley said. "At least compared to what we could be doing. Now you listen to me, Tim. You do what I'm telling you, and inside a couple of years you'll be wearing silk shirts and sleeping with fifty-dollar-a-night whores."

Shaughnessy smiled at the thought.

After Shaughnessy and McNamara had left, O'Malley poured another drink for Riley and himself. "I'm not so sure about those two, Jamie."

"They're okay. Just need a little supervision, that's all."

O'Malley shook his head. "Shaughnessy's such a hothead."

"Can't blame him much, what with Colin's gettin' killed like he did."

"I still don't like having to depend on them like we do."

"They're all right, I tell you. Tim serves his purpose and McNamara keeps him pretty much in line."

"McNamara's nothing more than a thug himself."

"We need men like them, Brian. Remember, we were thugs ourselves not so long ago. If we don't have men like McNamara and Shaughnessy to run in the streets with the gangs, then we'd have to do it ourselves. And you told me a long time ago that you can't work both sides of the fence at the same time."

"I know, I know. Still, I don't like having to depend on them." O'Malley downed what was left of his whiskey.

Shaughnessy and McNamara had done their work well. The word of the meeting spread throughout San Francisco gangland and the great mass of unemployed men who had nothing to do but mill in the streets.

By six o'clock that night the sandlot began to fill up with men. Workers had erected a platform in the middle of the large lot. For a while there was an almost carnival air, as the weather had fortuitously taken a rare turn for the warmer.

The men occupied themselves, wrestling, gaming, joking. It was not a good year for any of the men who gathered in the sandlot that night. The rest of San Francisco was prospering as the stock market continued to climb. The market soared higher and higher each day. Fortunes were being amassed by common waiters in restaurants. But to have money you had to have a job, and to have a job you had to have a skill. The men who had come to hear Riley speak had neither.

They were unskilled workers, the men who were hurt most by the massive Chinese labor force. They were ripe for Riley's words.

By eight o'clock there were more than three thousand men at the sandlot. O'Malley saw James Riley walking through the crowd, making his way toward the stand. Most of the men in the audience realized that the featured speaker had arrived. Many of them broke into cheers as Riley stepped onto the stage.

The cheers were led by Shaughnessy and McNamara's gang, which had spread throughout in the audience. Others around them, not knowing what they were applauding, applauded anyway.

Riley stood before the podium, waving, smiling. At length, things settled down a bit. He spoke in a loud voice, trying to be heard by each and every one of the more than three thousand men on the sandlot.

"I'm glad all of you men could come tonight," Riley began. "I'm glad and at the same time I'm sad."

He paused for a moment as the crowd seemed to hone in on his words.

"I'm glad," he continued, "because it means a show of

strength here. It shows that there's a whole lot of us who're in the same boat. But I'm sad because there are so *many* of us."

Riley stopped again, watching the bobbing heads. "I'm not going to pretend to you that I'm poor and unemployed. I'm luckier than most, I guess. I managed to save a few dollars during my life and I've got a small livery stable to show for it."

His voice rose again. "But I do *know* what it's like to be poor and unemployed because I've been there." He shook his head sadly. "I'm afraid some of the fellas who've been talking to you the past months, at meetings like these, don't know too much about that. Some of these politicians come from wealthy families up on the hill, learned what they know at eastern schools, wear fancy clothes, and then come out here and expect to lead poor folks."

The crowd rustled its agreement.

Riley held his hands out to them in explanation. "Now I ain't sayin' they aren't well intentioned. I'm just saying you got to know about being poor to help the poor."

"Right!" someone shouted.

"You got to know about being without a job to help those who don't have a job."

There was a louder chorus of agreement.

Again Riley's tone softened. "Now I want to say, right from the very start, that I ain't no candidate for any office. I never will be." He laughed. "Takes a smart man to make up laws, work in government, represent people. I know I ain't smart."

Riley let his gaze travel over the crowd. "I may not be smart enough to run for office, but that don't mean I ain't smart enough to tell who should, does it?"

There were a few murmurs.

"You men," he said, pointing back to them, "you may be out of jobs, flat on your back. You sure as hell aren't going to run for governor or senator or mayor or dogcatcher. But that doesn't mean you ain't got the brains to tell who *should* be governor or senator or mayor, does it?"

The men were turning to each other, nodding in agreement.

Riley leaned across the podium, resting casually on both arms. "Ya see, it seems to me that we've been letting the wrong people get elected around here for too long. We've been letting the wrong people tell us what to do.

"And do you know why?" He paused, then said, "Because

we don't think we're worth a damn in the first place. Well," he said, straightening, "what are we, anyway? Nothing but working stiffs, and that's only if we're lucky enough to have a job. Most of us ain't even that. So what good are you?"

His hands lashed out at the men as he spoke. "I'll tell you what good you are. Each and every one of you is a vote. You men are worth *three thousand* votes tonight. You know what a politician would do for three thousand votes? Why, he'd run jay naked down the middle of Front Street."

The men roared with laughter.

"And I'll tell you another thing. I'd vote for 'em. I'd vote for any one of 'em if I thought they'd keep their promises. But they won't."

Again there were heads nodding in agreement.

"I remember listening to a whole passel of speeches four years ago. I remember listening to them makin' all sorts of promises back then. They were gonna see to it that everybody had jobs. Have you all got jobs?"

"No!" someone shouted.

"They were gonna see to it that we got paid a special bonus for working on the railroad. Any of you men ever get that bonus?"

"No," they roared.

"They were gonna stop the Chinks from coming into California," he said in a loud voice. "Have they stopped the yellow horde?"

The crowd erupted again—"NO!"—and Riley nodded in agreement.

"You're damned right they haven't! Them Chinks keep steaming into San Francisco Bay every day. Every day there's more and more of them here to take jobs away from white people. And why? Because they can work for less, because of their heathen diet and sick ways."

Riley folded his arms. "No," he said, shaking his head, "they ain't gonna keep any of those promises. Only people they're concerned about is the men who own the railroads— the capitalists. Them big shots living up on Nob Hill.

"Well, I say it's time *they* start worrying. I say it's time *they* start getting a little scared. Them capitalists may have the money, but we've got the vote, and without us they're gonna find themselves out of office!"

"Yeah! Yeah!" the voices slapped.

"We aren't asking for a handout," Riley declared. "All we're asking for is what's due us. That's all we've ever asked for—a fair shake. But the word better go out to all the politicians and all the rich capitalists that if the common folks don't get that fair shake, then we're gonna show 'em what a real shake means!"

Angry fists shook in the air in agreement.

Riley nodded. "It's time for us to get organized. It's time for us to get together. It's time for us to start working like a team. That's what I want from all you men tonight. All I want is the promise that we'll get together again, talk again, work together. Do I have it?"

The question was answered by a massive ovation from the three thousand men who had thought they had nothing when they came to the sandlot. Riley had showed them different. They had something; they had numbers.

The cheering went on and on and the reporters scribbled furiously in their notebooks.

Chapter 36

By the time darkness fell on the evening of the twenty-third, the news of the impending tong war had spread throughout Los Angeles's Chinatown. In point of fact, the news had been circulating for days. There had been scattered incidents throughout the week—shots fired, a few more knifings than usual, rumors, threats—and it was simply a matter of speculation when the war would break out.

When forty-six highbinders of the Suey Sing tong had seized the left side of Nigger Alley the day before, the question had been answered. And yet, although it was to be war, to many of the residents of Chinatown it was almost a relief. For it meant that, for once, most innocent people were safe. This was tong against tong.

Accordingly, Nigger Alley, which was little more than a narrow path that stretched a few blocks, was virtually deserted except for the highbinders of the Suey Sing tong. Flanking either side of the winding alley were dozens of storefronts and lodging houses.

The Suey Sing highbinders waited in the shops on the left

side of the alley, groups of three and four in each shop. Up on the second floor of the buildings there were balconies and windows. People fortunate enough to live in the alley were to get a firsthand view of the entire battle. They stood by the windows or sat on the balconies eating pork and rice, detached spectators.

The high double doors on the front of the Kwong Dock house on Fort Street opened and, by twos, the hatchetmen of the tong filed out. They were led by Po Dung, followed by his two fellow warlords, Chou Chang Gung and Gwai Bu Tai. Each of these warlords commanded a force of fifteen highbinders.

Po Dung himself, in addition to having command over all the soldiers of the tong, had a personal elite squad of ten warriors under his direct command.

After these three squads had filed onto the street, out came Yang at the head of his eleven novices. As he stepped out onto the cobblestones, Yang felt his heart pounding, his chest swelling with pride that he was at the head of the young soldiers. He was determined that he would be triumphant in his first command.

From windows above, from cracked doors, from vantage points at the end of the block, dozens of people watched as the fighting tong assembled its soldiers for battle. They were an impressive lot, fierce in their appearance.

Each highbinder wore pajamas which were black as the night. About each man's waist was a pure white girdle. The initiated members of the tong wore the blood-red scarf of the T'ai T'sing rebels wrapped about their heads.

Yin Yip drew up to Yang's side. "It will be a night of glory."

Yang nodded in agreement. "A night that shall be sung of for centuries to come. We are fortunate to be a part of it."

"It was your performance in dealing with the hated Bei Ting that prompted the swordsman to allow us to participate in this battle."

Yang smiled slightly, accepting the praise. "We will all share the triumph this night, as we did when, together, we slew the Suey Sing warlord."

"And if we do," Yin Yip said, "it is you to whom the novices owe their thanks."

Yang looked at him and said, "Give me thanks only by distinguishing yourself in battle."

Yin Yip responded by clutching the butt of his hatchet. He returned to the ranks. Yang watched as Po Dung talked with the two warlords, going over last-minute details. He wished that he could be included in the final conference, but he remained in his place.

He looked over at Ho Huan. "You are ready?"

"Fully," Ho Huan answered.

"I ask only that you show the valor you displayed when we washed Bei Ting."

"That and more," Ho Huan pledged.

Yang nodded. "Good." He looked at the other novices. "The rest of them are not battle-hardened. They will need a strong example to follow. I am depending on you and Yin Yip to provide it."

"You shall not be disappointed."

Yang nodded, then turned as he heard Po Dung's voice.

"Warriors of the Kwong Dock tong," the swordsman called. "It is the time of battle. We have invoked the favor of Kwan Kung, the mighty god of war and protector of this tong. He shall be at our side, his scimitar with ours. Tonight we destroy the Suey Sing tong."

The highbinders cheered, many pulling their weapons from their waistbands and brandishing them overhead.

Po Dung's voice lowered conspiratorially. "Keep your enthusiasm, keep your energy. But remember to follow your warlords. Remember to follow the plans of battle and respond, unquestioningly, to the orders you receive during the conflict."

The swordsman paused, then finished by saying, "Do this and we shall surely emerge victorious. Now to the battle."

Again the men cheered. Then, led by Po Dung, the fifty-four highbinders of the Kwong Dock tong turned and headed toward Nigger Alley.

It was past eight o'clock when the first of the Kwong Dock warriors arrived at the mouth of Nigger Alley. The squads had long since split into smaller groups of four and five men. They filtered into the alley, occupying shops on the right side of the gangway.

The Suey Sing tong signaled their occupancy by an occasional knife whooshing through the night. When it became impossible to advance up the alley any longer because Suey Sing warriors were in the stores across the street, the highbinders of the Kwong Dock tong entered the stores from doors on the next street back.

Shortly before nine o'clock the battle lines had been fully drawn. All members of the tongs were in place. Sporadic gunfire rang out, but there were no real injuries yet. Mostly the gunplay was just preparatory bravado.

Several times foolhardy white reporters had dared to show their faces at the edge of the alley, eager to record the spectacle. They had been sent running by bullets whizzing close over their heads. This was a Chinese matter, both tongs agreed, and it would be witnessed and settled only by Chinese.

Yang jumped back from the window as another shot ripped past him, shattering glass onto the floor of the butcher shop he knelt in. He looked at the three men in the shop with him, all novices. From the clothing store next door he heard Ho Huan's men returning the fire. He pulled the pistol from his waistband and jerked three rounds of fire through the window.

Suddenly there were shouts from outside. Yang listened. It was English.

"This is the police. This is Captain Charleston of the Los Angeles Police Department."

The firing stopped; both tongs' highbinders were surprised by the white voice.

"Now I'm only going to say this once. I want you men to lay down your weapons, come out and go home. I won't stand for any more of this. You're going to shoot some white man and then you'll have to go to jail."

Yang felt blood surging through his body, his face hot with anger.

"How dare they interfere?" one of the men in the room with him said.

"Fan quay!" another highbinder barked. "What business have they here?"

Charleston's voice blared again. "You men just all go home and there won't be any problems. Come on out now."

From across the other side of Nigger Alley, Yang heard a Suey Sing highbinder yell, "Leave us alone, white man! Be gone!"

Then a Kwong Dock hatchetman called, "This battle is between the Kwong Dock and the Suey Sing!"

From across the alley another enraged Suey Sing yelled, "It is none of your affair!"

"Leave us! Leave us!"

Yang listened as the angry chorus sang from both sides of the alley, and suddenly he heard himself yelling, joining in the shouts.

The air cracked with a tremendous explosion as Captain Charleston let off a double blast from his shotgun. At the edge of the alley, with fifteen of Los Angeles's finest behind him and at the ready, the captain cracked the barrel of his shotgun and let the shells clatter loudly to the street in the silence that now engulfed Nigger Alley.

Behind the policemen was a phalanx of white citizens who had been quickly deputized to reenforce the lawmen's ranks. Charleston reloaded, smoke still snaking from the barrels. The smell of cordite was heavy in the air, mixing with his anger and refueling it.

"I'm not going to stand for this one minute longer!" the captain shouted. Unused to defiance, particularly from the Chinese, his voice seethed as he continued, "If you Chinks aren't out of here in the next ten seconds my men are going to come in there and pull you out. You can all spend the night in the calaboose!"

Yang stood by the window, looking out into the alley. Across the way he could see members of the Suey Sing tong standing in windows of shops, too. It occurred to him that he could easily pick off two or three of them.

Strangely, it no longer seemed to matter. All anger at the enemy tong had dissipated, and in its place was rage at the white men who had the arrogance to interfere with Chinese affairs.

He turned to see the white men advancing up Nigger Alley now, their weapons raised. Then Yang caught sight of a door opening across the alley. A Suey Sing highbinder stepped into the dim circle of light cast by a street lamp. Yang saw the tension in the man's face, saw his cheeks glistening with sweat. He prayed to the gods that the man would not give in to the whites' orders, and as if some gift of insight was suddenly bestowed on him, he sensed that that was not the man's intention.

Instead, the highbinder turned suddenly and faced the whites at the end of the alley. He pulled his pistol and fired a shot over their heads. Cheers rose up from the soldiers of both tongs.

The white band was well into the alley now and they were unsure how to react to the shot. Charleston urged them forward and the mass surged down on the man. As they began to beat the man, other highbinders poured out of the doors and windows on both sides of Nigger Alley, brandishing their cudgels and hatchets overhead. As the melee escalated windows above were slammed shut and spectators on the balconies ran inside for safety.

One of the white men, a citizen named Bob Thompson, had knocked down a highbinder and was about to bring his club down across the highbinder's skull when the shot rang out. No one ever found out who fired the shot, but it was a clean one, drilling a neat hole just above Thompson's left temple.

Seeing the killing and knowing that his forces were hopelessly outnumbered, Captain Charleston issued his orders.

"Pull back!" he cried. He grabbed one of his lieutenants. "Get the men out of here! Pull back!"

"Retreat!" the lieutenant cried. "Fall back!"

The order was hardly necessary. Intimidated by the fierce warriors, half of Charleston's men had already taken to their heels. At the first word from the lieutenant the remainder took flight.

In the streets of Nigger Alley a celebration had begun. They had given the whites a taste of their own medicine, and any antipathy between the two warring tongs was temporarily put aside. Suey Sing highbinders bowed to those of the Kwong Dock and instead of an exchange of bullets between them, now there was merry conversation.

"Did you see the whites run?" a hulking Suey Sing warrior asked Yang.

"Yes!" Yang replied. "And a good thing for them that they did!"

There was much clapping from above as the spectators came out onto the balconies again. Torn shreds of brown paper filtered down through the air and the highbinders bowed to their audience.

For once the opposing tongs and even some of the frightened onlookers were united in celebration.

"The die has been cast!" Po Dung declared. "The whites now know that we will not tolerate their forced control of our lives!"

The highbinders of both tongs stood in a circle in Nigger Alley, intoxicated by their unexpected victory, listening to Po Dung speak. Yang, standing by his side with Ho Huan and

292

Yin Yip, was proud of the role he and his novices had played in the declaration of defiance.

"We have repulsed the whites," Po Dung continued, "and we may rest assured, this night, that they shall not return." He clenched his battle-ax. "They know we will deal more harshly with them if they do. They fled like women and like women they will be afraid to do battle with us!"

The highbinders cheered.

"My highbinders will not war with the Suey Sing this night. We must all put aside our contempt for one another," Po Dung said. "For we are all brothers of blood this night and we have a common enemy, a common victory to celebrate."

The highbinders waved their weapons overhead in agreement. The celebration had begun.

Yang was in a restaurant on Olive Street with Yin Yip and Ho Huan when he heard gunshots in the distance. At first he thought it was still part of the celebration that was sweeping the quarter. The mood, after they had repulsed the police, was a festive one.

Not one of the highbinders had thought the police would dare return. The two tongs departed from Nigger Alley, having resolved their differences for that night, and Po Dung had even exchanged bows with the chief swordsman of the Suey Sing. There would be no more fighting among Chinese for the present, they decided.

All these things Yang glowed at. What he could not know was the rage that had swept through the white citizenry of Los Angeles, the mad frenzy that took hold of the entire city when it was learned that a gang of Chinese brigands had not only repulsed the police but actually killed a white man. Like crazed dogs, the white mob swept into the Chinese quarter. All manner of men came—clerks and clergy, thieves and bankers, businessmen and the unemployed. Blood lust had infected them all.

Yang turned as the double doors of the restaurant burst inward. Three white men stood in the doorway, pistols in their hands. Yin Yip turned as the first man fired. The bullet struck Yin Yip's right temple and seared into his brain.

The restaurant turned into a hell as dozens of white men poured in from the streets. The Chinese who had been eating in the restaurant began running wildly, like terrified animals, heading for the doors, the windows, the second floor. The white men were upon them like hunters upon seals.

Clubs flew like stalks in wheat fields. From a corner, with Ho Huan, Yang stood transfixed, watching Chinese heads being split open. One of the diners pulled a revolver and got off a shot. But then four whites were upon him and all Yang could hear were the wolfish growls of the men as they tore at the screaming Chinese.

Wave after wave of whites raced into the restaurant. Yang snapped to life as a white sailor grabbed hold of his arms. He whirled and jammed his thumbs into the man's eyes, drawing a scream of pain from his attacker.

Ho Huan kicked at the sailor as he fell, writhing, on the floor. Yang turned and grabbed an oil lamp from one of the tables and threw it, as hard as he could, toward the draperies on the front window of the restaurant. The crash of the lamp sent flames spreading quickly, and the white men began retreating, amenable to finding other prey elsewhere.

Yang looked at Yin Yip on the floor only long enough to see that he was dead. He turned to Ho Huan, as the flames spread around the restaurant. "We must leave. It won't be safe for long in this place."

"Where will we go?" Ho Huan asked, knowing it was not the flames alone that Yang feared.

"Out of the city. We'll have to make our way out of Los Angeles." He edged toward the rear door of the restaurant. "Nowhere will be safe." He grasped the handle of the door and opened it. "They've all gone mad."

Yang and Ho Huan crept through the streets like scores of other Chinese who had realized that they had a better chance being outside. At least outside they could run.

Twice the two men passed within fifty feet of bands of whites, but the fates were with them for they were not seen in the shadows. Once one white man had started toward them, but the rest of his group called to him and he left Yang and Ho Huan alone; he was apparently more interested in some Chinese prostitutes his friends had stumbled on down the street.

Ho Huan would peer around a corner before they would negotiate it, making certain that the way was clear. They retreated into buildings when whites bore down on them. From inside one of the buildings they rested in, Yang watched as a group of about thirty whites strode down the street. One man had half a dozen queues hanging from his belt, like so many black snakes.

As the band passed by, Yang and Ho Huan left the building and continued their trek. Up Hope Street, at the end of the block, Yang could make out a Spanish hacienda that marked the beginning of the white section of the city.

A group of half a hundred whites had surrounded it and it was apparent that a good number of Chinese had holed up inside, seeking to use it as a refuge. The idea of a siege appealed to the mob and they began storming the hacienda.

Some of the men were trying to batter the door down with a small tree. Kindling and small piles of wood were being laid around the foundation of the building at various spots as the men prepared to set fires.

The more industrious, perhaps ten or fifteen of them, had scaled the walls of the hacienda and now were astride the roof, working on it was axes handed up to them by the cheering mob.

Yang and Ho Huan watched from a safe distance. Neither spoke.

Finally the men on the roof succeeded in pulling up some of the tiles and breaking through the wood ceiling. They fired down into the building where the Chinese were crowded, and Yang could hear the screams from within.

The door of the hacienda suddenly opened and Chinese ran out into the streets. They were mowed down by the gunfire of the whites who were waiting for them. Other Chinese were set upon by the mob and quickly tied up. The unfortunates were dragged across the street to Goler's blacksmith shop.

One of the mob had thought to bring his children along so they could take part and learn how to deal with Chinamen. One of his brood, an eleven-year-old whose eyes sparkled from the excitement, had busied himself setting up a makeshift gallows, and by the time the men arrived he had five hangman's nooses laced over the beam of the blacksmith shop.

After congratulating his son on his work, the man slipped the rope over the first Chinaman's neck and, to the cheers of the mob, hoisted him in the air. Not content with merely hanging him, some men moved in to kick and beat the man, working quickly so they could inflict pain before he was dead. In a moment the man felt no more and swung limp in the air.

Another Chinese was noosed, but when he was pulled into the air the noose gave under his weight and he fell to the ground. The next rope worked better, and soon he was swinging alongside the man who had preceded him.

Nine Chinese were hung over the beam, and when finally there was room for no more, the men left, dragging the remaining Chinese with them to find a more suitable lynching site.

With the flames of the hacienda casting dancing shadows on his face, Yang turned to Ho Huan. "Quickly, let us leave this hell."

Chapter 37

For a while the actions of the tongs grew less overt. They returned to illicit dealings, sensing that it was best to bide their time until the white man's memory of the Los Angeles affair receded somewhat.

Economic conditions worsened in California in 1873. A declining European market for American farm produce, over-speculation in industry, a minor panic in securities speculation, all were portents of far greater trouble on the horizon. Wealthy men were getting worried. They were starting to lose money on investments. With prosperity still on their palates, failure was an unfamiliar taste.

For the poor, however, existence was much more difficult—unless one could offer special services which, through good times and bad, were always much in demand.

The bedroom was unlike any Ling had ever known. It had been her bedroom for more than a month and she was still stunned by it—stunned by the contrast between her cell in Bartlett's Alley and the golden paradise she now lived in.

It was a large bedroom, fifteen feet by fifteen feet, and carpeted in a most luxuriously thick pile. Three of the four walls were covered with champagne-colored silk. Neither were the walls lacking in ornamentation, for on each of them hung finely drawn scrolls.

The bed was the most magnificent she had ever slept on—befitting the wife of a mandarin. Its base was a single piece of oak carved in the shape of an oyster shell. The mattress was of down, as were the pillows. And both were covered with sheets and casements of black satin, which was changed daily by chambermaids so that she would not be offended by the wrinkles.

The bedroom was brightly lit with five lamps—three on the walls and two sitting on the marble tops of the bedside tables, which had been imported from Italy. The room lacked only cooking facilities. This was no hardship, since servants brought food whenever she required it.

For that matter, virtually anything Ling wanted she was brought, whether it was food, opium—which she used frequently—or cats, like the two snow-white Angoras in the room with her at present.

She sat on the bed, stroking one of the animals, looking at her ruby- and emerald-ringed fingers as they laced through the cat's billowy white hair. Ling was pleased by the display of colors, pleased by the contrast of the sparkling red and green jewels and the ivory fur of the cat.

The animal purred.

Ling purred back.

She felt her head grow light and she remembered that she had smoked a pipe of opium not too long ago. How long ago? She could not remember. It didn't matter.

She looked at the nightstand and saw the gold pipe sitting on the tabletop. Her head spun again for a moment and then it cleared.

Memories of the filth of her bagnio on Bartlett's Alley shot through her mind, and she forced them to flee. In their place came the image of drooling white and yellow faces—curiously somehow all the same—the memory of rough hands on her, of bites and pinches and whippings and beatings.

She reached up for the opium bowl but felt a hand on her own. She looked up to see Ah Toy standing over her.

"You still cannot forget?" Ah Toy said, seeing the tension lines in her friend's face.

Ling nodded.

"Try not to think about it." Ah Toy sat on the edge of the wonderful bed.

Ling looked at the red and white and blue and green silk of the jacket her friend wore. Resplendent, Ah Toy looked like a princess from a parable. Ling reached out and touched the garment. "Nice."

Ah Toy smiled. "Thank you. I have heard you did not eat anything today."

Ling turned on her side, away from Ah Toy's gaze. "Not hungry," she said. The opium made it difficult for her to form complete sentences.

Ah Toy laid on the bed next to her. "Why not?"

Ling giggled. "I think I smoked too much."

"You should not smoke so much opium. There's nothing to be afraid of now."

"Just memories."

Ah Toy stroked Ling's long black hair. "I shall chase them away. They won't return. There are only happy times to come."

"Happy . . ."

Ah Toy leaned forward and gently kissed Ling's neck, letting her tongue taste the sweetness of Ling's skin. "Yes, happy. Only happy times. We're safe now."

"Safe . . ."

Ah Toy's hand slipped to Ling's breast just as the gong began to sound. She drew her hand away and turned at the sound. Ling's eyes fluttered open, the sound piercing through the veil of opium.

"The gong," Ling said.

Ah Toy nodded, sitting up on the bed. The door of the bedroom opened and a middle-aged woman looked inside. "Hurry, you two. He comes, he comes!"

Ling knew what was happening and she fought for control over the opium. She could feel Ah Toy helping her stand up and for a moment she wobbled on her feet.

"Stand by yourself while I get you a cloth."

Ling steadied herself, holding one of the posts on her bed. Then Ah Toy was by her side again and she could feel the damp cloth being swabbed across her face and brow, could feel the sense returning to her head.

Again the gong sounded. Led by Ah Toy, Ling walked from her bedroom down a short corridor and into the large parlor which was the central room of the bordello. The chamber was worthy of the emperor's palace. The walls were covered with silk brought all the way from Beijing. Polished marble covered the floor and an enormous red, black, and white rug covered the marble. Finely sculptured dragons and tigers flanked low lacquered sofas, on one of which Ling now reclined.

All eighteen girls were assembled in the main chamber, awaiting the arrival of the Suey Sing warlord. It was one of a number of bordellos in Chinatown the Suey Sing controlled, along with *Fan-tan* parlors, opium dens, and other illicit operations. The bordellos were highly profitable; each was run by an experienced manager and protected by a permanent guard. Nonetheless, the Suey Sing were wise enough to know the dangers of absentee ownership, and accordingly, once every two or three weeks one of the tong's warlords would make an inspection. For that occasion all of the girls were turned out for review by the warlord, while the bordello's books were turned over to the tong's bookkeeper.

For Ling it was a ritual which helped mark the passage of time, and for that she was grateful. There were few other events in her life that she could regularly depend upon. Rather, everything seemed to blend together, obscuring the weeks, the months, the seasons.

She could still remember when it was not so. She could still recall her childhood, when time was such a clear thing; the summer and the spring, the fall and winter were as different as four strangers. Memories of her father and brothers laboring in the fields, planting, harvesting, setting up storage for the winter—all these things still flickered faintly in her mind.

She tried to think of them less and less lately. To think of them was painful. There were too many questions that needed answers. She had been young when her brothers left for California. She could barely recall what they had looked like, yet she hungered for news of them.

Her father had explained why she had to be sold and she had felt his pain—mistaking the shame for remorse. Ling somehow thought that Yang was more responsible for her slavery than Chin. She could recall how Chin had always been more sympathetic to the pain her feet had suffered from binding. But even that was not something she knew for certain.

What made matters even worse was that she was living in California now—the land they had journeyed to. It was possible they were even in this very city. And yet she was powerless to learn of their whereabouts. Once she had asked a man if he could help her locate her brothers. Outraged, the man complained to the master of the bordello, and Ling was caned for her efforts.

Rather than endure the torture of questions she could not have answered, then, she sought refuge in her relationship with Ah Toy and the relative safety and security of the bordello. It was not so bad, Ling convinced herself. After all, Ah Toy was an enthusiastic and gentle lover. The men she entertained ceased to trouble her. They were nothing more than blurred faces passing before her eyes.

She drank deeply of the lascivious rewards offered to those who did their job well. Ling indulged in opium and hashish and anything else that helped dull her senses. There was safety in that. Anything else had only frustration to offer her.

The door of the main chamber was thrown open. Two Suey Sing highbinders, emerald silk sashes about their heads, entered the room. The master of the bordello moved forward and bowed in greeting. The pair of warriors scanned the room for a moment before they turned back toward the open door.

Ti Ben, one of the two warlords serving under the Grand *Ah ma* of the Suey Sing tong, strode into the room. The bright blue silk tunic he wore said he was not dressed for combat this day; but the scars on his neck and face and the missing finger on his left hand answered that he was prepared if it was necessary.

Following in behind him were two more highbinders—the rear guard of the four warriors assigned to always be with the warlord. The last pair stood guard at the door as the other two searched through the rooms of the house. While the search for assassins took place, the master of the bordello greeted Ti Ben with appropriate deference.

"I am honored to have you grace my house, noble protector."

Ti Ben cast a cold eye on the man. "You lie worse than you flatter, old man. It would please you if we never visited you. Then you could steal from the tong as much as you wished."

"Never! I have never stolen even a—"

Ti Ben silenced him with a single gesture, his eyes taking in the women. "I did not say that you did; only that if the opportunity presented itself . . ." His voice trailed off as he looked at the women. "It is of no consequence. You shall never have that opportunity to end your life."

There was a knock at the door; one of the highbinders

opened it to admit the tong bookkeeper. His arrival, unescorted, symbolized the separate yet equal relationship between the elder scholar and the warlord. Ti Ben's rank was established by virtue of the personal guards who escorted him wherever he ventured. The bookkeeper had no guard, traveled alone. Yet he was privileged to arrive at this appointment after Ti Ben.

The two men bowed to each other. Then, to emphasize his importance, Ti Ben turned to the master of the house and said, "Now let him see your books, weasel."

"Certainly," the master said. "May I offer you some tea or wine while you wait, warlord?"

"Go with the bookkeeper," he snapped, his eyes roaming the room again. "I shall entertain myself."

Bowing again, the master left the room with the bookkeeper. Now the women were alone in the main chamber with only the highbinders. Among themselves, the women tittered. It was customary that Ti Ben would take one of them to bed. After he was finished, each of the other warriors would be allowed to take a woman.

It was something for which the women eagerly competed. For while certainly none of the highbinders was expected to pay for the women's favors, they would still give them a few coins if they proved truly proficient in their profession.

Ti Ben strolled about the room, his walk stiff and militaristic. As he walked past them, the women would flare their hips, smile seductively, pucker their lips with invitation. Seeking to make an impression, one of the women let drop the fabric of her blouse, exposing a dusky nipple to the warlord. Amused for a moment, he kept walking.

He stopped in front of Ling. Ah Toy, standing next to her, stiffened at the attention the warlord was giving to her lover.

"Your name, little flower?"

Ling looked at him, focused on his face. "Ling."

He nodded. "The opium is good?"

She nodded back.

Ti Ben smiled and she returned it.

He touched her hand. "Come with me, little flower."

Ling glanced at Ah Toy, caught the expression of pain on her face, then followed Ti Ben as he led her to the hallway and the bedroom beyond.

Ling lay on the bed, the sticky proof of Ti Ben's manhood drying between her legs. She watched him as he splashed water on the shriveled snake that was his penis. The water fell in droplets from the sac which, moments ago, had crashed against her thighs as he plunged again and again into her.

Pulling on his trousers, Ti Ben caught her staring at him. "It interests you to see a man naked?"

"Not all men," she answered.

He laughed shortly. "The opium has dissipated enough for you to know how to speak to a warlord, I see."

"I speak honestly. I am not interested in seeing most men dress."

"You speak in hopes of squeezing a few more coins from me," he said. Ti Ben reached into a pouch and tossed a handful at her. "Here. You've done well, woman."

Ling swept her hand across the bed, scattering the coins to the floor. She saw Ti Ben's eyes go wide. "I do not need your coins," she said. "I have no need for money!"

Ti Ben pulled his hatchet from the dresser top, raised its blade, and stared at Ling. "Speak quickly, woman, and convince me that you were honest in what you said. Convince me that you did not speak to get those coins."

Ling laughed. "What do I need your money for? Will I spend it on vegetables in the marketplace, or buy jade in a shop, or passage back to China on a ship? I have no need of your money, warlord, because I have nothing to buy with it."

He lowered his hatchet a degree. "The other women would scratch your eyes out for those coins."

"That is because their vision is short. They will send someone to buy them a dress or jewelry. Those things matter little to me. What matters is that I can speak with honesty. You see, warlord, that is all I have left."

Ti Ben lowered his hatchet as Ling said, "So you can believe me when I told you I am not interested in looking at most men."

"Why aren't you?"

"Because most of them look the same and . . ."

"And?"

"Another reason," she said.

"What reason?"

Ling averted her eyes.

"What reason?"

"I have said more than I wanted to."

He took a step forward, his voice firm. "Tell me the other reason."

She looked at him. "I am a lover of women."

He cocked his head at her, one of his eyes narrowing. "The woman-lover." He nodded. "I have heard of you."

For a moment a look of surprise bloomed on her face. It was a strange feeling and she realized it was one of pride. If she could still feel that, Ling thought, then she was still alive. If, even in this life of degradation and hopelessness, she could gain recognition, then perhaps there was still a chance she could . . . what? Escape? Survive? Know happiness? Happiness. It was not truly happiness she had with Ah Toy. It was an existence, preferable to the one she had known in the bagnio. But there was a price to be paid for it. Shame, and humiliation, and the only way payment could be avoided was through the deadening of her mind.

She didn't understand exactly what the pride she had felt at the warlord's remark had meant. But she knew it meant she still had hope and she knew, somehow, that that hope was to be found in him.

Ling looked deep into his eyes and there she saw that her words had touched something, a gentleness within himself that Ti Ben had all but forgotten ever existed. She smiled as the warlord placed his hatchet back on the dresser and reached out to touch her. His touch was warm this time, his lips soft, his lovemaking less rushed.

For a moment she wondered if he felt some small feeling for her or if it was only curiosity, his desire to see if he could make such a woman feel. Either way, Ling thought, it did not matter. All that mattered was that Ti Ben, warlord of the Suey Sing, was interested in her. For now, that was enough.

Chapter 38

In San Francisco the morning after the Los Angeles Massacre Chin stood in the large two-story foyer just outside the chamber of the Meeting Hall of the Middle Kingdom. The delegates milled about in groups of three and four, their voices lowered with respect and filled with concern.

The news had reached San Francisco that morning by telegraph. The Chinese soon learned the gruesome facts and the emergency meeting was hastily called.

Standing with Chin were Shao Kow and Tai Pien. Tai Pien, through merits he had proved he possessed in recent months, had been nominated and accepted as a delegate to the Kong Chow Company.

Chin glanced at Tai Pien's hard, set features and decided that the man was also well suited for his new position as chief if the Chinese Protective Police. He still served Chin as head of Chin's gambling interests. The irony was not lost on Chin. But Tai Pien's appointment as head of Little China's private militia gave even more security to Chin's own operations.

As Tai Pien spoke casually with another delegate, Chin took in more of the man's features. There was something, he thought, that Tai Pien had in common with the white policemen he had known—a fierceness, a certain indefinable strength—and he realized that in some ways all policemen were brothers. It was something that transcended the distinction of skin color.

Tai Pien had been exhilarated when he had heard the news of the resolution Chin had placed before the General Assembly of the Six Companies. More than anything else, Tai Pien had seen the Chinese Protective Police as a force to reckon with the tongs, a force which could once again bring law and order to the quarter. And this time, he had thought with pride, it would be a law and order brought about by Chinese, not bought from white vigilantes.

All these things Chin had seen in the man's face on the day he had accepted the appointment as head of the Protective Police. Tai Pien had taken to his job with a zeal that was still apparent today, as he stood in the Meeting Hall of the Middle Kingdom with Chin.

Chin turned to look at Shao Kow, on his other side. Strange, he thought, that it was the usually passive Shao Kow who had finally convinced him that force was the answer to dealing with the tongs. Chin wondered if he would have listened if the argument had come from Tai Pien. He remembered the discussion well.

It had been the night after he had brought two businessmen to observe a Chinese Protective Police raid. Donations were what kept the Chinese police force's coffers filled, and periodically they would let influential merchants observe their maneuvers. On this particular night Chin watched as Tai

304

Pien's militia swept down on a band of Kwong Dock high-binders they learned would be robbing a warehouse.

Tai Pien's men had moved efficiently, beating many of the highbinders bloody before carting them out of town. The businessmen had been impressed and Chin had obtained a sizable donation for the Protective Police.

But later the next day he had spoken morosely with Shao Kow. He confessed the burden of responsibility he felt and Shao Kow was wise enough to realize it was partially the loss of the white woman that weighed on Chin. Chin spoke of the letters he had written to her, all unanswered, of the warnings of her physician not to attempt to visit her.

Over tea, he confessed to Shao Kow that it was more than Rebecca Ashley that troubled him. He feared that the distinction between himself and the tongs was blurring. Never could he have imagined himself pontificating to businessmen about the virtues of club-wielding Protective Police regulars, supervising the apprehension of a band of villains as if he himself was a warlord.

It was in that morning of doubt that Shao Kow served as the vessel bearing the words Chin needed to hear—the words he knew himself, but had to hear another speak. Chin had accepted the mantle of leadership, Shao Kow told him. In so doing he had pledged to lead his people through both prosperity and adversity, through both peace and war.

The people drew their strength in part from him, Shao Kow explained. And because they did his resolve he must be firm, his determination unquestionable.

With resignation and relief, mixed with the slightest tincture of remorse, Chin had nodded and poured himself another cup of tea.

Now, standing in the foyer of the Meeting Hall of the Middle Kingdom, Chin realized how little he and the Chinese Protective Police had actually accomplished. He and Tai Pien had felt pride at the drop in the crime rate in the quarter. They had felt that some progress against the tongs was being made. But now, with the news of the Los Angeles Massacre, Chin realized just how pervasive a force the tongs really were. The actions of two warring tongs in a city hundreds of miles to the north could fan the flames of anti-Chinese sentiment throughout California. For the first time, he fully understood what the tongs were, and what it was that he had to do.

"What was the final count?" Shao Kow asked.

Tai Pien said, "It depends on whom you believe. The San Francisco papers say thirty-five Chinese killed. The Los Angeles accounts put the figure closer to twenty-five." He shook his head. "In either event, scores were seriously injured."

Chin rustled the pages of the special edition of the *Golden Hills*. A hundred advance copies had been delivered to each of the Company houses.

"It would appear that the Los Angeles newspapers' estimates are closer," Chin said. "The *Golden Hills* claims twenty-three Chinese are dead."

Communication between San Francisco and Los Angeles was sometimes less than accurate. But the Los Angeles chapters of the Six Companies tried to keep their brothers to the north advised of events unfolding there. One of the bits of information that was transmitted concerned the assassination which had triggered the tong war. It was reported, secondhand, that the murderer of Bei Ting Hwa had been a hulking monster of a highbinder who bore a horrible scar on the left side of his face.

This information was not lost on Chin.

The double doors opened and the sergeant at arms bid the delegates enter the hall.

Nang Lo, the elder of the Hop Wo Company, spoke from the floor with an anger that was felt by every man in the assembly.

"And it is my feeling, cousins, that our formal protest to the governor must be worded in no uncertain terms, in language that clearly expresses our rage. We must demand an inquiry into this crime against our people."

There was hearty applause from the delegates.

"And so," Nang Lo concluded, "I suggest we appoint a special committee to work on that project."

The committee was formed in a matter of moments.

Lu Tsai of the Yun Wo Company pounded his gavel on the director's podium. "The floor is open for discussion of how to prevent the massacre which happened in Los Angeles from repeating itself here."

Demands for recognition burst forth from several delegates, but Lu Tsai had made up his mind who he would call upon before he had even opened the discussion.

"The directors recognize Chin Wong, noble delegate of the Kong Chow Company, and solicit his opinion in this matter."

306

The great chamber fell silent as Chin rose to speak. He spent a moment looking at the other delegates. Then he began.

"Cousins, today is a day of mourning for us all. Many of our cousins have died in that city to the south. While we mourn for them, it is only right and wise that we concern ourselves with combating a similar occurrence here in San Francisco."

Chin listened to his words echoing in the meeting hall and he prayed that the gods were watching over him, guiding him, his words and thoughts.

"Although all the details are not yet known, I have read enough to understand what happened in Los Angeles, and what I understand is that the whites were not to blame."

Gasps sounded throughout the assembly and several of the delegates took to their feet in angry protest.

"Here me out," Chin said. "The white men pulled the trigger." He silenced the delegates with his hands. "The white men tightened the noose about our people's necks. But it was yellow men, our own cousins, who provided the gun and fashioned that rope."

"No, no!" the cries sounded.

"What are you saying?" another delegate called.

Chin turned toward the question. "I am saying that it was our people who provoked the incident." He nodded. "Granted, the whites wanted an excuse; but we did not fail them. As with every ill that has befallen our people in the recent years, the tongs are responsible."

The delegates sat listening, their eyes following him as he walked up the aisle.

"The tongs, cousins; they are like a cancer which we can barely contain. And like a cancer they erupt in places where we least expect them."

He turned to look at the delegates. "The whites we can deal with. Through the work of Tai Pien and the Chinese Protective Police, we have set up networks of officers who can warn our people when gangs of white hoodlums approach. But we cannot endure with the menace of the tongs in our midst—particularly when they themselves antagonize the whites."

He stopped pacing now that he had reached the front of the auditorium. "So what is our action to be? I tell you, cousins, it can no longer be one of defense. It can no longer be one of containment."

He shook his head. "You all know me. I am a man of peace. I have stood before you many times and pleaded for peace. But I do not think it can be any longer. I do not think the tongs have peace in them. No," he said, "I do not think we can settle for defense any longer."

Chin spoke with deliberation. "We must turn our Chinese Protective Police into an army. We must dedicate more money to it. We must look toward moving against the tongs. We must begin to think of an offensive; for if we do not, if we remain complacent, then the tongs shall either move against us or cause the whites to be further drawn into our affairs so that the hoodlums of both colors are brought down on us. We shall be caught in their midst.

"We must," he said, "begin to think of war."

On the long wall that ran behind Chin's desk in his office on California Street there was a large map. It indicated each street and alleyway in Chinatown. On the map there were clusters of pins, red and blue. The red pins noted Chin's various businesses—laundry houses, import shops, gambling dens, opium parlors.

It was the blue pins that Chin was interested in this afternoon, for Tai Pien was in the office with him. Each blue pin represented a two-man Chinese Protective Police team. There were twenty-six such teams in the quarter and they effectively patrolled the area, moving into strike positions as quickly as needed.

"Four Chee Tung highbinders were apprehended here," Tai Pien said, tapping the map, "last night when they tried to break into a jewelry store."

Chin nodded. "Good." He turned to look at the chief of the Chinese Protective Police. "Have you learned anything about the assassination last week?"

Tai Pien frowned. "We're certain that it was the Suey Sing. No proof, of course, but the method of the killing was a clear signature."

"Are you worried about a war here between the Suey Sing and the Kwong Dock?"

"No," Tai Pien said. "Not after what happened last night in Los Angeles. They'll cool down for a while." He looked at Chin. "It would be a good time to mount the offensive you spoke of."

Chin frowned. "Words only, I'm afraid. Something to keep the juices and donations flowing."

"Perhaps we could . . ."

"With seventy-five regulars? How far do you think your men would get against a hundred Suey Sing warriors and a hundred and fifty Kwong Dock highbinders and eighty Hep Sun hatchetmen—all of whom have been trained in battle for many years?"

Tai Pien sat on the edge of Chin's desk.

"Besides," Chin continued, "I am not certain if the assembly would sanction such an action anyway. They are reluctant, as I once was, to directly confront the tongs, to take the offense."

"They must be convinced that this is the only way," Tai Pien said. "The tiger is already at the gate."

"I will do what I can to convince them. And in the meantime you must redouble your efforts to build our forces. We must have a strong army if what you wish for is to come to pass."

Chapter 39

Ah Toy let the tips of her lacquered fingernails run lightly across the nape of Ling's neck. She smiled, watching Ling's puffed lips form a red *O* as a moan of pleasure escaped from deep in her throat.

She pressed herself closer, bringing her thigh against Ling's, the satin sheets covering the bed cool and slick beneath her. She looked into Ling's eyes; the lids drooped lazily in opium stupor.

Ah Toy's voice was a sweet whisper. "Do you like it when I make love to you, Ling?"

Ling's eyelids lowered and did not open as she said, "Yes . . . yes . . ."

Now her tongue expertly glided along Ling's neck, drawing fresh groans of excitement from her. Ling writhed, feeling the moist snake that slithered along her skin.

Ah Toy moved her mouth to Ling's ear and paused there, her hands stroking where her tongue had just been, feeling the rumble of mounting anticipation as Ling purred.

"Soon," Ah Toy said, "soon my tongue will travel where you crave its presence."

"Mmmmmmmmm . . ."

"Show me," Ah Toy said, "show me where."

"Ohhhh . . ."

"Show me . . ."

Ling moved her own hand down over her hips, across the flat plain of her belly and brought it to her pleasure mound. She stiffened as her hand brushed against her own hot vulva.

At that moment Ah Toy's tongue gnashed into her ear. Ah Toy's hands began massaging Ling's breasts, pulling, tugging gently at her nipples. "Touch yourself," Ah Toy urged. "Please, Ling," she whispered in her ear, "please, my precious . . ."

Her mind giddy from the combination of opium and the attentions Ah Toy lavished on her, Ling gave in once again and began massaging herself, moving her fingers up and down, from side to side, in circles, her legs parting to her own ministrations.

And then, somehow, her pajama bottoms were off her and her hands were again moving on her own body, twitching, flicking at herself, spreading so she could gain access to her most private treasures.

She could feel soft teeth bite into her hand now and she looked down to see Ah Toy's head below her, looked down to see Ah Toy's womanhood exposed to her, close enough for her to bathe in the perfumed fragrance that her friend had applied to her black-tufted love hair.

Ling's legs rolled outward as she felt her lover's tongue gently tease across her unhooded passion. Her hips began to quiver, begging for more attention. But Ah Toy was withholding it.

"Please," Ling begged, "please, Ah Toy . . ."

"No."

"Please; I can't stand it! *Please*! I'll do anything, anything you ask!"

Softly, Ah Toy said, "Do me."

Driven wild beyond control, Ling's mouth sought her lover's mound. She began greedily licking at the juices and throbbing womanhood that waited there for her and in a moment, true to her word, Ah Toy began to return the ecstasy.

And now, both women's hips were jerking spasmodically, undulating out of control, their legs thrashing, their heads bobbing, devouring, consuming like two wild animals. At last

310

they exploded with a frenzy and passion that was so shattering in its intensity that both women cried out, screaming, tears flowing, nails scratching, teeth biting from the power of their mutual climax.

Then, spent, they collapsed around each other, their hearts pounding against each other's bodies, their souls one with each other.

On the other side of the window that ran along the length of the special room in the bordello, the eight men felt the release and broke into speech for the first time since Ah Toy had entered the chamber half an hour earlier.

Their trousers tight from the almost unbearable excitement of the show, they eagerly went out into the main parlor of the whorehouse to select a prostitute whom they could finish with. Each man felt satisfied that the fifty dollars he had paid to be a part of the audience had been money well spent.

James Riley was one of the eight men who had watched Ling and Ah Toy, and he had enjoyed the experience immensely. He had equally enjoyed the fact that he was capable of paying fifty dollars for the privilege.

He left the house an hour later, having satisfied himself with one of the women. Outside, O'Malley was waiting for him.

"What are you doing out here?" Riley asked. "I looked all over that whorehouse for you."

O'Malley exhaled, his breath frosty in the night air. "Too warm in there. I wanted some air."

As the two men walked along the street, Riley said, "You could have told someone you were leaving."

"Sorry."

They rounded Kearney Street, heading out of Little China.

"Weren't those little Chinks something?" Riley said, a leer coming to his face.

"Aye."

"Did you see them lickin' at each other?"

"Aye," O'Malley repeated.

Riley laughed. "Looked like they were about to go crazy." He turned slightly to look at O'Malley, then he stopped laughing. "What's wrong, Brian?"

"Nothing."

"Come on, boyo; what is it?"

"Nothing, James."

Riley looked skyward, whistling loudly. "Whoo boy! When

you start calling me James then I *know* there's something wrong. Now what is it?"

O'Malley cracked a smile for a moment, then turned slightly toward Riley as they walked along. "I'm worried," he admitted.

"You know, I've never known you when you weren't worried about something."

"*You* asked me what was bothering me."

"All right, what is it this week?"

"It's the whole setup. It's going too fast."

"That should only be our biggest problem."

"Our biggest problem," O'Malley said, "is going to be controlling ten thousand unemployed thugs if you ever get them too worked up with those speeches."

"I know how to handle them, Brian. It's taken us a long time to mold them into a strong group. Now the word's getting around to the people who matter. With the election coming up they'll be a big bloc of voters some politician's going to want, and he'll have to come to us if he wants 'em."

O'Malley shook his head. "They won't be worth a nickel if they ever get out of hand and start a riot. Look what happened down in Los Angeles."

"That was Los Angeles. And besides, the Chinks had it coming. Shot a businessman, I read."

"I tell you, Jamie, I don't like it. McNamara and Shaughnessy are only interested in running wild. I don't think they give a damn about—"

"They're bringing in the take every week, just like clockwork. They'll do what I tell them."

O'Malley was silent for a moment, then he said, "I hope they aren't more powerful than you think they are."

Riley looked at him, deadly serious. "They take their orders from me. They always have and they always will."

The two men crossed Pine Street and entered the white section of the city.

O'Malley said, "Harcourt sent a messenger by this afternoon."

Riley turned and grabbed him by the jacket. *"What?"*

"I said Harcourt sent a messenger—"

"I heard what you said! Why didn't you tell me earlier?"

"Because I like to keep secrets."

Riley started laughing. "Well, if that don't beat all! The future mayor of San Francisco sent a messenger to see me." He returned his gaze to O'Malley. "What did he say?"

"He wants to meet with you tomorrow, at noon."

Riley let out a yelp of excitement. "I knew it! I knew damned well it would work." Riley broke out in a jig, bursting with glee. He slapped playfully at O'Malley and O'Malley began laughing, sharing his enthusiasm.

"You see, Brian? It's working out just the way I said it would!"

"Yeah, sure," O'Malley said. "Exactly the way you said it would."

Riley looked at him. "I swear, Brian, if an angel descended from the heavens and told you that you were going to sit at the Lord's right hand when you leave this world you'd still be down in the mouth."

"I'm just worried—"

"Well, *don't* worry," Riley said, cutting him off. "This isn't a night for worrying. The news is too good."

But Riley could see that his words weren't having any effect. He had come to depend on O'Malley over the years, to respect his judgment on certain things. O'Malley was a conservative man, and that was why Riley had depended on him, knowing that his own nature was not so disposed.

If O'Malley was truly worried, he thought, then maybe there was something to be concerned about.

"All right," he said, wrapping an arm around him as they walked up the street, "all right, I'll tell you what, Brian. I'll have a meeting with Shaughnessy and McNamara tomorrow. We'll talk the whole thing out. That satisfy you?"

"It'd make me rest easier knowing that everything is really under control."

"Then it's a meeting we'll have," Riley said. "Should have one anyway. Important that we talk to those two more often—particularly with us moving along as fast as we are now."

"It's just that everything's getting so big, Jamie."

"I know. But that's the only way we'll make it." The more he thought about it, the more he realized that O'Malley had a point. "You're right, Brian. We should keep a little tighter rein on them, though—just for safety's sake. Can't let them forget who's the boss around here."

Andrew Harcourt didn't like James Riley. He didn't like what he had heard about him and now that he was sitting across from Riley's desk he was certain that he didn't like the man.

There was an odor of the commoner about Riley and, al-though Harcourt reflected that that was probably what had endeared Riley to the unemployed and the ordinary laborers of the city, the candidate for mayor of San Francisco found it repulsive to have to deal with such a man.

None of this was apparent in anything Harcourt said or did. He sat in the straight-backed chair, his black pin-striped suit giving him a dignified air. A great gold chain, with a fob, extended across his vest, adding to the image of respectabil-ity. Muttonchop whiskers flanked the politician's face, meet-ing the edge of the black and gray mustache that stretched across his upper lip.

Harcourt smiled. "Nice office you have here, Riley."

Riley rocked back in his chair. "I done all right for a simple man."

"Simple, indeed." Harcourt laughed. "You seem to have at-tracted a large number of followers at those speeches you give."

"Probably because I'm so simple," Riley said, as though he had read Harcourt's mind.

Instantly, the politician's appraisal of the Irishman changed. Riley had been reading right through the facade.

"You're very perceptive, Mr. Riley."

"A compliment, coming from you, Mr. Harcourt. Now if you could tell me why you've honored me with a visit."

"I intend to win this election, Mr. Riley."

Riley sat, unmoving.

"That will happen," Harcourt said, "regardless of anything. Nothing can change that." He waved his hand casually. "Oh, I know there's been a lot of talk about James Otis running strong. But I'll beat him when the time comes."

"Go on."

"I'll come straight to the point, Mr. Riley. What concerns me is how much it's going to cost me to win this election—both in time and money." Harcourt smiled. "I've got a pretty large following, you know."

"I know."

"Well, I can go out there and start talking on every street corner in San Francisco and spend a lot of money plastering posters all over the city and work like the devil at this. Or," he said, "I can win this election without too much damned effort and money. I'd prefer to do it that way."

"And?"

"Well, sir, it must be fairly obvious to you that the reason

I came here today was to ask for the support of you and your followers." Harcourt lowered his voice a degree. "If you endorse me, combined with the supporters I already have, I'll sweep into office."

"Keep talking."

"That's it," Harcourt said.

"What's the offer?"

Harcourt raised an eyebrow. "Offer?"

Riley smiled, humoring the man. "Yeah, the offer. What have you got to offer me in exchange for my endorsement?"

The man's cheeks puffed out in surprise. "Do you mean, sir, that you are soliciting a bribe for your endorsement? Are you attempting to *sell* your support?"

Riley closed his eyes. "Enough, enough. Let's get serious."

"I can't believe what I'm hearing, Mr. Riley. You claim to represent the interests of the common worker and the unemployed, and at the same time you are trying to sell your approval to the highest bidder? The mere fact that I will fairly and justly represent the unemployed and the laborers should be enough to—"

Riley rocked forward in his chair, placed his hands on the table, and looked squarely into Harcourt's face. "Look, will you please stop all this crap before I have to call my darkies up here to shovel the shit off the floor?"

An expression of stunned surprise came over Harcourt's face. "I've misjudged you, Riley."

"No, you underestimated me. Now look, Harcourt, you wouldn't come into a stinking stable and see a lowly redneck like me unless you needed my help, so you can forget all that stuff about winning the election with me or without me. You need me, right?"

Harcourt weighed, judged, decided. Finally, he said, "Yes; yes, you're right."

"That's better." Riley smiled. "To tell you the truth, I need you, too." He laughed. "There, see? It didn't bother me that much to admit it to you."

"All right, Riley, what do you want?"

Riley leveled his gaze at Harcourt and said, "I want to be chief of police."

"Jesus," Harcourt said, exhaling a great gasp of air. He drew in again, regaining his composure. "You don't mince words, do you man?"

"I'm not a politician. I fire straight from the hip. You

asked me a question, I answered it. Now I'll ask you one: do we have a deal?"

Harcourt rose, looked at James Riley, and said, "We have a deal."

Chapter 40

Yang stood before the steel door of the large brick building in Spofford Alley. As he waited for someone to answer his knock he looked up and down the alley. He wasn't happy to be in San Francisco.

"It's cold here," he said to Ho Huan.

"We are accustomed to the warmth of Los Angeles. But you once lived here."

"Briefly."

A small viewing window in the door slid open and a pair of deep-set eyes stared out at them. "What is your business?"

"The red hair of the eagle," Yang said.

"Who sent you?"

"I travel by night like the tiger."

The window slid closed and Yang listened to the bolts being loosened behind the portal. In a moment it swung inward and a man as wide as the doorway stood before them.

"Yang Wong and Ho Huan," Yang said.

The man nodded and moved aside. They entered the house of the Kwong Dock tong. As the door closed behind them Yang looked about. He looked at the high ceiling of the foyer they stood in, the paneling on the walls. Instead of windows there were narrow viewing slits in the walls, which were nineteen inches thick. Clearly, Yang thought, this house was a fortress. He would learn that it was large enough to house all hundred and fifty of the Kwong Dock highbinders and that ample stores of food and water were kept on hand in case of a prolonged siege.

Yang turned to the man. "We are from Los Angeles."

Again the man nodded. "You are not the first," he said, leading them across the foyer toward a door. "They began arriving weeks ago."

"We made our way slowly so as to ensure that we would arrive."

"A wise path," the man replied. He opened the door and walked into the waiting room, Yang and Ho Huan following. It was a much smaller room than the foyer, the ceiling not as high. Like the foyer, there were no windows in this room. Four chairs, a desk, and a pair of lamps were the only furnishings.

"Wait here," the man said, then left.

Ho Huan paced the room for a moment. Finally, he said, "What do you suppose will become of us?"

"We'll have to wait and see."

"Do you think they will look harshly on our leaving Los Angeles?"

"I doubt it. Evidently we are not the first."

"Still," Ho Huan said, "perhaps we should have remained there. Perhaps they will feel that . . ."

The answer to Ho Huan's question came as the door opened and Po Dung walked into the room. After they had exchanged greetings, Po Dung said, "It is good to see you two again. I was worried that you had met harm in the riots."

"The gods were with us," Yang said.

"Indeed." Po Dung sat and bid the two novices do the same. When the three were settled, Po Dung said, "Tell me of your escape."

"There is not much to tell," Yang said. "After we had repulsed the whites we assumed, as did everyone, that the matter was over."

Ho Huan said, "We were having victory dinner in a restaurant when the whites burst in on us."

"You were fortunate that you did not meet your death in that restaurant."

"Yang dealt with attacker after attacker."

"There were not that many of them," Yang said.

Po Dung nodded. "How did you escape?"

"Yang threw a lamp at a window and the restaurant burst into flames. We made our way out after the whites fled."

"And straight out of town?"

Ho Huan nodded.

"We saw much death," Yang said. "The whites had gone mad."

"We lost many brothers that night," Po Dung said. "You were wise to flee, rather than to wait in the area just outside the city."

"What will happen to the Los Angeles chapter?"

"It is in limbo for the time being. Perhaps it shall reband eventually. But for now it is far too dangerous to risk organized activities down there. The climate is not right."

"What will become of us?" Ho Huan asked.

Po Dung turned to look at him. "You will remain here, in San Francisco. You will be members of the San Francisco chapter of the Kwong Dock tong."

Ho Huan looked to Yang. "Members?" He looked back to Po Dung, who now stood.

"Yes." The swordsman smiled. "Your probationary period is over. The council here feels that you both performed admirably—both in the matter of Bei Ting and in the battle against the Suey Sing."

Po Dung stood before them. "You are both to be admitted to the tong, as highbinders, on the morrow."

Yang and Ho Huan both felt their bodies throb with excitement, for the announcement was something neither of them had expected.

"Are we worthy of this honor?" Ho Huan asked, showing the proper humility.

Po Dung said, "It is the tong's decision that you both are. Accept the honor with grace."

Both men bowed their heads for a moment, symbolizing their humble acceptance. When they looked up again Po Dung's back was to them.

"You must both steel yourselves against the ordeal that is yet to come," the warlord said. He turned back to face them. "I pray, for both of your sakes, that you have each learned well the secret chants and other instructions you studied while novices."

Both men nodded, hoping along with Po Dung that they had mastered their lessons.

"Your conduct during the rites," he continued, "must be one of complete respect and reverence for those who conduct you on the passage." The swordsman's voice all but trembled as he spoke. "These men who see you through the rites of passage are to be obeyed to the letter. Whatever they ask you to do you are to do. There can be no refusal, not even the hint of hesitation, once you enter the Hall of Admission.

"If there is any reluctance detected, then you shall forfeit entrance to the tong and leave, forever disgraced. Do you understand all these things?"

Yang and Ho Huan nodded solemnly.

"Do not speak during the entire ritual unless you are instructed to by the brothers of the tong. Do not ask any questions, do not utter so much as a sound."

Po Dung strode about the room, speaking as he did. "You will be asked to perform certain acts. Your ability to succeed will weigh heavily in your ultimate acceptance and status in the tong. You will face challenges during the ritual. Face them boldly and without fear."

Po Dung paused, then said, "I have confidence in both of you. I am close to you in this hour and I shall be close to you tomorrow. We are of the same chapter and I know you will honorably reflect the training you received in months past."

The swordsman's voice was no longer that of an instructor, but that of a friend, a mentor. "You have performed well in the past and it has pleased me to speak of your merits to this chapter's council. I know that you will distinguish yourselves as much in the ritual of initiation as you have in the battlefield against our enemies.

"Proceed with the courage and bravery that I know is in your hearts and by the time the moon is high tomorrow night I will welcome you as full brothers of the tong."

It was difficult for Yang to sleep that night. For many hours he tossed and turned in his bunk, his mind filled with thoughts of the day to come. He was proud that he had achieved distinction among his fellow novices, and prouder still that he was being admitted to the tong as Po Dung's prized protégé.

It was what he had worked and trained and labored for. And it was not just physical labor, he admitted to himself. There was a great deal of mental exercise involved as well. He had had to study chants and ritual induction procedures and the history of the tong.

He knew that much lay before him in the day to come. Having arrived at this point was a great accomplishment, but the next day would prove a test of all that he had accumulated so far. It would test his strength and his will and his determination to become a member of the Kwong Dock tong.

He had every confidence that he would emerge from the initiation ritual a full member, with the privileges and honors due such a man.

At the first light of dawn three highbinders of the Kwong Dock tong whom Yang had never seen before appeared at his bedside and pulled him rudely from it. Chasing sleep from his head, Yang quickly donned the trousers and jacket of the Manchu dynasty—these had been provided for him for the ritual.

Having fortified himself the night before, on Po Dung's advice, he hardly missed the morning meal. With great and deliberate speed he was rushed down the hallways and corridors of the Kwong Dock house until at last he stood before a black door.

It was at this point that a scarlet blindfold was fixed over his eyes. Yang allowed this, as he had been instructed to allow all things, without the slightest resistance. As the light was cut off, as Yang stood motionless, he was suddenly struck by his vulnerability. In response, the muscles of his stomach tightened, as if anticipating a blow, a test.

None came.

Instead, there was a faint whisper in the air, like the soft beating of a robin's wings. He strained to hear it, at first thinking that perhaps he had imagined it. It was quiet for a moment, but then it came again—clearly the sound of two men speaking. In front of him? Behind him? By his side, he decided—to his left. He listened.

It was quiet again, but just for a moment. Whispers again—off to the right, this time, and behind him. He felt his head spinning, his ears straining first in one direction and then in the other to hear the sounds. He felt his body sway slightly to the sounds and he checked himself.

Suddenly there was a burst of loud clapping coming from all sides. But it was short-lived and, having succeeded in startling him, the clappers quickly fell silent. In its place was the sound of a door being opened, and he remembered the black portal he had been standing in front of.

A voice, deep and low, said, "Enter, novice, and begin the sacred Ritual of Admittance."

With a confidence that was born of his allegiance to the Kwong Dock tong, Yang stepped forward and entered the Hall of Admission.

Yang's ears picked up the sound of the door closing behind him. It was an airless, soundless vacuum of a room that he was in now. The only sensation he felt was one of engulfing warmth. He luxuriated in it for a moment. Then the spell was broken and he felt hands about his face.

The blindfold was removed and Yang blinked. It was a large room, the ceiling rising up twenty feet. The walls were all black, adding to the feeling that he was in a cave. A few torches set on the walls were the only source of illumination. Four men were in the room with him.

Each of the men shimmered with reflections of the flames, their bodies glistening with oil. They wore nothing but loin-cloths and a red sash about their heads.

Two of the men moved forward and raised Yang's arms out to the side. He stood, his arms outstretched, his legs spread, waiting, submissive.

The other two men moved in and began removing the garments he wore, the garments of the Manchu. In a moment he stood naked in the chamber, his eyes staring straight ahead.

One of the men began undoing his queue, and after it was unplaited it was combed out. Another one of the attendants brought the clothes of the rite and Yang was dressed in them.

He stood, now wearing the costume of the Ming dynasty, a five-colored outfit. Wrapped about his waist was a wide white girdle. The man who had unplaited his queue fastened a red cloth about Yang's head—the distinguishing mark of the T'ai T'sing rebels of the Great Chinese Rebellion.

After all these ministrations had been completed, the attendants took him by the arms and moved him forward to the next portal. On the next door he rapped—once, three times, once, then once again.

The door swung open and Yang passed into the Chamber of the Gauntlet.

It was much smaller than the room he had just come from, narrow, and dimly lit. As in the other chamber, the walls were blackened and the air was warm and musty.

The *sing fung*—the introducer—stepped out of the shadows, looked at Yang for a moment, and then turned his back on him.

"This man," the *sing fung* began, "comes to this place to begin the Ritual of Admission. He willingly runs the Gauntlet of Purification."

Yang listened to the *sing fung*'s voice. It was almost a song, the words a chant. He strained in the soft light, trying to see who the introducer was speaking to. He could make out three, perhaps four, faces in the room, but he felt there were more.

"All who have claim for grievance against this man take it now, while he is in submission, and forever grant him pardon when he leaves this chamber."

The *sing fung* turned back to face Yang and motioned for

321

him to move forward. As Yang did he looked down and saw the gauntlet in front of him. It was a low tunnel, running fifteen feet up the center of the room, formed by a fixed arch of forty swords in a row. The blades of the swords pointed downward, like a great dragon's teeth, so that a man would have to crawl through the tunnel they formed on his belly.

The *sing fung* touched Yang's shoulder and Yang dropped first to his knees and then to his stomach. He bent his head and began crawling, entering the gauntlet.

Yang had not crawled five feet under the swords when he felt a wooden club strike down hard on the back of his leg.

"He has too much pride!" the man who struck him called out.

Another yelled, "Let him learn humility!" and brought a club down on Yang's arm.

Yang blanked his mind against the pain and crawled, concentrating on finishing the gauntlet.

"He enjoys the fame that slaying Bei Ting brought him." The speaker rammed a club into Yang's rib cage. "Learn to bring praise to the tong, not to yourself, novice!"

Still he crawled along, knowing that the razor-sharp points of the swords were just above his head and that the slightest jerk or reaction to the beating would mean a slash on his body or neck.

At last he came to the final sword and pulled himself out from the gauntlet. He lay on the ground, passive, until the *sing fung* bid him rise.

The *sing fung* spoke to Yang and to those brothers of the tong in the room who had wanted to be present for the purification.

"This man is forever expiated of offenses against any man in this tong. You are pure to us all. Is this not true, brothers?"

From behind him, Yang heard the voices of agreement from those who had gathered for the gauntlet.

The introducer pointed to the right. "Proceed."

Yang walked forward and passed through the next portal. The huge chamber he came into was ablaze with light; the walls were covered with red-dyed silks. In the far corner of the room was an eight-foot-tall statue of Kwan Kung. The god of war stared stonily over the proceedings. A *mon war* crackled with offerings that had been made to it before Yang's arrival.

In the center of the room, on a raised platform, sat Hung Ma Kung, the Grand *Ah ma* of the Kwong Dock Tong. He sat on a lacquered throne, clothed as a god, with emerald and diamond rings on every one of his fingers. The Grand Master, whom Yang had never seen before, looked the part of a ruler.

Though Hung Ma Kung was rumored to be near seventy, his face was smooth and hairless except for his unbraided queue. Not a wrinkle, not a line creased his noble visage. The only mark to be seen on his body was a single scar which began where the right side of his jaw met his neck. This scar continued down to his collarbone and was the badge of a distant battle.

Yang looked at the brilliant colors of the *Ah ma*'s Ming dynasty robes, the gilt threads shimmering in the light of the torches. The *Ah ma*'s eyes stared at him as though they were two bits of smoldering coal.

On either side of the *Ah ma* stood three men, stripped to the waist, whose muscles rivaled those of Yang himself. These officers each carried a spear, and a sword was to be seen sheathed in scabbards that rode both of their hips.

Seated along the side of the chamber were eighty-nine highbinders of the Kwong Dock tong. They waited in silence as the novice approached the Grand *Ah ma*.

Yang stopped in front of the throne and bowed his head. One of the officers stepped in front of Yang, holding a cup of wine in his hand. The man held Yang's hand over the cup.

A second officer came forward and took hold of Yang's finger. With a single motion the man pierced Yang's finger with a silver needle. Yang stood, unflinching, as his finger began to bleed, the drops falling into the cup of wine.

The man with the cup retreated and passed it to the first of the hatchetmen, who took a small sip and passed it to the man to his right. Each member of the tong drank from the cup, thus binding themselves in blood to their new brother.

During this time, the *Ah ma* recited the twenty-one sacred regulations of the tong.

". . . bound to do everything in your power to take the life of any man who has taken the life of one of your brothers. You shall hold secret all signs, passwords, and ceremonies of the tong. You shall owe your ultimate allegiance to the Kwong Dock tong; this above all others—whether they be family, friend, or state. You shall follow, without question, the orders of your superiors. You shall . . ."

His head bowed in submission, Yang let the words wash over him, penetrate to the innermost recesses of his mind. He entered a dreamlike state in which the words were, at the same time, unfocused in their meaning and yet more meaningful than any he had ever heard.

When the *Ah ma* had finished the recitation of the twenty-one regulations, he said, "Lower yourself, Yang Wong. Lower and subjugate yourself. Be reborn. Speak the words and be reborn."

Yang lowered his body to the floor and began crawling up the platform where the throne sat. As he did, he said, "I renounce all other allegiances except that to the Kwong Dock tong. I renounce my parents, I renounce my brother, I renounce my sister, I renounce all kith and kin."

He came up on the platform and crawled beneath the legs of the throne on which the *Ah ma* sat, speaking the prescribed words, acting out the rite as it had been taught to him.

"I renounce my allegiance to the Emperor of Mother China. There is only one Emperor and that is the *Ah ma*. There is only one mother and that is the Kwong Dock tong."

When these words were spoken he had completed the crawl through the legs of the throne. As he stood, the *sing fung* appeared at his side. The introducer led him to the towering idol of Kwan Kung. An attendant held a box in front of Yang. Yang opened it and pulled out the wad of money which represented his month's stipend.

He walked to the *mon war,* opened the steel door, and fed the paper money into the flames as a tribute to the god of war. He turned to face the idol and bowed. Yang began a series of silent worship chants to the five monks who had founded the Kwong Dock tong. This completed, he offered prayers to the ancient kings.

As Yang completed the invocations, attendants lit candles and burned incense and gilt paper. Tea and wine were poured into offering cups and set before the idol of Kwan Kung.

Yang raised his head and turned to face the brothers of the tong. He fought to concentrate and, at the signal of the introducer, began chanting the thirty-five ancient oaths of the tong. As he did this, one of them placed a table with a glass basin in front of him. The other man held a bound-up rooster.

The cock tried to flap its wings, but they had already been clipped. Its legs were fastened together by a wide band of wire.

The tong brother set the rooster down on the table and held it, and while Yang continued to recite the oaths the other officer drew his sword and severed the cock's head with a single swoop.

The officer then held the bird over the basin, allowing the blood to flow into it, chanting, "Let the penalty for violation of these sacred ancient oaths you utter be the fate of the cock."

When Yang finished the chanting of the ancient oaths, the introducer ushered him to the throne again. He was quizzed by Hung Ma Kung. The Grand *Ah ma* asked him how a queue was to be braided in order to allow a fellow tong brother to know that he was one of them, and so avoid harm coming to him in a street encounter.

Yang proceeded to braid his queue in the prescribed manner.

A table was set before him and he was told to set the cups and tea kettle in the secret arrangement which would tell Kwong Dock highbinders that he was one of them. This, too, he accomplished.

For more than an hour he was asked questions about secret signs, passwords, code words. All of the questions he answered properly, and it seemed to him that he could sense the excitement and tension in the chamber as the brothers of the tong felt him moving closer and closer to being one of them.

"You have completed all the requirements of membership, Yang Wong." The *Ah ma*'s voice seemed distant, far away from where Yang was. "Are you prepared to receive the mark of the tong?"

Yang nodded.

From the corner of his vision he saw the attendant approach, saw the crucible in which the iron rested. He raised his arms toward the heavens, calling on Kwan Kung to give him strength in this moment of final testing.

He felt the warmth of the approaching red-hot iron, felt it touch his flesh, sear into it, smelled the fetid odor of burning skin, as the sign of the tong ate into him, marking him now and for all time as a brother of the Kwong Dock tong.

Perspiration poured down his face, pain lashed his body,

the flame held him in its horrible fiery clutch. Then the attendants moved away, removed the iron, and returned it to the crucible.

Yang had not cried out.

Chapter 41

Riley had been true to his word. He worked hard during the spring and summer of 1873, trying to drum up votes for Andrew Harcourt. He was careful not to appear too much in favor of Harcourt because he didn't want it to appear that he was only a puppet.

But the message was clear to the men he spoke to. Harcourt began to emerge as the politician who had the backing of the common worker and the unemployed. He wasn't going to have an easy time beating James Otis out of the mayor seat, though. Otis had a broad base of support in San Francisco and it was going to be a close race.

Moreover, Harcourt wasn't the only candidate who had the workers' sympathy. Most of the men who were running for the office of mayor were anti-Chinese and anti-railroad.

Sandlot meetings became a weekly affair in the summer of 1873. A dozen men, like Riley, began drawing large crowds. Some of them were candidates. Others, like Riley, had other interests and purposes in mind. Still others were merely fanatics who enjoyed the attention of a crowd.

James Riley was the smartest of the noncandidates, and he pulled the heaviest attendance. He was wise enough to realize that he could never hope to win an election on his own—as a candidate. There were certain powerful forces in San Francisco, like Charley Crocker and Leland Stanford, who would not permit that.

But being a noncandidate had a certain power attached to it. It meant that he was, supposedly, without self-interest. It gave Riley a sort of rough halo of honesty, and the power this bestowed on Riley made the men who lived on Nob Hill quake for fear that he might influence the election.

This was precisely what Riley had set out to accomplish.

By aligning himself with Harcourt, he reasoned, he might be able to swing enough votes to tip the election in the politician's favor, and thus advance his own cause.

On the morning of September 16 that year the steamship *Idaho* passed through the breakwaters and made its way into San Francisco harbor. On the bridge was Captain Ambrose Hutchinson. He carried, among other things, a cargo of seven hundred Chinese.

"My God," Hutchinson said when he caught sight of the dockside, "what in hell is that?"

His first officer, Thomas Sproule, raised his eyeglass and looked at the harbor. The wharf was lined with hundreds of men, their arms waving. Had Sproule not known better, he would have thought they were waving in greeting.

The thin row of San Francisco policemen in front of the spectators told the tale.

Sproule lowered the eyeglass and turned to the captain. "Looks like things have gotten worse since the last time we were here, sir."

Hutchinson nodded. It had been six months since they had landed in San Francisco. The memory was still with him. A hundred men had lined the pier then, protesting the landing of the Chinese. It had been a dangerous situation. Hutchinson had watched from the ship, grateful that he wasn't one of the coppers on the pier.

"Bad enough then," the captain said. "But this looks like it's out of control." He turned to the first mate. "Better issue belaying pins to the men, Mr. Sproule."

"Aye, aye, captain."

"Tell them to restrain themselves. I don't want any of our men going onto the dock until after that crowd is gone. Tell them to keep those pins in their pants. They're only to be used if those landlubbers try to board the ship."

Hutchinson looked back to the wharf. "Our only job is to deliver the cargo. Once those Chinks get on the dock it's their problem." He looked at Sproule. "But I mean to unload our shipment."

"Aye, sir." Sproule touched the tip of his cap and left the bridge.

The shouts of the men on the dock were thunderous. McNamara and Shaughnessy were in the midst of it, at the front of the men. Coppers' arms, linked together, formed the line that held them back.

As the crew of the *Idaho* tossed their lines overboard to the dockworkers below, the hoodlums surged forward. In unison the fifty coppers on the other side of the line pulled their nightsticks and held them at the ready.

San Francisco Police Captain Dearborn, standing at the front of the police officers, spoke through a megaphone. "You men settle down," he ordered.

And, in response to the order and the sight of the clubs, the gang did quiet some—at least enough for Dearborn to be heard.

"I won't tolerate any rioting here. I'll have the lot of you run in if I have to. I'll have order here, by the saints!"

Tai Pien and the Chinese Protective Police were a convenient solution to a problem which had been vexing City Hall. As the mobs that greeted the Chinese became more and more violent, it became clear that some sort of protection had to be offered the immigrants or they'd be torn to pieces.

Beyond that, there was a powerful element that was pro-Chinese—namely the men who realized that they provided a large and cheap labor force.

On the other hand, city government didn't want San Francisco police to escort the Chinese to their quarter because they didn't want to seem pro-Chinese in this crucial election year. Aside from that, City Hall didn't want to take the chance of local police getting into a riot with citizens over Chinamen.

The mayor elected to let Tai Pien and the Protective Police take over the task of guarding the immigrants on the trek from the wharf to their quarter. It even sounded good—Chinese guarding Chinese.

The city government went to pains to set up certain rules. Tai Pien's men were only allowed to carry protective equipment, such as their leather shields. No weapons, sticks, or knives of any sort were to be carried by the Chinese. Moreover, Tai Pien had been personally advised about the risk the entire Chinese community would be taking in having the Chinese Protective Police present at the dock. If there was the slightest action taken against a white man—no matter how great and justifiable the provocation—the city would assume no responsibility for the result. The Los Angeles Massacre did not have to be specifically mentioned.

Tai Pien brought his officers to a halt in front of the *Idaho*. For a long moment he watched as the ship disgorged its passengers. His eyes swept over the crowd of angry whites, who were waiting for him . . . for the "run."

When all the Chinese had left the ship and were counted, Tai Pien approached the San Francisco policeman in charge. He signed a claim for incoming Chinese, thinking about his orders. In effect, what these orders meant was that the Chinese Protective Police were only allowed to escort incoming immigrants to Little China.

In light of the manner in which newly arrived Chinese had been greeted lately, this meant an exercise in the greatest restraint on the part of Tai Pien's men—each of whom, by now, had been trained to a considerable degree of expertise in numerous of the deadly Chinese martial arts. That they were able to control themselves in the face of abuse, both physical and verbal, was a tribute to their training.

The men advanced at a trot. As they drew closer to the demonstrators, Tai Pien heard the shouts of the white men on the other side of the police line.

One of the sergeants stopped him again and Tai Pien presented the papers.

"Wait here," the sergeant said, shouting to be heard over the crowd.

A moment later Captain Dearborn appeared. The captain looked at Tai Pien and his men. "You got a job for yourself today." The police captain turned to look at the crowd of angry whites. "In a damned uproar over the *Idaho.*"

"It is no different from any other time."

"Maybe worse," the captain offered. "We aren't going to be able to hold these men forever. One of these days they'll . . ."

Tai Pien nodded as the captain signed and handed the papers to him. This done, Tai Pien took his position at the head of the line, blew a single loud shriek on his whistle, and began moving the line, at a trot, along the length of the pier.

It was a procedure the whites were used to by now. The coppers moved their line to block the whites from following the Chinese. Most of the whites, though—veterans of previous "Steamer Days"—had already bolted from the dock as soon as they heard Tai Pien's whistle blast.

For some of them it was sport; for others it was deadly serious. All of them, however, knew that there were certain unwritten rules, and for the time being they abided by them. As the whites ran from the pier Captain Dearborn knew that, at least this time, he had gotten away without a riot.

One of the rules was that the protesters couldn't harm San Francisco police officers. Once, months earlier, a copper had taken a cuff on the jaw and had a tooth knocked out by an overzealous protester. The man was quickly thrown into a police wagon. The following day the news hit the streets that he'd been booked, put before a judge, and sentenced to a year at hard labor before the sun had set.

Out of this grew the second rule. There was to be no violence on the wharf. It was just too dangerous—too much chance of accidently hurting a copper. So as soon as Tai Pien blew his whistle signaling time to move out, the whites did the same, taking up a position half a dozen blocks away.

There were three routes the Chinese Protective Police could take to escort the immigrants to the relative safety of Chinatown. One was up Commercial. The second was along Drumm Street and then up Washington. And the third was to take Drumm to California Street and then go up California to the quarter. It was this that added sport to Steamer Day: the whites had to guess which route Tai Pien would take.

Even if they guessed wrong, however, all was not lost. So large a group of men—usually over five hundred Chinese with each arriving shipload—could not conceal their path for too long. After missing them a few times the whites adapted and stationed lookouts at the two routes they didn't occupy. If the Chinese column was seen by one of the lookouts he quickly ran to inform the rest of the protesters.

While the demonstrators would not catch the whole Chinese column, they were usually able to arrive at the new route in time for some action.

This day the whites had guessed right. Tai Pien was taking them straight up Commercial Street. The two hundred whites waited, occupying both sides of the street. Some people gathered just to see the spectacle. Others took flight, not wanting to be involved.

It was a credit to McNamara that the protesters tried their utmost not to do injury to the regulars of the Chinese Protective Police. McNamara recognized that the Chinese Protective Police had certain ties to the police department and City Hall—ties probably helped along by influence-buying by wealthy white capitalists up on Nob Hill.

Still, McNamara knew that it was too early to outrage everyone. So he had instructed the men to avoid injuring the regulars. They tried.

Tai Pien cursed himself as he slowed the trot. The mob

had guessed right. He saw the whites waiting for them just across the intersection of Samson Street. Some of them were up on balconies, leaning over, baskets at their feet. Others were on the sidewalk of the broad avenue. They stood about, waiting and twitching like a pit of vipers who know an impotent mongoose has to cross their path.

He tightened his grip on his arm shield, looked over his shoulder and cried, "NOW!"

The Chinese column burst into a sprint up Commercial. The whites tensed, coiled, and, when the first tip of the yellow column of humanity crossed Sansom Street, struck. From both sides of the street a hail of rocks and stones pelted the hapless new arrivals. Rock slashed skin and skin yielded blood.

All about him Tai Pien heard the cries of his cousins. He didn't bother to look back. He knew what he would see. Instead, he held his shield up, an occasional stone glancing off of it. His concern was not so much for his own safety as it was to move the column through the white assault as quickly as possible.

Behind him the line of Chinese screamed out as the barrage of rotten vegetables and rocks continued. Blood streamed down the faces of the wounded, and when they fell, many were trampled by those who came after them. Some were helped to their feet and carried along.

As the wounded passed out of range they were replaced by fresh immigrants. These were even less fortunate than those who had preceded them, for by now the whites had run out of stones to pelt them with.

In groups of five and six, bands of the men would rush out into the moving yellow column wielding clubs and bats over their heads, picking their victims at random. Chinese after Chinese fell as the beatings began in earnest.

Shaughnessy swung his club again and again and again. So blind was his frenzy that he nearly struck a white man on more than one occasion. Finally he picked out a particular Chinese, and after he had felled the man with a single blow he set upon him. He worked on the man with a passion, bringing the club down first on the man's unguarded left kneecap, then the right; then the man's left foot, then his right. Shaughnessy moved to the man's arms, breaking them with his weapon.

He was about to slam the club down on the screaming man's head when he heard McNamara call out.

"Enough, Shaughnessy!"

"The hell you say!" Again he raised the club.

"Tim!"

Shaughnessy paused, the club over his head, and looked at his partner.

"Don't do it," McNamara pleaded. "You'll ruin the day."

"Ah hell," he said, tossing his club aside. Shaughnessy reached into his belt and pulled his hunting knife. He reached down and slashed into the flesh of the beaten man's head, circling the queue. When he was finished he pulled hard and the queue ripped off, pulling a chunk of scalp with it.

The scalped man fainted.

Shaughnessy laced the prize through his belt and turned to batter more of the newcomers. He picked his club up from the ground and moved through the column, numb to everything but the clubbing, everything but the feel of his bat striking a skull, the feel of bone cracking and giving way. And still he clubbed until his arms ached, still more.

Chinese lay everywhere. Some tried to carry the wounded on their backs, but they were set upon by whites for their efforts. The gutters of Commercial Street filled with a crimson flow of Chinese blood, as their cries echoed pitifully off the walls of buildings just four scant blocks from the safety of Chinatown.

But as Shaughnessy made his way through the crawling, bleeding mass of humanity he felt an emptiness, for his revenge could not be fulfilled. He could never beat enough of them, could never inflict enough pain on the Chinese to avenge his brother's death. There was something he found about the Chinese that was both puzzling and infuriating.

While there were screams of pain and suffering—sweet music to Shaughnessy's ears—most of the Chinese submitted to the attacks with incredible passivity. Once struck they fell to their knees, bent their heads, and accepted the beatings as if they were a matter of course. To Shaughnessy it made bitter the nectar of revenge.

He wanted a fight, wanted for them to struggle so he could force himself on them against their will. But it was not to be so, and Shaughnessy hated them all the more for it. It was as though they were salvaging some measure of dignity out of the beatings.

Shaughnessy was determined that some day he would savor

the full measure of revenge. But for the time being he contented himself with the brutality at hand.

He raised the club again.

Some of the seven hundred Chinese in the courtyard were lying on the ground, being tended to by volunteer nurses from San Francisco hospitals. Others were squatting. All were exhausted from the ordeal. Some of the men—those who had managed to come through unscathed—were trying to help the nurses, but they were hindered by the language barrier.

Chin surveyed the courtyard as he walked through it. It was like the aftermath of a war. Moans filled the air and everywhere there was blood—still flowing from some. The nurses bandaged man after man. Antiseptic was applied, drawing fresh cries of pain.

Chin walked among the wounded, his voice rising, speaking loudly, but in Chinese so the nurses would not understand him.

"Listen to me, all of you! Listen to me!" His voice dripped with sarcasm. "Welcome to this golden land! I trust your greeting at the dock was equal to the pleasure of your ocean voyage."

As he walked one of the wounded spit at his feet and Chin looked at the man. A rock had split his forehead and tissue was exposed, stained red. Chin saw a mixture of pain and hatred in the young man's eyes.

He bent and whispered low and hard. "Good," Chin said. "You hold on to that anger, young one. You harness it and keep it and feed it and let it grow. Hold on to it and listen to me, for I shall tell you what to do with it and how to use it."

He rose and continued walking, continued talking, the sarcasm gone from his voice now. "You have met one of the enemies who await you in this new land," he said. "He is white and he is poor and he is out of work and he blames you for all of these things except the first.

"The first, being white, is what gives him the right and the power to vent his anger and frustrations on you. You had better hasten to reconcile yourselves to this fact, or else rise and quickly run back to the docks, for the *Idaho* sails on the morrow. You'd best be on it if you hold any illusions about being equal to the whites in this land."

Most of the men were turning to look at him, listening as he spoke.

"Do not think that the white man is the only foe you have

to face in this land. There are other devils besides the white one. You think that just because you are no longer in China that you have escaped the barbarism of evil Chinese? Perhaps you came here believing that Chinese bandits cannot exist in this land because their actions will not be permitted by the whites.

"Well," Chin said, "put this thought out of your mind as well. The bandits exist in California. The only difference is that here they are more organized. The tongs are here, cousins. They operate with considerable freedom, because, you see, the whites really do not care what we do to each other.

"There are no mandarins here, there is no Chinese government—no matter how corrupt it may have been—to ride herd over the tongs. They have free rein and they reign with hatchets and cudgels and guns, and they will terrorize all who stand in their way.

"The tongs will accost you in the street, rob you, beat you, perhaps kill you, and you will have little recourse.

"If you are successful in business someday, through your industry, if you manage to open a shop, the tongs will exact a heavy toll both in theft and in protection money which will be extorted from you."

His eyes fell on a badly beaten boy at his feet. Teeth were missing and blood was caked all about the boy's mouth.

Chin predicted, "Today is but a specter of what is to come." He paused, then said, "There is, however, hope. It lies in unity among the Six Companies. Although each of our Companies is separate, the Companies have realized that we must unite in order to protect ourselves, and so the Chinese Protective Police was formed to deal with the terror that is visited upon our people."

He turned and looked over the wounded. "You have an opportunity to be a part of that police force. We are looking for men. We need men who will not stand for the oppression of the tongs and the whites.

"You were escorted from the wharf by members of that police force—regulars of the Chinese Protective Police."

"And a marvelous job they did of protecting us!" one of the injured cried out.

Chin leveled a finger at the man. "Be thankful that they were there, cousin. If they had not been then your bones would likely be on their way back to China for burial."

Chin walked a few more paces, drawing alongside Tai Pien, who had been listening to his address.

"But what this young man says is also true. We *should* have been able to afford you better protection. You should have been able to make the journey from the ship to this house unharmed. We could only assign a pitiful score of regulars to the reception squad.

"Why?" Chin asked. "Because others were needed in other parts of the quarter to guard against the violence of the tongs, to protect businesses, to ensure that ciitzens are not randomly beaten and robbed by the marauding bands of the Kwong Dock and Suey Sing tongs."

Chin shook his head. "We cannot be all places at once. We cannot fight against the tongs and protect against the whites. We have a difficult enough job just trying to protect the citizens of our community who had resided here for two decades. Even this job we do not do well enough. And during the night the quarter falls prey to dozens of incidents and beatings."

Chin paused for a moment, then said, "And that is precisely the point I make to you this day. We desperately need new men to join the Chinese Protective Police. That is why I am here today. To urge you to work, either full- or part-time, as regulars of the Protective Police."

He turned to Tai Pien. "Here with me is Tai Pien, the chief of the Chinese Protective Police. Through his efforts, though the force is understaffed and fighting against a superiorly armed opponent, Tai Pien and his men have saved dozens of lives, thousands of dollars in loss, and"—he paused for effect—"dealt with scores of tong terrorists.

"He will tell you more about his force, how you can join, and what you can do to make certain that what happened to you today will not be just a prelude to a continuing nightmare in this new land you have come to."

Tai Pien stepped forward and began speaking about how to join the Chinese Protective Police as Chin turned and headed for the large door that led back into the house. Once inside he made his way to the basement and there, alone, he was sick.

Chapter 42

James Riley was in a foul mood. Maybe, he thought, it was because of the company he was in. He didn't particularly like losers, and Andrew Harcourt was a loser.

Riley was in Harcourt's campaign headquarters and the whole place smacked of failure. The place had been a bakery before Harcourt had leased it and the smell of dough and yeast still clung to the walls. Bakery showcases lined the rear of the store. Behind the glass, on the bakery shelves, sat stacks of fliers and leaflets and rolled-up posters with Andrew Harcourt's picture on them.

A chalkboard that covered another wall showed the election record. There were smudges now where earlier numbers had been. To the right was a wall covered with more posters of Andrew Harcourt, proclaiming him San Francisco's next mayor. One of the posters had come partially loose and was drooping toward its inevitable fate on the paper-strewn floor.

Andrew Harcourt was in none too good a mood himself, and with the election over he didn't have to choose his words carefully with the likes of Riley.

"I should have won that election," Harcourt said. "I *would* have won it, too, if you'd brought your votes in like you were supposed to."

Riley looked at the man—a grain dealer who would be mayor. At least he looked the part, Riley thought. He was fat enough. And the vested suit was cut properly, with the ever-present watch chain and fob stretching, it seemed endlessly, across the man's belly. Even in defeat, Harcourt looked like a candidate.

"If every one of my men had voted for you you couldn't have won that election, Harcourt."

"The hell I couldn't have."

"You didn't have a pig's chance and I was a fool not to have seen it."

That much was certain, Riley thought. He had misjudged Harcourt's strength, had gone with the first offer he'd gotten.

Still, Harcourt was right. Not enough of his men *had* turned out, and that wounded Riley's pride. More importantly, though, Riley had been thinking, was why Harcourt wouldn't have won even with his men's votes.

Harcourt leveled a finger of accusation at him. "And I was a fool to throw in with you. Your men are the scum of the earth, Riley."

Riley smiled, then laughed.

"What's so damned funny, you Mick?"

Riley stopped laughing, but the smile remained. "I'm laughing at you, you fat old bastard."

Harcourt's face turned scarlet. His hands were on his wide hips. He looked around the room at the few supporters who had remained till the end. Then he turned back to Riley and said, "I don't have to take guff from you. I'm—I'm—"

"You're a man who's just lost an election, Harcourt, that's who you are. You're a nobody. And nobody cares about you, least of all me."

"I've listened to enough."

"And so have I," Riley said. "I suppose I owe you some thanks, though."

"Why's that?" Harcourt sneered.

"I learned at least two things out of this. First, dirty hands don't mix with clean, any more than oil mixes with water."

"I've no argument with that."

"And second," Riley said, "never depend on someone else. Especially when the someone else is wearing a suit."

Riley turned and walked from the room.

Chapter 43

Yang stood alone inside the circle of five men. Each man in the circle held an ax exactly like the one Yang clutched in his right hand. He was constantly whirling, his eyes fixed on the hatchets, never looking at the men's eyes, only focusing on their weapons.

They moved in on him, feinted, swung at him with their

axes. But Yang anticipated each movement, each attack, and he eluded them with a leap into the air, a lunge to the left, to the right, a drop to the dusty ground, and as quickly as he dropped, that quickly was he back on his feet, whirling again, his eyes on his attackers' weapons.

He let out a cry and moved forward on one of the men, slipping out of the arc of the man's swinging hatchet. The butt of his own broadax caught the man a blow in the stomach, doubling him.

Yang moved from the circle, the four men advancing on him. Then he moved back toward them again, and this time the flat of his blade made a loud clap as it caught one of his attackers flush on the leg, sending him to the ground.

Yang rolled, his weapon rolling with him, and the polished handle of his battle-ax cracked one of the men's shins. Only two were left then. He rose, backing to the wall as these two moved toward him. One of the men raced at him, his hatchet flashing in the noonday sun. Yang moved his head and the weapon bit into the stone wall behind him. He brought the handle of his ax into the man's ribs, crumpling him.

The final attacker brought his weapon over his head and down at Yang. Yang's hand moved like a hawk, catching the weapon in mid-flight at the handle, holding it in the air with one hand against the man's two. For a split second he held the weapon's descent and then he lashed out with his foot, catching the man in the gut, breaking his grip, driving him back.

Yang tossed the weapon aside and moved on the man, his feet and hands striking out with a precision that was honed to perfection, landing blow after blow. The man fell on his back and Yang flew upon him, the death cry piercing in the air, his battle-ax cast aside so his hands could do the work. Yang slashed down on the man, his hands ripping through the air and then freezing but scant inches from the man's face.

The man on the ground looked up at the hands that he knew could send him to his ancestors if they so desired. His breath was held, his face was wet, and for a moment he forgot that Yang was his instructor.

Then Yang straightened and moved off the student, to the applause of those members of the Kwong Dock tong who had been watching and studying the demonstration.

Yang turned to the dozen novices and half-dozen highbinders and said, "That is how one deals with a multiple attack. It matters not if you face two attackers or five, so long as you

338

are constantly moving, constantly flowing from defense to offense. Your offense must be a combination of your skill with a hatchet and your skill with your hands."

He dusted off his trousers. "Now practice these things you have seen today."

The men broke into groups and Yang walked toward the water bucket. He saw Po Dung making his way across the Kwong Dock courtyard.

Po Dung nodded as he drew up alongside him. "You train the novices well. And many of our experienced brothers appreciate being able to hone their skills under your tutelage."

Yang sipped from the long-handled cup he had pulled from the bucket. "They are good students. They learn well."

"Only because they have a good instructor."

"You have an assignment for me." It wasn't a question.

Po Dung arched an eyebrow. "How did you know?"

"I know." He dipped the cup and handed it to Po Dung. "When?"

"Tonight."

"Not much time to prepare."

Po Dung drank, then said, "We are acting on information we received only moments ago. A large sum of money is stored in a shop on Clay Street."

"How large?"

"Twenty-five thousand American dollars."

Yang pursed his lip in surprise. "Why do they keep such a sum of money in the store?"

"It cannot be deposited in the bank today because it is a holiday—Thanksgiving, an American festival. The banks are closed." Po Dung glanced away for a moment, watching as the novices practiced their war games. Then he turned back to Yang. "The shop made a sale of a spectacular diamond necklace this morning."

Yang smiled. "Perhaps we should have tried for the necklace."

Po Dung shook his head. "It would only fetch us twenty percent of its worth on the black market, and besides the necklace itself only arrived in the shop today. It was custom-made and shipped in."

Yang nodded.

Even from Po Dung's office on the third floor of the Kwong Dock house, Yang could hear the cries of the students as they practiced. It filled him with a feeling of well-being and pride.

Po Dung's quarters were small but well appointed, with walls of dark brown wood. Yang would have preferred to see his superior in a larger apartment, more fitting to his rank. But Yang reminded himself that Po Dung, though still one of only three warlords in the tong, was not the chief swordsman.

Though Po Dung was powerful, he was not so powerful as he had been when he was in Los Angeles. They were in San Francisco now, Yang reflected, and some of their strength had been diminished by distance.

Po Dung had been well received by the main chapter, but he would have to build his reputation here. Yang knew that it was important that he perform the assignments well when Po Dung gave them to him. Yang's star was firmly affixed to his mentor's; as one rose, so would the other.

Po Dung unfurled a roll of paper on his desk and Yang looked at the diagram of the shop.

"These shopkeepers are no fools," Po Dung said. "They guard their treasures well. In recent years they have done away with the show windows in the more expensive shops, and instead have thick walls to foil burglars. Indeed, some of these shops are like miniature fortresses."

He pointed to the two entrances of the building. "In addition, they have a strong force of guards from the Chinese Protective Police assigned to the shop."

"How many men?"

"Twenty to cover each door. All with revolvers and rifles."

Yang nodded respectfully.

"It grows even more difficult," Po Dung continued, pointing to the diagram. "Here, inside the shop, more regulars—again armed."

"And the money?"

"Here, inside a vault."

A light frown creased Yang's face. He looked at the diagram. "What is this?"

Po Dung looked closer. "It appears to be a skylight."

Yang nodded. "Have someone make certain. If it is, then we shall have eliminated the first problem."

"What of the young men inside and the vault?"

"I will have to think about that."

"You won't have long to think. Tomorrow they deposit the money in the Wells Fargo Bank. How many men will you need?"

"Ho Huan and three others."

"Five men?"

Yang nodded.

Po Dung stood erect, his hands on his hips. "You would take five men against a force of almost three score?"

Yang looked at his superior. "This is not a war, Po Dung. This is a mission. To move with a full force of men, just for the sake of doing battle, would accomplish nothing. We would still have the vault to deal with; and the commotion caused by gunfire and bloodletting would draw attention and, surely, reenforcement from the Chinese Protective Police. If I understand you correctly, it is the money you want here, not carnage."

Po Dung nodded. "You understand correctly. Do what you think is best." He paused, then added, "I can tell you that if you complete this mission successfully you will receive a generous promotion in rank."

"I am honored," Yang said.

Po Dung sat in his chair and looked at Yang. He thought about the first time he had seen him, in battle in a *Fan-tan* parlor. He had recruited him for his raw strength then, and little more. Muscle was needed for the tong to be powerful.

But, the warlord thought, Yang had exhibited more than just muscle after a time. He had cunning and wisdom—albeit a cruel cunning. He was a leader of men, in his own way; because he was indomitable, which inspired respect.

Briefly, Po Dung wondered what it was that drove Yang, then dismissed the question. "I have something to tell you of this mission, Yang."

Yang looked at him, noting the change in Po Dung's voice. "What is it?"

"I . . ." There was a hesitation in the warlord's voice now. "You know that you have sworn absolute allegiance to the tong."

Yang nodded. "Willingly and with a feeling of privilege."

"That allegiance goes beyond anything; beyond blood, beyond laws, beyond anything."

Yang remained silent, waiting.

"Yet . . ." Po Dung folded his hands. "Yet we are mortals, Yang, and sometimes, though we take a pledge, we cannot always honor it to the fullest in every moment of our lives."

Yang felt his heart begin to pound. He was puzzled by the words he had never heard from a highbinder before.

"What are you trying to tell me, Po Dung?"

"This is a very important mission we are sending you on. The tong wants that money badly. It can be used to buy weapons." Again his tone changed. "I will tell you—and this is of the utmost secrecy—that a great tong war is on the horizon. The different tongs of San Francisco cannot go on fighting against each other. There must be one ruling tong and a war will decide which tong it shall be.

"The money you will get from this mission will help purchase weapons and buy information to help us win that war."

Yang nodded solemnly.

"Therefore, anything which might stand in your way, anything which might diminish your enthusiasm on this mission must be considered."

"Truly," Yang said, "I do not understand."

Po Dung leaned forward. "You have been chosen because you are one of our bravest and most resourceful warriors. But there is a possible impedance that we must discuss."

"What impedance?"

"The store where the money is, the vault in which it is contained, the money itself belongs to your brother Chin."

"My brother Chin?" Yang looked down at the diagram. "My brother Chin?" He looked back up at Po Dung and then he smiled. He caught himself for a moment, out of respect for Po Dung, but there was no holding it. He burst into laughter, his whole body shaking, the laughter coming from his very soul. Po Dung watched him as someone would observe a madman.

Finally Yang reached down and rolled up the diagram. He placed it under his arm, looked up at Po Dung, and said, "You can tell the Council of the Kwong Dock tong that by informing me that it is my brother's business which I shall pillage they have increased my joy a thousandfold."

Yang turned and left Po Dung's office.

Shao Kow was in a nervous state as he approached the two-story building that housed one of Chin's import shops. It was difficult to see on Clay Street, for the fog was thick and shrouded the quarter completely by this time of night.

He didn't like the whole arrangement. It wasn't the proper way to do business. The manager of the shop had been fully reprimanded for the entire affair.

To Shao Kow's mind the only thing that would have made the money safe and secure would be to have it in Wells

Fargo's safe. Frustratingly enough, the bank was just two blocks from the import shop. And that was why the manager of the shop had been reprimanded—for not having realized that it was an American holiday and that the bank would be closed.

Shao Kow had spent most of the afternoon trying to get in touch with the president and vice-president of Wells Fargo. But both were out of the city for the holiday and couldn't be reached.

Had Shao Kow been in the shop he simply would have told the customer to return on the next business day. But the sale had been made, the money had been exchanged for the necklace, and now Shao Kow was left with a monumental security problem.

Tai Pien himself was stationed in front of the door that Shao Kow approached. With the chief of the Chinese Protecttive Police stood ten men, each bearing a sidearm.

Shao Kow stopped in front of him. "Just ten men?"

"And ten others you cannot see."

He looked around. "Where?"

"On the rooftops, in windows, their rifles all trained on you."

"And the rear entrance?" Shao Kow asked.

"The same."

"I hope they can see through this fog."

"Well enough to know if there is an attack on the shop."

There was little affection between the two men. Even in the beginning there had been more than a little resentment. Shao Kow was a businessman and prided himself on being Chin's top adviser. But during the last few years it was apparent that Tai Pien had gained considerable esteem in Chin's eyes.

Shao Kow could not help but remember that the chief of the Chinese Protective Police was involved with vice himself. Yet Tai Pien had worked hard at his job, managing Chin's gambling and drug interests while serving as the chief of the Chinese Protective Police.

Shao Kow had come to show a grudging respect for the work his rival did, and although their personal relationship did not blossom they developed a professional tolerance for each other. Tonight that tolerance was to be tested.

"Your men are inside?" Shao Kow asked.

The chief of the Chinese Protective Police nodded. "Your vault will be secure this night."

Terribly on edge, Shao Kow said, "I hope your men are up to the job."

"You wouldn't have to worry about it," Tai Pien snapped, "if you had done your job properly."

"I?"

Tai Pien nodded. "If you had been efficient enough to have realized that Thanksgiving is a holiday this would not have happened. Dealing with the Americans as you do, one would think you would have familiarized yourself with their customs."

Shao Kow felt his face flush with anger, but there was nothing he could say in return. Tai Pien was right. Shao Kow had to bear the ultimate responsibility for the error, because he was the man in charge.

He had already taken steps to ensure that the mistake didn't repeat itself. A list of American bank holidays was being printed and distributed to all of Chin's businesses.

He decided against telling Tai Pien these things. It wouldn't change matters and Shao Kow hated excuses.

Shao Kow looked at him. "Just see to it that your guards are alert."

"My men always are," Tai Pien said with a patronizing smile.

Shao Kow turned and walked to the door. After the viewing window had been opened, the door was unbolted. It swung inward and he walked inside.

The shop was constructed in the style of most of Chin's import shops. Three-quarters of the main floor was a showroom. There were four display cases. Behind a curtain was a small room where the manager could balance books and keep records. In this small office was a stairway to the second floor. The second floor was a loft where new merchandise was received, inventoried, and priced before it was put on display.

Three men were in the showroom—all of them regulars of the Chinese Protective Police. Shao Kow nodded to them. Another three regulars were in the back office.

Men Gwai Li, the manager of the shop, stepped through the curtains from the back room. He lowered his eyes as Shao Kow looked at him, still feeling the sting of the earlier reprimand.

Shao Kow approached him, knowing that there was nothing to be gained from further harshness. "By tomorrow this will be a bad memory."

Men Gwai looked at him. "I pray that you are right. It is my stupidity that has caused all this effort."

"We have survived graver errors," Shao Kow said. "We are adequately fortified. It would be a fool's errand to make an attempt on the shop tonight."

And yet, as he spoke the words, Shao Kow knew that twenty-five thousand dollars was a strong temptation, even to a wise man.

Two three-story buildings flanked Chin's import shop. One was a lodging house, the other a temple. These provided the high ground that Tai Pien wanted for his regulars. Sitting on the edge of the roof of the lodging house was Ning Ho Wa.

He had joined the Chinese Protective Police six months ago, spurred on by the jeering, rock-hurling crowds that greeted his ship in San Francisco harbor.

There were worse ways to earn a living, he thought, gripping the stock of the Remington that lay across his knees. To a large extent, Ning Ho Wa thought, he was his own master—or, at the least, had a hand in shaping his destiny. He was not the kind of man to sit idly by while yellow and white bandits beat him.

That was the final thought in his brain as the silvery edge of Yang's hatchet slammed through his back, through flesh and bone and sinew until it reached his heart, slicing it like so much raw meat.

Ning Ho's mouth had opened, but the blow had been so powerful, the death so sudden, that there was no time for a cry to escape. Instead, he fell lifeless to the floor of the roof.

At the same time Yang had swung his war hatchet, a regular on the opposite rooftop was meeting a similar fate at the hands of Ho Huan.

Yang motioned the two men behind him forward. Through the fog, he peered across to the other roof. They controlled the high ground now. Crouching behind the cornice, Yang looked down. In the street below he could make out all that he needed to know.

At the front and rear of the shop were a large force of regulars, armed to the teeth. He was pleased he wouldn't have to deal with them. Not that he was reluctant to fight; but as he had told Po Dung, the prize wasn't to be won by strength alone.

He thought back to the first time he had met Po Dung, in the *Fan-tan* parlor, and he recalled the man's words, remembered what it was that had interested him most. He had said that Yang was creative. And Yang thought of the pride he had felt at that time—pride that something he had done was more than just a physical thing.

Po Dung had given him great insight that day. From then on, he had realized that the physical must merge with the intellectual if one was to become truly great. He realized that while a soldier may only wield his weapon and fire his gun, a general does so for a purpose. Sometimes he holds back firing his weapon and sometimes he does not even fire the weapon at all. Physical and intellectual, Yang thought. With purpose. And that, he thought, was why he would be greater than his brother—because he had both.

His eyes focused on the skylight of the import shop below. His two cohorts drew up beside him. On his left was Mi San, one of the tong's most honored warriors. On his right was Tsau Tsau.

Yang glanced at Tsau Tsau. The man's skin gleamed, even in the fog. His eyes were black emotionless pools. He was an expert at what he did and the skill he performed was as vital as that of wielding a hatchet. And it could be learned and mastered only by a very few.

Yang felt chilled by the presence of the man, but he steeled himself for the mission and turned his gaze back down on the skylight.

Yang was pleased to discover that there were no regulars on the roof below to complicate matters further. He looked across to Ho Huan and the highbinder with him. Yang made a sign with his hands.

Yang turned to Mi San and motioned for the sack. He pulled the three grappling hooks from the sack and handed two of them to his men. Attached to each hook was a length of rope.

The three men secured the hooks on the inside edge of the roof and tossed the ropes over. They uncoiled, falling, stopping just three feet above the roof of Chin's import shop.

Again Yang dug into the sack and this time he produced three thick pairs of buckskin gloves, the palms reinforced with an extra strip of leather. These the three men slipped on and pulled tight.

Their weapons sheathed in their waistbands, the three highbinders grabbed the ropes just below the hooks and swung over the edge of the roof.

Below, on the street, Tai Pien and his men scanned the

corners and alleyways, looking for anything. On nearby rooftops regulars strained to see through the heavy fog. None of them saw the five black-pajamaed highbinders as they slid down their ropes, clinging close to the brick walls of the building until, at last, they landed lightly on the roof of Chin's import shop.

As soon as his feet touched the roof of the shop, Yang let go of his rope and fell flat. He watched as the other men did the same. For a moment he waited, making certain that their descent had gone undetected.

When he crept toward the skylight his slippered feet fell with no more sound than a butterfly makes landing on a flower's petal. Blessing the fog, he drew up next to the skylight. He brought his cheek and eye over the lip of the illumination that came from within.

Ho Huan handed Yang the suction cup and Yang gently pressed it against the skylight. Attached to the piece of rubber was a short length of twine. Next, Ho Huan handed him the glass cutter. Yang cut around the cup.

When the job was done he pulled on the twine and a circle of glass pulled free from the pane. Ho Huan sprung the latch on the skylight while Mi San handed out five more small grappling hooks and coils of rope from his sack.

In a moment's time the five hatchetmen were standing on the floor of the stockroom. Jang Ko Li carried his blowgun in one hand and a slender dart in the other. He lowered himself to the floor of the storage loft and crawled the last few feet to where the stairwell began.

There, at the top of the stairs, he looked down and saw three regulars in the back office of the shop. He raised the blowgun to his lips. Thrice he blew on the weapon, reloading with lightning speed between shots. Yang moved to his side, looked down at the three dead regulars in the office below and whispered, "We move closer to our goal."

Stealthily, the five highbinders made their way from the second-floor stockroom to the office below. The floor was silent; only the foul odor of death was in their way as they floated across it. In the far corner of the room Yang spied the vault. It was a meter high and easily as wide. It would take five sticks of dynamite to open it and then half the Chinese Protective Police regulars in the city would be summoned.

Yang stared at the combination dial on the safe, then

turned to look at Tsau Tsau. He had been right; there *were* times when men like Tsau Tsau were needed.

Yang motioned to Ho Huan, Mi San, and Jang Ko Li. Each of them pulled their hatchets, and Jang Ko Li also held his blowgun to his lips with his free hand.

Yang nodded, stepped forward with his men behind him, and pulled aside the curtain that separated the back office from the display area of the shop.

The five men in the front of the shop were so startled by the sight of the highbinders that they heard Yang's words before they had time to react.

"If one of you makes a move for a weapon his head will be split before his hands can close on it."

Shao Kow, the three regulars, and Men Gwai Li looked at the four men who opposed them, then at their weapons, which were raised and ready to be thrown. Yang, in return watched them. He saw what he wanted to see, the thing he always watched for. Each of the men let his shoulders slump and Yang relaxed slightly, knowing with animal instinct that they had surrendered.

Over his shoulder he said, "Tsau Tsau."

Tsau Tsau came into the room and, being careful to stay out of the line of fire, disarmed each of the regulars. Neither Shao Kow nor the shop manager was armed. The weapons collected, Tsau Tsau returned to the back office, leaving Yang to deal with the men while he readied the tools of his trade.

Outside the import shop one of the regulars, named Wa Chong, spoke to Tai Pien.

"I'm sure I heard something in there," Wa Chong said.

"When?"

"Just a moment ago. I was leaning against the back door."

"What did it sound like?"

"Like . . . something falling."

"You could not have imagined this?"

"No. I'm sure."

"It could not have been one of our men moving around?"

Now Wa Chong thought. He didn't want Tai Pien to think him an old lady, but still, he had heard the sound. "I am not sure. It seemed . . ."

Tai Pien dismissed him. "Back to your post at the rear. I will investigate."

Tai Pien pulled up on the collar of his jacket and walked

past two regulars flanking the front door of the shop. He pounded on the door.

Inside the four highbinders crouched, their weapons poised. Yang's mouth was a black slit as he looked at Shao Kow.

"Answer the knock. Say the wrong words and they shall be your last. This I promise you."

His body shaking almost convulsively, Shao Kow turned to the thick door. "Yes?"

"Shao Kow?" Tai Pien called.

"Yes?"

"How are things in there?"

"They are as they have been all night."

There was a slight pause in which Yang advanced, his ax held high, catching a glint from the light of a lamp on one of the showcases. If there was trouble this man would die first.

Again, from outside, came Tai Pien's voice. "One of my men at the rear heard a noise."

"Heard a noise?" Shao Kow asked. Now, sensing that his life was in the balance, Shao Kow summoned up all his strength to inject anger into his voice. "Are we mice that we are not allowed to make a noise? Would you have us sit in our chairs and not move all this night?"

Outside the door Tai Pien waved his hand in anger. "Ah, I should have known better." He looked at one of the regulars. "The two shopkeepers were probably dancing in the back office to pass the time."

Both regulars laughed. Tai Pien had thought for a moment about asking Shao Kow to open the door so he could inspect for himself. But even though it was unthinkable that anyone would mount an attack against the shop when they had such considerable forces on duty, Tai Pien didn't want the door of the shop opened unless it was absolutely necessary.

Inside, Yang lowered his weapon a degree. He motioned his five prisoners into the back of the shop.

As Men Gwai Li stepped through the curtain he felt his stomach begin to turn; the smell of death in the air sickened him. Shao Kow followed next. Finally the three regulars entered the room, and as they did Yang and his men thrust their weapons into them, in their necks so their death would be a quick and silent one.

The killings had been accomplished in an instant, and as the regulars fell to the floor, Men Gwai Li began to sob, for he was certain that he was next. Yang grabbed him by the queue and pulled his head back, whispering angrily in his ear.

"If you do not want to die, keep your mouth still."

Buoyed by the realization that he was to be spared, Men Gwai Li composed himself.

Shao Kow's reaction to the slayings was different. The sight of the men being butchered was no less shocking to him than it had been to Men Gwai Li, but in a strange sense he had been prepared for it. Not for the death of the three regulars, but for the arrival of death itself. For a long time Shao Kow had felt himself moving toward this point, toward a world of death and blood and destruction.

Yang looked at the corpses on the floor, then turned to look at Men Gwai Li. Crimson lifeblood dripped slowly off of Yang's battle-ax to join the scarlet pools forming and flowing on the floor of the shop.

"You do not want to die, do you, shopkeeper?"

Men Gwai Li felt fear choking in his throat, constricting it to the point that it was impossible for him to speak. Instead he shook his head, tears forming at the corners of his eyes.

"You shall not, then," Yang declared. "You shall live."

The shop manager could not believe his ears, until Yang lowered his hatchet and sat down on the desk in the room. If nothing else, Men Gwai Li knew that his life was safe for the moment.

Shao Kow glanced around. The four killers had all lowered their hatchets. If ever there was a moment to take them, he thought, this was it. But as quickly as that thought had occurred to him, so did the folly of the idea. They were highbinders, warriors of the tong. Without their hatchets, the highbinders would still defeat them.

He looked to the far corner of the room, at Tsau Tsau. The man was standing at the desk. The papers had been moved from it and were on the floor now. Tsau Tsau's back was to him, and he bent over his work. Shao Kow wondered what that work was.

He did not have time to think about it because Yang was moving them up the stairs to the loft now. As Shao Kow came up to the second floor, he looked at the skylight and realized how the bandits had gotten in.

The highbinder moved them to the far end of the loft and there bound the two men to wooden beams. When this had been done Yang spoke.

"You shall both live. I want only one thing. I want the

money in the safe. I require the combination." Yang's eyes narrowed like a panther's. "Which one of you has it?"

Neither Shao Kow nor Men Gwai Li spoke.

Yang smiled all the same. "Neither of you are regulars of the Chinese Protective Police. So far that has saved your lives. But unless I have your cooperation you shall die soon."

Still the two men were silent.

Yang placed his weapon against the wall and folded his arms. "You are both employees of the company which owns this store. One of you has the combination to that safe."

Yang regarded them both, silent as statues. They were not brave men, he thought—they were fools. Two hours, three hours from now he might call one of them brave.

"You choose not to cooperate." Yang nodded to Jang Ko Li and the highbinder moved to Shao Kow. He grabbed Shao Kow by the queue and pulled his head back. When his victim opened his mouth to cry out in pain, the highbinder pushed a wadded ball of cloth into his mouth.

When Shao Kow closed his mouth, the highbinder tied a gag tightly about him to insure that he could not cry out. During the time Jang Ko Li had done this, Mi San had tended to Men Gwai Li in the same manner, so that now both men were gagged.

"Very well," Yang said. "Perhaps we can persuade you to help us." Yang looked at Men Gwai Li, remembering the way the shopkeeper had wept when he saw the death downstairs. He turned to Ho Huan and motioned toward the bound man.

For a full thirty seconds Ho Huan beat the shopkeeper in the stomach. It was a pitiful thing to watch—Men Gwai Li straining against the ropes, jerking on the beam. When Ho Huan stopped, Yang approached.

"The combination?"

Men Gwai Li did not move.

"Fool," Yang said. Again he nodded to Ho Huan, but this time the highbinder produced more lengths of rope and these he used to bind the man's head back to the beam tightly, so he could not move it at all.

Shao Kow, tied to a beam opposite him, watched all this. The beating he had expected. But now, watching the highbinder tie the ropes about Men Gwai Li's forehead, he wondered what horrors lay ahead.

He did not have to wait long for the answer. The man Tsau Tsau was not a battle warrior. Shao Kow realized this when he saw the man coming up the stairs from the first floor, because he recalled that Tsau Tsau had not taken part in any of the physical attacks. Instead, he had been in the back office attending to . . . to what? Shao Kow wondered.

Tsau Tsau was carrying a metal tray and on it were a number of objects which Shao Kow could not clearly see. What he did see was Yang nodding to the man.

With this, Tsau Tsau walked toward the beam where Men Gwai Li was trussed. As he passed him Shao Kow saw what was on the metal tray: a razor and a number of small steel clips.

Yang leaned forward, looking into Men Gwai Li's wide eyes. "Once more. Will you tell me the combination?"

Again the shopkeeper failed to respond.

Tsau Tsau placed the tray on a crate and picked up the razor. He brought it to Men Gwai Li's throat and laid it tenderly there, against the skin. The torturer made a horizontal cut, quickly, so it would be straight and not affected by the jerk of pain from the man.

The bound and gagged shopkeeper did jerk from the pain of the blade and a muffled, barely audible cry, came from behind the cloth stuffed in his mouth. But it was more a cry of shock than of true pain, for the blade was very sharp and thus did its work with a minimum of resistance.

Too, the cut was not very deep, just a slight break of the skin—hardly enough to draw the thin line of blood that could be seen slowly oozing from the gash, which was less than an inch across Men Gwai Li's neck.

The purpose of the slash had not been to draw pain.

Again Tsau Tsau brought the blade to the man's throat, alligning the razor so it touched the left corner of the first cut. From here he made a longer slash, downward and at a forty-five degree angle from the first.

The blade traveled three inches. As soon as he stopped, Tsau Tsau put the blade to the right corner of the first cut and sliced down again for three inches so that from the edges of the first cut there now extended two downward slashes of three inches.

The cries from behind the cloth were more real now, for although Men Gwai Li had no idea what awaited him, it was apparent that these highbinders had not planned a swift death for him. His body shivered and pulled against the hemp and the post it bound him to.

But the highbinders had done an expert job in securing

him, and only his belly was free to jerk in and out, in and out.

Shao Kow could see his eyes, could see the anticipation of horror in them.

Tsau Tsau took one of the metal clips and opened it. His fingers sought the flap of the first. Knowledgeably, he attached the clip to the flap of skin and tightened it.

Tsau Tsau took hold of the short piece of twine that was tied to the clip and pulled, a quick, hard jerk. The skin of Men Gwai Li's neck gave way, ripping away from his neck in a long strip that now hung down to his chest.

Shao Kow felt the bitter taste of vomit rising in his mouth as he looked at the exposed red band on Men Gwai Li's neck. The shop manager's eyes were shut tightly and he was no longer in control of himself. His entire body convulsed from the pain of the torture, his legs kicking out but held by the cruel ropes. His stomach shrank and swelled, his chest rose and fell grotesquely from the air he sucked in and silently screamed out.

Through the cloth in the man's mouth, Shao Kow could hear the muffled shriek of unimaginable agony. He watched as tears flowed down from the man's eyes, as blood dribbled from the raw underskin of the man's neck, and he wished death and limbo for all the highbinders in this room and in this world.

When at last, after long minutes, the pain seemed to subside, when Men Gwai Li's jerking had abated, Yang again stepped forward and bent his head to the man's ear.

"The combination."

Weakly, Men Gwai Li looked up at him.

Yang said. "Clench and unclench your fist twice to end your pain."

Yang looked at the shopkeeper's fist, but it was balled. It did not unball. He turned to Tsau Tsau and said, "Again."

Long minutes turned into long hours. Shao Kow watched, awestruck. His sensibilities alternated between horror and numbness.

Nine long strips of skin hung from Men Gwai Li's neck. A remarkably small amount of blood had emerged from these wounds, but enough to stain the collar of the man's tunic a dull maroon. As Shao Kow looked at it he wondered how this man was able to bear up under the torture.

It occurred to him that Men Gwai Li had been given a

perceptiveness that came when one approached death. It occurred to him that the man realized that his life would be as forfeit as those of the regulars who lay on the floor below them the moment he gave these highbinders the information they sought. And so, no matter how painful it was, the shop manager clung to life and the information which would allow him to hold that life.

Twice Men Gwai Li had passed out. Now it happened again. Yang moved closer and pinched the man's cheeks several times, bringing him back to the terror of consciousness. Tortured eyes looked up at Yang.

"The combination," Yang hissed. "Merely unclench you hand, merely do this twice," he whispered, "and I shall know you will give us the answer. I will unbind you myself. I guarantee you shall live."

Shao Kow picked up a tone of urgency in Yang's voice that had not been there before. The manager had not been the easy mark the highbinder had planned on and now the hour was growing late.

Men Gwai Li's eyes fluttered closed as he slipped toward darkness again, but Yang's twisting fingers drew him awake.

"The combination!"

Yang looked at the shopkeeper's hands, but they were still clenched in a fist, albeit a weak one. His strength had all but ebbed by now.

Yang turned to Tsau Tsau. "We have not much more time. Soon it will be light."

"He is stubborn," Tsau Tsau said, the first words he had spoken this night. "But I have softened him considerably. Now I will pry the secret loose from him." The chief torturer of the Kwong Dock tong reached into his pocket and produced a suede pouch. "Make certain the gags about his mouth are secure."

This Yang checked personally and after tightening them he nodded to Tsau Tsau. Tsau Tsau stepped forward, opening the drawstrings of the pouch. He turned the pouch over and emptied the powder into the palm of his hand. The torturer stood before Men Gwai Li, raised his hand, and rubbed the powder across the raw strips where the skin had been peeled from his neck.

Men Gwai Li's body galvanized at the first touch. Shao Kow watched the man's dance of agony. Every part of Men Gwai Li's body was constricting, straining, shaking. The very beam to which he was secured groaned from the strength of his convulsions. His eyes threatened to pop from their sockets, the unheard screams puffing and stretching the skin on his cheeks so that it appeared they would burst.

When, after long minutes, the heaving in his chest subsided, the room hung in silence. Yang gave him time as would a fisherman to a fish that was tiring itself out from the run. For a moment Shao Kow thought that Men Gwai Li was either dead or unconscious. But Yang knew he was neither, and finally that was verified when the shopkeeper began to stir.

Filled with pain that was beyond pain, he slowly turned his eyes to Tsau Tsau and saw the fresh palmful of powder waiting for him. Then he turned his eyes to Yang and summoned a strength that existed only to stop the torture. Men Gwai Li unclenched his fist, clenched it, and unclenched it again.

Yang had the man untied. He would ask him the question, allow the man to answer, and then grant him the death he wanted more than life.

Chapter 44

It was just before nine o'clock the next morning when Tai Pien and Shao Kow walked into the foyer of Chin's house. Chin's houseboy told them to wait while he announced them.

The two men sat silently in the foyer, neither speaking, neither looking at the other. In a moment the houseboy returned.

"Master Chin will see you now."

The houseboy escorted the two men into the dining room where Chin was taking his breakfast. Light, diffused by the fog, broke through the windows. Chin was wearing a light blue morning robe and matching trousers.

He sat at the far end of the table and nodded as Tai Pien and Shao Kow walked into the room. The houseboy left.

"Will you have breakfast?" Chin asked, motioning for them to sit down.

Neither man replied, nor did they sit down.

Chin placed his napkin on the table. "It is a serious matter you come on. Tai Pien?"

"Robbers," he began, knowing that there was no easy way to deliver the news. "Highbinders came in the night."

"The tong?" Chin asked evenly.

Tai Pien nodded. "They got through the—"

Chin silenced him with a slashing hand. "It matters not how they got in. What of the money?"

"Gone."

"All of it?"

"All."

Chin looked down at the table, silent.

Tai Pien continued. "We did everything that was humanly possi—"

"Apparently that was not enough."

Tai Pien's words were bitter. "It was an unnecessary loss. It was something that shouldn't have happened." He turned to look at Shao Kow. "Were it not for the inefficiency of your shop manager—"

"He paid the price!" Shao Kow spit.

"What happened to him?" Chin asked.

Shao Kow turned to Chin. "Tortured! Tortured relentlessly. Tortured for hour on end while the regulars of the Chinese Protective Police stood outside and 'patrolled.' Strips of flesh ripped from his neck one at a time; salt worked into his wounds to finally pry the combination from his lips."

Chin lowered his head in remorse.

"A thousand men could not have guarded the shop better," Tai Pien said.

"Hah!" Shao Kow said. "Men inside, dozens more outside and highbinders still got in. Your men—"

"My men should not have had to be there. If you had—"

"Silence!" Chin ordered. "Enough. You sound like two old women blaming each other for a shared blunder."

The two men fell silent.

"The only thing that matters is that twenty-five thousand dollars is gone, ripped from our hands by these barbarians because we are too weak. The money will serve to make them stronger, to buy them better weapons." He looked at Shao Kow. "You have given Tai Pien your description of the man?"

"Yes," Shao Kow said with a shiver. "An awesome man, as

large as a bull and with a terrible scar running down the left side of his face."

Chin tensed at Shao Kow's words. "A scar, you say?"

"Yes. And this monster had a message I was to deliver to you."

"What did he say?"

"He said to tell you that the chess game only begins."

Chin leaned back in his chair, suddenly out of breath. Tai Pien asked, "Do you know the man, Chin?"

"Perhaps," he said, "perhaps." Then he looked at Shao Kow. "Your life was spared for a reason beyond the message. The tongs want you to be a trumpet. Your story of Men Gwai Li's torture, the details of which are burned into your mind—the tong spared you so you would tell and retell the story, so as to spread fear."

Shao Know nodded in understanding.

"Never speak of what happened." He turned to Tai Pien. "Instruct all of your men. If anyone asks it is to be said that there was a robbery and some men were killed during it. But do not give out any details. I want this event to be forgotten quickly. Also, lessen the amount stolen—spread the story that it was a few thousand dollars."

Tai Pien nodded at these instructions.

"I was wrong . . . all these months," Chin said. "We cannot hope to defeat the tongs."

Tai Pien leaned forward, his hands spread desperately on the dining table. "We cannot give in, Chin."

Chin looked at him. "I said nothing of giving in. I only said that we cannot hope to defeat them. There is a lesson to be learned from what happened last night."

Chin walked to the window. "It is not always strength that wins the day. A small force of highbinders stole a precious sum from us not because they were superior in men, but because they had a plan. They had a mission. Wisdom, not strength. If only I had, on our side, the man who planned this theft." He nodded his head. "That man had a plan."

Both Shao Kow and Tai Pien watched him, deep in thought.

"We have been going about this all wrong. I see that clearly now. We *cannot* hope to defeat the tongs . . . not with sheer numbers. They are too powerful." Chin turned to look at them. "But perhaps we can use their very strength against them."

Chapter 45

As dusk fell on the first day of summer in 1875, seven men walked into the most secret chamber in Chinese America. The room was a comfortable size, though by no means imperial. They sat around a long teak table. The elaborate trappings and appointments one normally associated with the presidents of the Six Companies were conspicuously absent.

This was a place where the most serious and secret work of the Six Companies was conducted—the Chamber of the Presidents. Its austerity was fitting, and the only concession to comfort was an ever-warm large-bellied kettle of tea.

In the two years since Shao Kow and Tai Pien had stood before Chin to tell him of his twenty-five-thousand-dollar loss, much had changed in the Chinese quarter of San Francisco. Numerous spies employed by the Chinese Protective Police had reported on Yang's rise in the Kwong Dock tong. There was a natural reluctance on Tai Pien's part to broach the subject, but when it had finally been discussed Chin had regarded the information dispassionately, as though it was just another report. Tai Pien realized that that was the only way Chin could hear the information and not be consumed with pain.

Change, too, had taken place within the Kong Chow Company, and not the least of the changes had been the death of Lo Chi, its president. Despite his protestations, Chin had almost immediately been raised to take his place. He was elected by acclamation of the entire company, and the cries for leadership from hundreds of people he had individually helped were too much for Chin to ignore.

So it was that Chin came to sit in this most secret of councils. Tai Pien, chief of the Chinese Protective Police, was the only man in the room who was not a Company president. But his business was so interwoven with that of the presidents that he was allowed admission to the chamber.

In the wake of a new wave of white violence against the Chinese, the business of the Six Companies was primarily one of law and order and how to attain it. The Chinese Protective Society had become the powerful arm of the Six Companies. Coupled with the attacks from the whites was the continuing threat of the tongs, which were once again growing in strength.

The system of advance warning worked out by the Chinese Protective Police proved effective against the whites. Streets were cleared as the bands of marauding whites moved into the quarter and the hoodlums were often shocked to find Chinatown little more than a ghost town when they arrived.

It was with the tongs, however, that the Six Companies realized their true battle was. They regarded the highbinders as men of the lowest order because they preyed on their own people.

In the aftermath of having lost a sizable sum of money, Chin went after the tongs with the fervor of a man bent on vengeance. Yet he did it with the wisdom he had always brought to his affairs.

The culmination of his plans were to come about in the next few weeks.

"The seeds of dissent have taken firm root," Chin said at the beginning of the meeting. "The plant has grown and now we are prepared to reap our harvest."

Tao Tsu, president of the powerful Ning Yeung Company, said, "It shall be a harvest of blood."

Chin turned to look at him. "It will require blood to wash ourselves clean of this cancer."

Tao Tsu shook his head. "You know I have never approved of your methods."

Sitting next to Chin, on his right, was Bu Syang Chr of the Yun Wo Company. "These methods have succeeded in weakening the tongs, Tao Tsu. You must admit that."

"That does not mean I must approve."

Chin sought to placate the powerful president. "We are at the threshold of the destruction of the tongs, Tao Tsu. If we remain firm in our conviction our people shall soon be able to walk the streets without fear of the tongs."

"And the white man? Will you deal with him next?"

Chin nodded. "But in a different way—just as a lion attacks a panther differently than he attacks an antelope."

Tao Tsu sighed and shook his head. "So wise for one so young."

Chin lowered his eyes.

"Perhaps it is best that you do things your way," Tao Tsu

said. "I sense leadership passing to your generation, and you must feel your own way . . . make your own mistakes. I only wish to guide."

Chin looked at him. "And I only wish to offer you safety, honorable one. I cannot abide the fear that one so respected as yourself could be the next victim of a beating or a robbery at the hands of these villains who happen to have the same color skin as we."

Tao Tsu nodded, closed his eyes for a moment, then leaned back in his chair, weary from the decades of debate and deliberation and decision.

Ma Fong, of the Sam Yup Company, said, "We have succeeded in turning the tongs against one another, Chin. Tell us why you have called this meeting tonight. I feel there is something momentous you want to ask of us."

Chin nodded. "I ask your permission to begin the final phase in the destruction of the tongs."

Sya Yu Shr, president of the Yeong Wo Company, asked, "What is this final phase you speak of, Chin?"

Chin turned to look at him. The president of the Yeong Wo Company was the only other conservative chief executive in the room. From Tao Tsu he expected nothing more than a perfunctory protest to what he was about to propose; the old man was too tired to argue anymore. If there was to be true opposition, he thought, it would come from Sya Yu Shr.

Chin glanced at Tai Pien, then said, "I ask you to authorize Tai Pien to send a team of his regulars to assassinate Low Sing, Grand *Ah ma* of the Suey Sing tong."

The room fell into a stunned silence and Chin felt grasped by it. He plunged ahead.

"Tai Pien's regulars will make it appear that the assassination was the work of the Kwong Dock tong, and a tong war will be the result. The two remaining powerful tongs in San Francisco will destroy each other in—"

"*No!*"

Chin turned, shocked at the volume of Tao Tsu's voice. The old president had risen in his chair and leaned forward to rest his hands on the conference table for support.

"No," the president of the Ning Yeung Company repeated, "I will not countenance this!"

Chin's tone was, once again, one of placation as he began to speak. "Honorable Tao Tsu, you—"

"I am speaking."

360

Chin's lips pressed tightly together; respect for the older leader mandated that he do so.

The wrinkles about Tao Tsu's almond-shaped face tightened, furrowing deep with anger. When he spoke again his voice was low and ominous.

"I have sat here for two years letting you all have your way. I have watched while you have plotted like evil generals, working your strategies. I have seen you turn the twelve tongs upon each other, like men who are pitting dogs. I have seen you send Chinese regulars, dressed as Hop Sing hatchetmen, to raid Bow On tong gambling parlors. I have seen you disguise our regulars as Gee Kung highbinders so members of the Suey On tong would think it was they who attacked their opium dens."

"And what is the result of it?" Chin asked. He could hold his words no longer, for he knew Tao Tsu to be a persuasive speaker and in years past he had seen him swing an entire delegation from an opposing point of view to his own.

"The result," Chin continued, "is that the Hop Sings and the Bow Ons are no longer even tongs. They number a dozen or so scattered renegades. The result is the Gee Kung tong has fled San Francisco to do their looting in isolated towns and villages in the mountains, and the Suey On have been eliminated altogether. We have planted dissension and the tongs have been torn apart by it."

Tao Tsu held Chin's gaze, held his ground, refused to back down to the younger man. "Why do you fail to mention the Kwong Dock and the Suey Sing tongs?"

"I have not failed to mention them. We are dealing with them this very night. As I have said—"

"And *why* have we waited until tonight to deal with them?"

"Because they are the most powerful."

Tao Tsu shook his head as though he couldn't believe that Chin didn't understand him. "How can one who is sometimes so wise be so ignorant at other times?"

Chin felt his respect for the man stretched to its limits.

Tao Tsu let his gaze sweep around the table. "Don't any of you understand? The reason, the very *reason* that the Kwong Dock and the Suey Sing are the strongest tongs is *because* of your actions. By eliminating the others you have allowed these two to climb in importance.

"They have pulled members from dissipating tongs and because they are all that's left, young hoodlums flock to them and swell their ranks." Tao Tsu grasped with his hand to emphasize the point.

"That will be over soon," Tai Pien said.

Tao Tsu turned to look at him. "By making the Suey Sings think the Kwong Dock have assassinated their leader?"

Tai Pien nodded.

"The only thing that is for certain is that a tong war will erupt and there will be the loss of lives—of highbinders and innocents alike."

"There are always casualties in a war," Chin said. "But when this action is done the tongs will be through."

"And if one snatches a quick victory? If one of the two tongs emerges as still powerful? What will you do then, Chin?"

"That shall not happen."

"You know this to be a fact?"

"I do."

"Tell us," Tao Tsu said with a measure of sarcasm in his voice, "tell us how you are able to know the future."

"It is simple mathematics," Chin said, returning the sarcasm. "The Suey Sing and the Kwong Dock are of almost equal strength. They will wage battle after battle and—"

"Perhaps they will have one great battle to decide the war."

"No," Chin said. "That is not the tongs' way. They will snipe and jab at each other, they will ambush and deplete each other's strength, as would two players in a game of chess."

"This is no chess game," Tao Tsu retorted.

Chin's voice grew stern. "And we shall not treat it as such. When they have all but destroyed each other the superior forces of the Chinese Protective Police will enter and finish the job."

"Annihilation?"

"If it is necessary. They will be given the choice of extermination or deportation to Mother China."

"You are certain of the cooperation of the mandarins?"

Chin reached into his pocket, pulling his trump card. He laid the document on the table for all to see.

"This is a letter from Lu Tsai, mandarin of Szechwan province. In brief, it states that his concern about the problem of the tongs in American is great."

Tai Pien interjected, "In part because of the fact that a cousin of his was killed here at the hands of a highbinder."

The presidents nodded in understanding.

Chin continued. "He agrees to accept all deportees and will be responsible for their resettlement and supervision in Szechwan."

Chin passed the document around the table. When it got to Tao Tsu the old president picked it up. He read it over and the men watched him. He looked at the official seal of the mandarin of Szechwan at the bottom of the page.

Chin waited until the president of the Ning Yeung Company had finished reading it, then softly said, "It will mean the end of the tongs in this country."

Tao Tsu folded the paper and passed it. He pulled his glasses from his tired face, sat down and said, "Do as you see fit." The old man looked at Chin. "I only pray that the gods will forgive us for the carnage we are about to provoke."

Chapter 46

The house of Low Sing, the Grand *Ah ma* of the Suey Sing tong, was worthy of the Emperor of China himself. This was fitting, for Low Sing was an Emperor in his own right. He presided over an empire of evil.

The interests of the Suey Sing tong extended to every vice known to Chinese-Americans—from gambling and drugs to prostitution, slavery, and smuggling. Over all of these interests, Low Sing presided with an iron fist. Beginning with a small sect of thirty-two followers, in little more than a decade he had created a tong whose warriors numbered over a hundred and whose workers numbered over a thousand. A legion of six hundred prostitutes labored, enslaved, in the Suey Sing brothels.

He waited, this summer night, for a woman to be delivered to him. His appetite was as voracious as his manner, and he employed a full-time procurer just to seek out the most desirable of women to fill his evenings.

A fine teak clock, imported from Mother China and as tall as a man, stood against one wall of his living room. And when it began to strike ten o'clock, there was a knock at the door.

A servant answered it and escorted Chi Do, the procurer, into the *Ah ma's* living room.

Chi Do bowed at the waist and Low Sing motioned anxiously for him to rise. "Tell me what delight you have brought tonight."

Chi Do approached the *Ah ma*. "A fine jewel from Changchung, Master Low Sing. Skin like olives and breasts like fine melons. And her skills . . ." He looked toward the heavens. "Of course I would not know myself, but I am told she has turned men to stone from the sheer pleasure of sharing her bed."

Low Sing smiled slightly, his black eyes gleaming in anticipation. "Have the woman brought in."

Chi Do nodded and left the room. When he returned, Low Sing saw that the procurer's description had failed to convey the woman's true beauty.

Her skin was clear and smooth, her eyes like those of a cat—comely, yet mysterious. Her ample bosom strained at the bodice that confined it and her gossamer pantaloons were tight, outlining the lips to which Low Sing would soon gain access.

Instead of bowing, the woman let the trace of a smile cross her mouth and now her lips parted to allow the dart of her tongue to be seen flashing, for a moment, behind ivory white teeth. Her eyes locked with Low Sing's.

The procurer cursed beneath his breath. "Fool. Don't you know who you are with? This is the *Ah ma*, Low Sing. Bow before your master."

"This is no master," she said, her eyes still on Low Sing. "This is a man."

Low Sing listened to the provocative voice of pure sensuality. It was an invitation to ecstasy.

The procurer raised his hand to strike her for her disrespect, but Low Sing raised his at the same time, halting him. His eyes still fixed on the woman, Low Sing said, "Be gone, Chi Do. You have done your job well. Now let me do mine."

The procurer nodded, bowed, and then left the chamber.

When the door was closed, the *Ah ma* said, "You are magnificent." He smiled slightly. "And brazen as well."

She stood before him, her hips flared. "I speak only the truth. Are you not a man?"

Low Sing laughed. "Of that you shall soon learn." Then

the smile left his face. "But you may find me a master as well."

"And you shall find me a willing servant." She lowerd her eyes. "Where may I prepare myself?"

Low Sing motioned his head toward the door at the far end of the room.

White marble, imported from Italy, greeted the woman as she entered the bathing chamber. She was not unaccustomed to luxury, as her clients were among the richest and most powerful in San Francisco. Still, this was more grand than the houses of more than a few of the railroad and business tycoons she had serviced.

She brushed rouge on her cheeks and checked herself in the mirror, then crossed the room to stand before the window. She worked open the latch and sprung it. Then she pushed out slightly and felt the rush of night air as it swirled in.

The fog was light, this night, and she could make out the hazy shape of a half-moon in the sky. She looked at the grounds below—sprawling lawns and a high stone fence around the perimeter. Her eyes focused on the guardhouse. She was unable to make out anyone inside, but she knew that Low Sing had an ample staff of guards, both in the guardhouse and on the grounds.

She shrugged her shoulders. That was not her problem. She had been paid a sizable advance to do the work she had done so far. If all went as planned she would be given triple that amount by the night's end—enough to pay her passage to Paris and set her up as an Oriental madame of the first order.

Tai Pien had decided to use six men for the assassination of Low Sing. He had learned well the lesson taught by the highbinders who had stolen money from Chin's shop years earlier. A larger force would draw attention. A swift, small force of men had the best chance of slipping in quickly, doing the job, and getting out.

The grounds around the *Ah ma*'s house were surrounded by an eight-foot-high stone wall. At the front entrance was a guardhouse where as many as half a dozen of Low Sing's personal bodyguards stayed. Additionally, twice that number roamed the five acres that comprised his estate.

Inside the *Ah ma*'s two-story brick house were another eight of the elite guards positioned at various points throughout the mansion.

Tai Pien's hands, blackened with charcoal, grasped the rope and pulled him upward. When he reached the top of the stone wall he threw his leg up over it and pulled himself over.

Within moments the rest of the regulars were inside the grounds and they knelt, keeping low to the grass, their black pajamas and charcoaled faces blending with the night.

Tai Pien looked at the objective, then spoke to his men. "The window is on the second floor of the north side. Keep low and to the hedges."

The men nodded and began making their way toward the rear of Low Sing's mansion. Only once did they see guards. Two highbinders came within twenty feet of them. But the regulars had fallen to their bellies and taken refuge behind the ornamental shrubbery that filled the garden.

It had taken Tai Pien but two tosses to secure the hook in the window left open by the woman. Then, like so many monkeys, they scampered up the rope, which had thick knots tied, for handholds, at various points along its length.

The six men stood in the bathroom, marveling for a moment at its splendor.

"A quick job of it," he said, his voice a whisper. "The swine should be alone with the woman, but guards may be nearby, so let us do it as quietly as possible."

Again the regulars nodded.

Tai Pien opened the door of the bathroom a crack, then further. The men moved out into the living room, their knives and swords at the ready.

But it was deserted.

Tai Pien stared at the doorway that opened onto Low Sing's bedroom. From within he heard love sounds, and he moved forward with two of his men. The others stayed back in case guards of the house surprised them.

The smell of incense curled into his nose as he came to the door. But he drove all other thoughts from his mind. Tai Pien clutched the doorknob and turned it slowly. Then he pushed hard.

In the dim light of the bedroom he could make out shapes in the bed. Low Sing, on top, almost blotting out the woman, his naked buttocks exposed and thrusting up into the air.

They moved into the room, their feet cushioned by slippers. Tai Pien caught the glint of the *Ah ma*'s eyes as he turned. A look of stunned surprise was on Low Sing's face. For a split second Tai Pien looked at the woman, at her naked beauty, the fine breasts, their nipples distended from arousal.

The second had been all Low Sing needed. His hand moved quickly beneath the pillow, grabbing for his knife. The blade lashed out, its poison-coated edge seeking Tai Pien.

It was Fu San, one of Tai Pien's lieutenants, whose sword saved Tai Pien's life. The flash of the lieutenant's sword through the air made a whooshing sound and the power of the stroke was not slowed at all by Low Sing's hand, which was severed with the knife still in it.

The *Ah ma* opened his mouth to scream from the pain and it was at that moment that Tai Pien lunged forward and drove his own blade down into Low Sing's mouth, skewering his tongue, driving forward with all his weight so that the blade was embedded in the man's throat. And instead of a scream of agony, all that escaped was the sickening gurgle of a dead man whose mouth had filled with his own lifeblood.

Chapter 47

"If you are not careful," the master of the bordello said, "you'll spoil her."

Ti Ben cast a piercing gaze at the man and was greeted with an appeasing smile that claimed the remark had been made in jest.

"Watch your tongue, procurer, or you shall lose it."

The man bowed. "I meant only to flatter you, warlord."

"I know full well what you meant."

And he did. The problem was that there was more than a grain of truth to what the man had implied. Within her small world, Ling had gained a certain notoriety. Whites and Suey Sing highbinders and their friends often came to see the "women who loved each other." Ti Ben came as well. But his visits to Ling did not include Ah Toy.

What had begun as a challenge to his manhood, he admitted to himself, had now developed into an attachment. She was not like other prostitutes. Somehow she had managed to keep alive that single trait which he most admired—pride.

Ling was a consummate lover, but this only served to fan the flame of jealousy in Ti Ben's heart. Away from her, he would agonize over the thought of her in other men's arms and, worse, in Ah Toy's. If this caused jealousy in him, it also made stronger the attachment he felt for Ling.

As his visits became more frequent and of greater length, Ling began to think of him as even more than someone who could give her hope. She began to think of him as a man, as she had not thought of any person, save her family, in a very long time. Otherwise for her there were no men—there were only bodies and hands and stabbing penises and pinching fingers.

It had been easier that way, there was only Ah Toy and the rest of the world. But now there was Ti Ben. And Ling was forced to think about her relationship with Ah Toy. It had become increasingly strained, and it was noticed by the master of the bordello and the patrons who watched the two women perform.

Certainly it was not lost on Ah Toy. She knew, all too well, of the warlord's visits to her lover. Ah Toy made Ling pay for those visits. When she made love to Ling it was with anger, with scratches and bites, and it was no longer love-making.

Ti Ben lay next to Ling on the perfumed sheets, their breathing returning to normal.

"Your master says I am spoiling you."

She nodded. "You are. You bring me too many gifts."

"That it not what he meant."

She looked at him questioningly.

"With Ah Toy," he answered.

Ling looked away.

"Is it true?"

"I don't know what you mean, Ti Ben."

"Do you still enjoy making love with her?"

"I never said I did."

"But you did, didn't you?"

She paused a long moment, then said, "Once, perhaps. Although it wasn't really enjoyment. Pleasure, maybe. Security, certainly."

"And now?"

She turned to look at him. "I get more pleasure from you. I feel more secure in your arms." She drew into his embrace. His arms were around her, yet not holding her. Ling pulled away and looked at him, resting her head on the satin pillow. "Tell me the reason you ask, Ti Ben."

He was silent.

Ling said, "I thought my words would please you."

"They do," Ti Ben said. "They flatter the man in me."

"And the warlord in you? How do my words make him feel?"

"There is an obligation I have, Ling. You must understand this."

She sat up in the bed, her muscles tensing. "I see. And part of that obligation is to keep me a productive whore?"

"Ling—"

"No. Please. I understand, warlord."

"You do not understand."

"But I do." She swung her legs over the edge of the bed and stood. "Bad business for the two of us to grow too close. That would affect my little performance with Ah Toy, correct?"

"Ling—"

"No need to explain, warlord. After all, the revenue I produce for the Suey Sing tong is far more important than—"

"Be still!" he ordered, his voice that of the warrior that he was. "Woman, sometimes I want to stick my hand between your legs to see if there's a stump there!"

She turned away.

"You talk more like a highbinder than a . . ." His voice trailed off. When he spoke again his tone was more gentle. "Now keep your lips still for a moment so you can listen to me. And face me when I speak."

Ling turned around, though she would not look at him.

"I was saying that I have an obligation," Ti Ben continued. "That obligation is to my tong. And, yes, you are the property of my tong. You do produce revenue. These facts may not be pleasant—either to you or me—but they are facts all the same."

She blinked, looking at him.

"You cannot deny that . . . that what we feel for each other has changed that which you felt for Ah Toy."

Ling cocked her head. It was the first time Ti Ben had actually acknowledged his feelings for her. "I . . . I told you my feelings for her had changed," Ling said.

"Then know that my feelings for you are strong, Ling. Know that it pains me, like a battle-ax creasing my skin, to think of you in her embrace or in anyone's embrace but my own."

Ling's eyes grew wet as she flew to Ti Ben's arms. Tears spilled forth as she felt his powerful warrior's arms wrap tightly about her.

Her voice choked with emotion as she spoke. "But . . . but you said . . ."

"I said I have an obligation and that obligation must be honored. The solution to this problem is to remove you from this place that causes my obligation and my heart to be in conflict."

"Oh . . . oh, Ti Ben . . ."

He stroked her hair. "It will take time and it will take money. Of the latter I have some and given the former I shall have more. Influence, fortunately, I have in abundance. I feel certain that when I have accumulated enough money and honor I shall be able to prevail upon the *Ah ma* to let me buy you." He paused, then added, "and make you my bride."

She looked up at him, wet rivers slicing through the white powder on her cheeks. Her lips trembled as she said, "I . . . I love you so much. I . . ." But she could not speak anymore, for Ti Ben's lips had silenced her.

They made love twice more that night. As the first shafts of morning light broke through the bars on Ling's window, Ti Ben rose gently from the bed. His eyes were on her as he stood, making an effort not to disturb her. He walked silently to the chair in the corner and pulled his trousers on. He slipped into his jacket and, turning to look at her, saw that she was looking at him, a smile soft and warm on her face.

"I woke you," he whispered.

"Fom one wonderful dream into another."

Ti Ben walked to the side of her bed and knelt. "You should sleep."

"Later," she said. "I want to be awake every moment you are here."

"I will return soon."

"Not soon enough."

He kissed her cheek. "Soon, though." He stood and slipped on his shoes.

Ti Ben was buttoning his tunic when Ling said, "I have a favor to ask of you."

He regarded her with surprise. In all the time they had

been together, Ling had never asked for anything, though the warlord frequently brought her presents.

"Then ask it. If I can do it, it shall be done."

Ling wanted to speak, but the words would not come. She knew that Ti Ben had no idea how difficult it was for her even to gather the courage to admit she had a favor to ask.

But Ti Ben sensed this. He crossed the room and sat on the edge of the bed, his voice now warm as the morning light filling the room.

"What is it, Ling? You know you have nothing to fear from me."

"I . . ." She looked away. "Once before I asked a favor of a man and . . ."

"And what?"

"I was punished for it."

"Who punished you?" he demanded.

"Who?" Her eyes widened, knowing Ti Ben would confront the master of the bordello if she told him it was he who had beaten her. And though Ti Ben was clearly the man's superior, it was Ling who had to live day and night under his thumb. The master could easily make life unbearable for her. "You do not know him," she lied. "It was a time long ago."

"This is now. And I am not that other man. Ask me the favor, Ling."

She looked into his eyes. "Many years ago, when I was a child, back in Mother China, I was separated from my brothers."

He nodded, gently urging her on.

"They journeyed across the sea, seeking gold in this country. My family was poor. My father could not afford their passage, so I was offered as security. When one of my brothers failed to meet his obligation I was sold into slavery."

"The pig!"

"No," Ling said. "Do not speak of them that way. I remember them kindly, though Chin more than Yang."

Ti Ben stiffened at Ling's words. "Yang, you say? Yang and Chin?"

She nodded. "My wildest dream is that they may be somewhere still in California; perhaps even in this city." Then the excitement in her voice lessened, as she looked away. "I know the chance of that is thin. I have heard men speak of the difficulties in the early years—the brutality, the thousands killed working on the railroads."

"Yang and Chin," Ti Ben repeated.

She looked back to Ti Ben, daring to hope. "Still, it is possible, isn't it, Ti Ben? Say it is possible."

He heard her words, felt her desperation, and said, "Yes, yes it is possible, Ling. I will look into the matter."

Ti Ben barely felt Ling's arms as she excitedly hugged him, her kisses of gratitude, her cries of thanks. He was thinking—thinking hard.

Chapter 48

The night of Low Sing's death marked the first anniversary of Yang's appointment to the rank of warlord of the Kwong Dock tong. The appointment had come just two month's after Po Dung had been promoted to his former position of chief swordsman of the tong.

In the year he had been a warlord, Yang had been a busy man, as was attested by the scars that crisscrossed his body. It was a time made for men like Yang. He led the men he commanded in killings, brutalities, and ambushes. No one knew for certain how many Chinese had been killed during the years the sporadic tong wars had raged. Some said it was near five hundred. Others, the *Golden Hills* for instance, claimed the number of deaths was closer to a thousand.

What was clear was that whole tongs had been completely wiped out. There was mourning; only for the innocents—children and old people—who got in the way of a flying hatchet or a stray bullet. Of these a precise count was kept. Thirty-two bystanders had lost their lives directly because of the conflagrations between the tongs.

They were battles for power, control, and territory. But mostly they were begun for vengeance. The Gai Chen Shez tong controlled prostitution and the Po Shin She tong was jealous, wanting prostitution for themselves. So the Po Shin She tong took to raiding the Gai Chen Shez brothels, beat their old hag wardens, loosed the prostitutes or, more often, took the women back to their own brothels.

Outraged, the Gai Chen Shez tong would retaliate with raids of their own, and war was the result.

Occasionally, there would be an assassination of a high-ranking highbinder and the opposing tong would deny having done the deed. It mattered little, for members of opposing tongs did not believe each other.

The result, duly noted in the *Golden Hills*, was that the tongs were thinning out. The news stories hastened to add that this did not mean that the tongs were no longer a force in Little China—only that there were fewer of them.

The two most powerful were the Suey Sing and the Kwong Dock. And, with the murder of the Suey Sing's *Ah ma*, it seemed that the war of wars was inevitable.

It was for discussion of this matter that Yang now sat in the War Council of the Kwong Dock tong. Presiding was Hung Ma Kung, the Grand *Ah ma* of the tong. Also present was the chief swordsman, Po Dung. Sitting on either side of Yang were To Ching and Mang Shao Shen, warlords of rank equal to his own.

Their attention was riveted on the *Ah ma*, Hung Ma Kung.

"The death of Low Sing was a timely one," the old leader said, "for it leaves them without an *Ah ma* to lead them into battle."

Po Dung said, "Ren Dai Ko, their most powerful warlord, will surely assume the role."

Hung Ma Kung nodded. "You are probably right, Po Dung. But Ren Dai Ko is a warlord, not an *Ah ma*. He may be familiar with leading a force of highbinders into battle, but he has not had experience in fighting a war."

The *Ah ma* turned to Mang Shao Shen. "Read the letter."

The warlord to Yang's right reached inside his tunic and pulled out a sheet of paper. He unfolded it and read:

"Whereas the scum of the Kwong Dock tong has undertaken the foul assassination of the revered Low Sing, it must accept the consequences of its actions.

"Accordingly, the warriors of the Suey Sing tong do declare a state of war against the dregs of the Kwong Dock tong, the end result of which shall be the annihilation of that most accursed group."

Hung Ma Kung smiled as the paper was passed around. "You see, Ren Dai Ko thinks as a warlord, not an *Ah ma*. Were I in his position I would have sent a force of as many warriors as I could muster to destroy my enemy. Instead," the *Ah ma* said, gesturing with his hands, "instead he makes an open declaration so as to put us on guard."

"Boldness," To Ching said.

Hung Ma Kung shook his head. "No. Stupidity." He settled back in his chair. "Do any of you have any idea who assassinated Low Sing?"

None did.

Yang said, "None of my men. That much I know."

"I know that, Yang," the *Ah ma* said. "No Kwong Dock highbinders killed him. Not that we haven't entertained thoughts of such a plan," he said, glancing at Po Dung. "But Low Sing's grounds were well guarded. It must have been someone who had friends within his tong. Someone who was not a member of any tong."

Hung Ma Kung threw his hands up. "It matters not. The deed is done and they think we did it and now war will come of it. Perhaps it is for the best." He looked around the table at his generals and said, "Now let us plan for this war."

For all of June and July and halfway into August, the streets of San Francisco's Chinatown turned red with Chinese blood.

From the beginning it was the Kwong Dock tong's war. Superiorly armed, in part due to the money they had stolen from Chin's import shop, the tong waged a relentless series of battles against the highbinders of the Suey Sing.

Bands of fifty and sixty Kwong Dock warriors would swoop down on a Suey Sing *Fan-tan* parlor and raze it to the ground, killing every Suey Sing employee and highbinder in the parlor. More than a few times innocent gamblers were mistaken for employees and met the same fate.

In July sixteen Suey Sing brothels were burned, their whore-keepers butchered, their guards shot, and the prostitutes taken prisoner to work in Kwong Dock bordellos. The gods spared the bordello in which Ling worked.

The Suey Sing retaliated in desperate ways. With less warriors in their ranks to begin with, and those ranks quickly being depleted, they fought a sort of guerrilla warfare.

In return for the burning of the brothels, the Suey Sing bombed half a dozen washhouses owned by the Kwong Dock tong. The Suey Sing were also masters of assassination. They struck quickly, usually with hatchets or cudgels, and often in the middle of the day.

They were selective in their assassination attempts, killing off lieutenants and better-known warriors of the Kwong Dock tong. But these did little but enrage the Kwong Dock tong even more.

In August a force of eight Suey Sings were caught in Beckett Alley by twenty-four Kwong Dock highbinders. It was over in a matter of seconds. Seven Suey Sings lay dead. One managed to escape to tell the story.

It was apparent that the war was going to the Kwong Dock. It was on the tenth day of that month that an emissary delivered a message to the Kwong Dock house calling for a final battle.

As Yang sat in the War Council, listening to the summons to battle, he remembered hearing the same summons not so many years ago in Los Angeles. This battle, he was certain, would end with the victory of the Kwong Dock tong.

". . . at Waverly Place at the hour of midnight," Ho Huan said.

Yang watched Ho Huan, pleased that a disciple of his had risen to the rank of warlord. Ho Huan had been elevated to that position to take the place of Mang Shao Shen, who had been assassinated in the second week of July.

Ho Huan was put in charge of a brigade of thirty Kwong Dock highbinders. This was the smallest of the tong's three brigades. To Ching, the veteran warlord of the tong, had seventy-eight men under his command—well down from the more than a hundred and fifty he had before the war started. Yang had fifty men in his command.

"So," Hung Ma Kong said, "it is to be the final night of the Suey Sing tong."

"Let us take care that it is not our own final night as well," Yang said.

All eyes turned to him and Hung Ma Kung's voice filled with anger as he said, "Does my own warlord doubt the strength of his men?!"

"No," Yang said, leveling his hand over the council table. "No. I know that we are destined to be triumphant over the Suey Sing. We would have beaten them in Los Angeles as well." He paused, then said, "But it is my memories of what happened there that trouble me."

Ho Huan looked at him, understanding.

To Ching asked, "What do you mean, Yang?"

He turned to look at the other warlord. "I mean the aftermath." Yang shook his head. "Sometimes . . . some nights it still haunts me." His words were soft and low and his eyes were far away.

"I will never forget it as long as I live. The whites were like nothing I had ever seen; more fierce than the fiercest wildcats, for no animal alive has ever been possessed of the bloodlust I saw that night. They were frenzied and nothing could stop them until they had drunk of Chinese blood until they could drink no more."

Yang looked at the men in the War Council. "I do not want to live through that again."

"And still," the *Ah ma* said, "we cannot avoid this night. If the Suey Sing are foolish enough to call for a direct confrontation, then we cannot miss the opportunity to finish them off."

To Ching said, "But as Yang says . . ."

Hung Ma Kung nodded. "Yes. There must be a solution, though."

"There is," Ho Huan said.

The three men turned to look at the newest warlord.

Ho Huan said, "The Suey Sing may be scum, but they are not fools. They have no more desire to die at the *fan quay*'s hands than we do. We need simply use Yang's words to remind them of the Los Angeles Massacre."

"But then they will decline the fight," the *Ah ma* said.

"We need only suggest different weapons." Ho Huan leaned forward again. "The whites in Los Angeles would not have gotten involved were it not for the gunfire on the warring tongs. We need to get the Suey Sings to agree not to use pistols for this battle. Let the weapons be confined to hatchets, knives, chains, cudgels."

Hung Ma Kung nodded, then turned to Yang. "You made a wise choice in choosing this warlord." To Ho Huan he said, "Send a messenger to the Suey Sing."

Ti Ben had wrestled with the knowledge he possessed all through the summer. The moment Ling had spoken the words "Yang and Chin," he immediately understood. The gods had selected him as a tool of fate. It was widely known throughout the corridor that the brother of Chin, the wealthy import merchant and Kong Chow president, was Yang Wong, warlord of the Kwong Dock tong. It could not be coincidence.

Ti Ben realized he had a powerful advantage in Ling. The sister of a Kwong Dock warlord was a prostitute in a Suey Sing bordello. It was an advantage which could prove invaluable to his tong. At the same time, Ti Ben wanted to make certain he used this information to his own benefit.

Thus it was not so much a question of whether or not to inform the *Ah ma*, but of the best time to inform him.

As Ti Ben watched the events of that summer unfold—the losing battle his tong was waging, defeat after defeat, and finally the decision to challenge the Kwong Dock to a final battle—he became more and more convinced that the time to make his relevation was approaching.

It did not occur to him to worry about Ling's welfare in all this. This was not out of callousness, but out of a feeling that she was merely a pawn. She had value only in that she was alive and could be used to threaten to buy the collaboration of Yang. Ti Ben was certain she would come to no harm.

Hung Ma Kung had guessed correctly that the Suey Sing would appoint Ren Dai Ko to take the place of the fallen *Ah ma*, Low Sing. While Low Sing had been a strong leader, he had not taken part in combat in many years and hence was not as battle-hardened as the warlord, now *Ah ma*, Ren Dai Ko.

Ren Dai Ko greeted the death of Low Sing with a mixture of sadness and pleasure, for he knew that, even though it occurred under less than desirable circumstances. the death of the *Ah ma* hastened his own ascendency to that position.

He sat in a War Chamber that was far less ornate than that of the Kwong Dock tong, for though the Suey Sing was the second most powerful tong in San Francisco, they still never approached the grandeur that was the Kwong Dock. Their coffers had been emptied to build the mansions and provide for the excesses of the former *Ah ma*, and not enough had been directed toward recruiting warriors and arming them.

"Although we appear to be at a disadvantage," he said to the two warlords in the room with him, "there are several things in our favor which the Kwong Dock have not considered."

Ming Lo San, one of the warlords, said, "Then tell Ti Ben and I what they are. Morale is low, Ren Dai Ko. We need some news to rally about."

The *Ah ma* looked to the other warlord. "Do both my warlords doubt our strength?"

Ti Ben shook his head. "Neither of us doubt our strength." He paused. "But we have sustained great losses. We have less than half the men the Kwong Dock tong does. It is as Ming Lo San has said. If there is secret cause for victory, now is the time to reveal it."

"Very well." Ren Dai Ko sipped from the tea in front of him. "The first thing for you to remember is that the Kwong Dock's *Ah ma* is an old man. He is not a warlord. Hung Ma Kung is their leader, but he does not lead a brigade of men. He has not been a highbinder for many years and, therefore, does not have recent experience in war."

More to himself than to his two men, Ren Dai Ko said, "Perhaps our ancestors guided the hand of the assassins of Low Sing so we would have a young *Ah ma* to serve as leader during this time." He looked at the two men. "In the final reckoning it will be my experience against Hung Ma Kung's, and I have the high side of the ledger there."

"Still," Ming Lo San said, "we are little more than a hundred against a force twice that number."

Ren Dai Ko nodded. "That may yet change."

The two warlords exchanged glances and then looked to the *Ah ma*.

Ti Ben asked, "How? How can the scales change so much when the battle is to be this very night . . . in less than six hours?" He would hear Ren Dai Ko's answer before he gave his own.

There was a knock at the door of the War Chamber and Ren Dai Ko said, "Even now events may be taking place which shall provide the answer to your question." The *Ah ma* looked to the door and called, "Enter."

One of the *Ah ma*'s personal guard, dressed in a black tunic, opened the door and looked inside. "*Ah ma*, a messenger from the Kwong Dock is at our gate."

Both Ming Lo San and Ti Ben sprang to their feet. Ming Lo San crossed the room to the guard. "Is he alone?"

"A trick!" the other warlord cautioned. "Remember the treachery with which they killed Low Sing."

"It is no trick," Ren Dai Ko declared.

Ming Lo San turned to look at him. "Perhaps a preemptive attack. Perhaps two hundred Kwong Dock hatchetmen lie in wait to surge forward at this moment."

"No," Ren Dai Ko said. "They would not be so foolish." He walked across the room to the guard. "Admit the messenger." Then he turned to Ming Lo San and said, "With a thousand hatchetmen they would not be able to storm this house. It is too well fortified; the gate is impregnable. They would lose all their men and still not put a dent in the walls."

Ti Ben said, "You seemed to expect this messenger, Ren Dai Ko."

He nodded. "Indeed. That is the telling difference between us and the Kwong Dock. Something even more than the fact that their *Ah ma* is not a warlord."

Ming Lo San could stand it no longer. "What then? What?"

Ren Dai Ko smiled. "Po Dung, their swordsman, Yang, and Ho Huan—three of the four on their War Council—all share a common heritage. All three are veterans of the Los Angeles Massacre of five years ago. They still bear the scars of seeing whites gone mad the last time our two tongs locked horns."

Ti Ben shook his head. "I don't see . . ."

"You shall," Ren Dai-Ko said, "very shortly."

Outside the massive gray steel portal that barred the entrance of the Suey Sing tong house, Yan Kwan, Ho Huan's lieutenant, shivered and pulled up the collar of his tunic. It was past six and it had grown cold in the city. But it was the sound of the bars behind the door being loosened that chilled him more than the weather.

Yan Kwan was filled with the knowledge that he was about to enter the innermost sanctum of his dreaded mortal enemy, and although he swelled with pride to have been chosen as the messenger, he still shook with the knowledge that he would be alone in the camp of his arch-adversaries.

The door swung inward.

Five highbinders of the Suey Sing tong stood with their hatchets drawn. Behind them Yan Kwan could see a score more with weapons in their hands.

He laughed defiantly. "We will make short work of you this night if you quiver so before the approach of a single Kwong Dock warrior."

But his laugh was cut short as one of the gate guards reached forward and pulled him in from the landing. The door closed shut and the wide steel bolts slammed home and locked with a clang of finality to them.

The guard who had grabbed him pushed Yan Kwan to a wall and began a rude search. "We take no chances with swine who strike at a man as he beds with a woman."

"A good lesson for him. He should have been leading his men instead of bedding a whore."

The guard spun him around and slapped Yan Kwan across the mouth with the back of his hand.

The young highbinder spit on the floor and looked at the

dozens of Suey Sing surrounding him. "How brave this mighty tong is when they are twenty against one unarmed man." Again he laughed. "We shall see how brave you are come morning when your blood flows like rivers in the gutters of Waverly Place. Now take me to your master so I may deliver my message and be gone; the stink of vermin in this place overwhelms me."

Four hatchetmen escorted Yang Kwan through the halls of the house. He walked in the middle, with two guards in front and two in back. His shoulders were held high, his arms swinging wide and proud. He would show these swine what a Kwong Dock warrior was.

The group stopped before the door of the War Chamber and one of the five men guarding the door stepped forward and again searched Yan Kwan. When he was satisfied that Yan Kwan was unarmed he nodded and opened the door.

Yan Kwan walked into the War Chamber of the Suey Sing tong. Seated behind the war table were Ren Dai Ko, Ming Lo San, and Ti Ben.

Ren Dai Ko said, "You bring a message?"

Yan Kwan held the envelope out to the *Ah ma* of the Suey Sing. Ren Dai Ko took it, opened it, read it. He nodded, knowing what it would say, pleased that he was so good a judge of his enemy.

There was truth in what his warlords had feared, Ren Dai Ko thought. They *were* greatly outnumbered. Ti Ben had not the boldness to admit that he doubted their strength, but the *Ah ma* himself doubted it. No matter how clever a general was, going against an enemy twice as powerful was no mean task.

Still, there were ways of evening the odds, even gaining the advantage. The Kwong Dock messenger had delivered one of those means. What the young warrior standing before him did not know, Ren Dai Ko thought, was that he would provide another means before he left the house.

Ren Dai Ko looked at the guards in the War Chamber. "Take this messenger downstairs and detain him."

Yan Kwan stiffened, fear clutching at him. He prepared to fight these men to the death, with his bare hands, if necessary.

The *Ah ma* sensed this and gestured to calm him. "You will not be here for long. But it is necessary that I take a few moments to consider my reply to this message."

That made sense, Yan Kwan thought, and relaxed. The

guards escorted him from the War Chamber. Again he was led down a maze of corridors and hallways. A door was opened and the smell of excrement from the basement sewer slapped up at him.

The men walked down the stairs and one of the guards opened another door. Yan Kwan walked into a small, dark room. The guard who had opened the door lit a match and touched it to a kerosene lamp on the wall. He walked to the other wall and lit another lamp. Light showed the bareness of the empty room. The only furnishing was a single straight-backed chair. The floor was hard-packed dirt, and the walls were of rough brick.

The guards left without a word.

Yan Kwan listened to the sound of the door being locked.

Ren Dai Ko smiled thinly as he watched Ming Lo San and Ti Ben reading the letter from the Kwong Dock tong.

When they had finished with the letter Ti Ben regarded him skeptically. "Surely you don't believe they are serious in this?"

"They are."

Ming Lo San agreed with Ti Ben. "You must know that this is a trick, designed to make us march into battle without pistols."

"It is no trick," Ren Dai Ko said confidently. "You will recall what I said about how the members of their War Council went through the Los Angeles Massacre."

Both warlords nodded, still not fully understanding.

Ren Dai Ko explained. "The Massacre happened because whites were spectators to the tong war and a prominent white was killed. The *fan quay* were drawn to the quarter by the sound of gunfire between our two tongs."

Ren Dai Ko poured himself another cup of tea. "No, it is no trick. The Kwong Dock tong wants a battle with no guns. So we will give it to them . . . for a time."

Now it was Ming Lo San and Ti Ben who smiled.

The *Ah ma* finished his tea and stood; the two warlords stood by on reflex. "We have business with our visitor." He handed Ti Ben the message. "Have a scribe write an answer to this, stating that we shall comply with the conditions outlined in their proposal—no guns."

Ti Ben nodded.

The *Ah ma* turned to Ming Lo San. "Send for the torturer.

Let's see what secrets we can rip from this young Kwong Dock devil's tongue."

Ti Ben stood silently, watching Ming Lo San leave to summon the torturer. He thought of what the torturer would do to the messenger, the pain the messenger would have to endure before he died. And then he thought of Ling.

Chapter 49

It was at the stroke of midnight that Hung Ma Kung stood in the courtyard before the almost two hundred warriors of the Kwong Dock tong. If a night could be made for death, this one was. The air hung heavy and still over San Francisco; the fog was unmoving.

"If the gods are with us," the *Ah ma* began, "the Suey Sing have already arrived in Waverly Place and wait for us. Your warlords have their orders. Obey them and return victorious."

Hung Ma Kung paused, then said, "After this night there shall be only one tong, only one power, only one glory, and its name shall be Kwong Dock!"

The warriors waved their hatchets over their heads, cheering. They were one hundred and seventy-one of the most efficient killing machines in the history of war. Each wore a red sash about his waist and forehead—the symbol of the T'ai T'sing rebels. Each man was skilled in a dozen ways of killing. Each man was primed for only one thing—Suey Sing blood.

Each of the warlords knew his role. The battle strategy had been largely designed by Po Dung, with the *Ah ma* offering only guidance and an occasional suggestion. Hung Ma Kung was wise enough and confident enough to depend on the wisdom of the men he had surrounded himself with—particularly when it was in an area in which they were acknowledged experts.

Po Dung had noted that they outnumbered the Suey Sing; that was a definite advantage. He felt certain the Suey Sing would arrive at Waverly Place early, hoping to establish the battle lines. This would spell their doom.

The swordsman decided that Ho Huan could lead his men through the south entrance to the square, while Yang's men would approach in a wide circle and secure the north entrance. Once the Suey Sing were trapped in the middle, To Ching's men would join Ho Huan's in a charge that would drive the Suey Sing into retreating into the blades of Yang's highbinders.

An hour earlier, Yan Kwan had been dumped at the doors of the Kwong Dock house, his body mutilated beyond description. From mid-thigh to the upper part of his body there was no skin to be seen, just shining crimson cords of muscle and tissue.

A terse note was pinned to Yan Kwan's corpse. It read, "We agree. No pistols."

Away from the other highbinders, Yang consoled Ho Huan on the loss of his trusted lieutenant. Yang insisted that the best way to pay tribute to the fallen highbinder was to avenge his death with Suey Sing blood.

It was Suey Sing blood that Yang himself wanted this night. He had offered his prayers to Kwan Kung and now he stood in the night, his battle tunic buttoned, a double-edge hatchet in his right hand, an iron cudgel in his waistband.

At the head of fifty-nine warriors, Yang walked through the open steel portals which guarded the courtyard of the house. Yang turned left onto Spofford Alley. Next came To Ching, accompanied by Po Dung. Their column of warriors turned right to take another route.

Finally, Ho Huan led his men out of the courtyard and followed Spofford Alley toward Stockton Street, which would lead him to Waverly Place. He didn't know the routes the other two columns would take. This information was known to Hung Ma Kung alone, who imparted to each man separate instructions.

Ho Huan's thirty warriors moved stealthily behind him, through streets that were narrow and deserted, for all the quarter knew that a battle was to be fought this night and that much blood would flow.

Like black panthers in the night, they moved with a slow grace, as though they were one. They moved a block at a time, securing each corner, massing, and then pouring over to the next block. And through it all Ho Huan thought of Yan Kwan and how he had died, and the pain he had gone through and how it had been he, Ho Huan, who had sent him.

He recalled the night they had broken into the import shop, watching Tsau Tsau torture the shop manager. It had hardly bothered him. Now the thought of his lieutenant being tortured in a similar manner made him feel weak and ill.

He rebuffed himself, recalling Yang's admonition. His men crept down the next street and Ho Huan formed a map in his mind's eye, realized that they were but half a mile from Waverly Place . . . and from the battle.

There was a stifled cry from the rear, then another . . . and another.

Ho Huan turned. His men were spreading out, confused. Wing Hip, another of his lieutenants, was at his side, and opened his mouth to speak as a hatchet came down like an eagle and embedded itself deep in his chest.

From above.

Ti Ben's men lined the roofs on either side of the street. Ho Huan looked up at the steel death that rained down on them and in that moment of terror he remembered that he had told Yan Kwan the route they would take to Waverly Place.

All of this took Ho Huan but a split second of thought. In another fraction of a moment he analyzed the situation. There was no fighting the Suey Sings. He was in an impossible situation—the Suey Sings above them, raining down death.

"Retreat!" Ho Huan cried.

The men, eighteen left from the original thirty, turned to flee up the street. They fled into a sudden barrier of more highbinders, more hatchets, more knives.

It had been quick—less than two minutes. Ho Huan had survived, had somehow fought through the line of Suey Sing at the end of the street. He had run as fast as his feet would carry him, through the streets of the quarter, back to the Kwong Dock house.

Four of his original force followed on his tail.

So far as Yang could see everything was going according to plan. Apparently the Suey Sing had arrived at Waverly Place at the stroke of midnight. He felt this because he and his fifty-nine warriors had made a wide circle around from the Kwong Dock house to the north. Waverly Place lay midway between the Kwong Dock house and the Suey Sing house on the north side of the quarter.

Yet as they circled north and into enemy territory, Yang

and his men encountered no Suey Sing highbinders. Thus, when his men were less than a block from the north entrance to the square, Yang felt confident that the strategy was going as planned.

The area of the battle was a large square which had but two entrances—one on the north and one on the south. Storefronts lined the square.

A forward scout reported to Yang that the Suey Sings were just in front of them, occupying the north entrance of Waverly Place.

Yang waited.

He had not long to wait.

At exactly twelve-thirty, To Ching and Po Dung arrived at the south entrance of the square with a force of seventy-eight hatchetmen. A signal rocket was shot and Yang's men attacked from the rear.

An encirclement and rear attack had been the one thing Ren Dai Ko and his high warlords had not foreseen. Yang's warriors sliced into their back side, hatchets and knives flailing, taking a toll quickly and driving the eighty-three Suey Sing highbinders out of cover and into the center of the large square.

At the moment they were flushed out, Po Dung and To Ching moved forward with the main force of Kwong Dock warriors. The two forces of Kwong Dock hatchetmen had effectively caught the Suey Sing in the middle of Waverly Place; it was there that the first engagement of the battle took place.

Ren Dai Ko ordered half of his men, those under the command of Ming Lo San, to turn and face Yang's faction. The remaining force, which had just arrived under the leadership of Ti Ben, turned to do battle with To Ching's men.

The Kwong Dock had succeeded in their immediate goal of splitting the battle into two fronts. Po Dung had pursued this strategy, knowing that the Suey Sing were not powerful enough to wage war on two ends for long.

For a time the Suey Sing were able to do just that, however. Under the foggy night sky of San Francisco, the death screams of dozens of men could be heard as steel clanged against steel, as blade broke skin, as lifeblood burst forth to stain Waverly Place.

It was during those moments that Yang knew best that he was truly in the favored sight of the god Kwan Kung. His ax felled a Suey Sing highbinder here, sliced a hand there; his iron cudgel slammed against a skull and he felt bone give. His black tunic was wet with sweat and blood—both that of his enemy and his own, for he had been slashed more than a few times by glancing blades.

But he knew not of pain or his bleeding wounds. He only knew of the battle, the killing, the bloodlust. He threw back his head in the middle of it and gave out a shriek as he bore down on his enemies, swinging his battle-ax, moving on through the night of death.

And then, when scores had been butchered, it seemed that Nature herself stepped in, because the two tongs shrank away from each other for a moment, weary from the battle, and regrouped.

The Suey Sing highbinders fled to the east side of the square and there they stood, surveying the carnage. Waverly Place was littered with bodies. Forces of the Kwong Dock tong stood at both entrances of the square, locking them in.

Ming Lo San took a quick headcount and reported to Ren Dai Ko. "Thirty-three men left."

The *Ah ma* nodded and turned to Ti Ben.

Ti Ben said, "I would guess the Kwong Dock have easily double that number."

Ren Dai Ko wiped the blood from his hands, shaking his head. "An attack from the rear. We should have thought of that."

Ti Ben nodded and said, "They have us sealed in."

"How many men do they have on the north side?" the Ah Ma asked.

"Thirty . . . maybe more."

"We could break through them," Ming Lo San said, clutching the pistol in his waistband, "with these."

"No," the *Ah ma* said. "We did not come here for a draw. We came for victory, and it is victory we shall have. We will not run." He glanced around the square. "Wait until they send another wave. When they are before us have your men draw their weapons and shoot."

The two Suey Sing warlords nodded and moved to give the orders.

Po Dung sat before a dry goods store with To Ching. Blood flowed from a wound on his arm and one of the warriors tightened a cloth about it.

To Ching stood before him. "Where can Ho Huan be? We need his men."

386

"Forget about him," the swordsman said. "He was either ambushed or fled like a coward. Perhaps treachery is even involved. We shall deal with that problem later."

He looked at the warrior tending to his wound. "Enough. I will survive this scrape." The highbinder retreated and Po Dung turned to To Ching. "Now, To Ching; now we deliver the death blow. Signal Yang."

A rocket shot skyward into the night sky and exploded, brilliant against the clouds covering the square. A battle cry rose from the highbinders of the Kwong Dock tong. On the north side of the square Yang's hatchetmen charged, their weapons raised. From the south side of Waverly Place Po Dung and To Ching led their men, war cries echoing against the walls of the brick battlefield.

A combined force of seventy-two Kwong Dock highbinders descended on the remaining thirty-two Suey Sing warriors. Ren Dai Ko stood in the midst of his men, watching the enemy tong advance on him. He saw the flash of their weapons in the night, the cruel slits of their eyes, the screams of their hatred, and when they were almost upon him he called, *"Now!"*

The thirty-two Suey Sing warriors drew their pistols, aimed, and fired, almost at point-blank range, into the charging enemy.

Yang heard the sound of the guns, almost as though it was a single sound, like that of dynamite charges he had heard detonated when he had worked on the railroad years ago. He saw the flash of their weapons, knew that they had fallen prey to treachery, saw his men go down all about him as though they had stumbled over an invisible wire.

On the other side of the square he saw To Ching's men falling, crumbling like paper dragons after the New Year's celebration had ended.

He had been played for a fool, he thought in that moment. In that instant he realized that he had given the Suey Sing a weapon when he had asked them to agree to exclude pistols from the battle.

He was a fool, Yang thought. The Suey Sing were the underdogs. They were desperate. They would use any device, take any risk to win this night. Let the white men come, they would think; by the time they arrived they would find only vanquished Kwong Dock, dead because Yang had been ignorant enough to believe the Suey Sing would honor a pledge.

Anger and rage bristled in him, and he responded to it rather than his intellect. It would cost him another ten men.

"*Forward!*" he roared, and his men obeyed as though Yang's mere command would make their charge of iron and blade a match for the bullets and powder of the Suey Sing pistols.

Ren Dai Ko, Grand *Ah ma* of the Suey Sing tong, could not believe what he was seeing. It filled him with a joy that was exquisite beyond anything he had ever imagined. The Kwong Dock were charging against his guns. They had hatchets and cudgels alone! And after the sides had become equal it would be his men, alone, who had pistols. They would make short work of whatever Kwong Dock were left.

"Fools," Ren Dai Ko whispered, then cried, "Fire!"

Another salvo went off from the Suey Sing side and ten of Yang's finest hatchetmen fell, to begin the journey that would end in the embrace of their ancestors.

Only then, looking at the dead that lay around his ankles, did Yang realize the depth of his errors. Error upon error; pride making him more of a fool than he already was.

"Retreat!" he cried. His men fell back to their former positions against the north entrance of Waverly Place.

By the south entrance of the square, Po Dung stood behind cover with To Ching. "How many?"

"We lost twenty men, at least. Guns! And they swore—"

"Forget what they swore," the swordsman said. "What is, is. We must deal with it."

Their words were punctuated by random shots being fired from the Suey Sing.

"I'm certain Yang suffered at least as great a loss; perhaps greater. If we have fifty men left that is a great deal."

Po Dung glanced about the entrance they were guarding. "The battle is not over yet. We still have the key point in our favor. We still have position. They are still caught in the middle. We have them blocked off at both ends."

"Unless they attack."

Po Dung turned and looked at To Ching. Another shot rang out.

On the east side of the square Ren Dai Ko and his warlords were exultant. All about them warriors of the Suey Sing tong cheered, raising their pistols, firing off shots of celebration.

"The tide has turned," Ren Dai Ko declared.

"Victory will be ours!" one of the warriors called. "Death to all Kwong Dock scum!"

Ming Lo San and Ti Ben crowded in close to him, eager to receive further word on the battle plan.

"What now?" Ti Ben called loudly, in order to be heard above the cheers of the men.

"The larger force," the *Ah ma* said. "We attack the south entrance." He turned to Ming Lo San. "Have some of your men fire against the warriors at the north wall to hold them at bay while we finish off the larger group. When we've done with them we will join you and destroy the Kwong Dock at the north wall."

Ming Lo San nodded.

The two warlords passed the word to their lieutenants and the lieutenants told the warriors. In a moment the battle cry broke from Ren Dai Ko's lips and the thirty hatchetmen of the Kwong Dock tong surged out into the square.

From their cover on the south side of Waverly Place, Po Dung, To Ching, and their thirty remaining men watched as the remains of the Suey Sing army charged for them, their guns blasting.

A bullet whizzed past Po Dung's head, missing him by inches, the sound of its buzz loud in his ears. A piece of brick bit at his face as another bullet barely missed.

The Suey Sing advanced and Po Dung and his men were helpless to stop them, could do nothing unless they could engage them in hand-to-hand combat. The gunfire kept them effectively pinned. Po Dung saw that a small force of Suey Sing were holding Yang's men back on the other side of the square. He cursed to himself.

The Suey Sing were twenty yards from them, their weapons blazing, ferreting out Po Dung's men with their pistols. The swordsman of the Kwong Dock tong saw his men beginning to fall.

"Throw knives!" he cried.

A flash of Kwong Dock blades flew through the air and several of these found their mark in the chest and bodies of the attacking Suey Sings. Startled by the attack, the Suey Sings slowed for a brief moment, falling back. But it was not long before they surged forward again, their guns blazing again, urged on for the kill by Ren Dai Ko at their head.

Po Dung knew that there were but minutes left to his life and that of the Kwong Dock tong itself.

389

To Ching appeared at his side. "What can we do? Should we retreat?"

"No!" Po Dung said. "They would hound us all the way back to the house. They would pick us off in the streets. We would never make it back."

"I say we retreat! I say—" Suddenly To Ching's face exploded in a crimson burst, skin and muscle giving way, as a Suey Sing bullet tore through his cheek, entered his throat, and ended his life. He fell to the ground.

Po Dung turned from him. The swordsman stood and raised his hatchet over his head. "Attack!" he cried. "Attack and kill!"

The hatchetmen under Po Dung's command rose and made the suicide charge. Fully half of them were cut down before they had made ten yards. More died with their hatchets overhead, trying to kill at least one of the dreaded Suey Sing.

Po Dung was among the eight men, out of an original force of nearly seventy-eight, who were able to get close enough to engage in hand-to-hand combat with the murdering Suey Sing highbinders. He drove his broadax deep into the stomach of a warrior who was aiming at one of his brothers and shrieked with delight as the deathblow struck home. He jerked the hatchet free and killed another Suey Sing who was charging for him.

Then Po Dung heard gunshots from behind him. Even in the heat of the battle, in the midst of the carnage, his mind worked. It couldn't have been the Suey Sing behind them; they would have attacked earlier. Who, then, with guns? Then a smile came to his mouth as he said, "Ho Huan!"

These words were his last. His life ended as Ren Dai Ko drove his blade deep into Po Dung's belly.

"*Die*, Kwong Dock slime!" The *Ah ma* of the Suey Sing twisted the blade cruelly, then wrenched it out, watching as Po Dung, swordsman of the Kwong Dock tong, dropped to the dirt of Waverly Place to his death.

Ho Huan led a force of eighteen men, each armed with pistols and rifles, the survivors of the attack on his brigade and the house guards. The Kwong Dock house was now left unguarded. He knew there would be no need to guard it if he did not act, for there would be no tong left by morning.

Standing on the other side of the square, Ti Ben watched the brigade of charging Kwong Docks. He heard their guns being fired, then felt the bullets as they struck him in the leg, arm, and chest. Volley after volley the Kwong Docks fired.

Ti Ben touched his chest, the blood warm and pulsing, and he knew it was a mortal wound. In his last moment he wondered if it would have made a difference if he had told the *Ah ma* of Ling's existence. It was in that moment that he knew he had made the right decision. Though he would die, she would live. He loved her. He knew that for certain now; because he grieved not over the death of the highbinders or his own death, but, instead, celebrated that Ling would live. As he fell to the ground he gave himself over to death without remorse.

Ren Dai Ko watched Ti Ben fall and Ming Lo San falling on top of him. A dozen more men crumbled before the Kwong Dock onslaught. The battle was turning again, Ren Dai Ko thought. All about him his men were falling, screaming, dying; when they had been so close . . . so close. His two warlords were dead, his army was in disarray, and he was in jeopardy of being annihilated.

He gave the order.

"Retreat!"

His remaining men turned and raced toward Yang's force at the north entrance of the square. Ren Dai Ko had eighteen highbinders left. He led them into Yang's force of twenty-two, and met a barrage of knives and cudgels flying through the air.

More of Ren Dai Ko's men fell, their wounds great and terrible. On instinct, he turned away from the wall of steel and into the bullets being fired by Ho Huan's men attacking from the south side of Waverly Place.

It was futile now. Ren Dai Ko made his gamble and he had lost.

The *Ah ma* of the Suey Sing threw his pistol down, raised his hands over his head, and shouted, "Surrender!"

His men followed suit. Suey Sing pistols hit the earth, some still loaded. The arms of the warriors went over their heads and they cried, "Surrender, surrender!" The words bounced back and forth off the walls of the square.

On either side of them, Yang and Ho Huan contemplated the fallen enemy. At length, the din subsided and quiet filled the square.

Yang shouted across to the other side. "Po Dung?"

"Dead!" Ho Huan shouted back.

Yang felt the pain stab in his belly, remembering his mentor—the man who had inducted him into the tong, the man who had guided him. He pushed it from his mind.

"To Ching?"

"Dead!" Ho Huan answered again.

So that was it. He, Yang alone, held the power now. He was the ranking warlord. With Po Dung's death, he was the chief swordsman of the tong.

He looked down on the eleven Suey Sing highbinders standing before him, their arms over their heads in surrender. He heard the moans of a dozen more Suey Sing who lay wounded, some dying.

There was no pity in Yang's heart, only hatred. He thought of the Suey Sing who had tortured Yan Kwan, who had ambushed Ho Huan, and of the treacherous Suey Sing who had sworn to bring no pistols. They had murdered Po Dung with those very pistols.

Yang raised his battle-ax over his head, strength flowing through his arms with the pulsing power of Kwan Kung, the god of war. In that moment the fog suddenly broke, and the ghostly moon looked down on him and glinted off Yang's hatchet as his voice cried out, *"Take no prisoners!"*

He descended on the Suey Sings.

Chapter 50

It was something the likes of which California had never seen before and would never see again. There had been Chinese funerals in the past—the funerals of the rich and powerful. But never anything like this.

The funeral cortege stretched for more than a mile. The mourners were legion, white-clothed, like a silent slithering ivory snake that made its way through the streets of China-town and down to the docks, where ships waited to take the dead men's bones back to Mother China.

It was a day of tribute, in which the distinction between tongs did not matter. Suey Sing shopowners walked beside Kwong Dock tong vegetable peddlers. Bow Leong tong cobblers walked alongside Bing Kung cigar-makers. Hep Sun highbinders walked with Hop Sing warriors.

At final count there had been a hundred and fifty-three

men killed in that terrible night. The number was awesome enough to wash away the hatred, if only for a day's respite.

The destruction of the tongs' fighting arms threw their regular workers into mass confusion. Those who made their living working for the tongs' legitimate enterprises—as bookkeepers, cashiers, clerks, and peddlers—felt that their very lives were in jeopardy.

They no longer had protection from the whites, from the police, from each other. For so many years they had worked under the aegis of the tongs. Now only a few dozen highbinders were left in each of the tongs. No longer was there an all-powerful tong.

The workers gathered for this final tribute to those who had been their protection. What would become of them after this day? No one knew.

Even more fearful were those who labored in the illicit businesses operated by the tongs. They stood in terror that they would be fought over, pulled in one direction and then another by the splintered factions that remained.

Not the least important of the underworld businesses thrown into turmoil were the brothels. As the funeral procession moved through the quarter it passed by one of the bordellos. The prostitutes stood by their open but barred windows and looked down. Curiosity, fear, uncertainty played on the painted faces of the women. One woman alone cried. Ling wiped at the tears with the backs of her hand as she looked down at the wagon carrying the body of Ti Ben. The sobs wracked her body and she shook with grief.

As she wept, Ling felt a comforting arm around her shoulder. She turned and, through her tears, saw Ah Toy standing next to her.

"He's dead, Ah Toy!"

Ah Toy shook her head. "I know, Ling. And I know that you loved him." She held her tighter. "That is the final price for loving a man. Women give men their hearts. Men take them and then, in their stupidity, they march off to be slaughtered. Love is not enough for them. They must have hate as well and, having it, they end up with nothing."

Ling fell into Ah Toy's embrace and shuddered in her arms. Ling had come home, Ah Toy thought, where she belonged.

Chin was enraged. His words echoed hard off the walls of

the secret chamber in which the presidents of the Six Companies met.

"This was not the plan!"

"You have fulfilled your mission," Tao Tsu said. "You have destroyed the tongs."

"They are not destroyed!" he insisted. "They are merely crippled. We must finish the job."

Sya Yu Shr, president of the Yeong Wo Company, said, "Chin, there are no more highbinders left."

"That is not true." He turned to look at Tai Pien. "Tell them."

"There are some pockets of highbinders left," Tai Pien said. "Not all were killed in—"

"We have a letter, received this afternoon," Tao Tsu said. "It comes from the *Ah ma* of the Kwong Dock tong. He pledges that the highbinders will forever lay down their hatchets; that they have lost the taste for war, that they only wish to live out their lives in peace."

"And you *believe* him?" Chin cried.

"Yes," Tao Tsu said. "I believe it is over. I believe we must—"

Chin pointed at the old president. "We had a plan. We were going to extradite the remaining highbinders to China after the battle. You agreed to—"

"We did not agree," Tao Tsu said. "We agreed only to let you send your assassins to kill the *Ah ma* of the Suey Sing. You sent them. They did their work. It is over now. Enough have died."

"More will die unless we wipe out these cancers."

"Chin!" Tao Tsu said, his voice stern. "It is over."

"It is *not!* It will not be over until they are eliminated to the last man."

"You are obsessed. There is no more battle to be fought, Chin. The work is done. Now let it die."

Chin said, "I want it to die more than any other man. But the tongs can only be ended when the last—"

"We will not hear any more of it," Tao Tsu said.

Chin looked around the conference table. He had underestimated the old president. He was neither as old nor as feeble as Chin had perceived him to be. He had been lobbying, talking with the other presidents, marshaling support to oppose Chin's final measure.

"Why do you stand against me, Tao Tsu? Why do you oppose this last step? Do you not want to be rid of the tongs?"

394

Tao Tsu stood, his voice strong. "Yes, I do! That was the only reason I permitted you to take the life of another man—because I thought you were right, that it would spell the death of the tongs. And you were right . . . they are dead. But this is no longer a matter of being rid of the tongs. You are becoming a warmonger, Chin. You have tasted blood and you have become addicted to it.

"We will not stand with you on this. We will not sanction the Chinese Protective Police in this matter. There will be no last roundup of the pitiful remnants of those hoodlum gangs. We will not spend our time and money searching them out in the cellars and alleyways of this quarter for the next ten years. It is over, Chin . . . over."

Tao Tsu sat down.

Chin looked at all of them and said, "Fools."

Chin was right. Earlier that morning, Yang had been given the title of chief swordsman of the Kwong Dock tong. After Hung Ma Kung finished the rites of installation, the *Ah ma* called for a meeting in the War Chamber. Yang's first action there as chief swordsman was to make a powerful and unorthodox proposal. One that would serve to maintain the vast business holdings still controlled by the meager remnants of the twelve original tongs. Thus it was that the union of the remaining warriors of a dozen tongs, the great tong of tongs, was formed.

Chapter 51

It had been a year of unprecedented growth and profit for James Riley. It had begun with the election of Andrew Jackson Bryant as mayor of San Francisco. Riley didn't particularly care who filled the position at the moment. Some people did care, though. One of them was Andrew Harcourt. His political star faded into obscurity, and the one-time mayoral candidate died of a heart ailment. Riley felt his own heart was strong and growing stronger.

James Riley had a plan of daring and genius, and if he was

successful he would end up sitting behind the desk, in the chief of police's office, his dream of chests filled with gold a reality.

While his master plan had proceeded well, it was not a year without problems. One of them was Tim Shaughnessy.

Shaughnessy's partner Billy McNamara was a fairly level-headed man; that was why Riley had teamed him with Shaughnessy in the first place. Shaughnessy was the hothead. Riley knew that he needed men like him—men who could lead hoodlums and kill ruthlessly. But the gang leader was getting a bit of greed in his blood, and that could make a man dangerous.

Things had come to a head on Christmas Eve, when Shaughnessy and McNamara had visited Riley at the livery stable. Reflecting back, Riley realized he could have explained the plan to the two of them that night. It wasn't that complicated. But it didn't matter; Shaughnessy wouldn't have understood it. The man had come to his stable with a single thought on his mind—more money.

In the end Riley had given it to him, because he was able to take the long view. That, he felt, was something men like Shaughnessy couldn't do. All they were worried about was the present. To Riley's mind the single most important thing was time—time for conditions in San Francisco to worsen, and for the robberies, burglaries, and beatings to grow so prevalent that the people screamed for law and order.

For a full year he turned the gangs loose, giving them open rein. It was a bad year for California. Summer had been disastrous. There had been a killing drought and the price of sheep dropped to a dollar a head. The Bank of California had failed to open in August and the economic repercussions were beginning to become more and more clear. Real estate values plunged overnight.

With winter came swarms of unemployed. They bloated the hotels and boarding houses as never before, and many were absorbed into the city's gang structure. They slept all day and came out at night to terrorize the local citizenry. Riley directed the gangs toward Chinatown, having them prey on cigar and vegetable vendors. When the police arrived on the scene, the the gangs would strike a deal with them, adding to the police corruption in the city.

An agreement was reached: the gangs would attack vendors and hold them until the coppers could arrive to check for peddling permits. The Chinese rarely bought the permits, so they were arrested. The coppers turned the merchandise over to the gangs and split the profits with them.

But the alliance between the police and the gangs was a shaky one. Often terrible gun battles broke out, with the better-armed side the victor. Public confidence in the city police sank deeper and deeper.

The catalyst came in January 1877. Riley was sitting in his office when O'Malley burst in.

"James, did you hear?"

"What's happened, Brian?"

"The Comstock dividend's stopped! They just broke the story in the paper. Value's dropped from eighty million to ten million—overnight!"

"Dear Lord!"

"Aye," O'Malley said, crumpling into a chair, dazed. "The stock market's paralyzed, bucko. They've suspended trading."

"Stopped trading? How can they do that? Every busboy and paperboy and waiter in San Francisco owns stock . . ."

He stopped talking. That was it. It was a crash. The Comstock dividend was the first to go. After all, there was no more gold. The rest of the stocks were following suit. That was why they'd suspended trading; if they opened the market, everyone would sell. The bottom was falling out of the market. People smelled the crash and the hard times to come. They wanted their money and they wanted it fast.

The big boys like Crocker and Stanton and Hartford had probably started the damned thing by selling off their large holdings. Other investors picked up on their lead and liquidated their holdings as well. But they couldn't keep it a secret forever.

As hundreds of thousands of shares owned by the big traders were sold, the value had to drop. And once the brokers were really on to it they'd be spreading the word themselves.

The ones who were going to really get burned, Riley thought, were the little investors. And with the way the market had been skyrocketing in the past few years, that meant everyone in San Francisco.

He looked at O'Malley. "How bad did we get hurt?"

"I won't know until the market opens for trading."

"The whole ball of wax. How much were we in for?"

"We may not lose it all," O'Malley said. There wasn't much conviction in his voice.

"Of course we're going to lose it all. This is a crash, damn it. We're going to lose every damned penny, right along with every other sucker in San Francisco. Now how much were we in for?"

"I'd have to look at the books."

"Take a guess, damn you."

"At least a hundred thousand. Maybe a hundred and fifty."

"Christ." Riley sucked in a long breath, thinking. "Did you get to the bank?"

"Aye. That was the first thing I did."

"Good thinking. Were you able to get our money out?"

O'Malley nodded. "And it was no easy task, I'll tell you. It's a madhouse at Wells Fargo, Jamie. There must have been a thousand people waiting to get in this morning."

"How did you manage it?"

"I bribed my way in. It was the only way. I must have spread five hundred dollars to guards just to get in to see the bank manager. Then another thousand to him to get ahead of everyone else in line."

"And the money?"

"All in our safe-deposit box."

"Thank God for that. Then the bribes were money well spent. See what you can do about the stocks. I think you'd better get down there and try to speak to someone. Save what you can. We'll be all right." Then something occurred to Riley and he smiled.

O'Malley couldn't believe that Riley had anything in the world to smile about. For a moment he worried his boss had cracked; there'd been stories of men blowing their brains out this morning.

"Jamie? Are you all right?"

"Aye. Sure I am."

"What is it?"

"I was just thinking." He looked at O'Malley and said, "This might be just the break we've been waiting for."

But it was a costly break. O'Malley's guess had been fairly accurate. The two of them had a hundred and eleven thousand dollars and some change wrapped up in assorted stocks.

Through five thousand in bribes O'Malley managed to save about thirteen thousand dollars. That was the first day the market had reopened. After that it was impossible. No amount of bribe money would do any good.

The market continued to plummet as stocks busted off the board altogether in the ultimate financial nightmare. Thousands of people went broke overnight. Life savings disappeared in a matter of hours, sometimes minutes. Fortunes were lost. The financial sector of the city was thrust into a paralysis as icy as the winter that gripped it. Business came to a standstill as San Francisco braced for the inevitable depression.

The wealthy up on Nob Hill—the Crockers and the Stantons and the few others who had held on to their fortunes—were worried, with good cause. They were a very small enclave of monied men in a sea of poor. They were incredibly visible, having built ostentatious Victorian monstrosities to live in that looked down haughtily on the poor below.

It was a situation ripe for revolution, and on more than one instance the police had to be called to break up angry mobs who had gathered before the palatial estates of the capitalists.

What was left of the working class was worried, as well. The hoodlums roaming the streets made a simple visit to the vegetable market a dangerous journey. Those who did have jobs worried most on payday. Beatings by gangs were numerous on those days, and most men walked home with a quick gait, anxious to get behind locked doors with their wages.

Into this chaos came Riley's Raiders. It was the second part of the brilliance that was James Riley's plan. Riley formed the Raiders out of the ranks of the gangs he controlled. In point of fact, he had McNamara send him one quarter of his men and, overnight, these men became vigilantes. Suddenly they were upholders of the law.

The newspapers picked up on it instantly. They still remembered Riley from the days of the sandlot speeches, and a city eager for hope embraced him enthusiastically. It appeared to the city that Riley's Raiders were waging a war against crime, and many times they did indeed "arrest" criminals in the act of breaking into warehouses and strong-arming citizens. Each act was glowingly reported in the newspapers.

What no one ever knew was that the hoodlums Riley's Raiders apprehended were never tried before a vigilante court, were never punished or beaten. No one ever knew that the salary and operating overhead for Riley's Raiders was supplied by the booty that Shaughnessy and McNamara's men pillaged from the city. But most important, no one ever knew that the hoodlums and vigilantes shared one common element—they both took their orders from James Riley.

There were a few stories about some of Riley's men being

former gang members. These weren't the ordinary, average citizens who had comprised the Vigilance Committee of 1856. But these were tougher times, and tougher men were needed for the job.

What people cared about was that Riley's Raiders were there, they were stopping some of the robberies, and the business community was damned glad to have them.

As the winter wore on, the rage of the public seemed to turn once again upon the Chinese. They were a convenient peg to hang the problems of the city on. Sandlot speeches became popular again, with thousands of men attending. The police were called out on dozens of occasions, and just barely managed to contain the incensed audiences.

The Chinese were responsible for unemployment, the line went. It was difficult to deny this, because most people didn't look beneath the surface. And what they saw on the surface was that the Chinese were working while they were unemployed. It didn't matter that the Chinese were working at jobs whites wouldn't do.

The Chinese, the speakers claimed, were stealing thousands of jobs from white's because they were willing to work for slave wages. Worse, they never asked their employers for wage increases.

Soon the newspapers began to buy the idea, and gradually there rose a call for expulsion of the Chinese and a return to law and order. This last plea, the newspapers said, could only be accomplished if police corruption was done away with.

It was during the first week of March that James Riley got the invitation, delivered to his office by a uniformed black man who said he had instructions to wait for a reply.

Riley sat in his office, O'Malley across from him. It was a short letter and it took only a few moments for him to read it. He placed the letter on his desk and looked up from it.

"Well?" O'Malley said.

"It's from Mayor Bryant." Riley smiled. "He wants to see me."

O'Malley stood and grabbed the letter off the desk, his eyes racing over it. "By the saints, Jamie! We just might pull it off."

On the appointed morning, James Riley's carriage pulled up to City Hall. He was in his best carriage, and as his driver pulled to the curb a police officer immediately approached it, tapping his nightstick on the rim of the wheel.

"No parking here," the officer said. "Pull away."

Riley opened the door of the carriage and stepped down. He handed the letter to the copper. "I've got an appointment with the mayor. I'd be grateful if my driver could wait for me."

The policeman looked at the official seal at the top of the letter, scanned its contents, then nodded. "No problem, Mr. Riley. No problem at all."

Riley walked across the broad plaza in front of City Hall. The sky was clear, but the air was biting and he had turned up the collar of his greatcoat. He had never been to City Hall before and he was impressed by its Romanesque grandeur.

He'd worn his best blue suit and he was glad of it. The meeting was called for ten o'clock and he'd been up since six getting ready.

It was warmer inside and he loosened the buttons of his coat. Everywhere worried little men in vested suits scurried about. He'd never seen people in such a hurry before; and with no apparent bosses lording over them, either. Hurry meant worry to Riley's mind, and that was good. He wanted them all to be worried.

He walked across the marble floor of the enormous cave that was the main foyer of the hall. Riley approached an information desk where a mustachioed police officer sat. He presented the letter and the officer hailed a cadet to escort Riley to the mayor's office on the second floor.

If the size of one's office was a mark of one's power, Riley thought, then the man sitting behind the immense oak desk was powerful indeed. The office of the mayor's *secretary* was larger than Riley's own substantial office. When the secretary had ushered him into the mayor's chambers Riley felt his breath suck in in spite of himself.

It struck him as quarters more suited for a king than a mayor. There were two fireplaces, a beamed ceiling sixteen feet overhead, and enough room to stable a score of horses. Soft couches, a bar with gleaming crystal, and bookcases occupied one side of the office.

The mayor's desk, a huge world globe, and more chairs sat before the far fireplace. As in his dream, two tall flags flanked the desk—one of the United States, the other the flag of the city of San Francisco.

Mayor Andrew Jackson Bryant was a burly man. He looked to Riley as if he was something of an outdoorsman, and that put Riley on guard immediately. Bryant, a big man, over six foot, looked like he could handle himself.

Riley doubted that Bryant could have gotten elected in a normal election. But when the field was thrown open by the combination of Harcourt's death and James Otis's death while still in office, Bryant was able to garner enough support from workingmen and a fearful public that he could carry the election.

Without knowing it, San Francisco had made a good choice. Andrew Jackson Bryant was an honest, God-fearing man, who genuinely wanted what was best for the city that had elected him. He would have no mean task providing it, though.

"I'll come straight to the point," Bryant said after the usual courtesies had been exchanged. "The work of your Raiders has come to my attention, Mr. Riley."

Riley nodded, deciding to let the mayor take the lead.

"A good many of them were former vigilantes under Coleman, I understand."

"I take my men where I can get them," Riley answered. "If they have experience, so much the better."

"Mr. Riley, you know that vigilantism is illegal, don't you?"

Riley smiled lightly. "Are you going to run me in, Mayor Bryant?"

Bryant laughed heartily. "Hardly." He opened his hands toward Riley. "Why, if I did I'd probably end up being lynched."

Riley felt safe in sharing his laughter. "You just might at that."

"But it is illegal, just the same. I only wanted to make that point at the beginning of our conversation. You'll see why in a moment." Bryant stood. "Legal or not, I'd be the last man to condemn what you're doing, Riley. These hoodlums have to be stopped. They've got the whole city in an uproar—robbing, beating, killing. God knows what they'll pull next."

The mayor paced at the side of his desk. "There isn't a day that goes by that I don't have some messengerboy running in here telling me that the revolution's started and his boss up on Nob Hill says we should come quick."

Riley laughed again, but Bryant wasn't laughing.

"Tell you the truth, Riley, it's not all that farfetched. What with things the way they are, anything could happen. Good thing we've got five thousand National Guard troops garrisoned here. Still, it could get mighty nasty."

"Mighty nasty," Riley agreed.

"I've got to confess that I'm not proud of the job our police have been doing."

"Not much to be proud of."

Bryant stopped pacing and stared at him. "You're a blunt man, Mr. Riley."

"Like you, Mr. Mayor, I believe in coming to the point. If you had something to be proud about then the city wouldn't need my Raiders, would they?"

Bryant nodded slowly. "That's true. And that brings me to the point. As I said earlier, what you're doing is illegal. That doesn't matter to me, because nobody's about to try and stop you. But it should matter to you, Riley.

"If you were working as a legal division of the city government you'd be eligible for city funds. We could pay your men a decent salary and . . ."

Sudden insight flashed its beacon on James Riley, and he realized that Mayor Andrew Jackson Bryant wasn't going to offer him the chief of police's job. It was a lesser offer. For a moment he felt his anger begin to flare, felt his neck growing red from it.

Ten years ago, five years ago, he would have leapt to his feet, cussed the man out, and stormed from the office. But he was wiser now. He had learned how to make concessions, how to deal. He was playing with house money. He'd come in with nothing, so no matter what he left with he was ahead of the game.

"What's your offer, Mr. Mayor?"

"We want you and your men to join the department."

Regular cops, he thought. Now his anger did boil over.

"No deal," he said, rising.

Bryant motioned for him to remain seated. "Now wait a minute, wait a minute. Listen to the whole offer."

Riley sat.

"I don't want you and your men to become just regular flatfoots. I know you and your boys are special and I'm offering you a special deal."

"What kind of a deal?"

"You'll have your own division and you'll be the head of it, Riley."

"Go on. I'm listening."

"Your men will be free to work in whatever way they see fit. You'll be your own boss."

"Responsible to who?"

"Only to my office."

"What about the chief of police?"

"I said you'll be responsible only to me."

Riley thought about it. It was a good deal; not as good as the one he had wanted, but a good deal all the same. If he had a separate division then he could pretty much write his own rules. There was one crucial question left to be asked.

"Where do you want my men to operate?"

"That depends on how many men you have."

Riley quickly calculated. He had forty or so vigilantes. He could easily draw off another forty or more from the ranks of Shaughnessy and McNamara's gang.

"Close to a hundred," he answered.

"That many?"

"Yes."

"I didn't realize," Bryant said, thinking. "That would be a tremendous addition, that many dedicated men. Well, I think we should split them into two areas. We can have half your men working the waterfront and the other half working Little China."

The waterfront appealed to Riley. There were dozens of shipping warehouses there. If his men were patrolling, it would be a simple matter to overlook Shaughnessy and McNamara's men making a break-in. Conversely, they could crack down hard on rival gangs, cutting the competition.

"Little China?" Riley asked. "Who cares about the Chinese?" he asked, thinking it best under present circumstances not to call them "Chinks."

Bryant said, "Ever since that riot down in Los Angeles we've been keeping an eye on them. You never know with these people. They've got a strong gang structure down there."

Riley nodded. "I know. I've heard of the tongs."

"Lot of white citizens going in and out of the quarter every day. Import shops, jewelry stores. There's a lot of shops there that carry expensive merchandise—jades, pearls. Even with the depression, there're still plenty up on the Hill who can afford those goods."

It was sounding better all the time.

"We have to keep some kind of order in that quarter,"

Bryant said. "Won't do to have one of our citizens getting in the way of a tong hatchet."

"Aye," Riley said, his thoughts still lingering on jade and pearls.

"Too many damned whorehouses and opium dens down there, too. I don't have a day that passes without some church or women's group coming in here and ordering me to close down some of those places. These Chinese have the basest moral standard of any race, I'll tell you."

"Shouldn't be too much of a problem," Riley said. "My men can handle it."

"Don't be too cocksure," Bryant warned. "There's plenty of those tong highbinders down there."

"They may be Chinks," he said, loosening, "but they aren't stupid enough to try to kill coppers."

"You'll get some help from the Chinese Protective Police—that's a Chinese-run civil police. They do a fairly good job of controlling things themselves. Chinese like to handle their own affairs, actually. The only reason that riot started down in Los Angeles was because white folks got into the middle of a tong war."

"We'll take care of our own," Riley promised.

The mayor stood. "Then do I understand that we have a deal?"

"I'll ask you only one condition, Mr. Mayor."

"What's that?"

"That my men are the only coppers in the area. I don't want to have to worry about corrupt police in my midst."

"Agreed."

Riley stuck out his hand. "Then we have a deal."

Bryant shook Riley's hand. "I'm glad," he said, standing next to Riley. "We've been needing a man like you for a long time."

"Well," Riley said, "I'm surely glad to be aboard."

Chapter 52

The presidents of the Six Companies would be haunted for years by their decision not to pursue extradition of the highbinders who had survived the tong war of 1875.

Had Chin but known that Tao Tsu had lobbied with the other presidents, had talked them out of pursuing extradition, he never would have put forth the idea of murdering Low Sing and fomenting the tong war. The result had been the creation of the tong of tongs. Together, the tattered remains of the fighting tongs were strong enough to protect their mutual interest; and in time; they grew.

It was a magnet of evil, attracting every young Chinese hoodlum in the city. Its ranks grew at a terrifying rate, and before long it numbered hundreds of highbinders. Before long the terrorism of the past reared its head again, and the presidents of the Six Companies knew that they had erred grievously.

At the head of the highbinders, with only the Grand *Ah ma* himself over him, was Yang. And it was clear that Hung Ma Kung would be succeeded by him. Hung Ma Kung was an old man now, and leadership was increasingly falling to Yang.

Chin realized that in large measure he was responsible for Yang's rise to power. This held the most bitter irony for him, for it had been his brother's bold robbery scheme that had forged his idea of revenge against the tongs. It had been Chin's idea to destroy them, yet he had made them even stronger through his efforts. He knew that the war and the resulting tong of tongs had lifted his brother to lofty heights in that syndicate of evil.

In April 1877 a meeting of the General Assembly of the Six Companies was called. It was the year of the Kong Chow Company's directorship and Chin, as its president, sat on the dais presiding over the meeting.

Chaos reigned in the Meeting Hall of the Middle Kingdom as five-score voices engaged in conversations of desperation and woe. When Chin finally restored order to the meeting, one fact emerged: that if the Assembly did not choose a course of action, a course would be chosen for the Six Companies and they would be destroyed by the tong of tongs. There were only two choices: either send the Chinese Protective Police against the tong and do battle, or make peace.

It was Shao Kow who suggested negotiation—to give total control of vice, the brothels and the opium dens, to the tong in return for the opportunity to run the businesses and lives of Little China in peace. He went on to take the liberty of his friendship with Chin to its extreme, broaching a matter that was on the mind of every man present but that none would dare to speak of. The animosity between the chief representative of the Chinese community and the power behind the tong of tongs was well known. Yet Shao Kow implored Chin to approach his brother and ask him if the tong would enter into negotiation; for blood could speak to blood in ways that no two ordinary men could do.

Chin searched his own soul, seeing in the encounter the personal conflict he had known all his life with the brother who had always exerted his physical superiority, who belittled Chin's own intellectual gift. It was as if they had been born to oppose each other. So it had gone for years, in China and in this new country. And as each brother had become stronger in his own right, it seemed to be the very will of the gods that they should clash, to decide for once and all who was the more powerful.

Yet if it could be avoided, resolved without conflict, then would not the gods be pleased? Yes, he thought; for power and might came from the mind as well as the arm.

The applause was deafening as Chin rose to agree to hold council with his brother.

It was a rice warehouse on Montgomery Street, not more than a quarter-mile from the Meeting Hall of the Middle Kingdom. Its walls were gray, paint chipping from them. A wooden door, also painted gray, stood in the middle and the hinges creaked, crying for oil, as Yang pulled it open.

He walked inside and shut out the noon sun behind him.

"I am pleased that you came," a voice to his left said.

Yang turned and looked at Chin, standing alone. His brother wore a simple blue tunic and trousers, a skullcap covering his head.

"No battle-ax?" Chin asked.

"Was one necessary?"

"No."

"You wanted to talk."

Chin turned his back for a moment. "Many years have passed since we have seen one another."

"I have not come for a reunion, brother."

"You have changed very little."

"And you."

"No," Chin said, "there you are wrong. I have changed greatly." He turned to look at Yang. "Two years ago I urged the Six Companies to send Chinese Protective Police against what remained of the tongs for the purpose of extradition to China."

"Then you *have* changed. They were fools not to have listened to you, Chin. It is too late for them now."

"Perhaps not. No more blood need be spilled."

"You do not understand. We are not afraid of spilling blood," Yang said. "We are not afraid of battle." He grasped the hem of his tunic and jerked it up to reveal the snakes of battle scars that covered his muscled stomach and chest.

"The medals of a warrior," Chin remarked.

Yang nodded. "Many of them thanks to you, my brother."

"To me?"

Yang lowered his tunic. "It was you who sent the assassin to kill Low Sing. It had all the markings of your skills—deceit and subterfuge; the desire to escape harm through cleverness rather than courage."

Chin leveled an angry finger at him. "And it was *you* who stole twenty-five thousand dollars from my store!"

"I am a warrior! I fought that battle by myself! I had the courage to lay siege! You did not."

Chin drew in a deep breath, calming himself. "I did not come here to argue with you. I came here to make a proposal."

"Propose, then."

"A truce. A treaty between us all."

Yang laughed a loud laugh. "To what end?"

"Peace."

The swordsman stood with his legs spread wide, his hands on his hips. "And how are we to gain this peace?"

"The Six Companies shall give the tong of tongs free rein in all areas of vice—prostitution, drugs, gambling, smuggling. In all these things we shall not interfere. Moreover, the Chinese Protective Police shall assist you in whatever way you see fit with regard to thwarting the intervention of the whites in your affairs."

"In return, what do you ask?"

"Assurances that extortion against businessmen and the general population shall cease and that order will be restored to the streets."

Yang looked at him. "No more protection-money demands?"

Chin nodded.

"You *have* changed, brother. You have become a fool."

Chin stared at him, suddenly knowing that Yang had not come to this meeting with any thought of reconciliation.

Yang continued. "Your proposal is a fool's errand. Do you think us idiots or children?"

"You would control all—"

"We already control most of these enterprises you speak of."

"There are many that you do not. We would turn over that which is controlled by the Six Companies' members. I myself own large gambling concerns. Hen Yok owns four brothels. Gen Kao has—"

"Why should we bargain with you?" Yang interrupted. "Why should we trade anything for that which we shall soon enough own? Why should we settle for peace," he asked, his voice dropping low, "when we can have victory?"

Chin held his brother's gaze. "Then it is true. You mean to destroy us all. You are a madman."

"A conqueror," Yang spat. "And you shall be the conquered. For all your wisdom, the battle still goes to the strongest. What good are all your money and brains, when I wield an ax and command an army that can wrench your riches from you?"

"You are right," Chin said softly. "I have come on a fool's errand." He paused, then said, "Why did you agree to this meeting?"

"Only because I had a message for you and I wanted the pleasure of delivering it myself. I want you to know that I will strip you of all you own, that I shall lay waste to your beloved Six Companies, that I, Yang, will be the mandarin of this country. You will cower before me in the end, Chin. You will lie before me like a slave before his lord!"

"What is it that has allowed this hatred to grow within you?"

"Look to yourself!" Yang cried. His voice dropped to a

whisper as he repeated, "Look to yourself. For so many years I had to bear my father's words—'Chin is so wise for one so young. Chin is so quick to understand. See how easily he masters his lessons, his books, his chess. Why can't you be more like him, Yang? Why can't you be more like your brother?' "

"But I was—"

"And *I*," Yang growled, "I, the older, I, the one who . . . who . . ." Yang's mouth grew thick with hatred, his face flushed, and his breathing became heavy and almost out of control.

Finally he drew a long, deep breath and looked into Chin's eyes, his own burning with hatred. "Begone from this land, Chin. Begone or I shall make you wish that you had never crawled from our mother's womb."

Yang turned and walked from the warehouse.

Chin stood in the warehouse for a long time after his brother had left. His eyes looked at the square of light that came through the open door and fell on the floor. But he wasn't able to focus on it.

Instead, he thought of Mother China, of his father and his village. He had the image, very clear in his mind, of a man old before his time; a man firm, yet filled with warmth and compassion and concern for his children. Then he realized that it was only an image in his head, and that the man had long since turned to dust.

Ling was the only reality left for him. How long had it been since he had thought about her? How many excuses had he made for not looking into her whereabouts? Why hadn't he taken the voyage back to China to learn who owned her, and buy her back? Was it shame, shame that he was the brother of a man who had allowed her to be sold into slavery?

That was part of it, he thought. He felt a certain guilt that he had not seen to it that Yang's payments were made regularly. He had known Yang was irresponsible. Yes, Ling's sale into slavery was partially his fault, and it was a fault he did not care to consciously face or admit.

Perhaps she had fared well, had been sold to a kindly master in China. Surely the gods would watch over one who had known only privation and suffering in her childhood. Surely . . . surely . . . He pushed her from his mind.

There was only he and Yang. Yang had become an animal.

And Chin was not completely pleased with what he himself had become. He wondered how unlike his brother he really was.

He remembered how idealistic he had been, how he had loved and worked for peace. Could the bitterness that welled in his chest have taken such root in just a few years? What had he become? He had driven away the only woman he ever loved. He had commanded Chinese police to do battle with highbinders. He had turned his face from peace. He had become filled with hatred toward his own blood.

And yet, Chin thought, he had not changed at all. He felt the coldness of the pistol he had concealed in his waistband, beneath his tunic, as it lay against his naked belly. Chin had had the opportunity to kill Yang in the warehouse in that moment. But he could not do it.

Yang, however, could have, and would have. What if it came to the final meeting, he thought. Could he? He didn't know. He would have to look to his soul, if that moment came, and he was terrified of what he would find there.

In that moment, he knew that his brother was right—that he would have to leave America or face that moment.

He would leave.

Chapter 53

When Chin left the warehouse he was shaking, both from the confrontation and from his decision to leave America. There were few turning points in a man's life, few landmarks, and he realized that this was one of them—the end of one period and the beginning of another.

Yes, he thought, it could be a beginning. He would return to China a wealthy man and live in splendor.

He began walking up Jackson Street, heading toward his house, thinking.

Hadn't that always been his plan? To make a great deal of money and then return to China, to his homeland? And yet, somewhere along the path, he had gotten sidetracked, had been led away from that plan. Politics and diplomacy and power had swirled about him like whirlwinds of dust, obscuring his vision so that the way was no longer clear.

He nodded to himself, hardly aware of the people in the street as he passed by them.

The way was clear now. And in large measure he had Yang to thank for it. Though certainly it had not been his brother's intention, he had, nonetheless, blown away the dust.

What did it matter if he was forced onto this path? Should he fight against that which he originally wanted, just because pride told him not to allow his brother to dictate to him? Everything he knew told him no. He would accept this road because, in reality, it was what he had always wanted. The gods had taken a hand in the matter, had sent Yang against him. He smiled at the mysterious manner in which they worked.

When he broke from his thoughts he realized that he was standing before the entrance to his house. He hardly remembered walking through the streets at all.

He stood for a moment, looking at the door of his apartment, hesitating. There was something else to do, something he must do quickly. Then he realized what it was.

Rebecca.

Chin sat in the back of the carriage as it creaked through the streets of white San Francisco. He knew quite well that it was madness for a Chinese to venture out of the quarter nowadays. It was dangerous enough in the quarter, let alone outside of it. The only Chinese who were tolerated were laundrymen carrying their baskets on the end of poles, and even they were accosted frequently by hoodlums.

The thought of the danger he risked hardly entered his mind. He was thinking about his stupidity, the time he had wasted sending her letters and speaking with her physician and heeding his warnings. He loved her and that was all that mattered. He thought about what he would say to her. She would be angry at first, perhaps even frightened. Too, he was violating a promise he had made long ago.

As he remembered pledging that he would never come to her house again, he felt himself growing uneasy, then angry. All that talk about the sanctity of her life, about how there were some things that had to be apart. Was she ashamed of him? Ashamed of a little yellow man coming to call at the door of a big white house? White woman and little yellow heathen, scum, foreigner?

Chin felt his neck growing warm and he shook his head

suddenly, clearing away the poisonous thoughts. He was reacting to Yang; that was all. Rebecca had nothing to do with that and he had to be careful not to take out his anger on her.

As they rounded a corner he looked out the window of the carriage at the fine yellow and white and blue houses, with their clean, expansive lawns, and wide front porches. Even though he lived in relative splendor, he knew it was nothing compared to the luxury of space these white people had to move in. He wondered again if she was ashamed of him. Different worlds: hadn't he said it himself?

He had been right; but in another way he was as wrong as a man could be. He closed his eyes and she played across the backs of his lids and he thought about them together in bed, the press of her naked body against his own. He felt his groin stir and tighten in response, and he knew that Rebecca Ashley was not ashamed of him.

The carriage jerked to a sudden stop, jarring his thoughts. He opened his eyes as the driver called down, "Howard and Price streets."

Chin opened the door, got out of the carriage, and looked up at the driver. The white man looked down at him as Chin dug into his pocket for money. The man was disgusted with him. He didn't take to carrying Chinese; but when Chin had agreed to the double fare the driver had relented. He could always wash his hands when he got home.

Chin handed the money up to him. The driver snatched the bills and gave the reins of the carriage a harsh snap. It pulled away from the curb and Chin watched it leave, like a ship. He was standing on the wharf alone, in a foreign land, and the ship had pulled away.

He felt his throat tighten, wanting to call out to the driver, to tell him to take him back to Little China where he and all the little Chinamen belonged.

The carriage rounded the corner and disappeared.

Chin turned and looked at the houses, their windows staring at him. He was glad that no one was on the street to gawk at him, point their fingers at him in amusement and hatred.

He had to get inside quickly, off the street. Rebecca's house was in the middle of the block, but he had told the driver to drop him on the corner because he had wanted to walk to the house, had thought he would want some last seconds to consider what he would say. He knew what he wanted to say, but he wanted to choose just the right words.

Now he realized that it was a mistake. It meant he had to walk the fifty yards to her house. He would never make it before a gang of whites bore down on him, their clubs swinging, their teeth gritted, their boots kicking. At the front of the gangs of whites, more ferocious than all the rest, his brother Yang . . . Chin swiped at the devils buzzing in his head, haunting his thoughts.

Could Rebecca agree to give up everything, this fine white house, her fine white friends, this fine white city? Would she move across a sea to China, to a strange land filled with strange people? Would she be his wife?

A Chinaman's chance, he mused with bitterness. Why should she? Because she loved him? The whites had a saying that love could move mountains. But could it traverse seas, heritages, and cultures? Could it bear up against the crush of two cultures which were so opposite?

He had to ask her; for if he didn't, it would haunt him all the days of his life. Always he would think that she might have said yes, thrown her arms around him, grabbed a single carpetbag and rushed to the harbor.

They would catch a ship that very night; be in China in a few weeks. They'd live in Hong Kong, in a fine house, three stories, with great eaves on it. He would buy her the finest house in Hong Kong and she would be the talk of the city. He thought with a start: There are British in Hong Kong; she would not be all alone.

She might go with him.

Chin turned to the sound of wheels and saw a large private carriage round the corner in front of him, coming toward him. He realized that he wouldn't make it to the house before the carriage passed him, and a shaft of fear shot through him. What if the carriage's owner ordered the driver to pull to the side? What if the owner got out and questioned him? What was he, a Chinaman, doing in the white part of San Francisco?

Chin cursed himself aloud. He hadn't felt such fears since he was a child, and even then he rarely had felt them. He was always confident, both of his ability and his dignity.

He was Chin Wong, a successful and respected businessman. He had friends in positions of power. He was well connected even in white San Francisco, and it was fully within the realm of possibility that the owner of the carriage could be one of his customers or the husband of one of his customers, at least.

He straightened. Let the carriage pass by him, let the owner order the driver to stop and confront him. He was Chin Wong, businessman and president of the Kong Chow Company . . .

The carriage stopped before it reached him. The driver had pulled it to the curb and was stepping down, his foot bracing on a sunburst that was a brass foothold. The uniformed man jumped to the sidewalk and landed there with the sound of leather against pavement.

The streets were so deserted, Chin thought; it was as though he was on a stage. Just he and the carriage and Rebecca's house.

The driver walked around to the back of the carriage and opened the luggage flap. He pulled out something with wheels and straps. He had set it on the sidewalk and was assembling it, pulling and pushing. It came into shape now, became a recognizable thing, a wheelchair.

Chin had stopped walking and stood on the street now, watching. The driver straightened the seat, then turned to the carriage, opened the door, and climbed halfway in. When he came out he had a gray-haired man in his arms, carrying him down from the passenger compartment with a smoothness that spoke of the many years the driver had performed this job.

In one motion the driver set the man down in the chair. The man in the wheelchair had a good face, Chin thought. There had been pain, but also the acceptance of pain, and the matter had been resolved.

The gray hair was not all from age: Chin was close enough to see that the man was not that old. But Chin saw a smile on the man's face.

There was a click, metal against metal, and Chin knew that the wheel of the gods was turning in that instant. It was not his decision to leave America that would signal the end of one portion of his life and the beginning of another; it was this moment.

Chin turned to see the door of Rebecca Ashley's home open. Rebecca stepped out onto the porch, smiled widely at the man in the wheelchair, and ran up the walk to swing open the gate.

He heard her call, "John! John!"

She left the gate open behind her and ran to the side of the wheelchair, smiling. She bent by his side, her arms around him, and he put his arms around her and kissed her, kissed the Rebecca who was no longer Chin's.

It was a play on a stage, and the audience was Chin. Then one of the players turned to look at him.

Rebecca turned to look at the small yellow man standing on her street. The smile of greeting was still on her face, the gladness was still there, her arms still around her husband. Then her eyes focused on him, and in one horrible moment her face went as blank as it had been the night he had asked her to marry him.

Chin turned, his legs like rubber, awareness turning in his stomach like a pack of rats. Then he ran, without looking back, not ever wanting to look back.

BOOK FOUR

BOOK FOUR

Chapter 54

Chin had put aside his plans to return to China. After the shock of seeing Rebecca with her husband and realizing that she could never be a part of the life he had envisioned there, Chin gave up that dream.

Many things began to grow apparent to him in the following weeks, and as the pain receded he saw that it was all the work of the gods. He had been reluctant to face Yang and the tong of tongs; it had been the gods who had sent him to Rebecca Ashley's house. It was their way of thwarting his plans to flee. But most important, it was their way of telling him that he had a mission still to complete in California: the resolution of the conflict between the tong of tongs and the Six Companies.

Things began to go badly.

It was during June that Shao Kow appeared at Chin's office with distressing news.

"Again?!" Chin said. "This is the third robbery in two months at that shop." He sat his teacup down. "How much did they get?"

"Five hundred dollars."

Chin stood angrily. "Why was so much money in the store? How did—"

"The robbery occurred immediately after a customer had made a large purchase—some porcelains."

"Perhaps the customer was involved with the thieves."

"Hardly," Shao Kow said. "It was Mrs. Wainwright. No, I believe the highbinders are watching the shops, waiting for customers to emerge with expensive purchases and then moving in."

Chin frowned. "I'll have to have a good talk with Tai Pien. I want officers close to that store all the time. We should at least be able to get protection from our own—"

"Chin."

He looked at Shao Kow. "Something else?"

"My . . . my brother was hurt in the robbery."

"Sun Sui Ta? Please don't tell me that." All concern about the robbery fled from him with the news of Shao Kow's brother. Sun Sui Ta served as manager of the Clay Street shop. "Is he—"

"No," Shao Kow said. "Nothing too serious. He tried to stop one of the robbers and was struck with a cudgel."

Chin turned his back, shaking his head. "I've told all our managers, dozens of times, not to interfere if there's a robbery. We tell them not to—"

"I know, I know. But he is young and the young don't always think."

"Where is he?"

"The hospital. Minor wounds really. He'll be released tonight. Do not worry about this." Shao Kow paused for a moment. Chin turned to look at him, sensing the importance of the pause.

Then Shao Kow said, "But this event has prompted me to make a decision I have been long considering. I am returning to China."

It was as if Chin had known that it was coming, had heard it before and was reliving it again. He was losing all of them. It had started years ago when he had left China. He knew that he would not see his father and sister again until the afterlife. Then he had lost Mei Peng; but Chin was able to accept that loss. After all, Mei Peng had lived a full and meaningful life.

He had lost Yang. There had always been an element of rivalry; but they had never been enemies, until they came to this land.

He thought lastly of Rebecca Ashley. He had had her and lost her, and through it he never knew that he had no chance of having her at all. It was a facade—a bitter reflection of his life.

And now Shao Kow was leaving. He remembered them sharing the same small room in the Six Companies' House when he had first come to California. Shao Kow had been the first person he had told of his appointment as Mei Peng's aid, about his appointment as a representative.

Chin had gotten him appointed to the Kong Chow delegation, had made him a wealthy man in his own right, had shared years of friendship with him. Now he was leaving for China, and Chin would never see him again.

"When will you leave?" Chin asked.

Shao Kow sat, surprised that his employer and friend offered him no argument. "In a few weeks. Will that be enough time for you to find my replacement?"

"I will never be able to find a replacement for you. You have been a good and honorable friend. We have been through much together. Your leaving will be an immeasurable loss."

"Why don't you leave with me, Chin? There is nothing in this land for you. The gold is gone from the mines and all that is left is the hatred of the whites."

"There is still much commerce to——"

"You care not for the commerce," Shao Kow cut in. "You have made a dozen fortunes. Take it all and return to Mother China where you can live in peace."

Chin smiled. "What makes you think there is peace in China?"

Shao Kow sat at the table and softly said, "At least there is sanity."

"That is true," Chin nodded. "And that is why I must stay here. Many of our people are not so fortunate as we, Shao. They cannot simply pick up and return to Mother China."

"So you will stay and nurse them all? Go down with them all? When did you stop being a businessman and become a priest?"

"I am no priest," Chin said. "Perhaps I am not even being honest with myself. You are right, Shao Kow. It is not for commerce that I stay. I have a sacred obligation, a challenge that I must meet."

"What challenge?"

"The tong of tongs," Chin answered. "I am not a man who likes defeat. I have done everything I can to strike a bargain with them. I have tried force and restraint and compromise and concession. But they are not the kind to be bargained with."

"But why you?" Shao Kow asked.

"Because it is my obligation. I owe it to my people, good friend, because the shame of the tong of tongs is the shame of my blood. I owe it to them because the devil himself is my brother." His words barely a whisper, Chin said, "I must stay until it is done."

Chapter 55

It was past nine o'clock when her carriage crossed into Chinatown. Rebecca had wanted to wait until dark. Somehow it seemed more appropriate. She wanted the business of the day to be finished.

Her driver pulled to the curb, familiar with the address. She got out and walked to the door.

Chin was sitting in his study, reading the financial reports of his businesses. He had taken terrible losses during the past year. Beyond the problems of the economy, a plethora of evil ate away at profits. Burglaries were a constant drain, as were robberies of messengers. Not a week passed that one of his men wasn't grabbed in the street and beaten, the day's receipts stolen. No matter how the route to the bank was juggled, the highbinders always seemed to figure it out eventually.

It was a personal battle. Chin felt that strongly. Yang was leading it against him. Times were difficult throughout the quarter because the tong of tongs had stepped up its extortion demands and its wave of crime. But it was Chin's businesses that were particularly singled out.

But in a larger sense, the tong was battling against the whole of the Six Companies through Chin. Chin represented all that the Six Companies were—power, respect, the central authority of Chinese law in America. The tong knew it had to topple the Six Companies if it was to survive.

It was a war, the battle fought week by week, day by day; the highbinders against the Chinese Protective Police, each soldier representing his own organization. And slowly but surely, the Six Companies and the Chinese Protective Police were losing.

Sometimes the attacks weren't even for gain. A dozen highbinders would spring on two members of the Chinese Protective Police, stab and kill them, and thereby lessen the forces of the enemy. Fear spread among the other members and more than a few left their posts and moved from San Francisco altogether.

Chin was losing his war.

He turned to the knock at the door. "Come in."

His servant came into the study. "Rebecca Ashley."

"Send her in," he said. There was no hesitation in his voice, no surprise. He had known that this day would come. It pleased him only that she had come to him.

Rebecca came into the study wearing a white shawl about her shoulders. Chin rose.

"Hello, Rebecca."

She nodded. "Chin."

"Please sit down."

She did.

"Can I offer you anything? Some sherry? Brandy?"

"Sherry, please."

He poured and handed her the glass. "You look well, Rebecca."

She sipped the sherry. "I'm sorry I didn't come sooner."

"You don't have to apologize." He paused a beat, then added, "For anything."

"I started to come dozens of times. But I couldn't. I was too ashamed."

Chin stood before her. In the moment he had seen her with her husband he had hated her. But hatred was no longer in his heart. He believed that she was a tool of destiny, and as such he could not dislike her.

"You have nothing to be ashamed of."

She looked up at him, a stranger now, so distant and detached. It seemed inconceivable to her that they had ever shared the same bed.

"I had much to be ashamed of. You're kind to say that, though."

Chin sighed and turned from her. "I confess I felt injured when . . . when I . . ."

"I should have told you."

He turned back to look at her. "Why didn't you tell me in the beginning? Did you think I wouldn't understand?"

She shook her head. "No. I knew you would understand. I . . . I just didn't want you to know . . ."

"That you were married?"

She nodded, unable to speak. Instead she sipped her sherry and let it warm her before she continued. "I don't want you

423

to think I'm a totally evil woman. I did not lie to my husband. He knew about you."

Chin listened.

"My husband John was injured many years ago in a riding accident. He was thrown. He's spent most of our marriage in a wheelchair."

"Then I was not the first?"

"No." She looked away. "John understands my needs. For a while I protested his suggestions, but eventually . . ." She paused, the words difficult for her. "He travels a good deal, seeing doctors, and as such he is away from home for times. I . . . I need the . . ." She paused again, and for a moment Chin almost spoke. Finally she said, "John insisted that I not be condemned to a life of celibacy."

She finished her sherry. "All the others I told. It was the first thing I discussed with them. Thus, the arrangement was clearly understood from the beginning. I love my husband," she said, looking at Chin. "I love him very much. He's very good and kind."

"And me?" he asked. "Why did you not tell me?"

"Because you were not supposed to happen. The others were all planned. We just . . . happened. The others fulfilled a need." She looked up at him. "I fell in love with you."

Chin smiled. "These are strange things you speak of, Rebecca. Your logic is confusing to me. You say you did not love the others and yet you were honest with them. You say you were in love with me and yet you deceived me."

"I deceived you only because of shame. I didn't want you to think . . ."

"That I was only fulfilling your needs?"

She nodded silently.

Finally she said, "What happened between us happened before I could stop it, before I could have any control. And then it was too late. I already loved you. There was no changing that."

"You must have realized that it would come to this eventually."

Again she nodded. "As you must have realized what would come, eventually, of your opposing the tongs; as a moth must somehow sense what will become of flying near the flame." She sighed heavily. "It was all too much to bear . . . hurting you, hurting me. Then . . . then having your child growing in me, a child I could never have gotten from John."

"Rebecca . . . don't."

424

"Well, I'm glad it's over." She stood. "I only wanted to tell you how sorry I am." She prayed that he would cross the room, sweep her into his arms, and carry her off to the bedroom to make love to her. But somehow she knew that it wouldn't happen, could never happen again.

She looked at him for a long moment. "I do love you, you know. I always have."

"And I love you," he said. "And you love your husband as well. I saw it the day I came to your house."

"I do love him. Can a woman love two men?"

"I think so. The gods are cruel sometimes. If things were different, if. . . . There are too many barriers between us, Rebecca. There always have been. I think we knew that even from the start."

Now he did cross the room. He took her hand, kissed it, and said, "Remember the good times we had. Forget about the bad. Always remember that I cared for you. If we keep that and hold it, then what we did was not wrong.

"Years from now," he said, "we will look back and feel warm and good about it."

He drew her close and kissed her softly on the cheek, his lips moist as they met her tears.

Chapter 56

Being a police captain agreed with James Riley more than he could have possibly imagined. He liked everything about it: the authority that came with the office, the being a part of city government, and the respect.

Respect was something new to him. He'd been feared before. He'd had men working for him because he paid them well. But he didn't really think he had ever been respected before—except maybe by O'Malley, who appreciated his wile.

That was the problem with dealing with common men— they didn't have the brains to respect anyone. All they had were fists, and because that was all they understood their only standard was who had stronger fists. It bred fear, not respect.

Now, when he walked through the halls of the precinct

headquarters, he was a man who was respected. His reputation had preceded him and regular police officers, weary of public condemnation, suddenly found that they had a hero, a standard-bearer. Cops who were on the take gave him a wide berth.

Riley rose to the role.

In the first months that his Strike Division, as it had come to be called, was in existence, he wrought havoc on the San Francisco waterfront. Riley had wisely instructed Shaughnessy and McNamara to have their men cut their activities in the area to a minimum. When Shaughnessy had protested, Riley told him to rob shops in a different area of the city for a couple of months.

What remained, after the gang leaders cleared their men out, were break-in men from other gangs and free-lancers. Toward these Riley was merciless. The crime rate on the waterfront dropped from epidemic proportions to practically nothing in a matter of weeks. A sea of letters, full of praise, flowed into City Hall from the owners of businesses and warehouses in the area.

Riley was once again hailed by a grateful press, this time as a legitimate lawman.

Mayor Andrew Jackson Bryant had kept his promise. Riley's men worked as an independent part of the police department, responsible only to the mayor himself—much to the chagrin of the chief of police. On one of the chief's angry visits to the mayor's office, Bryant had told him that he was in no position to argue, since his very job was in jeopardy, what with the rampant police corruption, so he'd better accept any help Riley could offer in raising the public's image of the police.

Riley had enrolled ninety-six men in the police department, ninety-seven including himself. Forty-two had been Raiders and forty-four had been culled from the ranks of Shaughnessy and McNamara's gang. It was a source of great amusement to Riley that the very men who had been breaking into warehouses a few months earlier were now arresting their counterparts in opposing gangs.

In a short time word got around that the waterfront was a dangerous place to pursue a criminal career. Free-lancers were dealt with especially hard, and more than a few broken teeth littered the dockfront.

With the area cleared of a good deal of crime, Riley let McNamara and Shaughnessy slowly filter men back into the waterfront. The number of reported burglaries began to rise again, but they were still considerably below what they had been before Riley had set upon the district, so there weren't too many complaints.

What none of the shopowners and warehousemen knew was that almost all robberies in the area were being committed by Shaughnessy and McNamara's gang and protected by Riley's police, with a portion of the proceeds eventually lining James Riley's pockets.

The system was simplicity itself—actually, the inverse of what it had been when Riley had been working as the leader of Riley's Raiders. Shaughnessy and McNamara just picked their hits, and sent a list of where and when the break-ins would be. Riley only had to instruct his officers to avoid these addresses and the burglaries went off without a hitch.

He enjoyed personally patrolling the waterfront and taking part in arrests. He was hardly opposed to a little physical contact, having been in hundreds of brawls in his life. With the law on his side, now, the fights were all the more fun. The press was, as they had always been, inordinately kind to him, eager for a hero in the midst of the adversity that was San Francisco 1877.

So it was not at all unusual that he himself was patrolling the waterfront on the night of June 16. He knew it was a night that Shaughnessy and McNamara had no break-ins scheduled, so he felt it would be a good time to make an arrest.

It was a cool night, but he walked his beat with his police tunic opened at the neck. Two policemen, Dwyer and Grady, walked with him. Both of them had been recruited from Shaughnessy and McNamara's gang.

"Beautiful night," Riley said, feeling not a care in the world.

"Aye," Grady said, adding, "for making a nab."

"And maybe to bust a few skulls," Dwyer offered.

Riley laughed and tapped the butt of his service revolver with one hand and the butt of his personal long-barreled Colt forty-five with the other. "Two-gun Riley," one of the papers had called him, and he didn't half mind the appellation.

"I guess we might run into some business tonight," he said as he sniffed the air deeply. "The scent is right."

Riley propagated many myths about himself, one of which was that he could smell when skulduggery was about. He

427

looked out to his right, at the bay, at the five ships sitting in the harbor.

"What we ought to do," he said, "is take fifteen or twenty men and go out in rowboats and sink those Chink-freighters."

"Someday those ships'll be takin' 'em all back to China where they belong," Grady said.

Dwyer looked at his partner. "Maybe soon, too. State Congress is ready to pass a law, I hear."

"That's gossip," Riley declared. "The Chinks will always be here. No getting rid of them."

"How do you know?" Dwyer asked.

"Because it's got nothing to do with Congress or the Chinks or the law."

"What then?"

"The people themselves, the unemployed bums in this city; they don't want the Chinks to leave."

For a moment the other two men were silent. Then, thinking Riley was making a joke, they laughed.

"You two think I'm kidding?" Riley asked.

Grady kicked a can from their path and it fell into the bay with a delayed splash. "Aren't you?"

"Hell, no. I mean it. You got to understand people, Grady. They'll admit to anything in the world except that they've failed. And that's what everybody in this city's done—failed. Everyone from the biggest speculator to the lowest bum on the street."

Riley listened to a foghorn sounding in the distance before he continued.

"They don't want to admit that it was them that failed, so they got the Chinese. They can kick them around and beat up on them and blame them for the unemployment."

Dwyer asked, "Then you don't think the Chinks are the reason there's so much unemployment?"

"No," Riley answered. "Maybe the Chinks got a little to do with it, but not everything. They just happen to be convenient to have around."

"Hell, you sound like you're standing up for the little Chinaboys."

Riley laughed out loud. "I'm not. I like beatin' up on 'em as much as the next man. Only with me they're for sport, not for makin' excuses. Besides, they . . ."

Riley paused; a light had caught his eye, off to the left. It was a wood frame building, two stories. A dim light was coming through a window on the second floor.

Riley stopped walking and squinted in the darkness. Thompson's Feed & Grain Store, he read.

Grady and Dwyer looked in the direction of Riley's eyes, saw the light, and also stopped walking. Riley's hand had instinctively gone to his gun butt and when he looked at Grady he saw that he, too, was clutching his gun.

"Easy," Riley said.

"Little late for somebody to be working, isn't it," Grady asked.

"Maybe, maybe not. Let's go find out."

The three men crossed the street and walked to the front of the building. Riley tried the knob. The door was locked.

He turned to Grady. "Let's try the back." Looking to Dwyer, he said, "You stay here."

"But I—"

"I said cover the front," Riley hissed.

Dwyer exchanged a look with Grady. Riley caught it and said, "Don't worry; next arrest you'll be in on it. Someone has to cover the front in case they try to beat it out of here."

The alley was pitch-black, but Riley could still see the light on the second floor of the building. He looked to the end of the alley and saw that there wasn't a lookout. To Riley's mind that meant that if it was a break-in it most assuredly was a free-lancer. No one belonging to a gang would be foolish enough to attempt a burglary without a lookout—especially in James Riley's precinct. So this meant the arrest would be that much more manageable.

He tried the handle on the door. It turned as he knew it would, and he pushed the jimmied door open. Riley turned to Grady and nodded. The two walked carefully into the back of the store. In the darkness it would be easy to knock over a chair or bump into a crate.

From above there came a faint light. Riley decided that it was coming from a single candle. He unsnapped the holster on his service revolver and fingered the butt, then glanced over his shoulder at Grady, who already had his pistol drawn. Riley nodded, then led the way up the stairs, creeping on his tiptoes.

The second floor was a storehouse, and against the far wall was a desk, some chairs, and a safe. The candle was sitting on top of the safe and a man, his back to them, was bent over it, working on the combination.

Riley pulled his weapon and leveled it. "Hold it right there, mister."

The man slowly turned around.

"Hands over your head," Riley ordered. "We're the police."

"Do say?" the man answered, his features coming into focus as the light hit them. "Wouldn't be running me in now, would you?"

Riley's eyes went wide with recognition. "Shaughnessy?"

"Aye."

"What the hell are you doing here?"

"What does it look like?" he said, his hands on his hips.

Riley relaxed. "I thought you and McNamara didn't have—"

"We don't."

Riley felt the hackles on his neck rise as cold steel pressed into the small of his back.

"I'll take your gun," Grady said from behind him. The police officer reached around and pulled the Colt from Riley's hand. "And the other one, too," he said, pulling it from the holster.

"What is this?" Riley asked, his eyes fixed on Shaughnessy, who was grinning widely.

"You're going to be a hero, Jamie, killed in the line of duty." Shaughnessy laughed. "They'll probably have a big funeral and all."

Riley's mind worked quickly; he knew he didn't have long. "You can't get away with this Shaughnessy. I've got another man out . . ."

He paused, realizing that the whole thing had been a setup. Both men had been pulled from Shaughnessy's gang.

"Does McNamara know about this?"

"Don't see how it matters," Shaughnessy said, pulling his weapon. "But I guess you got a right to know. No, he doesn't. This is me own little scheme, boyo."

"You're a fool."

Shaughnessy's grin turned to a grimace of undisguised hatred. "It's not me who's on the wrong end of a gun."

"What kind of deal do you want, Shaughnessy? A bigger split?" Riley kept talking, trying to stall.

"No good," the gang leader said, cocking the hammer of his gun. "It's too late. I want it all. Good-bye, Jamie."

Riley dropped to the floor as Shaughnessy fired. The bullet ripped into Grady's chest, catching him by surprise. Riley whirled and disappeared behind the tall stacks of crates.

"Give it up," Shaughnessy said, stalking forward.

430

Behind the crates Riley looked for an out. There was none. He had to settle it now. He moved back behind another row of the tall boxes and began climbing. He eased himself up on top of three crates and then looked down at Shaughnessy's shadow coming around the corner nine feet below.

"Make it easy on yourself," Shaughnessy said, the gun clutched in his hand.

Riley watched as Shaughnessy came confidently around the crates, his weapon in front of him.

"Shaughnessy!" Riley called.

Shaughnessy looked up and saw Riley's knife slicing through the air at him. The blade pierced the small of his throat before he could raise his weapon to fire.

Without a word, Shaughnessy fell to the floor, dead.

Outside, Dwyer had heard the single shot and knew that meant James Riley was dead. He'd get five hundred dollars for his part in the conspiracy. Shaughnessy would be out the back door by now. Grady would be on the second floor, out cold. When the rest of the coppers arrived, Grady would say that there had been three men inside and that there'd been a scuffle. A shot had been fired and Riley was dead. He'd taken a blow on the choppers and that had saved his life.

It was time to call for help, Dwyer thought, pulling a brass whistle from his pocket. He put it to his lips when he heard a tapping on glass behind him.

Dwyer turned and looked at the window in the door of the grain and feed store. He saw James Riley's smiling face. Dwyer felt his trousers turn cold and damp. It was the last thing he felt. The glass window shattered into a million pieces as both of Riley's guns flared.

Dwyer was caught full in the belly, at point-blank range. The powerful blasts lifted him from the ground, propelling him back through the air and out onto the street, where he fell in a bleeding, dead clump.

Riley kicked open the door and walked outside. Something glinted on the ground, catching the light from the street lamps. Riley bent to see what it was. He picked up Dwyer's brass whistle, put it to his still smiling lips, and blew long and hard.

Chapter 57

All that was lacking in the Chinese quarter by July was a formal declaration of war between the tong of tongs and the Six Companies. Every other element was present. Two powerful armies had been pitted against each other—the highbinders of the tong of tongs and the Chinese Protective Police of the Six Companies.

It was no longer just isolated incidents of crime and harassment. Now there were concerted offensive drives into what was clearly recognized as enemy area. It was no longer just a question of controlling certain businesses or enterprises, but of controlling territory.

The tongs controlled fully one-half of the Chinese quarter. Every shop, gambling parlor, furniture store, and barber shop in the south end of the district was controlled by the tongs. They were no longer a midnight organization. Many of their operations took place during the daytime, and hatchetmen boldly walked through the streets, brandishing their weapons as would the soldiers of a conquering army.

Their domination of the south side was total and complete. Each shopowner in the district paid a tribute, and a high one at that, for the privilege of doing business. Many times the tribute was so high as to drive the owner out of business, and the tongs took over the shop in that event, placing their own people in the stores.

But it was impossible to run every shop with their own men, so they allowed those who could afford their extortion to stay in business.

Hundreds of honest Chinese petitioned the Six Companies for relief. But the Chinese Protective Police found themselves withdrawing further and further, to the north side of the city. A clear line of demarcation existed that was moving further north with each succeeding week, moving closer and closer to the Meeting Hall of the Middle Kingdom and Chinese Protective Police headquarters itself.

Raiding parties of hatchetmen regularly entered the Six

Companies' territory and literally took it over, block by block. On notable occasions, minor battles erupted between the highbinders and the Chinese Protective Police. Invariably, the highbinders emerged victorious. This was in part because the Chinese Protective Police were fighting a defensive war and had to scatter their forces, whereas the highbinders, who were on the attack, could concentrate their efforts on a single point and break through.

Once a block was taken, the highbinders visited all the merchants and explained the realities of continued existence to them.

The Six Companies bent to the final indignity in the beginning of July. They sent a plea to the mayor of the city asking for assistance in stemming the incursion of the tong of tongs.

The reply came back that the San Francisco Police Department was already stretched to the limit trying to control the white hoodlums who roamed through the city. However, former vigilante chief James Riley had a division of policemen in the area and would meet with Tai Pien.

It did not take Tai Pien longer than fifteen minutes with Riley to realize that the police officer's only desire was to protect the whites who ventured into the area, and that he had only come to meet the Chinese Protective Police's chief at the mayor's request.

Shortly after their meeting, Tai Pien went to the house of Chin Wong and reported the results. For a long time Chin said nothing. Finally he looked up from the table, staring at Tai Pien with eyes of ice.

"We must move against them. We must destroy them, Tai Pien. There is no alternative." Chin looked down at the table, pausing in thought before he continued. "Perhaps it would be different if Yang were not one of them, but he is, and some insane jealousy . . . greed . . . hatred fuels him."

"You don't have to talk about it."

"I know I don't. But you and I know that that is much of the problem."

"The problem," Tai Pien said, "is what we are going to do."

"The time has come to march against them. We can no longer fight a war of retreat. We must move on them."

"The Assembly will never approve it, Chin. You know they—"

"Then we must move without their approval."

Tai Pien stared at him, unable to speak.

Chin leaned across the table. "The men will follow you, Tai Pien. They will follow me. They no longer take their orders from the weak women who sit in our councils. There is a time for debate and a time for action, and if the former stands in the way of the latter then it must be swept aside." Chin saw the look of total surprise on Tai Pien's face and said, "It is what you have always wanted, isn't it? To march against the highbinders?"

"I crave war no more than any rational man," Tai Pien said. "I gain no pleasure from spilling blood—even tong blood. But I, like you, am a man of my people. I do what must be done, and if what must be done is tending the field in peace, then that is what I shall do. But if what must be done is war and the spilling of blood, then that is what I shall do.

"We are the same," Tai Pien said, "flexible, sensitive to the needs of our people, protective of their right to live their lives." He leaned closer to Chin and said, "Now talk to me of this war that must be fought."

Chapter 58

In July Hung Ma Kung, the Grand *Ah ma* of the tong of tongs, was stricken ill. The elderly leader was confined to a sickbed in his suite on the top floor of the Kwong Dock house. For a full week the finest physicians Chinatown had to offer were escorted to the sickroom, where they examined the *Ah ma*.

It took more than two hours from the time a physician left his residence to the time he would actually see the *Ah ma*. This was not so much because of the distance between the two points—which, in fact, was always relatively short—but because of the intense security measures taken to safeguard the *Ah ma*'s life.

When Yang dispatched three highbinders to fetch a physician they were instructed to strip-search the doctor before he was allowed to come with them. Yang fully understood the

434

ways of treachery, and knew that even a physician had his price.

Once a doctor arrived at the tong house he was taken to a room where he was once again strip-searched. He was threatened with a most unpleasant and prolonged death should any harm befall his patient. Sufficiently terrified, the doctor would then be led into the apartment of Hung Ma Kung.

During the examination two highbinders of the *Ah ma*'s elite guard were always on hand. Also in attendance at every examination was Yang. It was during the examination that the *Ah ma*'s life was in the most danger, Yang felt. A poisoned needle, a potion, anything could be introduced, and thus the examinations were closely scrutinized.

The physicians agreed to perform the examinations more out of fear of reprisal for refusing than for the payment of triple their customary fee. And yet Yang knew that it would be impossible to keep the news of the *Ah ma*'s illness a secret. He knew, too, that it was the kind of news that the Six Companies could seize on. With the tong's leader ill, it would be an ideal time for the Six Companies to mount the counteroffensive Yang had long anticipated.

Yang had been preparing the tong for the ultimate battle for many months now. They had been procuring more and more weapons, drilling the warriors harder and harder, keeping tighter surveillance on the Chinese Protective Police's movements.

But with Hung Ma Kung disabled it would be more difficult to keep the chain of command strong, and that was vitally important during time of war. More and more, as the *Ah ma*'s illness wore on, Yang became apprehensive about the turn of events. It was as if the *Ah ma*'s very illness had been forced upon them to confound and hinder them.

After the tenth day of Hung Ma Kung's illness Yang began to feel great concern. They were a tong without a leader now, and that made him feel impotent and frustrated. Tradition dictated that each movement of the highbinders be approved by the *Ah ma,* and Hung Ma Kung was simply too weak to take full charge of his duties.

Just after dawn on the twenty-first, Yang sent for Ho Huan. When Ho Huan was ushered into Yang's apartment he found the chief swordsman hunched over a chair.

"Yang?"

Yang looked up at him through bleary eyes. "Sit down."

Ho Huan sat and for a long time neither of them said anything. Finally, Yang spoke.

"I have been awake all this past night."

"Something weighs heavily on you."

Yang nodded. "It is not good, this thing with Hung Ma Kung."

"A serious illness."

"Not the illness." He saw puzzlement in Ho Huan's eyes and said, "Of course the illness is serious, but I was not speaking of that."

"What, then?"

"His incapacitation. It is detrimental to the entire tong."

"In what way?"

"I have had reports that the Chinese Protective Police are massing men. Their patrols are less and less dispersed, more and more concentrated. They aren't even bothering to patrol the far perimeters anymore. Moreover, they no longer move in twos and threes, but rather in large groups of fifteen and twenty, sacrificing coverage for strength."

"What does it mean, Yang?"

Yang stood, pacing. "It means they no longer wish to have their men picked off. It means they care not as much for protecting the shops of their territory as they do for conserving their numbers. It can mean only one thing. They are preparing for an all-out attack."

"Can you be sure of this?"

"As sure as I can be of anything."

"Just from the fact that they—"

"More than that. The timing is right. The news of Hung Ma Kung's illness has not been kept secret."

"Who could have—"

"It doesn't matter. Maybe one of the doctors leaked it. Perhaps even one of our own men—a slip of the tongue. What matters is that it is known that the *Ah ma* is ill. The Six Companies will realize that this is the right time to strike against us."

"We will repel any attack."

"Perhaps," Yang said. "Still, Hung Ma Kung cannot be a strong leader while he is on his back. If there is a full battle he must be able to see what is happening.

"His mind must be clear to give the orders of war, analyze strategies. He must move quickly and he cannot do that now."

"You could assume command."

Yang turned. "No. You know the sacred laws of the tong as well as any warrior. The *Ah ma* is the absolute commander. All orders must issue from him. No other man may assume command." After a pause, he added, "So long as the *Ah ma* is alive."

The room hung in silence for a pregnant moment, before Ho Huan repeated, "Alive?"

Yang turned to look at him. "Yes, alive. While he is alive Hung Ma Kung is the leader of the tong. But if he were to pass . . ."

"That is in the hands of the gods."

"It need not be so," Yang said.

"What do you mean?"

Yang folded his hands. "This is a dangerous time. We are vulnerable, Ho Huan. We need a strong leader, someone who can order our warriors in the event of attack."

"What are you suggesting?"

Yang bored his eyes into Ho Huan. "You know what I am suggesting."

"The assassination of Hung Ma Kung? Our own *Ah ma*?"

Yang nodded. "For the good of the tong of tongs. No," he corrected, "for the very preservation of the tong of tongs."

"It is a crime punishable by death from torture."

"Sometimes the laws must yield to the times."

"Then let yield that law which says that only the *Ah ma* can assume command of the tong."

Yang shook his head. "That law is unalterable. The warriors would never follow me. I would not expect them to. I would kill any man who would follow anyone but the *Ah ma*. It is that law which preserves the absolute power of the *Ah ma*. If I am to assume command I must *be* the *Ah ma*."

Yang looked at Ho Huan for a long moment. "There is no other way. It must be done."

"If anyone should discover . . ."

"Only we two shall know."

"Why do you take me into your confidence?"

"Two reasons. You are my strong right arm. I need your counsel today as I did yesterday and as I shall tomorrow. We have traveled far together and we shall travel farther still. I need your strength, Ho Huan."

"You shall always have it. And the second reason?"

Yang looked away for a moment. "The method of death. I shall require a poison. It would be unwise for me to obtain it

437

myself. I am too well known, both to our brothers and our enemies. But you can . . ."

"I can get it for you."

"Yes. Will you?"

"I will." Ho Huan rose. "Were it any other man I would not do this. But the fates have conspired to make this thing right. What you say is true. We need a strong leader. The danger is all around us. You are that leader. The sacrifice is a right one."

"How soon can you have the poison?"

"I will return this afternoon."

"Good," Yang said, walking with him to the door. "Make haste, but be certain you are prudent and discreet in obtaining it. It would do us no good to reach our goal, only to meet death at the hands of the torturer."

Ho Huan nodded, then left.

Yang sat in the stillness of his apartment, thinking. Ho Huan was a good man, a good friend. Yang needed him for his counsel. It was true, also, that he needed him to get the poison. A man of his own stature simply did not walk into a chemist and ask for a vial of poison without drawing suspicion—particularly if the death of the *Ah ma* were to follow shortly thereafter.

But there was one other integral reason that he needed Ho Huan's participation, and a foul taste of bile rose in his mouth as he thought of it.

In the event the plot was discovered, Ho Huan's participation would serve as insurance. It would be Ho Huan who would bear the accusation, Ho Huan whom Yang would deliver to Tsau Tsau. And who would believe Ho Huan? Particularly when it would be learned that he had procured the poison. Who would believe a traitor over the word of the new Grand *Ah ma* of the tong of tongs?

Ho Huan had apparently heeded Yang's warning to exercise caution in obtaining the poison. Instead of returning to Yang's apartment in the afternoon, it was past the dinner hour before the knock came at his door.

Yang opened it and nodded to his guard. The guard stood aside and allowed Ho Huan to enter. The warlord made for a pair of lacquered chairs in the living room and chose one of them to sit on. Yang joined him.

"Did you have difficulty obtaining the poison?"

Ho Huan nodded. "Some."

Concern flooded Yang's face. "What kind of difficulty?"

"More of a preventive nature."

"Speak clearly."

"Twice I decided against purchasing the draft from chemists. Both times brothers of ours were nearby, once almost as I entered a store."

"But you were able to get it?"

Ho Huan nodded.

"From who?"

"Cha Pi Leng, a chemist on Powell Street."

"Good."

Ho Huan reached into his pocket and pulled a clear vial from it. He laid it on the table and pushed it toward Yang. Yang picked it up silently, looked at it, and then put it in his pocket.

"You have done well. Go to your apartment. I will take care of the rest."

Ho Huan rose and left.

Fragrant incense scented the air in Hung Ma Kung's room, but it did little to mask the pervading air of illness that hung like a heavy cloak, almost visible, making Yang's stomach turn.

Adorning every wall were brilliant red banners with elaborate lettering and paintings on them. Some of the banners bore dragons and tigers, to give the *Ah ma* strength to fight the illness. On a small stove tea brewed, and Yang kept an eye on it.

The old man's complexion was sallow. He did not look like a leader anymore. To Yang he only looked like an old man.

But he was a leader, Yang reminded himself, one of the most powerful men in Chinese America—absolute commander of the tong of tongs. Yang told himself that what he was doing was right because he wanted to keep the tong powerful. It was not for himself.

He would ascend to the throne and then he would defend the tong of tongs. No, he would take it against Chin. He would destroy the Six Companies, the Chinese Protective Police, and Chin. The last would be the most supreme delight. He paused in his thoughts, then pushed them aside.

"How are you feeling today, Hung Ma Kung?"

"The same," the old man said.

Yang had to listen hard. The *Ah ma*'s voice was barely a whisper. Beneath sheets of the finest silk, the Grand *Ah ma* lay waiting for a death that was now almost a palpable figure in the far corner of the room.

"You will get better soon," Yang said, moving to the stove.

"I do not think so."

Yang picked up the kettle and poured the tea into a cup. He felt his stomach tighten at Hung Ma Kung's words. The old man had given up. He was waiting for death. It made what Yang was about to do easier.

Yang reached into his tunic and pulled out the vial, his back to the *Ah ma*. He uncapped it and emptied the clear liquid into the teacup. Then he turned and walked to Hung Ma Kung's bed.

"Here is your tea," Yang said.

Hung Ma Kung took it and held the small cup in his hands for a moment, the feel of warmth good against them.

"Drink," Yang said, sitting in a chair at the bedside. "It will make you feel better."

But the Ah ma did not drink. Instead he just held the cup and asked, "How are things with the Protective Police?"

"They are unchanged."

"I think you deceive an old man."

"Be still, old one. Save your strength. Have some of your tea. It will improve your spirits."

"In a moment," the *Ah ma* said, an edge to his voice. "I will drink my tea in a moment . . . when I have finished what I have to say."

Yang bent his head in contrition, reminding himself that he was, after all, in the presence of the *Ah ma*.

Hung Ma Kung continued. "I do not think things are unchanged. They have worsened. Even before I fell ill, the Six Companies were pressed to the breaking point. I am told they are massing their forces. Is this true?"

"You must not worry about such things."

He nodded. "With my miserable condition keeping me on my back they will consider attacking us. Perhaps even as we speak they are mounting an attack."

"We have spies . . ."

"And what do they tell you? Tell me, Yang."

Yang looked away for a moment, but that was all the *Ah ma* needed. He nodded again, this time in understanding.

"Yes. Yes, you are right. I am too ill to be told of such things. I have not the strength to command."

"You will get better."

"I will not," Hung Ma Kung said, and then he put the cup to his lips and drank deeply, draining fully half of it.

When he rested the cup on his chest again, he asked, "Have I drunk death, Yang?"

It was only the second time in Yang's life that he had been totally shocked by a question. The first time had been many years ago, back in his childhood village, when his uncle had asked his father if Chin and Yang could join him on his journey to America.

Yang pulled his stomach in, his lungs hungry for air. He looked at the old man and slowly nodded in assent.

"I thought as much," Hung Ma Kung said. He placed the teacup to his lips and drank again. "How long?"

"Not long." Yang regarded him with more respect than he had ever felt toward any man. "You are a great leader, Hung Ma Kung."

"You shall be a greater one."

Yang bent his head.

"You have the courage," the *Ah ma* continued, "to seize that which needs to be seized. This needed to be done. Don't grieve over it. Now leave and do that which still remains to be done. Defend the tong of tongs against its enemies."

"To my death, I shall."

The wrinkles around the old man's eyes deepened. "Be wary of your brother, Yang."

Yang was shocked. "I will destroy him," he replied.

"Do not underestimate that man. He is powerful. He has not risen to such heights on good fortune alone."

"Nor have I."

The *Ah ma* nodded, his eyes closing slightly. "You have done it through force and ruthlessness. He has done it through beneficence and diplomacy. You possess the clear advantage."

"And I shall use it."

"So long as you do not let that force and ruthlessness fill you with so much pride that you fail to be wary of him. Keep your advantage," Hung Ma Kung warned. "Do not give him anything to become forceful or ruthless about. If you do, you shall place him on an even footing."

Hung Ma Kung, Grand *Ah ma* of the tong of tongs, closed his eyes and breathed no more.

Chapter 59

James Riley's control over nearly two thousand hoodlums in San Francisco was eroding. After McNamara had reported to him that the men on his payroll were uneasy about Shaughnessy's murder, Riley's response had been to lash out at them. He had cut their take by ten percent a month.

As he thought about it, Riley realized that he had made a fundamental error—he had isolated himself from his men.

Men such as those McNamara and Shaughnessy led were never satisfied. If they had a ninety-ten split they wouldn't have been satisfied. Shaughnessy had been able to maintain control over them by placing the blame for most everything on Riley's head. Riley was the reason they weren't getting more of a cut, Shaughnessy had claimed.

Shaughnessy had chanted this litany so many times that he had come to believe it himself, forgetting that James Riley provided the protection and most of the brains. So Shaughnessy had sought to remove his superior himself.

That Shaughnessy had been unsuccessful in his attempt only went to the gang leader's credit—if posthumously—in the eyes of the gang. His death served to further emphasize what he had claimed and made him a martyr. Rather than drawing the men into line, Riley's order to cut their wages by ten percent only further inflamed things.

When deterioration begins to take place in such circumstances it is usually rapid. The combination of Shaughnessy's death and the iron glove James Riley suddenly donned pushed things along at breakneck speed.

In the first two days after Billy McNamara made the announcement of the cut there was a wholesale drop of three hundred men from their ranks. By midweek almost five hundred men had failed to report to local saloons for their weekly orders. Local chiefs were reporting to McNamara that the men just weren't showing up. In fact, more than a dozen of the thirty chiefs themselves failed to show up.

"It's all right by me," Riley said, slipping into his police jacket. "They made their choice, now let them live with it."

O'Malley knew damned well that it wasn't all right with Riley. He knew that Riley was furious. Riley didn't like to lose . . . didn't like it at all.

"It's not a good idea for you to be at that sandlot speech tonight, Jamie."

"It's my job," he said, buttoning the jacket.

O'Malley laughed a humorless laugh. "All of a sudden you've got a dose of civic pride?"

Riley smiled at O'Malley's words, but the smile faded quickly.

"Look," O'Malley continued, "I just don't want you getting into anything you can't handle."

"I'll be all right. I can handle it."

O'Malley stood and walked around his desk, cutting between Riley and the mirror. "Jamie, there's going to be something like a thousand men at that rally tonight. And they're going to be angry. The speeches are going to be about the Chinks—kind of speeches you used to make, and remember how worked up you could get a crowd?"

"I remember. We'll keep it under control."

"Not in the mood you're in, you won't. I know you. boyo. I know you damned well. You're in a skull-busting mood, you are."

"I'll keep order, all right."

"That's exactly what I'm afraid of."

Riley edged him aside and looked at himself in the mirror. "Don't worry about it, Brian. I'll have fifty coppers with me tonight. More than enough to—"

"To stop a thousand men? Come on, man."

Riley glanced at him. "I'm not expecting a mass revolution, my friend. We'll keep a cool head."

"That's never been your strong suit, you know."

Riley smiled and placed his captain's cap on his head.

"And even if you keep a cool head," O'Malley continued, "that doesn't guarantee that the men coming to hear the speech will. Face it, Jamie, a lot of them were Shaughnessy's men. They're up in arms about you. So much so that they quit the gangs to free-lance."

O'Malley leveled a finger in warning. "You're going to show up there tonight with fire in your eyes. They'll be worked up over the speech, see you and . . . hell, man, anything could happen."

"It won't," Riley said, squaring his hat. "But I'll tell you one thing, Brian. I'll do my job. I had a fair deal with those men. They always got an even shake from James Riley. They pulled some dirty shit on me.

"They don't want any part of me, that's all right. They want me just to be a copper, that's all right, too. It's a copper I'll be, then; and God help the bum that looks at me the wrong way."

O'Malley had been wrong in his estimate of the crowd. More than two thousand men showed up for the rally on a sandlot near Mission Street. But then San Francisco was pregnant with unemployed men. The drought, the aftermath of the market crash, and a shriveled labor market had combined to swell the ranks of the unemployed.

Added to the considerable number of men without jobs was an equally large number of common workingmen. In fact, the meeting had been labeled a labor rally. Its primary purpose was to discuss the Chinese situation. "Discuss" was the word they had used on the handbills.

A long procession of speakers harangued the crowd over the Chinese curse, working them up to fever pitch. James Riley was one of three police captains attending the rally.

Each captain had a squad of fifty men assigned to him. A hundred uniformed officers were spaced around the perimeter of the sandlot, while another fifty—mostly Riley's men—drifted through the crowd looking to spot trouble before it began.

Anyone in the audience caught drinking liquor would be immediately arrested, the handbills had warned, and a caravan of paddywagons waited in plain sight to show that the warning was no idle threat.

There had been several close calls in the last few years and the police had made it clear that they would countenance no disorders. The right of assembly was a sacred one, but civil disobedience would be dealt with harshly.

Riley walked through the middle of the crowd and it was exactly where he wanted to be—out in the open, in full view of everyone. If someone wanted to make a move on him, let them try.

No one did.

"For too long we've tolerated the heathens in our midst,"

444

the speaker's voice boomed across the crowd, amplified by the megaphone he spoke through.

"They have stolen a hundred and eighty million dollars worth of gold from our country! They've raped America of her wealth. And what have they contributed in return? Nothing!"

The crowd cheered the speaker.

Riley closed his hand tightly over his nightstick.

"The United States has lost over four hundred million dollars because of Chinese immigration to this country. We have reaped a bitter harvest. These yellow scum have heaped their foul habits on our children—drugs, prostitution, reduced wages."

At the words of "reduced wages" the men roared their approval.

"Yes," the speaker bellowed, encouraged by the throng, "reduced wages. Or no wages at all!"

Again the men cheered.

"Through their insidious habit of accepting the lowest possible wages they have monopolized sewing, cigar-making, fishing, laundering. They've driven thousands of whites from jobs. They have pandered to the greedy capitalists and now both they and the rich capitalists will have to pay for the financial degradation they have visited on the decent workingman in this country!"

The cheers were deafening, pounding in around Riley as he felt for the butt of his gun with his other hand.

One push, one shove. Please; just one fist thrown at someone.

But it wasn't to be.

The speeches went on endlessly. The tirade against the Chinese continued on and on. The crowd swelled and rocked and cursed. But there was no violence in it. The anger wasn't aimed at the speakers, and a cool breeze off the bay allayed any danger of short tempers.

Apparently the handbills had done their work. There wasn't a bottle of beer to be spotted in the crowd.

It was past midnight before the last speaker had had his say. And by that time the crowd had thinned considerably. There were less than two hundred men left, and two of the police squads had already left. All that remained were Riley and his fifty officers.

Riley circled around and around the crowd. Some of the faces he recognized, and many of them recognized him. He

445

paced like a caged tiger and the attention of the crowd centered more on him than on the final speaker.

He grew tired of walking around them and decided to cut through their middle. They were a hated bunch. Scum of the earth. White Chinks, he decided, rather liking the label.

He hated them for opposing him, for caring more about Shaughnessy than him. He hated the fact that a fool like Shaughnessy was mourned.

"Ungrateful bastards," he murmured.

He shoved one of the men aside and the man turned to look at him.

"Come on, mate," Riley baited. "Try it. Take a swing. Take a swing. First one's on the house. Free swing."

But the man turned away.

Riley turned to the man standing next to him. "How about you, you miserable bastard? You want to be a hero? Come on; you can be the boy who decked James Riley. Avenge the death of your dear departed Tim Shaughnessy."

Twenty or thirty men had gathered to listen to Riley now.

"Any of you," he said, "any of you is free to take a swing. How about it, you miserable excuses for men?"

There were no takers.

"You dumb bastards. You had the deal of your lives and you blew it. All over some stupid Mick who had less brains than a cur. Well, if you want to go it alone, suit yourselves. But let me catch one of you so much as spitting in the street and I'll split your skull for you."

The men turned away and Riley called louder, "You hear that, you stupid jackasses? I'll split your lousy heads open for you!"

The speaker had finished and the crowd broke up. The group that had gathered to listen to Riley had, in fact, been a part of Shaughnessy and McNamara's gang. In that respect, Riley's words had found their mark. And they had had their desired effect. They had driven the men almost mad with anger.

Riley's appraisal of them had been fairly accurate as well. They were miserable bastards. They had few skills. There were thousands like them in the city. They had no prospects, and now, with Shaughnessy's death, they were without a leader.

Most of them had broken with Riley as much out of greed as out of respect for Tim Shaughnessy. Shaughnessy had been one of them. Riley, regardless of his connection with them, regardless of the fact that he was the real leader, had lost his ties with them when he opened up the livery business with O'Malley. He was a legitimate businessman and there was an unbridgeable gulf between him and the gang members.

Money speaks loudly, though, and the men would have forgotten about the death of Tim Shaughnessy. It had, after all, been a setup. But in his anger, James Riley wanted to punish all the men, give them a lesson they wouldn't forget. He had blindly cut their take at a time when they needed every penny they could lay their hands on.

Tonight, James Riley had rubbed it in their faces.

As they drifted away from the sandlot, anger and shame and hatred mixed and fulminated in them until it cried out for release. They had been pushed down in the mud, down to the slop beneath the mud, and what they saw in that stinking bog was themselves. It was too much to bear. There had to be a release.

They moved up Beal Street, a group of thirty of them.

"That no-good Riley. Did you hear him yelling at us like we was dirt?"

" 'Course I heard him," a thick Irish brogue answered. "Everyone on the damned lot heard him."

"Thinks he's too good for us," another of the men complained.

The man standing next to him agreed. "Aye; he forgets where he came from, that's what."

By the time they had crossed Market Street and into Chinatown, their group had grown to fifty, and the story about Riley had been rehashed again and again. All of them had been at the rally and all of them ached with a pain like that a man felt when he couldn't reach satisfaction with a woman.

They'd come to the rally out of pure boredom; it accounted for most of the turnout at huge mass meetings, and the politicians of the day never failed to seize on it. But as the speakers railed at the crowds they didn't realize they were setting emotions into play, emotions which would seek fulfillment.

When the men crossed over California Street they were more than sixty strong. Little China was quiet. It was nearly one o'clock. The streets were deserted. Perhaps if there were a few Chinese around to beat up on the group might have been sated. But there weren't, and that only infuriated them more.

The group turned onto Clay Street, raucously seeking to disturb the sleeping Chinese. But no yellow man went to his window. They knew better.

They passed by a lot where a building lay in ruins; a stove fire had gutted it. A few of the men drifted toward the charred remains. One of them climbed up on a pile of bricks and played king of the hill for a few minutes. He bent and picked up a brick in each hand, as if to fend off his attackers. There was more laughter as he feigned throwing the bricks at the other men and they fell back.

The man on top of the heap looked across the narrow street. His eyes fixed on a laundry house, its wide windows displaying stacks of neatly folded white sheets and towels and shirts on the other side. He looked at the sheets and towels and shirts and thought about the work involved in washing them, about how the Chinese would always have work because the bastards would scrounge for pennies.

Then his anger burst forth and he cocked his arm and hurled the brick. It sailed high across the street, over the heads of the men, and crashed through the window of the laundry house. The brick struck one of the stacks of laundry before it fell to the floor inside.

For a moment the sixty-eight men fell silent, staring at the broken window. A large, jagged shard hung down from the upper part of the window frame. Then, as if on cue, the piece of glass fell and crashed to the ground below.

It was as if the falling glass was a signal. They turned, one by one, and looked at the pile of bricks. Then they began moving toward it. Hands reached down and wrapped around the ocher and terra cotta slabs. The men hefted them, gave them flight. A barrage of stone pounded the building.

When they had finished this work the men surged forward and pushed through the door; some of them climbed through the windows. Inside the washhouse they stumbled around in the darkness for a while. Then, their eyes growing accustomed to the light, they began reaching for bundles of laundry, tearing them apart.

The men tugged on opposite ends of shirts and towels; the ripping of the fabric sounded like high squeals. Over and over they ripped the laundry, dragging it on the floor, kicking over equipment. Some of the men set about tearing the work counters to pieces, while others overturned the washing bins.

In fifteen mintues they had made a shambles of the laundry house and were swarming out into the street, a single machine of destruction giving vent to the most primitive instincts.

They began to pick up momentum. Others joined the group—white hoodlums who had been visiting the brothels and gambling parlors. Each street they crossed brought two or three new recruits.

They moved up to Tyler Street and stormed through another washhouse and left it in ruins. They rolled up the street, an unstoppable mass of eighty crazed men, and fell on still another laundry house. As they broke through the door they found the owner and his wife cowering at the rear of the shop, with a single lamp casting its light on them.

While most of the men began tearing the laundry house apart, a handful of them had their minds set on other pleasures. They pushed the diminutive owner aside and grabbed for his wife. While three of them held her, two of the others ripped her clothes from her body.

She screamed as the men pawed at her nakedness, struggling in their grasp. The men roared with laughter, pinching her, squeezing her, violating her in the foulest manner imaginable.

The owner of the laundry house was far from a brave man and he knew that he was no match for these white men. But finally there came the moment when he could no longer bear his wife's shrieks and the sight of the white men running their rough and greedy hands over her, unbuckling their belts.

He leaped through the air and onto the back of one of the tormentors. The white man he landed on had his trousers down around his ankles and was thrown off balance by the sudden attack.

Others in the group laughed, their laughter blending with the cries of the man's wife. They pried the flailing man loose from their cohort and pulled him to a wall at the back of the shop. There they began to work on him.

First they used fists, then their boots. Boards had been pulled loose when they had wrecked the washhouse and now they used them as clubs, beating the man senseless.

When they had finished they returned their attention to the man's wife. Playfully, the men let her go. She backed away as they closed on her. Her hand searched, searched for anything to use as a weapon. Finally it wrapped around the small lamp. She seized it and threw it forward.

The lamp hit one of the men square on the chest, shattering. The kerosene quickly doused his shirt and turned him into a burning, screaming pillar of flame. The man whirled away, ran through the store. Others tried to grab him, but it was impossible. He fell to the floor, rolling about in agony until he rolled no longer.

New flames sprang up; the laundry caught fire. The heat in the washhouse began building as the bone-dry wood crackled from the blaze.

The men poured out of the shop, furious that their friend had been burned alive. When the naked Chinese woman came running out of the door, four of the men grabbed her by the arms and thrust her back into the inferno, slamming the door shut.

Her screams died as the fire broke through the roof of the one-story building. As the flames burst through and leaped into the sky, so too did their anger soar. Incensed by the fire, they moved up the street in search of another laundry house.

After the rally at the sandlot ended, James Riley had felt as unfulfilled as the men who had attended it—albeit for different reasons. Riley had come looking for a fight and it had been denied him. He admitted to himself afterwards, that O'Malley had been right, as usual.

O'Malley had also known that provoking a fight wouldn't have been wise. No matter how many police he had with him, going up against a riot of two thousand unemployed men would have been a mistake. Still, his bravado had backed them down, so who was wrong? He had shown them the stuff James Riley was made of and they didn't dare move against him, even with a superior force.

Riley had thought about going back to the stables, but decided against it. He didn't feel like seeing O'Malley just yet. Sometimes O'Malley was right too often and it was a little hard to take.

The feeling of dissatisfaction hung over him and he decided to head back for the police house. It was odd, Riley reflected on his way back to the station—he felt as though the officers were more his peers than were the men of the streets. Tonight, when he'd been walking among the hoodlums of San Francisco, he had felt nothing but contempt and loathing, and he was glad that it was behind him.

He walked around the station house, joking with a few of the men, pacing, drinking a cup of coffee.

Then the news came in—indirectly, from the fire department. Four laundry houses in Little China were burning and a hundred whites were rolling through the quarters, rioting.

Riley knew then what he had been waiting for.

He was in the lead police wagon. Behind him more than a dozen wagons followed. Riley was the ranking officer in the station when the call came in, and Chinatown was his district. He leaped into action, ordering every available man to the wagons.

Riley cared for the Chinese no more than any other man of his ilk, but tonight he was grateful to them for providing this opportunity.

He turned to the young police lieutenant in the wagon with him. "Giles, I want every last one of those rioters locked up."

"Every one of them, sir?"

"Yes!" he rasped.

"The fire department estimated over a hundred, captain."

"I know what the . . ." Riley thought about it. The young officer was right. He only had forty men with him. They couldn't possibly arrest them all.

He looked at Giles, controlling his rage. "All right, lieutenant. Arrest anyone who puts up any resistance. You give one order to disperse and after that, cuff 'em and put 'em in the wagons."

"Yes, sir."

"I'm holding you personally responsible for those orders, Giles. I can't be everywhere at once and I expect some arrests made, Giles; you understand that?"

"Yes, captain."

"And don't be any too soft about it. These vermin need to be taught a good lesson." Riley lowered his voice and said, "I expect to see a few bloody sticks before the night is over."

Giles nodded, but Riley wasn't looking at him any longer. He was almost talking to himself.

"Bloody sticks . . . I want a few skulls split tonight, boyo. I want . . ." He turned to look at the policeman, conscious of being watched. "That's the only thing these sort of men understand, boy. Aye, a firm hand is what they understand."

The police wagon rounded a corner and Riley looked at the red night sky, lit by the flames of half a dozen fires. He could hear the bells of firewagons in the distance and the sound of horses' hooves on pavement. He looked at the horses pulling his own wagon, the sweat matted on their black sides, and he felt his muscles tense in anticipation.

The police wagons pulled to a stop in Portsmouth Square. The officers tumbled from the wagons and lined up. After Lieutenant Giles had issued preliminary orders, Riley said, "I want order restored in this quarter inside of an hour and I don't care how harsh you have to be to get it. I want order!" Riley shouted, pounding his fist into his palm. "And by God I'll have it."

Riley turned to his driver, nodded, and the driver pulled away from the curb, leaving Giles and the other men standing alone in the square.

The flames rose over Chinatown.

Chapter 60

If Riley had expected a short battle he was to be disappointed. As the police swarmed through the quarter the hoodlums reacted by moving down a few blocks and starting their riot again. Rioting and burning turned to looting, and soon store after store was being broken into and sacked.

Giles had tried to follow Riley's orders in the beginning, but it soon became apparent that he was not going to be able to arrest every resister.

The fires didn't help matters any. Aside from the dozens of firewagons that hampered the police's progress, the flames drew more and more hoodlums from white San Francisco who wanted to investigate the excitement. When they saw what was happening they joined in.

By four o'clock in the morning Riley had over a hundred police officers in the quarter, but the melee had turned into a full-scale riot by then. Riley's orders to go heavy didn't help quell things, and the police met with pockets of violent resistance. More than one officer was taken away with a bloodied face.

With daylight the riot ebbed. Both the police and the hoodlums seemed too tired to go on. It might have ended there, but Riley got in touch with the mayor and asked for reenforcements. He informed the mayor that there were rumors

452

that the rioters were talking about marching on Nob Hill, where the looting would yield better treasures.

The chief of police tried to take over at that time, but it was Mayor Bryant's feeling that Riley, who knew the area and the situation best and had had vigilante experience, would do best at dealing with this sort of men.

By nightfall the rioting had started again, egged on by the rough manner of the coppers under Riley's command. Hundreds of unemployed men poured into the quarter to take part in the pillaging. It was out of control.

The rioting continued for three nights. As the two violent factions clashed, Chinatown became a raging inferno. Twenty-five washhouses were razed to the ground. Factories employing Chinese workers were set ablaze. Lumberyards were torched. A dozen Chinese were brutally murdered and countless police officers and hoodlums were bloodied, in the worst riot in San Francisco history.

It wasn't until July 26 that Riley finally admitted that it was beyond his control. The news that Riley was in command had spread to every hoodlum in San Francisco and they flocked to Chinatown as a demonstration that they would not be spat upon—not by a man who had once been one of their own.

On the afternoon of the twenty-seventh, two companies of California National Guardsmen were mobilized. The Workingman's party, a political organization, had been blamed for inciting the riot with the sandlot meeting. To counter this charge the party took to the streets to aid the National Guard, putting three thousand men on the streets armed with pick handles.

On the thirtieth of July the last window was broken, the last flame flickered out, the last rioter dispersed. It was over.

The rioting had brought everything in Chinatown to a dead standstill. Yang had been proclaimed the *Ah ma* of the tong of tongs, but he had stopped worrying about the Chinese Protective Police for the present.

There was no way they were going to plan any sort of activity against the tong of tongs so soon after the rioting. A large number of uniformed white policemen still patrolled the district.

Instead, Yang continued to make slow progress in taking territory away from the Six Companies. Again his warriors began to push into the north side of the city.

When the news came, in the second week of August, that Lei Ko Lyio wanted to see him, Yang was elated. Lei Ko Lyio was the owner of one of the finest bordellos in the Chinese quarter, and Yang had had his eye on it for a long time.

This sort of thing had happened before. Lei Ko Lyio had once enjoyed the protection of the Suey Sing tong, which had owned the bordello. But after the final battle, with the Suey Sing scattered, he had grabbed at the opportunity for complete ownership, purchasing the bordello for a mere twenty five thousand dollars from the few remaining highbinders of that tong.

But now that the tong of tongs was pushing into the north side of the city, more than one businessman had contacted Yang, the powerful *Ah ma*, before their block actually fell. The idea was to make a deal ahead of time and thus salvage something.

Lei Ko Lyio was a rotund man of sixty-two. Watching Yang enter his office escorted by two of his personal guards, the old man paid fitting homage. He rose and bowed as Yang entered.

"Honorable *Ah ma* of the tong of tongs, my grateful thanks for your visit."

Yang bowed only slightly in return. He sat without waiting to be asked. "You said you have business with me?"

"You would like some tea, perhaps?"

"No." Yang felt no need to be gracious to this panderer.

The smile faded slightly from the bordello owner's face. "Very well. I would like to make you a proposal. I would—"

"You would like me to become your partner," Yang interrupted. "Is that it?"

"I—I—"

"That is precisely it," Yang declared. He smiled. "You businessmen all think you are dealing with children. You think because we wield a sword our brains have shrunk to the size of a pea."

"I never—"

"I know you didn't say it. You don't have to." Yang leaned back in the chair. "Make your offer, Lei Ko Lyio."

"If you would favor me with your protection I would be willing to offer you a twenty-five percent share in my business."

Yang's reply was a peal of laughter. Finally he said, "Why should I leave you anything? In a few weeks my soldiers will take over this area. Why shouldn't I just take it all and toss you out on your ear?"

"Because this is my brothel."

"Keep your mouth shut, old man, or you will lower my opinion of you." Yang shook his head and mimicked Lei Ko Lyio. " 'Because this is mine.' That is an old woman's cry as children in the street steal her vegetables. Are you an old woman?"

The man straightened in his chair. "No. You know I am not."

"Then don't give me an old woman's excuse. The answer as to why I should allow you to survive is because you have something of value, something of individual worth. You are a businessman. You know how to run this operation. Start sounding like it, at least."

"Then you accept my offer?"

"I accept your offer because I need someone who is capable of seeing that this concern operates profitably."

Lei Ko Lyio looked visibly relieved.

"But there must be a slight change in the terms."

"Change?"

"It is you who shall receive the twenty-five percent and I who shall take seventy-five."

Lei Ko Lyio stood up from his chair, about to speak.

Yang said, "Voice one word of opposition and I shall kill you tonight and place one of my men in this whorehouse to run it."

In fifteen minutes Lei Ko Lyio had calmed down. He was, after all, going to be able to stay in business. That was a better bargain than many who ran shops in the blocks that were taken over by the tongs. He had heard of laundry and restaurant owners who had been told to leave or die. Others had just disappeared. Tong employees were seen running the shops and stores shortly after.

Yang had requested the bordello's books and Lei Ko Lyio had turned them over to him. The tong's accountant would peruse them in order to make an estimate of what they could expect to gross from the operation.

Yang handed the books to one of his men and turned to Lei Ko Lyio as he walked from the office and out into one of the larger salons.

"I understand your house caters to the more unusual pleasures."

Lei Ko Lyio nodded. "That is true. We pride ourselves on being inventive."

"Mastery?"

The proprietor laughed, "Hardly the unusual. Perhaps that is something special at some houses. You forget you are in the finest house in this city—perhaps in all of America!"

Yang had humiliated him before. Now Lei Ko Lyio wanted to get back at him, by showing how much more knowledgeable he was in his own area of expertise than Yang.

"Come," the proprietor said, "I will show you what exotic really is."

They came into a smaller parlor. Low red davenports lined the walls, and the owner of the brothel bid Yang sit on one of them. When the *Ah ma* had complied, Lei Ko Lyio clapped his hands twice.

Two house attendants, stripped to the waist, wheeled in a black box two feet high and two feet wide. The two men unlatched the top of the box and lifted it off. Yang looked at the device in wonder.

The bottom half looked like a large cushion. It was covered in gold leather. Extending up from the middle of the cushion was a shaft which could be nothing other than a phallus. It, too, was gold: the shaft was brass, covered with a thin layer of gold leaf. It rose a foot up from the cushion, glittering lewdly in a steely erection.

In every way the tool represented manhood—ridged, the veins, imitating those of nature, the head bulbous and waiting. In size alone it differed, for it was as big around as a man's wrist.

When Lei Ko Lyio clapped his hands again music began to play from behind a curtain on the other side of the room. Moonharps and sweet bamboo fiddles played a hazy melody which carried a sensuous undertone. A single gong sounded and then the curtains on the other side of the room were pulled apart.

For a moment Yang tensed, his hand instinctively going to the weapon in his tunic. But then he relaxed, his eyes drinking in the most voluptuous creature he had ever seen in his life.

Her hair, black and silken and unbraided, fell down to the middle of her back. She moved with the grace of a gazelle, her feet barely touching the ground as she spun and danced

456

into the room. Her body was oiled from her cheeks to her toes.

The woman wore a silk tunic of gold and red and white. It was cut deeply in the center to reveal the full swell of her ample breasts. On either side of her breasts, sitting on the lapels of the jacket, were two brocade red dragons. Her pantaloons, of the sheerest silk, moved in the breeze as she swirled. The ghost of a naked body teased from beneath the gossamer garments.

A low, steady drumbeat picked up now and she followed it sinuously, twisting around the room. Yang's eyes were heavy on her. She rolled her hips as the *Ah ma* watched her, and with her free hand she reached in back of her and undid the clasp of her tunic. With a smooth motion she reached forward with both hands and the tunic slid off.

She spun to the music, turning as the beat picked up. Yang watched her breasts, like two fine melons, swaying to the beat. They were oiled, like the rest of her, the dusky twin points of her nipples erect and puckering.

Now she moved toward the enormous phallus that sat in the middle of the room. She twisted around it, her body in moving completely with the music. Her hands grasped it, snaked around it, squeezed it in feigned ecstasy. Yang watched as her mouth opened and the point of her tongue flickered across her lower lip, moistening it.

Twice she circled the phallus, her eyes fixed on it, regarding it as one would a lover—with anticipation and passion. Then the music picked up tempo and she raised one delicate foot into the air. She stepped up onto the cushion and in a moment she was poised above the golden phallus. Even Lei Ko Lyio felt his breath coming in jerks now.

The music had turned into a low, grinding moan and for the first time Yang heard her voice, her moan as she undid the waistband of her trousers and tossed them aside so that she was completely naked. He watched, hypnotized, as the oiled, slithering temptress before him threw her head back, her mouth agape, her hips grinding.

He watched as she slowly lowered herself down onto the golden joy, taking it into her.

Lower she went, down onto it, lower and lower, until it seemed impossible that she could continue. Her eyes were closed, her cheeks sucked in with pleasure he could only guess at. The woman's hands clutched at her own breasts, squeezing them, twisting her nipples so they stood out hard

457

and erect. Yang felt his arousal swelling to match the taut shaft that was now buried deep inside the dancer.

And then she was rising, the golden tool becoming visible as she released it. She stood all the way up, now, her body hovering over the phallus, her feet braced on the cushions. A ragged, lustful smile came to her lips and she moistened them again with her tongue. Then she began another descent.

But this time it was quicker, the shaft thrusting up into her as she bent into a squat, taking full pleasure from it. She stood, letting the rigid rod slide out of her. Again and again she took it into her. Again and again she stood.

Faster, and faster she worked, her passion mounting, her face glistening, dripping, until she let out a scream of culmination as she squatted down so low that her buttocks brushed against the cushion.

Her head fell forward, limp, in completion.

From behind him, Lei Ko Lyio said, "That, my friend, is what we call erotic."

Yang's eyes were still frozen on the girl, his undisguised excitement swelling lewdly against the fabric of his trousers. "I must have her," he said. "Arrange it. Arrange it quickly."

Lei Ko Lyio had shown Yang to a private room at the rear of the brothel. The dancer was already there, reclining on a large bed. In truth, Lei Ko Lyio had foreseen Yang's excitement and had arranged for him to have her afterwards. It was best, he learned, to have powerful men such as Yang as one's friend, even if it meant giving up a portion of one's income. The alternative was none too appealing.

The girl would keep him in good spirits.

Yang had taken her quickly, his passion almost uncontrollable by the time he was in the room. He took her with a force and brutality that was animal in its wantonness. There was nothing of love in it. There was only lust and greed and selfishness.

When he was through with her he stood before the bed and looked down at her. She smiled vacantly up at him and it occurred to him that she had been smoking opium.

"Which did you receive more pleasure from, woman—me or the golden spike?"

"You, my lord." Her eyes tried to focus on him.

"Lying whore," he spat. "Your mind is so fogged with opium that you would not feel it if an elephant ravaged you."

She still smiled.

458

Yang fastened his belt, reflecting that nothing was ever so sweet as its anticipation. "You are fortunate among all women," he declared. "Tell your whore-sisters that you had the honor of sharing a bed with the Grand *Ah ma* of the tong of tongs, Yang Wong."

She stared up at him, the smile still there, but not as vacant as it had been before. Yang was pleased. At least something had gotten through to her. He watched as the smile slowly left her face and he was more pleased. Reverence was the proper mood to assume, he felt, when one was in his presence.

"Yang Wong?" she said.

He buttoned his tunic. "Yes, Yang Wong, the *Ah ma* of—"

"Yang Wong?" she said, sitting up in the bed. She pulled the covers about her naked body, the veil of opium seeming to retreat as she became more alert before his eyes.

"Yang Wong whose father was Kung Lee Wong?" she asked.

He stopped buttoning his jacket, bewilderment sweeping over him. All power was gone from his voice. "How did you . . ."

The whore's hands covered her cheeks as her jaw fell open. "I . . . I am Ling. . . . I am your *sister!*"

"Ling? My . . ."

He looked at her, at the ghost-white China doll makeup that covered her face. He saw the raspberry lipstick that he had smeared with his own mouth; his mouth working against hers, his manhood penetrating her, taking her . . . his sister . . . Ling.

"It . . . it can't be . . . ," he began.

"But it is! I am Ling! I am your sister. Your *sister*, Yang! YOUR SIS—"

His hand slapped hard against her face, driving her back onto the bed, stunning her. He had to have time to think. This could not be. It was impossible.

He looked at her again.

And yet . . . there was something in her face, in her eyes, some distant resemblance to his infant sister that told him that it was true, that she was Ling, and the unthinkable had happened.

"It *is* you," she said, squinting, focusing, thinking back to her childhood. "Yang . . ."

"Shut up," he said, not looking at her. "Be quiet. I must think."

459

"I . . . I. . . ." She choked. "Our ancestors . . . our father . . ."

He turned on her then, his eyes wide, his nostrils flared like a panther about to strike. "Listen to me, whore! Listen well. What happened, happened. I do not claim to know the whims of the fates or the gods who look over us."

"But I am your sister."

"You are *not* my sister. My sister is an infant back in China, across the ocean. She sits in my father's house, her feet in bandages."

"I *was* an infant. I did sit in our father's house. My feet were in bandages. I am grown now. You must—"

"You are not my sister!" he bellowed, and she fell still from the force of his words. "Never say that you are related to me, whore. Never say this again. If you do," he said, turning away from her, "if you do I shall . . . I shall rip your throat out." His voice faltered, was barely a whisper as he opened the door and left the room. ". . . Rip your throat out . . ."

Chapter 61

Rebecca Ashley's recovery from the miscarriage had been a lengthy one. She had suffered emotionally and physically. But like all women of dedication and purpose, she was able to call upon a deep, inner strength during that time of trial.

Her first step to recovery had been to return to volunteer nursing work. In the beginning she chose to work at San Francisco City Hospital, avoiding contact with the Chinese, letting her own wounds heal. But she had worked for too long with the immigrants, she knew them too well, she felt too much compassion for them to turn her back on them forever. And when the tong wars raged, she began working in the hospital in the Chinese quarter once again. The final battle had stunned and shocked her. But in its aftermath, sewing wounds and ministering to the injured, she once again realized her worth and was herself healed.

She was making the rounds, checking on patients in the

460

ward, when three attendants brought in a woman who was screaming as though she had been dragged into the depths of hell. Patients and staff alike turned at the spectacle. She was a slight woman, but it required all three of the men to restrain her. Her arms flailed through the air, her nails clawing at them, drawing blood from at least one of the attendants.

Finally, a fourth orderly with a straitjacket grabbed the patient and forced her arms into it. Rebecca watched as the laces were tied. The woman struggled more now that she was immobilized. Her teeth snapped in the air like a crocodile and she kicked wildly.

Two of the attendants picked her up, carried her to a bed, and dumped her there. The woman kicked at them again with her legs, and soon restraining straps were fastened about them too. Still she struggled, shrieked, writhed.

The attendants walked away. Most of the patients went back to their own problems. The woman was kept company only by her sobs.

Rebecca walked to the bed and looked at her. The light over the bed showed a sallow face gazing up at her. The remnants of white makeup were streaked by rivers of tears. There was blood on her lower lip from where she had bitten herself.

"Be still," Rebecca soothed. "Try to calm down. Do you understand English?"

The woman didn't answer and Rebecca spoke in Chinese. "Try to control yourself. Are you in pain?"

The sobs had become jerky gasps now as they slowed.

"Take a few deep breaths," Rebecca urged.

"Can't . . . can't . . . can't do this . . ."

"What can't you do?"

The woman's eyes darted about the room, looking at unseen demons. "Can't do this . . . this horrible thing . . ."

"What is it that you can't do?"

"I . . . touched me . . . touched me . . . my . . . my . . ."

Rebecca bent her head lower, trying to make out the woman's words. "Who touched you? What happened to you?"

The woman screamed in response to the question. It was a sound unlike any Rebecca had ever heard before, the scream of someone forced to look at an unspeakable evil. Again the patients turned. One of the physicians came over to the bed.

"What's going on here?" the doctor asked.

"That's what I'd like to know."

461

The woman screamed again, tensing and thrashing against the straps and jacket that bound her.

"Look," the doctor said, "you'll have to leave her alone."

"I was only trying—"

He took her by the arm. "I know, I know."

"Please," the woman screamed, her eyes shut, "please don't . . . DON'T TOUCH ME!"

Rebecca looked at the woman on the bed, then to the doctor. "Maybe you should look at her."

"I'll get to her. You'd better leave her be. She's getting worked up and it's getting the other patients upset."

Rebecca turned to leave when she heard the woman's voice calling out.

"Please, father . . . help me, father, help me. Don't let him touch me . . . unclean . . . don't let him touch me. Help, help . . . Chin, help me . . . Chin, Chin, help me . . . *help me!"*

Rebecca pulled away from the doctor's hand and spun around to look at the woman. "Chin?"

The doctor turned after her. "Please, Nurse Ashley, you'll have to—"

"Be quiet!" she ordered him. Then she looked at the woman.

Startled, the doctor said, "I beg your pardon?"

"I said keep your mouth shut." She took a step toward the bed.

The doctor grabbed hold of her arm again. "Mrs. Ashley, may I remind you that you're in a hospital and that I'm the head physician here? I'll give the orders if you don't . . ."

Rebecca turned very slowly and looked at the doctor's hand on her arm. "Doctor, may I remind you that my husband donates fifty thousand dollars a year to this hospital? Your hand, sir, is on my arm."

The young doctor frowned for a moment, thought about it, and released her arm. "Just for a minute. Then you'll have to leave her alone." His voice no longer carried the authority it had. "We really can't have her disturbing the pa—"

But Rebecca was no longer listening to him. She had turned around again and was walking to the bed where Ling lay.

She bent by her side. "Chin?" she whispered. "Did you say Chin?"

For the first time since she had been brought into the hospital Ling stopped struggling. She half turned to look at Rebecca, her eyes still red and swollen.

"Ch—Chin?" Ling asked.

"Yes," Rebecca answered, her face not six inches from Ling's. "Chin Wong?"

Ling blinked her eyes hard, more tears spilling from them. She fought to clear her head. It was dangerous, dangerous to think too clearly. If she did then she would have to think about the horrible thing, and to think about it was enough to drive her to complete insanity.

Still, the white woman had said Chin's name. She knew him. She would have to think . . . just a little bit. Just enough to speak with her. Chin . . . Chin was the way. He was the way out of it. He could make sense of it . . . save her.

She opened her eyes. "Chin. My brother, Chin."

"Your brother?" Rebecca said. "You're Ling?"

Ling's mind cleared more. How could the white woman know Chin? Was it a dream? Had she already gone mad?

"You know Chin?"

Rebecca nodded.

She closed her eyes against the pain of memory. She was afraid to open them again, afraid the white woman would be gone and that Yang would be standing in her place.

"Get him," she gasped, her eyes still closed, "get Chin and bring him here . . . please."

It was close to six o'clock when Rebecca Ashley walked into the foyer of Chin's house. His servant asked her to be seated while he announced her arrival and she asked him to please be quick about it, as it was a dire emergency.

On hearing this Chin decided to break with ceremony. He walked into the foyer himself. "Excuse me for greeting you in the foyer, but Muong said it was an emerg—"

Rebecca was on her feet at once. "Chin, you must come with me! Please!"

He hadn't seen Rebecca Ashley in many months, but he knew instantly that something was seriously wrong. The mere fact that they hadn't seen each other in so long would have necessitated at least a civil greeting . . . unless, of course, something was so pressing as to obviate that courtesy.

Chin turned to his servant. "Pull the carriage around to the front." He felt Rebecca's hand on his arm and he turned.

"Please, Chin; I have a cab waiting outside. Hurry."

As the cab pulled away from the curb he said, "What is it, Rebecca? What can be so serious that you—"

"Your sister."

After a stunned silence, Chin said, "Ling?"

Rebecca nodded. "She was admitted to the hospital this afternoon."

He snapped his attention back to her. "The hospital? Rebecca, is she . . . ?"

"No. But she's in a terrible state."

"What's wrong with her?"

"The doctors aren't sure."

He looked out the window of the carriage. "Ling . . . How did she get to America?"

"Slavery."

He turned back to her.

"She worked in a brothel, Chin." She paused, then said, "I'm sorry."

He shook his head for a moment, closing his eyes, controlling himself. When he opened his eyes, Chin said, "Why was she brought to the hospital?"

"I asked around. One of the ambulance attendants said they were called to the brothel because she was hysterical. She was throwing things, biting people, pulling her hair out."

"Why, Rebecca?"

She shook her head. "I don't know. She's in restraints now." Rebecca looked at him. "Maybe you can find out something. She called for you."

Rebecca had seen that Ling was removed to a private room. There were only two private rooms in the small hospital. One was occupied by an elder statesman of the Hop Wo Company who had suffered a heart attack. Only the most powerful of Chinese could hope for such luxury, but Rebecca had used the Ashley name to get Ling transferred to the remaining room.

Rebecca had never used her standing before to get what she wanted in the hospital. Today she had used it twice.

Two Protective Police officers who were assigned full time to Chin escorted them to the hospital. They waited outside the door of the private room as Chin went in alone.

Ling was lying on the bed, her arms wrapped around herself. She was curled into a ball, much as Chin remembered her. She was bigger now, but that was all. She was as he had remembered her in their hut—vulnerable, full of pain. He wondered why it was that women had to bear so much pain in their lives, for so little in return.

He stood next to the bed for a long moment, stroking her head. She had watched him from the corner of her eye when he came into the room. She said nothing. But she had closed her eyes when he approached the bed, and some of the tension seemed to drain from her.

After a while Chin unbuckled the straitjacket and pulled her arms out. She still hadn't looked at him when she said, "You came."

"Of course I came. You called for me, didn't you?"

"I didn't think you would come."

"Why not?"

"I thought it was a dream."

"It isn't. I'm here." He took her arm and put it on his own. "Here, touch me, feel me. I am real. I am here."

"Thank you."

"For what?"

"For being here."

"I am your brother."

Her howl was that of a tortured soul bearing the agonies of hell. It pierced Chin's ears, raising the hackles on his neck from the shock. He had been startled for a moment, but now, as she continued her shriek, he reached forward and pulled her into his arms, holding her tightly.

"Easy . . . easy, baby sister. I'm here. Chin's here, baby sister . . ."

For a while he was afraid that she was beyond his help, but then she seemed to pull back as he repeated his own name over and over and over again. "Chin's here, Chin's here, Chin's here . . ."

And soon she began repeating his name over and over, drawing strength from it, as though it was a safe isle in a storm of madness. "Chin, Chin, Chin . . ."

"Yes," he said, rocking her in his arms, "yes, Chin's here . . ."

Finally she was still and he almost thought she was asleep. But when he let her out of his arms he saw that her eyes were still wide and he knew that it would be a long time before his sister would sleep. The horror that had brought her here would not let her rest. He had to know what it was.

"Tell me," he said gently, "tell me what's wrong, baby sister."

465

She began to whimper helplessly, the tears rolling again.

"No," Chin whispered. "don't cry. Chin will make it right, whatever it is. Tell me and I . . ."

She could not hear him. She was stretching out again, moving away from the light, moving toward numbness again.

The hard slap on her cheek brought her back from the edge.

Striking her was like driving a knife into his own chest. But it had been necessary. He had seen her drifting away and it had scared him in a way that was worse than being beaten by the white men posing as tax collectors almost thirty years ago. This helplessness was much worse. He felt he was losing her to some dark danger beyond the perimeter of the mind's reaches, and that if she ever went beyond that boundary she would never return.

She looked up at him dumbly.

"Tell me what it is," he ordered.

She spoke as if by rote. "At the house . . . at the brothel . . . I did my dance for him. I didn't know who he was," she said, shaking her head. "I didn't know who he was."

"All right," Chin said, his voice gentle again. "Just tell me."

She spoke, not hearing his voice, moving toward the numbness again. "Didn't know who he was. He came after the dance, came to my room. Lei Ko Lyio said he would . . . said I was to service him . . . important man. It would be good for me to service him . . . he was important . . . he—"

"Ling!"

"He didn't believe I was Ling. I should have told him before. Maybe then . . . maybe then he wouldn't have . . . taken me. Maybe he would have left me alone. Touched me," she said, her mouth curling terribly at the painful thought. "Foul . . . stinking . . . ripped my clothes off and took me like a dog, like two dogs in a dirty rut—"

"Who? Who, Ling?" Chin grasped her shoulders, shaking her, "*Who?*"

"YANG!" she screamed. "YANG! YANG! YANG!"

"Yang?" Chin roared, his mouth drawn into a snarl by the sudden flood of pain and hatred and disbelief.

"Yang, Yang, Yang!" She was beyond hysteria now, beyond reason. She began pulling her hair, ripping large clumps of it out by the roots.

466

"Ling!" he screamed. "Ling, no!" He grabbed at her arms and she twisted in his grip.

Her eyes bore into his with a black madness that chilled him to the bone.

"You," she cried, looking up at Chin. "You swine! Your own sister! You laid me open like a dog with your foul tool! RAVAGED YOUR SISTER!" she screamed, pulling one hand loose, battering at him, clearly seeing Yang's face where Chin's had been.

He backed away from the bed, the pain of her nails gouging his arm throwing him back for a moment. The attendants opened the door and hurried into the room. But it was too late. She raised both hands up into the air and brought them down across her face. Her long nails dug deep grooves in her face, starting just below the hairline, traveling down her cheeks, and ending at the jawbone.

For a moment Chin looked at the terrible deep furrows in Ling's face. Then the lines turned crimson and her face was bathed in streaming blood that poured down onto her white hospital gown and the straitjacket, onto the hospital attendants who grappled with her.

They held her arms, pushed them into the jacket, pulled tightly on the laces. But there was no need for them to struggle with her. She had stopped resisting. She was as one, now, with the numbness.

Chin was sick.

Chapter 62

Thursday had not started out as a good day for James Riley. For that matter, he hadn't had a good day since the July riots. But Thursday promised to be a black day even by the depressing standards of the last few weeks.

His popularity with Mayor Bryant and with all of San Francisco, seemed to be on the decline. Mayor Bryant had given Riley a free hand in managing the riots and had expected him to bring them under control in a matter of hours. Riley had expected the same thing.

That National Guard troops had to be called in was a disgrace to the police department and the local government alike. The message was clear—Mayor Bryant and his police department couldn't handle their own city.

Riley bore the brunt of this in the newspaper columns. Perhaps this was because he had gotten such wide exposure from his days leading the vigilantes and his first weeks as a police captain. Now he felt the press had turned on him.

But in the aftermath of the riots, something even more threatening happened. A reporter on the *Herald* got an anonymous tip that James Riley had at one time been associated with hoodlums. That association, the informant said, may have been more than a casual one.

When the story broke it made the front page of the paper. Riley responded immediately, denying the entire story. It was just so much claptrap, he claimed. Why would he have fought against the hoodlums if he was aligned with them? The mayor, too, dismissed the story. But the seeds had been planted.

Riley could see problems growing out of this. If someone, someone who really knew the details, began to talk there could be real trouble. As if reading his mind, Billy McNamara showed up at his office in the precinct house at ten o'clock that Thursday morning.

Riley showed him into his office. Once the door was closed he turned to McNamara. "What the hell are you doing showing up here?"

"Take it easy," McNamara said, sitting down. "Calm down, Jamie. I've never seen you like this."

Riley walked to his desk. "I've never been like this! That meeting, the men breaking away, the riot. It's a stinking mess, McNamara, and I hold you—"

"Hold your*self* responsible," McNamara snapped. "And don't go getting on a high horse with me. I'm here to tell you that you're not a part of us anymore. I'm leading the men, Jamie, and I don't want any interference from you."

Riley's first impulse was to leap across the desk and throttle McNamara. But then he thought of the implications. Still, his face was flushed red when he spoke.

"You must be mad, McNamara. How dare you—"

"I'm just telling you what's going to happen."

"And I'll tell *you* what's going to happen. I'm going to come down so hard on you that you and your men won't—"

"You aren't going to do a damned thing, Riley."

468

Riley was getting desperate now, as he felt the power pulling away, out of his grip. He fought to keep a calm exterior, and it took a concerted effort to do so.

"Maybe you forget the way that riot ended," he said. "Maybe you forgot about the National Guard troops. I can have them down here in a matter of—"

"But you won't." McNamara wasn't buying. He leveled a finger at Riley. "You're in trouble, Jamie. Or maybe you haven't been reading the newspapers. Even if you weren't linked to the gangs you'd be in trouble. You're supposed to run the police in the waterfront district and the mayor can't respect you too much when you have to call in the troops to handle your job."

"The riot was stopped and that's what matters."

"What matters," McNamara said, "is that your name has been linked to the gangs. People are starting to wonder."

"If I ever find the bastard who—"

"You're looking at him."

"You?" Riley bellowed, his eyes going wide. "You, McNamara? After all I've—"

McNamara closed his eyes, as if bored by the conversation. "Please, Jamie, no begging."

"Begging?" Riley sprang to his feet. "I'll show you who's begging. I'm going to have you locked up and—"

"Just sit down and shut up," McNamara ordered. "If you don't, me and the rest of the boys will start singing, Jamie, and an interesting melody it would be. The papers will be all over you. How long do you think you'd last with a couple dozen reporters sticking their nose into your connections?"

Riley regarded McNamara as a bird of prey would a field mouse. The look was not lost on the gang leader.

McNamara said, "And in case you've got any ideas about trying to put the kibosh on me, I've got half a dozen letters written up, giving all the details—I mean *all* of them—how you set up the robberies, Riley's Raiders, the works. If anything happens to me those letters get mailed to the chief of police, the newspapers, and the mayor's office. Before they get through with you you won't have an inch of skin left on your hide."

"Say what's on your mind, McNamara."

A smile bloomed on his face. "Ah, that's better, Jamie. I knew we'd reach an understanding. You'll remember I warned you it would come to this. I told you you couldn't push the men. If you only would have listened to me. Well, maybe it wouldn't have worked out anyway. Got to know when to let go of something. Even the best ideas—"

"Get to the point, will you?"

"The point is, we're finished. Our association is over. There's no more percentage for you, Jamie. You're out."

"I appreciate that, McNamara. After all the—"

"Hey, listen, it's not all my idea. I can't ride herd over two thousand men and force them to do something they don't want to do. Plenty of 'em were for blowing your brains out after that riot, I'll tell you.

"I had to do plenty of talking to stop it. You could have walked out of the stable one morning and into a shotgun blast if it wasn't for me."

"A true friend."

"You bet I am. I tried to tell you in the—ah," he said, waving a hand, "the hell with all that. Anyway, it's all over. Except one thing."

"What's that?"

"Once in a while we'll send you a note telling you about a job. Just make sure your boys stay away from the site."

"You've got to be kidding. You expect me to give you protection and you're not going to give me anything in return?"

"We're giving you something, Jamie."

"But you just said—"

"I just said you aren't getting your percentage anymore. What you're getting is your life. Hell, more than that. Not only aren't we going to shoot you, we aren't going to turn you in to the coppers.

"There won't be any more press leaks, either. Nothing about your ties to the gang. I talked them into it. Everything will be fine as long as you go along with us. Come on, it won't be that bad. You've made a fine buck over the years. It's our turn. Besides, you'll still have the Chinks to kick around."

McNamara rose and walked to the door. "Be seeing you, Jamie."

After McNamara left his office, Riley sat at his desk for an hour, thinking. If there was one thing he had learned from being around politicians it was that they spent a great deal of time thinking before they did anything.

The more time Riley spent thinking about it, the more he realized it wasn't as bad a situation as he had originally thought. What McNamara had said was true—he had made more than a few dollars over the years. Riley was a wealthy man from the years he had directed the hoodlums in San Francisco.

Moreover, the livery stable he ran with O'Malley had been a prosperous business, at least until the crash and the depression. That, too, had brought him a substantial income.

But it wasn't the money Riley would miss. It was the power. He would miss it, but he realized that it was time to end it. The one thing he had learned in life was to know when to walk away. McNamara was right about that, too. It was time. You couldn't hold on to power forever. Perhaps it was better to end it this way than ignobly, in some court or in a dark alley.

At a little before one, Riley found that he would have a date with a court anyway. A lawyer arrived and handed him a summons. The lawyer's name was Bolingsworth. He spoke with a marked New England accent and represented the city.

"What the hell is this about?" Riley said, looking up from the document. "The newspapers print one damned story, based on some anonymous informant, and all of a sudden—"

"This has nothing to do with the newspaper story," Bolingsworth said, "or with your alleged links to the hoodlums." He smiled. "Although I did find the story interesting."

"Then what's this summons all about?"

"We're running an investigation into the riots, Captain Riley."

"What kind of investigation?"

"Certain improprieties have come to the attention of the state attorney's office."

"Damn it, Bolingsworth, what kind of improprieties?"

"You'll find out in the investigation."

"What's this got to do with me?"

"Well, you were in charge of the police during the riots." He lowered his voice. "All I can tell you is that there've been some people saying your conduct at the rally wasn't exactly conducive to keeping the crowd calm. And during the riots you were a little heavy-handed, shall we say. Some of the orders you issued were . . . well, it'll all be discussed in the courtroom."

Bolingsworth stood and walked for the door.

"I'm a *police* officer," Riley blurted. "I handled it the way it was supposed to be handled. What did you expect me to do, just ask them if they'd stop rioting? I handled it the way it should have been handled!"

Bolingsworth turned, the door open, and said, "Then you've got nothing to worry about, do you, captain?" He left and the door closed.

It was coming apart. Riley could see that now. The whole thing was falling down around him like a house of cards. He was being set up. First Shaughnessy, then McNamara, and now the state attorney's office. He'd beaten Shaughnessy, come to a stalemate of sorts with McNamara. But he couldn't fight off everyone forever.

He wondered who had told the state attorney about the scene at the riots and about how he'd acted at the rally. A copper? An ambitious young lieutenant? Or had the mayor seen to it that the whole thing was observed?

That could have been it, Riley thought. The heat was on Mayor Bryant and he'd love to have a scapegoat. He'd love to hang the whole bloody affair on some fool of a captain. Official finding of the court of inquiry is that Captain James Riley overstepped his authority in ordering the police in his charge to beat the rioters, and so helped to inflame the rioting. That was the way it would go down.

Then he remembered what Bolingsworth had said about the rally, about how they knew he'd been looking for a fight. Stupid, he thought; it had been so stupid to act that way in public. He'd been baiting the punks and it'd come out in the hearing. Riley's fault . . . the whole thing was Riley's fault . . .

He jerked in the chair, pushing away the thoughts that grabbed at him with bony, clutching hands.

He was angry with himself. So things had gone a little poorly—so what? He'd been in tighter fixes than this before. Where was the Riley fight? He'd come out of it.

He stood up and paced his office, feeling better just from having resolved to fight. But how, he thought, could he fight it? He wasn't a lawyer. Once they got him in court he'd be on unfamiliar ground. Even if he hired an attorney it wouldn't come out good. They were clever bastards. They'd catch him in some lie.

He had to do something fast. He looked at the summons. The court date was set for next week. He didn't have much time. Hell, he didn't have any time. He had to do something spectacular, something that would make them forget.

Riley sat on the edge of his desk, thinking. There was something McNamara had said. He couldn't strike out at the hoodlums any more because they had the power to really sink him—especially with the inquiry coming up. But he didn't want to go after them. That was what had messed him up in the first place. They were too strong.

Something else that McNamara had said.

"The Chinks!" Riley declared, smashing his hand down on his desk. It was perfect. They were one of the reasons for the rally. He recalled what the speakers had said, how they had complained about the Chinese brothels and gambling dens and opium parlors. He thought about the tirade about cheap labor and about how the Chinese were the cause of the market crash.

It was perfect. All the hatred in California was directed against the Chinese. They had been the reason for the riot, the reason everyone lost their money, the reason no one could work. The Chinese.

One hundred and eleven uniformed officers stood in the assembly hall waiting for Captain James Riley. Five lieutenants and a dozen sergeants stood at the front of the hall. Not one of them knew what was on Riley's mind or what the meeting was about. All they knew was that an urgent order for an emergency assembly had been received. Riley's entire company had been called to the police station.

At a quarter past six that evening, Captain James Riley of the San Francisco Police Department walked into the assembly hall. The men stiffened for a moment, but Riley bid them relax.

He went to the raised platform and stood before his officers.

"Men," Riley began, "we're about to take part in an important mission. The nature of this mission has been kept secret until tonight so there would be no chance of word leaking out. I can now reveal the details to you.

"In a little more than an hour our entire company will move into the Chinese quarter. Our goal will be to clean out, for once and all, the blight these yellow dogs have laid on our city."

The officers stirred at the announcement, many of them nodding in anticipation.

"I don't have to go into details," Riley continued, "because you all know these Chinese scum for what they are and you all know what they've done to our city and state. Tonight we're going to take the first step toward correcting that."

Riley paced about the platform. "We're going to move

against three main objectives," he said. "The brothels, the gambling houses, and the opium dens." He turned to one of the lieutenants and said, "Avery, the map."

The lieutenant went to the wall behind Riley and pulled the curtain away. There was a large street map of the Chinese district.

"We'll divide into two platoons. I'll lead one, Lieutenant Heinz will lead the other. I'll come in from the here," he said, pointing to the map, "just below Market Street. Heinz, you and your men will come in here, from Drumm Street and up Washington."

The lieutenant nodded.

Riley turned back to the men. "Maps will be distributed to squad leaders. Each map will pinpoint various brothels, gambling parlors, and opium dens. Heinz, you'll have six sergeants under you, each with a squad of men. I'll have the same number. These squads will be assigned to specific targets within the quarter.

"The squads are to raid these objectives and arrest anyone found in them. I'm going to have paddywagons shuttling back and forth between the quarter and the station house to carry prisoners."

Again the men in the auditorium stirred.

"Let me emphasize that," Riley said louder. "I want *anyone* in those houses arrested. I don't care if they're customers, owners, or the whores themselves. We're going to clean up this area and we're going to start by making mass arrests."

Riley lowered his voice reverently, and said, as much to himself as the men, "If you boys bring this off like you're supposed to you'll all end up with commendations."

Chapter 63

Yang felt drained. Never in his whole life had he felt so weak—not after battle, not after the most arduous combat. It was a weakness not of the body, but of the mind, a kind of weakness with which he was unfamiliar.

He lay on his bed, the room darkened, his mind filled with

the recurring images of the afternoon: the dance, the music, the moonharps and the beat of the drum. He thought of the dancer moving with such practiced grace that it was obvious she had done the act a hundred times, a thousand times.

It was the most sensuous dance he had ever seen. In his mind's eye he could see her positioning herself over the phallus, lowering herself onto it, taking it into her.

And then he was on top of her, writhing about on the bed, taking her as he had taken scores of women—with greed and strength and wanton lust.

And then he had finished with her and he stood up from the bed, and it was no longer a whore lying on the bed before him, but his three-year-old sister, and she was naked and shrieking in agony, rivers of child-blood flowing from her womanhood. Yang turned away, revolted, and looked into his father's face, heard Kung Lee's accusatory voice saying, "Your sister. Blood of your blood . . . your own sister!"

Yang felt his body convulse and his eyes whipped open. He stifled a cry in his throat as the dream receded into the reality of the darkened bedroom. But reality had its own horror. There was no escaping what he had done. Worse, he knew, was the sin of how he had spoken to Ling.

He stood, lit a lamp, and caught a glimpse of his image in the mirror. He was muscled, naked, as powerful as any warrior who had ever lived. And yet he was a warrior no more. He had sinned the one unpardonable sin. It weighed on him like a rock too heavy for even the gods to bear, and he knew that they too were sickened by his deed.

He had not heard the first two times the guard had knocked on his door. The third time the man pounded harder, growing concerned that something was wrong.

Yang turned to the sound. "Yes, come in."

The guard opened the door, looked in, and said, "A messenger has arrived."

"Send him in."

Yang had buttoned his trousers by the time the messenger entered his bedchamber. He took no notice of the man's bow, and failed to return it; his thoughts were elsewhere.

"I come with a message of great urgency, *Ah ma*."

"Speak it and be gone. I have work to do this night."

"Work to do?" the messenger repeated. "Then you already know, *Ah ma*?"

Yang looked at the man. "Know? Know what?"

"They move against us. Already they are within the walls of the quarter."

"Who?" Yang asked, pulling on his tunic.

"The whites."

"Let them march. Let them burn the quarter for all I care."

"And not only the whites. The Protective Police, as well."

"The Protective Police?" Yang slipped on his shoes. "So, my brother has tired of being the whipping boy. Well, let him have it. Let him have it all. I don't care. Let him be *Ah ma*."

"Honorable *Ah ma*!" the messenger said in shock.

"Or you can be *Ah ma*, if you please. I don't care. Just get out. Leave me alone."

Too numb to speak, the messenger left.

The news of the two forces converging on the quarter had registered, but meant little to Yang. It was the message of another visitor this night that had overshadowed anything that ever would be. The visitor had come to his room bringing pain and anguish and anger with him. It was a visitor who would never allow Yang to know peace until he did what he must do. The visitor was shame.

Yang walked from the bedroom, called for one of his guards, and ordered the man to have a carriage readied.

Business was brisk at Lei Ko Lyio's brothel. It always attracted the powerful and the wealthy, men seeking the unusual and the erotic. They were men who could well afford to pay for their desires.

Lei Ko Lyio walked among the three parlors of his establishment, nodding to the patrons, watching approvingly as his twenty-three girls attended to the needs of the men. There were a dozen rooms on the second floor and another dozen on the third. Lust and money were the forces that kept those rooms in operation.

None of this would change when Yang and the tong of tongs took over the house, only the amount of money he personally would make from the house. The thought of running two sets of books had crossed his mind, but only for a moment. He had no desire to end up dismembered.

It was with surprise, then, that he saw Yang enter the main salon of his house that evening. Lei Ko Lyio felt he had handled the meeting earlier with great diplomacy and to the *Ah ma*'s satisfaction. He had granted all of his wishes, the deal had been made, and he had thrown in the whore to seal the bargain.

That she had gone raving mad after Yang left was of little concern to him. True, she performed well and worked the more erotic routines with a degree of expertise. But she was getting older and whores were a commodity in abundance. There were always replacements to be culled from the bagnios, younger women who would eagerly accept the chance to better their miserable lot, even if it meant agreeing to perversions that stretched the limits of depravity.

Yang came straight for him, cutting through the main salon. Lei Ko Lyio smiled, trying not to betray his fear.

"Good evening, honorable Yang. Your visit is—"

"Where is the woman?"

"What woman?"

"Ling. Where is she?"

"She—"

"Answer me."

"Why do you want to know?"

"Do not ask me any more questions, whore-master. Tell me where she is."

"She is in the hospital."

Concern filtered through his voice now. "Why?"

"She had an attack after you left."

"What sort of an attack?"

Lei Ko Lyio's hands began to shake. "I don't know! I'm not a physician. That's why I had her taken to the hospital."

Yang grabbed him by his lapels and pulled him closer. The brothel guards watched, not one of them so foolish as to make a move toward them.

"Tell me why she had to be taken to the hospital, Lei Ko Lyio. Answer my question or I'll spill your stomach on the floor!"

"After you left," he said, shaking in Yang's grip, "she was like a crazy woman, running around, knocking things over, attacking customers. She was pulling her hair out. We called the hospital for her own good! We were frightened for her."

Yang pushed him away, knocking him to the ground. He turned and walked from the parlor, out to the foyer. Yang was walking toward the door when it shattered before his eyes. The door crumbled inward beneath the impact of the police battering ram. Uniformed white officers flooded into the foyer of the parlor.

Yang shrank back from the foyer as the brothel guards

held the policemen at bay. Behind him Yang could hear the shrieks of whores. Men, patrons, were running, opening the windows, trying to escape the police net. A shot rang out.

Riley watched a Chinese guard slump to the floor, his tunic stained brilliant red from the gunshot wound.

Riley had been turned back by the hoodlums, but he wasn't going to let the same thing happen with the Chinese. They were his way out, his vindication. He'd be known as the scourge of the Chinese. He'd purify the city of these scum and the people would make him a hero . . . no, a god.

"Against the wall," he ordered, and the rest of the brothel guards obeyed. The Chinese stood with their hands over their heads as Riley's men moved in and handcuffed them.

Riley turned to the three officers behind him. "Come on, we've got work to do here. I want every whore and john handcuffed and led outside. There's paddywagons enough for the lot of them."

Riley strode into one of the salons. It was in complete confusion. Men and women were running, some of them trying to get out of the windows. It was exactly what Riley wanted.

He moved toward one of the windows, grabbed the queue of a man who was climbing out, and pulled back on the braid of hair.

The man screamed in pain as he was pulled back inside the brothel. He fell to the ground in agony and Riley lashed out at him with his boot, catching him on the side of the head. Riley kicked him again and again, blood and hair matting on his boot.

He turned and fell on another patron of the house. Riley looked around at the hell that was the main salon. His policemen were everywhere, kicking, punching, swinging their clubs, whipping hapless Chinese with their pistols.

"Upstairs!" he barked. "There's whores upstairs. Get them, arrest them, shackle the bitches and bring them down here." He leered at his men. "And handle them the way a whore should be handled, if you get my drift."

The men smiled back at him, buoyed by the power they wielded. It was a lust all its own and it spurred another craving.

Having handcuffed the men and women in the main parlor, the police officers took to the stairs. Riley stood in the salon, among the vanquished. He looked around at the beaten Chinese, their blood staining the carpet, and the handcuffed, broken men and women, and he felt arousal swell in his belly.

"I've won," he cried, "I've won!"

From the corner of his eye he caught the movement. He turned and ducked just in time; the knife whizzed past just to the left of his face. There was a thud as it struck the wall behind him, and a distinct twang as the blade and handle shook.

Riley looked at the man who had thrown it. He was a huge man, and something about him was familiar.

"You're gonna die, you stinking Chink!" Riley reached down for his holster as Yang leaped for him. It didn't seem possible that a man could cover so much ground in such a short time. But now Yang's hand clamped on Riley's wrist, stopping him from drawing his pistol.

Yang's attack was an act not of heroism, but rather of necessity. A general knows when to retreat, but the parlor he had run into had bars on the windows, in order to foil any escape attempts by the prostitutes. The only way out was through the main parlor.

Yang had lain in wait, watching the beatings, until all the police had left except Riley. It was apparent that he was not about to leave—he was drinking in the sight of the spoils of war. Yang had decided to kill him and flee, but the man had evaded his knife and now Yang's own life was in jeopardy.

Riley brought his knee up into Yang's groin, but Yang had anticipated this and pulled his own knee in to deflect the blow. With his free hand Riley punched Yang in the gut again and again, driving him back. Holding on to the hand that Riley used to clutch his pistol, Yang had no chance to mount an offensive of his own.

Riley drove Yang back further, against a wall, then brought his foot down across Yang's instep, drawing the first cry of pain. He wrestled against him, trying to free his weapon, but Yang held strong.

Riley grabbed Yang's face with his free hand and pushed it back, crashing his head against the wall. As Yang rebounded from the blow, Riley caught his face and again slammed it back against the wall. This time when Yang moved away from the wall there was a bloodstain on the plaster. Riley could feel Yang's grip on his pistol hand loosening.

Riley eased the assault for a moment, knowing that it would mean he'd have to take a blow from the man, but that was what he wanted. Yang didn't disappoint him. He hit

Riley as hard as he could and Riley felt a rib crack from the blow.

But the blow had sent Riley flying back. Yang's grip on the pistol hand was weak and now the white man tumbled away from him altogether.

As Riley stumbled backward he pulled his pistol. Yang started for him, but stopped as Riley pulled back on the hammer. "Come on—come on, you lousy yellow bastard. Make a move for me. Make your fucking move!"

Yang stood there, knowing that though he was a warrior of the first order there could be no battle against bullets. He would let the white man arrest him.

"You're going to die, you vermin. And it's going to be slow." Riley smiled, lowering his aim. "I think I'll start with your kneecap."

Riley tightened his finger around the trigger as the room exploded from the resounding clap. Riley's eyes went wide for a moment. He was still smiling as he reached out, tumbled forward, and fell, dead, to the floor of the main parlor.

Yang watched Riley fall, then looked to the door. Chin was standing there, a smoking pistol in his hand.

"Chin—you . . ."

"I saved you," Chin spat, ignoring the terrified patrons and employees of the brothel, handcuffed on the floor about them. "The *fan quay* had no claim to your life. I alone have the right to kill you, and I claim it. I claim it in the name of our sister Ling!"

Yang jumped back through the curtain, disappearing into the smaller parlor as Chin pulled off a second shot. Three white policemen raced into the main salon, saw Riley lying dead on the floor, and turned and looked at Chin.

"One of the employees," Chin said, pointing to where Yang had gone. "He shot Captain Riley."

Two of the coppers moved toward the curtained doorway.

"Yes," Chin bluffed, "he's in there. Get him! Be careful—he has a shotgun."

Immediately the two coppers stopped in their tracks. They turned stiffly, and looked at the pistol in Chin's hand.

Chin nodded. "You are right. It is a Chinese matter. Grant me the right to take him."

Gladly the policemen acceded to his desire.

Inside the smaller parlor Yang was bleeding. His jump had

not been quick enough this time. Blood trailed from his arm as he stumbled about the parlor in which Ling had danced.

Yang looked about the room quickly. The golden phallus was still in the room, the shaft still thrusting lewdly upward, taunting him, adding to his torment. He raced to the window, threw back the curtain, and saw the bars across it.

"You are about to die," Chin said from behind him. "Your whole tong is about to die. Tonight the Chinese Protective Police march against you. Already your tong house is in ruins, your warriors scattered to the winds. The gods have aided us, giving us the white police to combine with our own forces. Fate has conspired that we should both move against you on the same night."

Yang whirled to look at him. "How fitting that you would ally yourself with the whites."

"It is not the whites who will finish you, but I. They let me meet you alone in this final confrontation, in this place where your actions have caused shame to fall on the name of all our ancestors."

Yang's voice softened for a moment. "Chin, I came here to—"

"You came here because you wished to silence our sister forever. But it is too late. She has already told me and I shall avenge her."

Chin leveled the gun at him.

"You truly don't know why I came," Yang said, taking a step forward.

"I know all I need to know."

"Listen to me, Chin; listen to what I have to say." Yang came forward another step, his eyes locked into his brother's.

Chin blinked. "I have listened enough. I should have killed you when I had the chance."

"When you had the chance?"

"When we met in the warehouse that day. I came to talk of a settlement, but you would not hear of it. You had to have it all. You always had to have it all. Even when we were children, it angered you that I would win a chess tournament and so gain a moment's praise from our father. It was never Kung Lee's words that tormented you, Yang. It was your own, all-consuming selfishness."

Yang took another step; little more than an arm's length separated them. "You could have killed me then?"

"Yes," Chin said. "I came with a gun. It was inside my jacket. I knew I should have killed you; even as I talked to you, as I watched you go. But when the moment came I could not do it."

"You were a fool, then. You never had the courage a man needs."

"I have it now," Chin said, pulling back on the hammer. "I will kill you because you shamed our sister and our father and the very name of Wong. You must die."

Outside, in the main parlor, one of the white policemen grew impatient. All he could hear was the jabber of Chinese voices. He called out, "Hey, what's going on in there?"

Chin had not moved a muscle when the white man's question came, but his eyes reacted involuntarily to the sound, turning just a fraction of an inch to the left. It was all that Yang needed.

The kick was like that of a wild mule and Chin felt its force explode in his stomach, doubling him in pain. Yang sprang forward like a tiger, his shoulder wound completely forgotten.

His brother was nowhere near as powerful as the policeman he had battled out in the main salon. With a single twist Yang forced the gun from his hand. He buried his own hand in Chin's belly, driving the air out of him, pushing him to the wall of the small parlor.

Yang looked at his brother. The death blow. It was long overdue. His mind mapped it out, traced the movements his hands would go through. His left hand would slash sideways, catching the bridge of Chin's nose, as his right hand came up to drive the cartilege to his brain. Yang moved forward.

Driven with a hatred dredged from the charnel pits of hell, Chin did the one thing Yang did not expect. He jumped at him and into his arms. He wrapped his arms around Yang's massive sides, pulling himself closer, and screamed as he drove his mouth down and into his brother's neck.

Yang cried out in pain and rammed his fist into Chin's chest, pushing him away, letting Chin tear flesh and muscle as he did. Yang clamped his hands down on the wound, on the flow of crimson coming in great spurts. He looked at Chin, blood smeared around his mouth, as Chin spit the flesh to the floor.

Yang's cries were those of anger—the cries of rage from a terrible predator caught unaware by the prey it stalked. Though he could feel the strength ebbing from his body, Yang was still stronger than most men. But he sensed that time with shifting away.

He lunged again for Chin. This time he bent low and wrapped his massive arms around Chin's hips. Yang jerked his brother off his feet and into the air, straining every muscle to crush him in his grip.

Chin threw his head back in agony, feeling the shafts of white pain that tightened about his hips like a monstrous vise. Tighter, tighter still. Chin could feel his bones straining as Yang's arms constricted like steel bands, and knew that his hips would be broken in another moment.

He looked down at his brother, saw the blood coursing from the wound he had inflicted, then closed his eyes as the pain swept over him. Only seconds were left. He forced himself to look back down at Yang's sweating face, and raised both his hands up in the air. Then, with all that was left in him, Chin stabbed his fists downward, his outstretched thumbs ripping into both of Yang's eyes.

The hideous scream that came from his brother's throat was from a pain beyond the limits of human endurance. Chin fell to the floor as Yang's grip loosened. For unbearably long moments Chin watched Yang stumble about the room, blind, his hands unable to stop the flow of blood from the now useless sockets.

Yang's head lolled first in one direction, then the other, the scream traveling with it. Finally he fought no more. His arms dropped to his sides and he crashed forward to the floor, to move no more.

Yang was dead.

Chapter 64

It was a fine fall day. A cool breeze wafted in off the harbor and drove away the morning fog. The water seemed clean and clear this day and the *Clyborne* sat tall and proud by the pier, ready for her voyage.

Chin watched as Tai Pien supervised the loading of his luggage. There were sixteen trunks to be loaded. Already eleven crates of his household goods had been carried aboard. Finally Tai Pien turned to Chin.

"That's the last of it." The chief of the Chinese Protective Police laughed. "All you need is a house to put it all in."

"That won't be a problem."

"The financial arrangements have all been made. A voucher to your bank in China accompanies the ship." Tai Pein shook his head. "To transfer so much wealth across an ocean just by sending paper. Someday the whole world will be run on paper."

"You may be right."

"You will be all right, Chin?"

He nodded. "Shao Kow will meet me in Hong Kong. And you?"

"I will fight what must be fought." Again he laughed. "Who would have ever thought that I would become a missionary? Tai Pien, a policeman!"

Chin returned his laughter.

Then Tai Pien grew serious. "What did the doctors say about your sister?"

Chin's lips tightened for a moment. "It will be a long road to recovery." He glanced toward the ship. "She will have the best physicians in China to heal her. The doctors say going back to China may be of some help."

Chin looked back at Tai Pien, saw something in his eyes, and asked, "What is it?"

"I owe you so much, old friend."

Chin smiled. "You owe me nothing. You have repaid any services I may have done for you by helping our people. Continue to do this and your life shall be as full as mine has been."

Chin thought of the tributes, the farewells from the Six Companies. The news of his departure had prompted dinner after dinner in his honor. His fame would precede him to China, where he would be greeted by cheering masses who had heard of the young dragon who had gone to America and fought so valiantly for the betterment of the Chinese people.

"May good fortune follow you all your life," Tai Pien said.

Chin nodded. "And you." Then he turned for the gangwalk.

"Chin, Chin!"

He turned and saw Rebecca Ashley as she raced past Tai Pien, who was returning to the quarter and to his people.

Rebecca stood before Chin, the breeze blowing through her

484

hair. Chin took her hand. "You didn't have to come. We said our good-byes last night."

"I had to see you off."

"I'm glad you're here." He walked toward the gangplank as the ship's first mate made the last call. "I will always remember you, Rebecca."

"I . . ." She looked away.

"What is it?"

She turned back to him. "You were right," she said. "You were right about so many things that I was wrong about. I guess I'm a—a—"

"An idealist," he said warmly. "Thanks to the gods that there are still a few around."

She smiled, then said, "But you were right. Force was all they understood. It had to happen. It had to be that way."

Chin nodded. "Yes. But it is over now, and they will need goodness and kindness and compassion. Now they will need you, Rebecca." He kissed her hands. "I will miss you. Good luck to you, Rebecca Ashley."

She kissed his hands back. "Good-bye," she said. He turned and walked up the gangplank. "Good-bye," she repeated, her voice softer and softer, "good-bye, my love . . ."

The weather stayed fair for the first full week of the voyage. Only when they lost sight of land was Chin struck, for the first time, by the fact that he was actually going home to China. He wondered what it would be like, what changes had taken place, what new villains had replaced the old, what challenges would await him.

As he stood looking over the gunwale an old man approached him. Chin knew his name to be Jao Tai Sung. They had dined together on the ship. Chin had mentioned how different this voyage was, with its private cabins, from the voyage he had taken to California twenty-seven years ago.

Jao Tai Sung had nodded, and had recounted the story of his own journey. He too had come to America looking for a way to quickly make his fortune and return home. A few years had turned to a few decades before he knew it.

Chin smiled as Jao Tai Sung bid him good day.

"A fine morning," the old man said.

"Yes," Chin replied. "We have been blessed with good weather on this journey. A good omen, I believe."

"I pray you are right." He looked at Chin. "I see longing

in your eyes, Chin Wong. Is it for our homeland or for America?"

Chin laughed. "Strange that the question could even exist. One would think a man could only long for his homeland. Yet in some ways the land of the whites was my homeland."

It had been a harsh land, where the failure of his people to conform with Occidental ways had been rewarded with brutality and death. He thought of how the Chinese who had adapted had fared. Yang had tried it and it had spelled his undoing—for what he had adapted to was the greed of the whites. Chin realized that he, too, had acquired some of the whites' ways—though he had sought to add the best of what their culture offered to his own. For his efforts he had made a fortune, lost a brother, and nearly lost a sister, and would mourn all his life the memory of a woman he had loved but could never have.

Chin looked at Jao Tai Sung and nodded. "Yes. Like a man who has climbed the cruel mountain and come down again, I suppose I shall miss that land."

He turned and looked over the gunwale at the white-capped waves, the blue sky, the horizon. Then he smiled. "Still, it will be good, very good, to be home again."

About the Author

J. Bradford Olesker was born and raised in Chicago. He served in the United States Air Force and has traveled extensively throughout Europe, Africa, and the Caribbean. Currently, he lives in Los Angeles with his wife, Susan, and his cat, Grasshopper. He is also the author of *BEYOND FOREVER*, available in a Signet edition.

More SIGNET Bestsellers